SCORPION IN THE SEA
The Goldsborough Incident

P. T. Deutermann

GEORGE MASON UNIVERSITY PRESS

(GMu·77)

Copyright © 1992 by
George Mason University Press
4400 University Drive
Fairfax, VA 22030

Distributed by
National Book Network

4720 Boston Way
Lanham, MD 20706

3 Henrietta Street
London WC2E 8LU England

Library of Congress Cataloging-in-Publication Data

Deutermann, Peter T., 1941–
Scorpion in the sea : the Goldsborough incident / P.T. Deutermann.
p.   cm.
1. Title.

PS3554.E887S36   1992   813'.54—dc20   92–30827 CIP

ISBN 0–913969–49–4 (cloth : alk. paper)

 The paper used in this publication meets the minimum requirements of
American National Standard for Information Sciences—Permanence
of Paper for Printed Library Materials, ANSI Z39.48–1984.

For S.C.D., a keeper

My thanks to the many friends who encouraged this project and who read the manuscript and offered friendly fire; in particular, Peter and Patty B., Joan M., Royce L., and Cathy N., and to Barbara B. for shepherding the manuscript through the security review process.

This is a work of fiction; this particular incident did not happen. The principal ship portrayed in this book, USS Goldsborough, is named after a real guided missile destroyer, but the weapons characteristics have been changed to accommodate the plot. Other ships appearing in the book are, in general, portrayed with their real capabilities, although some adjustments have been made for security reasons. The setting for the book, the naval base at Mayport, Florida, and the north Florida fleet operating areas are described as they exist. The ocean environment and its effects on the conduct of naval Anti-Submarine Warfare (ASW) are accurately described. The U.S. Navy's real ability to cope with these problems is something that anyone who wants to mount the challenge must find out for himself. Any views or opinions regarding naval or military policy expressed in the book are purely those of the author and do not necessarily reflect the views or policy of the Department of Defense. Any resemblance between the principal characters of the book and real persons is purely coincidental.

SCORPION IN THE SEA:
The Goldsborough Incident

15 April, the fishing boat Rosie III; off the northeastern coast of Florida, near Mayport, 0445

    Christian Mayfield drew himself another mug of coffee from the battered pot secured to the back bulkhead of the pilothouse. The Rosie III was running east at six knots towards the edge of the Gulf Stream, passing through line showers every fifteen minutes or so, her bluff bows thumping into a short swell. The tiny pilothouse was completely darkened except for the green glow from inside the radar repeater cone, and the red glow of his engine instruments and the compass. He had the Rosie on the Iron Mike, as the auto-pilot was called in the trade. One deck below, his two crewmen were asleep in the truncated cabin above the engineroom. He would roust them out when they reached the Stream and began seining. Outside the night was warm and wet; visibility was two miles except in the line squalls where it went down to nothing. Humid gusts of wind blew in through the doors on either side of the pilothouse.

    Mayfield reached inside the small wooden cabinet next to the plotting table and pulled out a bottle of Jim Beam. He was a large, florid faced man in his mid-sixties, with the beefy build and mannerisms of a midwestern farmer, although he had been fishing for decades. He added two dollops of whiskey to his coffee, and restowed the bottle in the cabinet. Suitably fortified, he climbed back into the Captain's chair behind and to the right of the helm console, and squinted out through the rainswept windows, but there was nothing to see. One clacking wiper made a feeble effort to keep the window clear, but the accumulating salt smear from the seawater was winning between the rain squalls. Mayfield scanned the instruments, paying close attention to engine temperature. He had the nets out astern, dragging them in his wake to wet tension the lines. The mouth of the seine was still gathered shut, because six knots was much too fast for seining. It was somewhat dangerous to cruise with the nets out; they would lose the whole rig if the mouth happened to pop open. Mayfield made a practice of deploying the nets on the way out, however. It saved time once in the fishing grounds, or if he unexpectedly encountered evidence of a school. He could slow to trawl speed, pull a

1

releasing wire, and the huge net would open like the giant maw it was without ever having to stop the boat.

He scanned the relative wind dials; broad on the starboard bow at sixteen knots. Means we got beam wind coming out of these squalls, he thought. To confirm this he swung around in the chair, punched a button, and looked aft through the window in the back of the pilothouse. At the very stern, a small white light came on that illuminated the towing wire, a tough, plow steel, one and three quarter inch tow cable. The cable veered out to the boat's starboard quarter in the cone of light, confirming his appraisal that the boat was being set to port. Below them, at a depth of 150 feet, the long, closed bag of the steel and nylon net was trailing the boat at six knots, but offset to the starboard side.

Mayfield turned back to face forward and sipped his coffee, lulled by the warm whiskey and the steady drone of the diesel two decks below. Not a bad life, he thought. Don't have to commute, don't have to sit in an office all day, listen to a bunch of gabbing women, and work for some tight-assed "manager". Get to witness the glory of a sunrise at sea most every day. He would never admit such thoughts out loud; he made a point of bitching about every aspect of the fishing trade. Secretly, he wanted to do nothing else until the day he died.

He shifted in his chair to compensate for a slight heel to starboard on the boat. He glanced into the radar, and saw the two blips about eight miles ahead, with the fuzzy line of a rain squall between the Rosie III and them. He sat back in his chair, and suddenly heard the engine begin to strain, the throaty roar of the diesel changing tone as it came under a sudden load. He sensed a change in the boat's motion, almost a deceleration. He frowned and leaned forward to look at the engine dials, and saw the jacket temperature starting to climb slightly. What the fuck, he thought. Then the engine really started to lug, as the governor poured the fuel on in response to an increasing demand for power. The autopilot had sensed speed dropping off, and was trying to compensate.

Mayfield gathered himself to get out of his chair to check the tow wire, when the boat suddenly heeled sharply to starboard even as the bow jerked to port. Out of the corner of his eye, he saw the helm spinning to starboard, as the Iron Mike tried for a right turn to get back on course. Frightened now, and aware that the problem somehow involved the net, Mayfield struggled to get out of his chair as the Rosie III, its engine driving now at full power, heeled even more. From below decks Mayfield dimly heard a thump and a shout from one of the crew, but he was plastered by the boat's heeling moment into the side of his chair as it swivelled to keep him upright. He yelled himself as his coffee cup spilled its

2

hot contents into his lap. Try as he might, he could not reach the control console. He sensed that the hull of the boat was now banging sideways into the swell. Something big let go below decks, and he heard the galley drawers crash open and dump their contents. In the next instant, the boat went all the way over on her beam ends to starboard, the engine howling out of control as the screw momentarily came out of the water. A wall of warm seawater flooded into the pilothouse through the open doors on either side. The engine made a strangling noise, and then shut down as the sea poured into the engineroom through the cabin doors below. Mayfield thought he heard somebody yelling as the boat capsized, but then a second wall of seawater swirled him out of his chair and turned him upside down in the pilothouse, banging him against the steering console. Stone sober and frantically holding his breath, he flailed to get out of the pilothouse, flapping his arms and legs in the maelstrom, colliding with several hard objects, until he suddenly burst out of the water, gasping and spitting salt water, his eyes stinging and his ears roaring. He paddled in a circle for a few seconds, trying to regain control over his pounding heart and his pumping lungs. He could not see. He shook his head several times to get the water out of his eyes before realizing that they were screwed shut. He opened them in time to see the bow of the Rosie III being pulled *backwards* and down in a boiling froth of loose deck gear, a life ring, two potato crates and other topside gear that had not been tied down dancing in the roiling water. And then it became very quiet. Until, twenty feet away, his first mate, Jack Corrie, popped up out of the water like tethered buoy suddenly released from below. He subsided into a fluttering swirl of his own, inhaling deep gulps of fresh air, and hacking out the substantial piece of the Atlantic Ocean he had swallowed.

"Jack!" yelled Mayfield. "Jack, over here!"

He tried to wave, but the weight of his raised arm sent his head back under. He became aware that it was starting to rain, fat drops pattering audibly on the dark sea. He lost sight of Jack, but heard him calling from within the curtain of rain. He started to swim in Jack's direction, alternating yells with a few breaststrokes, until he collided with one of the Rosie's life rings, which smacked him in the lower lip, bringing tears to his eyes momentarily, and the salt taste of blood in his mouth. He grabbed for the ring before it got away in the night. Jack appeared then, dog paddling behind a five foot long plank, the bridge-wing nameboard, with its brass letters spelling out Rosie III glinting in the darkness. It had hung by two brass hooks on the bridge-wing, and being wood, had floated free.

"What the fuck happened!" spluttered Jack, crawling up the flat face of the board to get some buoyancy under him. He was dressed only in his skivvies, which clung to him now in ridiculous, wet folds.

"I don't fucking know," spat Mayfield. "One minute we're cruising along on the Iron Mike, the next minute I'm in the fucking water. Any sign of Buddy?"

Jack shook his head, turning his face up into the rain to wash away the stinging salt water. Mayfield noticed that Jack's face was a mess, with one eye swelling, and his forehead cut, the blood running in a black line down across his cheek. The rain was really coming down now, slashing the surface of the sea in sheets, and there was the flicker of lightning behind them. The rain came down so hard it seemed to flatten the ocean. Jack reached across his board for one of the cords on the life ring so that he, too, would not drift away. His face was gray-white in the dark, his breathing still rapid.

"He was in the bunkroom, same's me," Jack said. "I woke up outa my rack and bangin' on the bulkhead, and then the water came in like a fucking toilet flush; next thing I know, I'm in the water and there's no boat. Buddy—I don't know...what the fuck we gonna do, Cap?"

Mayfield shook his head to clear the rain out of his face, but it was no use. Jack was young; he scared easier. Not that Mayfield wasn't scared, but he had been at sea long enough to take stock when things turned to shit, and not let panic take over. Jack was close to panic. The rain was cooler than the ocean temperature, which was a Godsend. Guy in the water had a chance, if the water wasn't too cold. With Jack, there, bleeding, well, that was another problem, once the sharks got a whiff. The fucking boat had gone down *backwards,* not sinking, but making sternway. He remembered that one clear point of reference in the twenty seconds it had taken for her to capsize. He pulled out a handkerchief from his clinging pants. He stuck one arm through the life ring, and then tore the handkerchief in two, lengthwise. He whipped a quick square knot into two strips.

"Lean forward; I gotta close up that cut on your head," he ordered.

"What cut," said Jack, his hand going up to his head, pulling away, covered in dark blood.

"Oh, shit," he said softly.

He brought his plank closer, and bent his head down, almost into the water, while Mayfield tied the makeshift bandage on. The handkerchief was soaking wet, of course, but it might slow down the bleeding. Jack, a fisherman, did not have to be told that slowing down the bleeding was important.

4

When he was finished, Mayfield held his watch up to his face and pushed the light button. An hour until sunrise. He could barely see Jack's face in the darkness. The rain continued to fall. The fucking boat had gone down making *sternway*. He was sure of it. He tried to see if he could spy the lights of the two contacts that had been east of them, but the rain blocked everything out. He hunkered down in his life ring and tried not to think about sharks and Jack's cut forehead.

CHAPTER ONE
FIVE DAYS EARLIER

10 April, USS Goldsborough (DD-920); At sea, Mayport Fleet operating areas

The radio messenger came through the pilothouse door, blinking rapidly in the sudden blaze of sunlight reflecting off the polished bronze sea.

"Officer of the Deck," he called out, squinting hard.

"OOD, aye," replied Lieutenant (junior grade) O'Connor from the port bridge wing.

"Got a priority action, Sir."

The OOD came in from the bridge wing, pushed his dark glasses up onto his forehead, and took the steel message board. He scanned the top message briefly, initialled it, and then walked across the pilothouse where Commander Johnston Michael Montgomery was trying to stay awake in the warm morning sunshine.

"Priority action, Captain," said O'Connor. "A little bit off the beaten path, too."

The Captain stretched, and sat up in his bridge chair. The chair protested. Mike Montgomery was a large man, with an oversized, straight nosed, nordic face, permanently ruddy complexioned from years at sea, with bushy white blonde eyebrows and a shock of blonde hair tinged with gray brushed straight back from a wide forehead. He wore the regulation Navy at-sea working uniform of wash khaki trousers and short sleeved khaki shirt, with the tarnished silver oak leaves of a Commander, USN, pinned to the points of his shirt collar, and a gold command at sea star on his right shirt pocket. A pair of hand-tooled, black leather sea boots rucked up the hem of his trousers. He had large hands and massively muscled forearms; the metal message board looked like a piece of paper in his hands.

"Everything we do is a little bit off the beaten path, Tim. Lemme see it."

The Captain's voice had a booming quality even when he was calm. He scanned the message. The rest of the bridge watch looked on with interest. The Bosun Mate of the Watch tried to get the radio messenger

7

to let him in on the message. The messenger, a radioman who considered himself superior to all bosun mates, ignored him.

"Well, you're right, Timothy. This is indeed different. Get the XO up here, please. Quartergasket!"

The Quartermaster of the Watch stepped forward from his chart table. "Aye, Sir?"

"Plot this position, and give me a course at eighteen knots."

"Aye, aye, Sir."

The Captain turned back around in his chair, and reached for his lukewarm cup of coffee. Goddamn bosun mates were putting salt in it again; somebody had to talk to them. He knew the bridge watch was dying to know what was going on; he would let them eavesdrop when the Executive Officer, Lieutenant Commander Ben Farmer, arrived. He leaned back in the bridge chair.

Typical bullshit squirrel assignment for Goldsborough, he thought. The Coast Guard had forwarded a report from one of the Mayport fishermen claiming to have sighted a U-boat out on the edge of the Gulf Stream. Montgomery, a bachelor who lived in the fishing village of Mayport behind the Mayport naval base, knew most of the commercial fishermen personally. He could just see it. Some old fart like Christian Mayfield, stumbling out on deck in the morning twilight to piss over the side after a night-long session with Dr. James Beam and shaking with the predawn D.T.'s, sees a frigging U-boat. Right. Thinks he's back on the convoys. Lucky he didn't fall over the side in the excitement. And now Goldsborough, the one antique steam powered destroyer among all the new gas turbine powered frigates and destroyers in Mayport, would get to go out a hundred miles to the Gulf Stream and look for a U-boat. He sighed noisily. This was the kind of operational assignment which tended to confirm his suspicion that his career, just like Goldsborough's, was drawing to a close.

The Executive Officer appeared on the bridge from the doorway leading to CIC. Lieutenant Commander Ben Farmer was a chunky man, with a round face and a prematurely gray head of hair.

"Yes, Sir, Captain. Quartermaster called me and said we have to look for a—submarine?" The bridge watch team members pricked up their ears while trying to appear as if they were not eavesdropping.

"Yeah, XO. Another Weird-Harold mission for the Goldy-maru. One of the shrimp boats skippers called the Coast Guard on the Marine radio, says he saw a U-boat, gave a position. Group Twelve wants it investigated."

The Exec scanned the message. "But this was, hell, twenty-four hours ago," he complained. "Yesterday morning. That's a pretty big time-late. We were supposed to go in tonight. A hundred miles out, a hundred miles back, and some search time, we're looking at another day in the opareas."

"You broka-da-code, XO. I sense the slick claws of J. Walker Martinson, Chief of Staff to the Lord High Admiral George T., behind this little trip."

The quartermaster interrupted. "Sir, we need 085 to get to the original sighting posit."

"Very well. Mr. O'Connor, 085 at eighteen knots, please."

"Aye, aye, Sir." O'Connor gave the orders to the helm and lee helm. There was a jangle of engine order telegraph bells, and moments later Goldsborough swung her aging 4000 tons of steel around to the east and headed for the Gulf Stream. A light breeze began to stream through the pilothouse, rustling the charts on the chart table and stirring the general fug of cigarettes and stale coffee.

The Captain crumpled his paper coffee cup, and pitched it through the bridge wing door over the side. "XO, make an announcement to the crew that we're going out to investigate an unidentified submarine sighting report, and that our return to port will probably be delayed until tomorrow."

"Aye, aye, Sir." Farmer stepped closer, and said in a low voice, "Do you really believe that they saw a real submarine?"

The Captain shifted his large frame in the chair.

"No, XO. I don't. And what's more, if Group Twelve thought it was a real sighting, they wouldn't be sending us—they'd get one of the new Spruance class guys underway, send a real ASW ship out to take a look. But, what the hell; it beats boring holes in the ocean doing CIC non-maneuvering tracking exercises."

The XO squinted at the message again. He needed glasses, but refused to get a pair.

"Yes, Sir. I guess so," he said. "We'll have to hold an ASW brief this afternoon, say, 1330. If we're gonna do this thing, we'll need to post the blue and gold ASW teams. That's four on-four off watches, until we give it up. They say how long we're to look for this – er, U-boat?"

"Nope. So I'll mess with it all night, and then we'll do a Unless Otherwise Directed message and come the hell in. We've gotta get these boilers off the line; both of 'em are blowing steam, and I want to get those HP drain valves unscrewed by the end of next week so we can still go on the Fleet exercise."

9

The Exec nodded. "I'll tell Ops to file a new moverep."

"OK, XO."

The Captain sat back in his chair. The bridge cooled off noticeably as the ship picked up to eighteen knots and headed seaward. The bridge watch talked quietly among themselves about the sudden ASW mission. The word quickly spread through the ship, as the phone talkers chattered on their sound powered telephones to the lookouts and the main engineering spaces.

Mike Montgomery had been in command for almost two years. His selection for destroyer command had been exciting; his assignment to command Goldsborough had been something of a disappointment. Goldsborough was a twenty-seven year old, all-gun destroyer, armed with three automatic five-inch bore naval rifles, anti-submarine torpedoes, and even an ancient depth charge rack on the stern, courtesy of a senior admiral's pet project to get depth charges back into the fleet. She had four high pressure steam boilers which could drive her at thirty two knots if everything in the main spaces stayed steam-tight, which rarely happened. From the waterline up, she presented the classic lines of a large, modern destroyer, although her ability to defend herself against modern jet aircraft had long ago been eclipsed by high performance anti-ship missiles. Her Achilles heel was the elderly steam propulsion plant, compounded by an aging hull. Most of her class had been decommissioned when maintenance costs had begun to overrun operational capability. Goldsborough was now the sole remaining steam-powered destroyer based at the Mayport naval base, surrounded by the newer gas turbine driven Spruance class destroyers, which, at 8000 tons, were twice her size and one-third her age.

Because of her age, Goldsborough had been taken off the deployment list, which meant that she did not go overseas with the carrier groups on their six month deployments anymore. She stayed home and took part in fleet exercises and other training evolutions in the waters off Florida and occasionally in the Caribbean. She had inherited the role of semi-permanent duty destroyer, which meant that she was on call for all sorts of pop-up missions, like this one.

Mike had long ago realized that not being able to take his ship on deployment meant that he had become a marginal prospect for promotion to full Captain, USN. The selection boards for Captain paid a great deal of attention to fitness reports written by carrier battle group commanders on their destroyer skippers, especially during deployment operations overseas. On the other hand, Goldsborough was much sought after as an assignment by the enlisted men, whose promotions were dependent more on time in service and competitive examination than on deployments. For many, whose wives had found good jobs in the area, not having to go overseas for six months at a crack was as close as the enlisted could get to a homesteading situation and still be on regular sea duty.

Duty on Goldsborough was pleasant enough. The base at Mayport, placed at the mouth of the St. Johns river, near Jacksonville, Florida, was small enough to be friendly and personal. There were only two admirals, and one of those was usually deployed overseas. Career Navymen understood that the importance of petty regulations varied directly with the number and seniority of admirals present, and thus Mayport was a pleasantly laid-back naval station, especially when compared to the huge fleet operating bases up north in Charleston and Norfolk.

"It'll take us until 1530 to reach the datum, Captain," said the Quartermaster, interrupting his reverie. He re-focused on the submarine problem.

"Very well. OOD, we'll have an all-officers at 1330 for ASW action brief. I'm going below."

"Aye, aye, Sir. I'll get the word passed."

The Captain stood down from his chair, and stretched. The sea was absolutely flat calm, and its surface had gone from bronze to silvery gray in the haze of a typical late Spring day off the Florida coast. In the distance the surface of the sea was dotted with small fishing boats, cabin cruisers, and the occasional commercial fisherman or shrimper with nets over the side. On the horizon, one of the massive, 60,000 ton Toyota car-carriers was getting larger as she closed in on the entrance to the St. Johns river for the run up to the port of Jacksonville.

Mike wondered at the thought of a fishing boat Skipper seeing a U-boat. Most of the Skippers he knew would not recognize a submarine if they fell over one, and some were often not sober enough to know they had bumped into something. As a bachelor, he had spent enough evenings in the back bar at Hampton's Fish House with the fishermen to know something about their drinking habits. This was undoubtedly going to be a major waste of time. He let himself through the door at the back of the pilothouse and headed below to his cabin.

TWO

Washington, D.C., The Defense Department Photoanalysis Center, 10 April

Maryann Winters was fuming. Her boss, Harry Johnson, had groped her again, and she was getting sick and tired of it. It had been the usual scene—she standing over the optics of the analyzer table, which unfortunately pointed her curvaceous bottom at whomever might come into the lab, and Harry ambling over, ostensibly to see what she was working on. Maryann was twenty-six, single, and shapely, and Harry always managed to stand close enough to brush her backside with his right hand when she was running the photo analyzer. He had this really terrific technique: bend over with her, let his hand wander, and breathe heavily near her left ear. Unfortunately, he was a smoker, and his breath stank of stale cigarette smoke. He undoubtedly thought that he was being Mr. Cool. Maryann was ready to file a sexual harassment grievance against him with the Civil Service Board.

Rhonda from the adjoining central files office had suggested that she try stepping back on his instep with her high heels, which was how Rhonda had cured Harry when he played touchy-feely with her. Maryann, however, was determined to inflict some real retaliation through civil service channels, if she could only find a way to prove it. Her boyfriend, who worked for the Naval Investigative Service, had suggested putting some purple hands powder on the back of her skirt. This, he explained, was the invisible stuff they used to sprinkle bait, such as a wallet, for thieves. A thief would handle the wallet, and after a day or so his hands would turn purple, exposing him. Maryann was thinking seriously about trying it.

She bent down to look once more into the analyzer optics. The picture was from one of the new RQ-9X birds, and it was a sweep of the southern Mediterranean littoral. She loved doing the satellite imagery. This satellite swept across all the countries of northern Africa before moving up across the middle and eastern portions of the Soviet Union, the principal target. The Mediterranean pass was targeted to update North African naval and air orders of battle, but since Maryann worked in the naval section, she performed analysis only on the harbors and bases. She scrolled the image from left to right, duplicating the satellite's pass across its terrestrial footprint. She consulted her list of target installations, and then moved the crosshairs to stop at Ras Hilal, right on the coast, and initiated magnification. Counting carefully, she recorded the medium and small patrol boats, and noted that the six Foxtrot class submarines were still in place. Stepping away from the optics, she punched in a code on a computer terminal, and hit Enter. She bent back down to the eyepiece. In view now was the same pass, at the same coordinates, taken one month ago and superimposed on the current one, a standard photo-interpretation technique used to detect changes. She did the count again, finding one more patrol boat in the current frame. She entered that change into the computer, thereby automatically updating the appropriate naval order of battle file.

Harry Johnson came back into the analysis room, and Maryann turned her head to see who it was, almost defensively, but his hands were full of files this time. He nodded to her, smiling as if they shared some intimate secret, and left through the side office door. Just you wait, jerk, she thought. She went back to the analysis. Entering three more codes, she turned on the infra-red display, which depicted the targets in black-white contrast as a function of heat differentials. The satellite was a fancy bird: it shot visuals and infrared at the same time. She looked back into the optics, and found something unusual. Two submarines tied up across from one another at one pier were different. One showed the normal calico tones of hot and cool patterns distributed over the length of the hull. The other showed completely homogeneous heat, from one end to the other, as if the sub had been put in an oven and brought up to one uniform temperature.

That's weird, she thought. She called up the previous month's image, and found that both subs moored to that pier had similar calico hot and cold patterns. OK, so we've got a change, but what's it mean, she wondered. She knew, and suddenly dreaded, the next step. She was supposed to tell Harry. She thought about it for a moment. If she called Harry now, after he caressed her bottom this morning, he would think she was interested, which was the last thing she wanted to have happen. Old zoo dirt breath getting encouraged.

She thought about it. So the heat patterns are different. Ragheads probably painted the damn thing the day the pass was made. Who could tell what the crazy ragheads would do. If it showed up again on the next downlink she'd mention it to Bob Voss, the other naval imagery analyst. *He* could tell Harry. She looked at her watch. It was almost lunchtime; she could do Egypt before lunch. She called up the next set of images; she loved to see the pyramids on the stereo scope.

THREE

USS GOLDSBOROUGH, at sea, Mayport Fleet operating areas, 10 April

The officers all stood up as the Captain came into the wardroom. He nodded to the Exec, and took his chair at the head of the wardroom table. The Exec remained standing. The ship was rolling slowly as she made her way out across the continental shelf. The view through the porthole at the other end of the table alternated between gray sea and light blue sky. The Exec began the briefing.

"OK, gents, believe it or not, we're headed for a datum, a last known position of an unidentified submarine; courtesy of a commercial fishing boat's report at 0600 yesterday morning."

There was some murmuring around the table. More than twenty four hours was indeed a cold trail. The officers knew that the likelihood of finding anything was close to zero.

"Yeah, I know," said the Exec. "This is probably a drill. But. The message from Group Twelve was fairly clear: go out there, investigate, report. So we're going out there, and we'll set up ASW teams blue and gold, four hour watches, starting at 1600. Weps has made some changes in the watchbill, so check it out after this meeting. Ops, over to you."

The Exec sat down in his chair next to the Captain, and Lieutenant Wayne Foster, the operations officer, stood up. He walked over to a portable briefing easel at the end of the table, and flipped the first sheet into view.

"Captain, XO, I propose we execute an expanding square search around datum upon arrival, using plan four alfa, as shown here. The XO has said we have all night, so I recommend that we open the square to five mile legs, collapse it again, and then depart the area around 1000 tomorrow morning in order to get back into Mayport at around 1500. Captain, I have a movement change report ready for your signature."

He flipped to the next sheet, which displayed a matrix of status settings for the ship's principal sensors.

"I recommend that we make the initial approach with sonar passive, on the remote chance that there is a submarine still there or somewhere around there. We've been doing a cued electronic warfare listening sweep for the past hour, and we're looking, of course, for submarine band search radars, just in case he pokes something up to take a sweep, which, as we know, isn't likely."

Ensign Benson, the First Lieutenant, raised his hand. "Wayne, as I understand it, our 23 sonar doesn't have much of a passive capability. What's the point of being passive?"

Foster acknowledged the question. "Because if we started pinging now, and we're still about fifty miles away from datum, any submarine out there would hear it and know there's a tin can coming. If he's still around that position, it's better for us to drive in quietly, and then light off the sonar, when there's a chance of getting contact. This assumes that there is an unidentified submarine operating out here in the first place." He looked at the Captain.

"Good point, Ops," interjected the Captain. "What we have here, Guys, is a report from a commercial fishing boat skipper that he saw a

14

submarine, or, a U-boat to be precise about it. At a position that he thinks he knew. Now, we all know that these guys know generally where Mayport is, but never precisely where they are, so this datum posit we've got is suspect to begin with, as well as being very cold." The Captain leaned back in his chair. "My opinion is that this is a wild goose chase. On the other hand, I'd hate to go out there, look around in a perfunctory, half-ass fashion, and then come into port, only to have another sighting report in the message traffic the next day. So we go out there, and we do it right, OK?"

The officers nodded their understanding around the table. The Captain indicated to the operations officer to continue. He then tried to put an interested expression on his face. He hated wardroom briefings; the chairs were too small, for one thing.

"Yes, Sir," said the Operations officer. "That's why I picked the expanding square, because the initial data is probably pretty loose. Captain, I was going to ask: has anybody checked to see if this was or is one of ours?"

"No, and our masters ashore won't until we or another Navy unit actually makes a contact report. If we don't come up with a sniff, then the whole thing goes into the burn bag and that's it."

"Yes, Sir. So, basically, we go into the datum area configured as I've shown here, with sonar passive, surface search radar active, air search radar passive, TACAN off, torpedo decoys streamed at short stay, and off, fathometer off, and operating on both screws. Once at datum, we'll go active and ping around for the rest of the night."

The Exec spoke up. "What kind of water conditions we have here, Ops?"

"Medium shitty, XO," replied Foster. "We're right on the edge of the Gulf Stream, so we have a huge thermal interface between the 70 degree water inshore of the Stream, and the 82 degree water in the Stream itself. That's like a glass wall to the active sonar. Lots of mixing, boundary layer stuff, and tons of background acoustics from sea life. If a sub wanted to hide out, this is a beautiful area to do it in, except when the North Wall conditions form. Then things get pretty lively out here."

The Captain mentally nodded his head. Ops was understating the danger of the North Wall. The Gulf Stream, that magnificent, 60 mile wide channel of warm, tropical seawater which swept up the east coast of the United States until it reached the Hatteras area of the Carolinas, and then surged out across the Atlantic to make life possible in the northern Atlantic islands of Iceland and England, was a potent obstacle to any anti-submarine warfare problem, even when weather conditions were good. When certain atmospheric conditions prevailed over the continental United States, the north wall of the Gulf Stream became the ship-killing maelstrom which had given Cape Hatteras the sobriquet of Graveyard of the Atlantic.

Foster flipped to the next chart, which showed a variety of sonar ray diagrams.

"Linc Howard put these together for me this morning. They show the likely raypaths of ensonification in the environment we're going to see out there. This one shows the outside of the Stream conditions, this one shows the inside, and these two show what the boundary looks like, which you can see is dogmeat. And you have to remember that the boundary area can be five miles wide."

"Anyway," Foster continued, "There's not much else to brief. We don't know what kind of submarine this might be, or even if there has been one anywhere near this datum. And because we're searching along the side of the Stream, the water conditions are going to produce lots of false contacts and a great deal of background noise. The continental shelf begins to drop off there, too. The water depth starts to go from the 300 to 400 foot range on the shelf down to ten thousand feet in the Atlantic abyss, so we'll get reverberation in the active mode. About the best we can do is maybe spook the guy into running away, and pick up something when he moves. I wish we had a helo for this."

"There was no mention of any air support, Ops," said the Captain. "I think maybe if we got a contact which we could truthfully classify as something above ridiculous, they might bang a chopper out, but I wouldn't hold my breath, especially on a Friday morning. Nobody has been put on standby, that I know of."

He turned to the Anti-Submarine Warfare (ASW) officer, Lieutenant (junior grade) Lincoln Howard, the only black officer in the ship. "Link, you told me you were going to build a program on that desktop we bought for CIC that allows continuous recomputation of the sonar environment. Is that done yet?"

"Yes, Sir, it is. This will give us a good test, too," said Howard.

"Very good. Make sure we record the entire session, so we can show the Commodore. He was interested in what you were doing."

"Aye, aye, Sir. That's no problem."

Lieutenant Foster had nothing more to present. "Well, we'll at least get some ASW exercise time out of this," he said. "Captain, XO, anything else to put out?"

The Captain decided to preempt any further discussion from the XO, and stood up, followed by everyone else.

"These kinds of missions are just part of the job, Guys," he announced. "Let's just do it, take a good look, and get back in for the weekend. Try not to run into any fish nets or boats. Thank you, that's all."

The officers stood until the Captain and the Exec had left. Outside, in the wardroom vestibule, the Captain signalled the Exec to follow him up to the Captain's Cabin on the next level. He walked in to his cabin, pitched his Goldsborough baseball cap onto the bunkbed, and thumped down in a chair, motioning for the XO to sit down as well.

"Well, what do you think, XO. We getting picked on again, or what?"

The Exec grinned. They had had this discussion many times. The Captain was convinced that the Group staff, and, in particular, the Chief of Staff, Captain J. W. Martinson, III, had it in for Montgomery, and thereby Goldsborough. Mike was not an innocent bystander in the matter of his relationship with the Group headquarters. He had a penchant for writing messages that were openly critical of the local maintenance and supply organizations when they did less than good work, reflecting his conviction that the shore establishment existed solely to support the ships. Since coming to command, he had gained the distinct impression that some elements of the shore establishment found the ships to be a needless pain in the stern. Mike was also somewhat notorious on the waterfront for his rule that any staff officer who came on board his ship had to see him first. The staff officers were charged by their bosses to keep themselves informed about the material, administrative, and operational readiness of the ships in the Group. When staffies come aboard most ships, they were accustomed to dealing with their department head counterparts. In Goldsborough, they had to deal with a Commanding Officer, who always made it clear that he felt they were meddling. Which they usually were.

"You're getting paranoid, Captain."

"Shit, Ben, even paranoids have enemies." They both laughed at the old joke.

"But what bothers me," continued Mike, "Is that Captain J. Walker Martinson, the turd, knows that I really want to keep Goldy in this upcoming Fleetex. It's our one chance this summer to get out of Mayport, and the crew is really up for that. It would be just like that prick to find some screwy thing like this to use as an excuse for us not to go."

The Exec took off his own ballcap, and ran his fingers through his thinning hair. He was a senior Lieutenant Commander and nearly the same age as the Captain, courtesy of several years of enlisted time before he had won his commission. Ben Farmer was a no-nonsense, very experienced seagoing officer; he also had excellent political instincts for how things worked in the Navy. He had accumulated his twenty years, and thereby the rough confidence that the worst they could do to him was make him retire. He tended to speak his mind, but privately.

"I don't know, Skipper," he said. "I should think that the Group Chief of Staff has too many things on his plate to have time to hatch a plot like this, even if you do poke a sharp stick in his eye once in awhile."

"No more than once a day, XO."

"Yes, Sir," grinned Farmer. "I know. But, actually, this caper has only cost us a day, and the plant will take a few days to cool down anyway. We never really expected to be able to work those main steam valves over the weekend, so we're not in any jeopardy, schedule wise."

The Captain sighed. "I guess you're right, unless some other frigging fishing boat skipper starts seeing things."

The Exec grinned again. "You live next door to those guys, see them all the time. Why not put the word out to cool it?"

The Captain nodded. "I plan to do just that. I'll see Chris Mayfield—he's the daddy-rabbit skipper in the commercial fishing crowd. Tell him to change to a better brand of bourbon, stop these hallucinations."

Mike's choice of a home was another thing that somewhat disturbed the senior staff officers at the Group head-quarters. Mike lived on an elderly, refurbished houseboat down at the Mayport Marina. He was reputed to cut a reasonably wide swath through the nightspots along the Jacksonville beaches, whereas a proper Commanding Officer lived with his wife and children in quarters on the naval station. A proper Commanding officer was not a free-wheeling bachelor who drove a sports car and went on liberty like a sailor. No one amongst his contemporaries or on the staffs had ever come right out and said such things, but the expressions of prim disapproval were there if one cared to look, disapproval given impetus by some of the wives' appraising glances.

"Unless, of course," said the Exec, "Somebody really did see a submarine out there." He looked serious for a moment.

"Not a chance, XO, not a chance," snorted Mike. "This whole thing is bullshit, and Martinson knows it. Group's still mad about that message I sent in on the shipyard's main steam system valve work. It must really piss 'em off now when I report that they still leak. You watch—he's just pulling my chain."

The Exec had some opinions on the fine art of chain pulling in the Navy, but diplomatically kept them to himself whenever his CO got on to the subject of the Cruiser-Destroyer Group Staff.

18

"Yes, Sir, I reckon so. We'll give it a good run, and then get back to serious business."

"Right you are, XO. Whether or not this is Martinson and company, what we really need to be doing is working on the main plant and getting those steam leaks fixed. Let's go through the motions, send in a sincere message, and get back in."

FOUR

The Navy Relief Office, Mayport Naval Station, Mayport, Florida, 10 April

Diane Martinson sighed patiently, and decided to try one more time. She was on her third attempt to explain the fundamentals of basic household budgeting to the very young wife of a Petty Officer Third Class assigned to the frigate John L. Hall. She tried very hard not to show her exasperation. Her efforts represented the very essence of the Navy Relief work for which she had volunteered, but sometimes, Lord, it was very tough going.

"Mrs. Esposito, let me try again. This is important," she said. "We know how much money comes into the bank every month from the Navy allotment, yes?"

Mrs. Esposito, struggling to control a squirming baby on her lap while also preventing an energetic four year old boy from tearing pages out of one of the waiting room magazines, clearly did not understand.

"Señora, I know nothing this allo'mente; my hosband, he say to me how much money he get paid, an' how much I spend for everything. It is the bank, they say to me, no write no more checkbooks, why? There is no enough money this month. But last month, it was OK. Ernesto—stop that! Immediamente!

Diane curled her toes in frustration. The poor woman had not a clue as to how a checking account worked. The local banks were famous for this, happily taking the Navy enlisted wives' government allotment check, and then casting these innocents loose into a sea of overdraft loans, instant mastercards, and bounced check charges. The woman was bent over in her chair, berating the four year old.

Across the waiting room, a sailor and his wife watched in embarrassed silence. The woman looked nervous; her husband had been giving Diane's legs occasional appraising glances over the top of his magazine. She pressed her knees together under the table; her straight skirt was not especially designed for modesty. The small office was hot and humid in mid-afternoon; her sleeveless blouse was damp with perspiration, and her dark hair felt limp at the ends. She often wondered if it was such a

19

good idea to volunteer for Navy relief; her looks tended to distract some of the "clients". Sometimes she received not so subtle propositions, let's talk about my problem some more, say, maybe, at the EM Club. She would then let it slip that her husband was the Chief of Staff to the Cruiser-Destroyer Group Twelve, and, most of the time, the propositions died a natural death. She decided to give up on Mrs. Esposito.

"Mrs. Esposito, I think the thing to do here is for you to go back to the bank; they have experts there, some who speak good Spanish, who can explain this better than I can. If I call the bank for you, and make the appointment, will you do that?"

Mrs. Esposito finally cracked the four year old across the back of his head with a plastic hairbrush. Diane winced. The child began to howl. Mrs. Esposito threw up her hands in exasperation, as if the child had finally passed all limits of propriety by crying. She shook her head over the whole problem of checking accounts, agreed to go see the man at the bank, smiled sweetly at Diane, gathered up the baby, the squalling boy, her diaper bag and her two handbags, and left, thanking Diane profusely for all her help.

Diane sighed. Jenny Frames, the other volunteer on duty, came in from the back office at that moment, and motioned for the sailor and his wife to come over to her desk. Her husband was the Exec on the Dale, the guided missile cruiser based in Mayport. The sailor looked almost disappointed.

"You look like you could use a little Navy relief, yourself, Diane," she whispered as she went by. "I'll take care of these people. Why don't you call it a day?"

Diane nodded. "I think you're right. The time does fly when, etc." Jenny gave her a wry smile, and then greeted the couple as they sat down at her desk. Diane pushed back from the table and stood up; there were two splotches of perspiration on the blotter from her forearms; the lone air conditioner in the window struggled mightily, but cooled very little. She was conscious of the sailor's watchful appraisal as she walked into the back office for her things. She really ought to frump it up a little before coming down here, she thought. Diane Martinson was a tall, elegant brunette whose looks tended to turn heads no matter what the setting, whether shopping in the Navy commissary at ten in the morning, or decked out in an expensive cocktail dress for one of her husband's many Navy social functions.

She was not a beauty in the conventional, cover girl sense. She had widely spaced, dark eyes, a long and not quite straight nose, finely arched eyebrows, and generous lips; the total effect was to give her face a Latin cast. She was not athletic, which meant that her figure was softer, more lush than many of the wives who were part of the jogging and tennis set on the base. She would not wear shorts, preferring flattering skirts and simple blouses by day, and three-quarter length, designer evening gowns which accentuated her fine legs in the evening. On the beach she would wear a one piece, white maillot bathing suit rather than a bikini, and it was always a source of some frustration to other wives that Diane attracted more attention by covering up than they did by baring almost all.

Diane was by nature reserved; her face in composure projected a presence of cool indifference, especially to men. She had come to acknowledge long ago that she had a disturbing effect on men. It was now simply a fact of her life. She had also learned long ago that flirting always made things worse; now, at forty, she was finding that the shell of distant reserve she projected to keep men at a proper distance made her even more attractive to some of them, especially Navy men, often igniting just the opposite reaction, especially among her husband's immediate contemporaries, the senior staff officers and commanders of ships and tenant commands at the base.

Her mother, a tall and rather plain woman, had sympathized with her daughter as she tried to understand what all the fuss was about.

"You've got "it", kid," her mother would say. "You're just going to have to learn to live with it."

Nobody could quite explain to her exactly what "it" was, but boys, and later men, all seemed to know.

Diane gathered up her purse and car keys from the back office, and left the small, white Navy Relief building nestled at the foot of the St. Johns River lighthouse hill. She walked quickly across the sandy parking lot and opened both doors of her car to let out the accumulated heat. North Florida in Springtime was like mid-summer anywhere else. The heat from the car hit her like a steam blanket, deflating what was left of her hair-do, and molding her skirt and blouse to her body. She finally slid sideways into the still hot car, closed the doors, lowered all the electric windows, squirming around on the hot vinyl seat for a moment, and drove off, not bothering to turn on the air conditioning for the three minute drive to the senior officer quarters area along the beach.

She parked the car in the driveway of the quarters, a three bedroom, ranch style house nestled in tall palms, and went in. All the senior officer quarters in Mayport were centrally air conditioned, which made life bearable in the oppressive Florida humidity. She went straight to the bedroom, shucked her clothes, and stepped into the shower. She stood there for several minutes, letting cool water run over her skin, washing away the traces of desperation from the steady parade of enlisted wives who had taken on married life in the Navy with no idea of what they were doing. Why on earth would any young girl marry a sailor, she wondered. Her conscience responded: you married a sailor. She smiled. Not quite the same; I married an officer, who was already a Lieutenant Commander, and who is now a senior Captain, in line for selection to Admiral. J. W. Martinson, III, was many things, but no one would call him a sailor. She smiled again at the thought.

She did two stints of volunteer work a week, one day as a Gray Lady at the naval hospital over on the Naval Air Station south of Jacksonville, and a second day in the Navy Relief office here at the Mayport Naval Station. The hospital work was less taxing emotionally than Navy Relief, because the Gray Ladies were able to keep their work pretty impersonal. The nurses were the ones who became emotionally engaged with their patients; the Gray ladies, so named because of their utilitarian, non-descript gray uniforms, did the things the nurses did not have time for, and thus remained in the background. Working in the Navy Relief office, on the other hand, meant going one on one with people in trouble, and it was inevitably depressing, even for just the one day a week she spent down there. Navy Relief was the Navy sponsored charity organization whose dollars and counseling attempted to smooth out the many bumps encountered by young sailors trying to support a family. Navy pay for a single young sailor was pretty good, and it got better with seniority. But for the junior enlisted man who married, and inevitably produced children, Navy pay was simply not enough to allow them to rise much above the trailer courts and food stamps lifestyle. The Navy did not permit the most junior enlisted to live in Navy housing, hoping through this policy to discourage them from getting married until they had achieved a few chevrons on their tunics and better pay.

Senior officers' wives were expected to contribute their time to Navy Relief, as if by being senior officers' wives they had accumulated some spare wisdom which might be helpful to the often very uneducated and frightened enlisted wives. Diane found the contrast between her fairly gracious lifestyle as a Captain's wife, with beachside quarters, two cars, nice furniture and a great deal of social status within the close-knit Navy community a disturbing contrast to the plight of the besieged young women who came through the dilapidated doors of the Navy Relief office. On the other hand, she herself had no children, no career or job of her own, and not much else to do but to tend to house-keeping chores, do the shopping, and go out four evenings a week to dull Navy functions. On their last tour in Washington, she had briefly tried real estate, but J.W.

had objected to her being gone evenings and almost every weekend because it interfered with his heavy social campaign to maintain visibility at the Navy headquarters. Her new "career" had, therefore, not flourished. She then went back to school and earned a masters degree, which now languished, unframed, in one of J.W.'s file cabinets. She had wanted to hang the certificate on the wall with all of J.W.'s many certificates, but he had protested, claiming the wall ought to reflect his accomplishments; after all, he was the provider, and her MA in English literature would not put food on the table.

Good old J.W. The depression brought on by a day in the Navy Relief office translated smoothly to the familiar pit in her stomach about the future of her marriage. She had begun to realize a few years ago that her main value to this marriage was to be decorously present and politically acceptable, another block checked off in J.W.'s carefully fashioned mosaic of corporate rectitude, aimed as always, at being selected for Rear Admiral.

J.W. Martinson was more than just determined to make Admiral. He had explained to Diane from the first days of their marriage that reaching flag rank was his pre-eminent life goal. She had to admit: he had not attempted to disguise or minimize what was involved in a campaign to become an Admiral. He was going to do all the things required to make the coveted first star, which meant six month long separations when he was away on overseas deployments, fourteen hour days in the office when he was on shore duty, faithful attendance to Navy social requirements, and total involvement in whatever his current assignment demanded. He often remarked that a Cruiser-destroyer Group did not stop life at 1630; she was expected to understand and accommodate the round the clock aspects of his responsibilities. She would have the children and the household to take care of while he campaigned himself, with her help, of course.

Except the children had not materialized. The subject of children was now a carefully poulticed wound between them. After two years of trying she had suggested testing, but he had refused, declaring that it was almost always the woman's problem, and that testing would answer a question she might not want answered. She had thought about that for a while, and then had had herself tested, which proved that in this case, J.W. was mistaken. She had not told him, because it was evident to her by then that the ego beneath his smooth, highly polished exterior might not be able to sustain such a hit.

How smug I was, she thought, not for the first time. Thought I had the guy figured out. Their love life had settled down to a routine that had become, after a few years and the tacit realization that the marriage would be barren, more an act of consideration than passion. He attacked his assignments with energy and tenacity, and would often drop into bed late at night without a sound, exhausted by the day and the prospect of getting up the next morning before dawn to be in the office before the current Admiral.

While his career consumed and presumably fulfilled him, their marriage provided Diane with less and less. Without a family focus, she had become bored with Navy life. She disliked the highly structured and so very busy activities of the wives clubs on and off base, where too many of the wives slyly threw around their husband's rank while pretending to be just one of the girls. Diane did not care for bridge, did not have to jog, and was hopeless at tennis; she preferred to curl up with a good book. When she did get roped into the wives' functions, she would keep her distance and amuse herself by watching the political interplay.

J.W. had occasionally sensed her restlessness. He would offer up the refrain that they had to play the game, Diane, if we're going to succeed in this business; the top levels of the Navy have no room for non-conformists, characters, trouble-makers, or officers with controversial wives. But once they had come to Florida, she knew that if all she had to do was to lie around on the beach all day she would soon be driven to 11 A.M. vodka coolers like Mrs. Daniels next door, or to one of the bronzed young hunks who littered the Navy beach right behind her patio after four thirty. Hence the volunteering.

She had occasionally imagined what it would be like, to go out on the beach one day and signal some direct, uncomplicated interest, bring some guy back to the quarters, and screw his brains out. And then what? The fantasy always came apart at the "then what". But it made an exotic diversionary scene in her mind whenever her dear, dedicated, and extremely promising husband, *The* Chief of Staff, found a few minutes in his terribly exciting professional day to pay attention to his wife. Not that it ever led to much these days. And now she finally knew why.

J.W. most definitely brought the office home with him. The first hour of his return from work was spent in a sort of debriefing, and she was always fascinated by the attention he paid to gossip; it made her wonder if senior officers in the Navy ever did any real work in the office. From his conversations at night, when he stayed awake long enough to talk, she had the impression that he spent much of the day keeping track of which of his contemporaries was going where and getting what plum assignments. Maybe that was why be brought those two briefcases home at night, and closeted himself in the study until the wee hours. The Admiral seemed to have a more balanced approach to life; he was on the base golf course by five P.M. every day. J.W. always said that the reason the Admiral could play golf was that the Chief of Staff did all the work, which was how it was supposed to be.

She turned off the shower, and shook her hair out, attacking it vigorously with a hair dryer and styling brush, while she let the air conditioning dry her off. She could have pulled it off, the going through the motions, the dutiful wife routine, the polished facade, except for one little perturbation: the Wave Commander in Norfolk that had apparently been the real center of J.W.'s affections for *two goddamn years!*

She continued to brush her hair while letting the waves of anger recede. She had found out about her husband's girlfriend by accident. At first she had been terribly hurt, awash in feelings of inadequacy, bereft at the invasion of intimacy caused by another woman, wondering if he was compensating somehow for the absence of children in their marriage. But then the hurt had turned to anger as she had thought it through. J.W. was intimate with nothing but his own ambitions. She did not have a loving, caring marriage—she had a role, ironically much like the faceless woman in Norfolk had a role—written, directed, and produced by J.W. Martinson, III, in his pursuit of an Admiral's flag. The Wave Commander worked in the inner sanctum, the executive offices of the Atlantic Fleet Commander himself. Diane knew in her bones that her dear husband was probably using his girlfriend and her unique access in exactly the same way that he was using her, to further his career.

She had not decided what to do, if anything. Yet. She was pretty sure that J.W. did not know that she knew; he was sufficiently conceited to assume that she could not know. She had come to depend on the anger to sustain her when the hurt occasionally caught her unawares. She was finally recognizing that what really hurt was the lost opportunity to have had a real love in her life. At forty, the chances were getting pretty slim.

She glanced at her watch. She had two hours before she had to get herself dressed and painted up for yet another reception at the Officers' Club, in honor of yet another visiting fireman. She no longer kept track of who the various guests of honor were these days; J.W. always gave her a thorough briefing while he got dressed, and repeated it in the car. She would listen dutifully, fix a few key things in her mind so that she would have something intelligent to say to the great man of the hour, and then settle into the role of decorous prop while her husband cruised the party, getting his "face time" with the Admiral and checking the bases. Navy receptions, she had long ago decided, were designed to be exquisitely boring so that the men would ache to get back out to sea. Many of the other officers, inevitably married, who came on to her at the cocktail parties were dependably carbon copies of her husband, very busy, very important, and very interested in talking about themselves, their careers, their commands, and how everyone junior to them knew that they were someone to be reckoned with.

She decided to take a nap. She stood nude by the bedroom window for a minute, staring out through the sheers at the line of silver blue sea visible over the dunes behind the house. The discovery that even her marriage had been compromised by J.W.'s pursuit of promotion had accentuated her deep need for some *thing* that was missing from her life, some passion, some vital element that would make her life as a woman and an individual come alive. She knew that it was part sexual and part intellectual, and also partly a desire for something to happen before she ran out of time, and yet the revelation of her husband's infidelity had partially unnerved her, awakening doubts about her own self worth as a woman. She wondered if she would have the courage to go after whatever it was she was seeking, and the temerity to carry it through if she found it.

Maybe, she thought, there really is no way around it: maybe she should just go out and have an affair of her own. And then she laughed at herself, and recalled the episode last year when one her acquaintances on the base had "gone off the reservation", as J.W. phrased it, and spent a three day weekend at one of the south Florida resorts with a 'close friend' while her husband was deployed to the Mediterranean. The woman had eventually become a basket case, torn between her physical desire for a rematch and the terrible guilt, which was increasingly amplified by the everybody-knows syndrome inescapable on a small naval station like Mayport. The poor woman had eventually confessed all to her husband, against the somewhat cynical advice of her married friends (deny, deny, deny—it's what they're desperate to hear, dear), and then she, and her friends, had had to endure the emotional quagmire of their 'getting it back together'. Diane shivered.

She contemplated taking a Valium, but took an aspirin instead and slipped into bed, setting her alarm clock for four thirty. Fantasize, my dear, fantasize. Playing around was simply too hard, as J.W. was fond of saying, and J.W. ought to know, the son of a bitch. And, yet, she wondered. Her marriage was rapidly hollowing out to nothing more than going through the motions. But when she asked herself the vital questions, what would she do, where would she go, her mind failed open. She realized as she drifted off to sleep that she was going to have to come to grips with her problem, but had not the slightest idea of what to do about it.

FIVE

The diesel-electric submarine Al Akrab, off the northeast coast of Florida; 10 April, 1800

The Captain sat in stony silence at the head of the minuscule wardroom table. There were five other officers in the wardroom: his Deputy Commander, who was also the political officer, the Operations officer, and the two department heads, the Weapons Officer and the Chief Engineer. Behind the Captain's chair stood the Musaid, the senior Chief Petty Officer in the boat. The political officer was speaking. Still speaking.

"The error, therefore, is a collective error. The fact that the watch officer lost depth control and broached the sail is nothing more or less than the grand summation of training errors, admittedly poor discipline on his part, and insufficient qualification time in his training program aboard Al Akrab. It is not politically responsible to blame only the watch officer. The operational error has its antecedents in the doings of the collective organization: just as the organization's successes are always due to the efforts of the group, so are the organization's errors also attributable to the organization as a whole. That is my doctrinal position."

He sat back, and folded his arms. The Captain refused to look at him, but continued to stare straight ahead, his black eyes focused on the opposite bulkhead. There were times when every submarine commander had wanted to put his political officer into a torpedo tube and fire him into the abyss. This was one of them.

The Captain was a tall, thin man, with a walnut brown, hawk-like face, all angles, ridges of muscle, and corners of fine bone. His eyes were wide set and jet black under pronounced eyebrows, the legacy of some Turkoman in his Bedouin heritage. His nose was short and boldly hooked, reinforcing the resemblance to a raptor; his lips were thin and set in a rigid, flat line. There was an air of latent tension about him, in the way he stared at things and people, and in the way he carried his wiry body, leaning forward, hands in front and moving, as if ready to seize something.

His silence drew out the tension. The entire mission depended precisely and exactly on not being detected, and all the political officer's socialist cant did not change that fact. The Soviets had provided excellent training in their submarine school; they had offset that excellence by draping the burden of socialist political camel dung across the shoulders of every military commander in the form of his political officer.

"Does anyone else wish to speak?" he asked, softly.

The political officer, who simply loved to hear the sound of his own voice, sat forward as if to start again. The Captain held up one finger in

27

his general direction, as if in warning. Gauging the look on the Captain's taut face, the political officer subsided back into his chair.

"Does anyone *else* wish to speak?"

There was silence around the table. The hum of ventilator fans, and the occasional creaking of the hull from the pressure of 85 meters depth were the only sounds. Outside the curtained entrance to the tiny wardroom, a steward was arranging plates and cups on the tray table, waiting to set up the wardroom for the evening meal. The Captain looked at each one of them in turn.

"Then I shall speak. And you shall listen. The mistake may be collective, but the punishment for the next such mistake shall be individually extreme. Most extreme." He paused, while the four officers at the table looked at him in growing apprehension. Once again, the Deputy Commander opened his mouth as if to speak, and then shut it abruptly. The Captain continued, training his eyes around the table like a stereo-optic gunsight.

"As all of you know, our mission here is to lurk in the sea, and to await the arrival of the American aircraft carrier Coral Sea, the carrier that bombed our homeland in 1986. Bombed the Jamahiriya, and killed a favorite child of The Colonel. Our sacred mission is to surprise that carrier, and to sink it if possible as it makes its way into port. The Coral Sea is now in the Caribbean. It will return soon to its base at Mayport. Our intelligence service knows approximately when the carrier is due back to this port, but not precisely when. We shall be informed in time to prepare. Until we receive that signal, our mission is to explore our attack patrol area *and to remain undetected!*"

He paused for an instant.

"I have told you all this before," he reminded them.

He paused again to sip from a glass of cold tea. None of the others moved.

"If we are discovered before that date," he continued, "All of this is for nothing. Our journey of four thousand miles, the hours and hours of training, the deception of all the Soviet advisors in our homeland, the stress of living submerged for endless days, the danger of discovery from all the American warships which train in this area, all for *nothing.* This crew has been handpicked, carefully indoctrinated, confirmed to be politically reliable, and supposedly trained to the highest degree of operational readiness. This submarine has been given every piece of replacement machinery we needed, and the other five boats of our Navy have been stripped as required to do this. We have their spare parts. We have their working torpedoes. We have some of their crew."

His voice was controlled, but flat with menace. The tension in his face made the words seem like bullets.

"This mission has been three years in the planning. Three years. In great secrecy. At great expense. No one in the rest of our Navy knows where we are. Our Soviet advisors do not know—they think only that we are loose in the Gulf of Sidra. All of the Soviet submarine advisors have been taken to the South for a special hunting expedition, away from the base, away from the decoy that lies at our berth at Ras Hilal. If we are discovered out here by the Americans, 100 miles off the American coast, hiding in their own Navy operating areas, it will all be for nothing. *And they will kill us.* They will hunt us down and kill us, because our very presence will be an affront to the pride of the great American Navy. So."

He paused, moved back in his chair, and unsnapped the holster on his right hip. Behind him the Musaid tensed. Every Commanding Officer in the armed forces carried a sidearm, even aboard ship. He withdrew a large Russian automatic pistol, and set it down on the wardroom table. Four pairs of eyes looked down at it, and then back at him. He gestured towards the pistol with his chin.

"I will personally execute," he declared, "The next individual who does what the watch officer did this morning: exposes this mission, and this boat. He lost depth control less than a mile from a fishing boat at morning twilight. If anyone on that boat crew saw us, we may be in desperate trouble. Our only possible salvation is that their Navy will not believe it, and we must depend on their arrogance for that. Do you understand me? Shall I demonstrate my resolve for you?"

The officers did not know whether to shake their heads or nod. They remained silent. Finally the Deputy spoke up.

"Your orders are clear. We shall inform the entire crew. It will not happen again."

"Very well. I have nothing more to say."

They were interrupted by a tapping on the wardroom door coaming.

"Enter," ordered the Captain.

A petty officer from the control room pushed aside the curtain, and entered nervously. The tension in the room was palpable. He handed the Captain a contact report, his eyes widening as he saw the pistol. The Captain opened the piece of paper, and scanned it quickly. His face darkened.

"Very well. I have seen it. I will be there at once."

The messenger withdrew, fumbling with the curtains as he did so. The Captain looked around at the four faces again.

"Now we shall see. We have detected an American destroyer which has begun to ping, to the north of us, where we were this morning when this *collective* mistake was made."

The political officer wet his lips, and seemed to shrink in his chair. There were no telephones to the political security directorate at headquarters out here, and that pistol was still on the table. The Captain was staring at them.

"Go and tell every man what I have decreed."

They scrambled out of their chairs, and left the wardroom one after the other, being careful not to get too close to the Captain. When they were gone, the steward poked his head in through the curtain. He saw the Captain, and then he saw the black pistol. He made a squeaking noise, and hurriedly withdrew.

The Captain sat there for a moment, gathering his thoughts. The fools. The simple fools. The contact report had caused his stomach to grab with cold fear. He felt sick that the whole thing might already be over. He forced himself to take a deep breath, and then another. Behind him the Musaid moved discreetly. The Captain pushed back his chair, and turned in it to look up at the Musaid.

The Musaid was a bulky man with a coarse, Turkish face, a full black beard and moustache, and fierce eyes. He was not so much tall as broad, and he was ten years older than the Captain. He had been the Captain's bodyguard and shadow for nine years, and had been his trusted confidant since he took command of the Al Akrab. They had gone through submarine training together in Sevastopol. The Captain looked up at him for a moment, and then nodded.

"Musaid. You have something to say."

"Pasha," he said, using the archaic title. "The crewmen are volunteers. This edict will make them something else. For fear of making a mistake, they may do nothing when the situation demands that they do something." He seemed ready to say more, but then fell silent.

The Captain had great respect for the senior Chief, who held a position roughly equivalent to what the American submarine Navy called Chief of the Boat. The Musaid had served in the submarine force right from the beginning, being one of the first non-commissioned officers recruited from the Army into the fledgling Navy, and one of the first group selected to be sent off for training in the Soviet Navy submarine force. He had more military experience than did the Captain.

Publicly, wherever the Captain went ashore, the Musaid was right behind him. Onboard, when the Captain arrived in the Control room or any other compartment in the boat, the Musaid appeared immediately, even at sea. But over the four years the Captain had been in command, the Musaid had become much more than a senior orderly, bodyguard and driver. He had become the executor of any policies affecting the enlisted crew, and he had become a trusted advisor. The fact that he was older than the Captain made it possible, in a delicate but substantial sense, for them to consider each other as professional contemporaries. The Captain valued this relationship, and was very careful not to do or say anything to disturb it.

"Musaid, you may be right," the Captain replied. "But for now, my edict stands. It concerns the officers more than the crew. I will weigh its effect upon the crew. It would be helpful if you explained to them that this is a matter for the officers to worry about. In a few days, I will seek your counsel. It would also be helpful in the meantime if you could spend much of your time in the control room to ensure that the watch officers do not make any more mistakes like that, at least for awhile. After my orders have been announced, we shall confer again."

"It shall be done, Pasha. I will be there until the mission is completed."

The Captain nodded absently as the Musaid withdrew. He made a mental note to keep an eye on the Musaid, who tended to take things too literally. He would more than likely post himself in the Control room until he dropped. He sat back in his chair at the head of the table, aware of the steward waiting outside, and of the need to go to the control room. He forced the distracting session with his department heads out of his mind for the moment, reaching for equilibrium. He reflected on the mission, harking back in his mind to the night they had departed, almost a month ago, trying to recapture the excitement, almost as an antidote to the dread he was now beginning to feel.

The submarine had glistened like a killer whale in the moonlight bathing the Ras Hilal base, her sides black and glossy, her conning tower raked above the rounded hull like a thick, unyielding dorsal fin. He had waited on the pier by the brow, raising his face to the cool air streaming in from the surrounding desert and breathing deeply, savoring the desert smells of sand and fading daytime heat. Behind him, the exhaust from the idling main engines had rumbled at the waterline, alternatively throwing up hot bubbles and steaming spray as a low swell rolled up the submarine's sides from the harbor entrance. Pungent, wet clouds of diesel exhaust wafted over the conning tower above him, sending the two lookouts there into occasional fits of coughing. The Captain called it the conning tower, not the *sail* of modern parlance. Dhows have sails. Submarines have conning towers.

31

Where are these people, he had thought. It is time to begin. He stifled a sigh of exasperation. Staff officers. Always making a great commotion about nothing. Neither he nor his fellahin needed a sendoff. His pulse had quickened. It is time, he had thought, impatiently. It is time.

He had looked around at the submarine base buildings and the surrounding harbor, darkened and still at this late hour. Dim green and red lights from channel buoys winked and blinked around the harbor. The low swell washed quietly against the ballast rocks under the pier, stirring the flotsam. He had wondered how many people sleeping in the dusty barracks or on the patrol boats at the next pier had any idea of what was going on. Surely the engine noise must have aroused some curiosity, but there were no signs of life in the darkened buildings. He remembered shivering; the desert's night air threading its way into the harbor from the sand hills above the base reminded him of his proper antecedents.

To the east, the lights of Benghazi were illuminating the horizon. At each end of the pier there were two linehandlers sitting against the bitts, waiting for the order to cast her off. Both figures appeared to be dozing, their bodies dark lumps in the bright moonlight. A third man was waiting by the brow, sipping tea from a mug. Just forward of the conning tower stood the silhouetted and commanding figure of his Musaid, looking like a Janissary from the old times of the Turkish empire.

On the other side of the pier, his submarine's twin, the Al Khyber, lay silent and dark, like a dead ship. Not surprising, he thought. She and some of the others had been gutted to outfit the Al Akrab. Across the harbor, a tugboat had been standing off its own stub pier, its running lights dimmed, a long, familiar shape tied up alongside. At a nearby pier, the other four Foxtrot class submarines lay nested in two groups of two. There were a few figures visible on their decks; the departure of one of their own on an actual mission was an unusual event.

The Captain remembered scanning the single road that led down the hillside from the base main gate, but there was still no sign of the staff car. He had mentally cursed all staff officers again, and then had seen the headlights.

The car had come down the road quickly, moving faster than most vehicles would on the bumpy, poorly paved road. The base was not that old, but maintenance, on roads as well as ships, was fairly indifferent in his Navy. The car's headlights swooped erratically as the car negotiated potholes, throwing bright white light over the windows of the dark buildings and the storage sheds along the waterfront. The Captain had drawn himself up to his full height, just under six feet, a disadvantage in the cramped confines of a submarine, as if to give emphasis to his impatience.

He had glanced over his shoulder to make sure there was no one from his crew loafing about on the submarine's deck, but there were only the two faces visible up on the conning tower, and the motionless silhouette of the Musaid.

His orders from Defense headquarters had been specific. Wait for the official goodbyes, and then depart immediately. He glanced at his watch once more as the car drove down the pier itself. The two linehandlers sat up and rubbed their eyes as the headlights swept over them. The Captain had noticed that this was a large Mercedes, not an Army staff car. Strange.

The car had pulled up sharply and extinguished its headlights. The driver, a bulky man dressed in civilian clothes, had levered himself out of the car and looked around, inspecting the full length of the pier. The Captain did not recognize him, but then had been stunned to see who was getting out of the right front seat. *Him* ! He had stiffened to attention as the Colonel came over to him, dressed in the desert robes of his Bedouin tribe, his black eyes glittering in the moonlight. The Captain remembered feeling a surge of pride that the Colonel himself had come. He had been so excited that he had forgotten to salute.

Behind the Colonel, an elderly Army officer and a civilian had stood up out of the car, but they had not approached. The Captain had recognized the officer; he had been a Major General before the last coup attempt. Then all ranks had been reduced to satisfy The Colonel's dictum that Colonel was now to be the highest rank in the land. The driver had continued to look around, at the pier, the submarine, and the base behind them.

"Muqaddam Muhammad Al Khali! Greetings," the Colonel had rasped. "A good night to begin a hunt, is it not?"

The Captain remembered trying to find his voice. His throat was dry, and his heart had been straining with excitement. "An excellent night, Colonel. For a most unusual hunt."

The Colonel had smiled, turning his dark, angular face to survey the submarine, his eyes glinting with eager malice. The figures up on the conning tower had become motionless as they realized who was speaking to the Captain.

"This hunt must succeed, Muhammad Al Khali," the Colonel had declared.

He had turned back to lock those malevolent eyes on the Captain, his syllables precise in that dry, almost whispering tone familiar to everyone in the land.

33

"The cries for justice echo still on the desert air. This mission—do you doubt its success?"

"No, Colonel," the Captain had replied. "The justice of it is clear. But success will depend on several things. The American Navy is many and strong."

The Colonel's face had clouded, his mouth setting in a bitter line. The Captain could not look away from this face, with its intense, black eyes and jagged creases and wrinkles. A jackal's face, he thought; and like the jackal, the Colonel was cruel, tough, intelligent, and a merciless survivor. The Captain had felt a thrill of fear, while wondering if he had gone too far with his comment about the American Navy.

"The American Navy must be made to pay for the crimes they have committed, crimes against the Jamahiriya, the people, the revolution, my family," rasped the Colonel, his voice rising. His eyes transfixed the Captain. "Your kinsmen, too, do not forget."

"Yes, Colonel. I have not forgotten."

The Colonel had looked again at the submarine. "This ship, this Al Akrab, it is ready?" he had asked, and then continued before the Captain could reply.

"Al Akrab," he had mused. "The Scorpion. A most fitting name for what you are preparing to do. To go to the Americans' coast, to lurk in the sea, hidden but with stinger ready, and the strength to stab when the time comes. We have given you all that you need for the voyage and the mission?"

"Yes, Colonel," the Captain had replied. "The provision has been generous. We are indeed ready."

The Colonel had nodded. "This is good. This is a worthy hunt. You will surprise them, never fear. Our security has been excellent. They will never, ever expect such a thing."

"That is our vital advantage, Colonel," the Captain had replied, now suddenly anxious to be away. "But we must depart, and submerge before the next satellite."

The Colonel had grimaced again, grinding his teeth. "Their satellites are the devil's work. But I wanted to speak to you personally, to confirm the trust. You are my kinsman, Muhammad Al Khali, and I yours. The blood of our tribes is the same. It is for this reason that you command this mission. You are zealous, and you are trusted. And you must trust me, as I trust you. You and your crew are not being dispatched to die, but to avenge the great American crimes. The Jamahiriya will ensure that you return safely."

The Captain had nodded his head in appreciation. "Our trust is complete, Colonel. We shall exact justice, as it is written."

"Go then, Scorpion, and strike the Godless Americans. It is God's will." The Colonel had stepped forward and embraced the Captain in the traditional kiss of greeting and departures.

"Inshallah," the Captain had intoned. "As God wills it."

The Colonel had turned away, his robes floating silently around his feet, and the waiting men had scrambled to get back in the car even as the Colonel climbed in. His door had been barely closed before the driver started up, turned the big car around in one smooth motion on the pier, and drove back towards the shore. The Captain had released his breath, resisting an impulse to wipe his brow. He had turned to look down the pier.

"Linehandlers!" he had roared, and the two men at either end of the submarine sprang to their feet. Two petty officers rose out of a hatch on the submarine's deck, one heading forward, the other aft. They must have been waiting right below the hatch, he remembered thinking. Watchful, as they should be. As they would all have to be for this mission. The nerves had thrummed in his arms and legs as he strode quickly up the brow, turned forward, nodded once to the Musaid, and climbed the ladder to the maneuvering station at the top of the conning tower, rising through the cloud of exhaust fumes from the engines. The man on the pier had hauled on the short, steel brow, pulling it back onto the pier with a screech of metal on concrete. Up on the conning tower, the watch officer had been speaking on the intercom circuit. Forward on the hull, the Musaid supervised the linehandlers as they unwrapped their lines in preparation for casting off.

"We are ready?" he had asked, wedging himself into the tiny cockpit at the top of the conning tower, his eyes stinging from the diesel fumes.

"Yes, Captain," the watch officer had replied. "More than ready. I have given main engineering control a one minute standby. That was him? I did not dream it?"

"Himself. It is a great honor. An auspicious beginning." He had surveyed the pier. "Very well. Take in the lines."

The watch officer had given a hand signal to the men on the pier, and the petty officers on deck slacked the mooring lines. The submarine had been rolling very slowly, a few degrees from side to side, almost imperceptibly, as if anxious to be underway. Deep in her guts, the tone of the three main engines changed as the engineers reconfigured the control boards, producing a fresh blast of smoke along the pier. The men on deck had pulled the lines onboard quickly, hand over hand to keep them out of the water. The watch officer stood high on the foot railing of the cockpit, leaning out and looking forward and aft to see the lines.

"All lines clear," he had announced. Behind and above them, the two petty officers stationed as lookouts slipped large, black Russian binoculars around their necks, and clipped their safety belts to the periscope mountings.

"Very well. All engines back two thirds together," ordered the Captain.

The engine noise changed to a full throated roar, and a wash of foaming water had roiled back along the submarine's hull as the propellers bit in. Harbor debris boiled up between the submarine and the pier, and then the sub began to back out, slowly at first, and then more quickly as she gathered sternway out into the harbor. After thirty seconds her bows cleared the head of the pier, and the Captain stopped the port shaft, and ordered it ahead to begin the twist. The sub had come about slowly, vibrating as the narrowly spaced propellers opposed each other in their effort to twist the boat in place. As her head came around, beginning to point for the harbor entrance, he stopped the twist, and ordered both engines ahead. The Captain remembered glancing over to the shore; he had thought he could just see the dark staff car, stopped at the top of the hill. The submarine had gathered speed quickly, the night air pushing the diesel exhaust clear over the side.

The Captain had swept his binoculars around the harbor entrance, looking for anything out of the ordinary. Behind them the tugboat had started up, a large cloud of gray smoke hovering above her, as she headed for the pier which they had just left. The Captain had nudged the watch officer,

"The decoy," he had said. "Our stand-in."

"I hope it is authentic," replied the watch officer, correcting the course by one degree to avoid a buoy. "They say those American satellites can count the shoes on the front porch of a zawiya."

The Captain had laughed.

"They probably can, but what does it tell them? Only how many shoes there are on the mosque's porch. Increase speed to twelve knots. We must get out to the dive point before 0200."

The submarine had begun to pitch very gently as she met the first deep sea swell rolling in from some distant storm out over the Mediterranean. The petty officers on the foredeck finished turning the bitts under, folding each mooring line attachment point upside down and stowing it under the deckplates, while keeping an eye on the bow for any sudden waves. Each in turn made a hand signal to the conning tower, and then

36

disappeared down the forward hatch. The Musaid had checked everything again, and then stepped down into the forward hatch, clanging it shut behind him. The Captain could remember hearing the search periscope turning in its greased tube above him as the Navigator took bearings from his station down in the attack center. The sea breeze had felt fresh and clean, containing no hint of sand and dust for a change. Their wake made a broad path behind them, parallel to the shine of the moon on the black waters. The base had remained dark, sliding aft and dwindling now as they left the harbor, with everyone there oblivious to the steady rumble of diesels carrying the submarine out of the harbor.

The Captain remembered breathing deeply, a rush of adrenaline filling his veins. It had begun. They would have to run for about an hour in order to reach deep water. Time enough. The decoy would have been in place by then, and his sub would have vanished into the black depths of the Gulf of Sidra on its way out into the middle Mediterranean Sea, safe from the probing, hostile eyes in space. Assuming the satellite could see in the dark, there would still be six, old, and inactive Soviet Foxtrot class submarines tied up to their piers, as they had been for nine months. Their entire submarine force, thought to be barely operational, and therefore no threat. He remembered baring his teeth in the dark. The Americans would be five-sixths right. The Scorpion was loose in the sea, and unaccounted for.

He was startled back to the present when the steward dropped a handful of silverware on the deck outside the wardroom curtain. He rubbed his face with both hands as he considered his next move while the subdued sounds of life in a submerged submarine intruded on the edges of his thinking. He knew that his threat to execute the next person who made a major tactical mistake was extreme, and that probably he would have to soften it in the near future. But this mission was too important. If he had to keep their attention by death threats, he would do it. Their Navy would never get another chance like this one to strike a blow against the arrogant imperialists.

He retrieved and holstered the pistol, and headed for the control room, followed silently by the Musaid who had been waiting outside in the passageway. He climbed the short steel ladder leading up into the attack center, and looked around. The watch was in place, planesman, helmsman, diving officer, conning officer. They greeted him normally. The word was not yet out, then. He swept the gauges quickly. The boat was on level keel, depth 85 meters, on a southerly heading, away from the dangerous contact to the northwest. The Musaid went to the diving officer's position, and stood behind the planesmen.

"Report," ordered the Captain, taking his station near the periscope well.

"Depth 85 meters, trim stable, on one shaft, speed 3 knots, quiet condition two established," reported the watch officer, a young Palestinian. The Palestinians made the best officers, he reflected; smart, quick, and eager. And vengeful. That was important.

"We have one contact of interest," the watch officer continued. "It appears to be a destroyer to our north and west, with sonar active."

The Captain walked over to the sonar stack. "Audio," he commanded.

The operator, a Bedouin boy whose ears were the most discriminating in the whole submarine force, was listening on headphones. Continuing to concentrate, he reached up and flipped a switch. Immediately the full spectrum of the ocean's sound flooded the control room, the hissing susurration of the sea itself, the clicking and snapping of marine life, and there, in the distance, the distinctive ri-i-i-i-ng of a searching active sonar. The Captain cursed silently.

"Audio off," he ordered. He turned to the watch officer, noticing that the Deputy had come to the control room.

"Did he approach pinging, or did he just suddenly start up from his current position?"

"We detected the screwbeats of an approaching ship, along with those of other shipping; there are many ships coming and going from the river," replied the watch officer. "Suddenly, this one began to ping."

The Palestinian looked over at the Deputy; he seemed to be aware that this exchange was out of the ordinary.

The Captain cursed aloud. That meant that this warship had come out silently, and then had begun to look for something. If the ship had come out from its base pinging, it would signify no more than an operational testing of their sonar. To have one come out and begin pinging in the very area where they may have been seen meant something else entirely. It had to be the fishing boat. They must have been seen.

"Make your course east, 090, into the Gulf Stream. When we encounter the sidewall temperature boundary layer, remain in that layer, and turn south, away from this destroyer. Maintain present depth."

"It shall be done, Captain."

The watch officer snapped out quick orders to the helmsman. The submarine, dead silent when running on its batteries, heeled very slightly as she came around to port. The watch officer was using his head—no large rudder angles, and therefore no residual vortex left in the water for the enemy sonar to find. The Captain nodded approvingly.

The Captain went back over to the sonar console, and tapped lightly on the petty officer's headphones. Without a word, the petty officer took them off and passed them back to the Captain, who put them on. He listened intently, absorbing the ping pattern and frequency.

"What model sonar is this?" he asked the petty officer.

"American, SQS-23," replied the young man. "An old sonar." The boy had been to the Soviet Navy sonar school at Sevastopol, and even the Russians had been impressed. He had acutely discriminating hearing, and genuinely loved his work.

So: this must be an older ship, thought the Captain. The newer American ships carried lower frequency sonars, which they rarely used in the active, pinging mode. The Russians said that the Americans were using exclusively passive sonar now, letting their sophisticated computers listen to the low frequency spectrum, to the inaudible sounds made by motor bearings and pump motors and transmitted as tiny vibrations through the hull into the dark sea, where they travelled for miles due to their relatively long acoustic wave lengths. Most navies had also recognized the beaconing effect an active sonar created: the pinging could always be heard by the submarine at nearly twice the distance that the submarine could be detected by the active sonar. Active pinging indicated an older ship, probably with poor or even no passive capability. Twin screws meant a destroyer, not a frigate. A frigate would have been passive. An old destroyer also meant no accursed helicopters. Their luck might still be holding.

He forced himself to concentrate, to squeeze out the background noises of the sea. The frequency of the pinging was even, not rising or falling. No discernible doppler effect. So, they were in omnidirectional mode. Not cued. Just...looking. And not going silent periodically to listen on passive equipment. No matter, he thought. For a diesel boat on the battery, passive was a waste of time. Compared to their nuclear powered sisters, with their noisy high pressure pumps and whining steam turbines, the diesel-electric submarines were quieter than the ambient noise of the sea itself. The only time they made noise detectable by passive equipment was when they went fast submerged and the screws cavitated, or when they used their diesel engines to recharge their batteries. Then they had to either surface, or to stick up a special pipe called a snorkel pipe, to get air for the diesel engines. The Foxtrot class could stay submerged for up to ten days without recharging the huge battery banks stuffed under and aft of the control room, but if they did the batteries would be seriously depleted.

The requirement to snorkel every few days was one of the reasons he had picked this area to hide in. The Jacksonville naval fleet operating areas were filled with diesel powered fishing boats, pleasure boats, and transiting merchant shipping. A submarine's diesel engine breathing on the snorkel at night would sound like any other marine diesel to a listening passive sonar. As long as the oceans were filled with small and medium sized marine diesel engines, it was perfect cover, unless one happened to broach in full view of a fishing boat. He felt like rousting out the morning's watch officer and shooting him right now, while this destroyer was up there, except that the enemy would probably hear it.

He pulled off the earphones and handed them back. It was time to think. Like any submariner, he wanted to put the scope up and take a look, but that would be madness now, at the beginning of a search. Perhaps later, say at 0300, when their pursuers would be tired and bored.

"The layer?"

"Sir, the layer is at 25 meters, with a secondary gradient at 80 meters."

The Captain pondered. Good, two layers. The young Palestinian had again used his head, maneuvering the sub right beneath the second layer. The ocean tended to settle itself into horizontal thermal layers, especially near the surface, like a vast, liquid parfait. In the warm waters off northern Florida, the first layer was normally only 20 to 25 meters deep, containing water whose temperature hovered around 80 degrees. The next layer was much colder, and its thickness varied. The layers beneath the first two became progressively colder and denser. The boundaries between the layers acted like the boundary between air and water, refracting the probing sound beams of an active sonar, much like the image of a fish seen just beneath the surface in a pond is not where the fish actually is. The layer effect could thus be used to mask an object that was able to maneuver to keep the layer between itself and a searching sonar. With two layers, they were safe, and would be even safer once they merged with the vertical sidewall of the Gulf Stream, where there would be vertical thermal gradients as well as the two horizontal ones.

He pursed his lips. Maybe then they would slip back, and take a look at this destroyer. He had an urge to see who his pursuer was, if indeed he was being hunted at all. It was risky, but in these sonar conditions even the active sonar up there would be blind beyond a few thousand meters. The sound conditions were impossible. He made his decision. They would listen for awhile. Keep their distance from the destroyer, and remain invisible in the swirling layers on the edge of the great ocean current. If they could find another surface contact to mask the radar image of their periscope, he would drift back, staying east of the destroyer, close to the shield of the turbulent Gulf Stream, and take a look. Practice; yes, it would be practice for the day when the Coral Sea came home. Practice makes perfect. Even the Americans believed in that.

He saw that the Deputy was watching him carefully. The Musaid had taken up his station in the control room, as he had promised. The Captain decided to leave the control room, to let the word be spread.

"I will be in my cabin," he announced. "I will have supper in my cabin. Begin passive bearing analysis; I want to know his range. Call me if the pinging appears to be closing, or if there is sustained doppler."

"Yes, Captain," responded the watch officer.

"You have placed her well, Yassir," he said to the watch officer.

"Thank you, Captain."

SIX

USS Goldsborough, Mayport Fleet operating areas; 2000, 10 April

"Captain's in Combat," sang out a chorus of voices, as Mike stepped through the door into the darkened Combat Information Center. The ASW team was in place around the central plotting table, where the search plan had been laid out for the night's operations. He walked over to the table. The Weapons officer, who was the Evaluator, greeted him.

"Evening, Cap'n, Sir. We're at twelve knots, on the fourth leg of the expanding square search." He pointed to a spot of light that was projected from underneath the glass top of the plotting table. The spot marked the Goldsborough's true position relative to the search plan track that had been traced out on the sheet of plotting paper taped to the top of the table.

"Sensors status?"

"SPS-10 surface search is in radiate; SPS-40 air search is in standby, TACAN is in standby, all fire control radars are in standby, the sonar is active, the fathometer is off, and the Pathfinder radar is radiating."

"Very well. What are the sonar conditions."

"Piss poor and getting worse," said the Evaluator, with a wry grin. "All we're doing out here is pissing off a million snapping shrimp, and probably energizing a few acres of bioluminescence around the bow."

"Don't sugar-coat it, now, Weps. Tell it to me straight."

The Weapons Officer shook his head as the plotters grinned around the table. He pointed to the raypath diagrams glimmering on the screen of a PC set up next to the table.

41

"We've got a layer at 80 feet, and another layer at around 240 feet. To the east, about ten miles by our navi-guesser's best estimate, is the western edge of the Gulf Stream. Injection temperature is still holding at around 76 degrees, but we get an occasional whiff of 82 degree water, so we're right on the edge of the boundary layer. That means vertical layering. The sonar girls tell us we're getting max reverberation."

The Captain pulled a three legged stool over to the table, and sat down, his large frame perched precariously. The rest of Combat was quiet, as the watch team concentrated on the ASW picture. The large, plexiglass plotting boards used for displaying the air picture were dark. The plotting table was manned by two enlisted people, a plotter, who marked the ship's position at three minute intervals to construct the trace, and a phone talker, who communicated with sonar control four decks below. The Evaluator, who was also on sound-powered phones, was linked to the conning officer on the bridge, and the sonar watch officer down in sonar control.

"Any surface contacts?"

"Just a few—night fishermen, the occasional merchie going in or out of Jax, and the usual collection of pleasure boats, smugglers, and dope runners. Nothing exotic."

"Any other Navy around?"

"One K-mart frigate fifteen miles north, doing a full power run, according to the weekly op-order. Otherwise, nothing. We are the proud owners of the op-areas tonight."

"Us and our submarine."

The Weapons Officer snorted. "Yes, Sir. Right. Our very own submarine. Captain, if there is a sewer pipe around here, and he wants to hide, he's gonna stay hid."

The Captain leaned over the plot, absorbing the picture of surface contacts and the planned search track. The expanding square search was the classic technique if one had only the vaguest notion about where the object of the search might be. If properly computed, the track would cover the maximum area in a minimum of time. The ship would proceed two miles in an easterly direction, then turn right to the south and go three miles, and then turn to the west, and go four miles, and so on. The track was adjusted for the predicted effective sonar range, so that a broad path on either side of the ship would be swept for submerged contacts throughout the night.

"It kind of depends, Weps," mused the Captain. "If it's a nuke, the only clue we're going to get would be hydrophone effects if he happened to kick it in the ass within range of our sensors. Since we're banging away in the active mode, he would have to be pretty dumb to give us that much noise. If it's not a nuke, then our chances of detecting him are slim to none, unless he does one of three things: go fast and cavitate, stick a scope up to see who's out here pinging, or, stick a snorkel mast up sometime tonight to put some amps in the can."

"Yes, Sir, but all of that assumes there is, or ever was, a sub out here, and, second, that he's still somewhere nearby the original sighting position."

They were interrupted by an announcement over the 29MC system, a voice activated announcing circuit controlled by the sonar operator.

"Sonar contact, bearing one-one-zero, range, 2450, doppler no, definition medium, classification to follow."

The plotting crew marked the contact in red pencil on the trace, and waited for the follow-up classification.

"Bridge reports bearing is clear on the surface," said the Weapons officer. Then the 29-MC came to life again.

"Sonar control evaluates the contact as non-sub; probably marine life."

Everyone relaxed. The Captain stood up.

"We'll probably see a lot of that throughout the night. Maintain that track—it's as good as any. Have the surface search radar watch pay close attention to pop-up contacts, especially on the pathfinder. I'll be in my sea cabin."

"Aye, aye, Sir."

The Captain left the CIC, and went back out to the bridge. It was a clear night, the sky glittering with stars, and a gibbous moon behind them. The night air was twenty degrees cooler than it had been at midday. The lights of some of the surface contacts twinkled on the horizon. By morning there would be mists and fog as the dew point reached saturation over the warm expanse of the Gulf Stream to the east. He climbed into his chair for a few minutes.

Who could this be, he wondered, if indeed there is a pigboat out there. Submarines simply did not come and go out here. American subs made transits all the time, providing exercise services to the surface units and the squadrons of ASW aircraft at Naval Air Station Jacksonville on their way to other business. Submarines from allied nations sometimes made a trans-Atlantic crossing to participate in fleet exercises, but this was fairly rare. The fisherman's report made it sound like the sub had been seen on the surface. A U-boat. That suggested a conventional diesel-electric boat, as opposed to a nuke which almost never would come to the surface—there was simply no need. And, the fisherman had reported a submarine, not a periscope.

The Bosun mate brought him a paper cup of coffee, two sugars, no cream, as he liked it. Murmuring thanks, he settled back into his chair. So, a diesel boat. Whose diesel boat? And what was it doing out here, practically in the Gulf Stream? Jacques Cousteau got himself a sub, maybe? Doing some marine research? The whole thing didn't compute. The Soviets wouldn't send a diesel boat across the Atlantic for some offshore intel work—a nuke attack boat was more like it, and Navy intelligence kept a pretty good handle on where the Soviet nukes were operating.

There was another announcement of a sonar contact, followed moments later by the same classification of marine life. The Gulf Stream was like the aorta of the Atlantic, thrusting a teeming flood of living organisms up the east coast of the United States to sustain a food chain that stretched from Florida to beyond Iceland. But it was no place to do active ASW, he thought. Like listening for a single conversation in the crowd at a football game. The swirl of marine life, the surging canyon of water moving north at up to three knots, and the kaleidoscope of temperature gradients refracted and deflected the sound waves from their sonar, creating three dimensional shadow zones in the sea in which a large object could hide with impunity. An active sonar in these conditions was like a boom-box in a deep canyon. As he well knew, the submarine, which lived in that environment instead of trying to look into it, had a much clearer picture of what it looked like than a surface ship, which had to rely on hourly bathythermograph soundings to plot the ocean structure beneath them. He sighed out loud. They would play the game, find nothing, and go back in. A perfect assignment for a couple of has-beens, Montgomery and Goldsborough.

He reflected on the twilight of his naval career. It hadn't always been like this. He had graduated from his mid-western university with a degree in business administration, compliments of a Navy ROTC scholarship, and varsity letters in football. His parents had fairly burst with pride at his commissioning, the first of their family to gain an officer's gold bars. He had been assigned to a destroyer in the Pacific Fleet, where he had enjoyed the exotic pleasures of being a single, junior officer in the exotic Orient for his first year in the fleet. He had married a beguiling blonde from San Diego in his second year in the ship, but then Vietnam had come over the western horizon like a fast moving storm, and the deployments for his destroyer had turned into a gruelling grind of six months in the States, and seven, sometimes eight months overseas on the shore bombardment gunline off north and south Vietnam.

His young marriage had become a casualty of the deployment cycle. His new bride soon tired of being left alone when Mike had gone to sea for months on end. He had come back from a deployment to Vietnam to find letters from a lawyer informing him that his wife had filed for divorce on grounds of mental cruelty, and was planning to remarry, to said lawyer, no less. She had moved out of their rented apartment in San Diego, leaving behind his civilian clothes, a hi-fi set and his budding book collection to gather dust until he got back. The lawyer letters told him that she wanted nothing from him in the way of alimony or possessions; her new husband would see to the better things in life. His one attempt to contact her had resulted in a severely strained conversation with what seemed to be a perfect stranger. He had been stunned by her efficient, calculated departure, and had not been overly consoled by the observations of more experienced officers in the ship who told him he had gotten off lightly.

In reaction to the sudden, almost surgical demise of his marriage, he had thrown himself into his career with the dedication of someone with nothing else to do with his life. After a second, two year ship tour, he had volunteered for the riverine gunboat force that was forming up for operations in-country, against the advice of his Executive officer and Captain, who looked on the brown water Navy as a career sideline. But after nearly four years in the increasingly paper bound ship Navy, the excitement and novelty of the river gunboats had drawn him into the exotically alien land war in southeast Asia. Instead of doing his war from the safety of a ship offshore, with three meals a day at the wardroom table, clean sheets and fresh laundry, and off-hours of paperwork, he would be on the ground in the thick of things.

His first night fire-fight in a narrow waterway of the notorious Rung Sat secret zone had disabused him of any notions of being simply out on some kind of Hollywood adventure. The sudden roar of machine gun fire flashing out at his boats from the black jungle ten feet on either side of him, the crash of shattering windshields amidst the whining buzz of bullets, the rain of hot brass casings into the pilothouse from the twin fifties mounted above, and the screams of wounded men afloat and in the bush ashore had shocked him into the reality of close combat, and nothing was ever the same after that night. He had completed his full thirteen month tour, grimly intent on surviving and ensuring that his boats and his people also survived.

Following his in-country tour, he was assigned to another destroyer on the gunline for two years, and then a missile cruiser, where he made

45

Lieutenant Commander and added another row of ribbons to his already impressive collection, the fruits of six years service in the seemingly everlasting Vietnam conflict. At the end of his second year in the cruiser there came a collision at sea in which he had a role, followed by transfer to yet another ship in the Pacific fleet. By the end of his twelfth year in the Navy, he had accumulated more years on sea duty than most officers would see in an entire twenty year career, and the Bureau of Personnel had wanted him to come ashore. But the stigma of the collision at sea was obstructing his selection for an Executive Officer assignment, so he wrangled yet another sea-going job, this time on a carrier group staff. Two years on the staff had broadened his horizons immensely and helped to wipe away the stain of the collision. He had been selected on his next to the last look for a Lieutenant Commander Exec's job, to which he proceeded directly from the carrier group staff and six months at the prospective XO school in Newport.

The Exec's job had come in the Atlantic Fleet for a change, but the deployments ground on. His ship made two, six-month deployments to the Mediterranean, where the emphasis seemed to be on fresh paint, polished brass, and shined shoes in contrast to the rough and ready Pacific Fleet after years of wartime operations. It was a stark contrast to the freewheeling days of Vietnam, and Mike Montgomery's rough edges became evident despite the paternal attentions of two successive Commanding Officers, who had tried with varying degrees of success to align Mike's professional talents with the niceties of professional political behavior as he drew closer to command selection. His second CO talked him into taking his first shore assignment in nearly fifteen years, at the headquarters of the Atlantic Fleet destroyer force, with the intent of exposing Mike to what the Captain called the grownup side of the Navy.

Mike spent three years at the headquarters, where he was promoted to full Commander, but not selected for command until the third year, and then only because his Admiral was President of the selection board. After the board's command selection list had been published, the Chief of Staff had shared some of the Admiral's observations about Mike's record, pointing out that his seagoing career, and especially his war record, was stronger than almost all the other candidates, but that the taint of the collision at sea, combined with Mike's own intolerant views towards the Navy's vast shore establishment had almost done him in. He advised Mike not to try to negotiate for a better offer when he was finally offered a command, but to take it and run because there would not be a second offer. Which was how he had ended up on Oldy Goldy, a ship that was headed for decommissioning in less than a year, and was out looking for a U-boat, of all things, in the Florida op-areas this fine night. He sighed again. He began to look forward to the weekend as he rose from his chair.

"I'll be in my sea cabin, OOD."

"Aye, aye, Sir. Do you want to be called for contacts?"

"Only if they classify it as possible sub, Frank."

"Aye, aye Sir. We probably won't be calling you then."

"Probably not."

SEVEN

The submarine Al Akrab, submerged; 0315, 11 April

The Captain, his lean face tightened by lack of sleep, made his way through the central passageway to the control room. The dim red lighting rendered his face in spectral hues of gray with darker tones under his eyes. He climbed the short ladder into the control room, and at once perceived the change in atmosphere. The watchstanders tensed in their chairs, and only the watch officer, who was the same individual who had broached the boat the previous morning, would look directly at him, his face a pale mask. The word had been put out. In one corner of the control room was the Musaid, hunkered down on a stool like a stone palace dog, watching the actions of the planesman and helmsman. He did not look like he had slept, either.

"Report."

The watch officer cleared his throat nervously.

"Sir: the enemy ship remains to our west by northwest. Passive angle tracking constructs a current range of about 22,000 meters. Sir: this is a composite range. He is executing a search pattern, which at times takes him farther away, and then later brings him back in our direction. My depth is 100 meters; the secondary layer descended one hour ago. There is 92 percent power available in the battery. Sir."

The young officer, of Bedouin and Egyptian extraction, was perspiring, even though the control room was no more than 80 degrees.

The Captain did not acknowledge the report, but stared instead directly at the watch officer. The rest of the watch, aware of the lengthening silence, remained intent on their instruments. A full half-minute passed before the Captain unlocked his eyes from those of the watch officer, having reinforced the death threat which had already pressurized the entire crew some hours before.

"Surface summary."

"Sir," continued the watch officer, swallowing and glancing at a status board above the torpedo control console. "There are five active surface contacts, excluding the enemy destroyer. They appear to be stationary, or drifting, possibly fishing. Only two have engine noises."

"Very well. Is the destroyer approaching now on an easterly leg of his pattern?"

"Yes, Sir. By the plot, he should come within 15,000 meters, and then turn away, to the south. He appears to expand his square by 2000 to 3000 meters on each leg."

His Deputy Commander came into the control room from back aft. The watch must have called him, the Captain decided. The Deputy did not look well; the night time did not agree with him.

"Where is the nearest surface contact?" he continued.

"Bearing 010, range approximately 4000 meters. No engine noises for about one hour, but there is a generator running. Sir: all of our ranges are derived from passive tracking. They will be inaccurate."

"Yes, I understand. We are at 100 meters, after all."

He looked down again at the plot. The plotting crew stood back to give him a clearer view. The Deputy remained to one side.

"These are my orders," declared the Captain. "Come to course 010. I wish to move to the vicinity of that contact, and to pass beyond him, so that his sound line is between us and the destroyer. Then I will come to periscope depth and take a look, but only after the destroyer makes his next turn to the south. We must pay strict attention to the doppler from his screws to detect the turn. I will use the contact to radar-mask my periscope. Maintain your present depth; increase speed gradually to 8 knots, slow to 3 knots when we have passed under the contact."

"Aye, Sir."

As the orders began to flow, the Captain went over to the sonar stack.

"Focus the receiver to 010; I wish to listen to this contact."

The sonar operator complied, and then handed up his earphones. The Captain slid them over his ears, and concentrated. The putt-putt sound of a small diesel generator was audible on the bearing, along with another noise, a grinding sound. He pulled off the earphones.

"Amend my orders: come to course 035; get past the contact in two legs. He is operating deep nets—I can hear the winches."

The watch officer acknowledged, with a look of further embarrassment. He should have checked for net winch sounds in making his original classification of the contact. The submarine might have become entangled in deep sea fishing nets.

48

"Deputy."

"Sir?"

"Set attack condition one."

"Sir! *Musaid!* Pass the word. Attack condition one!"

The Musaid rose immediately, and hurried forward. Unlike on surface ships, where the general quarters alarm would have rousted everyone out of their racks, the word to set the attack condition was passed quietly and quickly by word of mouth, so as not to transmit any dangerous sounds into the listening sea. Within five minutes, all of the attack positions were manned up, and the boat was closed off into four watertight compartments. The temperature in the control room began rising immediately. The weapons officer took charge of the attack director console. The Deputy Commander took over the main plot, and two chief petty officers manned the planes. The Musaid resumed his station to supervise the planesmen.

"Put the fishing boat's noise on the speaker," ordered the Captain.

There was a crackling hiss from the speaker above the sonar operator's console, which was punctuated suddenly by the distant ping of the destroyer's sonar. The Captain put his hand on the sonar operator's shoulder.

"Tell me when you think we have gone past the contact to the north. Raise your hand when you hear the bearing shift."

The operator nodded soundlessly, intent on his earphones.

The submarine was headed in a northeast direction, attempting to pass the fishing boat to port. Once past, they would turn due north, thereby executing a dogleg, to keep the fishing boat between themselves and the destroyer. Once the destroyer made its turn to the south, the submarine could come up to expose a periscope. The fishing boat would mask any sonar echoes in the direction of the submarine, and by turning away from them, the destroyer was pointing his screws in their direction, thus fouling his own listening sectors. Any radar echoes off the periscope would be confused with those returning from the fishing boat. The Captain reviewed his plan, and found it workable.

He listened to the pinging sound, audible over the putt-putt and winch noises from the fisherman, and waited for a doppler shift in the ping. As the destroyer closed in from eleven miles, the frequency of the pinging would appear to the trained ear to rise; once he turned away, it would decrease, much like a train whistle does as the train rushes by a stationary observer. The Captain was counting on three factors to keep him undetected. It was just past 0300 in the morning, the daily ebb of human performance and acumen. The fishing boat would provide a dis-

49

traction, both on radar and sonar. And as the destroyer turned south, she would point her screws and rudders in the direction of the submarine, increasing her own self noise in the very sector where the contact, if made, would be. The sonar operator raised his hand.

The Captain nodded. "Come to 000, speed seven knots. Make your depth 50 meters, gradually."

The boat took on a slight up angle, and heeled perceptibly to star-board as she came around in the left turn. The atmosphere in the control room had become very stuffy, with all the men at their battle stations. Everyone seemed to be wide awake, intent on their instruments.

"Request permission to open outer doors," said the weapons officer.

"Denied. I want no noises until I know he has turned south."

The Captain knew that if the destroyer did happen to have a wide-band passive array, the sound of the outer torpedo doors opening would print out in a heartbeat, as long as the array had a clear bearing on which to listen. He had to get the fisherman into proper blocking position before doing anything that would give up an unmistakable classification to their opponent. He knew that ASW was full of ambiguity; it was always best to create some more whenever that was possible.

"Captain, the doppler."

The Captain listened. The doppler shift in the pinging was clearly audible. The destroyer had turned south, away from them.

"Bearing to the destroyer."

"250 degrees."

"Bearing to the fisherman."

"300 degrees, Sir."

"Make your depth 25 meters; speed three knots. Maintain present heading. Deputy, inform me when the bearings are within five degrees of each other."

"Sir."

They waited for the tactical geometry to develop. The Captain watched the depth gauge, as the senior chief brought her smoothly up to 25 meters, five meters shy of periscope depth.

"Bearing spread."

"Twenty-two degrees," answered the Deputy.

"Very well." They waited some more. The Captain tried to gauge the attack crew's emotional state, but everyone was fixed on his console or station. If his edict had indeed been promulgated, it was having no visible effect now. This was the superbly trained crew he remembered from the weeks before departure, when they had exercised and exercised until everyone was dragging.

"Nine degrees, spread, axis is 245."

"Very well, come to course 065; make your depth 20 meters. Now you may open outer doors forward."

The submarine swung around slowly to the new course. This would put the destroyer directly astern of her, but it would also keep the fishing boat on the same bearing as the destroyer.

"Fishing boat entering the baffles," reported the sonar operator.

The maneuver to line up the submarine, the fishing boat, and the destroyer had put the destroyer and the fishing boat in the submarine's sonar deaf zone directly aft, where the propellers were. Both the destroyer and the submarine were pointing their deaf zones at each other.

"Very well. Depth."

"Twenty two meters; approaching twenty meters," responded the Musaid. "The boat is stable. Twenty one meters. Preparing to trim. Trimming forward."

Pumps whined in the bilges as seawater was transferred to bow trim tanks to level her out at periscope depth.

"Twenty meters."

"Up scope." The Captain bent down to wait for the viewing handles as the shiny brass tube rose silently on its hydraulics. He stood on the bow side of the optics, facing directly aft down the bearing of the destroyer. When the optics appeared from the well, he grabbed the viewing handles, and folded them down. His eyes were focused in the optics when the scope broke the surface above.

The first thing he saw was the fishing boat, a good sized shrimper, with white lights shining down from her booms into the water, and large lines leading aft.

"Range to the fisherman, is, mark!" He had focused the optics stereo-optically on the shimmering image of the fishing boat; the focus was translated by prism angulation to an estimated range, which appeared on the side of the periscope control dial.

"10,000 meters estimated range," read out a plotter.

He looked in vain for the destroyer, but the white lights adorning the fishing boat booms blinded him. He quickly walked the periscope 360 degrees to make sure there was nothing else up there. The scope remained dark. There was only faint moonlight showing through light cloud cover. He swung the optics back to the fisherman, and then to one side. There, one white light. He focused the optics, and clicked on high power.

"Range to the destroyer is, mark."

"12,500 meters."

"Target angle is 240."

"240. Plot started."

"Enter notional speed ten knots; course is 180."

"Plot is running."

"Very well." He scanned the image in high power magnification.

"Come left, make your course 300."

He needed to move the fisherman to the left in order to get a better look at the destroyer. The white lights were still too bright. Slowly, the warship's image materialized. It was a large destroyer, but not one of the new ones, with their boxy, voluminous shapes. This one had masts, and at least two large gun mounts. He was seeing a port quarter, almost a stern aspect. The key feature were the two guns on the back of the super-structure. A Forrest Sherman class destroyer. Old indeed. That explained the active sonar.

"Target angle is 223; range is—mark it."

"13,800 meters."

"Classification is Forrest Sherman class destroyer; pendant number is not visible. Down scope!"

The periscope sank into its well with a hiss as the Captain stood back.

"Come right to 090, make your depth 100 meters, make turns for ten knots."

It was time to leave, to seek the turbid depths of the Gulf Stream again. The scope had been up long enough to have attracted some attention on a radarscope. He could visualize what was going on in the destroyer. If they had seen the brief radar pop-up contact, they would argue about it, consider the presence of the fishing boat, the possibility of radar ringing, and then develop a consensus, and then call their Captain. It would take time. They would be long gone.

"Closing outer doors," declared the weapons officer.

It was standard procedure to prepare to make an attack when classifying an enemy warship. More than one submarine had been sunk in the act of taking a look at a prepared and alerted destroyer. There was nothing like a torpedo to disrupt such an attack, even one that was just fired into the bearing wedge of the approaching destroyer. His attack team had set up and maintained a firing solution on the destroyer the entire time he was at periscope depth.

"Stand down from attack condition one," the Captain ordered. The word went out at once over telephone circuits, and the men began to secure their consoles, reducing the crowded control room to the basic maneuvering watch. The Deputy approached.

"It was smoothly done."

"Yes, it was. They have not lost their edge. Now we will see if this destroyer is a hunter or a target."

He eyed the depth gauge, which was passing 85 meters as he spoke. Nearly back to two layer protection, and acoustic safety. The old hull creaked under the increasing strain of sea pressure. The Captain frowned. One of the propeller shafts had a rumble in it. They listened to the pinging sounds from the distant destroyer. The doppler was consistently down. He was not turning around.

"A target," declared the Captain, contempt in his voice. Allah be praised were the words echoing in his mind, however.

EIGHT

USS Goldsborough, Mayport Naval Station; Friday, 11 April, 1500

Mike watched impatiently from the bridge wing as the harbor pilot talked his tugs through the mooring evolution. Mayport was a very crowded mooring basin, with ships nested three and sometimes four deep at each berth, with only fifty feet from the bow of one to the stern of the nest ahead. There was little maneuvering room for the practice of traditional landings, which meant that most ships came into the basin, stopped, tied up a tug at each end, and then let a harbor pilot use the tugs to push the ship sideways into one of the tight berths. Goldsborough was moving compliantly, if slowly, sideways alongside one of the new Perry class frigates. The frigate's Skipper was out on his bridge wing, watching the evolution. He waved to Mike, his voice echoing in the rapidly narrowing space between the steel sides of the ships.

"Have a nice trip?" he called.

"Yeah, it was OK," responded Mike. "Until yesterday; then we had to go out to the edge of the Stream to look for some unident. Waste of time, naturally."

The Goldsborough landed softly against the camels, the floating wooden fenders positioned between ships in a nest. The camels groaned as they were squeezed by Goldsborough's 4000 tons for a moment.

"Yeah, I saw the message in my traffic yesterday," replied the other Captain. "Somebody smoking dope."

The line handlers passed over Goldsborough's mooring lines to the other ship, where sailors quickly made them fast to bitts on deck.

"At least dope. Probably whiskey-soaked dope. Anyway, nothing seen or heard of any pigboats. Like I said, waste of time."

"Sir, the ship is moored," called the Exec from inside the pilothouse. "Request permission to secure the special sea and anchor detail."

"Permission granted," Mike replied. He waved at the other CO, and went back inside his own pilothouse, stopping next to his chair. "What've we got for the rest of the afternoon?"

"Well," said the Exec, consulting his notebook. "We have to get the plant shut down so those boilers can begin cooldown. Porkchop says he has some stores on the pier. And you wanted to go over and call on the Commodore. Other than that, we'll do a freshwater washdown tomorrow with the duty section—Saturdays are good for that—and let the guys go on liberty as soon as the stores are onboard."

"Right, OK. I'll give the Commodore a call as soon as they get the phones hooked up, and walk over. Verify that Linc was able to make those tapes, so I can tell the Commodore we got some good out of this little wild goose chase."

"Aye, aye, Sir."

Mike took a last look around at the berth and the mooring lines before going below. In his cabin, he changed into a clean set of wash khakis, and replaced his seagoing boondocks with shiny black corfam shoes. The Commodore, Captain Eli Aronson, Commander Destroyer Squadron Twelve, was a stickler for military appearance, of both ships and CO's. Captain Aronson was the immediate boss for every destroyer commanding officer in Mayport, reporting, in turn, to the Admiral, who was the Commander of Cruiser-Destroyer Group Twelve. Although Aronson was a four striper, he was called Commodore because he commanded a squadron of ships. There were two other Commodores in Mayport, one who commanded the squadron of frigates, and the other who commanded the Squadron of Service force ships, replenishment ships, fleet tugs, and the single repair ship.

The phone rang. An IC-man was testing the circuit, and reported that the shore lines were now open. Mike called the Commodore's office, and was told that Captain Aronson was available. He hung up, grabbed his Commander's hat with the brass scrambled eggs on the visor, and left the cabin, walking directly aft through the narrow passageway which led out onto the midships replenishment deck. His crew was busily pulling aboard the heavy, black shore power cables, which, when connected, would plug the ship's 2000 amp electrical load into the pier, thus permitting the main steam plant to be shut down for maintenance. He nodded to the men as they heaved and wrestled with the heavy cables, and continued aft on the weatherdecks until he reached the quarterdeck area, where there was the usual crowd of people present whenever a ship came back into port. The Officer of the Deck saw him coming and cleared the quarterdeck so that the Captain could get through the milling crowd. The ship's loudspeakers blared out four gongs, and the words, "Goldsborough, departing." Mike saluted the Officer of the Deck and then the American flag flapping at the stern, and then walked across the narrow brow to the next ship, whose own announcing system was proclaiming "Goldsborough, crossing," to the world at large.

He crossed the frigate's quarterdeck, and walked down her brow to the pier itself. The Commodore's office was up on a small, man-made hill above the piers, less than a half block away. The office had a large plate glass window on its pier side, with darkened one-way glass. Mike was conscious of the probability that the Commodore was sitting up there at his desk watching him walk down the crowded pier. It was a typical Mayport afternoon, clear, sunny, and hot, with an afternoon breeze pumping some loose papers along the waterfront street. It being Friday, there was already a steady stream of sailors walking down the street with the Captain, their beach outfits in vivid contrast to his pressed khakis and shiny shoes. Hope Himself is in a good mood, thought Mike. He was always a bit nervous when he went to see Captain Aronson, whose mercurial temper was legendary on the waterfront.

He was met in the Commodore's outer office by Commander Bill Barstowe, the Chief Staff Officer of Destroyer Squadron Twelve. Bill was a good friend, which was fortunate, because he was in a position to make life much easier or very much harder for any CO. He had already finished his command tour, and was thus an experienced filter of both good news and bad news to the Commodore.

"Michael," he said, warmly, standing up as Montgomery walked into his office. "How's the deep blue sea, Sir?"

"Deep and blue, Bill. And empty of submarines, I might add."

"Sit down. The Commodore's talking to some guy in Washington. Want some coffee?" He reached for his own mug on the corner of his cluttered desk.

"No thanks; it's almost Miller time. I'm coffee'd out, anyway."

"Right; hang on a minute while I refill."

Mike looked around while Barstowe went to refill his coffee cup. The Chief Staff Officer's desk was literally piled high with paperwork. For all the hassle of being a destroyer commanding officer in the peacetime Navy, it had to beat being a staff officer, even a Chief Staff Officer. Or a Chief of Staff, he thought, darkly. He was still convinced that his nemesis on the Group staff, Captain J. Walker Martinson, III, had been behind the little trip out to the Gulf Stream. Barstowe returned.

"So," he said, sitting down again. "No U-boats lurking out there amongst those upstanding citizens of the real Mayport, our shrimpy friends?"

"Nary a one," replied Mike, stretching his long legs out in front of the overstuffed chair. "We could have made better use of our time back here going cold iron and working steam leaks."

"Yes, Sir, I know. Even the Commodore thought that was a little strange. But the Chief of Staff—"

"I knew it!" exclaimed Mike. "I just frigging knew it. That guy has a hardon for Goldsborough, and takes every opportunity to jerk us around. He's just trying to cut us out of the Fleetex."

Barstowe grinned. "Now, now, you can't make a federal case out of it just because he sent Goldy—you guys were already out at sea, and you are technically duty destroyer this week, until 1600 today as a matter of fact."

Barstowe, along with almost every other Commander on the water-front, knew of the antipathy between Montgomery and Martinson. It was just one of those things—the two officers had taken an instant dislike to one another at their first meeting. It was Mike's bad luck to be one grade junior, and two levels in the chain of command beneath Martinson. Martinson's reputation as a jerk was secure; it was commonly acknowledged that the only thing good about him was his beautiful wife. But the burden of comity was on Mike to get along with his seniors. As the old Navy saying had it, a personality conflict between a Captain and a Commander had two elements: the Captain had a personality, the Commander had a conflict.

A yeoman put his head into the office. "Commodore will see you now, Captain Montgomery."

"Thanks," said Mike. "Bill, be good. See you around this weekend, maybe."

Barstowe stood up. He was a year senior to Montgomery, and also senior by virtue of his staff position, but he affected a reverse rule of military courtesy, calling all the commanding officers Sir, and acting generally as if they were all senior to him instead of the other way around. It was a small flattery, but it was one of the secrets to both his popularity and his effectiveness as the Chief Staff Officer.

"Don't forget, Mike—reception for P-3 guys tonight at 1800. You were planning to be there, right?"

Mike groaned. He had forgotten all about it. On purpose. Another goddamned reception. This one was one of the Admiral's pet rocks—to get the ship drivers and the antisubmarine patrol bomber guys together to build "inter-community spirit". Just what everyone needed on a Friday night. Barstowe was watching, his eyes amused. Mike settled his face into a polite smile.

"Why, of course," he said. "I wouldn't miss it. It will be the perfect cap to a perfect week, talking to a bunch of overpaid aviators. Arrrgh!"

Barstowe laughed, and pointed him down the hall, to the office with the plate glass window. Mike walked past the junior staff officers' cubbyholes, and knocked on the Commodore's door, or actually, door frame. The Commodore had a set of wooden bat-wing doors, reminiscent of a western bar, the legacy of a past incumbent who had tried to make the office look like Chester Nimitz's World War II Pacific Fleet headquarters office.

"Yeah, come in," called the Commodore. Mike went in and walked over to the imitation leather chair positioned exactly in front of the Commodore's large desk. The Commodore did not stand up, nodding instead with his head for Mike to sit down. Eli Aronson had an oversized head and upper body attached to legs which yielded a grand total of five feet, five and one-half inches of overall height when standing very straight. He would have had to crane his neck up several degrees if he stood up to greet someone as tall as Mike. He was Jewish, and pugnaciously proud of it. His hooknosed face reminded Mike of one of the ancient patriarchs, missing only a flowing white beard to bring a picturebook image of Moses to mind. He was reading a message, marking certain lines with a yellow hi-liter, as Mike sat down. He read on for a minute, and then discarded it into a pile of messages. He looked up, fixing Mike with his bright, dark eyes.

"So, a good week at sea? The plant all right?"

"Yes, Sir. Pretty productive, although I've got to chase down some HP drain valve leaks this weekend. We're looking forward to going on the Fleet-Ex."

Aronson nodded. "Yeah, I suspect you are. Beats sitting around here. How about that submarine report—anything to that?"

Mike shook his head. "No, Sir. We discovered the Gulf Stream, but that's about it." His attempt at flippancy appeared to fall flat.

"That's been done, already," said Aronson. "Figured it was a waste of time, but you never know about submarines."

"Did anyone cross check with our guys, or with the intel people, to see if—"

"No," interrupted Aronson. He had a habit of cutting people off in mid-sentence.

"Fisherman reported seeing a sub, and the Coast Guard forwarded it to us. If the Coasties had just called on the phone, we'd have told them to pack it. But they send a formal message through channels, so we send a ship out. You guys file a message closing it out, and we're done. OK?"

"Yes, Sir."

"So, anything else? You coming to this reception tonight, I presume—Admiral's going to be keeping score."

"Yes, Sir," replied Mike, his face neutral. Aronson studied his face.

"You'll be there, but you don't want to be there, do you."

Mike squirmed a little. "Actually, I don't mind; I just—"

"Yeah, stow it. You just don't want to play the game, that's your problem. You're a good enough Skipper, but when it comes to Navy politics, well, you're hopeless."

Mike bridled at that hopeless label. "I thought my job was to be a good Skipper."

Aronson snorted. "Don't give me that 'my job' shit."

He leaned back in his chair, studying Mike for a moment before continuing.

"I'm trying," he said patiently, "to get your ignorant ass promoted. Being a good skipper gets you into the selection boardroom. Being politically adept gets you selected. And that means putting on an enthusiastic face when you show up tonight, and not cutting out after the first thirty minutes like you usually do. You ever gonna get married, by the way?"

This last question caught Mike off guard. "I suppose if the right woman—"

"Yeah, right. OK. So, go get your steam leaks fixed, and get me that closeout message on the street tonight. See you at the club." He picked up a new message, and began to hi-lite it.

Mike got up, and left the office. Halfway down the hall he remembered that he had not told the Commodore about Linc's new environmental conditions system. Barstowe was waiting at the end of the hall.

"Everything OK? Anything I should know?" he asked.

"Yeah, I'm supposed to get married before I come to the club tonight."

Mike jammed his hat on his head and left the staff offices, oblivious to the quizzical look on Barstowe's face.

"Anybody special?" asked Barstowe.

NINE

Commissioned Officers Club, Mayport Naval Station; Friday, 11 April, 1830

Mike stood at the main bar in the Officer's club, nursing a beer. He had come prepared to be bored, and had not been disappointed. The large reception room was already getting hot and stuffy, its air conditioning overwhelmed by the growing crowd of officers in summer whites. The crowd was a mixture of aviators and surface ship drivers. Two thirds of them were trailing wives, and Mike, having nothing better to do, conducted a faintly indifferent appraisal of the women as he scanned the room.

The Admiral, a tall, ascetic looking man in his mid fifties, had just arrived with his wife, creating the appropriate stir amongst the faithful. He was followed closely by the Chief of Staff and his wife. The Admiral's wife was a kindly looking lady, with a ready smile for everyone she met and the ability to convey the impression that she remembered each and every one. The Chief of Staff's wife, on the other hand, was something else again. Mike remembered her from previous official functions. In her case, one could not be indifferent. He was intrigued by her fine dark eyes, which she focused neutrally on a point about five feet ahead of her husband as she accompanied him through the crowded room. If she was conscious of the stares and glances of the room full of men, she gave no indication. He watched her progress through the crowd with her husband, moving with a cool, detached grace, causing almost a ripple effect, like an elegant yacht entering a marina through the crowd of smaller day boats. He wondered how a woman who looked like that had ever hooked up with J. Walker Martinson, III, cold fish non-pareil.

"Now that's worth staring at," said a voice behind him. Mike turned to see who it was. A Commander wearing gold wings on his shirt was looking past him at Diane Martinson.

"Amen to that. Too bad she's taken," he replied.

"I see that look on her face, I have to wonder how often she's being taken. That guy looks a lot more interested in the Admiral than in giving her the time of day, and she's definitely scouting."

Mike laughed. "You can tell all that from twenty feet and a port quarter view?"

The commander smiled. "That dolly is transmitting on the SEX band, my friend. I have a permanent watch on that band, even if I am married."

They both turned back to the bar as the Martinsons disappeared into the crowd of officers and their ladies clustering around Admiral Walker.

"Name's Don Pringle, by the way; I'm skipper of VP-4." Pringle was a handsome man of medium height, with a fierce-looking moustache sprouting aggressively from his tanned face.

Mike shook hands. "Mike Montgomery; CO of Goldsborough."

"Is that one of the Spruance-class ASW ships? I don't recognize the name as one we work with."

"No, we're not really in the ASW game. We specialize in AAW, like in shooting down aircraft. Goldsborough is a straight-stick tin can, with guns."

"Shooting down aircraft! Bite your tongue! No wonder we don't play with you. You guys are dangerous!"

Mike laughed. "We don't shoot down P-3's unless we absolutely can't help it, and then we always pick up the survivors, so there's no break in their per diem..."

"Only communists and other undesireables would have the gall to shoot at, much less hit a P-3, Blackshoe," Pringle responded amiably. "We're much too valuable. Bad enough that the Sov subs are supposedly putting SAMs in their periscopes; we don't need our own tin cans getting hostile. Ready for another beer?"

"Ready as ever. What do you think of this little gathering?"

They moved together down to the bartender's station, snagged two beers, and then made their way to one of the French doors opening out on to a veranda to escape the rising tide of cocktail party noise.

"I think it's an OK idea," said Pringle. "We never really see you guys, except at sea, or on a radio net, or maybe at an exercise prebrief. It gets kinda impersonal, you know? I talked to one guy, skipper of one of the Spruance DD's, and he's going to set up an exchange day, my officers aboard his ship for a day at sea, and then we're gonna let his guys come fly on one of our patrols. Walk a mile in the other poor bastard's moccasins, you know?"

Mike nodded. "Yeah, that's good stuff. We've got all the heloes out here at Mayport, but you guys are all the way over at NAS Jax. Besides, Goldsborough does ASW as sort of an add-on mission; she's a quarter of a century old, and her sonar is strictly an active beast. We're out of it when it comes to sophisticated passive work, and that seems to be the game these days."

Mike was scanning the crowd as he spoke, hoping to catch another glimpse of Diane Martinson, but she was not in sight. He wondered what made Pringle think she was on the prowl.

"Yeah, well, of course, that's all we can do from the airplane," continued Pringle. "Unless we drop a pinger buoy, but we don't do that until we're pretty freaking sure we got the sewerpipe in a box. We use an active pinger, we usually drop a torpedo on the next pass. But before that, we'll work a guy for hours on end, getting him localized. It takes lots of sono-buoys and lots of time and lots of patience."

Mike turned back to the bar. "Yeah, I hate that about ASW. From the ship's point of view you spend hours and hours processing ambiguities, all the time wondering if you really got a guy or a whale."

Pringle nodded. "You know what they say: ASW means anti-submarine warfare; it also stands for awfully slow work."

Mike finished his beer. "Roger that. Look, nice talking to you. I've got to let my boss see that I actually came, and then, with any luck, I'm outa here and on the beach."

"You single? I thought all you blackshoes were married." Pringle looked surprised.

"Free and easy, as the song goes. Which is why I feel the urge to blow this popstand. See you on the radio."

They shook hands again, and Mike turned to find the Commodore. He needed to make his manners to the Admiral, and then convert a trip to the head to a sneakaway into the parking lot, the Commodore's instructions not withstanding. He pushed gently through the crowded room, careful not to take advantage of his relative bulk, and oblivious to the buzz of conversations and the thickening atmosphere from the smokers, greeting fellow CO's as he headed for the second reception room. There he found the Commodore, the Admiral, and the Chief of Staff clustered in one corner, surrounded by mostly surface officers who were trying to look extremely interested in what the Admiral was saying. Since this was business talk, there were no wives in the group. He noticed that the alluring Mrs. Martinson was not around as he joined the small crowd, and eventually worked his way close enough to nod to the Commodore, who acknowledged him with a brief nod of his own, and to say good evening to Admiral Walker. Out of the corner of his eye, he could see Captain Martinson eyeing him, but he decided to ignore him for the moment. The Admiral was asking him a question.

"Well, Captain, did you find any submarines out there last night?"

"No, Sir." He went on to describe the search, emphasizing the wretched sonar conditions in that part of the operating areas, as the officers around them listened attentively. "I think maybe somebody was seeing things," he concluded.

The Admiral nodded. "I suspect that's possible; fishing can be a tedious business."

Captain Martinson broke in. "So can ASW; are you sure you looked hard enough, *Captain* Montgomery?" Martinson pronounced the word "Captain" in a manner designed to let everyone know how improbable he found the title. An officer was always called "Captain" if he were actually in command of a ship, even if his actual rank was only a Lieutenant. Mike turned his head to look directly at Martinson.

"We looked as hard as the report warranted, Chief of Staff."

There was a sudden pause in the surrounding conversations. The Commodore shot Mike an exasperated look from behind the Admiral's right shoulder, confirming Mike's own sudden realization that, once again, he had gone a little too far. The Admiral, aware of the unintended impertinence, gave him an amused smile.

"I'm sure you did your best, Captain. If there really is a sub out there, we'll probably be hearing more about him. Gentlemen, I need a refill. Eli, you look like you're out, too. Come on."

The two senior officers moved away, breaking up the attending circle. Mike turned with the rest of the officers to go, but Martinson wasn't finished.

"Smooth move, there, Montgomery. You just told the Admiral that you make the decisions as to which missions are important and which aren't. How clever of you," he said, with a superior smile on his face.

Mike flushed with anger, mostly with himself for letting his mouth run without his brain being engaged, but he held his tongue. By Navy protocol, Martinson, being senior, could call him by his last name like a sailor if he wanted to, even though it was a deliberate insult for the Chief of Staff to do so. Martinson finished his drink. He was almost as tall as Montgomery, with a receding hairline, and fine, aristocratic features which were marred by the perpetual, faint sneer on his face when talking to subordinates. He was known in the surface ship community as a "killer", one who promoted only his favorites and who killed off their competitors with exquisitely crafted fitness reports. He spoke with an acquired New England accent.

"I understand," he said, "That you live in the actual village of Mayport. As I remember, that's right next to the commercial fishing piers. Perhaps you can speak to some of the commercial fishermen this weekend, and perhaps see what that was all about." He pronounced the word perhaps in the British style, p'raps.

"The Coast Guard," Martinson continued, "Was less than forthcoming. It might be useful to explore the antecedents of this report. Think you can manage that? I mean, if I ask you to do it, will that be sufficiently important?"

He stared down his nose at Mike, as if peering haughtily over reading glasses that were not there. The effect was diluted somewhat by the fact that Mike was taller than the Chief of Staff.

"I think I can manage that, Chief of Staff," said Mike, evenly.

"Oh, very good. Do let us know what you find out."

He gave a frosty smile, turned and walked away to find the Admiral. He had said "us" as if there were a royal triumvirate to whom this minion would report on Monday. Another ship CO who had been standing nearby and listening wagged his index finger gently at Mike as the Chief of Staff strode away.

"You do have the gift of gab, Michael," he said sympathetically, albeit with just a hint of professional relief that someone else was on the Chief of Staff's list. Commander Brian Thomas Duffy had command of a Perry class frigate. He was of medium height, red haired and had a round, red Irish face.

"Win some, lose some," shrugged Mike. "That guy's been on my case since the first time I sent out a message saying the basin gave the ships lousy support."

"Yeah, I remember hearing about that," Duffy said with a chuckle. "That was like, what, over a year ago, wasn't it? It needed saying, but I was glad you said it instead of me."

Mike looked down at him, trying to keep any hint of contempt out of his voice. He had little respect for the go-along guys, the Commanding Officers who chose never to criticize anything, although in his more reflective moments he realized that they were going to get along a lot better than he was. Duffy caught his look.

"Yeah, yeah, I know," he said, finishing his drink. "If more of us bitched, maybe things would get better. But let me ask you—did you get any better support from the base after you blasted them? I'll bet you didn't."

"If everybody keeps quiet," replied Mike. "It never gets better."

"Nope, I think you have it wrong," said Duffy, shaking his head. "It's peacetime. The shore establishment is never going to support the Fleet in peacetime the way they should. It's you that has the unreasonable expectations. All you accomplished was to get yourself some instant notoriety as a troublemaker, and now the big guys treat everything you do with suspicion."

"Perhaps," said Mike. "But I think it's our job as CO's to call a spade a spade."

"Again, I disagree," said Duffy, looking past Mike at someone across the room. "It's our job as Commanders in command to conform to the expectations of our superiors, not piss them off. That way we stand a chance of getting promoted, and thereby gaining a chance of fixing some of the things that are wrong once we get senior enough to do it. I have to go. Take care, Michael."

Mike finished his beer as Duffy walked away. He knew that Duffy was probably right, but it still rankled him. One of his CO's during his XO tour had said the same thing. The Navy is monolithic; it is neither bad nor good—it just is. It succeeds because it makes its officers, especially its commanding officers, conform to a professional standard. You can buck the system if you want to, but be prepared to experience some pain for the privilege.

It was time to go. The Commodore most certainly knew that he had been there. Mission accomplished, sort of, he thought wryly. He made his way through the crowd to a side door, and out into the hall. Some of the party had spilled out into the hallway, slowing him down as he headed for the main entrance to the club. He made a pit stop on the way out. Coming out of the men's room, he spotted the destroyer squadron Chief Staff Officer standing by the front door, in animated conversation with two aviators. He reversed course, and trying to look inconspicuous, walked back down the hall, made a right out through a side patio door, and collided with Diane Martinson.

They touched briefly, and stepped back away from each other in confusion. He was aware of a subtle perfume, and the soft feel of her body. The back of his right hand had momentarily pressed against her belly. They both were startled, and began apologizing simultaneously. He thought of a dozen flippant things to say, but was distracted by her dark, appraising eyes. They stared at each other for one second longer than was appropriate, a visceral, subliminal channel opening briefly between them, and then she half smiled, half frowned, stepped around him and was gone.

He stood there, feeling like a tongue-tied teenager. She had been nearly as tall as he was; probably just her high heels. Part of him wanted to turn around, go after her, apologize again, do something to maintain contact. Then his better judgement reasserted itself, told him to get gone while he could. The Chief of Staff's wife, for Chrissake! He fled through the side door, and went out to the parking lot, a mosaic of images still imprinted on his mind of her disturbing beauty.

He unlocked the door of his car, a white, 1966 Alfa Romeo hardtop coupe, known by aficionados as a "big Alfa". He slid in, and lit off the engine, which came to life with a satisfying vrooming noise. He drove out of the O-club parking lot a little faster than was necessary, aware that the Chief Staff Officer probably had seen or heard him leaving.

What had that woman been doing out there alone on the patio; maybe she had been as bored with the reception as he was. He wished he had been able to keep her there for a moment. He made his way across the base, past the piers and the repair buildings, and out the main gate. Turning right, he drove down past the long fence which bordered the airfield for a mile and a half. The Naval Station itself was collocated with the Mayport Naval Airfield, home to four squadrons of anti-submarine warfare helicopters. The tops of the hangar complex were visible above the palm trees and dense palmetto groves which framed the landing strips. To get to the village of Mayport, he had to drive almost all the way around the perimeter of the naval complex, a distance of some four miles.

Mayport itself was a tiny fishing village at the junction of the St. Johns river and the Intracoastal Waterway. The St. Johns flows north up the east coast of Florida, through the city and port of Jacksonville, and then east to the Atlantic, while the canal-like Intracoastal Waterway parallels the east coast of Florida. The two waterways joined in a Y-junction a few miles inland from the mouth of the St. Johns on the Atlantic. A ferryboat ran from the Mayport side to the opposite side of the St. Johns, to allow the coastal highway to continue up the Florida coast to Georgia.

Several commercial fishing boats were based in Mayport, tied up to aging wooden piers on the Waterway. There was one large seafood restaurant, an historical tourist attraction called Hampton's Fish House, which was perched directly on the point defining the intersection of the river and the Waterway, and right next to the ferry landing. The village of Mayport consisted of a few stores selling bait, tackle, and beer, and one gas station. Between the ferry terminal and the main river were two sandy dirt roads embracing a collection of ramshackle wooden houses. On the other side of the fishing piers lay the Mayport marina.

Mike drove down the hard packed gravel road to the marina, parked, made his way past the marina office and across several floating pontoon piers, and went aboard his houseboat, named the Lucky Bag. As soon as he opened the door, he was greeted by a raucous "Shit-fire!" from a large African grey parrot who was roosting on an A-frame perch in the main lounge. The parrot stretched his neck and began the bowing routine parrots do when greeting their bonded pair mate. Mike dropped his briefcase on the leather room couch, and walked over to the perch. The parrot was dipping and weaving, and Mike bent his head over to one side, and then the other, much to the parrot's delight. They then recited the parrot's repertoire of unsavory language, and, when all the formal amenities were over, he pitched the parrot onto his shoulder board and headed for the bedroom to get out of his Navy uniform and into his marina uniform of khaki swim trunks, a t-shirt, and ancient tennis shoes.

The Lucky Bag was a converted commercial fishing boat, eighty feet in length, with a proportionally deep beam and draft. The interior had been gutted and rebuilt to accommodate a large central lounge amidships, two guest cabins and a bath forward, a galley just aft of the lounge, and a spacious master's cabin which took up the entire after section below deck. The engines had been removed, and the engine room, located beneath the galley area, now contained a diesel generator, an air conditioning plant, and the remaining utilities. The deckhouse had been modified to retain the pilothouse and a companionway ladder to the lounge forward, but the entire after section of deck had been made over into a large, covered, screened in porch area which reached all the way to the stern. With the boat moored bow-in at its pier, the porch overlooked the entire waterway and river junction area.

Mike fixed himself a gin and tonic in the galley, and then he and the parrot went up the after companionway ladder to the porch to watch the sun go down over the river junction. After an evening of serious Navy, and a week at sea, the view from the porch deck was particularly lovely. The western sky over the palm trees across the waterway was filled with red and orange hues and light, stringy clouds. The waterway itself was a shimmering sheen of orange, sparkling light, cut repeatedly by a steady parade of small craft going in both directions. There was a slight onshore breeze from the Atlantic ocean, coming from behind the marina and the naval base hidden in the trees. The screeing noises of the gulls, the puttering hum of small boat engines, and a mixture of music from the radios on passing boats provided a soothing contrast to the metallic environment of a warship, with its tight, confined spaces and atmosphere of anxiety over old machinery and often dangerous evolutions. He found it wonderfully ironic that he could slip out of the Navy entirely by simply stepping onto this old houseboat on the river.

Upriver there came a loud honk of the car ferry's horn as she got underway from the far shore and headed for the Mayport side. The ferry's horn was echoed by the lesser blat of a commercial fisherman standing into the junction. The two skippers were exchanging signals about how they were going to pass in the junction of the two waterways. The St. Johns was navigable to large, ocean-going ships from its mouth next to the naval base all the way up to Jacksonville, which meant that considerable care had to be taken when operating any kind of boat in this busy intersection. Mike put Hooker, as he called the parrot, down on the back of a rocking chair; Hooker promptly cussed him and dropped a bomb on the newspaper that Mike kept spread around the rocker to protect the rattan carpeting. Mike retrieved his binoculars from their box by the companionway door, focused them, and identified the incoming fisherman as the Rosie III. Good, he thought. Chris Mayfield. Now maybe I can get the skinny on this stupid submarine business, as well as some fresh snapper for supper. He put the binocs down and retrieved Hooker; the bird walked down his arm and took a slug of gin and tonic, getting a beakfull and then putting his head back to swallow.

"You're going to get fucked up, there, Bird."

"God Damn!" croaked the parrot, helping himself to one more shot. He wobbled a little on the return trip to Mike's shoulder.

"Idiot bird," grumbled Mike.

Mike left the porch via the port side main deck, and went down the brow to the pier. He waved to a couple of girls who were opening up their boat for the weekend. The big chested blonde invited him to stop by; he acknowledged the invite without actually saying yes or no. With Hooker on his shoulder, he walked across the floating moorings to the sand parking lot, and headed down the dirt road towards the commercial piers.

The Rosie III was docking in a cloud of diesel exhaust and shrieking seagulls, who were anxious for whatever scraps might be coming their way as the crew finished cleaning out the nets. Mike could see old man Mayfield in the door of the boat's pilothouse. Christian Mayfield was about seventy, and he had been fishing almost his entire life on the Jacksonville fishing grounds. He affected a poverty-stricken demeanor, always complaining about the high cost of everything, but Mike happened to know that he owned a third interest in Hampton's, as well as many of the house lots in the village. He normally would not give a Navy officer the time of day, but had been intrigued by Mike's choice of habitat, and his habit of bringing Hooker into the back bar at Hampton's.

The front bar of Hampton's was where the tourists went; the back bar, separated from the main dining room by the kitchens, was reserved for locals, and the bartender, an enormous black man called Siam, made sure that this rule was observed. The day he had moved onto the houseboat, nearly a year and half ago, Mike had decided to check out the action at Hampton's. He had gone into the tourist bar with Hooker on his shoulder. The hostess had been flustered by the bird, and especially after Hooker started up with his salty language. She had told Mike he had to leave because no pets were allowed in the restaurant. Mike had objected on general principles, and then Hooker helped things out by proclaiming a word which genuinely embarrassed the waitress at the top of his durable lungs. The waitress had called Siam, who doubled as bouncer. Upon discovering that the offending customer was almost as big as he was, and being even more intrigued by the parrot's language, Siam had invited Mike to the back bar. He later told Mike he was curious as to the extent of the bird's vocabulary, cursing being something of a fine art in Siam's opinion. Siam and Hooker had compared notes on profanity apparently to Siam's satisfaction. The bartender then tried to pet the parrot, who promptly took a chunk out of his hand, much to the delight of the regulars. Mike had been a local ever since. Thereafter Siam had great fun trying to induce the uninitiated to go down and pet Hooker on the head. He also kept a small, wooden box with a towel stuffed in it under the bar for those occasions when Hooker drank too much and passed out.

Mike used the side entrance near the kitchen into Hampton's, thereby avoiding the fancier front foyer. The back bar was a small, plain room, with only five booths along the water side, and a long bar with a steel foot rail made from the steam exhaust piping of the original ferry, and stools running down the length of the landward side. Most of the long wall on the waterway side was glass, which overlooked a railed deck, and a floating pontoon to which boats could tie up. Waterborne regulars could moor to the pontoon and come directly into the back bar for a beer if they wanted to. Behind and above the bar ran panels of mirrored glass, which let the serious drinkers enjoy the view outside without having to execute dangerous maneuvers on their barstools.

Siam was polishing glasses and ignoring the one other customer when Mike came in. When he spotted Hooker, Siam got out the wooden box and slid it down the bar, and began mixing a gin and tonic for Mike, putting in extra lime. Hooker was partial to lime. Mike took a seat at the end of the bar, and waited for Mayfield. He wondered if he should call the ship, to make sure the shut down of the main plant was going all right. The Chief Engineer would stay aboard until fires were pulled under the two boilers and the ship was on shore power. Another good deal for the snipes, to stay aboard after everyone else went on liberty. He decided to give it another hour, so as not to appear that he was worried about what was going on in the ship, even though he usually was. Mayfield banged through the side door, and yelled for a beer. He spotted Mike and joined him at the end of the bar.

"Hello, you ugly fuckin' bird," he rasped, scowling at Hooker.

"Fuck your Mama," squawked Hooker, aiming a bomb at Mayfield's right boot. Mayfield shied his boot away at the last instant. He smelled of sweat, fish, bourbon and diesel oil in equal proportions.

"Dirty little fucker," he said. "Hey, Siam, this fucking bird just crapped on the deck, for Chrissakes. What kinda place you runnin' here, anyway."

Siam just shook his head; he was not much for conversation. Mike had been letting Hooker suck on the gin and tonic for a few minutes, and the parrot was now rapidly developing a starboard list. A cocktail waitress came in from the front bar to get a steel tray of ice, saw the wobbly parrot staggering around the bar, and shook her head disapprovingly. Mike, figuring enough was enough, laid Hooker down in the towel box, where he promptly closed his eyes and passed out in a heap of feathers. Mayfield looked over into the box.

"You're gonna kill off that little fucker, he keeps drinkin' like that," said Mayfield.

"Hasn't hurt you any, best I can see," replied Mike.

"I've been going to sea longer; toughens up your liver and lights. What's happening with the fucking Navy these days? I thought I saw number 920 out there along the Stream the other day."

"You sure did. Some wiseass called in a report of seeing a submarine out there, and we were elected to go see. You don't happen to know who that was, do you?"

"Yeah, I do. It was Maxie Barr on the Brenda. He called me about it the other morning on the marine; him and me sailed in the Liberties in Willy Twice, so he figured I'd recognize a U-boat if I saw it. And he said it was a fucking U-boat, came up on the surface, sorta halfway up, and then went back down again. Scared the shit outa him."

"He called it a U-boat?"

"I just said that, didn't I? Yeah, he called it a U-boat. Said them fucking Nazis were back, and that he was gonna tell the Navy, get somebody out there to kick their asses."

Mike stared at his drink, shaking his head. It was almost dark outside; the lights in the bar were reflecting against the glass, dimming the silhouettes of the boats along the waterway. Siam eased down the bar.

"Hit 'em again?" he asked, tipping his chin at their glasses.

"Yeah," said Mayfield. "But give this sailorboy a sody pop, so he stops getting his parrot fucked up. Lookit that bag a shit in there, that's disgraceful." Hooker opened one eye, yawned, and went back under.

"Well, we went out there and spent the night killing fish with the sonar," said Mike. "I think Maxie must be getting the DT's or something. If he did see a submarine, then it was a diesel boat from that description. We don't even own any more diesel boats."

"Them fuckin' Russians, now, they got diesel boats, yeah?"

"Yeah, but they don't send diesel boats across the pond to fart around in U.S. waters—they might send one of their big nukes, but, man, you won't ever see a nuke on the surface like that."

Mayfield nodded. "Well, he saw something out there; he was jibberin' like a goddamn Portigee on that radio."

Siam brought their refills. The bar was starting to fill up, as the crewmen from the fishing boats gathered for some serious drinking. Mike didn't need another drink, but it was Friday, and it was bad manners to refuse. He would now have to buy Mayfield a drink, so he slowed it down to make the next round a single.

"Navy gonna keep looking?" asked Mayfield. His tone of voice was indifferent but his old eyes were serious as he looked sideways at Mike.

Mike shook his head slowly. "Nope. We didn't even file a report on it. If a Navy unit doesn't make the sighting, it never happened."

"Shit. Just like the fuckin' cops," grumbled Mayfield. "Some asshole cuts you off on the road, you get his license, report it, cops give ya the same story. We don't see, we can't write it."

Mike agreed. "Well, that's how it is. You catch that U-boat in your nets, bring his ass in, we'll seize his butt and take all the credit."

He looked at Mayfield for an instant, and then both said, simultaneously, "Just like the cops."

They laughed. Mike finished his drink and ordered another beer for Mayfield, leaving money on the bar. He stood up, and picked up the parrot, cradling the inebriated bird in his left elbow.

"You want a fish?" asked Mayfield, over his shoulder.

"Sure."

"See Jack; he's got some nice snappers in the chill box."

"Appreciate it, Cap. And look out for U-boats."

Mayfield finished off his second beer, and started in on the third. Wiping a line of foam off his upper lip, Mayfield belched loudly. "I'll do her, Michael. Count on it."

Mike left the bar and headed back down the sand road along the commercial piers. He stopped by the Rosie III, where Jack, the cleanup man, was hosing down the after deck, blowing bits of fish, viscera, and seaweed from the nets through the limber holes along the deck. A few hundred seagulls swirled overhead in the spotlights. Jack pointed with his chin indicating that Mike should help himself. Mike went into the deckhouse to the ancient refrigerator that was secured to the bulkhead by flimsy looking chains, and picked out a nice one and a half pound red snapper, stuck his finger through its gills, and headed back out on deck to the gangway. Buddy handed him a plastic bag with a dozen large shrimps.

"Kept too many for me to eat," he yelled over the noise of the gulls.

Mike thanked him, and carried his fish and bag of shrimp back to the marina, Hooker sleeping soundly in the crook of his arm. It was almost fully dark as he walked down the sand road toward the marina; a pair of tourists going towards the restaurant gave him a strange look.

Back on board the Lucky Bag, he put Hooker in a duplicate of the box in the bar to sleep it off in the lounge, and cleaned the shrimp and fish in the galley. He walked back to the short ladder leading up to the back porch, where he turned on the gas grill set up on bricks. Returning to the galley, he put the cleaned shrimp in a glass plate and poured Catalina dressing over them; he brushed down the fish with olive oil. He removed a half loaf of old French bread and a bottle of Kendall Jackson Chardonnay from the refrigerator, uncorked it, grabbed a glass and the fish, and headed back out to the porch deck. He settled back in a deep rattan chair, waiting for the grill to heat, and enjoyed a glass of wine while he watched the boats go by in the dark.

He picked up the phone and dialed the ship's number and told the OOD to have the Command Duty Officer call him back. He sat back in the creaking chair, and sipped some wine. Maybe later he would slip down to one of the clubs along the waterway, see what was shaking. Or see if the big blonde next door had been serious; or maybe he would just eat his fish and hit the rack. A week at sea, with countless calls about contacts at night and ship exercises early in the morning, was taking more of a toll than it had when he was a Lieutenant. The phone rang, and the CDO gave him a status report on the plant. Mike dictated a wrapup message on the submarine search, which the CDO promised to have out that evening. When the grill was hot, he put the bread in one corner and then placed a well blackened cake rack criss-cross on top of the steel grill. He broiled the marinated shrimp for two minutes on one side, a minute on the other, before picking them off the grill. He then raised the grill, turned down the heat and put the snapper on.

He sat back on the porch while the snapper slow roasted, and thought about the mythical submarine while snacking on the shrimp. A U-boat. Maxie had apparently used the term U-boat. Both Maxie and Chris Mayfield had served in the convoys during the big war; they would know what a U-boat was supposed to look like; Mayfield had told him that he had seen one on the surface after a destroyer had cracked it open with depth charges. He said it had looked like a gutted big fish rolling on the surface, all covered in red rust, and blowing diesel oil and bodies out of huge gash in her side before tipping up her bows and sliding out of sight. Mike knew that modern nuclear powered submarines didn't look anything like that; even modern diesel-electrics tended to be streamlined and tail finned like the nukes. Except for the older Russian boats, which were, after all, copies of the last class the Nazis had put out in 1945 before their thousand year Reich derailed.

He poured some more wine, went back to the lounge to check on Hooker, and came back out to the porch deck. He turned the snapper over. A U-boat. He had hoped to hear a vivid tale about a big something coming up out of the water in morning twilight, something a drunk or a near-sighted old man who had been up all night might feasibly confuse with a surfacing submarine. But if Maxie had called it a U-boat, then he had seen something else altogether.

He retrieved the fish and the hot bread from the grill onto a wooden platter, broke out some lemon wedges and a doubtful looking tomato from the refrigerator, and returned to the table on the screened porch to have his dinner. The traffic on the river had thinned out by now, with only an occasional small boat putting by in the dark, the faint noise of its engine competing with the sound of bugs flying into the screen. He washed up after dinner, thought briefly about going out, and decided to call it a day instead. Definitely showing his age, he thought.

TEN

The Mayport Marina, Sunday, 13 April, evening

Mike unlimbered himself from his cramped position on the pier up under the bow of the Lucky Bag, and began to gather up his painting materials. He had spent three hours attacking a section of paint along the waterline that had begun to peel. The section had started off being three feet long, and had grown, as such projects do, to a ten foot long scraping, sanding, undercoating, and finishing effort which ended up taking the entire afternoon.

He was ready for a beer. The late afternoon sun was still hot, and he had the beginnings of a headache from the turpentine he was using to clean up. His hands were covered in paint, and his body glistened with sweat over the sunblock he used on his chest and back.

He heard a low wolf whistle from across the pier. Looking over, he saw two guys in a sloop staring at someone at the end of the bulkhead dock. Shielding his eyes from the sun, he was surprised to see Diane Martinson standing at the top of the steps, some fifty feet away. Coming down the steps was her husband, the Chief of Staff. Diane was dressed in a tight, white skirt and sleeveless blouse, with some kind of colored scarf in her hair. The low angle of the sun illuminated more of her figure than she probably realized. She was wearing dark glasses, and was standing next to the gatepost at the top of the steps. She was fooling with something in her purse, oblivious to the interested looks she was attracting.

Her husband walked gingerly across the float to the Lucky Bag, concentrating on where he was putting his feet. Mike stood there as he approached, feeling slightly uncomfortable dressed only in his bathing suit and sneakers. The Chief of Staff was decked out in a white linen summer suit, complete with boater. While many American men would have looked faintly ridiculous in such an outfit, Captain Martinson presented himself with sufficient style to carry it off. He paused about twenty feet from the Lucky Bag to turn around and wait for his wife. She gave him a long look, and then, with evident reluctance, started down the stairs to the float. Captain Martinson waited for her, and then together they made their way towards the houseboat. Martinson looked the Lucky Bag over as they approached.

"So this is the famous houseboat, eh?" he said.

"Yes, Sir," replied Mike, glancing over Martinson's shoulder at Diane.

She was clearly uncomfortable, and Mike wondered if it had anything to do with his working uniform of the day. She seemed to be trying not to look at him. Having made daily use of the Goldsborough's weight room for the past year and half, Mike knew he cut a manly enough figure, but he still sucked in his gut an inch or so. He wondered if she remembered their encounter in the doorway at the club. The Chief of Staff was saying something.

"We were going to dinner at Hampton's, and I thought I'd stop by to chat for just a second. Did you get to talk to any of the fishing people about that sub sighting report?"

Mike put down his paintbrush, and picked up a rag to begin wiping his hands. "Yes, Sir, I did, although not to the guy who made the sighting—he's still out there. From what Chris Mayfield tells me—he's sort of the senior fishing boat skipper around here—the guy swears he saw a U-boat. He specifically used that term."

Diane was definitely looking right at him now; or maybe he was just imagining it; her eyes were hidden behind by the sunglasses.

"A U-boat," said Martinson, musingly. "Strange term to use, unless the individual is fairly well along in age."

"Maxie Barr is the Skipper who made the sighting. He's probably Chris' age, late sixties, maybe seventy. I guess he's old enough to have seen a U-boat in the big war."

Diane was standing nervously behind her husband, looking out over the waterway now at the parade of boats. The two men in the sloop next door were staring openly at her, making no attempt to be discreet about it. Mike pulled himself back with some effort to what Martinson was saying.

"Well, if in fact he did see something, then we're talking about a conventional boat, not a nuke," reflected Martinson, looking thoughtfully out over the waterway.

Then he became aware that his wife was fidgeting behind him. He frowned. He had asked her to accompany him to the houseboat but she had been strangely reluctant. Mike felt foolish standing there with more sweat than clothes on, his hands still covered in turpentine, as an awkward silence developed.

"Diane, This is Commander, or rather, *Captain* Michael Montgomery, CO of Goldsborough. Michael, my wife, Diane."

Diane took off her sunglasses and stepped around her husband to nod at Mike.

"Captain," she said, quietly, looking not quite at his face.

Mike smiled and looked at her directly, and suddenly her eyes flashed recognition. Mike had the feeling that she did remember him, but was trying to hide it.

"Diane," he said. "I'd shake hands, but—" He held up his paint covered hands.

She gave him an awkward smile, but said nothing.

"You're rather famous amongst the destroyer Captains, Michael," said Martinson. "Living in sybaritic splendor aboard this grand old boat. You must spend many an hour on maintenance, especially with a wooden hull."

"Yes, Sir. Chipping paint tends to dilute the splendor somewhat. Would you like a tour?"

"J.W., we have to go; the reservations—" interjected Diane, looking over her shoulder at the restaurant in the distance as if it might escape.

"I'm sure they'll hold the table, Diane," said Martinson. "Yes, I'd love to see it. If you don't mind the intrusion, that is."

"No intrusion at all; it's actually quite a comfortable home. C'mon aboard."

"Are you sure you don't mind, Captain?" Diane asked anxiously. "We can do it another time."

"Not at all," replied Mike, intrigued by her obvious desire to leave. "Right this way."

Mike showed Diane the stepped gangway up to the deck of the Lucky Bag, and followed her up the ladder, with the Chief of Staff in trail. His heart skipped a beat as he watched her smooth hips rise in front of his face as she went up the three step ladder. Once aboard, he took them down through the forward hatch, showing them the two guest cabins and adjoining bathroom, and then into the main lounge.

The lounge was surprisingly large, thirty feet long by twenty two, occupying the entire center of the boat below the main deck. There were four large, brass-rimmed, curtained portholes on either side, and both the walls and the overhead were panelled in various grains of dark veneer. There was a large oriental carpet taking up the entire deck, and comfortable leather furniture placed centrally to face a gas-fired fireplace on the starboard side. The port side walls were inset with bookcases, and the after part of the lounge contained a sizeable dining room table and six armchairs, with a brass, ship's wheel chandelier centered over the table. There were three doors in the after bulkhead, one leading to the galley area, one to the Captain's cabin, and the third to a companionway leading up to the porch deck aft.

"Oh, my word, this is quite posh," said Martinson. "It's much larger than I expected."

"Well," said Mike, trying not to shiver in the air conditioning, "This was a commercial fishing boat at one time, so there was a lot of empty room below decks for the catch."

From a corner of the room, Hooker sounded off with an epithet, startling Diane.

"A parrot!" she exclaimed, momentarily seeming to forget her discomfort. "This is really too much. Did he just say something?"

Mike felt his face begin to redden.

"Don't pay any attention to what that bird says; his vocabulary isn't very polite."

He desperately hoped that Hooker would not launch into any more profanity. He showed them the galley area, and then let them peek into the Captain's cabin which took up the entire area under the stern porch.

The master bedroom was also panelled, containing a large bed, its own bathroom on one side, and rows of drawers built into the bulkheads on the opposite side. There were three portholes on the after bulkhead which allowed bright yellow light from the setting sun to stream into the room.

The Chief of Staff made appreciative noises about everything, ignoring his wife's evident desire to be on her way. Standing in the doorway to his bedroom, Mike suddenly became aware of her perfume.

"This is indeed all quite posh," Martinson repeated. "I think I can understand its attractions." He turned to his wife. "Maybe we ought to look into buying a boat, for when I retire, Diane. Do you think you might enjoy something like this? I think it might be fun."

Diane raised her eyebrows. "Retire? I presumed that that's still a few years away, Dear."

Martinson frowned again. "Oh, well, yes, of course," he said, hastily. "I wasn't implying that I'm ready to retire. It's—oh, well, forget it. I guess we'd better be on our way."

Mike was aware of an undercurrent of conflict in their brief interchange on the subject of retirement. He led them up the narrow companionway steps to the stern porch area, where they could see the entire waterway shimmering before them. The stern porch was screened in on all sides and had a fiberglass roof built on to a tubular steel frame. The deck was covered in rattan carpeting, and the porch furniture was a mixture of wood and rattan armchairs, a table, and some ancient bar stools. There was a gas grill in one corner, set up on a square of bricks. A large fan was suspended from the overhead, and a wooden railing surrounded the porch area inside the screen. They had a panoramic view of the inland waterway in both directions, and the sounds and smells of the water swept over them in tangy contrast to the aseptic air conditioned atmosphere of the cabin below.

Mike offered to fix them a drink, but Martinson, in belated deference to his wife, now firmly insisted that they had to go. Mike led them through the screen door on the port side of the porch and back up the main deck to the gangway steps. The Chief of Staff apologized for intruding, thanked Mike for the tour, and stepped briskly down the gangway, turning to wait for his wife. Diane stood for a moment at the top of the steps. Mike tried not to stare at her. He could not figure out what it was that made her so attractive—she was not beautiful in the conventional sense of the word, but she had a physical, utterly feminine presence unlike any American woman he had met. He was reminded of the French women he had encountered in his travels, who always seemed to project an almost blatant femininity before he noticed anything else about them. She offered her hand this time, and Mike took it, turpentine and all.

"Thank you so much, Captain, for the tour," she said, her face neutral. "I think your boat is marvelous."

Still holding her hand, Mike looked directly into her eyes. "It was good to meet you, Diane. Come again."

She seemed about to smile, but then let go of his hand abruptly, and stepped down the gangway. He watched them walk across the float pier and up the steps. She walked slightly behind and to one side of the Chief of Staff, as she had done in the Officers Club. At the top of the steps, she turned to look back once, but did not wave. One of the guys in the adjacent boat mimed a fainting spell as she left, swooning in mock despair into the sternsheets of the sloop.

"I'm in lo-o-o-o-ve," he moaned theatrically.

I think I know the feeling, thought Mike, wonderingly.

ELEVEN

Mayport, Hampton's Fish House, Sunday, 13 April, 1900

Diane put her sunglasses back on to counteract the glare flooding the main dining room. They had a window table. J.W. always insisted on a window table. The evening sun streamed through the tinted plate glass windows over-looking the river junction. The glare was amplified by reflections glinting off the dancing prisms of choppy waves on the waterway. J.W. was looking around the room to see if anyone of importance was there while he sipped a martini. Diane was nursing a glass of chilled white wine. She was thinking about Mike Montgomery.

She held the picture of him in her mind's eye, standing straight, muscled and tall on the pier, his undressed, athletic body glistening with perspiration and daubed with paint, and his eyes frankly appraising her from across the piers. She had told J.W. that she would wait at the head of the pier, but J.W. had insisted she come along, wouldn't be a minute, just a quick word with this fellow. J.W. had gone down the steps, unaware that she was hanging back, conscious of Mike's stare and her own growing reaction, and then she had been drawn across the floating pontoons to the houseboat like the proverbial moth to the flame, a delicious sense of anticipation flooding her mind, tinged with the knowledge that there was danger in what she was doing. She had been aware of the juvenile antics of the two young men in the sloop, but Michael Montgomery had filled her sights even as he had set some strings in her belly vibrating that had been too long stilled by her husband's indifference. J.W. has his career and his girlfriend, she mused. I wonder...

"Diane?" J.W. was looking at her.

"I'm sorry. My mind was drifting. All this sunlight. You were saying?"

"I was saying that Commodore and Mrs. Taylor are here. We should probably go over and say hello."

"You go ahead," she replied. "I'll waggle my fingers at the appropriate moment from here."

"That's not particularly friendly of you."

"She's not a particular friend of mine," replied Diane stiffly.

J.W. made a 'well, excuse me' expression, pushed back his chair, picked up his martini and threaded his way through the rapidly filling dining room. Diane dutifully waggled her fingers in the Taylors' direction at the appropriate moment, and returned to her musings, staring out over the inland waterway.

She wondered when, if ever, she would confront J.W. with what she knew. Actually, she didn't "know" anything—she had only overheard the women talking about the pretty Wave Commander in Norfolk. But it fit. Another notch on J.W.'s image stick. If she really wanted to get even, she would wait until a month or so before the next flag selection board, and then cause an eruption on the base with a messy, noisy, tell the whole world divorce action. But, like her fantasies about snaking some hunk off the beach for some afternoon delight, the 'afterwards' scenarios were usually all pretty depressing. What would she do with a divorce? Where would she go? Even a senior Navy Captain didn't make enough to provide a decent alimony. As J.W. would say, what's the objective.

She also felt in her heart of hearts that she could not derail J.W.'s Navy career just for the satisfaction of it. He was so entirely a creature of his career that it would destroy the man himself. She should have seen him for what he was from the beginning, that underneath all the glittering uniforms and the sophistication and worldly charm was the sterile soul of a devoted bureaucrat, a mandarin who advanced for the sake of advancement, who played the game with consummate skill, and who wanted to win, not for the sake of achieving power to do something, but because winning showed off how well he played the Navy career game. The 'special friend'—that was the term the woman in the bathroom had used—was consistent: another facet of the good life to be added to the collection of successful career, presentable wife, nice cars, the right suits...Navy men were a lot alike in that regard—they often sought the values of upper class English gentlemen in their pursuit of the right things, an expensive ethic born of the Royal Navy's profound influence on the American Navy. A naval officer, no matter what his social origins, was acceptable in polite society by dint of his commission. The waiter hovered tentatively, but she dismissed him with an order for another white wine.

And now in what she recognized was a critical juncture in her life, Michael Montgomery had risen above her horizon like a racing powerboat approaching a small sailboat. She was aware of his latent physical power. He apparently lived as he chose to live, and was not above sticking an occasional sharp stick in the eye of the naval establishment, judging from J.W.'s occasional comments. A bit of a rogue male on the political waterfront, and evidently all man from the sight and size of him. At the instant of that collision in the doorway she had felt his hand press against her for just the briefest instant, and she could still feel it down there. An accidental, random touch, but a part of her had wanted to turn around, go back out there on the patio and grab him. She smiled at the thought. Poor man would have gone over the wall in fright. And yet, he had reacted, too; she was certain of it.

She was used to men reacting to her physically, but this had been spontaneous and uncontrived, a flash of undisguised desire before the necessary social modalities had been dropped back into place like gunports coming back down over a sudden display of cannon by a ship of the line. And again, tonight, on the dock and yet again on the boat, a subliminal channel of sexual energy had existed. And all of it right in front of her oblivious husband. She had wanted to bolt even as J.W. had insisted that she go with him to the boat. It would never cross J.W.'s mind that his dutiful wife could be sexually interested in another man, even as he deftly managed an affair of his own with his peculiar brand of smooth efficiency. He was coming back to their table.

"Taylor's an important player in the ship repair world," he announced as he sat down. "We depend on a good relationship with them to keep these exotic Spruances going. I'm sorry you didn't come over; she's not that awful to talk to."

"She's undoubtedly a perfect Navy wife; my problem is choosing what script we'll act out when we go over pretending to be oh, so glad to see them."

"You don't have to be that way," he complained. "We need connections like that, people to feel comfortable with, people to do business with when we have to. Here, have a menu; we probably should order. This place is getting crowded."

Diane studied the large menu indifferently. The waiter had reappeared. She decided she was hungry.

"I'll have the stuffed lobster," she declared. J.W. raised his eyebrows, and began to reconsider his own choices. She knew that J.W. always fixed in his mind a total amount that he would spend on dinner before going into a restaurant. When she ordered an expensive meal, he perforce selected a lesser entree in order to get back on budget. She watched him squirm out of the corner of her eye as he mentally ran the numbers.

"And we need a good wine to go with this, I think," she announced. "Perhaps a Pouilly Fuisse; that goes nicely with lobster, don't you think, Dear?"

J.W. swallowed and nodded, trying to figure out what his normally compliant wife was up to. The budget was rapidly going out the window. After the waiter left, he leaned forward in his chair.

"Are you feeling all right, Diane? You normally don't indulge yourself at a restaurant this way."

"What way, J.W.?" she asked innocently.

"Well, I mean, lobster, Pouilly Fuisse—are we celebrating something?"

She laughed out loud, a melodic sound that caused the heads of some of the men who had been looking surreptitiously at her from behind menus and over their wives' shoulders to turn in her direction.

"It was your idea that we go out," she replied, airily. "I'm just going to enjoy myself and not worry about the budget for a change. With all that per diem you've been accumulating on your trips to Norfolk, we should be able to afford it. Where do you stay up there, by the way—that awful B.O.Q.?"

"Yes, as a matter of fact. Although it's not so awful. They've spruced it up quite a bit. The only drawback is that the dining room's closed at night, so one has to make, ah, other arrangements to go for dinner."

She almost gave it away as she looked at him over her wine glass, but he had turned his face to stare out the windows, missing the glittering look in her dark eyes. Other arrangements.

"Odd fellow, that Montgomery," he mused, still looking out the window.

"How so?" asked Diane; it was her turn to look away.

"Well, living the way he does. What must his JO's think? All the other CO's are on the base in quarters, and he lives like some bohemian down here in this dirty little village."

"Well, perhaps he likes it. And that boat was no bohemian's nest; it looked more like a living room out of Country Life. What's his background?" she asked, staring down at the table and toying with her wine glass.

J.W. shrugged. "Well, nothing too exotic. NROTC commission, of course; he's hardly the Academy type. Spent a lot of time in the Vietnam theater, gunboats, destroyers, that sort of thing, as I recall. I looked his record up after we had that first spot of trouble from him. He sent out a message to God and the world saying how bad the repair work was at one of our local civilian shipyards. Caused quite a flap. I had to spend several hours soothing ruffled feathers amongst the repair world."

"Was he correct—did they do inferior work?"

"Well, it's always hard to tell, isn't it. So subjective. But the point is that in peacetime we need these civilian shipyards possibly more than they need our work, so we have to be temperate in our criticisms. Some constructive criticism would have been more useful than many of things he said. And of course he made it info to the destroyer Type Commander back in Norfolk, so we had to placate them as well. He's sent out one or two other messages of the same ilk. Comes from having no Washington shore duty, I think. Spent all his time at sea, with only one shore tour in Norfolk on the Type Commander's staff. Has zero political sense, in my opinion. I'm frankly not quite sure how he got command, although all those years in Vietnam probably helped; he does wear a lot of ribbons. But, the ship's on its last legs, going to be decommissioned next year, I think, so he's been given just about the right kind of command. All in all, however, a bit of a pain in the arse."

Diane digested J.W.'s description while the waiter brought their salads.

"He seemed pleasant enough when we toured his boat," she continued. "I didn't get the impression of a fire-brand."

"Well," smiled her husband, indulgently. "I suppose women would find him attractive. He's young and fit, and probably very popular with his crew—they can identify with someone who so obviously doesn't fit into the establishment mold very well. But he'll never get to full Captain that way—the troops don't sit on selection boards, do they."

"Pity," she murmured.

"Whatever do you mean?"

"Well, I think the Navy might benefit from having one or two, I'm not sure of the word I'm looking for, unconventional, I suppose, Captains in its ranks. If all the Navy's Captains are cut from the same cloth, an enemy in wartime would have a pretty easy time of it. From what I've read, they certainly weren't all the same in World War II."

"Once it got going, that was probably true, but at the beginning of the war they were very much alike."

"Maybe that's why we had Pearl harbor," she countered.

He laughed. "Touché, I suppose. But nowadays the Navy's influence is felt on a much wider spectrum of our foreign affairs, which means that what we do bears close scrutiny at the highest levels of government. Our ships carry more firepower now; in some cases, more firepower than was expended in all of World War II. So it becomes very important that our

Commanding Officers are indeed predictable, and also sensitive to the politics, Navy or otherwise, of what they do and say. And I'm never quite sure of what Commander Montgomery is going to do or say next, so I'm uneasy with him or people like him in command. We limit the potential damage he can do by taking his ship off the overseas deployment list, ostensibly for other reasons, and generally confining the ship to odd jobs, like this silly submarine business. I'm sure he thinks that the Group staff has it in for him; but we really don't have time for that sort of thing. We get the occasional lone wolf, the non team player, and we just put them in a box. Like the Sicilians say, it's not personal, just business."

"Suppose he were to turn over a new leaf and become respectable, in your terms. Would you change your opinions of him and his ship?" Diane tried to make the question sound unimportant, as if she were just making conversation.

Martinson pursed his lips as if thinking seriously about her question.

"No, I don't think so. Mostly because that type does not change its stripes; they usually become increasingly belligerent, and eventually provide their superiors with the means of levering them out of command. I think he has only six months or so to go in command, anyway, so it's not very important. Do you find him interesting?"

It was Diane's turn to dissemble; J.W. might be indifferent, but he was not entirely stupid.

"Not particularly; I just thought it was interesting how the naval establishment reacted to a man like that. I wondered if he posed some sort of a threat."

J.W. laughed. "No, Diane. The potential for threat is all on our side. We have him under control. He bears watching and occasionally, disciplining. It's really all just part of my job as Chief of Staff. Ah, here's the wine."

TWELVE

The submarine Al Akrab, Mayport Fleet operating areas, Tuesday, 15 April, 0435

"Sonar, this contact continues to close us?" The Captain swung the periscope around, from south to west, straining to see some lights in the darkness above.

"Yes, Captain. The three around us are dead in the water; generators, but no mains running. This one closes at slow speed, from the southwest. He is passing through rain squalls."

"Yes, I know. I can see the lights from the three, but I cannot see this one. Prepare to secure snorkeling."

The order went aft over sound-powered telephones. After a moment, the sound of the big diesel engine changed, as the generators were taken off the charging circuit. They had been snorkeling since 0100, continuing the pattern of finding some fishing boats, positioning themselves so that the fishermen were initially between them and the coast, and then coming up to periscope depth, sticking up the snorkel mast, and lighting off the diesels to recharge the battery. If there were hydrophone arrays on the bottom near the naval base, they would not hear another diesel engine light off amongst all the other diesels of the fishermen who carried out a nightly pattern of moving and drifting. The relative position was important only for the initial light-off; after that, they only had to stay near the fishermen to mask the diesel. After three hours, they were now surrounded on three sides, north, east, and south, by the commercial fishermen, who were blissfully unaware of the 3000 ton fish lurking nearby. This night they had the added advantage of passing rain showers, which further muddied up the sound picture.

The Captain took another full circle look with the scope. He could see the lights of the nearby fishing boats lying a few miles away on three sides, white spots on tall booms, topped by red and white hazard lights. He had lingered in this area for the good sound masking, but the new contact approaching from the southwest was going to spoil the temporary nest. Time to go. And since there were nets down on three sides, he would have to make his exit initially to the southwest before turning back out to sea, east away from the coast into the safety of the Stream.

"Down scope."

The periscope hissed down into its well, the arms folding up with a metallic snap.

"Secure snorkeling."

"Secure snorkeling, aye."

Immediately, the sound of the diesel died away, and everyone felt a squeeze on their ears as the pressure changed in the boat.

"Main air induction valve cycling. Main air induction valve is closed; lowering snorkel mast," reported the diving officer.

The lights on the hull apertures status board went from red to orange to green, indicating apertures closed and locked. The pressure in the boat stabilized. Everyone in the control room opened and closed their jaws several times to equalize their ears.

"Main control reports the drive motors aligned to the battery, turns for three knots, ready to answer all bells. The diesel engines are secured."

The Captain rubbed his eyes and thought for a moment. The watch was waiting for a course order, as the boat crept along at three knots at sixty feet. He saw the Musaid shift on his chair, his eyes haggard from his continuous watch in the control room. He would have to do something about that; the senior chief was making a religious vigil out of this. He missed his shadow. His edict was taking other tolls around the boat as well. He brushed away the intruding thoughts and concentrated on the surface picture above.

"Come left to course 230, speed six knots; make your depth forty-five meters."

"Course 230, speed six knots; making my depth forty-five meters, aye."

The sub tilted downward, and the shafts vibrated slightly as the engineers responded. The planesman kept his planes aligned in the shallow dive position, the foreplanes on the bow tilting down, the after planes slightly up, like an airplane making a dive. The diving officer was using the boat's speed to settle down to the ordered depth, rather than flooding tanks.

"Bearing to the approaching contact."

"Sir, bearing is 250, but the bearing is indistinct due to surface weather."

"Very well; course 230 is good enough separation."

"Passing thirty meters," announced the diving officer.

"Very well," responded the Captain. He grimaced to stretch the muscles in his face. He too, was tired.

Snorkeling required precise depth control, or else the boat might dip a few feet under the surface, which caused the float valve in the snorkel pipe to slam shut, pulling an instant vacuum in the boat as the engines drew on the boat's atmosphere rather than the outside air to sustain combustion. When the pipe broke free, there was yet another hard pressure change. The snorkel pipe system was identical to the tube used by skin-divers to keep their heads just below the surface. It operated on the same principle—if the top of the tube went under, a ball was forced onto its seat to prevent water ingestion. It was very hard on the crew if depth control was not just about perfect, which, in the Al Akrab, meant that the Captain had to be present in the control room. There was also the added danger of sticking the snorkel mast too far up, which might attract the unwelcome attention of a passing radar. They needed three to four hours a night to keep the battery up to 98 percent. In normal circumstances, the Captain could leave snorkeling to the watch, but there were too many possibilities for things to go wrong, either with depth control, surface contacts, or even a problem with the diesel. And the consequences of error were now severe enough to warrant his presence. He was beginning to wonder what he would do if someone else made an egregious error, and he had to follow through on his threat. He now realized that he would have to speak to the crew; he had to defuse this building crisis, a crisis of his own making. The red rimmed eyes of the Musaid reproached him every time he looked across the control room.

"Depth is forty five meters; the trim is stable; we are steady on 230."

"Very well. Bearing to the approaching contact."

"Bearing is 255, drawing slowly right; doppler is up doppler."

"Very well."

Good, he thought; drawing right meant that he would pass near the fisherman but not under him, in case he was dragging a net. But the net was not likely, as the boats seemed to go much slower when seining than this one was going. Someone coming out to join the rest of the crowd.

"I will have some tea," he announced to no one in particular. The messenger of the watch scrambled aft to rouse the cook.

THIRTEEN

The Submarine Al Akrab, submerged, 15 April, 0455

They had ten seconds of warning as the Rosie III's net tow cable screeched its way along the submarine's side from the bow to the base of the conning tower. Then the submarine lurched into a momentary up angle as the off-axis pull of the cable and the fishing boat above exerted a sudden 80 tons of force. Everyone in the control room went sprawling except the sonarman, the planesman and the helmsman, who were all belted into their console seats. The Captain's hot tea splashed down the sonarman's back, evoking a howl from the startled sailor, but his cry was overwhelmed by the noise of unsecured gear crashing about in the control room and the hideous screech of the wire cable against the steel outer hull of the submarine. The lights in the control room blinked off, then back on, and a cloud of dust billowed momentarily above their heads.

The Al Akrab quickly levelled off, causing a second round of scrambling as men tried to regain their balance. The submarine, displacing almost three thousand tons submerged and going ahead at six knots, had pulled the 80 ton fishing boat under in less than thirty seconds, assisted by the fishing boat's autopilot, which had tried to compensate and instead had sealed the boat's fate by commanding a turn which had become her death spiral.

The Captain was the first to recover his wits. He half rose from the deck, wedging himself into a semi-upright position by the attack director as the submarine levelled.

"All stop!" he roared. "Right full rudder! Maintain up angle on the boat!"

The planesman pulled his yoke all the way back, trying to maintain the up angle caused by snagging the tow cable and the net. The simultaneous right turn had the effect of turning the face of the conning tower into the direction of the pull, allowing the net and cable to be stripped off with a great metallic, slithering noise. The momentary up angle on the boat kept the tangled mass out of the submarine's screws; the steel cable in the screws would have been fatal to their own survival. The Captain heard the mess pull free, and moved quickly to restore dynamic stability. An ominous rumbling, bubbling sound could be heard aft for a few seconds.

"All ahead together, standard! Rudder amidships! Steady as you go. Depth?"

"My depth is passing through thirty meters, Sir!"

"Make your depth twenty meters." He pulled himself fully upright, and grabbed the intercom box, as the boat once again began to level off.

"Main engineering, report!"

There was a moment of silence, punctuated by the noises of the watch team in the control room regaining their feet and their efforts to pick up some of the equipment rolling around in the control room. The Captain felt an enormous pit in his stomach at the thought of what had just happened. Without ever having experienced such a thing, he knew that he had snagged a fishing net. He wondered if they had capsized the boat above.

"Sir, main engineering reports all systems functional. We are doing the compartment check now, but there is no report of flooding or fire."

"Very well." He switched off the intercom. "Depth?"

"Sir, my depth is twenty three meters, coming to twenty meters."

"Recommend we slow to three knots, Sir," said the Musaid, from his corner perch by the diving officer's station. Idiot, thought the Captain. I ordered a standard bell, and then failed to take it off. At twelve knots, we could broach at this depth.

"All ahead slow together, make turns for three knots. Prepare to surface."

The watch team jumped to configure their boards for surfacing. He looked over at the senior chief, and nodded. Thank you for thinking when I stopped thinking, the look said. The Musaid, his mahogany face impassive, nodded back. Voices could be heard throughout the boat as the crew picked themselves off the decks and restored order. The Captain watched the depth gauge and the pitometer log, waiting for the speed to come down to three knots. When it finally did, he ordered the scope up, and took a look around as it broke the surface above. Darkness. Darkness and rain; he could see the trails of raindrops sweeping across the glass optics of the periscope. Twice he thought he could see white lights on an easterly bearing, but they might have been raindrops on the scope. He swung the scope through 360 degrees, crabbing around the shining brass column. Still looking around through the scope, he called to the sonar-man.

"Sonar, what do you hear?"

"Rain, Captain. Nothing else."

"Bring up the ESM mast."

Behind the periscope rose another steel tube, this one with an electronic listening array mounted on the top. The watch officer across the control room energized a panel as the ESM mast came up, and three oscilloscopes wavered into life. A junior officer slid into the console seat, and adjusted the displays.

"Search for radar—airborne or surface ship radar."

"Sir, I detect a Raytheon device, bearing 095, classifies as a fishing boat radar." The petty officer twirled two knobs as he searched the spectrum. "Another at 140; nothing else, no naval emitters."

"Very well. ESM mast down."

The Captain rotated the periscope to 095 and then to 140. He still thought he could see white lights, but the heavy rain obscured everything. Now he had to decide. He had given the order to prepare to surface because he had to know what had happened to the fishing boat. But the green digital clock display in the scope told him that it was only an hour until nautical twilight. Should he wait until daylight to see what he could see? He thought he had seen lights; in rain, it meant that the three fishing boats were probably not more than five miles distant; one at least had his radar on. But would anyone be looking at the radar while handling nets? Pulling his face away from the scope, he saw his Deputy watching him from across the main plotting table, a neutral expression on his face. He probably wonders who will be shot for this. He is frightened, thought the Captain. So am I.

"Down scope! What do you recommend, Deputy Commander?"

The startled Deputy looked uncomfortable for a moment, but then appeared to stiffen his resolve.

"Sir. We should surface, I think. Yes. We need to examine the conning tower for damage, and we must find out if we capsized that accursed boat. And if there are survivors."

The Captain's eyes narrowed, and he swallowed. Survivors. Yes, he had forgotten that possibility. Some of the control room crewmen were looking at him. Survivors.

"Up scope."

The periscope came back up, and he looked around again, going slowly. No lights. More darkness and rain. A flash of lightning startled him, causing him to flinch with a muttered curse. The officers watching him in the control room saw his eyes reflect the blue-white flash from above, as if he had looked at a welder. The flash momentarily destroyed his night vision.

"Down scope!"

He subconsciously waited for the rumble of thunder, which they could sometimes hear at periscope depth. Decision time. Dawn was coming.

"Up scope! Surface," he commanded. He pressed his face to the optics as they rose and continued to watch through the scope, turning it constantly, as the boat tilted up, her ballast tanks blowing noisily. He did not look away from the eyepieces until he felt the boat level on the surface, the wash of a heavy rain squall audible now above them. While he scanned the dark horizon he listened subconsciously to the routine reporting sequences of valve lineups and the final announcement from the diving officer.

"Sir, the boat is stable on the surface."

He pulled his face back from the periscope. The watch officer was looking at him. "Sir, do we want to take a sweep with the radar?"

The Captain glared at him, transferring his anger at what had happened to the hapless watch officer.

"Don't be a fool! The one thing that can confirm our presence here, even more directly than a visual sighting, is an intercept of our radar. There is an entire naval base full of ships who might pick that up."

He was shouting now, and the men backed away from him.

"I have told all of you a thousand times: the radar is a fire control device! It is for killing, not for looking!"

He felt his hands gripping the periscope handles painfully hard. Control, control, get yourself under control.

"No," he growled, restraining his breathing. "We must use our eyes." He turned to look directly at the watch officer.

"We must use our heads, above all, our heads."

He looked around at the white faced men in the control room, staring at each one, seeking their assurance that they understood the peril of any emission from the submarine. There were nods. He turned back to the watch officer.

"Open the hatch. Watch officer, we shall remain on the battery. Helmsman, reverse course 180 degrees. I want to go back down our track. Increase speed to five knots." He turned to find the Musaid.

"Musaid, assemble the special team. Make them ready to come on deck through the forward hatch at my command. Deputy, reconstruct our track for the past fifteen minutes; I wish to retrace it exactly. Adjust the course so that we do. Fire Control, raise the ESM mast. Keep the ESM system manned, and alert me at once to any military radar intercepts."

As the control room watch scurried to carry out his orders, he walked forward to the conning tower ladder, and began to climb. Two lookouts scampered up the ladder ahead of him. A stream of warm and wet fresh air flowed past him into the boat as he neared the open hatch above. Salt water pattered on to his face. The noise of the rain was more pronounced in the conning tower.

His eyes were not night adapted when he rose up into the conning station, making him doubly blind. The rain rebuked him, soaking his face and hair, and then his uniform. He had not thought to get raingear. The two lookouts on either side were equally blind, having preceded him from the white light of the interior. The three of them waited patiently as the boat came around in a slow turn, the noise of the rain drowning out any other sound. Without the diesels, the boat was silent as a ghost, a dark shadow in the sea.

After five minutes, they could begin to see again. The Captain leaned over the front of the conning tower. He realized from the way that the rain blew over his face that the windscreen mounts were gone, as well as the pedestal for their running lights fixture. There was one scrape mark running up the full height of the conning tower, the bruised steel glinting in the rain. He thanked Allah they had not had a scope up. The rain suddenly began to diminish, and the visibility began to extend in every direction. As the rain dwindled, all three reached for the binoculars the lookouts had brought up with them. After a few more minutes, he could begin to see the twinkling lights of the fishing boats on the eastern horizon. He also sensed that the sky was beginning to lighten in the east.

"Captain," came the quiet voice of the Musaid over the intercom. "The special team is assembled under the forward hatch."

"Very well. Keep them ready. Night adapt their eyes."

The special team was a seven man squad of naval infantry. They lived by themselves in one corner of the forward berthing compartment, having little to do with the rest of the crew. They were big, silent, and hardened soldiers, disdainful of all sailors. Trained in the Palestinian commando camps, they spent most of their time doing physical exercise and cleaning their AK-47 assault rifles. Their leader was a ferocious looking black Algerian from the Atlas mountains. A few words from the Musaid, and they would deal with any survivors.

"Captain," came the Deputy's voice over the intercom. "We are on the reverse of our track. At this speed it will take ten more minutes to cover the area of the—ah—incident. We have about thirty minutes until nautical twilight."

"Very well, come up to seven knots."

The speed order was acknowledged. Now, he thought, how do I find one or more men swimming in the ocean, if there are any. He swept the area ahead with his binoculars, as did the two lookouts. Thirty minutes to nautical twilight, the official time for star fixing, when the horizon would be just visible against the night sky. The air was cool and the visibility clearing rapidly in the wake of the rain squall. It must have happened very quickly for them. A light. He needed to show a light. Men in the water would make themselves visible if they saw a light. He ordered the control room to raise the search periscope, train the optics down into the water, and then to turn on the periscope interior tube light and begin sweeping the periscope from side to side. The prisms in the periscope would project a beam of dim white light down into the water. It would not be visible to ships or boats on the horizon, but, thirty five feet below, on the surface of the sea, a swimming man might see it.

He heard the tube hiss up to full elevation behind him, and begin to swivel from side to side like a cobra seeking prey. He kept his eyes pressed into the optics of his heavy, Russian binoculars in order to keep his night vision intact, and continued to scan the arc of black water ahead.

They had gone for six minutes back down their under-water track when one of the lookouts touched his sleeve, and pointed in the direction of the port bow. He trained his binoculars in that direction. There. He saw something white in the water. The pungent smell of diesel fuel was suddenly noticeable. The Captain reached for the intercom switch.

"All engines stop. All engines back slow together. Bring the special team on deck." He turned to the senior of the two lookouts. "Well done. You may go below now."

The men looked at him blankly for an instant, and then they both unstrapped their binoculars, and climbed down off their perch, disappearing into the conning tower hatch at the Captain's feet. A moment later, the Musaid's head appeared above the hatch coaming.

"Permission to come on the bridge," he requested formally.

"Permission is granted," replied the Captain, not taking his eyes off the bobbing white objects coming slowly into view ahead.

Up forward, on the wet, black foredeck of the submarine, seven bulky shapes rose up out of the dim red light showing through the forward hatch. Each shape carried an assault rifle.

"Come left twenty degrees; all engines stop. Secure the periscope tube light," ordered the Captain into the intercom.

The orders were acknowledged below, and the boat turned toward the white things in the water ahead. The Captain continued to adjust the boat's heading as they closed in on what appeared to be two men in the water. The big submarine began to wallow as her speed through the water dwindled. Twilight was coming fast now that the rain had moved out. The fishing boats on the horizon were still visible only as lights, but the lights were dimmer now in contrast to the lightening horizon. Fortunately, they were several miles distant. Time was running out. This had to be done quickly.

The two survivors began to wave as they saw the dark shape of the submarine approaching. One of the men in the water stopped waving, and held his hand near his face, as if trying to make out what kind of vessel was silently approaching them. The submarine, which had slowed to bare steerageway now after the backing propellers dragged her way through the water down, was rolling slowly in response to some unseen swell.

They looked so small in the sea, with seven eighths of their bodies under water, like tiny ice floes in the black sea. The Musaid turned to look at the Captain from the side of the cramped bridge area. The special squad were in line, their rifles at formal port arms in the darkness. He could hear the men in the water shouting now, their voices a mixture of anxiety and relief at being found. The boat was close now, moving through a slick of diesel oil and debris from the fishing boat. Suddenly, the men in the water stopped shouting, as they saw the soldiers and their rifles, and realized what that silent line of men on the foredeck might mean.

The Captain raised his right hand, waiting for the submarine to pull almost alongside the swimming men, and then dropped it. The night erupted in automatic weapons fire, the hammering sounds penetrating to flinching men below decks. Ten seconds later, there was nothing on the water except the oil slick and some bits of debris from the Rosie III, including a life ring that was floating very close to the submarine's side.

"On deck," called the Captain. "Retrieve that ring!"

The sergeant in charge handed his rifle to another man and ran back along the deck, past the conning tower, his boots clumping on the deck. Just aft, he stepped out onto the swell of the ballast tanks, putting his foot into a limber hole along the submarine's water line, and reached out to retrieve the life ring that was bumping its way aft along the side. The Captain watched from above, approvingly. The life ring would have a name on it. The rest of the debris would be dispersed in a few hours, but the life ring would have floated and been proof that the fishing boat was sunk.

"Prepare to dive," he ordered over the intercom, as the men on the foredeck went back down the hatch, one by one, passing their rifles before them.

The sergeant, clutching the white life ring, waited for them impatiently. The Captain turned to look at the Musaid, who was staring impassively down at the oil streaked water.

"Well, Musaid? This was a necessary thing, yes?"

The Musaid nodded grimly, trying to erase the sight of the thrashing figures in the water as their faces were obliterated by the AK-47's.

"Very well, then. Clear the bridge," ordered the Captain softly.

He then took one last look around before keying the intercom and giving the command to dive. The Musaid dropped down the hatch, slithering down quickly in the manner of old hand submariners, letting the tips of his boots just brush the rungs while sliding the ladder rails through his gloved hands.

The Captain suppressed a stab of guilt at what they had done to the men in the water. It violated the law and every tradition of the sea. Would that be their fate when the final encounter came with the American carrier? The mission, he reminded himself. You must keep the mission in the forefront of your mind. Let nothing distract you. He conjured up the cold fire in the Colonel's eyes on the pier. This is a mission of vengeance, to be carried out in the old way, by the precepts of the Book. This killing of innocent men was necessary; these two men had to die in order that his men and this holy mission would live. He felt a chill, despite the tropical warmth of the air. He knew the real reason for his guilty feeling: he should not have passed so close to the fishing boat in the first place.

These men had died because of his stupid error. His second major error of the trip—the first was that equally stupid edict about shooting the next man who made a major mistake. By rights, he should go shoot himself. The sounds of the ballast tanks spewing air and the sudden downward tilt of the bow snapped him back to reality. He shook his head and looked around again, before turning to the hatch as the submarine leaned into the dive.

FOURTEEN

The Mayport Marina, Wednesday, 16 April, 1830

Mike Montgomery parked the Alfa in his usual spot at the Marina, and sat in the car for a minute, rubbing his eyes. It had been a tough three days. Daylight was fading quickly because of a low overcast and a drizzling rain that had set in Monday evening, one of those systems which made commuters wish they had bought intermittent windshield wipers. Goldsborough had been a veritable zoo, with engineering repairs, four unannounced staff inspections, two Captain's mast sessions, briefings for the upcoming fleet exercise, and all of the end of the month reports. Monday had gone late enough to warrant his staying on board in his cabin rather than driving home.

He became aware that the rain seemed to be turning into a steady affair, judging from the sound on the car roof. He jammed his brass hat on his head, zipped up his khaki windbreaker, and climbed out of the car. He noticed a small knot of men standing under the streetlights at the head of the commercial pier. There seemed to be something wrong. Curious, he walked over.

One of the younger men he recognized nodded in greeting. "Eve'nin', Cap," he said.

"Evening," replied Montgomery. "What's happening?"

"Chris Mayfield is overdue," said one of the older fishermen, in a broad north Florida accent. "S'posed to be in fust thing this mawnin'; nobody's seen hide'ner hair of him or the Rosie, neither. Been on the marine radio all day, ain't it, boys?" There was a subdued chorus of yeahs.

A black government car pulled up out of the wet darkness, and stopped at the head of the pier, its windshield wipers scraping noisily. Two Coast Guard officers got out, one a Lieutenant, the other an Ensign. The Lieutenant came directly over to the group on the pier.

"Afternoon, gents, I'm Lieutenant Barker from the District," he announced.

He saw Mike, turned and saluted. "Commander," he said, and then turned back to address the fishermen.

"We've received the boat overdue report, but there have been no reports of incidents or accidents in the fishing areas for the past twenty-four hours. If any of you can show us on a chart where the Rosie III might have been operating, we'll initiate a search at first light."

"Why ain't y'all goin' out now?" asked one of the men, his white hair and red face in stark contrast to his black foul weather gear.

"Because the weather is below minimums for helicopter operations after dark," replied the officer, patiently. "All the fishing boats that are out there have been alerted on marine radio, as have a couple of Navy destroyers who are out in the op-areas for training. That puts a pretty good mix of eyes out at sea; we'll get a helo up at first light, if the weather permits, and do the aerial surveillance. But we do need a better idea of where they might have been."

The older fisherman spat noisily over the side of the pier.

"Shit, Mister," he said. "They coulda been anywheres. Ole Mayfield, he go where he damn well pleases, same's the rest of us. Ain't none of us goes around tellin' where he's hittin' good fish, neither." There was another muttering of agreement from the rest of them.

The Lieutenant looked annoyed. The Ensign was waiting to write something down in a small notebook, which was getting wet in the rain. Montgomery decided to intervene. "Lieutenant," he said, "Are you new in this district?"

"Yes, Sir. Two months. I came from Seattle."

Mike nodded. "OK, the way it works, these guys go out and do most of their fishing between the Gulf Stream and the coast, depending on what they're after. Mayfield works the margins of the Gulf Stream, where the mixed water is. Your best bet is to draw a line from the entrance of the St. Johns river directly out to the Stream, and then a construct a search box along the inside margin of the Stream, north and south, say, for thirty miles. If he ran into trouble fishing, that's where he probably was. If he had a problem on the way out, he'll be on that easterly line somewhere."

"Much obliged, Sir," said the Lieutenant. "Are you here for the Navy?"

"No, I live over there," Mike said, indicating the Marina with a nod of his head. "These guys are my neighbors."

"I see, Sir. Well, we don't have much info here, as you can see. The boat's overdue twelve hours, which doesn't necessarily mean there's a problem. As I understand it."

94

The Ensign had closed his book and was looking longingly at the car.

"Mayfield don't come in on time, he gits on the marine," said another of the fishermen. "Man loves to talk on the goddamn radio, don't he?" There was more agreement all around.

The Lieutenant shrugged. "Well, I guess that's all we're going to accomplish here." Turning to the cluster of fishermen, he said, "If any of you people come up with any additional information, please call us."

The fishermen just looked at him; fishermen did not love the Coast Guard, inspectors of licenses and safety regulations. Until, that is, they were in trouble at sea. The Lieutenant saluted Montgomery again, and he and the Ensign got back into their official car and drove off. Mike hunched his shoulders; the rain was definitely settling in for the night. The far shore of the waterway had dissolved in a gray mist; even the sea birds were quiet. The knot of men under the streetlight looked as if they were trapped in the cone of light shining down in the rain. Mike pulled up the collar of his jacket.

"We're going out tomorrow for some sea trials," he said. "I'll work the area so we cover as much of Chris' stomping grounds as possible. Hopefully, those guys'll get a helo up."

"Thanks, Cap," said the white haired fisherman. "Goddam Coast Guard, they ain't too quick on the draw, it comes to fishing boats. Some big banker on his Chris Craft, now, that'd be a different story." Some of the men had begun to drift away towards Hampton's back bar.

"Well, Hell, Whitey," said Mike. "Chris probably busted his radio and is just not going to come in until he's ready. He's probably found a good hole full of fish and isn't telling. He's not going to worry about it until he runs out of Jim Beam."

The old man didn't laugh. "I donno, Cap. Ain't like him, three days now, you count the Monday and all, and he went out on a Monday. Ain't nobody heard nothin' from the Rosie. Can't figure it. We had rain and everything, but nothing bad. Like some damn thing et him up."

Montgomery patted the old man on the shoulder. "You start seeing sea monsters, time to give it up, Whitey. Tell that fat bartender over in the back bar to buy you guys a round on me. Chris'll hear about it, and come in to get his share."

"Yeah, he would, now, wouldn't he," grinned Whitey.

Mike walked back to his car, retrieved his briefcase, and started walking towards the Lucky Bag. He had a few hours of paperwork to do, and then an early start tomorrow for two days of sea trials. If the steam seals forward held tight, they would be able to go south on the fleet exercise next Tuesday. If not, well, he did not want to consider that possibility.

Goldsborough was showing her age; they were welding on top of welds in some areas of the boiler room.

Funny thing about Mayfield, though. He was infamous for jabbering away on the marine radio. It was not like him to go completely silent. On the other hand, these fishermen were an independent breed. He boarded the boat, let himself in through the pilothouse door, and secured the alarm. From down below in the lounge came a familiar squawk.

"Shit fire," said Hooker bird.

"Save matches, Bird," replied his owner, turning on the lights.

FIFTEEN

USS Goldsborough, Mayport operating areas, Thursday, 17 April, 1730

The Captain sat in his chair, glowering out at the persistent rain and the gathering darkness. The ship was headed at slow speed into the wind, which gusted noisily through the open doors. The bridge watch did not exactly tiptoe around the pilothouse but there was none of the usual banter. The red light came back on the bitch box in front of his chair. He leaned forward.

"Bridge, Main Control," announced the box.

"Bridge, Aye," Mike responded.

"Cap'n, that feed pump is not responding to the control system; she comes up on the governor, but trips off the line when the first demand signal hits. We're gonna have to bring it down and have another go at the controls."

"What's that leave you with, Snipe—one feed pump operational forward?"

There was a slight pause. "Yes, Sir. 1A is feeding 1A boiler; 1B has a 1200 pound steam leak, and now 1C won't respond to control system signals."

"OK, Snipe. Look into the possibility of taking the controller off of 1B and putting it on 1C; if we don't have two feed pumps forward, we're not going anywhere next week."

"Snipe, Aye. I'll talk to the Chief."

Mike sat back in his chair and watched the red light blink off. His sense of gloom deepened; there went the fleet exercise and their chances of getting out of Mayport for awhile. Fucking main feed pumps; over-hauled only a year ago by the Philadelphia Navy Shityard in their endur-ing tradition of half-ass work. That, plus another couple of high pressure steam leaks back aft, and a sick lube-oil purifier, and an intermittent water chemistry problem in 2B boiler... None of them individually fatal, but collectively, enough to convince the Group Commander to pull him out of the Caribbean trip. And his dear friend in high places, Captain Martinson, would be delighted to do just that. Mike finished the last of his cold coffee, crumpled the paper cup, and pitched it through the bridge wing door straight over the side. The bosun mate, about to offer him a refill, thought better of it. The Officer of the Deck took a sudden interest in the radar repeater. Outside, there was a sudden burst of heavier rain against the windows. A bright, narrow wedge of late afternoon sunlight low on the western horizon was being squeezed into the sea by the overcast.

Fuck it, he thought; we do the best we can. Old ship, dwindling parts support—which made sense, when you thought about it. Goldy was going to the mothball fleet in a year. Good people, but not the very best people. The very best people traditionally went to the brand new ships as precommissioning crews, which also made sense. All very sensible, and right in line with how we do business, but... disappointing.

It's peacetime, he kept reminding himself. What do you want, a war? He realized that he was condemned to spend his entire command tour doing nothing but routine training evolutions in home waters. Might as well have gone to a reserve training ship. He wondered what it must have been like to skipper a tin can in wartime. Had to beat this dull business. Unexpectedly, his mind conjured up the image of Diane Martinson standing hipshot at the top of the float pier at the marina, her lovely body silhouetted in the afternoon sun, unconscious of her effect on mortal males while she rummaged through her purse for something. Or was she? Was a beautiful woman ever unconscious of her effect on men? Forget it, dickhead—she's married, she's Navy, she's the Chief of fucking Staff's wife, and you don't go crapping in your own foxhole, as the Army guys daintily put it. Lots of pretty women out there on the beaches. Still the image persisted, stirring him. It was more pleasing than main feed pumps.

"Captain?"

He sat up, surprised by the appearance of the Operations Officer. "Yeah, Ops?"

"Sir, remember we're supposed to be keeping a lookout for that missing fisherman while we do the sea trials?"'"

"Yup. As I recall, you've worked up a general search area track, right? We've been executing that track?"

"Yes, Sir, we have, and we've covered about seventy percent of it. Two extra lookouts topside all day, too. Well, now there's a formal missing vessel report in from Coast Guard District. We're action on it, 'cause they know we're out here. There's a coastie coming out to assume on-scene commander for a real search tomorrow, and then we got this in from the Group." He handed Mike a message.

Mike fished in his jacket pocket for a red flashlight, switched it on, and scanned the message. He sighed, and handed it back.

"OK," he said. "So we go on over there and do a concentrated search, but I don't think we're gonna see anything at night in the rain. And I think they've got the area wrong, too. Mayfield works right here on the edge of the Stream, not thirty miles inshore of it. How'm'soever, get the XO to set up a track to rendezvous with the Coastie. If Group Twelve wants a concentrated search, we'll give them a concentrated search. About all we're good for these days, anyway. Tell the XO."

"Aye, aye, Sir." The Operations officer left the bridge.

Ten minutes later, the bridge phone talker announced that one of the topside lookouts reported smelling diesel oil. The Officer of the Deck went out on the bridge wing, which was the upwind side. The rain had dwindled again to a mizzle. The ship was creeping along at five knots while the Engineers worked out the problems in the steam plant.

"Cap'n," he called in from the bridge wing. "I think we got an oil slick out here. All engines stop!" he ordered. "Spin main engines as necessary."

"All stop, spin as necessary," repeated the lee helmsman, snapping the brass handles of the engine order telegraph back to the straight up and down position; the engine order telegraph bells rang in response.

Mike got out of his chair and went out onto the bridge wing. The stink of diesel oil was suddenly strong. The oil slick could not be seen in the gathering darkness, but the smell was unmistakable on the normally pristine sea air.

"You're right, Jimmy, that's smells like a slick. Have CIC mark it down, and let's take a look around here."

He felt the beginnings of concern in his belly; from the smell of it, this was more than somebody pumping a dirty bilge over the side.

He called up to the signalmen on the next level to light off the two twelve inch searchlights. "Sweep either side, Sigs—we're looking for anything floating."

"Sigs, aye," came a voice from the gloom of the 04 level above the bridge.

Moments later, a yellow cone of light stabbed out into the darkness, the light rain glinting in the beam as it jerked this way and that, until it pointed down onto the sea surface. The telltale multicolored sheen of oil sprang into view. The ship drifted slowly to a stop, and then began to roll slowly as she lost steerageway.

"Put left full rudder on, Jimmy, and then bring her up to three knots. We'll do a slow spiral right here, see what we get."

"Aye, Cap'n."

The Officer of the Deck called in the orders. It took a few minutes for the ship to respond; they had to look over the side to watch the trail of an overboard discharge to see that she was in fact moving. Three knots; think you can handle that, Mike asked mentally. Oldy Goldy, the crew called her. Then he saw something in the water, as the light flashed over it from the level above.

"Hey, Sigs, go back, forward there," he called out. "I saw something."

The signalman pointed the searchlight beam back up to the bow illuminating a sea of heads on the bridgewing; most of the bridge watch had come out on the wing to help look. They strained to see what had caught the Captain's eye. A small crowd had also gathered up on the forecastle as the Bosuns passed the word that a slick had been found. Finally, two men saw it at the same time. "Hold it," they yelled simultaneously, but by then the signalman had seen it too, and was holding the beam steady, right on the bow. It looked like a plank of some kind, shiny and dark in the oil stained water. The ship's head was slowly swinging past it.

"Get the big dipper up on the forecastle; back her down easy, so we stop right here, Jimmy."

The word went out over the phones for the boatswain mates to bring up the big dipper, a large dip net attached to a long handle, designed to scoop up debris from the sea from the ship's weather decks. Destroyers were often tasked to recover debris, especially when a carrier plane went down. The dip net was easier than putting a boat down. The ship trembled gently as the Officer of the Deck backed the offboard screw, keeping the propeller wash on the other side, and pulling the bow slowly back towards the plank in the shimmering water below. There was a flare of light on the forecastle as the hatches came open, and a crew of boatswain mates came topside, carrying sections of the dip net handle and the net itself.

The Executive Officer appeared on the forecastle. Mike smiled mentally; the XO had the right instincts—always go where the action is. He was lucky to have Ben Farmer for an Exec. Finally the forecastle crew had the big dipper assembled and pointed over the side. The net was six feet deep, but the plank was still an awkward object to retrieve. They pulled it up on deck after another few minutes of bad language and lots of direction. The signalman kept the searchlight centered on the net as it came up, and everyone saw the brass lettering at the same time.

"Oh, shit," said the Officer of the Deck. "That's a name board."

The deck crew turned the board face up, and the brass letters gleamed out the name of Rosie III. The letters were big enough to be read clearly on the bridge.

"I'm going down there, OOD," said Mike, his face grim. "Instruct the bosun mates to put an anchored marker buoy over the side; water's not that deep, and I want to mark the spot where we found that."

"Aye, aye, Sir. Quartermaster, gimme a depth of water under the keel. Sir, shall we tell the Coast Guard?"

"Yes, right; tell them we've got a datum," ordered Mike as he left the bridge.

He went down two sets of interior ladders and out onto the main deck, and then forward through the breaks to the forecastle. The boatswain mates made way for him as he walked up the sloping steel deck. The oil smell was even stronger down here; the wet plank was covered in a thin film of oil; it looked like a corpse of some kind, lying on the deck in the folds of the net. The Chief bosun saluted as Mike stopped at the net.

"That who we're looking for, Cap'n?"

"That's him," replied Mike.

What the hell have you done here, Chris, he thought. These were the signs of disaster. He stooped down to inspect the board, as if looking at it might somehow undo the stark import of finding a name board in an oil slick. Three bosuns began affixing a boat anchor to a coil of manila line, while a fourth disconnected an anchor buoy from the lifelines. The Chief pointed to the edge of the board.

"That looks like a bullet hole, Cap'n."

Mike bent closer. Six inches to the right of the last roman numeral was a round hole with smooth edges. He reached into the net and turned the board over. The hole came through the other side with very ragged edges; there was a long splinter of wood missing on the back side of the hole. He looked up and down the length of the board, but there were no other signs of damage. It did look like a bullet hole, about a thirty caliber round, with enough energy to have torn the wood up on the other side pretty good. He stood up, wiping the oil off his hand on a handkerchief. There was a splash as the bosuns threw the anchor over the side, and the manila coil whistled as it uncoiled to the bottom, 350 feet below.

Mike returned to the bridge and summoned the operations officer.

"Make a report, Ops; we've got the Rosie III's nameboard, and an oil slick. We're going to stay in the area tonight and search for people and any other debris. Tell 'em we've put an anchor buoy down and give 'em the posit. I assume that Coastie will come out here and take over, so include a local weather summary so he'll understand there's no real big hurry; we're not going to see anything tonight, and I strongly doubt that we're going to find Mayfield and his two guys."

"Aye, aye, Sir. Should we set up a fathometer watch? The water's not deep here, and maybe we can detect the boat on the bottom."

Mike nodded. "Yeah, we can do that, although our bottom charts aren't going to show the level of detail we'd need to pick the boat out of the normal bottom return. But go ahead; we'll plot anything we find, and let the Coasties follow it up. Set up an expanding square search around this position, slow speed, real tight—I don't want to go more that five miles from this position."

"Aye, aye, Sir."

"And, Ops—tell 'em we found what looks to be a bullet hole in the nameboard. Make the message classified, and make it op-immediate. Info the Group and the Commodore."

"Aye, aye, Sir. A bullet hole? Rosie mix it up with some drug runners or something?"

"I don't know, Ops, and the sea isn't telling."

SIXTEEN

Cruiser-Destroyer Group Twelve headquarters; Friday, 18 April, 1800

Mike shook out his raincoat as he entered the Group headquarters building, a white, World-War II "temporary" building one block down from the Commodore's office. A yeoman sitting at a desk literally covered in papers showed him where to put his hat and coat, and then pointed him in the direction of the Admiral's office.

"Everybody's down there, Sir," he said, returning to his typewriter. "Just waiting for Goldy to get tied up."

"Thanks," he replied, and headed down the hallway.

He wondered who 'everybody' was. The messenger from the Commodore's staff had been waiting on the pier; meeting at Group Twelve as soon as Goldsborough is tied up. He had left at once, leaving the remainder of the return-to-port operation to the Exec.

He found the door to the conference room open, and went in. The conference room contained one long table with ten armchairs in the center, a podium and screen at one end, and chairs around the rim of the room for straphangers. Two air conditioners hummed quietly in the shaded windows. The Admiral, sitting at the head of the table, was talking to the Commodore and the Chief of Staff when Mike walked in. Some of the Group Twelve staff officers were sitting around in the chairs against the wall. The DesRon Twelve Chief Staff Officer, Commander Bill Barstowe, saw Mike, and pointed a finger at the chair opposite the Commodore. He then caught the Commodore's attention discreetly, and indicated that Mike had arrived.

"Captain," nodded the Commodore, as Mike sat down. The Admiral and Captain Martinson broke off their conversation, and the Admiral turned to greet Mike.

"Captain," he said, formally. "Thank you for coming right over. This meeting concerns the Rosie III and your schedule. The Commodore and I have been digesting your engineering sitreps; you've turned up quite a few main plant casualties. I was hoping that Goldy could go south next week, but I'm thinking now that might not be such a good idea. Comment?"

Mike was aware of the smug look on Martinson's face, and he felt a tinge of anger creeping into his face. The Commodore was giving him a significant look. Not the time to light fuses. He took a deep breath.

"Yes, Sir; no one of our problems is fatal, but the aggregate makes at least the forward fireroom a doubtful proposition for a three week operation. My guys have gone 'round the clock on the feed pump controls, but we're down to needing parts now, and parts take time. The purifier in two engineroom presents the same problem."

The Admiral nodded sympathetically. "I know you and your crew were looking forward to getting out for some fleet time, but I think what would happen would be that you'd limp into Gitmo or San Juan and clamp on to a pier for the better part of the three weeks. I'm afraid that Goldy is simply showing her age, and I fully understand that parts are becoming hard to find for that steam plant. I think you'll agree that that's simply not worth it."

"Yes, Sir," sighed Mike, resignedly.

He had half expected this, but the reality still disappointed him. The Commodore was looking down at the table. It was his job to ensure that his ships were ready to meet their commitments, even his elderly training destroyer, so there was some professional egg on his face as well. But the Admiral was also being realistic, and did not seem to be condemning anyone.

"Now," the Admiral continued. "This business about the fishing boat. That was a good job on finding the wreckage—your instincts on where to look were better than ours, but then I understand that you are acquainted with the Mayport fishermen."

Two of the staff officers sitting in the wall seats exchanged a smirk, as if to say what kind of a nut lives down in the village of Mayport, on a boat no less.

"We have something of a mystery on our hands now, though," continued the Admiral, holding a sheaf of papers in his elegant fingers. "You've heard about what the Coast Guard found?"

"No, Sir, I don't believe so; we did a turn-over with them this morning, ran some more engineering trials, and came straight back in."

"They carried a Tethered Eye on that cutter; are you familiar with that system?" said Martinson.

"Yes, Sir," Mike nodded.

He had read about the Eye some six months ago. It was a miniature submarine television pod which could be sent underwater to depths of 600 feet, trailing a fiberoptic control and data wire. In addition to a tiny sonar transceiver, the pod had a high intensity light surrounding its spherical glass nose, and the camera lens inside gave the front of the pod an eye-like appearance. The Coast Guard had begun to use the Eye to do quick surveys of sunken vessels, to determine if there were signs of life from men trapped in a hull.

"Well," continued the Admiral, "They found the fishing boat, lying on her side on the bottom about a thousand yards from where you put down that buoy. She had her nets deployed, and not a mark on her. No signs of a collision, fire, explosion or any other kind of damage."

Mike frowned. So why had she sunk?

"The complication," said Martinson, "Is your report that there was an alleged bullet hole in the nameboard that you turned over to the coastie. We haven't released that to the press, yet, and we're waiting for the coastie to get back in. We're going to turn the board over to the local police labs to get their opinion on that purported bullet hole. The problem is, of course, what do we do about it, if it does turn out to be a bullet hole."

Mike sat back in his chair. Alleged? Purported?

"It sure looked like a bullet hole," he said. "Smooth entrance, ragged exit, long splinters of wood torn out on the back side. And no other damage to the board."

"We appreciate your opinion, Captain," said Captain Martinson. "But we still intend to have forensic experts look at it. It makes a difference as to what happens next."

"How so, Sir?"

"Well," said the Admiral, "Absent the bullet hole, the Rosie III is a closed case as far as the Navy is concerned; misadventure at sea. The sea is full of mysteries like that, and they are a Coast Guard problem, not a Navy problem. If there's a bullet hole in the board, however, then there's more to it, and there's going to have to be an investigation of some kind."

"Yes, Sir," protested Mike. "But that's a Coast Guard matter, too—law enforcement within 200 miles of the coast. I suppose they can raise the boat and take a look, if they want to. Chris Mayfield was a friend, but what does this have to do with the Navy?"

"Because," said the Commodore, speaking for the first time, "The locals are saying that it might have been the submarine that did it."

"Submarine? What submarine?" asked Mike, forgetting for a moment that he had conducted a search for a submarine the previous week. "Oh, for Chrissakes, that submarine report?"

He laughed in disbelief. But nobody else in the room even cracked a smile. The Commodore leaned forward and explained it to him.

"Yeah, well, you think it was somebody having a bad dream, and, frankly, so do I, but the local fishermen, especially Mr. Barr, skipper of the good boat Brenda, swear that it was real. The way they see it, we couldn't find it; if we had found it, Mayfield might still be around. They think the bullet hole in the nameboard proves he mixed it up with someone."

"But we haven't released anything about a bullet hole, have we?" asked Mike.

"No, Mike, we haven't," said the Commodore patiently. "But you know those guys—they have a way of knowing what's going on. Somebody's been running his mouth; or the Coastie talked to District on his marine radio. Who knows. But that's why we're going to get the cops to have a look at the nameboard."

Mike shook his head. The others in the room were looking at him. He still didn't get it. What was the Navy's involvement?

"It means, Captain," said Martinson, a faint hint of triumph in his voice, "That if the police say it's a bullet hole, we have to send a ship out there into the op-areas to look for a submarine again."

Now it all fell into place. Martinson had convinced the Admiral to use the excuse of his engineering problems to keep him here for this little sideshow. Mike looked at the Commodore for a moment as if expecting some help.

"Does anybody here believe," he asked, rhetorically, "that there is an unidentified, diesel-electric submarine operating offshore who's going around sinking fishing boats?"

"No, Mike, none of us believe that," responded the Commodore, heading off the Admiral. "But if the fishermen believe it, and the newspapers pick it up and spread it, then we have to be seen like we care and that we're proactively doing something about it; the Coast Guard doesn't do windows or submarines."

"We are reporting this situation up the Navy's public affairs chain right now," said the Admiral. "I want to be out front on this one, rather than waiting for the local papers to clamor for action. We are also pulsing the intelligence system, to see if there are any Sov's unaccounted for. Now, your engineering casualties preclude you from going on a three week fleet exercise, but not from local ops. So, on a contingency basis, we're announcing that we're going to assign Goldsborough to go back out Monday. By that time the police lab either will or won't have corroborated the bullet hole theory, and Goldsborough will, or won't, spend a week looking for our phantom submarine."

Mike looked down at the table and nodded. "Aye, aye, Sir. Only fair—we found the problem. But might you not want to send out a real ASW platform for this? Goldy is hardly a front-line subhunter."

"Goldy is as much ship as we want to commit to this effort, Captain," said Martinson politely. "As even you made clear the other night, we don't think there's a whole lot of merit in this submarine theory."

Stung, Mike sat silent. Goldy was good enough for the shit details; that was what the Chief of Staff was saying. But not for fleet ops. The staff officers, taking their cue from the Chief of Staff, were smiling openly while looking innocently down at the floor. The Commodore, aware of the currents of antagonism flowing in the room, finally intervened.

"It's a shallow water operation, Mike," he said. "The big sonars on the Spruance's aren't worth shit in shallow water in the active mode. Searching for something in these op-areas, especially a diesel-electric on the battery, takes an active sonar, and you've got a 23; the 23's were made for active work, and this calls for active work."

"And if you find one," said Martinson, "You've even got depth charges, as I recall. You can classify him with an oil slick, like they did in World War II."

The staff officers smiled at his wittiness when Martinson looked around the room as he enjoyed his little joke.

"You giving me permission to use depth charges to classify, Chief of Staff?" asked Montgomery, his face neutral. The Admiral made a sound of exasperation.

"No, Captain, he is not. C'mon, Mike—this is a shit detail, OK? We're not even bothering our bosses about it—just the public affairs people. Go out there, go through the motions. You get a contact, do the regulation peacetime drill to find out what it is and who it is. Peacetime rules of engagement all around. Come in next Friday and it's over and done with, and we've made the effort. Sorry about the fishing boat, and all that. Let's not make this thing into a bigger deal than it is; this is all just peace-time public affairs damage control. OK?"

Mike sat back. Straight talk, at last.

"Yes, Sir," he replied. "Got it. We'll be ready to go Monday morning."

The Commodore intervened again. "Let's make it Monday afternoon—that way we can see what the midday supply run from Jax brings over. Maybe get some of your parts in."

"Good idea," said the Admiral. He began to gather up his papers, signalling that the meeting was over.

Mike had a fleeting thought, about something Mayfield had said in the bar. Maxie Barr had called it a U-boat, not a submarine. Do you suppose... But the Commodore got up at that point, breaking up the meeting.

"C'mon back to my office, Mike. I want a full brief on your engineering problems. Maybe we can expedite some of those parts." He turned to Commander Barstowe. "CSO, you work with Captain Martinson here on that other matter we were talking about."

The two officers took their leave, and headed back to the DesRon Twelve office. The rain had stopped. The ships tied up along the bulkhead pier glistened in the glare of the quartz halogen streetlights. Neither of them spoke on the walk back. Mike was still angry about the whole thing, the decrepit machinery in his engineering plant, cancellation of the cruise to the fleet operations in the Caribbean, and embarrassed that his ship didn't run. And now getting stuck with this submarine charade. If this is what command is all about, they can stick it. He belatedly remembered his crew; they had worked hard, inspired by the prospects of real fleet ops and some Caribbean liberty ports. They would be really pissed off, too. He would have to go back and put the word out tonight. The Commodore must have been reading his thoughts.

"Sometimes command gets pretty disheartening, Mike," he said, as they entered the darkened offices. There was only one yeoman working late in the squadron staff building; the rest of the staff had long since gone home. The Commodore made a quick phone call to his wife, telling her he'd be home in a few minutes. They went into his office, and the Commodore sat down at his desk, indicating a chair for Mike.

"Now, on all these engineering casualties: I want a composite report made up in a message. List the top ten hard spots, describe what's wrong, and what you need to fix it. Get that on the street tonight, so the Type

Commander guys up at headquarters in Norfolk get it in their Saturday morning message traffic. You keep the plant steaming this weekend, so you can get back out there Monday, let's say for a 1600 departure. That'll give you time to refuel, load stores and all that stuff Monday morning."

"Yes, Sir," Mike nodded. "The engineer should have that message done already. But I need to call the ship and let the snipes know right away not to shut down."

The Commodore pointed to his desk phone, and Mike made the call.

"Now," he continued, as Mike hung up. "I'm going to assume you were correct about the bullet hole business. You must have seen one or two in all those years in Vietnam, yes?"

"Yes, Sir, I certainly did."

The Commodore sat back in his chair, looking at him. Only his shirt-front was visible in the desk light; his face was in shadow. Mike could not see his expression. The Commodore was silent for a long minute. Then he leaned forward, his face showing his age in the light of the desklamp.

"You don't have a lot of friends over there, you know," he began. Mike knew that over there meant the Group Twelve headquarters.

"That Martinson fella keeps making remarks," continued the Commodore, "like Goldy is on a downswing, can't make her commitments, even the easy ones like this Fleetex, and now all this bullshit about a fishing boat and a submarine."

"We didn't exactly start that one, Commodore," bristled Mike.

"No, but you are firmly associated with it; somehow this whole Weird-Harold is tied to Goldsborough. What I'm telling you is: take care. Martinson has the Admiral's ear, lots more than I do. He obviously dislikes you, and you surely know his reputation as a career killer. If he puts a drop of poison on your name every time it comes up, eventually the Admiral starts to get sick when he hears your name, and then Martinson will try to get him to yank you offa there for something that doesn't warrant it."

Mike sat back in his chair, shaking his head in disbelief. "I know I've done some things to get on their shitlist, Commodore. But the problems I've been squawking about do exist!"

The Commodore sat silent for a moment. "You're in command, Mike," he said, his voice flat. "You're in command, in peace-time, in an old ship without a mission. You're competing with guys in newer ships who are in the mainstream of fleet ops, who get to go overseas on deployment. That alone puts you at a real disadvantage. Also, you haven't helped your case with some of those shittograms you've sent out over the past year, blasting the supply department and the repair department and the shipyard and anyone else who didn't measure up to your standards of support to the Fleet. I cautioned you about that after the first one, but then you let another one go three months after that."

"But everything I described in those messages was true. They—"

"Yeah, yeah, you told it like it was. But you put some senior Captains on report in the process, and they don't care for that shit. They call Martinson and bitch and moan about how they have problems too, and they don't need shit from some guy on the waterfront when there's lots of ships that need support besides Goldsborough, etc. The Admiral pulls me aside at a party and says to get Goldsborough under control, that the way to get along is to go along—shit, you know the drill. But your biggest sin in the eyes of our very traditional Navy is that you're different—you aren't married, you live on a houseboat instead of in quarters, you go on liberty down at the beaches, you drive an expensive sports car—I know, I know," raising his hand, as Mike sat forward in his chair, ready to protest.

"But the Navy is a very conservative, straight-laced organization," the Commodore continued. "In peacetime, it values conformity over just about everything else, and appearances even above conformity. In peacetime, when nothing very real is going on, appearances take on the role of reality, because all the Services go into a defensive mode—trying to stave off the budget cutters who want to gut the military now that the country doesn't need them. I stress that word peacetime."

He got up, and began to pace behind his desk, looking out through the plate glass window at the basin full of gray warships. "I know what I'm talking about. I wanted one of the Norfolk DesRons, close to Fleet headquarters. For visibility purposes. Visibility is the key to promotion in peacetime, especially when you're trying to go from O-6 to O-7 and an Admiral's star. Instead, I'm down here in what is, relatively speaking, this Florida backwater. On top of that, I'm Jewish and I'm a little bit aggressive about that; that makes me different, too. I'm a short guy in a tall man's world, and I've always been a little pugnacious about that, too. I've got a bad temper. And therefore, I have little hope of becoming an Admiral, not because I'm any of those things, but because in the aggregate, I'm different—do you understand the distinction there?"

He paused for a moment, looking at Mike, a bitter smile on his craggy face.

"Probably not," he sighed. "Well, here's a rule you can get promoted by: you can afford to be different as long as you—you meaning your command, whether it's a ship, a squadron, or even a shore station—as long as you don't have any problems. Today's peacetime Navy doesn't have any problems, see, and if we do, we keep them in-house, thank you very much. When I was a ship CO, I went up the line and got help with problems from a reasonably sympathetic Commodore. Now that I'm a squadron commander, now that I'm the Commodore, I get some not-so-faintly veiled threats when I take problems up the line. When you sit where I sit, the word that comes down from on high is: so you got problems? We don't want to hear that, OK? So you take just care of 'em. Or we'll get somebody in there who can, OK? That's what so-called major command is all about. It's important that the System sees whether or not you can play the game when you're a Commander. But when you're a Captain in command, or a squadron Commodore, they want to see if you can play the game without depending on going up the line for help."

"Surely," Mike interrupted, "the big guys know that the ships have all sort of problems—people problems, machinery problems, supply problems. They don't really believe that everything's just fine and dandy down here on the waterfront, do they?"

"Of course not; but remember, they came up the same road you're walking, and they all got by the command hurdles without having problems they couldn't solve, one way or another, either by fixing them, with or without help, or even by hiding them until the next guy came along. They understood early on that the key is to keep the problems, whatever they are, behind the scenes. By all means, work the problems, work 'em hard, and get help from the system, but do it discreetly, and do not make the Navy look bad."

The Commodore stopped again in front of his big plate glass window, looking at the ships through the darkened glass.

"We're getting more and more like the Marine Corps, where the gravest sin is to bring any kind of discredit upon the Corps. Now: this submarine thing has the potential to blossom into a real story, and thereby make the Navy look bad, or worse, foolish. So you pay attention, and do it right—lots of tactical sitreps, search plans, fast paced operations razzle-dazzle: make it look really good. Write your sitreps using unclassified language which can be released to the newspapers, so the Public Affairs wienies don't have to think, not that they could. Remember what this drill is all about. Because if you don't, and this thing ends up making the Navy look bad, you are very vulnerable, because you're on a ship that's got problems, and because you are known as a guy who pours gasoline on the support fire instead of water, OK? Martinson and company are going to be looking for the first sign of intransigence from

Goldsborough to put the axe into your command tour. You get the picture?"

"Yes, Sir, I sure do," replied Mike grimly, getting up from his chair. He stared out the window for a moment. Goldsborough was just out of sight to the left. The Commodore returned to his desk and sat down.

"And, Mike—remember something else, before you tell me that they can take command and stick it. Remember that you're the Captain. You feel like the world is picking on you, and maybe you want to say fuck it, and hang it up. But that would leave your guys, your officers and crew, hanging out there, at the mercy of some hotshot who would be brought aboard to fix everything up, and a lot of people would get hurt professionally by a guy who has nothing to lose, and no way to go but up, see? You accept command, you take it on for the whole trip, for the good times and for the bad times. They say a ship is like a woman—costs a lot to keep her in powder and paint. But command is really like marriage in the Roman church: you're married to that gray bitch until one of you dies or your relief shows up on the pier."

Mike stood silently by the window for a long moment. "Yes, Sir," he said, as if talking to his reflection. "I hear you. And thanks for the advice."

The Commodore grinned at him in the semi-darkness of the office. "Yeah," he said. "And other than that little unpleasantness, Mrs. Lincoln, how did you enjoy the play?"

Mike grinned back. "Right, Commodore. Good night, Sir."

Mike left the office and headed back across the waterfront to the ship. He hoped the XO was still onboard; knowing Ben, he would be hanging around until his CO got back with the word. Ben was a damned fine Exec; there was none of the eight to four-thirty mentality he found in many of his junior officers. The young ones today considered shipboard duty just a job, not a life, as he had been brought up to do. Maybe in peacetime, especially in an old, non-deploying ship, it looked more like a job than a life. A trio of his sailors came by, dressed in the liberty uniform of jeans, sneakers, and T-shirts. They greeted him politely in the darkness, but their thoughts were obviously on the beach. The ship was back there and out of their minds. For him, the ship loomed ahead and was very much on his mind.

The quarterdeck watch saw him walking down the pier, and, moments later, the four bells and "Goldsborough, arriving" rang out over the waterfront. The rain started up again as he walked up the brow. He could hear the old ship stirring against the pier, her steel sides scrunching the log camels against the heavily creosoted pilings. Hello, Gray Bitch.

110

SEVENTEEN

The Mayport Marina; Saturday 19 April, early afternoon

Mike was stepping out of the shower after an hour long workout with his weight set when the phone rang. Grabbing a towel, he stepped into the master's cabin to reach the phone.

"Captain," he answered, forgetting for an instant that he was ashore on his boat and not in his cabin.

"Yes, Sir, Captain, CDO here. We've had a motor vehicle accident, Sir."

"OK," Mike sighed, opening the towel out on the bed and sitting down. "What happened?"

"Best we can tell, Fireman Quigley in B division—he's an after fireroom guy—wrapped his Harley around a bridge abutment over in Orange Park. I don't have any more details on how it happened. We got the call from NAS JAX hospital."

"Is he alive?"

"Yes, Sir, but he's racked up pretty bad. The B division officer is on his way over, and I can't raise the XO."

"OK, I'll go on over there. Send out the personnel casualty sitreps and all that. Does he have family?"

"He's single, Sir. Parents in Fall River, Massachusetts. I can give you their phone number; the hospital has it already and is going to call 'em. He's like, twenty, maybe twenty one."

"OK, thanks. Make sure you inform the Squadron duty officer, and have him notify the Squadron Doc. Tell them I'm on my way over to the hospital."

"Aye, aye, Sir. Sorry about this."

"Not as sorry as Quigley probably is; he a good guy?"

"Engineers seem to think so; at least he's not one of their shitbirds."

"OK, thanks."

He hung up and looked at his watch. He was suddenly cold in the air conditioning. It was not all that hot outside, but the humidity was still up around 1000 percent. His body ached from the workout, but he felt better. Nothing like pumping iron to dissolve stress.

He found a clean set of summer whites, rigged a shirt with shoulder boards and insignia, and headed topside. As he was closing up the boat, he noticed that the clouds were blowing in again. More rain coming. He stepped back into the pilothouse and grabbed a plastic raincoat, just in case. Jamming his officer's cap on his head, he headed for the Alfa.

111

He drove out of the marina and headed south on A1A. Traffic was light for a Saturday afternoon; everybody was already at the beach if they were going, although the overcast skies were not inviting. He drove down through Mayport Beach, Jacksonville Beach and Neptune Beach and then west to the Jones Point bridge across the St. Johns, which was two miles wide at the bridge crossing south of Jacksonville. He could see the Naval Air Station off to his right as he crossed the hump in the middle of the bridge built to allow river boat traffic.

Just what Goldy needed, he thought, was some more attention. A kid wrecks his motorcycle, and the ship gets its traffic safety program inspected. Don't have problems, the Commodore had said. Then his thoughts turned to the young sailor in the hospital, and all the administrative burdens precipitated by a traffic accident ashore were reduced to their proper insignificance. Twenty year old kid on his Harley, money in his pocket and the weekend still young, and now he would be seeing stainless steel tables, white lights, and people in green masks through a fog of pain. He grimaced. Poor bastard.

On the other side of the river he intercepted Route 301 for about two miles, and then turned off into the back entrance of the Naval Air Station, where the signs indicated the way to the naval hospital. A light rain was starting as he drove into the parking lot. He looked for a spot reasonably close to the main entrance. As usual, there were none to be seen, and he began circling the lot, waiting for someone to leave. Sections of the parking lot were covered by wide sheets of standing water from the previous rains. The shimmering image of the main building of the hospital, surrounded by palm trees, was reflected in the wide puddles. Finally, he saw a car leaving and steered the Alfa into a parking spot. Grabbing his raincoat, he headed for the main entrance.

He asked for directions to the emergency room at the main desk, and they pointed him down a long green hall to the right of the waiting room. There was a steady procession of hospital staff, active duty patients, retirees, dependents, and an occasional man in uniform milling around in the corridor. Saturdays were apparently a busy day. He followed the signs to the emergency room, where he identified himself to the admitting desk corpsman.

"Yes, Sir, Cap'n," said the Corpsman, a tall, thin black man, who eyed the gold star on Mike's right breast pocket. "He's in recovery four; they took him right up to surgery when he came in. That's gonna be on the fourth deck. Elevators right over there."

He thanked the corpsman, and took the elevator upstairs. He was met at the surgical admitting desk by a nurse. The ER had called them to alert her that the CO of Quigley's ship was on his way up. The nurse, a Navy Lieutenant, was being harried by two ringing phones and an impatient looking young doctor. She looked at Mike anxiously as he walked up, but he waved her off. "Take your time; I can wait."

She gave him a grateful look and returned to the three-ring circus at her charge desk. Mike looked around. The surgical admin area was at the junction of two halls. On one side were the swinging metal doors to the hallway containing the operating theaters; on the other a hallway led through swinging doors to wards and the special recovery rooms. There were several signs on the wall giving directions to various rooms and wards, along with faded safety precautions posters and hospital regulations. Mike had the sense that all the real action was behind the swinging doors. There was an uncomfortable looking wooden bench against one wall. He decided to remain standing. There was no one else in the desk area, until Diane Martinson came walking through the doors leading back to the recovery rooms.

Their eyes met across the waiting room. For a moment, neither of them spoke. She was dressed in the traditional Gray Lady hospital volunteer uniform, so called because the starched full shirtdress was a utilitarian gray with trim white borders. Diane wore no makeup and had her hair pulled into an efficient bun at the back of her neck. Mike still thought she looked like a million dollars. She walked over to him, her face carefully composed. He could not decide whether to call her Diane or Mrs. Martinson. Her face grew serious as she approached, and he belatedly remembered why he was here.

"Captain Montgomery. You're here to see about Fireman Quigley." In her hospital flats, she had to look up at him.

"Yes, I am," he answered, ducking the first name issue.

The nurse hung up the phone with a bang and groan of exasperation.

"Damn these infernal bureaucrats. They forget what we're supposed to be doing here!"

She composed her face and turned to where Diane and Mike were standing.

"Captain. Thanks for being patient. We've got kind of a zoo going here."

"No, problem, Lieutenant. I encounter zoos occasionally. How's my guy, Quigley?"

The nurse pulled a steel chart clipboard from a rack on the wall, and opened it up.

"Not terrific, Sir," she replied. "He's got two broken legs, some broken ribs, a possibly punctured lung, a dislocated shoulder, and several square inches of hide missing. Typical motorcycle accident, I'm afraid."

She looked up, wondering if her offhand comment might have offended the tall Commander.

"Can I see him?" asked Mike. "Is he, uh, awake?"

"Yes, Sir, I think he is—Mrs. Martinson, you've been back in recovery—is Fireman Quigley awake?"

"Yes, he is, although they have him pretty well sedated. Shall I show you back to recovery, Captain?"

She was keeping it formal, as if they had never met. Once again, she seemed uncomfortable in his presence. He decided to keep it all official if that's what she wanted.

"I'd appreciate that, Mrs. Martinson. I'm not going to try to take up a lot of his time or energy."

He turned to the nurse.

"His division officer, Lieutenant (JG) Sorento, is supposedly coming in. I want to see him before I leave, and then I'll need a phone with an outside line to call his parents."

"Of course, Sir. You can use Doctor Henry's office, right over there. Don't be too long in there; that kid is going to need his strength."

Mike smiled mentally at the twenty-four year old nurse calling the twenty year old sailor a kid.

"I understand. Mrs. Martinson, if you'll lead on..."

Diane walked in front of him through the swinging doors into the recovery area. He was conscious again of a faint perfume amongst all the antiseptic smells of the hospital. Her uniform dress rustled as she walked. He realized that he was a half a head taller than she was, and that her hair, even pulled tight into a bun, was thick and luxuriant. They stopped outside of yet another set of swinging doors, marked Recovery Four.

"There are two patients in here besides Quigley," she said, quietly, over her shoulder. "One appendectomy, a dependent wife, and one child who had to have her gall bladder taken out, of all things. Quigley is in the way back, behind the closed curtains. He's—he's not very pretty to look at."

She paused in front of the closed door to see if he had any questions.

"Do you volunteer here often?" he asked.

She looked up at him for a moment, seeming to weigh the propriety of a personal question under these circumstances.

"Yes, once a week, but usually on a weekday. They needed help today, so I came in. Shall we go in?"

He nodded, and they pushed through the door. The recovery bay contained four sections, each with a single bed backed up a bank of tubes, monitors, and steel tables with medical equipment in steel trays. The beds were ringed by freestanding screen curtain racks on wheeled frames. The light was subdued, owing to the deliberately dimmed lights and growing darkness outside as more clouds moved in. Diane pointed to Quigley's bed, and stepped aside to let him approach. Mike shivered. He hoped he would never have to spend time in a recovery room.

Quigley was on his back, his arms taped to splints at his side. His pale face seemed to be painted with blue, green, and yellow bruises all around his two very large black eyes. There was a great red scrape mark all the way across his forehead. He had tubes going down his nose and into both arms; his arm splints were taped to the bedside to ensure he did not disturb his IV's. His legs were also on splint boards, and they stuck out from under the covers like marshmallow man legs. Mike recognized the man, but he looked very much smaller in the bed, enmeshed in all the paraphernalia of life support systems. One swollen eye was partially open, and suddenly he realized that Quigley was looking at him. Forgetting Diane Martinson, he bent down closer to Quigley's face.

"Hey, snipe. You don't look like you're gonna be ready for the 20–24 in two firehouse tonight."

Quigley tried a grin, but his puffed lips barely managed a painful twist.

"Don't try to talk," Mike continued. "There's ladies present, and they're probably not used to snipe talk. Now, listen: Mr. Sorento is on his way in, and he's going to hang around until we know that you're stable and on the mend. The hospital has notified your parents, and I'm going to be calling them as soon as I'm done in here. If they want to come down, the ship will arrange for a motel room nearby. OK?"

Quigley blinked his eyes a couple of times; tears were welling up. Mike took Quigley's hand in his. It felt hot and dry.

"It hurts; I know it hurts, son. But they'll take good care of you, and we'll leave somebody back when we go out next week. You're not going to be alone. Diane—Mrs. Martinson—can I have a kleenex or something."

Her hand appeared next to his, and he took the sterile paper towel and dabbed Quigley's eyes a couple of times. From behind, Diane watched, marvelling at this big man's gentleness with the sailor. Her only contact with senior officers had been in circumstances where a certain amount of professional posturing and a polished, almost macho image was the order of the day. Montgomery was holding this young man's hand and wiping away his tears like he would a son, all the time reassuring the injured young man. For the first time, her attraction to him was infused by something besides the unmistakable sexual currents which seemed to flow when they met. She had to recompose her face when she realized he was getting ready to leave.

"Ok, snipe," he said. "The doctor'll be in soon. I'm gonna call your folks right now and let them know what's going on. You hang in there."

Diane escorted Mike back to the swinging doors. He smiled at her briefly; his eyes were not all that dry, either, she noticed.

"Will you stay with him for awhile?" he asked.

She nodded. "My relief comes in in about twenty minutes; but I'll stay with him until she shows up."

He nodded again, thanked her, and slipped out the door to make his calls. From across the recovery room bay, the young wife recovering from her appendectomy asked Diane if the big officer was the Captain of a ship.

"He sure is," said Diane. "In the best sense of the word."

The woman frowned, not quite sure what Diane was talking about. The woman asked her for a glass of water.

EIGHTEEN

Naval Air Station Jacksonville; Saturday, 19 April, 1630

By the time Mike had made his calls, checked back on Quigley, and talked to Lieutenant (J.G.) Sorento, it was well after four o'clock. He made his way to the entrance of the hospital and found that it was raining hard, the skies darkening even as he stood in the vestibule. He slipped into his plastic raincoat, pushed his hat down over his forehead, and made a run for his car. His shoes were soaked after about twenty feet by the standing water in the parking lot.

He made it to the Alfa and piled in, fighting the flapping raincoat as he wedged himself into the car. The rain drummed down on the car roof vengefully, as if angry that he was finally under cover. He lit off the engine, and waited for the rain to let up so that he could see where he was going. After a few minutes of increasingly harder rain, he decided to go.

Turning on his lights, he threaded his way out through the lanes of parked cars. The main hospital building was no longer visible, blotted out by sheets of rain; he had to stop in the lot periodically to get his bearings. Using a line of streetlights as a landmark to find the narrow exit road, he crawled along in first gear to make sure he stayed on the road, which was rapidly becoming indistinguishable from the flooded drainage ditches on either side. It was a serious, tropical rain, and he knew that those ditches were four feet deep. A sheet of lightning glared in the dark clouds overhead, followed by a boom of thunder. He turned his wipers on high, but without much effect. The entire area of the road ahead was a yellow white wedge of thrashing raindrops.

Coming around the second bend in the road he nearly ran into a car that was stopped ahead. Stopped and listing to starboard. As he closed in, he saw the car lurch even more to the right, its brake lights flaring in the rain. It ended up hanging at a precarious angle, half on the road, halfway into the ditch. It was a Volvo station wagon. As he slowed, the driver of the Volvo tried to pull it out to the left, but the rear end slid the last few remaining inches over into the ditch. The entire rear end began to sink down into the deep ditch, the drive wheel churning the water as the right brake light submerged, canting the front of the car up high enough for its headlights to illuminate the tops of the palm trees on the other side of the road. Then all the Volvo's lights went out as the water shorted the system. Scratch one Volvo, he thought, as he pulled up as close as he could get, turned on his flashers and set his hand brake.

He kept his engine running to provide lights. As he prepared to get out, he saw the driver's door open on the Volvo and a woman climb out. In the glare of his headlights he recognized Diane Martinson. She had no raincoat on, and the rain quickly soaked her Gray Lady uniform as she went around to look at the rear end of the car. She banged a fist on the back window of the Volvo, and then stumbled back as the car lurched even deeper into the ditch. She lost her footing and sat down hard.

Mike got out, forgetting his hat. He ran forward to where she was sitting in two inches of water in the pouring rain. Mike fought down a sudden wild impulse to laugh, and offered her his hands. He pulled her up off the road. She stood there, eyes blinking, not yet recognizing him.

"Dammit!" she cried. "I couldn't see the road. Look at my car. His car. He's absolutely going to kill me!"

Then she recognized him, and became aware that she was gripping both his hands. She let go, and turned to stare at the car. The rain came down even harder, as if it were proud of what it had done.

"Hey," he shouted over the noise of downpour. "Grab your purse and get in my car. I'll take you over to the Exchange garage and we'll get a tow truck."

He started back to the Alfa, but she just stood there looking at the Volvo. He went back, took her arm, and pulled her along to the Alfa, where he handed her into the right front seat. He went back to the Volvo, gingerly opened the driver side door, and recovered her purse; the car was still settling into the ditch. He ran back to the Alfa, opened the driver's side door, handed her the purse, and then went back to the Alfa's tiny trunk and extracted a flare. He tried for a minute to get the thing going, but the striker became soaked the moment he ripped the top off.

"Screw it," he said, throwing the flare into the ditch.

He got back into the Alfa. Diane sat there, soaked to the skin, her mouth tight and her eyes very close to tears. The rain drummed hard on the roof.

"Shit," she said.

"Shit, aye," he said, putting the Alfa in reverse.

He backed away from the Volvo, and then pulled out around the sinking sedan. He crept along the road even more carefully now; the ditch that could take one third of a Volvo could eat an entire Alfa. Diane remained silent for the next fifteen minutes as he navigated in first gear across the golf course perimeter roads towards the Exchange Service Station area. The rain continued, although not quite so hard.

They arrived at the Exchange gas station to find it dark. An attendant inside the small office waved him off as Mike figured it out. Power failure. He maneuvered the Alfa alongside the office door, and rolled his window down. The man stepped reluctantly into the doorway.

"We're shut down," he called. "No electricity."

"I don't need gas, I need a tow truck," Mike shouted over the noise of the rain on the metal overhang. "Got a Volvo in the ditch over by the hospital."

The attendant shook his head in the doorway.

"Truck's already out; we got a three car pile-up on the main drag. You can leave a work order if you want, and we'll get it when we can. But it's gonna be awhile. Like tomorrow, maybe."

"OK, we'll do that."

Mike rolled up the window, and pulled the Alfa under the gas pump line overhang. He looked over at Diane. The front of her hair was plastered to her forehead, and the Gray Lady dress was a sodden mass of wet cotton. He found himself staring again. She looked back at him for an instant, and then down at the floor.

"I have to call J.W.," she said, resignedly. "Might as well get it over with. I take it they can't help us."

"Not right now, but they'll go pull it out sometime tonight, or maybe in the morning, after this rain lets up a little and they get power back in this part of the base. I'll go in and call the cops on a base phone, and get the guy to work up a towing order. There's a pay phone over there you can use to get off base. I can run you home, and then you'll probably have to

118

come back over tomorrow morning. That's the best we can do, I'm afraid."

She nodded, and fished in her purse for a coin. She got out, and went to the pay phone. Mike got out and went inside to call the base police to report the Volvo. The rain on the tin roof of the gas line sounded like hail. The attendant wrote up the towing order, which Mike signed. By the time he came back out, she was standing at the edge of the office apron, with her back to him. He could see her shoulders shaking. Alarmed, he went over to her. She was crying silently, her arms folded over her stomach, her chest heaving in short gulps. He put his right hand on her shoulder.

"Hey. What happened?"

She did not turn around, but stood there, trying to get control of herself. He remained silent, his hand still on her shoulder, until she could speak. The attendant was watching through the window of the office. A car pulled into the gas islands, saw that there was no power, and pulled out again, its headlights sweeping across the two of them for an instant. Finally she spoke.

"He said—he said that I'm to stay here until they get the car out. He said I should have waited for the rain to stop before leaving the hospital. He said—I should have taken my car, and now that you've destroyed my Volvo, you get it fixed, and don't come home until you do. That's what my dear husband said. Among other things."

She closed her eyes in frustration. Mike shook his head.

"Hey, Diane," he said, speaking to her left ear over the noise of the rain on the roof. "They're probably not going to get that car out of there until tomorrow morning—they won't work those ditches in the dark. You can't make it happen any faster by hanging around here. I'll run you home—just give them a credit card, and let's get out of here."

She half turned towards him, leaning into him a little bit, her face still wobbly. She smelled of damp cotton, that perfume, and wet hair. He suddenly ached to take her in his arms. He steered her instead towards the office. They went in and she handed over a credit card for an imprint. The rain continued outside, but it was now a steady, Florida rain instead of a tropical monsoon. The attendant was obviously trying to figure out why the card said Captain, but the man with her was a Commander. He started to ask, but then looked at the woman's face and decided to mind his own business.

When they were finished in the office, they walked back to the Alfa. He started off again, headed for the back gate. Diane remained silent as they left the base and made their way towards the Jones Point bridge back across the St. Johns. She fussed in her purse for a comb and made a desultory pass through her wet hair before sighing and giving it up as a lost cause. He watched her out of the corner of his eyes; her dress was plastered to her lush figure. He concentrated on keeping his eyes on the road.

"I can't go home," she declared minutes later, as they turned north on A1A after crossing the bridge. "Not after what he said. I just can't."

He was silent for a long minute, and then took the plunge.

"I can offer a hot shower, a washer and dryer, and a drink back at the Lucky Bag. I'm the guy with the houseboat, remember?"

He kept his eyes on the road. What the fuck was he doing. A voice in his mind was telling him that he was being incredibly dumb. A second voice said, you want her. Her husband doesn't. You've rarely wanted a woman as much as you want this one. She can always tell you to take her to a neighbor's house.

"Thank you. I think I'll just take you up on that. It sounds like just what the doctor ordered," she said, her voice neutral.

It was her turn to keep her eyes on the road. They remained silent, alone with their thoughts all the way back to Mayport. A new band of heavy rains swept through as they arrived at the marina parking lot. They made a another dash through the downpour to the boat. He was glad that it was raining, that no one would see him with this woman. His heart was pounding as they climbed aboard, and it was not all from the quick sprint across the bulkhead pier. He flipped on lights and showed her below to the main lounge. She stood in the middle of the room, soaked and uncomfortable, looking around. Hooker roused himself on his perch when the lights came on, and stared at Diane. He bobbed his head back and forth a couple of times, and then gave a long, loud wolf whistle. Diane smiled.

"That bad, hunh, bird?" she said.

"That was a compliment," Mike laughed. "This way to the amenities."

He took her to one of the forward guest cabins, produced a full length, terry-cloth bathrobe and showed her where the bathroom shower was, checked towels, and handed her a Navy style laundry bag. She took her purse with her, gave him a brief smile, and closed the door. He went aft to get out of his own wet clothes and to shower. He dried off in his bathroom, and then paused for a moment, wondering what to put on. She would be in a bathrobe; it wouldn't do for him to get dressed up. He pulled on a pair of swim trunks, and then his own terrycloth bathrobe. He was setting up the bar when she reappeared a half hour later. He tried mightily not to stare.

The white bathrobe came down demurely to her ankles. She was carrying the laundry bag with its limp, wet contents. The bathrobe was made of a thick pile material that revealed nothing, but the flash of white lace in the laundry bag confirmed what he already guessed. Her dark, wet hair was pulled straight back in a limp mass covering the collar of the robe, accentuating the fine arch of her eyebrows, the lush contrast between her creamy, white skin and her dark eyes. She smiled tentatively before glancing away, clearly reading the interest in his eyes.

"I think I'm going to live," she said.

"You look—marvelous." He almost blushed. "What's your preference," he asked, nodding towards the bar.

"A brandy, I think," she said, coming closer. "Yes, a brandy. It's not cold, but it's been a brandy sort of day."

"Brandy it is. There's a washer-dryer set in the galley, just back there, if you want to get that stuff going. Soap's in the cabinet above the washer."

He poured two snifters of Courvasier while she attended to the laundry, and started to take them over to the leather couch.

"Goddamn," said Hooker. Mike diverted to the perch.

"Yeah, Bird. Goddamn is right. You want a hit?"

He tipped the snifter so that the bird could get his beak in the glass, but at the last moment he shook all his feathers and backed away from the fumes.

"You don't really let that bird drink alcohol, do you?"

She came over to the perch, where he handed her the other snifter. They stood side by side, watching Hooker as he weaved from side to side to keep them both in view. Mike was very much aware of her nearness. He could smell her wet hair, and a trace of perfume that had eluded the downpour outside. Part of his mind did a whirlwind comparison between this woman and the occasional dates he had brought home from the Jacksonville Beach bar scene. Diane projected the self assurance that all attractive women have, exuding a mature awareness of sexual competence without the coy trappings and flirtatious devices of the young single set. She was looking at Hooker, who continued to shift from one leg to the other, looking back at both of them.

"This parrot is a natural born boozer," Mike said. "But he mostly likes fruity sort of stuff—wine, gin and tonic, rum and tonic."

"Doesn't it make him drunk?"

"Absolutely. Once he starts to weave around, I have to put him in his drunk bird box until he sleeps it off."

She reached out to pet Hooker on the head. Mike held his breath. Hooker was into amputations. But this time the parrot bent his head sideways, looking at Diane first with one eye and then the other, and then, miraculously, bent his neck forward and let her scratch the bright green feathers on his neck.

"He must like you," said Mike. "Normally you would have been chomped by now."

"Where did you get him?" she asked, sampling the cognac.

"Bought him in Norfolk two years ago. Always wanted a parrot, but they tend to bond to their humans, and you can't leave them. When I found out I was coming to a ship that didn't deploy, I figured it was safe."

"What happens when you go out to sea for more than a couple of days?"

She sipped her cognac carefully, using one hand to hold the snifter, and the other to run a fingernail lightly through the bright plumage on the parrot's neck. Hooker kept his head down and made small sounds. Her robe was partially open at the top, revealing the swell of her breasts. Mike was torn between looking at her breasts and watching that fingernail slide up and down the parrot's neck feathers.

"He goes along." He smiled down at her. "As Captain, I can get away with that; couldn't do it before."

They stood together by the perch, not touching and yet within each other's personal space, she stroking the bird's head, he trying to tamp down a sense of building physical excitement, trying hard to pretend that something wasn't happening between them. A sudden burst of heavy rain drummed on the cabin roof. The boat moved slowly in the wind sweeping off the intracoastal.

She watched the parrot for a long minute, and then stepped away from the perch, walking towards the after end of the lounge, towards the couch. She stood before it for a moment, as if trying to decide something. He watched her carefully, excited by the way the robe clung to her hips. The muted grind of the washing machine in the galley tried to compete with the noise of the rain overhead. She gave her head a little shake, and then sat down, pulling the robe modestly around her legs. Mike discovered that he had been holding his breath. He relaxed, and moved to join her on the couch.

"Aw, shit," croaked the parrot.

They both broke up, laughing a little louder than necessary. He sat down and looked at her. She smiled.

"For a moment there..." she said.

"Yeah. Me too. It's the cognac, I guess."

She looked at him. Her eyes were almost purple in the dim light of the cabin.

"No, it's not the cognac. I wanted—I mean, we're both grownups here. You've been very nice to me, and J.W., my husband, is not very nice to me. It's kind of complicated. I've just recently made a discovery: my husband has a girlfriend." She lowered her eyes in embarrassment.

Mike did not know what to say, so he kept his silence. She looked back up at him.

"You're an attractive man, and over there, standing next to you, I felt—something. Part of me would very much like to indulge my desires for awhile, but the part that's been married for sixteen years keeps surfacing the usual consequences."

She looked directly at him for a moment before continuing, her eyes luminous.

"I don't think I have what it takes to have an affair, to sneak around, to manage the deception. I'm the type who would just come right out with it one morning, admitting all, and I'm not prepared to put up with what would follow. That's what I meant by consequences; I've seen it too often in the Navy."

She looked away again. He started to say something, but she put a finger to her lips.

"Let me finish, before I lose my nerve. I wanted—I still want, actually—for you to make love to me. When we ran into each other at the O-Club, and again when you gave us the tour of the boat, I felt the attraction. I think you feel the same thing."

He waited, his mind whirling.

"As you've guessed," she continued, "my marriage is not, I don't know—working? Is that the word these days? No, that doesn't quite describe it."

She tossed her head impatiently, and sipped some cognac. She continued to keep her eyes averted from his face.

"J.W. and I are at the going through the motions stage. When we first got married, he explained to me that his career in the Navy would come first and foremost, that he was determined to make Admiral, and that getting to Flag rank would take a hundred percent effort. I went along with that. I was supposed to have the family, and do what was required to support his career. We tried hard to have kids, but that didn't work out. Which meant that the career became everything. And even that was pretty interesting, at least for awhile. He was on the fast track, and people seemed to think he was a comer."

"But—?"

"But. I found out that his career didn't leave much of a role in life for me. I tried a couple of things—real estate in Washington, going back to school, and that filled in the empty space for awhile, but J.W. made it clear that I could do anything I wanted as long as it didn't interfere with my support role."

"And, of course, everything you tried did just that."

"Yes. That was made clear, always in a subtle manner, but clear. And now, I find out he's been seeing some woman on his trips to Norfolk. I realized that I was an important part of the frame but not part of the picture. I should have guessed, of course; the wife's the last one to figure it out."

Mike wanted to reach out for her, to hold her. Her discomfort was palpable.

"Is the woman someone you know?" he asked.

"No. I found out quite by accident. I almost wish I hadn't. She's in the Navy, of all things. A Commander, on the Fleet Commander's staff in Norfolk. J.W. goes to Norfolk to meetings all the time because the Admiral hates to go to conferences. She has a condo out in Virginia Beach. He gets a room at the BOQ, but stays with her. It's apparently been going on for nearly two years."

"How did you find all this out?"

She laughed, a short, bitter sound.

"At one of those awful receptions at the O'Club. I was in the ladies room, and two women came in while I was in a stall. They were talking about J.W., how good looking he is, and all about—her."

Mike leaned back in the couch, unsure of what to say. He was sorry for her pain, but at the same time aware that the fact of her husband's infidelity somehow changed the equation. He remembered the aviator's comments that she was scouting. He wondered if she was, behind all the protestations, ready to have an affair of her own. She looked across at him and smiled a bittersweet smile, as if reading his thoughts. He felt himself beginning to blush.

"Does he know you know?" he asked, trying to divert his own thoughts.

"No," she said, shaking her head. "I was very hurt for awhile, but I'm not sure what a confrontation would prove. He has his career, his nice office, the staff at his beck and call, a mistress, and a presentable wife. I have my volunteer work at the hospital and at the Navy Relief Office, the nightly round of receptions, a very nice set of quarters on the beach, and a presentable husband. Most women in America would think I was pretty well off. But lately it's gotten pretty lonely inside; I keep thinking that there's something else—you know the song, is that all there is?"

She smiled ruefully and sipped her cognac again.

"And then I say to myself that I'm being stupid, that there are thousands of women who have not one tenth of what I have and to grow up and shut up. Maybe even he will grow up one day."

She shook her head again, as if to clear away the complexity of what she was trying to say.

"I think that what I desperately need is to be, well, wanted. As a woman, as a wife, as even a friend. And now, here I am, on a bachelor's boat, with nothing on under this robe, and a very attractive and considerate man a few feet away, and part of me is saying, Diane, he wants you, you want him, do it for God's sake, let go, and the other part is saying, don't be an ass—married women who fool around always, but always, get nothing but pain out of it, even when their husbands are cheating on them."

She shook her head again, slowly.

"I'm not doing this very well. Maybe I better just get the hell out of here."

He moved closer to her on the couch. He leaned across the space between them, reached out and brushed her cheek with the back of his fingers. She turned her face slightly.

"You must live right," he said, softly.

She looked at him, a question forming in her eyes. He cupped her face in his hand for a moment, and then leaned back.

"My turn. I was married briefly to a girl I thought I knew; came back from a deployment to find out she'd left me for a lawyer, for God's sake, and that I didn't know anything, not anything, about her, and probably not about women in general. I've been single now for, what, almost as long as you've been married, sixteen years; in all that time, I've made it a hard and fast rule never to go after another man's wife. I have this superstition, see: if I take up with another man's wife, it will come back to haunt me. One day, maybe, I'll fall in love, and get married, and then some evil bastard will come along and seduce my wife, and I'll find out, and there won't be shit I can do about it, because I will have been guilty of the same crime. It's silly, probably, but there it is. And it's a bitch, lady, because when an attractive, married woman sends out that "I want" signal, all the sweet young single things get blown right out of the room. I don't know what it is, exactly—basic biology, I guess."

He threw up his hands in a gesture of exasperation.

"So, yes," he continued. "I would dearly love to take that robe off, but, right now my stupid conscience would get in the way. But not for lack of inspiration."

They looked into each other's eyes for a long moment. She made a small sound, deep in her throat as tears welled up in her eyes. He slid over then and held her while she wept, great wracking sobs, punctuated after a few minutes by the beginnings of hyperventilation. He patted her on the back and calmed her, telling her that it would be all right, to breathe slower, until she quieted. He left her on the couch and went to the bathroom, returning with a cold cloth. He wiped her face gently, erasing the smudged remains of mascara, and reducing the blotches of color on her cheeks. She kept her eyes closed while he did this; he was glad that she did, because he did not think he could restrain himself from loving this woman whose need was so strong. He continued to smooth the skin of her face with the cloth, tracing her features, marvelling at the folly of a man who could ignore this woman. He suddenly found himself to be ravenously hungry.

"Are you hungry?" he asked.

She opened her eyes and looked at him blankly for an instant, as if she were trying to fathom the question. He tried again.

"I'm not a bad cook, and I've just decided that I'm starving. Let me fix something, and then we'll get you home."

She nodded quickly.

"Yes. That would be nice. And thank you—for everything."

Her voice wavered, as she understood what he was doing—breaking the tension. They were both very close to being overwhelmed by their separate desires. He looked down at her face for a moment.

"I think I might be kicking myself in the tailfeathers when you're gone," he admitted, smiling. "I'm pure hell on what might have been's."

She looked back at him, the beginnings of a smile playing across her face.

"Sex without intimacy is usually a disaster, Captain," she said. "I read that in a book somewhere, so it must be true. The fact that you did not take advantage of me inclines me to think that I don't—I don't want to just drop things, if you can understand that. I'd like to build, well, intimacy. Yes. That's the right word. I think that's my basic problem, the absence of intimacy. I desperately need a—someone. Can you put up with that idea?"

He paused for a moment, his face serious.

"Yes, I think so, but you have to understand that I don't believe in adult men and women being just friends when there's sexual desire

126

between them. That's just an exercise in mutual frustration. I'm all for the intimacy, but only because that makes the loving that much more profound."

She nodded her understanding.

"Yes. I'm not sure I know what I'm doing just now. But I'm going to do something. I can't just let things keep drifting, now that J.W. has stepped over the line."

"Well, you probably already know that I don't stand very high on your husband's hit parade, and professionally I don't think very much of him or his tactics. I hope to hell he doesn't make Admiral, although I'm finding out that he's more likely to make flag than I am to make Captain. I guess you're going to have to decide whether or not you're a free agent. If you are, I'd love to take up your option."

"The ironic thing," she said with a sigh, "Is that I suspect he's taken up with her as much for her access to the Fleet Commander's inner sanctum as for any other reason. But maybe I'm just rationalizing. He may actually find her more attractive."

"I find that kind of unlikely."

"Thank you, kind Sir," she said with a smile. "You better go make us dinner before we talk ourselves into trouble."

She got up from the couch, and went to the porthole, staring out over the inland waterway in the rain. He walked up behind her, aching to put his arms around her, but he stopped himself. He could see the reflections of their faces on the porthole glass, pale blurs in the indistinct light of the cabin.

"I'm very much attracted to you," he said in a low voice. "I'd call it falling in love, but it probably isn't, not yet, anyway. But I think I'd like it to be love, and when it is, I want to hold you and love you and keep you. Until then—"

She turned to look at him over her shoulder.

"Until then," she finished for him, "I want to see you, and get to know you, and maybe sort out in my own mind what's going on. I know I can't keep going on like I have been, or I'm going to go crazy."

He toyed with the tips of her hair, if only to keep his hands off the rest of her.

"Good," he said. "That way we can both make sure this feeling is not just a temporary short circuit between our brains and our groins, as my XO says."

She turned all the way around and stared at him for a moment, and then her face began to work, her mouth forming the words short circuit and before she dissolved in helpless laughter.

"OK, OK, people, it's chow time in the city," he announced in a loud voice. He left her standing by the porthole, still laughing.

"I'll have you know that I am a chef of some repute," he called from the galley door. "I will now make you a goor-met dinner. But first, we gotta get some atmosphere in here."

He came back in from the galley with a bottle of white wine and two glasses. He motioned for her to return to the couch. Opening the wine with much ceremony at the bar, he filled the glasses, and brought them over to the couch. He put the wine down on the coffee table, went over to the stereo and fired up a Vivaldi tape. Then he went over to the fireplace, turned on the gas log and adjusted the flame. He turned out two of the three table lamps, and returning to the couch, he bowed theatrically as she clapped silently at all the accoutrements of seduction.

"A little late, but de rigueur," he said. "Just so you know that I know how; I have my reputation to protect, after all. Now, you just relax, and I will go see what's available."

"Then we have to figure out how you're going to get me home tonight," she called, as he went into the galley.

"No sweat," he called back.

Half an hour later he brought back a tray of shrimp sauteed in seasoned butter, hot French bread, and a salad. They ate hungrily, relaxing, finally, to enjoy each other's company, lingering over dinner until the lights suddenly went out as the power failed. The gas log continued to burn, providing the only light. Vivaldi died with the lights, as did the air conditioners. The sound of the rain grew louder in the sudden silence.

They ignored the power failure, absorbed in each other's company. They sat on the couch in the flickering firelight for another hour, talking, exploring each other's pasts and present. She described her years as a Navy wife, the long separations, the envy she sometimes felt when she saw other Navy wives wrap themselves up in their children while their men were gone to sea, trying as she did to pick her way through the slow desiccation of her own marriage, speculating on precisely when her husband had sought another woman's companionship, or perhaps even love.

He described to her the years following the loss of his own spouse, his own absorption with career, and the subconscious decision to shut any permanent relationships with women out of his life, and how that decision, which he had always termed "for awhile" had solidified over time into years. She mused about the parallels, how they both had defined their personal existences in terms of careers and what was missing from their lives, consciously at first and then, as with much of life, by sheer force of habit.

Mike listened avidly, content to watch her face and to be with her. It seemed to him that they were communicating on two levels at the same time: the first filled with the medley of necessary but superficial things two people ought to know about one another, and the second a thrumming reinforcement of desire, the small, vital moves of body language and nuance of expression, the touching without touching that creates the delectable prelude to joining. He was surprised to find himself beginning to experience an exquisite anticipation of love in a way he had not felt for years. They were both careful not to look directly at each other for very long, as if both were aware that even a long look would be a sufficiently volatile conduit, once established, to allow passion to flare in defiance of their careful approach to each other's feelings.

They talked about the Navy, and how it had both surprised and occasionally disappointed them. He told her of his years in Vietnam operations, first as skipper of a gunboat on the rivers, and then later on the shore bombardment gunline and in the Tonkin Gulf, and how he had thought that building a combat record was the most important thing he could do to further his career. But then you found out, she said, that the clever young men who had positioned themselves close to rising Admirals and not necessarily the sea-going operators were the ones who snapped up the early promotions and the elegant assignments close to the seats of power in the Navy. It's just the system, he told her; once I had it figured it out I could have gone along. I chose not to, stayed at sea, and now other guys have the big new ships and go out on deployments.

She asked if he was going to stick it out in the Navy for a full thirty years. Mike shook his head thoughtfully. "I don't think so. All my Navy career I worked to get command, and now that I have it, I'm finding out that I may have aimed a bit too low."

"But lots of officers never get command," she reminded him.

"Yeah, but the truth is that command isn't at all what I thought it would be. My image of it was formed as a junior officer: the Captain this, the Captain that, the Captain God Almighty in his cabin and on the bridge. They ring the bells on the quarterdeck when you come and go, and they all stand up when you come into the room. For the first few days after I assumed command I kept mentally looking behind me to see if the Captain was behind me when everybody got up, and then it finally sank in. And then you read the Navy Regs, what the Captain is personally and finally and ultimately and irrevocably responsible for, and it curls your hair. I started out by lying awake nights wondering what I would do if this situation or that situation arose; I had dreams about getting into maneuvering situations, and having the whole bridge watch freeze as they waited for me to give the magic order that would keep us from colliding or going aground or hitting the pier. I got over it, but it took awhile and the responsibility took the bloom off the rose of command at sea, let me tell you."

She smiled sympathetically. "Sounds like some romantic notions just being worn off by reality. And maybe just a bit of an overactive imagination."

He laughed. "I keep forgetting you're a Navy wife; you must have heard all this before."

"No, not directly. J.W. took his first command tour all in stride, as if it were his natural due. He is a vain man, I finally figured out. He never let command worry him very much, but, then, he also short-toured. He told me that his mentors told him to "limit his exposure in command", as they put it. I think in retrospect that he lacked the imagination to be particularly apprehensive about the burdens of command."

Mike began to feel uncomfortable with this talk of her husband; that first voice was back. He got up and went over to Hooker's perch, put the parrot on his left hand, and came back to sit down again on the couch. He began to scratch the bird's head while he talked.

"Well, Goldsborough is all work and very little fun. I mean fun in the professional sense—all we do is churn through the peacetime drill of training, replacing personnel, doing maintenance and mostly boring operations. It'd be different if we got to go overseas with the deployed fleets, to go out and do something real, but Goldsborough is too old. Everybody knows she's going out of commission next year, so nobody cares too much about the ship. We end up going through the motions of maintaining readiness, but the whole crew knows it's a drill. You can't fool them, and I'm no longer inclined to even try. I wish that I had gotten a better command, a deploying ship instead of the Oldy Goldy."

"Why did you get Goldsborough," she asked, remembering J.W.'s revelations about putting non-conformists in special boxes. "All those decorations you wear usually mean better things than a training ship."

He nodded and sighed.

"Because on my third ship I fucked up—excuse me—because I made a significant professional error one night, and there was a collision. The Bureau told me when I got command that the only reason I was being given a ship was because of my war record. Goldsborough wasn't the greatest assignment, naturally, but you know how it is with a command: you can take it or leave it, but if you ever decline one, you'll never get another offer. So I took it."

"I'm curious about this collision incident," she said quietly. She was leaning back on the couch, her face obscured in the darkness. "Frankly, you don't strike me as the type who makes mistakes like that."

He stared down at the parrot's shiny feathers, his eyes becoming unfocused as he thought back to that night years ago. Then he stood up from the couch, and walked over to one of the portholes.

"I was the Evaluator in CIC, the senior officer on the watch team. We were in a night carrier screen formation, a little after one in the morning. The OOD lost the bubble and got confused over a change of station tactical signal. While he was trying to sort it out with the Junior Officer of the Deck, the Officer in Tactical Command on the carrier signalled to execute the maneuver. The OOD called the Captain, told him he was in trouble, and then, finally, and much too late, he called me. I came out onto the bridge to help him sort it out; the Captain came out on the bridge about a minute after I did. He was angry at being called, and even more pissed off when he found out his whole bridge watch team had lost the picture."

"He was a screamer, so, naturally, he started yelling, without really knowing what the tactical maneuvering situation was, and chewing everybody's ass in the process. The OOD went into the parrot mode: tell me what to say, Boss, and I'll parrot those orders. I was pissed off at getting yelled at, especially because I hadn't done anything wrong, and was actually trying to help. So I clammed up and said nothing. While all of this was going on, ships were going everywhere. It was pitch dark and windy, so everything was being done by radar. If it had been daylight, if we could have *seen* the other ships, it would probably never have happened."

"What happened?"

"The Captain finally started issuing maneuvering orders, which, by the book, meant that he had assumed the conn. The rest of us were now legally superfluous. He told the OOD to come left; I knew in my guts that that was the wrong order. They hammer it into you in maneuvering and emergency shiphandling school: never turn left in a situation where there's risk of collision. But. Because I'd been part of the initial problem, and was now too afraid or too pissed off to speak up, I held my silence. The next thing I knew there was a big shape fine on our starboard bow showing a red running light and a hell of a crash and everybody and everything went flying. Three of our sailors in a forward berthing compartment were crunched into dogmeat by the bow of a cruiser."

Mike stared off into space for a long minute. Not for the first time did he see again the darkened pilothouse, the faces of the watch officers, pale green in the illumination from the dim radar screens, their eyes wide with apprehension as the Captain shouted questions and curses, and then gave the fatal order. Not left. Tell him, don't just stand there. You don't ever turn left. Tell him. Tell him!

"And they blamed you for this?" she asked, bringing him back to the present. He was silent for a few moments before going on.

"Not exactly. The investigation, and then the eventual court martial officially blamed the OOD and the Captain. The OOD for not calling the Captain sooner, when he first got into trouble, and the Captain for turning the wrong way when he was in extremis. The Captain was relieved for cause. I was a made a "party" to the investigation—that's what a Board of Investigation calls accessories to the crime. In one sense, I was exonerated: the original maneuvering recommendation we had sent out from CIC had been the correct interpretation of the signal, and both the OOD and the Captain had ignored it. But. The investigation board took a swipe at me in their official report for not speaking up when I thought that the Captain's final maneuvering order was wrong. They said that I had, and that I probably knew that I had, a better picture of the maneuvering situation than the Captain did. The President of the Board gave me a lecture about an officer's responsibility to speak up regardless of the possible consequences to himself. Because the Captain legally had the conn, they couldn't legally blame anything on me. But as you've probably heard, the system neither forgets nor forgives. It was never put into a fitness report or anything, but the taint of having participated in a disaster tends to linger in the Navy for a long time."

She shook her head in disbelief. "And you're convinced to this day that you did own a piece of it."

"Yup," he said, looking down at the floor. "For awhile, I tried to rationalize it, say I tried and all that, but I remember, all too vividly and all too often, a little voice inside me on the bridge that night telling me to do *something,* just don't stand there because you just got your tail bit..."

"But what would have happened if you had spoken up—would the Captain have countermanded his order?"

"Probably not. He was always more of a transmitter than a receiver. But there was always the chance that he might have hesitated, and then maybe we might have had a near miss instead of a bang in the night and three body bags. So that's the part I own."

She was silent for a few minutes. He came back to the couch, pitched Hooker up on his shoulder, and reached for his wine.

"And now you're the proud owner of Goldsborough?"

"For my sins, yes. I mean, hell, they could have told me no for command altogether, so I guess half a loaf, et cetera. But a lot of the professional satisfaction that ought to come from destroyer command is missing from this old girl. Like this stupid submarine thing."

"I've heard J.W. talking about that. He acted like it was some kind of joke. A joke on you, if you must know."

"That doesn't surprise me," he sighed. "The Commodore tells me that the Chief of Staff disapproves of me and my life style."

He paused for an instant as the irony of the Chief of Staff's wife sitting here in the darkness with him sank in. He wondered if she caught it, too. He quickly continued.

"And it's a typical mission for Goldsborough. Some fishermen reported seeing a 'U-boat'; that's what they called it. Made it sound like they actually saw a surfaced German submarine from World War II out in the fleet operating areas. Gimme a break. So we get sent out to have a look, and, of course, find absolutely nothing. The chances that a foreign conventional sub would be operating off the coast of Florida is almost zero. Maybe in wartime, but these days? Bullshit. Nobody would have any reason to do that. Then last week one of the local fishing boats went missing; we were told to conduct a search, and we find an oil slick and a name board. The Coast Guard found the boat on the bottom using a robotic TV system. No damage, no holes, signs of fire or anything. Big mystery. But certainly no plausible connection to a submarine."

He told her the various theories of why the boat was lost, and something about Chris Mayfield and the missing crew. He told her about the bullet hole in the nameboard. She listened intently.

"Now some of the local guys are saying that the phantom submarine got Mayfield, because of the bullet hole in the nameboard. So the Admiral decides to do some public relations damage control to make sure the local Navy doesn't look as if it doesn't care. Goldy gets to go back out next week and look for the phantom submarine again. It's stupid. If Mayfield did mix it up with somebody, then druggies would be the most likely answer."

She turned to face him.

"What if it's true," she asked. "What if there is a submarine out there, and it did sink the fishing boat?"

"C'mon," he protested, sitting up. "It's all sweetness and light between the Sovs and us; what would be the point?"

"What if it's not a Russian submarine? Don't other countries have conventional submarines? Diesel boats, I think you call them?"

He got up from the couch again, and put Hooker back on his perch. He began pacing around the dark lounge.

"Yes, of course. Our NATO Allies have exclusively diesel boats, except for the Brits and the French—they've got some nukes. But—"

"You keep labelling this thing as if it came from, I don't know, a known source, like the Russians or NATO Europe. I think I've heard J.W. talk about other countries, like the North Vietnamese, and the Israelis, and some of the Arab countries—you know, some of the bad guys. If there really is a submarine out there, could it be one of theirs?"

He turned to look at her in the firelight; her body a white form on the leather couch. A Captain's wife, talking shop. A sudden apprehension filled him. What the hell was he doing here, messing around with a senior officer's wife? He was glad that she couldn't see his eyes in the darkness at this moment. But she'd made a point—what if it were one of the crazies? He thought about it for a minute.

"I suppose," he said. "I suppose it could be done...I mean, the Germans ran 12,000 mile patrols during the war; so did our guys in the Pacific. Diesels are economical as hell; long range is what they do best. I suppose if somebody wanted to deploy a diesel boat all the way over here, from, say, the Med, it could be done."

He shook his head before continuing.

"But what the hell for? Yassir Arafat going to start a war of shipping attrition against the United States fishing fleet? Most of those rag-heads only have three or four boats, max, and most of them don't work. Hell, Diane, it doesn't wash. Dispatch a boat all the way to the east coast of the U.S. to start sinking the Mayport shrimping fleet? What's more likely is somebody's smoking dope or drinking too much Jim Beam. Some old fart dreaming about being in the convoys during World War II, waking up, and seeing U-boats."

She got up and went over to the porthole. The storm was playing out, the lightning moving offshore, creating a vivid sound and light show among the piled clouds over the ocean.

"Well, at least you get to go out," she said wistfully. "I have to stay at home. Which reminds me, we need to get me home before my sweet husband sends out the base police to check on his missing car and possibly his missing wife."

He joined her at the porthole, and looked down at her.

"Last I heard, he didn't seem to give much of a shit where you spent the night, just as long as he got his Volvo back in one piece."

She smiled sweetly. "Which is one of the reasons I spent the best part of it with you, kind Sir."

Before he knew what was happening, she turned and put her hands on his shoulders and kissed him, withdrawing before he had time to react.

The momentary press of her body against his had transmitted a promise that made him ache.

"What time is it?" she asked then, matter of factly.

He looked at his watch, while trying to find his voice.

"It's 1230. I guess it's story time."

"Yes," she said, smiling ruefully. "Story time."

He collected the wine glasses and the remains of dinner, and headed for the galley.

"No biggee," he called over his shoulder. "We keep the essential elements as they happened, with the exception of you having come here. I did find you at the car, took you to the gas station, and then we waited around for them to do something. When they didn't, we stopped for dinner in Orange Park, went back, waited some more, and then I brought you straight home to the quarters. I had reason to be out there at NAS because of the motorcycle accident, which the Group knows about by now."

"I need to do something about my clothes," she said.

"Take 'em out of the washer and put 'em in the dryer for ten minutes; put them on all wrinkled—it corroborates your being out in the elements."

"Or I could always tell him I got picked up by a super horny sailor, taken to his pad, and ravished repeatedly. It'd be worth it to see his face."

She kept her voice light, but there was an undercurrent of bitterness in it. He paused with a dish in his hands.

"Well, you can always call. If you're going to burn some bridges, the boat's right here," he said.

His voice had carried a hint of worry. She laughed at him in the darkness.

"I don't even know your phone number," she said.

"I don't give it out to just anybody. They have to qualify."

"That might take some time," she whispered.

"Then you probably shouldn't burn bridges. Yet," he said. "Makes it hard to get back across the creek."

The quarters were dark when they pulled up. There was not even a porch light on. She got out of the car. Her hair still damp from the trip from the houseboat to his car, her gray lady uniform a wrinkled, damp sack. She bent to look back at him in the window.

"I can't thank you enough, Commander," she said, loud enough for ears to hear if any were listening. "We'll go recover the car in the morning, as soon as they get it out of that ditch."

He smiled at her in the door. She closed it, and walked briskly up the walk to the quarters. A light came on inside the house as she unlocked the front door. Story time.

NINETEEN

USS Goldsborough, Monday, 21 April, 1730

Goldsborough swayed slightly as she cut across the afternoon ebb tide currents in the St. Johns river and pointed fair for the open ocean. The afternoon sunlight was a welcome relief from a weekend of rain. The beach sand gleamed in golden tones on either side of the river entrance. Seagulls swirled at the edge of the rip currents, and the rocks on the jetties along the base perimeter were spotted with fishermen in pursuit of flounder. The temperature was hovering in the mid-eighties, and everyone seemed to be in a better mood now that the rains were over and the ship was headed back out to sea.

Mike sat in his chair on the bridge, watching the Officer of the Deck conn the ship out through the river buoys. A warm breeze flowed into the pilothouse through the bridge windows, and the whine of the forced-draft blowers made a comforting sound after all the normal confusion of getting underway. He was glad to get free from the basin and all of its hectoring "support".

Monday morning inport had been a zoo, with several stores trains appearing alongside, a visit from the Commodore and his engineering staff to take a look at the main plant, and the usual complement of last minute people problems that always seemed to crop up on a departure day. Some of the crew had acted as if the ship were going out on deployment instead of week's operations, and there had been a larger than usual complement of wives and girl friends on the pier when they pulled out.

Mike had still not briefed them on the details of their "mission"; he was not sure he had the right words together yet. The word was out in the ship that they were going after the mysterious submarine again, and that it was somehow connected to the sinking of the Rosie III. Make it look real, the Admiral and the Commodore had said. Appearances über alles. The ship put her nose down into the first Atlantic roller as she cleared the St. Johns bar, and the men up on the forecastle stepped back handsomely away from the sides in anticipation of a blast of spray, but none appeared. The sea surface was almost flat calm under a big Bermuda high building in the southeast.

Mike reflected on the weekend, savoring his, what should he call it, encounter with Diane. He recognized that he was firmly in lust; he feared that he might also be falling in love. It had only been two days, and he wanted her so badly that he almost hoped something else would break down so that they would come back into port early. His face reddened at this disloyal thought; he called for coffee. The boatswain mate jumped to rig him a cup. Acting just like any other sailor fresh from a good liberty, he thought. He wondered how many others in his ship had set sail this afternoon with the perfume of a woman lingering in their faces. The Chief of Staff's wife, Dummy, the little voice in his head said. I know, I know.

He had brought Hooker aboard Sunday afternoon to avoid being too flagrant about having a pet aboard the ship. The crew joined him in a conspiracy of silence because having a parrot gave their Captain a little extra panache. He tried not to flaunt it, however, and always brought Hooker aboard hidden in his drunk box, and then only on weekends when there was a minimum number of people onboard. His cabin steward had told him that there was always a sudden increase in the number of visitors to his cabin when Hooker was onboard. Electricians needed to check the lights, A-gang snipes wanted to check the air conditioning, and the yeomen cleaned out his outbasket hourly instead of once a day. Hooker's vocabulary was much admired, and Mike suspected that the sailors had expanded it somewhat during their visits.

"Sir, recommend we secure the special sea and anchor detail," said the XO, who was also the ship's navigator.

"Yeah, OK. Wrap it up. What's the start point for this caper?"

"O85 for eighty miles," replied the Exec. "Then I propose we work a box, north and south along the Stream."

He eyed the Captain for a moment, and then stepped closer to the chair, out of earshot of the bridge watch.

"You plan to brief the crew, Cap'n?"

"Yes, I suppose I must."

Mike got down from his chair, and moved over to the chart table at the back of the pilothouse. The XO went with him, and they looked down at the chart for a long moment.

"Soon's I figure out how to describe all of this without laughing out loud."

The Exec nodded thoughtfully.

"It does seem strange," he said. "I can't quite get my mind around the possibility that there's some kind of hostile submarine dicking around out here and whacking fishing boats."

"Don't spend a lot of brain fuel on it, XO," Mike snorted. "What we'll really need are some inventive sitreps to send back in which we show how hard we're trying. I gave Ops an addressee list for the messages. First one ought to go out, say, 1800 tonight. Maybe put a general plan of intentions in it, hunh?"

"Yes, Sir. Any suggestions as to what our intentions are?"

"No." Mike grinned down at the XO. "I'm waiting for my executive staff to tell me. You guys use your fertile imaginations. I'll approve it, OK?"

The Exec shook his head.

"OK, yes, Sir," he said.

Mike was silent for a moment, looking down at the chart of the Jacksonville operating areas.

"Maybe *you* ought to brief the crew, XO. I think if I do it, my attitude about this whole deal is going to show through. I don't want to infect the crew with the way I feel about it. We have our orders, and we should carry them out, no matter what I think about it. You get on the 1MC and give 'em the word, with as many facts as we have. I'll go down to my cabin and pout."

The Exec laughed. "Pout, aye. I wish to hell we were going south."

"Yeah, me too," said Mike ruefully. "That's the thing that really pisses me off. We're up here doing this birdshit op while the real players go do Navy stuff. I almost wish there were a submarine up here so I could sink something and kill somebody."

The Exec was mildly surprised at this uncharacteristic blast of bitterness from his normally upbeat CO.

"Other than that, Captain, did you have a good weekend?" he asked innocently.

Mike gave him a look. There was no way the XO...

"Yeah, other than that," he said, "My weekend was just fine. Rain day and night, power outages to help the air conditioning in my boat, one of my guys gets creamed on a bike, yeah, all in all, terrific weekend. Aarrgh."

"Uh, yes, Sir. Got the picture. We'll call you when we've worked up the search plan and the first sitrep."

"Thanks, XO."

At 1900, Mike was in his cabin giving Hooker a head scratch when the Exec knocked on his door and came in. Mike looked up.

"Evening, XO. Got the plan?"

"Yes, Sir. Plan, first sitrep, and some notes on what I'm going to tell the crew."

"OK, lemme see. Back on your perch, bird."

Mike flipped the parrot back onto the wooden A-frame perch standing next to his desk. Hooker complained and gave the XO a dirty look, and then began to sharpen his beak on the perch. The XO handed over the folders, keeping his distance from the bird; he did not care for birds. Mike read through the general plan for the search, and then the draft of the first situation report, nodding his head as he skimmed the material. "OK, this looks good."

He initialled the release line on the message draft and handed it back to the Exec.

"You're opting for a southern orientation, which is as good as any, I guess."

"Yes, Sir, six of one, half dozen of the other. One thing the ASW officer pointed out: we should map the bottom of the areas we search, you know, record the wrecks, pinnacles, and things like that. We've got a bottom contour chart, but we ought to tie the sonar picture we see to each anomaly in case we ever have to chase this guy around the area."

"This guy? Careful, XO, you're gonna have yourself believing this fairy tale."

The Exec grinned self-consciously.

"Well," he said. "I guess I'm getting into character. Seeing as I have to brief the crew..."

"Yeah, yeah, OK. Somebody has to be Joe sincere. Might as well be you. And I agree with that business of building a bottom chart. The mine hunting guys call it bottom conditioning—they work over harbor areas and the approaches to our major naval bases all the time, and map and map and map—everything on the bottom that sticks out. That way when some bad guy lays a mine out there, they can pick it up because it's new. Takes time, though."

"Yes, Sir, but Linc's got that computer program, remember? He's got a PC up in Combat that we can use to generate the maps; he's been dying to use it for something, and this seemed like the perfect deal."

"I agree. Then we can write it up and put him in for a tactical improvement program award. Kid's pretty sharp."

"Yes, Sir. Now the other things have to do with the watches: I can't see putting the ship at ASW condition two for something we both think is a figment. We're going to be doing this for at least a week, and we'll exhaust the watch officers pretty quick if we put them up on port and starboard, six on, six off, watches. We get a contact that looks like something, well, then we set the 1AS detail. Otherwise three sections on the bridge and in CIC. That sound OK?"

Mike swiveled in his chair and thought for a moment. The Exec's reasoning made sense, as long as the premise was correct, namely that there was nothing out there. Out here, he corrected himself. But if they did turn up something, and this mythical submarine started a fight, the ship would be less prepared to defend herself than if a fighting watch was posted. A Captain could be forgiven many things, but being surprised was not one of them. The staffies at Group would just love to see the trouble-maker of the Goldsborough get caught with his operational pants down.

"Let's do this, XO," he replied. "I'll grant you the three section watch instead of port and starboard, but I want the torpedoes and the depth charges ready to go, and enough people in sonar and CIC to execute a snap defensive move if something happens, OK?"

"Yes, Sir, that's no problem," nodded the Exec. "The sonar people are going to be six on, six off anyway to do that bottom mapping. We don't have enough sonarmen to do a three section watch. And it's no big deal to have the weapons consoles lit off and ready, as long as we don't have to man up the tubes. It does mean having charged flasks in the torpedo tubes, and initiators in the depth charges, though."

Mike nodded his head.

"I know, and I'll sign the weapons fuzing sheet. We'll also have to brief up rules of engagement pretty thoroughly—tell the guys no shooting unless I say so, and either positive ID or a hostile act before we let something go. I'd hate to whack a transiting U.S. sub, or a Soviet, for that matter. I just want to have a brick or two to throw back if something comes our way. Not that it will."

"Yes, Sir, but something got the Rosie III."

"I know, but I'm damned if I believe it was some frigging submarine. It just doesn't compute. Submarines don't fool with fishing boats; they like big stuff, like carriers and super tankers."

"Unless part of its mission is to stay hidden; then it might whack a fisherman."

Mike turned to look at his Exec.

"You are beginning to think there might be something to all this, aren't you?"

The Exec rearranged his stack of papers for a moment. Then he met the Captain's eye.

"It's like what they always teach about intelligence, Cap'n" he said. "You go on capabilities, not intentions. It is *possible* that there is a hostile diesel-electric boat operating out here. We've had a sighting, guy who saw a U-boat in the big war called this thing a U-boat, and an unexplained accident with a commercial fishing boat with indications of violence—as you know, the cops confirmed that that was a bullet hole. On the surface, the brass think enough about it to send out a ship, for a week, if necessary, to have a look. It's just, well, it's way out and all that, but it is *possible*."

The Exec's expression was serious. Mike frowned.

"You weren't at the meeting with Admiral Walker, XO, but I will spot you the feasibility part of it. Yes, they're sending us out, but they haven't told Norfolk—it's all for local PR consumption. Anyway, let's play it straight, and I'll keep my opinions to myself so you can fire the guys up to do a good job. Let's do it."

"Aye, aye, Sir." the Exec replied, gathering his papers.

Mike caught the note of relief in his voice, along with his unspoken request to at least act like he took it seriously, because if the wardroom and the crew thought otherwise, they would blow it off.

"I'll get on the 1MC in a couple of minutes and brief the crew," said the exec. "Then we'll start the search at around 2100 when we get to the initiation point."

"Where Rosie went down, right?"

"Yes, Sir. It doesn't mean anything tactically, but it's sort of symbolic. The crew can relate to the fact that some other guys died and that's why we're out here."

"Good thinking. I'll come up around 2200 to see how it's going; tell Linc I'll want a demo of his new toy."

At 2200, Mike went up to the Combat Information Center. The control center was in darkened condition, with only the green lights of the scopes and the dimmed red lights around the overhead illuminating the crowded room.

"Captain's in Combat," sounded off the watch supervisor when he saw Mike coming through the door.

Mike walked over to the main plotting table. The search track was laid out on the tracing paper, with a bottom contour chart taped underneath the tracing paper. The anti-submarine warfare officer, Lieutenant (Junior Grade) Lincoln Howard, had his PC up and running by the side of the table.

"Show me how this works, Linc."

"Aye, Sir. Basically, I can take the video presentation on the sonar scope down below into the PC on a scanner channel: just as if I were scanning a document, only I get an image. I have the bottom contour chart already scanned into a file, and I keep the part of the chart we're steaming over in a window. I have another window active, with nothing in it. When we pass over some feature on the bottom that's marked on the chart, I get the sonar girls to freeze frame the scope display, and then I call for the scan. The scan comes into the second window, and I merge that video picture with that section of the chart, and store them. Anytime we come back to this area of the chart, I can call up the video scan for our present position, and put it in a window, and then call up the current video presentation from the sonar, and we can see if they're different. If they are, something's there that wasn't there before."

The Captain nodded in appreciation.

"That's pretty slick; I suppose we have to be making our pass over the bottom feature going the same way as we did when you first recorded it, right?"

Linc grinned. "Yes, Sir. You got it. Otherwise, the feature would be painted by the sound waves from a different angle, and therefore maybe look different. So I also type in the course, speed, and the water sound layer conditions into each file. You can see one here that we just did."

Mike looked over at the PC screen. In one window was a segment of the bottom chart. In a second, larger window, was a collection of squiggly white lines painted against an amber background. It looked like one of those Rohrsach tests psychologists used.

"Um,—"

"Yes, Sir, I know," said the ASW officer. "That's what you get; it's not like a clear outline. According to the chart, that happens to be a pinnacle. It's like a knob of rock sticking up off the surrounding flat bottom some 120 feet high above the ocean floor. When the water depth is around 380 feet, that could look like a sub either sitting on or real close to the bottom. Since we know there's a pinnacle there, we can ignore it."

"But suppose the sub knew it was there, and was trying to hide. Couldn't he park next to the pinnacle, say in the acoustic shadow of it if he knew which way we were coming? Might we not mistake the contact for just the pinnacle?"

"Yes, Sir, precisely, but that's what my little windows will tell me; especially if we can make two passes from different directions on the pinnacle. I don't know what it would look like with a sub parked next to it, but I do know it will look different; then we can circle it and ping his ass out of there."

"Very good, indeed. So while we're searching, we ought to take at least two "pictures" of any feature where a bad guy might want to hide out here, as long as we have the time."

"Yes, Sir," said Linc, appreciatively. "Most of this area on the continental shelf is pretty flat, although when you get too close to the slope, there's a jillion canyons and stuff. But it would be pretty hard to duck into one of those because the water tends to flow down them and make a hell of a current, not to mention the danger of mudslides."

"I want to concentrate along the interior margins of the Gulf Stream," mused Mike. "Everything that's happened has happened just inside the Stream. The water is turbulent, and the boundary layers are a tough problem, acoustically, but that's where a sub would hide. He can look acoustically into the fleet operating areas, but he's nearly invisible to surface ASW forces. Somebody bring me a big chart of the whole area."

The surface supervisor went to the chart table and rustled through the large charts, finally pulling one out that covered the approaches to the St. Johns river and the operating areas for one hundred miles either side. He laid it out on the plotting table.

Mike picked up a soft lead pencil and drew a two inch wide band down the seasonal interior edges of the Gulf Stream.

"There," he said. "There's where our bad guy would hang out, if he had some kind of business in the operating areas. Now, gimme the lat-lon of the position where Rosie III went down."

The quartermaster read out the latitude and longitude coordinates, and Mike made an X on the large chart. He pointed to the pencilled X-mark.

"Let's sweep this sector, south from where Rosie went down, for 48 hours; then let's make a sweep up through the middle of the operating areas, going by any really prominent bottom objects—as I recall there's some ships sunk and a dozen or so humps and pinnacles. Then we'll take the northern sector of the band along the Gulf Stream."

He stood back from the chart, taking in the whole picture, assessing in his mind the magnitude of the search.

"The other thing we need to do is to take fathometer readings each time we draw a picture," said the Exec, who had, as usual, materialized in Combat because the Captain was there.

"Hiya, XO. Yeah, I agree, if you're thinking what I'm thinking. You're looking for initial search depths for torpedoes, right?"

"Yes, Sir. If we get into a contact situation, we call up Linc's pictures, and at the same time set up one of our fish so that it's programmed not to try to go below the actual water depth." He noticed Linc's face. "What's the matter with that, Linc?"

"Well, Sirs, the basic problem is that our anti-submarine torpedoes will acquire the bottom every time at these depths—it's just too shallow. But what that depth reading would be really useful for are the depth charges. See, if the chart says the water depth is 400 feet, and we're trying for a target sitting on the bottom, we'd set the fuzes for 400 feet. But if the real depth was 375 feet, they'd never go off. The data on this chart is over forty years old; lots could've happened since then. We definitely need accurate depth dope."

Mike nodded thoughtfully. The other members of the ASW team stood around, listening in to the discussion.

"OK," he said. "Make it so. Get a good picture of the anomalies. XO, maybe we shouldn't have the torpedo tubes charged, hunh?"

"Well, Captain," Lincoln Howard interjected, "The beauty of the torpedoes is that they can be fired fast. We hear a fish incoming from a certain bearing, we can shoot one down that bearing. It might go after the bottom, and it might even blow up on the bottom, but it will disrupt maybe the second and third fish the guy's trying to shoot at us, and it might even acquire him and kick his ass. The depth charges require that we go right over the guy, and that takes time, especially if he runs for it. I think we ought to keep one on each side ready, anyway."

"OK, XO. I'm convinced. You guys sound like you have your stuff together. Let's give it a try. XO, I'm going out to the bridge—you got anything else for me?"

"No, Sir, nothing that can't wait till morning."

"OK."

Mike walked through the forward door of the CIC and out onto the darkened bridge; it took a moment for the Bosun to spot him and announce him. It was a clear night with a bright moon, so it was not all that dark. He crossed over to his chair and swung himself up into it. The Bosun mate appeared with a cup of coffee, which Mike took but did not drink. It was too late at night for coffee; he wanted to be able to go to sleep. Not wanting to hurt the bosun's feelings, he held the cup in his two hands.

Those guys were setting this little operation up exactly right, he reflected. The ASWO had a super little toy in his PC system; whatever came of this, he had to make sure Linc got some credit for it. He sat back in his chair. The sea was shiny black, with a broad avenue of moonlight reflecting on the overhead of the pilothouse. The ship was cruising along at 10 knots, barely moving for a destroyer, and the sea winds were calm. Of course it's all bullshit, he thought. We'll go through the motions, and we'll get a really good bottom contour chart. Maybe I'll get all those fitness reports done that have been piling up in my inbasket. And then, there was this weekend, yes, this weekend.

He wondered how he and Diane could get together. If they would get together. He had simply assumed that they would. Somehow. He digested for the hundredth time the news that his nemesis on the Staff was playing around, and that Diane knew about it. He had wrestled with the problem of feeling good or bad about that situation, but the consensus among his voices was that J.W's mid-life penile indiscretion had opened a very wide door for Mike Montgomery. He fantasized about the possibility of his making Diane his wife. She was his age or maybe even a little older than he was probably, but what did that matter. J.W. didn't want her, and Mike was discovering that he certainly did want her. Everybody said he should settle down, get married, have a family, live on the base. Well? He laughed silently. If he and Diane Martinson linked up, neither one of them could stay around the Navy. He would be roundly condemned for "breaking up" the marriage of a senior officer with his wild, bachelor ways. Martinson's girlfriend would be conveniently forgotten. But, hell, he was going probably going to have to retire from the Navy pretty soon anyway, and she was certainly sick of Navy life. He knew that Diane was not a woman to be enjoyed and discarded like the pneumatic beach bunnies who occasionally inhabited his houseboat. He sensed that a relationship with Diane would be a serious undertaking. He had tried to fluff the whole thing off under the guise of a mature bachelor's attitude—woman's available for a fling, go have a fling, but nothing more. The problem was that he was more than a little smitten.

He sipped some of the coffee after all. The next weekend might be the most interesting thing he would deal with all week. Certainly more interesting than this mickey-mouse tasking. He yawned and settled back in his chair to watch the night sea. A submarine. What a laugh.

TWENTY

Mayport Naval Station Commissary, Tuesday, 22 April; morning

Diane Martinson pushed her shopping basket past dry cereals and headed for the meat counter. She was doing her biweekly shopping somewhat on autopilot, getting the same things she always bought, making the identical circuit of the base commissary store that she always made.

She was still preoccupied with Mike Montgomery. J.W. had listened to her story about the car impatiently, frowned when she told him who her rescuer had been, but focused more on the Volvo and when it would be salvaged than on the fact that she had spent some time with the maverick CO of the Goldsborough. He had just turned off the lights when she arrived, and had gone back to bed without much more than a complaint that his Sunday would probably be completely occupied screwing around with the damn car, and thank you very much for the repair bill. Diane remembered thinking that he could go screw around with the car and she...she smiled at the outrageous thought, and smiled wider at the thought of her actually saying such a thing to J.W. She wondered if J.W. would splutter.

"Hamburger that amusing, Diane?" asked a woman's voice.

She turned to find Admiral Walker's wife making her way down the meat counter. Diane forced a quick laugh.

"I was thinking about our episode with the Volvo over at NAS Jax," she said lightly. "We've always called that car a big boat and it very nearly was."

"George told me about your weekend travails," said Mrs. Walker. "J.W. said you had a very harrying experience. Wasn't it lucky Commander Montgomery was right there and everything."

Diane wondered if she detected just the hint of a meow in Mrs. Walker's words.

"Yes, it certainly was. I don't know what I would have done out there with my car sinking before my very eyes. Although in that downpour that little sports car he was driving needed a periscope."

"Yes, I've seen that car. George thinks it's a wee bit flashy for the Captain of a destroyer, but Commander Montgomery seems to lead a—different life than most of us."

Diane picked up some items from the meat case, moving slowly down the display line. Mrs. Walker did the same, staying close enough to talk as they moved along.

"Different?" asked Diane. "He drives a sports car, and he told me he lives on an old houseboat at the marina, but otherwise he seemed pretty normal, although I don't know how he fits in that sports car."

"Yes, he is a large man, isn't he. But George says he has some rather, unconventional, I think he said, ideas about how to get along with the rest of the Navy in Mayport. I've heard him come home in the evening griping about another Montgomery-gram. Apparently Goldsborough complains a lot. But you know how it is with these young CO's. I'm sure it's nothing. George was very pleased that he took the time to rescue you and see to it that you got home. But wherever did you hide out during that awful weather—George said J.W. told him that you had to wait at the gas station for most of the night?"

Diane's female antennae began to quiver. She sensed that there might be more than just passing interest in this question. Without putting too fine a point on it, Diane knew that her looks would always be grounds for suspicion among the more ordinary looking wives on the base. She would have loved, for just once in her decorous life, to smile sweetly and say that she and Commander Montgomery had gone to a motel for eight hours for some serious fucking. Even as she made her reply, she realized that she wanted to do something very much along those lines with the 'large' Commander. She also realized that almost instinctively that she would have to be the initiator if something was going to happen, and surprised herself when she realized that this would not necessarily be a problem. Her subconscious mind had apparently made a decision. But now it was story time, part two.

"We waited for awhile at the gas station, but they were blacked out in the storm, so we went over to Orange Park and found one of those awful roadside restaurants to wait it out. They tell me Orange Park used to be a pretty little town, but it's just one big neon strip now. We went back to NAS at around ten again and waited some more."

Mrs. Walker finished with the meat counter and prepared to turn away into another aisle.

"Orange Park was never pretty, my dear. Little, but never pretty. Anyway, I'm glad the car's going to be all right. We wouldn't want you to stop your volunteer work for lack of a second car, would we. It does make a difference, believe me. See you later."

She waggled her fingertips in Diane's direction and steamed off down the soft drink aisle. Diane continued to walk along the meat counters as Mrs. Walker disappeared. Prying old biddy. Actually, she wasn't that old, and was actually well regarded by most of the wives on the staff. Some Admirals' wives wore their husband's stars quite prominently, but Mrs. Walker almost never did. But that had been an unmistakable probe; *wherever did you hide out*...meaning, watch it, babe, this is a small town and a thoroughly Navy town.

Diane tossed her head and headed for the checkout counter. In for a penny, in for a pound. We did nothing wrong, but maybe we should have. If the upper stratum of Navy society could look aside while J.W. attended to another woman on his trips to Navy headquarters in Norfolk, they could damn well look aside if Mrs. J.W. decided to take a walk on the wild side. A part of her knew this was all wishful thinking; the Admiral probably was very well informed about his Chief of Staff's girlfriend, but had not told his own wife. If Diane were to be found out straying from the reservation, there would be an immediate scandal. Do as we say, not as we do, dearie. The Navy is a man's world.

"Good morning, Mrs. Martinson," said the young man behind the checkout counter. "A light basket today."

"Good morning," she replied, "Yes, you're right, I'm not getting much today."

She turned a thousand watt smile on him, daring him to pick up on the double entendre. He promptly scanned the same sack of oranges three times.

TWENTY ONE

The Al Akrab, 600 miles east of the Gulf Stream, Tuesday, 22 April, 0100

"Surface sonar contact bearing 100, range undetermined, closing, composition one, single screw. Evaluate merchant."

"Very well." The Captain hung up the phone by his rack, and glanced at the depth gauge above his bunk. Sixty meters. The submarine was in the rendezvous position, as she had been for two nights. There had been no contacts; this position was not on any routine sea lane. But now, in the third day of the rendezvous window, a single ship was closing the position. With any luck it would be the tanker, Ibrahim Abdullah. They would know in an hour, if the contact created the recognition signal. Precisely at midnight, local time, the tanker was to throw three hand grenades over the side. The noise would propagate for miles, and the submarine would come up. The weather had been perfect at the last periscope observation taken at sundown. The sonar station buzzed him again.

"Yes."

"Sir, the contact has slowed to 20 rpm; she's closing still, but very slowly now. Bearing still 100."

"Very well. Protect your ears at midnight."

"Yes, Sir. We are ready."

"Tell the watch officer that I will address the crew at midnight, if this is the one."

"It will be done."

He looked again at his watch. 2320. Forty minutes more or less. He lay back in the bunk. Their transit out to the rendezvous had been uneventful. They had spent the time making an inventory of small repairs needed, pumps, motors, valves—the usual laundry list. The tanker had been fitted out with a machine shop for this mission. She also had food, diesel fuel and fresh water for them, which was very fortunate because one of their evaporators had broken down. Submarines, like surface ships, had to make all their potable water from seawater, using distillation plants called evaporators. A submarine had small water reserves to begin with; the loss of even one evaporator was serious.

If the weather held, they would be able to get the men off the sub and onto the tanker for a few hours, for hot showers and a good meal. He wondered if there would be women. The Russian advisors had told him that their support ships were crewed almost entirely with women; full service support ships, they would say with a leer. He had seen some of the Russian women, and wondered how one told the difference between them and the machinery. He had never married and had no particular interest in having a permanent relationship with a woman. They satisfied sexual needs, but were nothing but trouble for anything else.

He had to control himself from going to the Control Room. He sensed that the mission was at midpoint. there were still times he could not believe that they were doing what they were doing, that he, of all the submarine Captains, had been chosen for this mission of all missions. He had come a long way indeed.

His parents had been servants in the mansion house of a British businessman in Tripoli. He had grown up with four other children in a one room hut built into the back wall of the mansion's compound. His "duties" as a child were limited to helping the groundskeepers; none of the children had ever once been allowed inside the main house. He had grown up knowing only what his father would tell him of the many rooms, the fine furnishings, and the incredible amounts of food. His mother had taught all of them to read and write Arabic, but he had never set foot in a school until the Revolution had upended the colonial order of things and changed everyone's world dramatically.

He had joined the Army as soon as he was old enough, and had flourished, applying his native intelligence in a manner that quickly caught the attention of superiors who were desperately looking for indigenous officer material. He had been assigned to the artillery, where he was schooled by grim-faced Soviet advisors in the lethal mathematics of ballistics and the intricacies of surveying. Because his tribal origins were the same as the fledgling nation's leader, he was promoted somewhat faster than many of his fellow officers.

His political education paralleled his technical training. He learned that the entire world, led by the United States and its allies, had turned against his country for the sin of throwing off the yoke of colonialism, and that they were now attempting to isolate his country to the desert sands of North Africa. Only the Soviets had been their steadfast friends on the world scene, providing armaments, training, advisors, and a market for the precious oil when the Arab world executed its first oil embargo. He had learned Russian through a combination of association with the advisors and formal schooling.

Ten years into his career, the Soviets had provided six submarines, and a call had gone out through the Army and the Air Force for volunteers to become submariners as the leader added a new and deadly dimension to the country's armed forces. He had been encouraged by his Commanding Officer, a Colonel of his own tribal group, to volunteer on the basis of political reliability, mainly to extend the family's influence into this new and exciting facet of the country's armed forces. With his grasp of the Russian language and innate technical ability, he had been accepted easily, and then had come the intensely alien experience of living and going to submarine school in the Soviet Union. Upon completion of the year's training, he had been put in command of a Foxtrot class Russian submarine, and had been its Captain ever since.

Mechanically, his submarine was no easier to keep running than the other five, but he had patiently assembled a capable crew and reliable officers over the years, many of them volunteers from different Arab countries or nationalities. More importantly, they remained with the submarine permanently, as his country did not subscribe to the policies of rotation that other navies used. As the international climate grew increasingly hostile to his country, the submarines were given more and more resources against the day when they might have to go out into the Mediterranean to defend the country against the growing power of the imperialists, or to strike a blow against the hated Zionists. The Al Akrab achieved a reputation for readiness that made her the natural candidate for this incredible mission to restore his country's honor after the American sneak attack.

The phone buzzed again.

"Yes."

"Sir, the contact has stopped engines."

"Very well; turn off axis to 010; begin a passive plot on him for the next thirty minutes, and estimate the range."

"It will be done."

He climbed out of his rack and found his sea boots. A thirty minute passive plot was a waste of time, but it would give them something to do while waiting. This had to be the support ship. He needed to tell the whole crew what was going on. But he would have to wait for the signal, to be sure. He went aft to the control room.

Arriving there he found the tactical team hovering over the plotting board. Every three minutes the sonar operator would call the bearing to the contact, derived by listening to its engine noise, to the table plotters, while the submarine travelled north, perpendicular to the initial bearing, at a steady speed of five knots. After thirty minutes, the bearings would begin to converge, and a very rough range could be measured. If the contact was also moving, the procedure was more elaborate, and took much more time. But for a stopped or almost stopped target, one leg would do it for a very rough estimate. It was good practice for the watch officers; the submarine could determine the all-important range to the target without making a sound or revealing a periscope. He looked at his watch. Ten more minutes. He sat down on his steel stool by the periscope, and waited.

At midnight, he asked for the estimated range.

"Three thousand, five hundred meters," replied the watch officer. The quartermaster logged the number in the contact log. They waited.

"Turn back to 110," ordered the Captain. He would begin closing the ship.

At five minutes past midnight, three evenly spaced, metallic clanks were heard throughout the boat. The Captain smiled.

"Prepare to surface," he ordered.

Five minutes later, the Deputy announced that the boat was ready to surface. The Captain acknowledged, and picked up the ship's announcing system microphone.

"Be silent," he began, using the traditional admonishment which preceded any important announcements. "In the name of Allah, the Merciful: in a few minutes, we will surface to make rendezvous with our mother ship, the Ibrahim Abdullah, a national tanker. She has been sent by our Leader with fresh provisions, fuel and water. For the fortunate, she may also have mail."

"Our plan is to remain alongside for twenty-four hours. This depends on the weather remaining calm, and no other contacts coming near. Everyone will be allowed to go aboard the mother ship, to bathe and to enjoy some fresh air, and perhaps other things. All clothing and bedding will be cleaned. But first there is work to be done. We must take on a full load of fuel and water and food before anyone goes anywhere. That way, if we are forced to dive, we will have done the essential things."

"We have completed the first half of the mission. We have journeyed to the enemy's coast, we have learned his patterns of operations there, and we have scouted the bottom in preparation for the second phase. This rendezvous is the vital intermission point: from here, we go back to the patrol area, and await the American carrier."

"Remember, our mission is still a secret. The crew of the Ibrahim knows only that we have been dispatched to America to carry out an important mission of reprisal. They do not know the target, nor the timing. Keep silent about the final objective. If they wish to speculate, smile with them, let their imaginations run, but do not confirm our mission. A failure of surprise will mean the death of every one of us. Surprise is our only protection from the American Navy."

"Now, surface. Allah be with us. That is all."

Fifteen minutes later, the boat was nosing into position alongside the tanker, her diesels rumbling, filling the diminishing space between the tanker's high, slab sides and the submarine with their noise. The tanker was an old Greek multi-product carrier, bought in Piraeus three years ago for the specialty fuels run along the north African coast, and modified for this mother ship mission six months ago by the military shipyard at Benghazi. She looked like any other medium sized tanker in the world, with a superstructure and funnel aft, a long, flat deck running forward, where another superstructure containing the bridge and the cabins rose close to the bow. She was of 25,000 dead weight tons displacement. Nothing in her outward appearance would have revealed any special capabilities.

She lay to now, a dark silhouette in the light of a full moon, as the submarine maneuvered alongside. There were special fenders already deployed along the tanker's side, and they creaked and groaned as the sub slid alongside and backed down. Heavy ropes snaked down to the sub's deck, and the crew then pulled down wire mooring hawsers to make her fast. The submarine kept one main engine on the line, charging batteries and maintaining readiness to cut away quickly if they were discovered.

Once alongside, the tanker deck crew passed down a fuel hose and a water hose, and the vital replenishment began. There was some back and forth shouted conversation between the tanker crew on deck up above and the submariners, but the essential transfers were the main order of business. A steam winch blew clouds of exhaust steam over the side as it hoisted pallets of food and spare parts down to the submarine's deck. The crews worked until 0330 before the fueling and watering was completed, and most of the stores had been brought onboard. Then, with the weather still flat calm, everyone secured until later in the morning. If the submarine had to be cast off in an emergency, the main replenishment was completed.

At 0900 that morning, the tanker crew dropped an accommodation ladder down over the side, and one half of the submarine's crew went topside for the first time in five weeks. They were a smelly, scruffy lot, carrying their accumulated dirty laundry and bedding up to the mother ship. Once onboard, they were delighted to find out that there were women onboard, along with unlimited quantities of hot water for baths, and a special meal available in the dining room all day long.

The remaining half of the crew stayed aboard the boat to keep watch, and to stow the fresh provisions. They also passed up the items for repair, taking care to disable no system entirely in case they were scared off the mothership. The rendezvous position had been picked to avoid shipping lanes, so the chance of another ship coming along was very remote. The position, as best their intelligence services could ascertain from their Russian friends, was also off the track of surveillance satellites.

The Captain went up the ladder at 1000, following the first increment of his crew. He was greeted by the master of the tanker, who introduced the political officer, a Lieutenant Colonel in the security service. The Captain recognized him as the officer accompanying the Colonel on the landing the night they had left. The political officer was several years older than the Captain. He indicated that the Captain should come with him to his cabin. He instructed the master to keep a vigilant watch while the two military officers conferred. By his manner, he was clearly in charge of the entire replenishment operation.

They went up to the forward superstructure, climbing a set of ladders to the third level above the tanker pipe deck. It was a bright, sunny day, with almost no wind. The submarine was hidden in the shadow of the Ibrahim created by the easterly sun. They made their way to the Lieutenant Colonel's cabin, which was a spacious affair, especially when compared to the Captain's tiny quarters aboard the submarine. There was a sitting room with conventional furniture, and a bedroom and bath off to one side.

The Lieutenant Colonel politely offered tea, and inquired after the Captain's health and personal well-being in the traditional manner. He was a swarthy, powerfully built man, who looked more like a Turk than a Bedou, which he was. He had been a Major General until the last coup attempt had provoked Khaddafy to reduce all ranks to something below full Colonel. He was of Khaddafy's tribe, and therefore to be trusted. He smoked noxious French cigarettes continuously.

The Captain reviewed the events of the transit across the Atlantic, and the first few weeks off the Florida coast. He did not at first describe the broaching incident, but he did give full details of the sinking of the fishing boat. The Colonel's eyes grew narrow.

"What was the enemy's reaction to this incident?"

"Nothing that we could tell. We heard a destroyer operating in the area later the next day, but there were no indications of a real search. They must have concluded that it was an accident. I am convinced that they have no idea we are there."

"And there were no survivors, correct? You took care that no one was left in the water to tell the tale?

The Captain swallowed, and sipped some tea to hide his discomfiture. He had still not quite come to terms with what they had done. It offended many precepts of the desert code. In a sense, the sea was not much different from the desert. Even your enemy was given succor if he was helpless on the sands. Later you might kill him, but always the fundamental courtesy of rescue would be extended. To shoot the men in the water had been inescapably necessary, but very much against his instincts.

"Yes, Effendi. There were two survivors, and we machine-gunned them in the water. The sharks took them as we watched."

"You are confident then that you have not been actually sighted?"

The Captain thought quickly. It was likely that the Colonel would interview the Al Akrab's political officer when he was done with him. That worthy would surely reveal the broaching incident.

"Yes, we may have been sighted. It was on the second day in the patrol area. The watch officer lost depth control briefly, and we broke the surface momentarily. It is called broaching. There were fishing boats nearby, but it was dark; morning twilight. I doubt that any of them saw us."

"Was there any Navy reaction?"

"By coincidence there was a destroyer that came out and pinged around the area that day, but they do that all the time. This is their training area. Destroyers, frigates, they are always out there pinging, practicing ASW. We watched him from the shelter of the Gulf Stream, and he went away after a while, going into port that Friday morning as they always do. They are very predictable, these Americans. They come out Monday, they go back Friday by midday. They must be very religious."

The Colonel, who had been an Attaché in America many years ago, snorted. The Captain obviously had no concept of the American weekend.

"Did you discipline the watch officer who exposed you?"

"I issued a decree that the next such mistake would be punished by death."

The Lieutenant Colonel's eyebrows went up. This young officer had steel in him. Killing the surviving witnesses, and now this threat to his own crew. The Colonel had chosen well.

"And there were no more such mistakes?"

"Not until I made the one which resulted in snagging the fishing boat," he said evenly. Might as well tell the truth, he thought. The older man might actually respect it.

154

The Lieutenant Colonel looked out the porthole for a long moment. Then he got up and went over to his desk. He retrieved a thin envelope, and handed it over to the Captain.

"This contains the latest intelligence estimate of when the carrier will return to its base. And a new part of the plan."

"A new part?"

"Yes; we have some additional weapons for you. This is most secret. It is described there, in the instructions. Why don't you just read them. I will have some food sent in when we are through."

The Captain opened the envelope and scanned the operations order. He looked up. "Mines?" he asked, incredulously.

The Lieutenant Colonel sat back and smiled at him. "Yes, mines. We are going to take two shots at this carrier. The first will be when you attack him on the approach to the base. The second will come when he actually enters the harbor."

The Captain's face flushed. "You mean, if we fail."

The Lieutenant Colonel looked at him for a long moment. Then he stood up, and began walking around the cabin. The sunlight streamed through the portholes now. The Captain, after weeks in the dim light of the submarine, found the light to be almost unbearably bright. The Lieutenant Colonel stopped his pacing and faced him.

"Captain, this is an audacious plan. An outrageous mission. To strike back at the American Navy for the crimes they committed against the *Jamahiriya*. If it comes to nothing, for whatever reason—they catch you before the carrier comes back, or during your attack—we will have expended a great effort only to be embarrassed again."

He leaned forward, staring down at the Captain. His black eyes were bright. "It must not fail," he said, his voice full of menace. "Do you understand that?"

He calmed himself for a moment. "Look," he said. "You and I are military men. The politicians always think that, because we can march in close formation and our uniforms are pressed, we can make everything happen according to a plan. Military operations are not like this, yes? You have already had two close calls—perfectly reasonable incidents, considering the dangerous operation you are carrying out. Predictable, even. You are probably going to have others before this thing is over. We hope not, but we know better, you and I, eh? Inshallah, yes? As God wills it. But the politicians, they think that this whole adventure will go boom, boom, boom, right by the plan. The mines are simply a way of adding depth to the plan. You may take your best shot at this carrier, and you may even hit it and damage it. But we both know you probably cannot sink it."

155

He paused to light another cigarette from the embers of the last one. He pitched the butt into a trash can. The room filled with stinking smoke, blue in the bright sunlight.

"The Colonel demands that the carrier be destroyed. A ship, even an American super-carrier, is not destroyed if it can get to harbor, however badly damaged. We military men would be satisfied with putting it out of action, killing hundreds of their men like they did to us in their little sneak attack. Kill them while they are sleeping, yes? That is justice, and justice is a good enough reason for a mission like this. But Dey Khaddafy says "destroy". Tell me if I am wrong: a ship is not destroyed until it is put down beneath the sea, yes? This is the way of it?"

The Captain nodded. He was beginning to see the logic of it. If the Americans drove him off, they would relax; they would have won, after a fashion, they would feel safe. They would never expect mines, not in their own backyard. The Lieutenant Colonel watched him carefully, saw him work it through, accept it, even appreciate it.

"You see it now, don't you. Mines. Little assassins, lying in wait. You will make your attack, and hopefully tear open his belly with torpedoes. Then you will make your escape, God willing. The carrier will be helped into the nearest port, which is her home base. And then the assassins will finish the job. Come, I want you to see them. Then I must show you some other things, and then you can rest, have a decent bath and a good meal. You may use my cabin for as long as you want. But first, come see."

They left the cabin and retraced their steps down to the long flat deck between the two superstructures. The air above the tank decks stank of fuel oil. Between the forward and after deckhouses, the midships winch operators were clustered around two pallets, each containing two brown cylindrical shapes. They looked like torpedoes without propellers, each being about eighteen feet in length, almost two feet in diameter, and painted a dull, sandy brown color. The Lieutenant Colonel pointed out some of the mines' features, while the workmen stood around, waiting to lift them down to the submarine below. The Lieutenant Colonel pointed with pride.

"They are made in France; the French are wonderful people—they never let their alliances or their rhetoric interfere with business, eh? Only the Germans are better. You see the sensors, yes? Pressure, magnetic, and the ear of the ship counter. I am an Army man, but these things have been explained to me. You know all about them, I suppose."

The Captain nodded. He had been schooled in the Soviet Union, but not on French mines. But a sea mine was a sea mine: the principles were the same the world over. Mines lay in wait on the bottom until they were activated by a prescribed target. They could be set to explode when the magnetic field of a ship's steel hull passed over them, or when the mine sensed the pressure differential created by a large hull moving through the water over top of the mine. The counter listened and counted the number of ships, which allowed minesweepers to make several passes over the mine without effect. The mine might be set to activate after ten or fifteen ships had gone overhead, or it could be set on a combination: lie still until ten ships had gone by, and then activate on the next contact which exuded a sufficiently large magnetic and pressure field. The really sophisticated mines activated and became torpedoes, rising off the bottom and pursuing their targets. The thing that caught his attention was the size of these mines: these were very big mines.

"The warhead?" he asked.

"Very special. They have 1800 kilos of gas enhanced Semtex. This should be sufficient to lift even an aircraft carrier, yes? And four of them? I think these assassins will be valuable allies."

"The trick will be to place them," mused the Captain, awed by the size of the warheads. They were monsters. And the Semtex was gas-enhanced.

"The channel entrance to the carrier basin at Mayport is only 60 to 70 feet deep," he continued. "We will have to go in on the surface. And there is the problem of the river; the river currents mingle with the tidal currents at the mouth. The mines may not stay where we place them. I shall have to think about this."

"Load them to the submarine," ordered the Lieutenant Colonel, and then he took the Captain by the arm, propelling him back to the forward superstructure. The Captain knew there was something important he was forgetting. They were intercepted on deck by the master of the Ibrahim and the Al Akrab's weapons officer. The weapons officer spoke first.

"Captain, I did not know about these mines."

"Neither did I, Lieutenant," replied the Captain. "But there has been an addition to the plan."

"Where shall we put them, forward or aft?"

The Captain now knew what had been bothering him. The addition of four mines to their warload presented a problem. They had a full torpedo load onboard, which meant that all ten tubes, six forward and four aft, were loaded, and all the reload slots were also full. They would have to download four torpedoes to accommodate four mines, because mines were deployed from the torpedo tubes. It would mean unstowing four large, warshot torpedoes, assembling the torpedo loading path trays through the submarine, opening the weapons loading hatches, and then carefully extracting four live torpedoes out of the submarine, all from alongside another ship. Each fish would take several hours, at least. The Captain explained the problem to the Lieutenant Colonel.

"You cannot just put them aboard—lash them down somewhere?"

The Lieutenant Colonel had never been aboard a submarine, that much was clear. The Captain shook his head. "That is impossible. They have to be in one torpedo room or the other, and all the stowage bays are filled. My crew sleeps literally on top of the torpedoes, Lieutenant Colonel; it is that crowded."

The Lieutenant Colonel sighed in exasperation. Somebody had screwed up.

The Lieutenant spoke up. "Captain, if we must take these things onboard, there is a quicker way, although it is wasteful."

"Yes?"

"We cast off the after part of the boat, and we safe and fire the four torpedoes out of the stern tubes. We then load the mines into the after torpedo room. It will still take several hours, but we will not have to drag out the warshots. It would be the safe way, but, as I said, most wasteful."

"Do it," ordered the Lieutenant Colonel. "The mines are essential to the plan."

The Captain shrugged his shoulders. The Lieutenant Colonel would bear responsibility.

"I will need certain people back in the boat for this," he said to the Lieutenant Colonel. "I will have to put off your offer of hospitality until this evening, Sir."

"Cannot your people do this thing by themselves?"

"No, Effendi. I must be present whenever we handle large weapons such as torpedoes or mines. If there is an error or accident, the Ibrahim could go to the bottom along with the boat. And we need to do this thing before the weather turns."

The Lieutenant Colonel was impressed. "As you wish, Captain. We have some more things to discuss when you are finished with the mines. Can you spare your political officer while you are loading the mines?"

The Captain had guessed right. He was relieved that he had admitted the broaching incident.

"I will send him aboard at once," he said.

He longed for a hot bath, but the loading of the mines, and the firing of four torpedoes demanded his personal supervision. The crew would be unhappy, losing the afternoon.

Half an hour later, with her stern pointed off at an angle of twenty degrees from the side of the Ibrahim, the submarine fired the first of the four torpedoes. The Captain had ordered the arming wires disconnected; the two ton torpedoes, their propulsion systems and warheads disabled, plummeted harmlessly to the bottom 10,000 feet below. The weapons officer had wanted to fire them hot, but the Captain, ever mindful of the possibility of a circle runner, had elected to safe them instead.

On deck, the crew had unbolted the weapons handling hatch on the submarine's deck aft of the conning tower. The winch operators on the Ibrahim had lowered all four of the mines down to the deck. Once the crew had the torpedo handling slide assembled, and the submarine was back alongside, the winch operator picked up the sling on the first mine, and dangled it, nose tipped down, at the upper lip of the slide. With six men pushing and shoving, the mine was landed on the slide and started down into the after torpedo room. There was no stowage for reloads in the after room, so each mine was loaded directly into a torpedo tube. By sunset, all four were in tubes, and the crew began the task of disassembling the weapons loading slide and re-bolting the hatches opened through the pressure hull to permit the operation.

In the after torpedo room, the weapons officer and the chief electronics technician sweated over the technical manual, which was written in French. They had to back each mine partially out of the tube to make the activation settings, one for magnetic field strength, one for pressure, and then the counter. In each case, they set the field strengths for the maximum setting, on the theory that an aircraft carrier, at nearly 100,000 tons, would create the biggest field the mine would see. They set the counter to zero, which meant that the mine would activate and explode upon first sensing a field of pressure and magnetic flux equal to or greater than its minimum settings. To make sure, they set an 'and' gate on each mine's computer, which meant that it had to sense both maximum pressure and maximum magnetic flux.

They successfully set up three of the mines, but the fourth would not accept the combination settings. They called the Captain, who came aft to take a look. The after torpedo room was the next to the last compartment in the submarine, with only the steering machinery room behind it. The overhead curved down at the back end to match the hull contours. The compartment was hot, being right behind the motor compartment. With tube doors being opened and closed, there was some oily seawater in the bilge, and the tiny space was extremely humid. The overhead was full of piping and electrical cables; three men could barely fit in the room.

The torpedo tube inner doors, glistening in chrome and brass, filled the after bulkhead. During an attack action, one man was stationed in after torpedo; he could manually fire each tube once if the remote firing mechanism, controlled from the weapons direction console in the control room, failed to work. Four high pressure air flasks, with piping capable of holding 3000 pounds per square inch pressure, bulged out of the bulkhead over each tube door. A firing signal released the compressed air in the flasks into the back of the tube, blowing the projectile out into the sea. In the case of a torpedo, the arming lever on the torpedo was attached to a hook in the torpedo tube by a short length of tungsten wire called the arming wire. When the fish was expelled, the wire tightened and tripped the lever on the back of the torpedo, allowing the torpedo's propulsion system to fire and its gyro to spin up to control speed. In the case of a mine, the wire simply activated the mine's battery and computer. The mine itself would travel about fifty feet aft of the submarine before settling to the bottom, arming itself on the way down.

"What's the problem?" asked the Captain, bent over to avoid hitting his head. His uniform wilted at once in the extreme humidity.

The weapons officer and the Chief were stripped down to shorts and their hats. The temperature in the cramped compartment was nearly 100 degrees. The pages of the technical manual were curling up in the wet heat.

"This pig-fucker will not take settings," complained the weapons officer. "It remains on default settings, which is counter zero, and pressure or magnaflux of the minimum setting."

He squatted down on his haunches.

"If we put this bitch in the river mouth, it would arm immediately and get the first good sized fishing boat that came along, if not us in the process."

The Captain nodded. "We've already got one of those," he mused. The Chief grinned; he had no particular scruples about killing Americans, civilian or otherwise.

"I recommend we safe it and shoot it; get rid of it. I don't trust it, especially with a faulty computer," said the weapons officer.

The Captain thought about it for a minute. Perhaps there would be a use for this final mine. He hated not having any torpedoes in the after tubes. A brace of fish into the face of a pursuing enemy destroyer was always a good diversionary tactic for an evading submarine. Everything they were going to do would be in shallow waters. A hair-triggered mine fired in front of a pursuing destroyer might be just the thing. If the submarine was able to get far enough away from it. That much Semtex would

160

blow the front half of a destroyer right off, but it might also smash a submarine's propellers and rudder if it went off within a few hundred yards. A stinger in his tail, albeit a very dangerous one, but one befitting a scorpion.

"No," he decided aloud. "We will keep it. Load it at default settings, and mark the tube door for manual firing only. I don't want that one capable of being fired from the console."

He saw the concern on his weapons officer's face.

"Consider," he said. "We have jettisoned the stern shot torpedoes. With this we regain a stinger in our tail. You are correct that we cannot use it for the carrier attack. But against a pursuing destroyer?"

He saw the comprehension in their eyes.

"It will be done," said the weapons officer.

The Chief was not so sure. How far would such a weapon go before arming itself, and was that far enough to keep the submarine safe? But he held his silence.

TWENTY TWO

Aboard the mothership Ibrahim Abdullah, Tuesday, 1700

The Captain lay back in the luxuriant warmth of a hot bath. The Lieutenant Colonel's cabin actually had a bathtub; merchant tankers, unconstrained in volume above deck, had cabins that were much larger and more comfortable than most cruise ships. The cabins were built in proportion to the superstructure, which in turn was sized in proportion to the ship's 25,000 ton capacity hull. He relaxed in the hot water, letting the strain of the past five weeks soak away. He could hear the taped sounds of an Arabic language radio station being played over the outside announcing system for the benefit of his crew, who were lounging about on the tank deck, enjoying the sunset.

The sea remained flat calm, which was exceedingly fortunate. The big ship moved very slowly, hardly disturbing the ugly, black object lying alongside. He drifted, partly listening to the tape of the radio outside, and partly dreaming of home. A noise in the cabin bedroom intruded.

"Who is there?" he called.

"Jenan, Effendi," answered a soft voice. "I am the Lieutenant Colonel's masseuse."

The Captain did not know what to say to this, so he said nothing, a habit which had helped him become a Captain. The Lieutenant Colonel's masseuse. He looked down at his long, lean body, wavering in the ripples. A massage. That would be very pleasant, as long as she wasn't one of

161

those Turkish 200 pounders who enjoyed tenderizing their clients. If she was, he would dismiss her.

"I'm coming out," he called through the bathroom door. There was no reply. He wondered if she was still there. He rose from the tub, stepped out, and slipped into a full length, towel-like bathrobe hanging on the bathroom door. He dried his short, wiry hair vigorously, and then stepped out into the bedroom of the cabin.

Jenan was not a 200 pounder. She was very young, dark skinned and black eyed, and slender. She was dressed in a one-piece, white cotton gown which draped all the way to the floor. She did not look directly at him, but kept her gaze demurely downward. She stood to one side of the wide bed, next to a small, wheeled table, which contained small vials of oils. There were towels spread on the bed. She was not beautiful, but she was not plain either. He thought he saw the barest trace of a smile on her face, and then he realized she was waiting for him to lie down on the bed. What to do with the robe? He had not wrapped a towel around his middle before putting on the robe. Fearing embarrassment more than nudity, he finally walked over to the bed, turned his back to her, and took off the robe, and then lay face down on the towels. She immediately draped a towel across his buttocks, and then knelt on the bed alongside of him, and began to rub his back.

His muscles were tense and tight, partly from nervousness about being on a bed and alone in a room with a strange woman. She probably had other skills besides massage, but he was apprehensive. He had stopped seeing the prostitutes near the submarine base two years ago, not for any moral reason but because of this new, American disease. His abstinence had been vindicated: two middle grade officers at the submarine base had been removed suddenly to the military hospital in the past year, where they had reportedly died of mysterious pneumonia complications. The Americans made much noise about the Colonel's chemical weapons program, but, according to the Soviet advisors, this new virus borne disease had reportedly escaped from one of the American's own biological weapons laboratories. They spoke of thousands of deaths in the United States.

The girl's probing fingers, replenished with warm oils, worked their magic down his back. She was obviously a professional masseuse. She worked whole groups of his muscles, going from one to the next along connections he had not known existed. She performed her ministrations in such a way as to not excite him sexually, for which he was grateful. She also did not speak, which was a wonder in itself. He did not need any more complications in his life just now. He drifted off to sleep.

162

Waking an hour later, he found himself still on his belly, a light sheet draped across his back. The night was at hand, and the only sounds were those made by the air vents washing humid Atlantic air through the cabin. Then he became aware that someone was knocking, softly, on the cabin door. He rose up on his elbows.

"Yes?"

"I have your evening meal, Effendi." The girl's voice again.

"One moment."

He got up, switched on the table lamp, and pulled the robe around him again. "All right, come in."

She brought in a tray table which had been covered by a cloth. She wheeled the table to the main dining table, and set his meal out. She left as quietly as she had come. The telephone rang. He looked at it for a moment and then picked it up.

"Captain, this is the Master. The Lieutenant Colonel asks that you call him in my cabin when you have finished your evening meal. He wants to discuss some more of the plans, whatever that means. The extension is 201."

"I shall, thank you. Are all the transfers complete?"

"Yes, they are. But we have one surface contact now, which may be a problem. She is still thirty-two miles out, and her closest point of approach will be more than nine miles, but we have to watch her."

"Tell the Lieutenant Colonel that I thank him for his consideration in allowing me to use his cabin and dine alone, but I will be pleased to see him now. That way..."

"Yes, I understand." The Master broke the connection.

Five minutes later, the Lieutenant Colonel let himself into the cabin, greeted the Captain, and helped himself to a cup of tea.

"You are rested and refreshed?" he inquired, taking a seat on the couch while the Captain finished his meal.

"I am indeed. You have been very gracious."

"Good. Jenan was—satisfactory?"

"She gave me an excellent massage. I'm afraid I fell asleep right in the middle of it."

"Yes, that happens. If you wish, I will send her back after you have eaten. In case there is anything else she can do for you."

The Lieutenant Colonel raised his eyebrows in a sign of inquiry. The Captain smiled at the Lieutenant Colonel's not so subtle suggestion.

"That will not be necessary, Lieutenant Colonel. You have already been most accommodating. You have more information to give me?"

"Yes," replied the Lieutenant Colonel, getting up and going to his desk, firing up a cigarette on the way. "I want to review the basic plan, and then give you the date we expect the carrier to return to port. I have deliberately held that back until just before you depart; that way the secret remains a secret, yes?"

"Most wise. So, the plan: we have completed the first phase, which was to make the transit to American waters, and to scout the operating areas around the entrance to the carrier's base. This we have done, including making a good chart of the bottom areas for places to hide should we be pursued."

"There are such places?" asked the Lieutenant Colonel, puffing vigorously on his cigarette.

"Yes, there are some shipwrecks—tankers torpedoed in the German war, some of which are large enough for us to lay alongside in an emergency. There are also topographical features—underwater wadis, if you will, and hills. On a sonar they look like contacts, but when the American checks his chart, he will see a pinnacle, as it is called, and then ignore it. We spent a great deal of our waiting time checking our charts for these things."

"Did you have to operate your own sonar to find these obstacles?"

"No, we would never do that. A submarine sonar is a very distinctive sound. Any sonarman listening on a surface warship would know it at once. No, we used our fathometer—our depth measuring device; it sounds like all depth finders everywhere; fishermen use them all over the world, and the sound is propagated straight down, which helps. Would you care for more tea?"

"Thank you. And your instructions also said for you to establish operating patterns of the defensive forces; were you able to do this?"

The Captain laughed, and pushed away from the table. The cigarette smoke was strong in the air, and suddenly he wanted one, but he resisted.

"There are no defensive forces," he said. "The Americans are not like us. There are many ships which come and go in the operating areas, but all for training. We were told that they never patrolled their own coasts; I did not believe our Russian friends, but it is true. There is no defense."

The Lieutenant Colonel thought about that for a moment. "But that almost makes it more difficult, does it not? If there are no regular patrols, then you must deal with irregular encounters with warships, yes?"

"Yes, precisely. But the American warships are never silent when they come out of port; they fire up all their electronics and their sonars, and usually run up their engines too. We can always hear them; any submarine could. I think that if they gained contact on us, they would pass right by; they are that confident about their own waters. And there are many fishing boats and merchant ships around, and they, too, use radars and sonars and fathometers; as long as the Americans are not alerted, we are reasonably safe."

"This is amazing, really," said the Lieutenant Colonel, lighting a second cigarette off the first one. "This does not offend you, I hope," he said, gesturing at the cloud of blue smoke.

"I used to smoke, but am now being very self-righteous."

The Lieutenant Colonel laughed. "I'll blow some your way. I have tried to quit many times, to no avail. So, you have scouted your target area, prepared escape and evasion tactics, and determined that you can operate there with relative impunity."

"The key word is relative, Lieutenant Colonel. There are over twenty destroyers and frigates at that base; if they ever suspected—"

"Yes, I understand. Now, the mine scenario: this is a new element; you will need time to plan it."

The Captain got up from the table, and stared out of the porthole into the darkness.

"That is going to be a very dangerous operation. We are going to have to go in on the surface, at night, and probably in bad weather if Allah provides it. It will have to be done very late in the operation; perhaps one or two nights before the carrier comes."

The Captain returned to the table. The Lieutenant Colonel stood there, nodding.

"I agree; seeding the mines will present the first real opportunity for them to know that you are there. They would make the connection between the carrier's return and your presence very quickly. But would not the mines keep them locked up in the harbor?"

The Captain shook his head.

"No—they are set for an aircraft carrier. A destroyer would not set them off. Except for one."

"One?" asked the Lieutenant Colonel, alarmed.

"One would not take settings; it is programmed to its default settings, which is first ship, first encounter, and a minimum signature. I kept it as a defensive weapon."

The Lieutenant Colonel shook his head.

165

"Wouldn't you know it; one out the four does not work correctly. This is the way of military operations; the politicians never understand that."

"I view it differently: three of the four do work; that's pretty good, for modern weapons. Even for French weapons."

"I know what you mean," the Lieutenant Colonel laughed. "All right; let's assume you get the mines planted, and then you take up an attack position. Once we give you the date for the carrier's arrival, where do you station yourself?"

"There is a line of shallow submarine valleys and submerged seamounts southeast of the river entrance. They are on the line of approach for a ship coming from the Caribbean. The water depth is just over one hundred twenty meters, which is deep for this area. My plan is to deploy to the surface two British electronic direction-finding buoys tethered on wires from the bottom, to pick up the electronic signals of the carrier when it comes over the horizon. The carrier has a unique radar, which the buoys are set to search for. I will space them three miles on either side of us. From the air or surface they will look like fishing buoys—the area is full of them. The submarine will be between them, on the bottom."

"If they are tethered to the bottom, how will they communicate with you?" asked the Lieutenant Colonel.

"When they make a detection, they transmit a low powered signal through a transducer in the bottom of the buoy. We have a decoder in our sonar receiver that can extract the bearing information from that signal."

The Lieutenant Colonel nodded his understanding.

"Initially," continued the Captain, "The bearings from the buoys will be almost parallel; as the carrier approaches, they will begin to point inward, which will give us a rough range, and we can begin setting up our torpedo fire control solution. Eventually they will get so close that the bearings will merge, and we will then come up, take a look, and take our shot. After that, we will run like the devil."

"As simple as that, Captain?" The Lieutenant Colonel was smiling. The Captain turned from the porthole.

"No, of course not. It might in fact be that simple, but there are many factors which can disrupt the entire thing. We might be seen; the buoys might be picked up. The carrier might be closely escorted— destroyers and frigates riding in close, so that our torpedoes cannot get in. There could be fog, or helicopter escorts. Any number of things can go wrong. But we are counting on complete surprise. They will be coming home after several weeks away. The destroyers will probably go in first, because the carrier will take the most time getting into that tiny basin. There may not even be any destroyers, if she releases them out at sea and they go to other homeports—that is a question to ask intelligence: which escorts will be with her, and where are they homeported?"

The Lieutenant Colonel pulled out a notebook and made a quick note. "It shall be asked."

"They will probably have to time her arrival to meet high tide in the basin, and the time of the least river currents in the entrance. This fixes the attack window more precisely than just a known date. If I can get into 6000 meters attack range, and fire six type-50 torpedoes, I will tear her guts out. If they all hit on the same side, we might even capsize her. Inshallah."

The Lieutenant Colonel stood up.

"In God's hands; yes. What a coup this will be. Especially if you can get clean away, so they have no way of knowing who did it. We owe these arrogant bastards. It was the American Navy which first came to Tripoli in the early 1800's to "suppress", that's the word their history books use, our corsairs in the Mediterranean. They have been coming ever since. Now it is our turn to come. Well, let me get you the sealed envelope, with the date of the carrier's arrival. And then you should probably go. There is a ship coming, the Master informs me."

"I must get the word out to my crew to re-board the boat."

The Lieutenant Colonel worked the combination of his desk safe.

"I have already done that, if you will pardon my presumption," he said, over his shoulder. "Your ship should be ready to go. Here."

He gave the Captain a single, brown envelope, sealed across the back with red sealing wax. The Captain fingered the oily wax. The Lieutenant Colonel smiled.

"Very traditional, yes? Someone saw this stuff in a movie, I think. But now only you know the date; I have not been told, and I have not opened that envelope. It comes from Him."

The Captain did not have to ask who Him was. He took the envelope, and shoved it in his trousers pocket.

"One final matter," said the Lieutenant Colonel.

"Yes?"

"I have been instructed to remind you of the final paragraph of the mission orders and to obtain your acknowledgement."

The Captain's face hardened. The final paragraph of the mission orders had been short but explicit: if the mission failed, and the submarine did not achieve an attack on the carrier, the Captain was directed to ensure that no physical evidence could be obtained by the Americans that would point to the origins of the mission. He was directed to destroy the submarine and everyone in it if that were necessary. Outside, he could hear the sudden rumbling of the submarine's main engines coming to life.

"I alone onboard the Al Akrab am aware of those conditions," he replied carefully. "And I will do what must be done if and when the time comes."

The Lieutenant Colonel nodded. "I am sorry to have to bring it up. But we cannot afford any more fingers pointed at us."

He looked down at the carpeted deck for a moment, as if trying to remember his lines. Then he looked up with a brief smile.

"We are of course confident that no such measures will be necessary," he said.

The Captain looked at him for a moment, but said nothing. He stood up, put on his hat, and opened the cabin door to leave. The Ibrahim's Master was waiting outside in the passageway.

"That contact will pass within ten miles, it appears," he said. "That should not present a problem, yes?"

The Captain nodded. "We will depart anyway; your hospitality has been excellent. You will go back home now?"

The Master laughed. "No, we go to Aruba, for a load of specialty crude. Part of the cover. The Americans track us now, ever since the Red Sea mining business. They track every one of our ships, harbor to harbor. So we must show up somewhere on the other side of the Atlantic, to keep this business secret."

They began the walk back to the ladder on the starboard side, crossing the empty tank deck.

"How will you prevent your crew from talking?" asked the Captain. "In Aruba, I mean."

"We do not go ashore; we mate to an offshore pumping terminal buoy. Load up in 18 hours, and then head home."

They arrived at the sea ladder. The Captain turned to the ship's Master.

"My thanks to you. It was good to get a hot bath, and my crew appreciated your hospitality."

The Master smiled and nodded. The Captain turned to the Lieutenant Colonel.

"Tell Him that we understand how this mission must end, one way or the other, and that we trust in God to see justice done."

"God go with you, Captain," said the Lieutenant Colonel. "Your mission is just; strike them hard."

"I shall." They embraced in the traditional fashion, and the Captain went over the side to the submarine waiting below in the darkness.

TWENTY THREE

USS Goldsborough, Jacksonville operating areas; Friday, 25 April; 1200

The sound of eight bells, ringing out in four groups of two, echoed through the ship, marking the official arrival of noon. In the wardroom, the officers were finishing lunch, turning over coffee cups in their saucers to let the mess attendant pour coffee. At the head of the table, Mike declined dessert. The Exec, sitting next to him, accepted; it was banana cream pie, his favorite. Bright sunlight streamed in through the front portholes, and the ship rolled gently in generally calm seas.

"That shit goes straight to your middle, XO," said Mike.

"Yes, Sir, it does; it's nice to see at least one system that's efficient on this ship. But so far, it doesn't stay there."

"Just you wait, Henry Higgins; one day it will."

"You seem to be avoiding it pretty well, Captain. All that pumping iron doesn't hurt, I'll bet," said the Operations officer.

Mike winced inwardly; Ops tended to be obsequious at times.

"Yeah, well, the iron keeps the muscles fit, but I need to run to keep banana cream pie from settling in; kinda hard on a tin can, though. Maybe this weekend."

"We going in today, Captain?" asked one of the Ensigns. Mike stirred his coffee for a moment before answering.

"We sent out a sitrep at 0900 this morning; if they want us to stay out over the weekend, we should get the word in the next few hours. It kind of depends on how the PR guys have been playing this thing. Lord knows we've given them enough purple prose to work with."

"My guess is we'll go in this evening," said the Exec. "We phrased this morning's sitrep to sort of conclude things, and they'll have to come up with a pretty good reason to have us stay out into the weekend. With this new policy about saving fuel and impacting personnel retention with weekend ops, my bet is we'll go in."

"Maybe they'll redesignate Goldy as a hydrographic research ship," grumbled the Engineer.

"Well, they might. That thing Linc dreamed up has produced a pretty interesting collection of bottom data. I had no idea there were so many wrecks out there, for one thing," said Mike.

"The east coast was a tough place for tankers in 1942," said the Exec. "They say they used to be able to see them burn from the beaches up and down the coast. Damned U-boats had a field day for awhile."

"What finally beat 'em?" asked the Supply Officer.

"Radar and convoys," replied the Exec. "As long as they sent tankers out by themselves, the Germans picked them off one by one. When they sent them out in groups, with some tin cans and maybe a light carrier with radar equipped planes, the free ride was over. Then it was the U-boats that got picked off. There's a sunken German submarine in our collection, by the way. The sonar girls had a lot of fun mapping that one."

The Weapons officer joined the conversation.

"I've heard there's a dive charter guy up in Charleston who'll take you out to a U-boat off the Carolina coast; you can go inside and crawl around, at 160 feet. Still has torpedoes onboard; dead Germans're still in there, too."

"Really terrific," said the Engineer. "Just what I'd like to do—bump swim fins with skeletons. They ought to just leave them alone. A sunken warship is a national tomb, for Chrissakes."

"Yeah, the German government complained about that charter guy; I was in OpNav when we worked the action to get him shut off; he used to keep some skulls from the sub in his dive shop window. Kinda insensitive."

"Well," observed Mike. "That's what happens when you lose an ASW action; one or the other of you gets to spend eternity in a drowned ship."

The officers at the table shifted uncomfortably at this reference to death at sea.

"There's some tin cans out there along the coast along with those U-boats," Mike continued, "not to mention a lot of dead merchies who were deep fried in burning oil when the U-boats got lucky. A torpedo hit on a destroyer is usually the end of the world; our training battle problems, where the script reader calls out, Torpedo hit, forward, does not begin to convey what it would be really like. We have to train for it, of course, but in most cases we'd have a minute or so to collect our hat, ass and overcoats and step into the sea."

"Well," interjected the XO, "If you got hit on the bow or stern, you could do some damage control and probably keep her afloat. But for a torpedo amidships, I agree, we'd be wasting our time trying."

"Kinda like this little witch hunt we're on, XO?" asked Ops.

He had apparently remembered the Captain's initial comments about the fishing boat incident. Mike glanced at the Exec before answering.

"Well, it's true we haven't found any submarines; on the other hand, let's review the facts: we've had a fishing boat Skipper sight what he thought was a submarine, and then we've had another fishing boat, skippered by a very experienced guy, go down for no apparent reason with no survivors or even a trace of the people onboard. Both of these events are unusual, and maybe, remotely connected. Some of what we're doing is window dressing, of course; make the Navy look like it's at least a little concerned. But, if nothing else, it's been some good training, as well as producing some very unique knowledge about the local operating areas. If we ever had to fight our way out of Mayport in wartime, this stuff Linc's team has put together would be invaluable, especially for shallow water ASW."

The sound powered phone under the table at the Captain's chair buzzed twice. Mike picked it up, as the table went quiet.

"Captain."

"Yes, Sir, Cap'n, Evaluator in Combat here; Linc's guys think they have something worth looking into."

"Like?"

"Yes, Sir. Sorry. An active sonar contact they're classifying as possible, confidence low to medium, definition metallic. The guys got onto it about five minutes ago, and were about to drop it when it appeared to take off. Doppler went from no to audible down. Linc wants us to head back east, 110, to take a better look."

"OK, I concur. Don't change the keying interval or make any other indication that we might have detected something. And make no reports to the beach yet; if this is another false alarm, I don't want to interfere with the come-back-home message we expect any time now."

"Roger that, Cap'n."

Mike replaced the phone under the table. He looked up at the officers.

"Linc thinks they have something," he announced to the table. "We're gonna go take a look."

He turned to the Exec as he pushed back from the table.

"XO, let me know when we hear from the Group. I'm going up to Combat."

TWENTY FOUR

The Al Akrab, Jacksonville Operating Areas, Friday, 25 April, 1215

"Idiot!" hissed the Captain, bursting into the control room. "Reduce speed to four knots! At once!"

The alarmed watch officer relayed the order swiftly, and the boat quickly began to decelerate from the sudden burst of speed ordered only two minutes ago.

"Make your depth 120 meters; flood negative—we must get some more layers above us."

The control room watch was tense, every man sitting upright in his chair. The Musaid, his face drawn and haggard, loomed over the planesman, coaching him softly as they worked to get the boat deeper without making any telltale noises. Any further telltale noises. The distant destroyer had changed its search pattern suddenly, and headed directly towards them. The Watch Officer had reacted by ordering a burst of speed to get away, followed by a depth change. Only then had he called the Captain, who was already on his way to the control room when he sensed the boat surging forward on the electric motors.

The Captain scanned the gauges swiftly. "Sonar, report."

"Sir, the enemy destroyer is closing from the west; I hold him on the port quarter, but he's drifting in and out of my baffles. His speed appears to be unchanged. He's still in omni transmission mode, no frequency change. No new keying rate."

The Deputy looked up from the sound plot at the back of the control room. "Bearings indicate he has altered his pattern of search; bearings have steadied."

The Captain cursed again. They were on the battery, so engine noises were not the problem. Doppler was the problem. If the enemy sonar operator had suspected he had a real contact, and focused on it at the same time the Al Akrab increased speed, the audio on the destroyer's sonar would have shown down doppler, and thereby, motion away from the destroyer. Doppler was one of the crucial classification cues; marine life rarely showed doppler. As soon as he had entered the control room, the Captain had taken the speed off, and dived deeper to get more acoustic layers of water between the boat and the destroyer.

"Range?"

"Estimate the range to be 12,000 yards; there is no way to tell if he is closing or not," said the Deputy from the plotting table.

"Bearing 280. Steady bearing."

The destroyer was coming their way. Something had attracted his attention. Much would depend on what the destroyer did with his sonar. The next clue would be if he went to directional keying, pumping out all the acoustic energy in the direction of where he thought he might have a contact, rather than his present mode of banging out the ping in all directions.

"Sir, depth is passing through 70 meters. Negative tank is flooded."

"Make your heading 110; speed five. Level off at 120 meters."

"Planes, aye, 120 meters."

The Musaid was trying to get the Captain's attention. There was a distinct note of apprehension in the planesman's voice. Three hundred and sixty feet was approaching the submarine's extreme operational depth capability limit. The boat's hull was already beginning to make small groaning and popping sounds as the steel hull compressed under the increasing pressure of the sea.

The Captain cursed again, silently. This was partly his own fault: he had ordered the watch officer to stay within five to ten miles of this destroyer ever since they had returned from the mothership and heard the steady pinging of a searching sonar. He glanced over at the Musaid, who looked swiftly at the rate of descent dial.

"100 meters; preparing to blow negative," he said.

"No!" interjected the Captain. "*Pump* negative; increase speed if you must to hold her, but no noise. No air."

The men controlling the dive scrambled to line up the valve manifolds. The negative tank, a large seawater ballast tank with oversized water-admission valves, sat astride the submarine's center of gravity, and was used to make quick changes in the submarine's buoyancy. Flooding the negative tank made the submarine immediately heavy, thus rapidly accelerating a diving maneuver. When the boat approached its ordered depth, the normal procedure was to force compressed air back into the tank and thus blow the seawater out, thereby quickly restoring the submarine's neutral buoyancy. Depth was then maintained with careful use of the trim tanks, much like an airplane is trimmed up to stabilize flight once the climb to altitude has been completed.

The Captain was aware that the blast of compressed air from the flasks would send out a transmission of broadband noise. His order to pump out the negative tank with relatively silent electric pumps rather than using a blast of high pressure air was driven by the tactical necessity for silence. The price for silence was delay: pumping took much longer, especially against the pressure of almost 400 feet of depth. The delay, in turn, meant that the boat would settle past its ordered depth unless speed

173

was increased so that she could be held at depth by the force of the water flowing over the forward and after planes.

"120 meters," sang out the diving officer, his forehead glistening with sweat.

The hull was complaining audibly now, creaking and groaning throughout the boat. A fine mist had appeared in the air ventilating system, casting a thin aurora around the lights. The men in the control room tried hard to ignore the signs and sounds of the implacable grip of the deep.

"123 meters; I'm having trouble holding her. Request eight knots!"

"Eight knots," replied the Captain.

His eyes, like those of every man in the control room, were fixed on the depth gauge. The black needle was inching around clockwise, past 125, 126, as the diving officer manipulated the bow and stern planes to put a shallow up angle on the boat, using the increased speed. The needle went to 127, and then to 128, as the boat mushed down into the depths. The boat inclined more sharply, and then levelled slightly. The diving officer had to take great care. He could put too large an up angle on the boat and cause it to stall like an airplane and even slip backwards. The key was to get the negative tank pumped out.

"We cannot hold her," declared the Musaid softly. "You will have to blow negative."

"No. Continue pumping. Ten knots."

"Ten knots, aye."

The depth gauge now indicated 130 meters, over four hundred feet of depth. The temperature was rising in the boat. At the back of the control room, a sailor surreptitiously closed the watertight hatch. The mist effect was more pronounced.

"Steady yourselves," growled the Captain. "We have taken this boat to 170 meters before."

He continued to watch the depth gauge; the needle was holding at 131 meters, as the extra speed took effect. His mind raced. The problem was now, once again, doppler. He could not maneuver the boat off the destroyer's search axis until he had depth control back in hand, and the boat was now driving away from the enemy's sonar at a speed which was definitely not typical of marine life. He desperately needed to make a turn.

TWENTY FIVE

USS Goldsborough, Jacksonville Operating Areas, Friday, 25 April; 1230

"Captain's in Combat!"

Mike entered the darkened central control area of the CIC and went directly to the plotting table, where a small crowd of officers and enlisted operations specialists were staring hard at the plot.

"What've we got, John?"

The CIC officer scooted his stool forward and pointed down to the plotting paper, where the NC-2 plotter was marking a small dot in red pencil on the tracing paper. The dot was the most recent in a trail of red dots which began about five miles east of the Goldsborough, and which was now tracking southeast. The spacing between the dots was supposed to be proportional to the target's speed, but sonar was notorious for offering up ambiguous velocity data. The plot showed that the distance between the Goldsborough and the underwater contact was slowly closing, after remaining steady for five minutes. Mike stared down at the plot, and then reached over and keyed the intercom squawk box to sonar.

"Sonar, Captain, tell me again why you think this contact is any more valid that all the other ghosts we've stirred up out here this week."

Linc's voice came back over the box. He had been in sonar control for six hours, and had stayed past his watch time when this contact was detected. His voice was husky with fatigue.

"Captain, this one's got substance. I've got Chief Mac on the stack and the audio on the wall speaker, and this goblin's got some meat on him. We hold him in a stern aspect, going deep, with varying doppler—marked down doppler when we first turned to look at him, then much less, and then again down doppler, like someone's trying to peel off the clues while we're sniffing around."

Mike felt the first stirring of apprehension as he listened to the ASW officer. The classification of a sonar contact was an art; one added up the cues and clues and made the call, and even then, the guy could get away while you were still trying to decide what you had. A new thought intruded: if this turned out to be a hostile submarine, how prepared was Goldsborough for a surprise attack?

"OK. If he's going deep, you want to go to directional? It might be worth it to get a solid ping on this thing before the layers bury it."

Mike noted that he was speaking about the contact as if he had already decided that it was a submarine.

"Yes, Sir, I think we better. We've followed doctrine so far—no changes which might alert the target that we're on to him, but this is the Stream—"

"Right, OK: go to long pulse on the bearing and knock on his door; make sure you're taping all of this, too."

"Oh, yes, Sir, we have been. Video and audio. Sonar shifting to directional transmission."

Mike released the squawk box key, and turned to the Evaluator.

"Evaluator, set up condition 1AS; if we do have a live one out here, I want the underwater weapons ready. Tell Damage Control Central to set modified condition zebra below the main deck."

"Aye, aye, Sir."

The Evaluator picked up the ship's announcing system microphone, and passed the word to set Condition 1AS throughout the ship. Moments later, the Exec and the Weapons officer came hustling through the door to CIC, followed by the rest of the CIC team.

"We actually have something?" asked the XO.

"Don't really know, XO," replied the Captain. "But if we do I don't want to be sitting out here in condition Sunday drive."

The XO nodded, and went out to the bridge to check the setting of condition 1AS. Men continued to come into CIC as the increased manning of weapons and sensor systems was implemented.

Condition 1AS was a variant of general quarters, wherein all of the anti-submarine warfare stations were manned up, and certain watertight doors were closed below decks in case a contact turned into a fight. In Goldsborough, 1AS meant that CIC and Sonar control were fully manned instead of having just enough men to operate the basic equipment. The anti-submarine torpedo tubes were manned, and all the air flasks which propelled the torpedoes over the side were charged up with high pressure air. The depth charge rack station was also manned on the stern, where the men removed the covers on the ten 500 pound depth bombs and inserted arming plugs and hydrostatic fuzes. In the Sonar Control room down on the 3rd deck, well below the waterline, senior sonarmen took over the sensor consoles and the attack director. In CIC, the plotting team was doubled and augmented with more experienced and senior technicians. The three principal officers in the ASW tactical team put on sound powered telephones and established a control circuit, where ship maneuvers, contact information, and weapons control could be coordinated directly by the tactical team.

"Shifting to long pulse, directional mode," called Sonar control on the squawk box.

Mike walked over to his Captain's chair, which was set up at one end of the plotting table, and climbed in. The tactical team members closed in around the plot, and waited for the sonarmen below to report.

Mike thought about the contact. Young Linc had spent almost his every waking hour down in sonar, watching the watch teams as they probed the turbulent waters of the operating areas along the Gulf Stream for signs of something besides marine life and seamounts. They had mapped large portions of the bottom, refreshing charts and recording any larger underwater objects which might confuse a submarine search.

Mike was still convinced that this whole submarine thing was an enormous waste of time. He was also very disappointed about missing the fleet exercise, and now the maintenance world wanted him shut down for an entire week in order to work the main feed pumps. This meant another week alongside the pier coping with all the shoreside "help".

He recalled the Commodore's words of advice about command, and still had half a mind to ask for a short tour. He was probably going to have to retire just like his ship. He thought about where he might go after the command tour, and drew a complete blank. Most Commanders were promoted to Captain at the end of their ship command tours; those who were not usually went to dead end jobs, or retired as soon as they had accumulated their twenty years. He would reach the end of his command tour and his twenty at about the same time. He shook his head mentally to get himself back to the current ASW problem.

"Sonar contact!" announced the squawk box. "Definition sharp and clear, doppler is down, bearing 112, range 10,500 yards; echoes intermittent due to layers."

The Operations officer, who was the Evaluator for Condition 1AS, spoke rapidly into his sound powered phones.

"Bridge, Combat, increase speed to fourteen knots, come right to 112."

He looked over at the Captain. "Bearing's clear, Captain. I'm going to close him a little; Linc thinks he's going deep."

"He really got doppler on this thing?"

"Yes, Sir. Good down doppler."

"Evaluate possible submarine, confidence medium," reported the squawk box. "Bearing 110, range 10,000 yards."

Mike leaned forward.

"Change keying frequency, down one band," he ordered.

The Evaluator relayed the message to sonar. The plotters bent over the table, keeping up the marks with the red light from the NC2 plotter. Now that the sonar had contact, the plotting table's circuits were tracking the contact automatically. The other watchstanders in CIC were eaves-dropping hard on what was going on at the plotting table in the center.

"Keying frequency changed one band; contact remains strong; echoes still intermittent due to layering. Bearing 108, range 9700 yards."

"Is this an area we've mapped with the bottom recording system?" asked the Weapons Officer.

"Yes, Sir," replied the CIC Officer.

"What's on the bottom around here?"

The CIC Officer tapped in some search codes on the PC. "We're on the edge of the inner Gulf Stream boundary; we have the beginnings of several parallel, shallow canyons that run east west about ten miles out to the shelf. According to the PC, there is only one significant wreck, a tanker that went down in 1946."

"Can we get the bearing and range of the wreck from our present position?"

"Yes, Sir, I think so. Surface Supervisor, give me a lat-lon!"

A young operations specialist read the dials on the dead-reckoning tracer table, and called out the current latitude and longitude. The CIC Officer keyed in the geographic coordinates, and then rolled the cursor over to the charted position of the tanker.

"Sir, it's 130, eight miles from our current position."

The Weapons officer turned around in his chair to look at Mike in his Captain's chair.

"Right where this contact is headed, Captain," he said.

"If it is a submarine," mused Mike aloud. The squawk box erupted again.

"Sonar has no echoes, last bearing was 122, last range was 8500 yards. Attack director is in PK."

Mike acknowledged this report with a sigh. It figured; they had been lucky to hold on to this contact for as long as they had, given the water conditions. He had not had much faith in it to begin with, and now the contact had disappeared just like all the others. Linc had put the underwater weapons fire control computer in the Position Keeping mode, which assumed that the contact would keep going on the last computed course and speed. The computer kept the sonar's display cursor pointed at the predicted position of the contact, in case the echoes emerged again. Mike leaned forward.

"OK, guys, I think we've locked on to another hydro-spook. Weps, ask Linc if he wants to keep playing with this anymore."

The Weapons Officer picked up a handset and held a brief conversation with the ASW Officer, nodding as he listened. Mike heard the words "wreck" and ranges and bearings being exchanged.

"OK, Linc. I'll tell him."

He hung up the phone and turned to the Captain.

"Sir, Linc wants to go silent on the sonar and continue down this last bearing at twelve knots, below cavitation speed. He wants to drive in for about four miles, and then light off again, see what we turn up. He really thinks this was a valid contact."

Mike thought for a minute. The ASW Officer always thought that the last contact was a good contact, a possible submarine. This was normal; the ASW officer was supposed to be aggressive. But Mike thought he knew what would happen next: they would pursue the matter for another twenty minutes or so, light off the sonar again, and gain contact on the wreck on the bottom. The whole 1AS team was waiting for his decision.

"And what do you recommend, Weps?"

Mike had learned this ploy at the Navy's surface command school: if you can't make up your mind on what to do, ask your subordinates for a recommendation. One of them might know or illuminate the right answer, and it gave you time to think some more.

"We're out here, and this is the strongest contact we've had," said the Weapons Officer. "It doesn't cost us anything to keep screwing around with it. Linc thinks this guy is headed for the wreck, either to hide or to throw us off the scent. He wants to go ping around the wreck."

"OK, OK, you guys do what you want to. I'll sit here and watch."

The Weapons officer grinned. "Yes, Sir!"

Mike watched as the Weapons and Operations officers used the PC to refine a course that would allow the ship to pass over the wreck, some 500 feet below the surface. The Exec came back into Combat to see what was going on, and Mike brought him up to speed.

"Gonna let the guys screw around with it for awhile; there's nobody else out here, they like to do it, and it builds up their self confidence," he explained in a low voice, as the officers crowded back around the plotting table, and the Weapons officer sent new course and speed orders out to the bridge.

"They thought about how they'll distinguish between a wreck on the bottom and a submarine hiding nearby?"

"Presumably with Linc's PC magic, but they haven't thought that far ahead, XO. One thing at a time," smiled the Captain.

Mike knew that it was going to be hard enough to pass over or even near the wreck, given the vagaries of navigation when beyond radar range of land. If there were a submarine here, it would probably drive by the wreck, presuming the sub knew it was there, and then slip down into one of the canyons and disappear over the shelf into the deep ocean abyss while the destroyer went around in circles. He called for coffee, and settled back into his chair to watch his young ASW team work. It was one of the few remaining joys of being in a destroyer as opposed to a larger ship—the junior officers could be allowed to run an ASW search by themselves, or almost so, and he could observe without having to direct every detail. The Exec would go out to the bridge to make sure they didn't run over a fishing boat in their enthusiasm. And then hopefully they could go back into port for the weekend.

TWENTY SIX

The Al Akrab, submerged, Jacksonville Operating Areas, Friday, 25 April; 1240

"Eight knots," ordered the Captain. His forehead was damp with perspiration, and his uniform was getting sticky.

The depth gauge continued to hold steady; the whine of the pumps beneath the deckplates of the control room competed with the creaking and crackling noises coming from the pressure hull. The needle backed off to 129, and then 128.

"Get her level. Now. We need to turn."

The Musaid continued to coach the planesman as he adjusted bow and stern planes to bring the boat level. As the water was forced out of the negative tank, the boat became more responsive.

"Come port to 040, small rudder angles," ordered the Captain.

He knew that if he could bring the submarine's heading around to a course perpendicular to the oncoming destroyer's search axis, the net effect would be to nullify the doppler on any returning echoes, regardless of his speed. The tradeoff was that he would now present the whole length of the submarine to the probing sound rays, but he counted on depth and the swirling acoustic layers of the Stream to mask the larger target he presented.

"Depth unstable," called the Musaid urgently, putting his hand on the helmsman's shoulder to stay the turn order.

Turning without depth control could spell disaster because the planes would induce rolling moments. The Captain looked at the depth gauge needle, as it cycled between 128 and 130. The submarine was porpoising, creating a shallow roller coaster ride as her buoyancy changed. The pumps continued to mill and grind.

"Commence the turn! Now! I need to show him null doppler," shouted the Captain.

The Musaid removed his hand, his face stiff.

"Helm, Aye. Commencing the turn," responded the helmsman, his voice cracking. The other men in the control room were frozen in position, afraid to look at one another.

"Sonar, what is the destroyer doing?" demanded the Captain, his voice more under control.

"Sir, he continues to ping in omnidirectional mode; the bearing is beginning to draw right; I don't think he—"

The sonar operator suddenly opened his headset away from his ears, and then reached forward to the console to make an adjustment on the audio volume. He did not have to tell the Captain or anyone else in the control room why: the drawn out, ringing sound of a powerful directional sound pulse was reverberating in the control room. The men looked nervously at one another, and swallowed. A second long ping. The men had to hold on as the submarine rolled to one side, and then the other, as the rudder took effect. The Captain's face tightened.

"Prepare to release a decoy. Quickly."

The Deputy jumped from his station at the plotting table, and opened an air valve to arm the starboard decoy tube. There was a small hiss of air as the firing chamber filled to 3000 psi.

"Decoy tube is armed, Sir."

"Very well."

Now, thought the Captain, they would have to wait. It all depended on how determined this enemy was. He did not know how long this destroyer had been out looking around the operating areas. They had returned from the mothership in the early hours of Thursday morning and detected the pinging as they closed in submerged from the Gulf Stream. He had to know if this destroyer was actually conducting a search or just out testing his sonar. When his sonar officer had run back through his tapes and determined that this was a sonar they had encountered before, the Captain became suspicious. This destroyer's presence was no accident. He had determined to shadow it, staying outside the predicted sonar range but near enough to record the enemy destroyer's search patterns on the passive plot, to learn his tactics, and to appraise his vigilance.

The Captain's mind raced. Somehow this destroyer may have detected the Al Akrab. And he was sure enough that he had something other than a school of fish to switch to directional keying. The turn would nullify the doppler, but now the Al Akrab would present her full beam to the enemy sonar. Going deep and the swirling layers above them should take care of that. Should.

"Passing 070."

"Depth is stable; we can slow," declared the Musaid, straightening up.

"Slow to five knots; continue the turn to 040."

"040, Aye. Passing 060."

The Captain considered the timing of the decoy launch. The decoy was a miniature transponder. It was shaped like a tiny torpedo, three feet long and about four inches in diameter. It had an air driven propeller that would run for about three minutes. In the body of the decoy was a sonar receiver and an amplifier. At its nose was a miniature sonar transmitter. The decoy could detect the incoming sonar pulse from the destroyer's sonar, match its frequency, introduce some slight doppler shift, and ping back at the destroyer. The destroyer's sonar would see a solid echo since the decoy's response, however muted, was always stronger than the faint, real echo from the submarine. The destroyer's sonar tracking circuits would then lock on to the decoy, while the submarine stole away into the depths.

The key to success was the timing of the decoy launch: if the enemy was in firm contact, the decoy would show up as a second contact and be exposed as a decoy, thereby confirming the presence of a submarine. If the enemy sonar had lost contact, the decoy could trick the enemy operator into thinking he had regained contact. The Captain listened carefully to the directional ping.

"Passing 045; steadying on 040."

His new course was almost seventy degrees off the original course, enough to strip off most of the doppler effect, but not so far north that he would emerge back out of the protective thermal layers of the Gulf Stream. The long pings were not so loud now. The Captain made his decision.

"Release the decoy!"

There was a relatively loud thump as the decoy was expelled into the depths, pointed behind and below them. They could not know precisely which way the decoy would go, only that it would begin to transpond after thirty seconds. The Captain stared at his watch.

"Speed ten knots," he ordered when the thirty seconds was up.

He would make a dash to the northeast, while hopefully the destroyer would lock onto the decoy as it careened along to the southwest at random depths.

"Ten knots, aye."

The boat surged forward perceptibly. The long pinging was still audible, but its frequency had changed. Everyone in the control room listened and waited. Then the pinging suddenly stopped.

TWENTY SEVEN

USS Goldsborough, Jacksonville Operating Areas, Friday, 25 April; 1245

"Sonar is still passive," announced the Evaluator.

Mike sat forward in his chair. They had driven along at twelve knots down the last bearing of the contact, theoretically closing the range, for the last four minutes.

"How close are we to the wreck?" he asked.

"Sir, the wreck should be 075, at about 16,000 yards," answered the surface supervisor.

Mike leaned back in the chair, and stared up at the darkened ceiling. Now they would get contact again, this time on the wreck. It was entirely predictable. But, what the hell.

"Tell Sonar to go active," he ordered.

"Sonar is going active," announced the Evaluator.

"Sonar Contact!" announced the squawk box, twenty seconds later. "Contact bearing 090, range 10,450 yards. Echo quality sharp, doppler is up doppler, echoes are intermittent due to layering."

Mike sat up when he heard the report of up doppler. This was not the wreck; doppler meant motion—this contact was coming at them.

"Classification?"

The Evaluator consulted with Linc in the sonar room below.

"Bearing is clear," reported the Bridge.

"Linc says sonar thinks it's a decoy, Sir."

Mike closed his eyes for a moment. A decoy? Oh, come on, he thought. Then Linc's voice came on the box.

"Captain, this new contact is too good. It's coming in and out of the layers with a consistent echo quality, and its headed in our general direction. The last contact was going away like a bandit. That doesn't compute. I need to change pulse back to omni and mess around with him, but I think this is a decoy."

183

Mike considered this data. The officers around the plotting table were looking at him. He got out of the chair and reached for the squawk box key.

"OK, Linc, do what you want to with the sonar. I think we're stretching things a little here, but I'll go along with it. Check your contact out and advise."

"Aye, aye, Cap'n."

Mike thought for a moment. If this was a decoy, which he doubted, it implied two things. First, a decoy meant there had to be a submarine. And second, if this was a decoy, where was the sub? He stepped back over to the plotting table, and the officers made a space for him around the plot.

"What was the original contact doing when we lost him—where was he?" he asked.

The plotter pointed to the red trace with his pencil.

"He was going away from us, to the east by southeast, speed around eight, maybe ten knots. We lost him right here, Cap'n, and the new contact came up over here."

Mike could see that the new contact had appeared north of the original track. Which implied that the sub—there I go again, he thought, the sub—had turned left before putting out the decoy. Linc was back on the box again, his voice excited.

"Cap'n, Sonar Control: the echoes remain the same no matter what keying mode or frequency we lay on this thing: the Chief says that's the sign of repeater—this thing is pinging back at us with a constant doppler shift, and matching our freq so that we get consistent echoes. By our bearings plot it's going south now, across our track, but the contact's quality is constant. It's too good to be anything but a transponder."

"OK, Linc, how do we let this guy know we're onto his trick?"

"We go silent again, wait a coupla minutes, and then come up again—let the decoy run outa gas. Then we go back into search."

"Where do we look, Ops?" Mike asked.

Mike knew that this was the magic question. They had lost the original contact probably because he had gone deep enough to get beneath several acoustic layers. After that, the sub could have gone in any direction. Their chances of regaining him were slim to none, but the appearance of a possible decoy changed the whole game.

"Cap'n, I don't have a clue. He could be anywhere."

The Weapons Officer spoke up.

"Sir, the decoy came from north of the original track. He probably turned north, dropped the decoy, and then turned again. My guess he's gone out into the Stream because that's the best water to hide in. I recommend we go silent, turn northeast or east, wait fifteen minutes or so, and then resume omni pinging. That'll tell this guy we weren't fooled."

Mike thought about that. Tell this guy? What guy? If there was a sub out here, and that now looked to be at least possible, what did they want to reveal to the sub's skipper? That the U.S. Navy was now alerted to the presence of an unidentified submarine? Wouldn't it be better to break off, go somewhere else while they reviewed what they had, looked and listened to their tapes, and maybe asked for some more assets?

"Sonar reports no echoes; last bearing 094, last range 9400 yards."

No echoes. So now, whatever it was, it was gone. He stared down at the rubber matting on the CIC deckplates. Should he call in help from the specialized ASW forces? Maybe get a helo out here, or one of the ASW destroyers? If you find a fire, first call the fire department, then and only then you grab a bucket of water. He was aware that his officers were waiting for a decision. He felt a sudden need to consult with the Exec.

"Evaluator, turn off track to the south, resume omni pinging, resume the original search pattern. Wait one half-hour, then secure from 1AS. Tell Linc to bring his tapes up here to Combat and bring the Chief. I'm going to go talk to the XO."

The Evaluator raised his eyebrows and then acknowledged and passed the orders down to sonar over the sound-powered phones. Mike knew that Linc would be protesting that they would lose any chance of regaining contact. The Evaluator gave him a verbal shrug and told him to come up to Combat with his tapes. The CIC crew also looked visibly disappointed, but Mike ignored them. He headed for the bridge.

Stepping out onto the bridge, he had to squint in the bright sunlight. He saw the XO leaning on the Captain's chair, and smiled inwardly as the Exec stood upright suddenly when the bridge watch announced that the Captain was on the bridge.

"XO, step out here with me for a minute."

They walked out onto the port bridge wing, and the watch team made themselves inconspicuous on the other side of the bridge so that the two could speak in privacy.

"XO," said Mike. "Linc thinks that last contact was a decoy. If he's right, that changes everything."

"Yes, Sir, I overheard that report on the phone circuit. I'm having a little trouble with it, myself."

"Yeah," said Mike, looking out over the calm, entirely peaceful sea. Staring at the vivid red lines on the plotting table made it seem real. The placid seas of the Jacksonville operating areas, dotted with fishing boats and afternoon pleasure craft, framed the whole idea of a submarine in unreality. He shook his head.

"I still can't feature it, XO. Why would a submarine, any kind, ours, theirs, or a perfect stranger's, be skulking around the Jax opareas? What's the point? What's the likelihood of it? There's no intel, there're no out of area reports, there's really no hard sighting data, just one perpetually drunk fisherman's report, and one coincidental accident—and now our guys have talked themselves into "finding" something, which I'm convinced appeared because we've been looking hard for three days...Can you imagine what the Group Chief of Staff would say if I report that we have a sonar contact out here?"

"You seem to be arguing with yourself, Cap'n," reflected the XO, being careful to look into the distance. "If you really think this is a buncha shit, then we call it off, log the thing as a good drill, and wait for the come-back-in message."

The Exec's voice was neutral. Mike had heard that tone before, every time the XO went into his "You Chief, me injun" mode. It usually meant the Exec disagreed.

"OK, XO," Mike said with a sigh. "Let's hear it. What do you think's going on here?"

The Exec pulled out the clasp knife he carried in a leather sheath on the back of his belt, and began cleaning his finger-nails with the narrow blade. He wedged himself into a corner of the bridgewing bulwark, hooking one foot back up on the pelorus pedestal.

"I think we're not being entirely objective with all this," he began.

Mike noted the use of the "we" term; XO was being polite.

"I think, if we put aside the waterfront politics for a minute, we have a chain of events that bears investigation. We have the initial report, which came up with a fairly precise description—guy called it a U-boat. Not a submarine, not a periscope, but a U-boat. Now, Maxie's been out at sea for the whole time, and nobody's been able to ask him any questions about this sighting, but he called it a U-boat, and Maxie's old enough to have actually seen or at least remember what a U-boat looked like."

"Then, we have Chris Mayfield getting into some kind of scrape that gets his boat sunk, without a scratch on it, mind you, and in weather that, at max, would have been classified as a heavy rain, and we retrieve his nameboard with a bullet hole in it. No sign of any people—no bodies, no life-rings, maydays, no reports, no nothing. Just the boat on the bottom, with its nets out but closed, and the nameboard with a bullet hole."

The Exec shifted from one leg to the other, still not looking directly at Mike.

"Now, we search out here for three days, learn a lot about the opareas, the bottom, map some wrecks and pinnacles, get the ASW team oiled up pretty good, and then at the last minute we get a contact that's different from all the false alarms we've had all week. What is it? We don't know, except that it's different. And while we're screwing around with it, with the first team on the sonar stack, by the way, we lose the first contact and then get another contact, and this one exhibits the classic technical signal of a transponder decoy, just like the mini mobile targets we throw over the side to train with."

The Exec had turned to look at him now. "So," he continued, "that's two contacts out of the ordinary, and they could be related—a decoy's gotta come from somewhere. There's nobody else around throwing transponders over the side—nearest Navy unit is fifteen miles away—so how come this thing pops up when we're working the only unique contact we've seen all week? I gotta tell ya, Cap'n, if this were a homicide investigation, your famous detective's elbow would be tingling right about now—too damn much coincidence here. I realize it'll sound squirrely to the shore establishment, but this detective's elbow is tingling."

Mike took a deep breath and let it out. The XO was a devoted reader of mystery novels, and often spoke in the metaphor of police procedurals. Mike stared out over the serene seascape as the ship plowed south through the entirely familiar and ordinary looking fleet operating area on this sunny, Thursday afternoon. There were men out on deck below working on touching up the paintwork, the buzzing of their deck sanders and casual banter reinforcing the normalcy of the scene around him. He looked sideways at the Exec.

"You think this thing is real, don't you."

"Like I said before, I think this thing is *possible*. I can't prove it, and I can't explain it. But I think the facts point to the possibility that there might be a submarine out here, messing around in the Jax opareas, and that, somehow, is important. And there's something else."

"What's that?"

"I think some of our officers and troops feel the same way. Linc is going to come up to CIC armed for bear. He's gonna try to persuade you that they had something, and he's gonna be pissed off that we broke it off. We both know how dumb this would look if we filed a contact report, but have you figured out what you're gonna say to Linc and his sonar team?"

Mike squinted at the Exec in the sunlight.

"I didn't think so," continued the Exec. "I don't know what to say either, other than it's your best judgement that there was nothing there, and you're the Old Man. But you've always been pretty straight with them up to now, and that's going to sound phony."

Mike was stung; the Exec was right, as usual. Any superficial excuses he offered for breaking off the search would be phony. He would be violating yet another old Army maxim: you don't shit the troops you march with. And yet he knew that his superiors ashore would hit the overhead if he came in now with anything resembling a contact report. They had not been sent out to find a submarine, only to go through the motions of looking. But then an idea began to take shape in his mind.

"OK, suppose I punch the I-believe button, which I haven't done yet, by the way, and accept the existence of an unidentified submarine lurking in the Jax op areas. You know and I know that we'd be laughed out of the harbor if we took this notion back in with us. Martinson would probably be able finally to convince the Admiral that Goldsborough needs a new CO. But let me run this by you: suppose I believe it—what's the next move? The smart move? Nobody else will believe it until we can bring back some hard evidence, some proof, *and* some reason for a sub to be here. Right?"

He began to pace back and forth on the narrow bridge wing, while the Exec listened, and the watch team tried to.

"When we lost contact back there, he could've gone in any direction, and we're close enough to the Stream that our chances of regaining contact are lower than whaleshit. So: doesn't it make sense not to let the guy *know* we know he's there? If he thinks we're on to him, he'll really hide, but if he thinks he fooled us, maybe we can find him again. I don't know, I'm wingin' it here, but we do know what the reaction to this would be if we report it. So, this is what I tell Linc and his guys: I broke it off because I want to study the tapes, and I want to kick this thing around here in the family, so to speak, and then figure out what to do next and who to tell, all the while not revealing to the potential bad guy that we know his ass is out there. How's that sound?"

The Exec slowly grinned at him. "Not bad, for wingin' it. I suppose you want me to tell 'em."

Mike grinned back. "Yeah, I do. I want them to build a case—tapes, plots, contact characteristics: as much hard evidence as they can, and come convince me why they think it's real. If they convince me, I'll take it up the line."

The Exec nodded. Mike felt better. He still did not believe there was a sub out here, but now he had a way of facing his ASW team, at least for the moment. Then they both noticed the radio messenger standing just inside the pilothouse door.

"Cap'n," he said, "I got an Oboe from Group Twelve."

Mike took the message and scanned it. The message directed Goldsborough to break off the ASW search and return to port that afternoon.

"Goldy-come-home?" asked the Exec.

"Yeah. Get together with the ASW team and tell 'em what I said, and to keep this under wraps. Under tight wraps. Tell their people not to yap about it. Impress on the officers and Chiefs in CIC and Sonar that it's not over, but if this gets out we'll look like turkeys, and that the only way we'll get to pursue it is to keep it quiet. They'll take care of the troops. I've got to decide whether or not to tell the Commodore—I think he would be an ally, as long as it's not out in public."

The Exec nodded his understanding. "I'll get 'em together in CIC right now."

He looked at his watch.

"It'll take us about four hours to get back into Mayport. Next week we're in for maintenance, and the week after that we're slated for sea trials after the engineering plant work. So we have a week to figure this thing out."

Mike nodded. "Yeah, and like your famous detective, we still have to come up with a motive, XO: why is this guy out here? Who is he, and why's he sneakin' around the opareas? And will he still be here in a week? I'm not going to talk to anybody off the ship until we come up with that."

"Aye, aye, Sir. We'll get on it. I'll tell the crew we're going back in."

Mike remained out on the bridge wing after the Exec left the bridge. The bosun brought him a paper cup of particularly evil looking black coffee, and Mike dutifully thanked him. He would hold it in his hands for five minutes and then drop it quietly over the side.

He thought about this submarine problem. He would of course have to talk to the Commodore after they got in, but he would have to hear his people's case first. Maybe Monday afternoon, or Tuesday. He'd get on the Commodore's calendar when he got in. The main focus next week would be work on the engineering plant—the parts ought to be waiting for them on the pier this evening. Three days to cool the plant down, and then a week's worth of repair efforts, followed by a weekend light-off—another good deal for the engineers—and back out the following week to see if the stuff worked.

He and the Exec had had an argument earlier on a message Mike had drafted about the steam admission valves. Mike had wanted to excoriate the Mayport repair superintendent, and the Exec had argued against it. Mike had been forced to admit the Exec had a point: it did not make sense to blast the guy whom you were then going to ask to help fix the problem. He had given in to the Exec's counsel, but with the mental reservation that he would blast them all when they finally fixed the valves. It was because of their sloppy work that the snipes would have to light off over the weekend, thus losing what little time they had with their families.

And, in between, they had to thrash this sub thing out. He thought about the weekend. It would be pleasant as always to get back to the Lucky Bag, kick back, maybe hit the beach clubs. Then the vision of Diane Martinson materialized in his mind. He had been half keeping her memory at bay, half saving it for last, ready to savor the thought of being with her, and yet conscious of that inner voice that told him in no uncertain terms that his seeing Diane was trouble.

How could they meet? Where? Under what pretext? He couldn't call her, and she might not call him. He felt a moment of panic at the thought that she might not call. Christ, like being a teenager again. He could go back out to the hospital to visit Quigley. But she said she normally didn't volunteer on weekends—that Saturday had been a fluke. He needed a way to make it happen.

Squirming in his bridge chair, Mike let out a deep breath. He couldn't keep his mind off her: she was firmly embedded in his psyche, and unless his instincts betrayed him badly, available. No. Wrong word: available implied something superficial, a one night stand, some kind of temporary indiscretion. Diane represented something of value, a woman of substance, a human edifice that was moving off its foundations. He was beginning to recognize that his involvement with this woman might have consequences beyond the difficulties arising from the fact that she was already married, and married to his boss' boss. But thinking about the possibilities gave him a thrill, not unlike the first time he had given a conning order on a destroyer, and felt 4000 tons of steel begin to move in response to something he had said. The Chief Engineer came out on the bridge wing, a sheaf of work requests under his arm. Thoughts of Diane vanished as Mike went back to work.

TWENTY EIGHT

The Al Akrab, Jacksonville Operating Areas; Friday, 25 April; 1330

The sudden silence was almost deafening. The enemy's sonar had gone quiet. The creaking and cracking noises were audible again. The Captain turned to the sonar operator.

"Report."

"Sir: the enemy destroyer is audible on the starboard quarter. He has stopped directional pinging. He is barely cavitating. I—wait! He's gone back to omni!"

The distant ringing sound permeated the control room, distinctly different from the long and much louder directional ping.

"The ping has down doppler; he's moving away from us, Captain."

The Captain nodded silently. He found his hands were gripping the railing around the periscope rail tight enough to hurt. He forced himself to relax.

"I will have some tea," he announced. His statement had the desired effect of breaking the tension. The Captain would not call for tea if the action were not over.

"Recommend we come up in depth to 80 meters," called the Musaid.

"Permission granted. Make your depth eighty meters. Proceed to the east for one hour at five knots, and then turn south."

There was a collective if discreet sigh of relief in the control room; no one liked to be at 400 feet of depth unless they had to; there was little margin of safety if something went wrong, with as much danger from a collision with the bottom as there was from a sea water leak at depth. It was much easier to get back to the surface from 260 feet if something gave way than from 400 feet. The Captain ignored their concerns; by the book, the Al Akrab was capable of withstanding the pressure of 200 meters, or more than 600 feet. If the water had been that deep, he would not have hesitated to go down to 200 meters just to show the crew that the boat could take it. He accepted the mug of tea, and went over to look at the plot. The control room personnel were changing the watch, and talking quietly among themselves about the encounter with the destroyer. The Deputy was clearly concerned. The Captain glanced over at him.

"Yes?"

"Sir," the words tumbled out. "Sir, the decoy: now they will surely know—"

"Lower your voice! They will know nothing," said the Captain harshly. "If they thought that was a decoy, they would not just turn away and resume their aimless searching. They would have gone into lost contact procedures, initiated a close area search, continued directional pinging, called for a helicopter—anything but a turn away. They are not hunting. They are not hunters. They are not even warriors. I will predict that they will go back into port for their long sabbath."

The Deputy wanted to believe, but his years as a political officer had given him a more suspicious mind. He leaned forward.

"Sir," he said, his voice an urgent whisper. "They were doing nothing, and then they turned toward us. Changed their sonar's pulse. Came directly down the bearing towards us. We evaded and released a transponding decoy. They pinged on it for a minute and a half, and then went silent. And then they turned away. The ending of this sequence is not what we would expect, but the sequence itself is significant!"

The Captain shook his head impatiently. "I tell you it is not. No destroyer searching for a submarine would break off an action if he even *thought* that a decoy had been fired: it would confirm the existence of the submarine. This ship is not even searching, I tell you. He gained contact, classified it as possible, lost contact, gained another contact, and classified it as nothing, and broke off. That is all. We remain undetected, and we remain free to operate where we want and when we want. Our next operational objective is to plan for the seeding of the mines in the river's mouth. We will receive a signal soon telling us the attack date. We will plant the mines one or two nights before the attack day. Your primary duty now is to plan the approach and the maneuvers to lay the field. Is that understood?"

The Deputy stood back. "Sir. As you command," he said, formally. "Very well."

The Captain dismissed the Deputy with a jerk of his head. The Deputy went forward to find the operations officer. The Musaid approached. The Captain saw that the older man was very tired. He felt a wave of guilt over the fact that the Musaid was taking his request to supervise the control room watch too literally. He had forgotten his own mental note.

"You must get some rest, Musaid," said the Captain.

"My place is here, as you commanded."

The Captain waved his hand, dismissing his previous command, and the dire threats about shooting people who made mistakes.

"I command that you go to sleep for eight hours. Rest. The crew is tight again; the officers are reacting."

His eyes narrowed momentarily, as he remembered the watch officer's maneuver of forty-five minutes ago.

"Except that Achmed should have called me first, and then increased speed. He created doppler where there was none. He should have dived first."

The Musaid gave the Captain a wry look.

"But he acted, Captain. He did not just sit there, and by moving away he maintained the range when the enemy closed us. If you chastise him now, none of them will act with initiative again."

The Captain gave the Musaid a hard look, but then nodded.

"What you say is true. I will hold a debriefing of the incident, and we will discuss it. I have instructed the Deputy to plan the mining operation. I will want your views when the plan is laid."

"As you command."

"Go then; get some rest. I need your brain alive when we plan the next move. I feel that the attack day is approaching. Do you think the decoy was a mistake?"

The Musaid stared down at the plotting table. The question had come suddenly.

"It was a calculated risk," he replied. "The enemy did not react as if he had detected a decoy, but only another contact. One among many, and one on the edge of the great Gulf Stream. It was a risk, but it appears to have worked."

The Captain felt reassured, as he always did when the Musaid agreed with him. The whining Deputy was a political officer, not a submariner. The Musaid was, like him, a warrior at heart. Warriors took chances.

"But we did not set the attack condition," observed the Musaid, and the Captain's sudden surge of euphoria dissolved.

The Senior Chief was entirely correct. They should have set the attack condition—if it had come to it, they might have had to fight, and he had become so engrossed in the problem of evasion that he had forgotten to prepare the boat to fight. It had been a major omission. The Captain nodded slowly, grateful that the Musaid had kept his voice down. Had the other officers noted the error? They would, later. He would have to bring it up at the debriefing session. They all needed to hone their procedural awareness. Someone should have made a recommendation to set the attack condition.

"You must compliment them, encourage them again," said the Musaid, as if reading his mind. "They fear you, and your threat of shooting the next one to make an error smothered their initiative. Encourage them to speak out with recommendations, and they will remember the things you might forget in the heat of the moment. It is the proper way."

The Captain nodded again. He would reflect on it. The Musaid saluted him, and left the control room. The Captain walked back over to the sonar console, and tapped the operator on the shoulder. The operator passed back the earphones. There, in the distance, the drawn out ringing sound, succeeding pulses ranging gently down the doppler scale as the destroyer moved away from them. The raucous background noises of the Gulf Stream were steadily overcoming the enemy's ping, even as they enfolded the Al Akrab in a cloak of living noise, reinforcing the submarine's great advantage of being immersed in the sea instead of upon it.

TWENTY NINE

Mayport Naval Station, Friday, 25 April; 2100

Mike walked rapidly down the waterfront towards the Group Twelve headquarters building. The piers were darkened by the bulk of gray warships tied alongside as he passed from the light of one amber halogen streetlight to the next. The Squadron duty officer had met Goldsborough when she tied up and relayed the message that Group wanted a final debrief from the Captain upon Goldsborough's arrival. He had said that the Group public affairs officer had been told to wait around until he had seen Goldsborough's Commanding Officer. Mike had wanted to talk to the Commodore before seeing anyone at the Group, but the Commodore was at sea grading an engineering trial on another ship, and would not be in until tomorrow afternoon. Mike had asked the duty officer if the public affairs officer could come over to the ship, but the duty officer had recommended Mike go over there.

"He said he couldn't come over to the ship;" the young Lieutenant had said. "There might be something else going on, because he said the Admiral and the Chief of Staff were still in the office."

That changed everything. Mike had done a quick shift into a fresh uniform and headed for the white headquarters building as soon as the brow was over. If the heavies were staying late because of Goldsborough, Mike did not want to be the cause of any further night hours.

But when he arrived at the headquarters he was surprised to find a great deal of activity. Most of the offices were still open, and a number of staff officers were coming and going. The Group staff yeoman at the front desk gave him the news that there had been a collision between one of the carriers and a replenishment ship, and that there had been considerable damage and a number of personnel casualties. Mike acknowledged this news with a grimace; a collision at sea was always nasty business. He did feel a momentary and almost guilty sense of relief that all the commotion was not about Goldy.

The yeoman pointed him in the direction of the PAO's office. He walked down the hall, acknowledging the greetings of two staff officers who were headed into the Admiral's office. Mike knew that Captain Martinson's office was right next to the Admiral's office. As he walked past the two executive suites he hoped that he could just make his report to the PAO and get out of there without having to see Martinson or the Admiral.

He found the PAO's office at the end of the hall. The PAO, a tall, thin Lieutenant Commander who needed a haircut, was on the phone. He waved to Mike and indicated a chair. From the conversation Mike deduced that the PAO was talking to his counterpart at the Navy headquarters staff in Norfolk. He waited patiently for the conversation to end.

"There," said Lieutenant Commander Fishburne, banging the phone down onto its receiver. "Norfolk is just about as much of a pain in the neck as the so-called working press. You heard about the Coral Sea?"

"Just now," replied Mike. "How bad is it?"

"Well, first reports aren't terrific. They were alongside the Susquehana, and the oiler lost power. They drifted apart initially but then came back together, side to side, with the oiler scraping her way down Coral Sea's starboard side. Some fuel hoses parted and started a fire, and some guys were knocked over the side from the oiler, and a helo on the number one elevator was also knocked overboard with a flight deck crew inside. So we're gonna be here awhile; the press already has it, and the families are starting in on us now."

"I'm sorry to hear it. My phantom submarine seems like pretty tame stuff compared to all that."

The PAO gave him a twisted grin. "Only as long as you didn't find one."

"You got my last sitrep—this morning?"

"Yes, Sir. We put out a final statement to the local press at noon, and hopefully terminated the whole thing. Unless you've got something to add to that—"

"Nope," said Mike quickly, getting up. "And you've got your hands full here, it looks like. I'll just get back to my ship."

The PAO stood up also.

"Thanks for coming over, Cap'n; normally I would have come to you, but—"

He stopped as the phone began to ring again. Mike waved goodbye and left the office. He went down the long hallway and out the side exit in order to avoid going past the executive suites again. He was walking through the darkened Group Twelve parking lot when a voice called to him out of the darkness.

"Hello, Stranger."

Mike turned to see Diane Martinson smiling at him from the front left window of the Volvo. He made a quick course change and walked over to the car.

"I see you've got this hummer dried out and running again," he said.

She was sitting behind the wheel, her features only dimly visible in reflected light from the office building.

"That's literally what they did," she replied. "They took it to a paint-shop and put it in the oven for several hours, and it runs fine. I'm waiting for J.W.—there's some sort of flap on."

"Right; I've just heard about it. The Coral Sea and the Susquehana have managed to lock horns. It may be a late night for the Staff."

"Oh, dear," she said with a sigh.

She knew full well the import of a collision at sea, especially one involving an aircraft carrier. There was a moment of silence between them. Mike felt an urge to fill it, before the silence gave his real feelings a chance to escape.

"So, the Volvo runs and now you're no longer guilty," he offered.

He wanted to bend down to see her better, but felt exposed in the nearly empty parking lot. She smiled up at him, a cool if somewhat mischievous expression on her face.

"Not for the car, anyway."

He laughed nervously at this.

"Story time went OK?" he asked.

His voice unintentionally revealing his discomfort. He was suddenly angry with himself: he had thought about her at sea, and now that she was right here, all he wanted to do was bolt before someone looked out an office window and saw them together. Her face became neutral.

"Story time went just fine. I felt bad about the lie, but it didn't change the fact that I want to see you again."

She reached out a hand and covered his resting on the window sill of the door.

"And I would very much like to arrange that before you get any more spooked and go loping out of this parking lot."

He felt his face flush at her accurate intuition. Her hand was warm on his, and despite himself he covered hers with his other hand. Her eyes were large and luminous in the shadow. His desire welled up and he suddenly wanted to make love to her right there. She saw his expression change, read it accurately. They stared at each other for a long moment, mutual doubts evaporating in the presence of a suddenly urgent need. She put a finger to her lips.

"Don't say it, don't say anything—just when."

"Tomorrow night? At the boat?" he said softly.

"Yes. I'll be there. I don't know when, but I'll be there." Her voice was husky.

196

Suddenly there were voices coming from the headquarters building doors, and a flare of white light from the hallway inside. Mike straightened up, squeezed her hand, and walked away into the darkness between the buildings, his mind awhirl. What was it about this woman? He had come within a few seconds of climbing in the car with her and damning the consequences. His desire struggled with his fear: had anyone been watching from the office? Had Martinson looked out his window to see if his wife was waiting for him, and seen them together? How much of her allure was due to the illicit nature of their attraction? And, if so, what of it? He knew that some people carried on affairs precisely because it was illicit and therefore more exciting than the routine of marriage.

But Diane was different, he told himself. That long look they had exchanged had changed everything. Their sincere discussion of her needs for a friend, for someone to confide in and to provide comfort, had been shoved into the background. At this moment, it was all much simpler. He wanted her. She wanted him, and the look they had exchanged through the car window had transmitted and acknowledged a message that transcended any mere words. He felt a thrill of anticipation.

Shaking his head as if to clear his thoughts, he strode rapidly back down the piers to the ship, trying to refocus on the business of settling the ship in for the next week. At least he had some control over that; his personal life seemed to be slipping swiftly out of control.

THIRTY

USS Goldsborough, Mayport Naval Station, Friday, 25 April; 2200

When he returned to the ship, Goldsborough was tied up port side to the pier. Mike crossed the quarterdeck and made his way up the outboard side to avoid the press of sailors passing shore power cables and steam lines between the pier and the ship. The Exec caught up with him on the 01 level amidships as he was picking his way through the snarl of cables.

"That go OK, Skipper?" asked the Exec.

"Yeah; they weren't interested in us after all," replied Mike. He related the news about the Coral Sea as they walked forward.

"Damn. Sounds like they really got into it out there. She was due back here in a couple of weeks; I wonder if they'll bring her home early. My neighbor's the MPA. His wife is always a nervous wreck when the ship's gone for a couple of months. Now she'll be a basket case."

They walked together through the radio passageway and up to the Captain's cabin. The Exec had to walk behind Mike; there was not room for two men to walk abreast in the cramped passageway. Mike pitched his hat onto the bunk shelf and sat down. Hooker croaked some obscenity from the corner of the cabin.

"Up yours, bird," said Mike. The XO remained standing; he had a folder of papers in his hands.

"So. We shut down?" asked Mike.

"Yes, Sir. We're on the diesels right now, and expect shore power in about a half hour. Here is a bunch of paperwork that I've accumulated over the week which needs to get signed out by Monday, and also Linc wants to come see you before you shove off, tonight, if that's possible."

Mike frowned. It was after 2200, and he was tired. He did not feel like getting into a discussion with his ASW officer, especially since Linc would want him to explain why they had broken off the contact that afternoon. The Exec saw Mike's expression.

"I told Linc he could have five minutes tonight," he said hurriedly, "And that he was not to come in here all hot and bothered."

"He was disappointed that we quit, wasn't he?"

"Yes, Sir, but he's a pretty professional guy for a junior officer. He got wound up in this thing, and he really believes we had something out there."

"How do you recommend I handle this?"

"Like we discussed earlier—I think he wants reassurance that you're not blowing this thing off. He's got all his charts and tapes ready, but I told him that had to wait."

"I can come back in tomorrow morning," said Mike. "But I hate to make him and his Chief come in on a Saturday after a week at sea; the wives get an attitude about that."

The Exec laughed. "Tell me about it."

The Exec, like all Exec's in the Navy, came in almost every Saturday morning for a few hours of undisturbed paperwork.

"OK, I'll see him. Then I'm going to take this impolite bird and my weary ass home to the houseboat. Leave that stuff in my in-basket. You want to sit in on this?"

The Exec thought about it for a moment, trying to determine if Mike wanted him to stay or was just being polite.

"I think it's you he really wants to hear this from, Captain. I kind of set the stage this afternoon, but I think he wants to be sure we're not putting him off."

Mike nodded and put on an injured expression.

"You're a hard man, XO, making your poor, ole CO deal with this all by himself, abandoning me to the slings and arrows of an offended J.O. I guess nobody loves me but my parrot, and he craps on the rug all the time. I'll remember this at fitrep time."

The Exec grinned back at him. "Yes, Sir. I'll get him up here."

He left the cabin, and Mike went over to the perch and picked up his parrot.

"Hello, Bird," he said.

He scratched the bright feathers on the bird's neck. Hooker looked up at him sideways and then closed his eyes to concentrate on the neck rub. Mike stood by the single porthole in his cabin, staring out over the twinkling waters of the harbor basin in the moonlight. The bulk of the supercarrier Saratoga loomed against the carrier bulkhead across the basin, the detail of the 96,000 ton monster lost in the shadow of her own overhanging flight deck.

Once again he sympathized with the Captain of the Coral Sea, the other Mayport carrier, who was now going through all the hell of an accident investigation, although it sounded like it had been entirely the oiler's fault. Still, he had lost some people and an aircraft. He remembered the pit in his stomach during the days of his own collision investigation. There was a knock on the door behind him.

"Come in," he called.

Lincoln Howard stepped through the door. Howard was the sole black officer in the ship. He was of medium height and slim build, and he carried himself with a quiet dignity that belied his age. He was a Naval Academy graduate and an extremely sharp young man. Both his mother and father were civil servants in Washington, and every one of their five children had achieved success in professional careers. Mike thought he was one of the best officers in the wardroom, and so did most of his shipmates.

"Linc, sit down, please," said Mike. "I'm pleased that you wanted to hang around tonight and talk about our little mystery out there."

Howard cleared his throat nervously. He was always extremely polite and respectful around the more senior officers in the ship, to the point where they were careful not to kid him too hard because he tended to take it literally. He sat almost at attention on the edge of the couch which concealed the Captain's folding bunk bed.

"Thank you, Sir, for seeing me tonight."

He appeared to be working up to a prepared speech, so Mike cut him off. He remained standing, the parrot in the crook of his left arm.

"I know you guys were disappointed when I broke this thing off today, but it was not a frivolous decision, as I think the XO explained earlier."

"Yes, Sir. He did, and I understand what you want to do."

"OK, then, and if you can come in tomorrow morning, or Monday if you want, I'm ready to hear your rationale and look at the evidence that we really had a contact. But for now, I want your personal, professional opinion: do you really think that contact was a submarine?"

Linc cleared his throat again, and then plunged in.

"Yes, Sir, I do. I know I haven't been at this very long, and I have to admit I've never seen a diesel electric submarine on the sonar. But that contact was different from anything else we'd seen out there. We'd had some solid contacts before, but they always kind of melted after a few minutes of pinging. The senior sonarmen, they know the difference; they can usually tell by the audio that a contact is marine life or a mud bottom or a heavy thermal layer. But everybody in sonar sat up on the first ping we got on this guy, Cap'n, and the Chief got on the stack himself after only a couple of pings. It was just like at ASW school—you know those trainer tapes, where the contacts are always perfect—it sounded like that. And we had a change in doppler, *after* we gained contact. That's significant. The contact responded when we got on him."

Mike paced the narrow space between his desk and the end of the cabin.

"And then you lost him," said Mike. He regretted his terminology almost immediately. It sounded like an accusation, and he saw the flare of concern in Linc's eyes.

"I didn't mean that the way it sounds: you were unable to maintain contact."

"Yes, Sir. We did. But the Chief said we would. We were right there on the margins of the Stream, so any solid contact was something of a fluke in that water—we knew he could slip into a thermal vortex and disappear. You remember we reported that the contact was intermittent due to layering. But when we had him, it was solid. The echoes damn near clicked at us. The fact that we got a contact of that quality in the Stream margins almost has to mean it was a real contact, because the other stuff we get out there would not have persisted for more than just a few pings. And then, of course, we had the decoy."

Mike nodded again, and sat down in his desk chair. He held the parrot out over his trash can, and the bird obliged with an accurate bomb. "Good bird," said the parrot, and Linc grinned, relaxing a tiny bit.

"What we're gonna need, Linc," Mike said finally, "Is a reconstruction of this episode that is convincing, extremely convincing, because if you think I'm skeptical, wait till I run this by some of those staff officers."

"We could have done a better job of that if we'd held him longer," said Linc, his hands suddenly clenching the creases in his khaki trousers as he realized that his last comment sounded like a rebuke to his Captain.

"I understand, Linc. But I had my reasons. First, it was unlikely that you could regain contact; second, I wanted to think about this thing. I had never given any credence to this mystery submarine thing from day one—now all of sudden, sonar is telling me you think you have a real contact. Third, if we had gone booming around in a lost contact search, which I think both of us realize would have been something of a futile exercise because of where we were, and this was a submarine, we would have given away the fact that we were on to him. Now, think about this: we're not at war, so why would some guy be out there in our fleet training areas? If it is a submarine, whose is it? What's his mission? Could it maybe be one of ours, on some secret operation? And if it isn't, were we walking into some kind of ambush? And finally, what do you do first when you think you've found a fire?"

"You call the fire department," replied Linc.

"Right, and we're not the ASW fire department. We're a straight stick gun destroyer with an antique, active sonar."

Mike paused to gather his thoughts.

"What I want to do next is for you guys to build a little presentation, a briefing, that shows where we wcrc, the contact track history on a chart, and then some audio-visual stuff, where you show the kinds of contacts we had all week, and then this one, and, of course, the one you thought was the decoy. You need to show that both these contacts were unique. For my part, I'm going to start by telling the Commodore. He may or may not want to pursue it, and his decision will turn on our credibility and the likely political reaction he would get from Group and the higher-ups in Norfolk. You should realize that, if he takes it up the line, you'll have to send your tapes off to the classification center in Norfolk for real technical analysis."

"Second, depending on how far we take this, we'll have to prepare something of a defense: if we thought we had an unidentified sonar contact, why didn't we report it through the normal reporting channels for such an incident."

Mike could see that the same question had occurred to Linc, so he answered it himself.

"The basic answer is that ASW classification is a commanding officer's function; that's official Navy doctrine. And at the time, this commanding officer didn't believe the data. Now, there's some behind the scenes politics involved in all this: we were sent out to look for a sub, but it was kind of a wash, OK? Even the Admiral felt the thing was ludicrous, so we were sent out mostly to placate the press inquiries caused by a commercial fisherman reporting a submarine sighting, and their linking it to the loss of the Rosie III."

"You mean this is news the Admiral won't want to hear."

"You got it. And, I think, from a political standpoint, the result may well be an evaluation that the CO was right, this was not a contact, and life goes on. We both know how ambiguous sonar contacts are."

"But, Captain," protested Linc, "This *was* a contact. When you see the tapes and hear the audio, I think you're gonna be convinced. Then what do we do if the higher ups clamp a lid on it?"

"That's the tough question, Linc. But we're not there yet. You do the first part, and gen me up a convincing briefing. Factor in things like the nature of the bottom in the area, that business about the water conditions obscuring everything except a real submarine, the nearest wrecks, our bottom chart project: I want a show that will convince the Commodore that we've thought the thing through, and now we want maybe to go back out there, this time with some real ASW ships, and maybe take a harder look. That will also allow the staffs to query the U.S. submarine operations people, who may tell us to just forget the whole thing."

Mike looked at his watch, and Linc quickly stood up.

"We'll have a briefing ready for you tomorrow, Cap'n."

"That would be fine, Linc. But don't work on it tonight. Let everybody get some sleep so you start fresh. I'll be in late, mid-morning, so we can do this in a civilized fashion."

"Aye, Aye, Sir."

THIRTY ONE

USS Goldsborough, inport, Mayport Naval Station, Saturday, 26 April; 0900

The assembled group of officers and chief petty officers rose in unison as Mike came into the wardroom. There were more people present than he had expected. Besides the Exec, the Weapons and Operations officers, the Combat Information Center Officer, Linc Howard, and the principal chiefs in CIC and Sonar Control were gathered around the green, felt-covered table. Mike greeted everyone and sat down, turning his coffee cup over in its saucer to allow the mess attendant to pour coffee. The others resumed their seats. The Exec opened the meeting as the mess attendant withdrew.

"Captain, the combined CIC and Sonar control officers are present this morning to brief the contact we had in the opareas last week. Our focus is on evidence which would indicate that it was a submarine and not something else, as you directed. The Senior Chief Operations Specialist, Chief Marnane, will present Combat's material, which consists of a recapitulation of the track charts from the first three days of operations, our findings during that period, and then the track charts during the contacts of interest. The Chief Sonarman, Chief Mackensie, will present a set of audio tapes which have been edited to show the contrast between the general garbage contacts gained in the first three days and the contacts we're interested in. Petty Officer First Class Magruder, the leading sonarman, will present the sonar video tapes, again contrasting the general, run of the mill contacts with the two contacts of interest. I'll present a wrap-up and conclusions, if that's acceptable, Sir."

"Sounds fine, XO. Before you proceed, I want to apologize to everyone for your having to come in on Saturday morning. I'm going to see the Commodore first thing Monday morning, so there's no other time to do this. Go ahead, please."

The faces ringing the table were serious; some of the petty officers looked as if they were uncomfortable being in the wardroom.

Senior Chief Marnane, a slender and balding man whose face looked older than his forty one years of age, rose and went to the briefing easel at the end of the table. He carried a stained and chipped coffee mug held loosely in his left hand; he was never without it. He folded back the cover sheet.

"Cap'n, XO, this first chart shows the whole operating area that we laid out from day one, with the planned tracks. You can't see it from that end, but we also highlighted the major bottom topography features—seamounts, holes, wrecks, pinnacles—that we expected to see on the search and survey. We made detections on all of the expected features, and some we didn't know about, and we entered all of them into Mr. Howard's PC program that correlates bottom contours and features to the sonar picture. We spent Monday here, Tuesday in this area, here, Wednesday going along here, and Thursday, up to noon, in this sector, here."

Mike nodded his acknowledgment.

"At around 1230 on Thursday, we gained contact on goblin Alfa Three," the Chief continued. "Initial contact was gained at this position here on the overall track. I'm now gonna shift to my second chart, which expands the contact of interest area." He flipped the easel paper to the next chart.

"We picked up Alfa Three here, that's the red line, and held him for six minutes. He initially displayed no doppler, and then he displayed down doppler, which correlated with both his track away from us and his computed speed. We lost him right here, at a last bearing of 137 and range of 8200 yards. We reacquired Goblin Alfa Three, or at least we thought we had, four minutes later at bearing 110 and range 8900 yards. After a minute or so, we recategorized the reacquisition as a new contact, goblin Alfa Four, because it came up too far away from the tracking probability lines of Alfa Three. It also was showing up doppler, indicating a track towards us, and some features which we'll talk about in the audio part of this pitch that caused both us in CIC and the guys in Sonar Control to call this contact a decoy. Any questions so far, Sir?"

Mike leaned forward. "Yeah, Senior Chief: what were the nearest bottom topographical features to the contact area of both goblins?"

The senior Chief pointed to the area of the chart where the background area changed from light blue to dark blue.

"The nearest plotted feature was a wreck, bearing 080 at a distance of 14,000 yards from us. We had plotted that wreck once before, and it was in our PC survey data base system."

He shuffled the charts around.

"It's right here on the big area chart. Directly east of the contact area, which is under the inshore margin of the Gulf Stream, is the edge of the continental shelf. This area has a series of submarine canyons, oriented east-west, where the edge of the shelf fractures and drops off from an average of 500 to 600 foot depth to about 10,000 feet."

"Is it possible, Senior Chief," asked Mike, "That either of these contacts could be vortices spinning off the Gulf Stream in the area of those canyons? You know what I'm talking about?"

"Yes, Sir, we've looked at that, and the area handbooks talk about them, sorta undersea versions of a dust devil. But Chief Mackensie is gonna show you why we don't think that's what these guys were."

"OK, continue."

"Yes, Sir. I gotta say we got a lot of useful data on the PC project—Mr. Howard's program to correlate the visual image on the sonar stack with the feature that's plotted on the bottom contour charts. In some cases, we had to correct the chart because the feature, a pinnacle, a wreck, whatever, wasn't where the chart said it would be. But the unique stuff we got is the comparison between what the contact looked like on the sonar display, from a couple of different directions, too, and what the feature was. The mine hunting people already use this technique; they call it bottom conditioning, but they're working with very precise, high definition, and short range sonars, not an SQS-23 like we got. So, anyways, we got some video images to go with specific features on the bottom. We didn't cover every feature out here in the opareas, of course, but we got quite a few. And we got some on the contacts of interest, only because we had the video cameras running for the PC project when we made the contacts."

"Very good, Chief. I want to have this project written up for the tactical improvement program, regardless of what comes of these two contacts."

"Yes, Sir, Cap'n," said the Operations officer. "We've got that project underway."

The Chief continued his briefing.

"Yes, Sir. OK. I've shown you the overalls and the local tracks. Chief Mackensie will now run through the audio stuff; I'm gonna help him with the PC side of it, and we'll leave the track charts up, because we need to show where it was we heard what, if you follow me..."

Chief Mackensie got up, as did Linc. Linc had a portable PC set up on the wardroom table, and the sonar chief had two bulky reel to reel tape recorders sitting on the serving counter next to the wardroom table. A tangle of wires led from each recorder to one of the wardroom's hi-fi speakers in a corner. The sonar chief, an intense technical specialist who was ten years younger than the Chief Operations Specialist, began his presentation.

"Captain, XO, I'm gonna let you listen to a series of contacts we got during the first three days of the operation. Mr. Howard, here, will run the PC display in parallel with what we hear, and Chief Marnane will show you on the overall track charts where we recorded each of the contacts we're gonna listen to. We've selected a sample of contacts so we can show you a wide variety of things: disassociated marine life, a whale, a surface contact, a wreck, marine life around a bottom feature, and the turbulence of the Stream itself. I'll let you hear active and passive takes on these kinds of sounds, and I can let you compare the two. Then I've edited a tape which will let you compare the sound of Alfa Three and Four with the contacts from the spectrum which would most likely be confused with a real contact. OK. This first contact is what we call disassociated marine life: a school of fish, a swarm of shrimp, even a cloud of plankton. The first segment is passive: audio in the range of the human ear that this kind of sound source makes over an open speaker in sonar."

The Chief turned on the tape, and the eerie, reverberating sussuration of life under the seas boomed out into the wardroom. Mike was startled, as were the other listeners, by the scale of it. He had heard sounds like this in ASW training as a junior officer, and on National Geographic television specials, but the incredible diversity of the individual noises was impressive. The Chief let it run for about thirty seconds, and then shut it off.

"OK," he continued, "That was passive. Now we're gonna hear that same sound source reacting to an active sonar pulse. And this is weird, because a swarm of shrimp, for instance, can feel the hydrodynamic pressure of the sonar pulse as it expands through the water, and they react to it. Scientists call it a biomass: a big gaggle of living things reacting as if the gaggle itself was the living thing, not the individuals. You'll hear the ping as a click, 'cause, of course, the sonar receivers are blanked during the active transmission so's to protect them from the outgoing power."

He turned the tape back on, and a low hiss came up on the speakers. There was an instant of silence, and then a distinct click, followed by washing sound, followed by the sound of thousands of different sized combs being stroked by human fingertips. The chirring sounds died out as the pulse travelled farther from the ship. There was another click, followed by the same response from the swarm.

The Chief took them through the rest of his underwater sound show, first with the passive audio, and then the response of the living organisms to the punishing pulse of acoustic energy generated by the ship's sonar dome. In one case the Chief played the frenzied response of a pod of porpoises as they scrambled to get away from the painful sounds of the sonar, which was powerful enough to be a designated defense against underwater swimmer attack. The porpoises literally screamed and wailed as they darted frantically away from the ship and its deadly blast of noise. A trio of whales, audible at a great distance from the ship on the passive bands, stopped their unearthly singing after the first few pulses from the active sonar, as if to protest this alien acoustic intrusion.

Most interesting to Mike, however, was the sound of the echoes coming back from sunken ships. Every marine life target had a blurry characteristic to the echoes, a there-but-not-quite there quality to the sound. The wrecks, on the other hand, especially when caught side-on against a reasonably flat bottom topography, came back with a crisper sound. The Chief made a point of playing samples of this contrast, with the mushy echo of a reasonably good sized whale clearly different from the flat, metallic nature of the steel sides of sunken ships.

Linc Howard ran the video display of the sonar scopes, pictures of what the operators had been seeing during the collection of the audio segments. The display was amber in color, and circular, with the ship positioned in the center, and the sonar pulse represented by a ring of expanding light opening out from the ship. Contacts appeared as crescent-shaped smears of light, tiny croissants blooming on the bearing of the contact, persisting for a few seconds, and then fading out as the pulse travelled out beyond them at 1800 feet per second. Everyone could see what the problem was with the scope video: every contact looked like every other contact, except for the biomass swarms, which looked like cloud formations on the amber scope.

The Chief moved between the tape recorder and the video display, pointing out what each contact looked like. Mike and some of the other officers had to get up and stand in front of the television to see better, and, after a while, Mike could begin to see the difference between a school of fish and a bottom wreck. But it was very difficult. But there was no mistaking the crisp, metallic sound of the sonar hits on Alfa Three; even the video was brighter and stronger. The decoy was even better, too much better, than everything else.

The session in the wardroom was interrupted by the quarter-deck messenger, who told Mike the Commodore's office had called in on the quarterdeck phone. The Commodore wanted him to call.

"Let's break for coffee, guys," said Mike. "I'll be right back." He left the wardroom and went to his cabin to place the call.

"Morning, Mike," said the Commodore. "My duty officer tells me you wanted to talk to me last night. Whatcha got?"

"I need to come see you first thing Monday morning if that's OK, Commodore: I need to talk to you about—"

"No can do, Michael," interrupted the Commodore. I'm outa here for Norfolk tomorrow for the Fleet Commander's conference. The Admiral, the Chief of Staff, and the other two squad dogs—we've all got to go to this thing. Can't it wait?"

Mike thought fast. From what he had seen already, Linc and his people had indeed found something out there. But he had not yet seen their entire presentation, nor had time to think about it, nor to make a full appraisal of the entire problem.

"Mike?" asked the Commodore impatiently.

"Yes, Sir: is there any chance you can come over here, say in about an hour? There's something I need to show you, and I can't really bring it over there."

"What the hell, Mike: what's this all about?"

"That mystery submarine, Commodore."

"What?! Are you telling me you think it's real? That there's some sewerpipe screwing around in our opareas?"

"Commodore, I'm not positive, myself. But I think you should see what we've got before I do anything further with it."

207

"Well, you got that part right," said the Commodore. "What'd you tell Group last night?"

"Nothing, Sir. Besides, they were focused on the collision. Goldy and the submarine were down in the noise level."

"Right. Good. OK—I'll be over at 1130. I've got a tee time at 1315, so let's keep it succinct. Jesus Christ, Mike."

"I know, Commodore, I know. But I need some more experienced eyes to see this. I'm no ASW expert."

"Everybody's an ASW expert," snorted the Commodore. "That's why there are so many opinions about it. I'll see you at 1130."

"Thank you, Sir." Mike hung up, and took a deep breath. This was going to be interesting. He headed back down to the wardroom.

THIRTY TWO

USS Goldsborough, pierside, Mayport naval base; Saturday, 26 April; 1130.

Mike waited at the head of the wardroom table until the Commodore had taken his seat, immediately to Mike's right. Mike remained standing when everyone else sat down. There was a lot of clearing of throats and shuffling of papers in the silence; everyone was nervous at the sudden appearance of the Commodore, especially since Mike had said he would not be seeing the Commodore until Monday. Captain Aronson's volatile reputation had been embellished repeatedly throughout the waterfront, especially among the enlisted people. Mike sensed that the wardroom suddenly seemed overly warm and stuffy.

"Commodore," he began, turning to speak directly to Captain Aronson. "Thank you for coming over this morning on such short notice. We had planned to run through this presentation a few more times, but, with your schedule, I think it's important to let you see what we have now so we can get your advice on how to proceed. Sir, we're going to take about fifteen minutes to show you what we were doing last week, along with some background tapes and some PC pictures to set the stage for what's got our attention. If it's a little unpolished—"

"I understand," interrupted the Commodore. "Go ahead."

Mike nodded to the Exec, who proceeded to walk the Commodore through the entire presentation, with the two chiefs doing their part with the charts and tapes, and Linc Howard running the video. The Commodore fidgeted at first, but slowly became absorbed in what they were showing him. He was obviously impressed with the bottom mapping correlation system developed on the PC, and complimented Linc on it. The Chief Sonarman finally came to the first contact of interest.

"Now, here," said Chief Mackensie, "Here's Alfa Three."

He switched the audio tape back on, and everyone listened with their breath held to the click, the washing sound, and then the sharp echo quality of the first hit on Alfa Three. Chief Mackensie put his pointer on the television screen to show the visual display of the contact, and the Commodore got up to look closer, as the second and third click-wash-contact echoed in the wardroom. The officers and petty officers watched closely, to see how the Commodore would react.

"I got on the stack at this point," continued the Chief. "Went to an expanded picture."

The video presentation of Alfa Three jumped to center screen from the perimeter of the scope. It was clearly a brighter and stronger image.

"It almost looks too good," muttered the Commodore.

"Yes, Sir," said Mike, from his chair. "That's what we thought, too."

"So then we went directional pulse: long and hard down the bearing," said the Chief. "Look at the image now."

The audio tape in the background gave out the standard click to indicate the sonar's receivers were blanked, but the ensuing washing sound carried overtones of the piercing ring of a high powered, directional sound beam. The sound of the returning echo was even sharper, as was the corresponding amber image glowing in the center of the screen, surrounded by clouds of noise and other interference from the tumultuous waters of the Stream.

"And, here, we changed down one frequency band on the sonar transmitter."

"Why?" asked the Commodore, who continued to stare at the video screen display.

"Uh, because the Captain said to—" answered the Chief.

"They were reporting intermittent layers," Mike volunteered.

"What you're really saying is that you didn't believe what you saw and wanted to see if the lower freq would make this thing maybe go away..." retorted the Commodore. And then, as if to take the sting out, "And I would have done the same thing. I don't quite believe what I'm seeing—it looks too much like sonar school."

"Yes, Sir, it does," said the Chief. "Then, after a few minutes, we lose contact—no echoes."

"Just too much acoustic shit in the water out there, wasn't there," said the Commodore.

"Yes, Sir."

The small knot of officers gathered around the television monitor continued to stare at the smears of light on the sonar display scope, as if trying to make that one bright contact reappear.

"What'd you do next?" asked the Commodore, straightening up from the television.

"We went silent, and closed in on the datum with the attack director in PK. We went in 4000 yards at twelve knots so's not to cavitate, and then we lit off and went active again. I'll fast forward this, 'cause there ain't nothin' to see for the next twelve minutes."

The Chief then took the Commodore through the second contact episode, with its sudden reappearance, up doppler, and even more perfect echo quality. The Commodore watched intently, and then nodded as if in recognition.

"This is a goddamned decoy," he said.

There was a stirring all around the room. Mike suddenly felt a flush creeping up his neck. He said nothing, and avoided looking at Linc Howard. The Commodore watched for a few more minutes until the second contact was lost, and the Chief related the sequence where they had broken off the search. He nodded again, this time more slowly, and then went back to his chair.

He looked around the room at the expectant faces.

"OK, guys," he said. "You have any more sound and lights for me?"

"No, Sir," said Linc Howard.

He appeared to be ready to say something else, but the Commodore shut him off with a wave of his hand. He looked around the room, taking in their faces. Mike sat at the head of the table, just behind the Commodore's line of vision. The Commodore began to speak.

"OK. First, I'm very impressed with the combination of the PC, the sonar video, and the sound recording system. I think it's a unique development. Dream up a catchy acronym, and write it up. I'll get it into the Fleet tactical improvement program. You'll be famous."

He grinned, and the officers and petty officers relaxed a little. Many found they had been holding their breath.

"Second," he said, his face becoming serious again. "Second, I want everybody here to clam up about what you found out there, and what you've shown me on these tapes. I don't mean by that that you go out of here and tell the mess decks you have a big secret, because that would draw attention to it. I want you to go out of here and say that the higher ups are skeptical, and we're gonna study it. And everybody knows that when the Navy says they're gonna study something, it means they're gonna bury it. Whatever people have heard about this, I want them to lose interest. You all understand me? Can you do that?"

There was a chorus of 'Yes, Sirs' around the table.

"OK. We are going to study it. I want all of this info put together as a complete briefing package, and I want Mr. Howard and Chief Mackensie to take it up to Norfolk to the ASW school, to their classification and analysis people. I'll have my staff arrange it. I'm going to ask them to analyze the video and the audio, and to give us a quick reading on what the two contacts are. When we get the answer, we'll reconvene and decide what to do next. OK?"

Once again there was a chorus of assent. The Commodore got up, followed by everyone else. He gave Mike a sign that he wanted to talk to the Captain alone in his cabin. Mike led him out of the wardroom and up the ladder to the next level. The Exec followed the two officers to the cabin. Once inside, the Commodore told the Exec that he needed to talk to the Captain alone, and the Exec started to withdraw.

"Commodore, I'd really like XO to stay," said Mike.

The Commodore, standing in the center of the small Captain's cabin, frowned. The Exec studied the carpet.

"The Exec's judgement is very important to me," Mike persisted. "Whatever you have to say will affect us both, so I need him to hear it firsthand."

The Commodore looked directly at Mike for a few seconds, and then said, "Very well," and sat down in Mike's desk chair. Mike took the only other chair, and the Exec sat on the edge of bunk bed. The Commodore was silent for a moment, and then he looked at Mike.

"Tell me why you broke it off."

Mike took a deep breath. He had been waiting for this question. He could tell the Commodore that he had not wanted to alert the possible submarine that they were definitely on to him, that breaking it off was a tactical decision based on cover and deception. That might get him off the hook in case the Commodore thought they should have persisted. But the Commodore was staring right at him, his black eyes looking like two gun barrels. Mike opted for the truth.

"I didn't want to believe it," Mike admitted. "I didn't really know what the hell to do with it, so I backed out. I told the guys that I broke it off so's not to alert the contact that somebody knew he was out there. But the truth is, I figured if we came in with a contact report and scrambled the whole ASW defense force, Group would have had my ass."

The Commodore sat back, his face unreadable. The silence in the cabin grew. Mike felt compelled to fill the void. He was having trouble meeting the Commodore's gaze.

"I still don't quite believe it," he continued. "But once we got in and I got to see all the evidence the guys put together, it's more convincing. Maybe Norfolk will find a hole in it, but I'm beginning to believe they won't. That's why I wanted you to see it."

The Commodore nodded slowly, as if deciding on something.

"OK," he said. "First things first. As the Captain of a destroyer, or any warship, you must always, and I mean always, sustain the elements of intellectual integrity inherent in your position as a Commanding officer. And then you have to stick by them. You broke off this contact because you were afraid of what the staffs back in port might think or say or do. That's not your job, and your decision fails the integrity test. You should have reported it. Straight facts, the reasons why the contact looked different from what you had been seeing, and then you should have stayed on the bastard until he was well and truly lost in the Stream."

The Commodore sat back in his chair. He seemed to grow larger in the chair as he continued.

"We give you, the Captain, almost unlimited authority over this ship and its people, but we expect unlimited accountability. Part of the accountability has to do with the consequences of a politically unfavorable action."

The Commodore got up then, and paced around the small cabin for a minute before continuing. The Exec, who was acutely embarrassed, stared hard at the deck.

"You are quite right in your estimate of how that news would have been received," continued the Commodore. "There would have been some ridicule around the morning staff meeting, and your dear friend Captain Martinson would have had some clever riposte to make."

He turned around to look at Mike.

"But that isn't your concern, Captain. Your job is to call 'em like you see 'em. To tell the unvarnished truth, and not to filter your operational reporting through the lens of what is or is not politically acceptable. I know there are lots of Pentagon E-ring ballerinas who would tell you different. The truth is that the system is every bit as politically sensitive as you're making it out to be, Mike, but it depends on at least one entirely rigid benchmark: the Captains of all the ships have to be consistently straight. Only if that is true does the system have the luxury to indulge in internal Navy politics. We assume that when we get a report from you that nothing was found, then nothing was found. As your people have pointed out down below, there is some disturbing evidence that something indeed was found. As your boss I now have two problems: what to do about Alfa Three and Alfa Four, and how to restore the system's faith in one particular Commanding Officer. Got anything to say? And do you want to excuse the XO now?"

Mike's heart sank. His face was flushed, and there was a pit in his stomach.

"No, Sir. I understand my mistake, and, no, I don't want the XO excused. He has to learn this, too, and I haven't been teaching him very well."

"That's for damn sure, Captain."

The Commodore returned to Mike's desk chair and sat down. He pressed his left hand up to his face and rubbed his lips absently, closed his eyes, and thought for a minute. The only sound in the cabin was from the forced air vent in the overhead. The bright sunlight streaming through the porthole cast a white circle on the locker at the end of the cabin. The Commodore opened his eyes.

"OK. Enough lecturing. We've had a screw-up. Now we have to recover. Have your people put that presentation together as a package today, and then I want Ensign Howard and Chief Mackensie to go with me on my trip to Norfolk tomorrow, Sunday. The Fleet Conference doesn't begin until Monday, but the Fleet Commander's giving a reception tomorrow night, so unfortunately we have to travel on Sunday. I'll get your guys into the ASW school's classification and analysis center—the CO's a friend, and we'll get an informal, quick read. Then, if it comes out like I think it will, you and I will go see the Admiral here; that'll be Wednesday, when I get back. We'll let your two guys give the brief, we'll show him the Center's opinion, and then we'll let him figure out what to do. I'll be back Wednesday noon."

Mike nodded. "Yes, Sir, can do. But I wonder—"

"If we should wait that long?" interrupted the Commodore. "Way I see it, we've had a series of incidents: the fishing boat disappearing for no apparent reason, the sighting report of a U-boat, and now your contact, all over a two week period. If there is a guy out there, he's hanging around. We have to figure out two more things: is it true that there is a gomer out there, and why is he hanging around. In the meantime, I've got the Deyo going out on engineering sea trials next week. I'm going to have him do his trials in that area where you were this past week, and I'm going to have him do passive analysis all week, in the diesel engine sound spectrum. We'll see what he turns up. I'm especially interested in the night time. If this is a submarine, I think this might be a conventional boat, a diesel electric. He'll have to charge his batteries, and he'll do that at night. With any luck we can catch him on the snort."

"But he'll be doing that amongst a dozen diesel powered fishing boats, Sir. It'll all sound the same."

"Maybe, but maybe not. If Deyo can record one diesel engine out there that is distinctly different from all the others, we get another clue. He won't be able to localize it amongst all the others, but we'll have another indicator that something is, in fact, out there. If we get lucky, he'll get something before Wednesday, and that will strengthen our case with the Admiral. OK. XO, now *will* you excuse us."

The Exec got up with alacrity and excused himself from the cabin. Mike sat back in his chair, and waited for some more incoming. The Commodore was looking at him again.

"OK, Michael. Here's the story: when this gets to the group, Martinson's going to take the position that you falsified an operational report. In a sense you did, but we have an out: ASW classification is a CO's prerogative, and you did not believe the data as it was presented to you. When you got back in, and the guys were able to put together a comprehensive analysis, you began to doubt your original decision, and then you did report it—you called me. I saw the presentation, and still doubted the data, but was willing to take it to Norfolk. Norfolk will decide what Norfolk will decide. If they say it's a big nothing, the matter will never come up. If they say it's possible, then, and only then, do we take it up the line. If they squawk, our defense is that we did not want to cry wolf until we were a lot more certain of our facts. Got it?"

"Yes, Sir. And I thank you for your support. I can see that I screwed this one up."

"That you did, Sunshine. And lest you think I'm a generous soul, you should understand that my support is more than a little bit in my own self interest: they may well ask why I didn't come to them as soon as I saw your sound and light show this morning. As we both know, classification of a sonar contact is a very subjective thing; in the absence of other indicators, we always tend towards caution. But the Admiral's no dummy, either, and he's going to see that the crucial part is the why: if there is a bad guy loitering out there in our opareas, there has to be a reason. Think on it, and remember what I had to say about integrity: senior officers' capacity to indulge themselves in Navy politics is only made possible if every CO always tells the truth. You need to talk to your XO, too. Right now he thinks I'm picking on you unfairly. You need to explain to him that I'm being entirely fair in picking on you."

Mike grinned. "Yes, Sir. And thank you."

"Don't thank me," said the Commodore, putting on his hat. "I'm only saving my ass here; saving yours is a lesser included offense. Now you can see me to the quarterdeck."

THIRTY THREE

USS Goldsborough, pierside, Mayport Naval Base; Saturday, 26 April; 1245

After seeing the Commodore off, Mike walked back along the main deck to the hatchway leading into after officers' country, as the group of officer's staterooms on the port side aft was known. It was getting hot outside, and the metal bulkheads of the ship were beginning to radiate their own heat, baking the salt spray of a week at sea into a fine, white powder around the fittings. The Exec's stateroom was the third door on the left in the narrow passageway. He knocked on the Exec's door and went in.

Lieutenant Commander Farmer stood up in surprise even as Mike waved him back into his chair. The XO had a small mountain of paperwork on his desk. The Exec's cabin was tiny, eight feet by seven, with a convertible couch bunk bed along the outboard wall, one porthole, a desk, a steel sink, and a clothes cabinet. Two people could not stand simultaneously in the patch of tiled deck space not taken up by the compact, steel furniture. The cabin was situated over the after fireroom, which, when the boilers were lit off, heated the steel deck to the point where bare feet were not a good idea. The only personal touches were a picture of the Exec's family on the desk, and a few novels wedged above the bunkbed couch.

Mike threw himself down on the couch, and rubbed his eyes. The Exec sat back down in his desk chair, keeping a watchful expression on his face.

"Well, XO," Mike said, with a sigh, "You win some and you lose some. I think today I lost one."

"I appreciate your letting me stay, Cap'n," said the Exec.

As soon as the Commodore had asked him to leave he had known that something bad was coming. Mike's asking him to stay, when he, too, must have known what was coming, had been a great vote of confidence. Mike looked at the XO from between his fingers.

"Yeah, well, you got to see the other side of command, young man. It ain't all glory, bells, and sideboys."

The XO laughed, especially at Mike calling him young man. The Exec, with his enlisted time, was actually a few years older than the Captain. Mike knew that as well, but it was a private joke between them.

"The funny thing is," Mike continued, "If I had gone straight in to the Group with a report of the contact, the Commodore would have clawed my ass for not consulting him first."

"I don't know if he would have done that, Cap'n," said Ben, "But it would have put him on the sidelines. Right now we have him as our advocate. For whatever reason, that's better than having nobody between us and Group Twelve."

Mike looked at the Exec for a long moment. "That's pretty astute, XO," he said. "I'm going to have to keep an eye on you."

"Yes, Sir. All us XO's bear watching."

"Damn right. OK. Now: we need to get Linc and his Chief prepped up to go to Norfolk Sunday with the Commodore. I want them to make duplicates of all their tapes, audio and visual, and the stuff they have on disc in that PC."

"You afraid Norfolk might just lose the stuff?"

"Not in the sense of some grand conspiracy, I'm not. Nobody in the Norfolk Navy is that organized. But their standard practice is to analyze the fleet's stuff and then discard it. They get so much submitted to the ASW lab that they can't store it."

"And if it turns out that we get told to go stifle," said the XO, "And if something happens, it wouldn't be all bad to have a copy of our original report."

"There you go, being devious again." Mike got up and stretched. "I'm going to head back to my boat." He nodded at the paperwork stack. "Anything in that mess needs my attention today?"

"No, Sir. We're in all next week; plenty of time for paperwork."

"OK, I'm gone. I'll be in town all weekend. My bilge alarms are both lit up, which means I've got another slow leak somewhere. That's usually an all day, Maryann, job."

The Exec grinned. "My wife's got a couple of those waiting for me."

"So get home. Like you said, we got all next week to do paperwork."

"Aye, aye, Cap'n. If you insist."

"I insist," Mike snorted.

Ten minutes later, Mike left the ship and drove back to the marina. He glanced at the fishing piers as he drove by. All but one of the commercial boats were still out. Saturday afternoons at the shrimp piers were always a big business day. He'd have to slip over to the bar tonight to see what the locals were thinking about the mystery submarine, if anything. He suspected that the Navy's failure to produce the "U-boat" would not be sitting well, especially in view of the still unexplained loss of the Rosie III.

Mike spent the afternoon in the bilge chambers of his boat, hunting down the source of a leak that had caused his bilge pumps to cycle during the week at sea. By 6 p.m., he was ready for a beer. Hooker, for some reason, did not seem to want to leave the boat, squawking loudly and trying to bite Mike's hand when he reached for him.

"So, the hell with you, Bird," said Mike, and left the main cabin.

He was wearing cut-off shorts, sneakers with no socks, and a Miami Dolphins T-shirt with the sleeves cut out. He walked across the marina piers, taking in the sights and sounds of a marina on a Saturday as all the weekend sailors came out to play with their toys. The sun was still well up in the western sky, and the first wet hints of the intense Florida summer were in the air. Mike did not care much for the muggy heat, but felt it easily counterbalanced by the reappearance of the ladies' summer costumes. Judging from some of the outfits, the boats were not the only toys at the marina. This observation reminded him that Diane had promised to materialize today, or, more accurately, tonight. He felt at once excited and apprehensive.

He was not prepared, however, for the woman who was waiting for him in Hampton's back bar. He let himself into the cool, air conditioned interior, adjusting his eyes to the magnified glare from the waterway through the big plate windows. Siam, the bartender, greeted him carefully, and nodded in the direction of one of the booths.

"You got a visitor," he muttered.

Mike looked across the room. In the last booth a gray-haired woman sat hunched into the corner of the booth. Her face was pinched, and her expression, magnified by coke-bottle thick eyeglasses, transmitted equal parts of anger and discomfort. She fastened her eyes on him as he walked over. He had never seen her before.

"I'm Mike Montgomery," he began.

"I know who y'are," she said, in a flinty voice. "You find that damn U-boat got my brother?"

Mike did not sit down. He was aware that a few of the regulars at the bar were listening hard while trying to look like they were not. The woman was tiny, and easily in her middle seventies. She was dressed all in shapeless gray, but the anger in her face gave her substance.

"No, we didn't," replied Mike. "You're Chris Mayfield's sister?"

"I am," she declared indignantly, as if he should have known that. "Why didn't you? How come you're back in, and not out there lookin'? You ain't gonna find no U-boat in this damn bar."

One of the men at the bar snorted, and she looked past Mike to give him a hard look.

"You shut your mouth over there; nothin' but a bunch a goddamned drunks call yourself fishermen."

The man ducked his head as his buddy on the next stool elbowed him. She looked back up at Mike. "Well?"

"Well, we did look," Mike said. "But we simply did not find anything that would indicate there was a submarine out there. You have to understand—"

"I don't gotta understand nothin'," she spat. "I already understand that you fancy Dans in your big ships ain't good for nothin' but eatin' up taxpayers' money. You don't produce nothin' but smoke and noise, and you foul up the fishin' with all your goings on night and day. The one time we need you to find some damn devil that's goin' around killin' honest fishermen, you go out Monday and come in Friday like it's a week's work, and then come over here for your liquor while my brother's bein' 'et up by the damn crabs."

She slid sideways along the booth's seat, her feet not quite touching the floor, pushing her way out of the booth and standing, with her head thrown back, to look Mike in the eye. She barely came up to his chest. She clutched a bag on one arm, and a walking stick in the other hand. She looked up at him with a disgusted expression on her wrinkled face, her eyes brilliant with anger. Mike was almost afraid she was going to swing on him with that stick.

"Fancy Dan's, that's all you Navy are. You mark my words, that damn devil's gonna do it again, and you're gonna be sorry you didn't find him. Only next time I hope it's one a yourn gets it."

She swept the room with a hostile glance. "You're all gonna be sorry, you mark my words. You won't think about that when you're in here with your damn liquor, but you go out there agin', it'll come to you. You'll see."

She swept out of the bar, her stick whacking the floor in an angry cadence.

Mike slipped onto a bar stool as Siam drew him a draft beer.

"Well, shit fire, as Hooker says," breathed Mike.

"Where is that bag'a shit today?" asked Siam.

"On the boat; little shit didn't want to come over here this evening."

"Got a psychic bird, there," said Siam, mopping the bar counter. "Enjoy meeting Ellie, did you?"

"Is that her name? She acted like she had been waiting for me."

"She's been in here since about four o'clock. Asked me if you were gonna come in. I told her Saturdays, you usually came around for a beer if the ship was in. She said you were in, she was gonna wait. Like to scared off half the regulars, starin' at 'em with them beady, li'l eyes."

This was as much as Mike had heard Siam say in a single afternoon, much less in one conversation. As if he had become aware of his sudden volubility, Siam shook his head and moved down the bar.

"Nothin' out there, hey, Cap?" asked one of the men a few stools down.

"Not a thing but lots and lots of water," said Mike, somewhat defensively.

He stared down at his beer, mentally grappling with the fact that his denials involved something more than the Navy politics involved. Mayfield's sister was convinced that her brother was dead and that something more than an accident had killed him.

"Don't let her get to ya," said the man. "Nobody believes that submarine shit, anyways."

"Maxie Barr believes it," offered his buddy, leaning forward so he could see Mike's face. "Maxie Barr says he saw a fuckin' U-boat, and that's all there is to it. Says the Navy's coverin' somethin' up, 'cause it can't find the goddamned thing."

"The Navy can't find the goddamned thing because it's not there," retorted Mike, angrily. "Where's Maxie think a U-boat's come from, the Bermuda triangle?!"

"Beats me, Cap," replied the fisherman. "But Maxie, he ain't backin' down none. Says he saw what he saw, and ain't nobody gonna tell him otherwise."

"Nobody could ever tell Maxie Barr otherwise," said Mike, finishing most of his beer and sliding off the stool.

He had come down to see what the locals were thinking, and did not care for what he was hearing. Deep inside, he knew that his anger was due at least in part to the fact that he was not telling the truth to these people. As he left the back bar, the aromas from the restaurant kitchens swept over him, and he realized he had not eaten all day. He ducked into the formal main entrance of the restaurant and booked a window table for 7:30, and then went back to the boat to change. He rarely ate out, but he did not feel like constructing a culinary production.

Returning at 7:30, he allowed a delectable blonde in a short skirt to show him to his table, and he was torn between admiring the view outside or the view walking away from him. He settled for the menu. His waiter was a bubbling young man who was so full of good cheer and enthusiasm as he chirped through the evening specials that he almost put Mike off his dinner. Mike ordered a dozen oysters on the half shell, a swordfish filet and a Caesar salad, and a bottle of Kendall Jackson chardonnay in place of a cocktail. He was halfway through his dinner when he looked up and saw the Squadron Chief Staff Officer, Commander Bill Barstowe, his wife, and Diane Martinson entering the dining room. Mike saw them from his window table in the corner, but they did not initially see him as they were shown to a table about twenty feet from Mike's table.

Diane was dressed in a peach colored, sleeveless sheath dress with a single strand of large pearls around her throat. Other men in the dining room followed her with their eyes as she followed the hostess to the table. She sat down, thanked the waiter who pushed in her chair, casually patted her hair, and, looking up, saw Mike across the dining room. Her eyes widened in surprise for an instant, and then she looked away at the water, giving no overt sign of recognition.

For the next half hour, Mike tried to keep his eyes off their table. Commander Barstowe's back was to him, and his wife had not seen Mike. Diane occasionally let her glance traverse Mike's table, and once he thought he saw the beginnings of a smile on her face when she looked directly at him across the room. Commander Barstowe's wife was a chatterbox, oblivious to anything that might be going on around her. Her husband appeared to listen attentively, but Mike decided that Commander Barstowe was actually a lot more interested in looking at Diane.

When Mike had finished his own dinner, he wondered if he should stay at his table until they were finished and had left, or just leave. Despite the glow of anticipation he felt whenever he looked over at Diane, he was not sure he wanted to encounter her in the presence of the Commodore's senior staff officer. He wondered where the Chief of Staff was, and then remembered that Captain Martinson was also supposed to go to this big meeting up in Norfolk. But why would he leave on Saturday? An instant later he remembered and knew the answer.

His waiter appeared with the bill, and a few minutes later came back and politely but pointedly asked if there were anything else he could bring. Mike could see a line of people in the foyer waiting for tables, so he paid the bill in cash, and followed the waiter across the dining room. He thought he heard Diane exclaim about something out on the waterway, attracting her table's attention out the window as Mike started across the dining room. And then Commander Barstowe saw him.

"Mike Montgomery: come say hello," he called.

Mike changed course and walked over to their table. Commander Barstowe's wife interrupted her monologue to gush an effusive greeting.

"And you know Diane Martinson, I'm sure," said Commander Barstowe. "The Martinson's are neighbors and the Chief of Staff had to go up to Norfolk this weekend, so we convinced her to join us for dinner. We're almost finished—join us for a cup of coffee?"

Mike hesitated. Diane had smiled an impassive greeting, but he was not sure of what he should do. The Commander's wife insisted noisily, and their attentive waiter brought up a fourth chair. He sat down, facing the Commander's wife, with Diane on his right. His knee bumped hers as he sat down, and, once again, he thought he saw the glimmer of a smile in her eyes. The Commander's wife had started up again, so Mike was spared the necessity of saying anything right away. Commander Barstowe gratefully turned to Mike to ask about the week's operations, leaving his wife to train her gossipy prattle exclusively in Diane's direction. It was Mike's turn to suppress a smile as he watched Diane's eyes begin to glaze over. The waiter brought Mike a cup of coffee.

"So no submarine, hunh?" inquired Barstowe.

Evidently the Commodore had not shared the morning's revelations with his Chief Staff Officer.

"Nothing to write home about," responded Mike.

"Damned strange, all the same," said Barstowe. "Guy reports seeing a U-boat, and then a fishing boat goes down for no apparent reason. The Group PAO said the local press were really trying to make something of it."

"I'm sure they did," said Mike, recalling his run-in with Christian Mayfield's sister. "Problem is that people get to believing it, just because it's in the local news."

At that instant, Mike became aware of a soft, probing sensation along his right ankle. Diane was playing footsie with him under the table. He almost missed what Commander Barstowe was saying.

"—checked with our own sub ops people, of course, and they said they had nothing going down this way. Sounded like they thought we were a little bit out of it. You know how the staffs in Norfolk view Mayport."

Mike laughed, partly in sympathy with Mayport's reputation as being in the sticks when compared to the big base in Norfolk, and partly as a nervous reaction to Diane's playful ministrations under the table. She was rubbing her stockinged toes up and down along the back of his right calf. Mike wondered if the table-cloths were long enough to conceal what was going on. He glanced at an adjoining table, and saw that they were. Diane saw him look and smiled again, nodding as if she were paying close attention to the other woman's conversation. Mike struggled to pay attention to the Chief Staff Officer's opinions on the likely sources of the submarine story. He was fervently hoping that Commander Barstowe would not become aware of the interplay going on literally under his

221

nose. Diane finally relented, and Mike made good his escape a few minutes later.

He hurried into the foyer. There was indeed a crowd of people waiting for tables. He lingered in the foyer, feeling a little ridiculous and not sure that he should wait, but hoping Diane might come out to the foyer. The restaurant had a raw bar off to one side of the foyer which was surrounded by illuminated tropical fish tanks all along the walls. Mike wandered into the raw bar area and pretended to examine the vividly lighted tanks, while keeping an eye on the entrance to the actual dining room.

The blonde hostess saw him looking and smiled at him. After five minutes he was rewarded by the sight of Diane stepping through the entrance. His heart rose and then immediately fell when he saw that the Commander's wife was with her. They went directly to the ladies' powder room; Diane gave no sign of having seen him. He mentally muttered a silent curse, and walked out of the restaurant. The young hostess, who had been watching him out of the corner of her eye from the reservations podium, glanced at him curiously as he left, shrugged and called the next party of four.

THIRTY FOUR

The Mayport Marina; Saturday, 26 April; 2300

Mike reclined in his chaise lounge on the back porch of the Lucky Bag and watched the occasional boat go by, its red and green running lights twinkling across the dark water in time with the light chop. The onshore breeze had come up when he had returned from the restaurant, and he had switched off the air conditioning and opened the boat up. He had turned all the lights off in the houseboat except for a tiny night light at the top of the companionway leading to the lounge, and was sitting in darkness. The only visible light on the stern porch came from the dim walkway lights along the piers between the rows of boat moorings. There was music coming from a party two piers over, but the people having the party were being considerate for a change and not sharing their musical tastes with the entire world.

Mike had shifted back into shorts and tennis shoes when he first got back, but then had shucked all of his clothes when he came out to the humid darkness of the porch. He lay naked on the cushioned chaise, his long, bulky body filling the length of it. He could feel the cushion buttons pressing indentations into the skin of his back as he waited. The night air moving across his skin was pleasant, and the apprehension he had been feeling subconsciously about what was about to happen seemed to peel away with each passing moment.

If she came, when she came, it would not be for talk. The breeze was cooling except when it faltered, and then the humid heat of a Florida night pressed back in, burdened with the briny scents of the river and the waterway.

He deliberately let his thoughts drift, smoothing over the earlier tension of the day. He had banished the mysterious submarine out of his mind, along with the embarrassment of being rebuked by the Commodore in front of his own Exec. He thought now only of Diane, how she had looked earlier, the hint of a smile playing on her lips at the table, and the promise he had seen in her eyes in the parking lot the night before. He had made himself a wine cooler, and absently ran his fingers up and down the sweating glass, oblivious to the condensation dripping on his bare chest.

His skin tingled like a freshly shorn pelt, and all the muscles in his body seemed to be poised for some great exertion. The Lucky Bag dipped slowly in response to a passing wake, and he could hear the slap of waves under the broad hull. Occasionally he could hear women's voices across the marina, but his hearing focused now on another sound, the sound of a woman's leather tipped, high heels coming across the pontoon piers, carefully, but deliberately, up the single step between pontoon and pier, and then down again, coming closer until they stopped at the Lucky Bag's diminutive gangplank. He had left the railing unlatched back at the top of the gangplank, and the doorway leading down into the main lounge was also open. He thought he could feel the boat shift slightly when she came aboard, followed by a moment of silence, and then she appeared in the doorway of the porch, a slim shadow that perfumed the night air with a tendril of Chanel and perhaps something more elemental. He felt like he was barely touching the chaise as he looked over at her in the darkness, the excitement building in his chest even as he remained motionless and silent on the chaise.

She walked slowly over to the chaise, and stood at his feet, her face a pale blur as she looked at him. He heard her breathing change when she realized that he was naked. She reached behind her and unhooked her dress, slipping out of it in a fluid, two step motion. She wore no bra, and he could sense rather than see the sway of her heavy breasts in the darkness. Her panties were visible only as a white triangle across her hips until she slid them down over her thighs. She stepped over the chaise, and then lay down full length on top of him, her arms stretching out over his head and her mouth closing hungrily on his even as he wrapped her in his arms and joined her to him in one powerful movement.

Much later, as they both lay spent on the chaise, he awoke to the sound of her gentle snoring in the hollow of his shoulder. He shifted slightly, and ran his fingers across her forehead, clearing the damp hair out of her face, touching her cheek gently. She murmured something unintelligible, and tried to snuggle closer. He carefully extricated himself from her warm body, and then gathered her up in his arms and took her to the cabin below, where they made love again.

The morning intruded with the long blat of the St. Johns ferry leaving the slip for her first run across the river. Bright sunlight streamed through the windows in the cabin as Mike rolled over and sat up, rubbing his face, smiling at the memories of the night. Diane was curled in a ball in the middle of the bed. He reached down and kissed her cheek, and then got up, pulling the sheet over her until only her face showed. He watched her sleep for a few minutes, marveling at her beauty and his great fortune, and then went into the bathroom to make his morning ablutions.

He went into the galley to make coffee, slipping into a bathing suit on the way. He carried the coffee up topside to the porch, and waved hello to his neighbor across the pier, an elderly and very dapper retired lawyer from New York named Nathan Goldstein. Mr. Goldstein was very New York and very funny in a waspish, big city manner. He lived for his Sunday New York Times and his pot of coffee laced with Schlivovitz that he enjoyed with some style on the fantail of his fifty foot Bertram yacht.

The waterway was already teeming with boat traffic of all descriptions making their way down the channel to the St. Johns river junction and the sea five miles downstream. The sailboats pitched and bobbed in the crisscrossing wakes made by the more numerous powerboats. Mike was exchanging criticisms on their sea manners with Mr. Goldstein when Diane appeared on the porch, fresh from the shower, her dark hair done up in a twisted coil high on her head, and the rest of her wrapped in a full length terry robe. She poured herself a cup of coffee. The sleep was disappearing rapidly from her face, leaving only a visibly contented glow.

"Oi-veh," called Mr. Goldstein appreciatively, when he caught sight of Diane. "You found yourself a woman for change, Mikey, instead of one of those little girls you bring home from the beaches!"

Diane smiled archly at him and then went over to one of the cushioned deck chairs and sat down. Mike, not knowing what to say, joined her, leaving Mr. Goldstein to try to read his paper while stealing surreptitious glances at Diane. Mr. Goldstein, long a widower, was reportedly a heavy hitter among the local Sunday bingo set.

"Morning, Sunshine," said Mike, taking in her freshly scrubbed face. He suddenly wanted to take her back down below. She smiled at him, and he was ready to forego even going below.

"We would give your friend over there a heart attack, Captain," she said with a grin, once again reading his face.

"He'd go out a happy man," replied Mike, grinning himself despite his sudden attack of desire.

"And you? Would you go out a happy man?" she teased. She rearranged her robe, letting Mike have a look at a luxuriant length of thigh. Mr. Goldstein rattled his coffee cup over on the Bertram.

"Happy, but not satisfied, Madam," Mike replied. "I need to go to the well again a couple of hundred more times. This morning, that is."

"My, how we do go on," she simpered. "Does that mean I can stay all day?"

Mike's face lost its playful cast. "You can stay forever, as long as you stay with me," he said.

She looked at him over the rim of the coffee mug, her eyes fathomless. "Don't go falling overboard, Captain," she said softly. "It's bad for appearances."

He leaned forward. "I'm not sure I care about appearances just now," he said. "Your husband is with another woman right now, and you are here with me. I'm officially sorry if your marriage is a wash, but I'm not embarrassed to tell you that I want you. After last night—do you realize how extraordinary that was? We didn't just click, lady, we welded. I know I'm not being practical or wise or even very smart, but there it is. I-want-you. I'm also falling in love with you."

Diane looked down into her coffee for a long minute. The light mood of the morning had been replaced by something else.

"Can we just try this one day at a time, Mike?" she asked, looking up. "I'm very new to this, and what I would really like to do is to sit around the boat all day and do not much of anything. You have to understand that just being here is pretty heady stuff for me. I'm not sure I can deal with freedom and love and your very warm desire all in one breath."

She saw the concern in his eyes.

"That's not a no, Mike," she said quickly. "That's not a turndown, or a put off. Last night was—fantastic. Right now you, the boat, last night, how we loved each other—it's like a puzzle I've worked on for years and I finally got the whole thing together on the table. I just don't want to break it by making a wrong move. OK?"

He sat back in his chair, feeling more than a little foolish. "Well, can I make you breakfast instead?" he said.

She laughed aloud, a bright peal of pure pleasure. Even Mr. Goldstein, thirty feet away in the bright sunlight, nodded and smiled when he heard that sound. It was the best sound in the whole world. Good for Mikey.

THIRTY FIVE

USS Goldsborough, pierside, Mayport Naval Station, Monday, 28 April; 1000

"Just how much has the Commodore told you about all this?" asked Mike.

He was speaking on the phone to Commander Pierce Marshall, IV, skipper of the Deyo, one of the eight thousand ton Spruance class anti-submarine warfare destroyers based in Mayport. Pierce Marshall had been aide to a Vice Admiral in Washington before getting the Deyo, and he was an extremely smooth operator. He came from a Navy family, and his contemporaries called him "the I-V" behind his back.

"Not much at all, Michael," replied Marshall. "Just that he wants us to conduct a passive sound survey of some sort against diesel engines, of all things, in the Mayport opareas, especially at night. And that we're looking for something 'different'. He said he did not want to tell me more because he wants a clean look, not something predisposed by our knowing what we're looking for. He did say it was for something connected to Goldsborough, and the only thing I've heard about Goldy lately is that you've been chasing down some mystery in the opareas about a U-boat, I believe. Any connection?"

"Well, yeah," said Mike. "You've got the most sophisticated passive acoustic detection and analysis gear down here; I think he wants to see if you can detect the presence of a conventional boat on the snort amongst all the fishermen out there along the Stream. I'm surprised that he wouldn't tell you that."

"Well, you know Aronson;" said Marshall. "I have to tell you that he sounded like this was a firefly."

"A firefly?"

"Yeah, you know, one of those issues that comes swimming up out of the grass and merits a passing swat, but not something we go worrying over for very long. Pentagon E-ring term. Anyway, this will give my sonar girls something to do while we work the bugs out of our new main engine. Although I'm not sure what we're going to hear among all the other diesels that bang around out there every night—there must be dozens of boats in addition to the fishing fleet. You guys find something out there?"

Mike thought quickly. He may have already said too much, especially if Marshall was to talk to one of his buddies on the Group Staff.

"No, not really. I think the Commodore wants to be able to say that we did a very thorough job of disproving the submarine myth, and since Goldy has no passive capability whatsoever, you guys run the drill out there, come up empty, and we can put the whole thing to bed once and for all."

"Right, got it. OK, Michael, thanks. The IC-man is here to cut the phone lines, so we'll see you Friday. Enjoy your boiler work, my friend."

"Thanks a heap, shipmate," replied Mike, hanging up.

Enjoy my boiler work, indeed. The Spruance community took great pride in not having the albatross of a steam plant hanging around their precious necks; the Spruance class ships ran on airplane engines, and when there was a problem, they simply changed out the engine and they were back in business in a week. Every steamboat skipper envied the gas turbine ships, who could light off their engines and be underway in literally thirty minutes, as compared to the steam plants which had to light off one or even two days before departure. Mike called the Exec.

"XO, I just got a call from Deyo; they're gonna do the passive sound survey on diesels, just like the Commodore said."

"That'll be a project, Skipper," said Farmer. "The passive environment out there has to be a real bear. I've got the engineering assist team assembling in the wardroom in five minutes. Do you want to come down and kick it off?"

"No, but I will. I don't suppose we've heard anything from the guys in Norfolk yet, have we?"

"No, Sir, not yet, other than that they got there OK and got rooms at the Dam Neck BOQ. Linc's gonna call me at 1700 today, let me know what's shakin'."

"OK, XO. Sounds good. I'll see you in the wardroom—call me when everyone's there."

He hung up, and leaned back in his chair, dismissing the engineering team and the submarine so that he could conjure up the memory of his weekend with Diane. She had stayed the entire day, not going back to her quarters until late Sunday night. After their first brief conversation in the morning Mike had backed off and given her some space, and she had relaxed. They had taken a nap in the afternoon, promising each other that they would just cuddle and ending up in an exciting bout of lovemaking. He had fixed her dinner again, and they had finished the evening on the porch, watching the sun go down over the waterway and talking quietly, holding hands.

She said that she would tell J.W., if he called, that she was driving down to Lauderdale during the week to see some friends, and that she would be out at the houseboat every night. Now Mike couldn't wait for 1730, when he could leave and get back to the boat. Just like a sailor, he mused, dying for liberty call. He firmly squashed the little voice in his mind that said he was playing with fire. The phone rang and the XO said everyone was ready. Mike pulled himself out of his reverie and went below to begin the week.

At 1700, Mike sat sprawled on the couch in the Exec's cabin while the XO talked on the phone to Linc, who was calling from Norfolk. He watched the Exec's face as Linc made his report, and tried to concentrate on the business of the possible submarine. His mind, however, was very much on other things, like his weekend with Diane. Two more days until her husband came back; two more nights and a day, to be precise. He tried not to think about that aspect, or how they would manage once J.W. Martinson III was back in town. Diane had told him that she would start cutting back on the Navy social life; she had been threatening to do that for some time, anyway, claiming terminal boredom. J.W., who spent most of his time at Navy functions allocating face time, had not seemed to care very much. He had said that he was happy she was finding other interests. Mike started to smile at the irony of that thought when he was pulled back to reality by the sounds of the Exec finishing his conversation with Linc.

"So—what've we got?" he asked, as the Exec hung up.

"A strong possible," said the Exec.

Mike groaned. The ASW Classification Center was living up to its reputation for ambivalence. The Center was known for contact classification fence straddling. Three years previously they had analyzed the sonar tapes of a destroyer which had capped off a NATO ASW exercise by colliding with a submerged British submarine, and the highest classification the Center would grant to the destroyer's contact tapes was "possible".

"Not very useful, I admit," said the Exec. "But Linc said the three master Chiefs who did the analysis of the tapes thought it was a real contact and not marine life or bottom. They just couldn't get their bosses to go out on a limb with a "probable" classification. You know how they are up there."

"I surely do," said Mike. "But now what the hell do we do with this thing? Group isn't going to jump through their hoops on another "possible submarine" contact that's, what, four days old now."

He sighed, and thought for a minute.

"Linc going to come home tomorrow? And he knows he's to bring those tapes back here?"

"Yes, Sir, to both questions. I guess now we wait for the Deyo's little witch hunt."

Mike shook his head slowly in resignation.

"They're going to go out and tape diesel engines in the fishing grounds. And nobody's going to be amazed when they find a dozen or so. Even if they record an unusual engine, or an out of pattern detection, it's not going to resolve the general ambiguity. We need something concrete."

The distraught face of Christian Mayfield's sister had popped suddenly into his mind, for no apparent reason.

"One way or the other," he added.

"Should we call the Commodore and give him the word?" asked the Exec. "I can't remember what the arrangement was."

"I'll call the Commodore's office here, although I think he was going to talk to the Center directly. I don't think the CSO's been cut entirely into the loop, so I'll just tell him that the verdict was "possible" in case the Commodore calls him. If the Commodore wants to share it with him, he will."

"Aye, aye, Sir," said the XO. "You going to shove off, then?"

"Yeah, I think so, XO."

Mike wondered if the Exec had detected his preoccupation during the day of meetings and planning sessions on the engineering work. He knew that he had been quieter and less intrusive than usual, his mind bemused with thoughts of Diane. But if the Exec had noticed anything, he was not revealing it. Which was good, because Mike was in no position to explain to his Number Two his sudden involvement with the Chief of Staff's wife. Just the thought of seeing her again excited him. He pulled his large frame off the couch, and paused in the doorway.

"Somehow I think this submarine business is going to rise up and bite somebody in the ass," he said. "I want us to pay enough attention so's to ensure it ain't us."

The Exec grinned.

"No sweat, Cap'n," he said. "We'll call it a UFO—underwater flying object, and then the Air Force'll get stuck with it."

"There you go, XO," laughed Mike. "Knew you could handle it."

But then his face grew serious.

"You know, the missing element in all this is still the motive, if that's the right word. If there is a foreign sub loitering in the Jax opareas, why is he there?"

The Exec sat back in his chair, staring blankly at the bulkhead.

"Maybe," he mused, "Maybe it's a test. Maybe the higher ups have plunked a guy down here to see how long, or even if, all these tin cans will stumble across it. You remember the Soviet tape incident."

Mike nodded. The Fleet Commander, a dynamic Flag officer with many pet projects, had positioned a Navy electronic warfare training van in the State park across the river and had it transmit the simulated radar signal of a Soviet missile cruiser into the base across the river. It had taken three days before one of the ships there, the Barry, had detected it, and another two for that ship to make a report. There had followed several homilies from Norfolk on improving electronic warfare readiness.

"Yeah, I suppose, but we don't own any conventional subs; ours are all nukes. Which would mean he would have had to get one of Allies' boats, like a Brit or a Canadian. That's stretching it a bit, I think. But maybe...shit, I don't know. This whole thing has me baffled. And I hate to be the guy who raises the issue—you remember how Barry got shit on for delaying his report, even though he was the only ship in the harbor that picked up the signal."

The Exec nodded slowly.

"Yes, Sir, on the other hand, you remember what the Commodore said—it's not up to us to sort out the political impact. We get a contact, we report it."

Mike snorted. "Right, and hang the consequences. Damn the torpedoes and full speed ahead! Easy for you to say, XO, but not so easy for me to do. I get the distinct impression that some of we commanding officers are tolerated, but only just so. You light enough fuses, one of 'em will get you a bang."

"Yes, Sir, I realize that," said Farmer. "But when you first took over, you lit fuses all the time. I would kind of think they'd be used to it."

"Not when you have somebody like Martinson in the backfield. I have it on pretty good authority that he would love to find a way to yank me offa here. I've been advised that if I want to complete my command tour, I have to be, what was the word, more circumspect, yes, that's it. Circumspect."

Like when screwing the Chief of Staff's wife, he thought. That's really being circumspect. The Exec saw Mike's expression change, and decided to drop it.

"Figure out the motive, XO," Mike said. "If Deyo comes up with something, and we can think of a motive, I'll pursue it. With whom, I don't know, but I will pursue it, at least until they fire my young ass. OK?"

"Yes, Sir. We'll think of something."

Mike went back up to his cabin and called Commander Barstowe. He waited for the yeoman to find the CSO. The late afternoon sunlight streaming through the single porthole cast peculiar patterns on the wall of his cabin. The noise level in the ship had diminished now that two hundred forty of his crew had gone ashore with the 1630 liberty call, settling into the occasional noises of the duty section sweeping down the passage-ways and getting ready to put her to bed for the night.

The CSO came on the line and Mike reported the gist of the word from Norfolk about the tapes. Barstowe gave no sign that he knew what Mike was talking about, but he promised to relay the message, and no, he had not yet talked to the Commodore. Mike asked when the Commodore was coming back to Mayport, and was told late Wednesday afternoon; the Commodore would return with the rest of the Mayport contingent on a Navy transport aircraft that would land at the Mayport naval air strip adjacent to the base.

Wednesday afternoon, Mike reflected, after hanging up. So we have tonight and tomorrow night. And after that? Whatever we can get, he told himself. The submarine thing seemed to be fading back into the shadows again, he thought, with some relief. Now that Diane was in his life, he would be only too happy to step back out of any limelight at Group headquarters and leave the face time to the more ambitious of his peers at Mayport. He suddenly realized that what he really wanted was to finish the command tour and then get out of Dodge and the Navy and all the bullshit with his twenty intact and a retirement check for life. And after that? He would probably follow the old adage and put Hooker on one shoulder and an oar on the other and walk inland. When someone finally asked what the oar was, he would be far enough from the sea to stick it in the ground and call it home.

But right now he had a warm woman on the near horizon and steam up. He got up, and went into the tiny head at the forward end of his cabin to change out of his uniform. As he stuffed the wrinkled wash khakis in his laundry bag, he looked at himself in the mirror mounted on the back of the door by one his predecessors. He was still in pretty good shape, all things considered. It suddenly occurred to him that Diane might already be at the boat. He had given her a key to the main lounge hatchway door. If she was, he did not want to appear in a five o'clock shadow and khakis that smelled of that unique Navy destroyer aroma of fuel oil, ozone, steam, galley grease, disinfectant, and metal.

He stripped down and took a quick shower, shaved, and then put on slacks, a sport shirt, and some loafers. He splashed a touch of cologne around his jaw, and grinned at himself in the mirror. Now I look and smell like most of my troops who are headed for the liberty trail. He wondered if the quarterdeck watch would notice the difference. He suddenly didn't care if they did.

As he walked aft to leave the ship, he thought about what might be going on up in Norfolk. It was up to the Commodore now to decide what to do next. He might wait for the Deyo to do its thing, but he also might tell the Group Commander what we've got so far. Maybe take the sting out if they get to think about it for a few days. Hell, he might even get the Admiral to go over to the Center to see for himself. But he doubted it.

The Exec was waiting on the quarterdeck.

"I told the CSO I'd be home in a half hour, in case the Commodore wants to talk."

"Aye, aye, Sir. If he calls here we'll forward the call."

"Thanks, XO," said Mike.

He was aware that the Exec thought he should not be going home until the loop had been closed with the Commodore. Barstowe would call Captain Aronson, and then Aronson would probably want to talk to him, and might even expect him to be aboard and not at home. But there was Diane.

Five minutes after he arrived onboard the Lucky Bag, Diane arrived, slipping into the lounge and giving him a breathtaking kiss. He promptly forgot about the submarine, the ship, the Commodore, and the rest of the world, until it intruded abruptly one hour later when the Commodore called.

"OK, Mike, CSO gave me the word," said Aronson, starting right in as if he and Mike had been talking for the past half hour.

"I'm gonna have to see the Admiral and fill him in; I'll try to do it without Martinson getting into it, at least initially, because he'll want to focus on you and not the submarine. Man's in a foul mood, anyway—says his wife took off for Lauderdale to go shopping again; last time she did that it set them back a coupla grand."

"Yes, Sir," said Mike, swallowing.

He was sitting at his desk in the lounge, looking at said wife on the couch ten feet away. He thought he felt the first faint tugs of the web of deception he was weaving. She was watching the evening news on television, apparently ignoring Mike and his phone conversation.

"I want you to send a message to the CO of Deyo—personal for, OK? And ask him to send you a sitrep on their passive search as of Wednesday at 0800; that'll give 'em two nights of search and analysis. You relay the dope to me at 1000 Wednesday through Barstowe; he knows how to reach me. If I can catch the Admiral for a few minutes tomorrow during the conference, I'll brief him on what we know so far, and what we're doing. If Deyo comes up empty, I think the Admiral will just drop it—the Center's evaluation isn't all that strong. But just to be sure, I'm going to talk to them tomorrow, too, in between these goddamn scheduling meetings. How's the engineering work going?"

Mike related the events of the day, and the prognosis for the pump repairs. It would probably take two weeks, not one.

"Yeah, well, that figures, Mike," agreed the Commodore. "You just push 'em to do a good job, and let's hope there are no more mysterious incidents out in the opareas for awhile. The Navy's got enough trouble trying to work up a fleet operating schedule against all these budget cuts."

"Yes, Sir, we'll do it. Thank you for calling, Sir."

But the Commodore had already hung up. Mike then called the Command Duty Officer on the Goldsborough and dictated a Personal message for the CO message to Deyo, telling the CDO to release it as a priority. He then joined Diane on the couch.

"Sounds interesting," she said, snuggling in under his arm.

"I didn't think you were paying any attention to all that," he said.

"Navy wives learn to tune in to those kinds of conversations even when they're talking to someone else, my love. Anything out of the routine usually means something's coming or someone's leaving."

"Well it certainly won't be Goldy-maru," he said. "We're in for the better part of the next two weeks changing out main feed pump steam seals."

"But the mystery submarine hasn't gone away, has it?" she asked. He turned to look down at her, to see how much she might really understand.

"No, actually, it hasn't, although it might well have taken off by now. What the Center found is a possible contact that happened last week. Now the Commodore has Deyo out doing a real needle in the haystack search for any peculiar diesel engines, on the theory that, if he's still there, he'll snorkel at night to recharge his batteries."

"What's a snorkel?"

"It's a pipe, basically, that a sub can stick up like a periscope and provide air to diesel engines without surfacing."

"Oh. OK. But if there is a submarine out there, why?" she asked.

"That's the million dollar question, Sweet Cheeks."

"Sweet Cheeks?" She sat up, a mock severe expression in her face. "Did you call me Sweet Cheeks?"

Mike stared hard at her face and then tracked somewhat lower on her anatomy.

"Well," he said, "That's just my memory speaking; it has been a long time, you know. Might be wrong...you know what they say—memory is the second thing to go."

"And the first, may I ask, is what?"

"Don't remember," he pronounced solemnly, and then he pulled her toward him to refresh his sadly failing memory.

"Remember, I get dinner," she said, her voice muffled in his shoulder. "And for calling me Sweet Cheeks, I also get dessert."

THIRTY SIX

The Al Akrab, submerged, Jacksonville Operating Areas, Tuesday, 29 April; 0130

"Bearing One. Mark!" The Captain swung the attack scope around to the right, and stopped suddenly. "Bearing Two. Mark! Down scope."

The glistening tube hissed out of sight into the periscope well below the attack center. The Captain straightened, and glanced over at the depth gauge. They were steady at 18 meters, despite the medium swells up above on the dark surface.

"Confirm the plot."

"Sir, the plot confirms as follows: two fishing boats are trolling into the seas, speeds at between two and three knots. There are no other major shipping contacts in the area, except for the large car carrier which is opening to the east," said the watch officer.

"Sound operator confirm."

The sonar operator turned in his chair.

"Sir, passive sonar confirms two contacts, diesel engines, bearing west and northwest, drifting right. No other nearby engine sounds. No other contacts except for the large ship opening to the east."

"Very well. Raise the snorkel mast. Make preparations to snorkel."

The control room watch officer called the engineering watch officer and relayed the order to configure the propulsion systems for snorkeling. He nodded to the diving officer, who began raising the thick snorkel mast, carefully eyeing the reference mark as the mast came up to ensure that it was well clear of the sea surface, but not so high as to create a large radar contact for any watching eyes above. The planesmen hunched over their controls, keeping the submarine precisely at eighteen meters of keel depth.

The Captain reflected on the surface plot, sipping on a mug of hot tea. Two fishing boats, both underway, meant good diesel sound coverage. His uniform was sweaty, the back of his shirt sticking to his back. He stank. They all stank. They had again lost one of their two fresh water evaporators due to a pump failure, and it had cost them dearly in terms of available fresh water. There was enough to drink and cook meals, and to wash one's hands, but no more. The crewmen, already strained by the mission, were growing short and ill tempered with each other due to the constant lack of water. The temperature of the Gulf Stream, hovering near 82 degrees, had slowly cooked the boat up to an ambient temperature in the low nineties, with effusive humidity. For men used to the dry heat of North Africa, this was real misery.

The sighting of a large destroyer, the USS Deyo by her hull pennant number, had added to the tension. Their intelligence books made it clear that Deyo was a first team ASW destroyer, equipped with all the latest technology that the older, unknown destroyer did not have. The one factor working in their favor was that Deyo was not using active sonar, and was also charging around the fleet operating areas at high speeds, apparently doing some kind of engineering trials. At those speeds, even her acutely sensitive passive arrays were useless. As long as the submarine remained very quiet, and as long as the Deyo remained occupied with other things, they were reasonably safe. It also helped that Deyo had disappeared up to the north a few hours ago.

But now they were going to make noise; the battery was down to seventy-five percent, and they needed to pump a charge into the banks of lead acid storage cells nested beneath the control room for about four hours to get them back up to ninety-five percent. This meant that they had to light off the diesels, and, using the direct current electric propulsion motors as generators, activate the direct current charging circuits. The diesels required huge quantities of combustion air, which meant they either had to surface or ingest all that air through the thick snorkel mast now jutting four feet above the waves on the surface up above.

The Captain walked back over to the plotting table, and rubbed his eyes before looking down once more at the plot. The watch officer stood back to give him room. The planesman and the helmsman concentrated on keeping the boat straight and level, so as not to dunk the snorkel mast once the diesels started. If the mast went under a wave, the weight of the water would seat a steel float ball in the top of the snorkel tube, keeping water out of the engines, but also forcing the diesels to gulp combustion air momentarily from within the boat, clamping a painful vacuum on everyone's ears, and then just as painfully reversing the pressure when the ball lifted off its seat as the wave went by. Snorkeling called for precise depth control, and it had to be maintained for hours on end.

The Captain verified the plot one more time. The tactical chart showed the track of the Deyo headed off the tactical plot to the north, with last contact being held three hours ago. The noise of just one fisherman should mask any sound of the submerged diesels in the submarine, but the Captain had made it a practice to find two boats, both with their engines running, before he would snorkel.

"Is the plant configured for snorkeling?" he asked. The watch officer nodded.

"Sir, main engineering control reports ready to snorkel. The main propulsion plant is split out. The switchboards are aligned to the battery. The battery compartment checks clear for hydrogen concentration. Hydrogen monitors have been purged. Request permission to open main induction."

"Open main induction and commence snorkeling."

Across the control room, the diving officer actuated a hydraulic control, and the twenty-four inch diameter main induction valve cycled open in the snorkel pipe. A glowing red warning light appeared on the valve console, indicating that the boat was now exposed to catastrophic flooding should something go wrong. The diving officer confirmed the valve open, and then spoke into sound powered phones to main engineering control. An instant later, the rumble of the mains shook the boat. The lights flickered momentarily as the boat's electrical load was adjusted, and everyone instinctively winced in anticipation of the dreaded pull on their eardrums. But the boat remained steady as a rock on its northerly course. The Musaid entered the control room, nodded to the Captain, and fixed himself a mug of tea.

"Crack the ventilation augment valves," the Captain ordered. A technician stood up and opened the large valve on the side of the snorkel pipe, which allowed fresh air from the sea surface above to blow into the control room for some temporary relief from the stagnant atmosphere of the boat. There was a similar valve back in the engineering spaces, which he knew the engineers had probably already opened to divert some of the precious fresh air.

"Raise the electronic warfare mast."

Just forward of the thick snorkel mast, the pineapple shaped head of the electronic sensor mast broke the sea surface twenty feet above. The Captain watched the EW console as the EW Chief Petty Officer scanned the screens. The Musaid came over to stand next to him, watching the console.

"No military surveillance radars," the Chief reported. "One commercial Decca bearing 290; correlates with the fishermen."

"Very well. Maintain a watch on ESM."

The Captain relaxed slightly and moved over to his chair. He would remain in the control room for the entire snorkeling cycle. His submarine was dangerously close to the surface, and, by tactical standards, had a large mast exposed and was also generating tons of acoustic noise into the water. They had to be alert to the sudden appearance of an airborne or surface search military radar signal on the EW console, which would be the signal to shut down the mains and bring down all the masts at once. Because an active radar could be detected at one and a half times its own detection range, an alert scanner should always be able to get under cover before the active radar would begin getting echoes. The key word was alert.

The Captain hoped and prayed to Allah that the Deyo or one of her kind was not up there somewhere operating under radar and acoustic silence. The Deyo was a professional sub killer, equipped with an air bubble belt around the submerged portion of her hull. The belt breathed a curtain of small air bubbles down the entire length of the ship's hull, effectively masking all machinery noises coming from within the destroyer. Her screws had a similar system, which meant that submarines listening for the familiar chopping sounds of high power propellers would hear only the hiss of the ambient sea. The Deyo was entirely capable of looming out of the darkness and spearing the Al Akrab with a brace of screaming antisubmarine homing torpedoes.

But the Captain had to weigh the likelihood of the initial detection: there had been some interaction with the American Navy, but every indication was that they had never been actually detected. Even when they had fired the decoy, which had been a near desperate measure, the old destroyer had turned away and gone back into port. Unless the Americans had actually concluded that there was something out here, the lack of the initial cues would keep the Al Akrab safe. The ocean was simply too big.

He glanced at his watch. It would be a long night, even if it all went perfectly. He gestured for more tea. One of the sailors scrambled to bring him some. He looked up at the Musaid.

237

SCORPION IN THE SEA

"Well, Musaid. Are we safe?" he asked softly.

The hum of instruments, rumble of the diesels aft, and the hiss of the ventilation augmenter were the only other sounds. The boat was actually rolling slightly in response to the waves above. The Musaid's face crinkled in a wry smile.

"Safe, Effendi? When were we ever safe?"

The Captain nodded. Here they were, hovering scant feet below the surface, radiating diesel engine noise, two masts exposed, and not fifty miles away from a major American naval base, and doing all this in an ancient Russian submarine that had more parts and pieces from her sister ships than original parts. A real sub-killer had been in their area only a few hours ago, and might have come back for all they knew. The Captain reflected on the Americans and their technology. It was all so unfair.

"The Americans," he muttered. "They're everywhere. They dominate the world. Even the Russians fear them, their technology, their designs to make the whole world over in their image. The kings of Carthage must have felt the same way about Rome."

"And today Carthage is a large open field, with lumps of marble here and there on ground still poisoned with Roman salt," said the Musaid. "I have seen it. I have often wondered if that is our fate, too. For all the advisors and equipment we have bought over the past ten years, the Americans came from the sea in one night and struck with impunity. They can do it anytime they want to. We are never safe."

"Well," observed the Captain, finishing his tea. "Two can play at a game, as the British say. This time it is we who shall come from the sea. I am convinced that they do not even dream we could do this, come this far, and wait patiently for our target like a scorpion in the sand. They call us rag-heads, did you know that? Rag-heads. Think of it."

The Musaid snorted.

"The Americans have a need to call other people names; it soothes their consciences when they exercise dominion. It is a trait they took from the British—wogs, gyppies, and now, rag-heads. Oppression of lesser people offends their Christian values; but it is no crime to kill a wog. It is the nature of imperialism to reduce its victims to names."

The Captain smiled, his eyes glinting.

"Which will make this mission so very satisfying; I wonder if they will be able to admit that it was a rag-head that put torpedoes into their aircraft carrier."

"I worry about that decoy, Effendi," said the Musaid, changing the subject.

The Captain looked at him sharply, and then away.

"I too worry about that decoy, Musaid."

He looked around the control room to see if anyone was listening to them, but the watch remained intent on keeping depth control.

"I am convinced that we had to do something, but I wish that encounter had never begun. If there is any connection between the killer destroyer Deyo today and that decoy, we may soon be the quarry instead of being the hunters."

"The key is to have the carrier return home soon," mused the Musaid. "The longer we stay here, the more chances we take. We need to do this thing soon." The Captain nodded.

"We can do nothing about that, Musaid. Inshallah. That remains in God's hands." He heaved himself upright. "But depth control remains in our hands. Watch officer!" he called. "You are half a meter low. Pay attention!"

THIRTY SEVEN

USS Deyo, northern Jacksonville operating areas, Tuesday, 29 April; 0145

Sonarman Third Class Francis McGonagle was trying hard to stay awake. It was always the same on a midwatch: the agony of getting up at 2330, the zombie-like walk through the messdecks for some coffee or, occasionally, hot soup, the climb through darkened passageways to the Combat Information Center, and then the turnover in sonar control, where he and his team-mate, Petty Officer Paul Barney, went through the motions of assuming the watch, checking the display equipment, adjusting their console chairs and the ambient lights, and then, finally, having burned up a grand total of twenty minutes of their four hour midwatch, came the realization that they had another three and half hours to go. Another cup of coffee to keep the heart turning over; five more minutes used up.

"God, I hate this shit," muttered Barney, blinking his eyes in the blue light of the CIC.

As usual the air conditioning worked especially well at one in the morning; both men wore jackets over their dungarees to ward off the chill. Barney sat the active sonar console, which contained three large black and white video screens and four panels of control equipment. The active console was side by side with the passive array console, where McGonagle sat, rubbing his eyes for the tenth time in the past ten minutes.

"Yeah, I hear that," said McGonagle. "This coffee ain't working, Man."

"Well, at least you have something to do," said Barney. "I'm shut down."

McGonagle grunted. Recording the passive displays on surface diesel engines was not his idea of modern anti-submarine warfare. The night orders, passed on to them by the 20–24 watchstanders, were short and explicit: keep the active sonar in standby, and conduct a passive search in the acoustic frequency bands where marine diesel engines emitted. The night orders did not say what they were looking for, only that they were to cover the entire internal combustion engine frequency band, and record everything, from 2300 until 0600. The previous watch had focused the passive array into the correct frequency bands, and now there was nothing to do but watch the displays and ensure that recorders did not run out of paper.

Sonar control in the Deyo was located in one module of the Combat Information Center, which was four times the size of the CIC in Goldsborough. The CIC in Deyo was compartmentalized into modules, with sonar control and the ASW weapons control center located on the port side of the CIC, which itself was only one deck down from the bridge. At general quarters there would have been twelve men in the sonar section alone, but for an independent steaming situation, there were only two watchstanders. One could have managed with the big, active sonar shut down; there were two to ensure that they both stayed awake.

The active and the passive displays were all synthesized digital video which looked nothing like the older displays in Goldsborough. In place of the expanding ring of light that Goldsborough's sonarmen studied, Deyo's active sonar equipment produced what were called waterfall displays, dozens of parallel light lines streaming down a grey screen display that looked very much like a computer graphics depiction of a waterfall. The sonarmen were trained to pick out changes in the gradations and character of the lines which indicated the presence of a return echo. The passive displays were also waterfall screens, but the screen remained blank until the sensitive passive detection array computers actually picked up a sound in the underwater environment, and began drawing a line down the screen. Each line represented both a discrete frequency of sound and a bearing, or direction from which the sound was emanating.

Deyo's sonarmen were trained to recognize certain frequencies, such as the unique line emitted by all Soviet Navy electrical equipment. Or the equally characteristic line generated by the Soviets' older, six bladed submarine propellers. Unlike Goldsborough, Deyo's main sonar armament was the passive array, which capitalized on the same principle that passive electronic warfare used: a signal could be heard well beyond the range at which that signal could tell its originator anything. Goldsborough's sonar had to push a sound wave out into the water, and then wait for that wave, which was dissipating in power with every spherical meter it travelled from the sonar dome, to hit a contact, bounce off, and return to the sonar receiver. Since the return wave also dissipated with every meter it travelled back from the contact towards the ship, the initial hit had to be pretty strong to complete the cycle. Deyo, on the other hand, listened for the tiny sounds emitted into the water by a submarine's own machinery or propellers. These sounds ranged in frequency from the very low frequency sound of a propeller beating in the water to the very high frequency, and inaudible to the human ear, squeal of a worn out bearing in a submarine's pump. These sounds only had to go one way, dissipating in power as they went, of course, but detectable thereby at ranges many times that of active sonar. The target had to cooperate for this system to work, which meant that it had to make noise. Modern, nuclear submarines, with their steam plants and pumps and turbines, were ideal candidates for passive tracking. Diesel-electric submarines, running on DC motors powered by silent batteries, made almost no sound at all. Unless they ran their diesel engines.

"Well, we've got at least two of these suckers out there," said McGonagle, looking up at his waterfall, yawning again.

There was a group of squiggly lines trailing down the paper on the recorder. The screen showed that the sounds being picked up were all similar in frequency, differing only in their bearing from the Deyo.

"Looks like they're all to the south of us, and pretty close in bearing," observed Barney.

"Yeah that's probably the Mayport fishing fleet; one guy finds a school of fish or shrimp, and the others drift over to where he's working and pretty soon you got a gaggle of 'em. There's no way we're going to break out individual contacts when they bunch up like that."

"You ever go over to Mayport and get a bushel of shrimp and boil 'em up in the backyard? They're cheap as hell that way."

"Naw, I hate shrimp. I guess I'm allergic or something. Shellfish tear me up inside, Man."

"That's too bad; makes for a good excuse to drink a pony of beer."

"I don't need any excuses to drink beer; wouldn't mind one right now."

"That's for damn sure," said Barney. "Look at all that shit, would you—"

Barney slid his chair over on its tracks to study the passive display. The lines were more numerous now, drawing over one another now, creating a black smear on the recorder's paper trace, and a confusing jumble of light lines on the video displays.

"I'm gonna have to expand this display," McGonagle complained.

He made some adjustments, and shifted the frequency scale, which had the effect of separating each line being displayed into a quarter-inch of vertical space. Several new lines began to draw even as he opened up the display.

"Look, there's another one," he pointed. "A lot bigger engine, too. Maybe there's a merch coming out of the St. Johns, and we're seeing it on the same bearing."

"What bearing is that?"

"From us, 170 to the centroid of the sound sources." Barney flipped down an intercom switch.

"Surface, sonar, gimme a bearing to the mouth of the St. Johns."

He waited for a minute while the surface plotter in the adjacent module ran the bearing, and then said, "Sonar, aye, thanks."

"That ain't the St. Johns, Man—river bears 195."

McGonagle squirmed in his chair. All the coffee was beginning to accumulate. He watched the lines drawing down the plot, beginning to merge again as the sound sources overlapped. He shook his head.

"I can't see anything useful in all that shit," he said. He took off his intercom headset.

"I gotta go take a piss. We'll let the recorder run; the Chief can make out of that whatever he wants. I don't even know why we're doing this shit."

"You know how it is, Man; the officers gotta pretend we're out here for some reason other than boring holes in the water."

"Right. Well, tell 'em we found the fishing fleet for 'em."

"Roger that."

McGonagle took off his intercom earphones and departed for the head. Barney watched the waterfall displays, and studied the last set of lines to begin drawing. Deeper tones in that stream, with some heavy harmonics in the low frequency bands. Bigger engine, he thought. Much bigger than the Jimmie V1271's they usually heard out here. He stood up out of his chair and flipped back along the paper trace coming out of the recorder. There. it had started up right there, after the other two began to draw. maybe a harmonic set adding from the sound lines of the first two. Naw. Too big. He extracted a red pen from his shirt pocket, and made a little tick mark next to the timeline on the left side of the paper trace. McGonagle would probably laugh at him, but he'd mark it anyway. That way if something came up, he could always say he did in fact see it. They had, after all, said to record any variations in the normal sound patterns. This one was fading in and out of the other two sound groups, like a deeper bass note thrumming in and out of an audience's audible consciousness. He rolled the paper trace back up to the current drawing, and sat back down to watch the maze of light lines squiggling down the video display like the streams from a leaking paint can cover. It was going to be a long freaking watch.

THIRTY EIGHT

USS Goldsborough, pierside, Mayport Naval Station, Wednesday, 30 April; 0900

"OK, Gents, let's hit it," said Mike, breaking up the morning engineering staff meeting.

The Chief Engineer, his machinist mate and boiler Chiefs, the ship repair superintendent, and the ship's department heads rose from their chairs and filed out, refilling paper cups of coffee on the way. Mike and the Exec remained seated at the head of the wardroom table while the officers and chiefs left. They had been meeting for almost an hour, as they did every morning during the week of repairs in the main propulsion plant. Mike got up and brought the stainless steel coffee pot over to the table and refilled both their cups, put the pot back on the warmer, and sat down again, rocking back in his armchair at the head of the table. The sound of a pneumatic chipping hammer could be heard chattering up forward on the forecastle.

"Well, XO, they gonna fix these main feed pumps or was this all smoke and mirrors?"

Ben Farmer reviewed his notes.

"An awful lot of wishful thinking going on," he said. "They're going through all the correct repair procedures and motions, but I haven't heard anybody say they've found the problem in each pump and that they know for a fact what's wrong and how to fix it. This is just a quick and dirty overhaul."

"Which is better than nothing, I suppose," Mike said. "I'm almost surprised they're doing it, given that Goldy's going out next year."

"I think that's because they're never sure about decommissioning—remember Vietnam, when all those old cans from Willy Willy Twice were extended in '67 for six months to go on the gunline? They were still all there in '73."

"Yeah, I suppose," said Mike, "But this has to be costing megabucks—new twelve hundred pound steam seals, new regulating admis-

243

sion valves, all that level one welding to get access to all this shit, the X-rays after the welds, and then they're not positive they know what's wrong with the goddamn pumps!"

"I think it's a case of age, Cap'n: those hummers've been turning and burning for twenty three years. That's main steam: 1275 psi and 980 degrees, pumping water at 1500 psi into a steaming boiler for two dozen years."

"Yeah, I reckon. Well, what else we got going on?"

"We have the preparations for the next 3M inspection, which I'm guessing is coming up pretty soon. Chief Taggart from Squadron has been nosing around the Chiefs' Mess, which usually means a "surprise" 3M inspection is inbound. The Chiefs all have the word, but we'll need an all-officers meeting on it. And then there's a medical assist team coming Friday for a sanitation inspection, and that will be followed by the TyCom medical officer's "surprise" inspection within the next thirty days. And then—"

"OK, OK—!" Mike threw up his hands in surrender. "That's enough inspections and assist visits for one day. Christ! I wonder how the 10,000 ships we had in World War II ever managed to win the war without all these staff assist visits and inspections."

Mike blew on his coffee, as if that might improve the taste. The Navy had been buying progressively cheaper coffee over the past few years; some of it was genuinely awful.

"I think it's what miners call overburden," said the Exec. "In those days they had one Admiral and his staff for every 200 ships in the Navy. Today we have one Admiral and his staff for every three ships. With no war on, we have to justify the existence of all those brass hats, which is where I think all these "command attention" programs come from."

Mike sighed. The constant stream of rudder orders from the high command on how to run every aspect of a command's daily life was the bane of every Commanding Officer's existence, ashore and afloat.

"Well, XO," he said. "It's a hard monster to get your hands on. Each of the Navy's mandated management programs is, in and of itself, justifiable and possibly even necessary. The problem comes when you aggregate them. I spent six weeks going through a Prospective Commanding Officer school in Newport prior to coming here, just like you spent six weeks in your Prospective XO course. The whole curriculum was focused on this enormous array of special management programs required of every ship. They did a good job of explaining where each program came from, and how each one evolved from the discovery of problems in the fleet, ranging from poor engineering maintenance to ineffective oversight of personnel records."

"So each time a fleet-wide problem is discovered, the Navy charges the Fleet Commander or the Type Commander to design a special management program to fix it."

"Right. And each program gets designed by a whole staff of people as if the ship were going to do nothing else but that one program. Nobody ever coordinates all the programs, and the resulting paperwork requirements. You read the directives: the Commanding Officer shall personally devote X amount of time and attention to seeing to it that the Personnel Qualification Standards program is, etc., etc. I keep hoping someday the CNO will sit down and add up the total paper requirements of all these programs."

"If he does," snorted the Exec, "We'll get another program, a paperwork reduction program, complete with reports, how many pounds of paper got reduced today, and so on."

"You got it, XO. Watch out, they'll make a staffie out of you for thinking that way."

They were interrupted by a knocking on the wardroom door, followed by the radio messenger bearing a steel clipboard.

"Personal For, Cap'n," he announced, passing the clipboard to Mike.

Mike opened the clipboard, initialled the record copy of the message, and then took the back copy, dismissing the messenger.

"It's from Pierce, in Deyo," said Mike. "Addressed action to the Commodore, info to me. And it says: "have recorded underwater sound survey in diesel bands for two successive nights. Not surprisingly, have detected several diesels, but nothing to indicate unusual characteristics or anything but the normal anomalies of the Jax opareas and fishing grounds. Unless otherwise directed, intend to continue survey for one more night prior to return to port Thursday, unless engineering trials completed Wednesday, in which case will return to port Wednesday P.M.." Rest of it is on his engineering trials, which went, unlike ours, swimmingly. "Very respectfully, etc, the IV." Mike tossed the message over to Farmer, who scanned it briefly.

"So nothing to write home about there, either, XO. I think now maybe this thing's dead. Or gone. Or both."

"I wonder what he means by 'normal anomalies'," muttered the Exec.

"Shit, I don't know. The professional ASW guys tend to speak in tongues," said Mike. "As everybody seems to know, ASW is an imprecise business."

The Exec put the message down on the table, and drank some more coffee.

"This stuff *is* getting worse," he commented, peering suspiciously into his cup. "Navy gets cheap on coffee; we're really getting down there."

He studied the message form, as if by looking at it he could compel it to explain the mystery submarine. Mike stared off into space.

"I wonder," said Farmer, "If we're not running into the same thing on Deyo that we got up in Norfolk."

"Like?"

"I mean that the IV may have dismissed this whole project a priori as something from fantasy land. Maybe we ought to send Linc and his Chief over to Deyo tomorrow when they get in to actually look at their tapes. Informally, of course. Let the Chief set it up; matter of fact, don't send Linc, just send the Chief. Chiefs are forever coming and going along the waterfront, so nobody would notice. See what we get."

Mike nodded thoughtfully.

"That's probably not a bad idea, although from the sound of things, he's coming in tonight, so we'll only see two nights' worth of tapes." He looked over at the Exec. "And if we see something on his tapes that he didn't? Then what?"

"Then we hold another skull session with the Commodore and we figure out what to do next. We're going to be back out there ourselves next week, *if* they fix these fornicating feed pumps."

"That's not on the schedule."

"Yes, Sir, but we'll need an engineering trial to prove that the feed pumps can handle steaming loads."

Mike pushed away the coffee.

"If the higher ups conclude that there is something to all this," he said, "They sure as hell are not going to send Goldsborough to deal with it."

"But if they conclude that it is all bullshit, we can go out and screw around some more, see what we turn up, and nobody has to know."

"The Commodore would have to know. But what the hell can we do that the Deyo's of the world can't do? I mean, shit, she's an ASW specialist. Sonars up the gazoo, carries a helicopter, and they can even process sonobuoys. All we can do is ping."

"Yes, Sir," said Farmer, leaning forward. "But that's precisely it: we can ping in shallow water where the Deyo's sonar is useless: it's too damned big. So far, everything that's happened has happened inside the continental shelf: the U-boat sighting, the fishing boat going down with a bullet hole in her nameplate, our two contacts, all in water 300 to 500 foot deep, and all inside the Gulf Stream, too. Spruance's like Deyo need water 6000 foot deep for their sonar's to reach out there and touch someone."

Mike sat back in his chair, a surprised look on his face.

"You're back to believing this shit, aren't you," he said.

Farmer nodded once.

"I go back and forth on it. I'll admit that. But I want to know what Deyo means by normal anomalies—that's an oxymoron. If our guys can see something on his tapes that might be a sub on the snort, then I think we ought to go out there and try to find the sucker, before—"

"Before what?"

Farmer sighed and started rubbing his eyes with both hands.

"I don't know," he said, his voice muffled by his hands. "We're still missing something here."

The wardroom door opened and the Chief Engineer came back into the wardroom with the shipyard superintendent.

"Cap'n, we think we've found out what's eating those steam seals," he announced.

Mike looked at Farmer for a moment, and nodded his head fractionally, acknowledging that the Exec might be right. He then turned to the Engineer.

"OK, Snipe, sit down and tell me all about it. You know how I love main feed pump steam seals."

THIRTY NINE

USS Goldsborough, pierside, Mayport Naval Station, Wednesday, 30 April; 1630

Mike sat in his cabin, and stared with distaste at the paperwork piled in his in-basket. Out in the harbor he could hear the sounds of horns as two tugs berthed the Deyo, which had just come into the Mayport basin from the sea. He was tired, and not just from the day's work of meetings, walking around the ship to check on the repair work, fitness report counseling sessions with two of his not so good junior officers, a training session with the department heads, and the latest discussion with the Exec on the submarine. He was also tired from two wonderful, marathon nights on the house-boat, where he and Diane had made up for their respective dry spells. He had been only half-joking when he had whispered in her ear that it was a good thing the Group staff was getting back because he was too old for this pace of affairs. She had proceeded to demonstrate that he was not that old, but it had been a close run thing.

He speculated on their relationship for the ninety-ninth time. It was not that she was any more demanding than he was; they were both taking as big a measure of loving out of the situation as they could, knowing that it would soon become more difficult to do so. But the fact that it was forbidden and even dangerous for both of them, if for different reasons, made it all the more exciting. Once in the early hours he had again professed his love for her, and she had laughed softly in the darkness, rolled over on top of him and told him the facts of life, her face a dim blur framed in the darker shadow of her hair hanging in his face.

"This is called fucking, Mike, not love. Love is something altogether different. Love is intimacy over a long time; what we're doing now might lead to love, or it might not. But right now, this is something more basic: I need it and you need it and we're terrific in bed and damned lucky to have struck the spark in the first place, because from what I can tell, most people don't even get close. But let's not call it love, OK? Not yet, anyway. Both of us have probably missed our chance for love, for whatever reason, which is why we're doing this and now kiss me..."

He had obliged and soon forgotten her rebuff, if that was what it had been. He had a feeling now that there was more to it, but he was unwilling to disturb what they did have. The occasional weekend with one of the beach bunnies was good enough to take the horns down a little, but this was, like the lady said, something different.

But now it was Wednesday, and her husband was coming back in a few hours, and the Commodore was coming back and even the Deyo was coming back and tomorrow he would still have to deal with this submarine issue. At the very least he would have to go see the Commodore, and then maybe even the Admiral and the Group staff. He did not relish either prospect, especially if it elevated to a session with the Group staff, which he dreaded. He could already see the knowing smirks, the amused looks around the table, as always orchestrated by the politely caustic and ever so patronizing commentary from the Chief of Staff as he dealt with Montgomery the Misfit. Boy, do I have the ultimate put down line for that bastard, he thought. Right, just as long as you're prepared to fall on your sword out on the headquarters parade ground once you've used it.

The tugs across the basin gave out two long, final blats on their horns acknowledging that the harbor pilot was finished with them and that the Deyo was safely moored. Mike had arranged for Chief Sonarman Mackensie to ease on over there this evening to get a look at the passive sonar printouts and video tapes. A lot would depend on what was really on those tapes. Deyo had said there was nothing there, other than 'normal anomalies', and the Commodore had not called him from Norfolk, so perhaps the great submarine mystery was a dead issue, after all. But the image of Christian Mayfield's sister's face hovered on the edges of his mind. He had a sinking feeling that this was not over. His outside line phone rang.

"Captain," he said curtly.

He had decided long ago not to answer his phone with the normal, "USS Goldsborough, this is not a secure line, Commander Montgomery, Commanding Officer, speaking, Sir" routine. He figured if someone called his outside CO's line number, they knew it was the CO's phone.

"Captain, indeed," said a throaty voice.

"Diane!" he said, in a too loud voice, glancing around the cabin almost furtively.

"Wow. I think he misses me. Does he miss me?"

He grinned into the phone. "If you were here instead of wherever you are, I could show you."

"And what if I were on a certain houseboat, with a certain ill mannered parrot calling me names because I'm not properly dressed...?"

"Are you out of your mind? That plane's due in here in an hour and a half!"

"I know that. You know that. Hooker might even know that. But I have no intention of going to meet that plane. My very important husband will go from that plane directly to the office in the Admiral's big, black staff car to make sure there are no 'smoldering embers', as he likes to put it. After all, he's been gone three full days and God only knows what those cretins on the Staff might have done or failed to do. And when every *thing* has been put to bed, when all the important papers are tucked in for the night, and the Great Man has gone home, then and only then will he call me to come and get him. And depending on how quickly you can get here, and how interested you are, I may or may not be there to get his phone call. By the way, you ever hear of Victoria's Secret?

"Are you kidding? One of the J.O.'s got their catalogue and it made the rounds of the whole wardroom."

"Well," she said softly, "I get their catalog too. I even buy things from their catalog."

"That's not fair," he said.

"Don't whimper. Why don't you climb into that little sports car instead and go fast, kind Sir, and let's see what Victoria and I can work out. So to speak."

"Here I come," he said, in a voice that was somewhat weaker than he wanted it to be.

"No, not there, Dummy. Here," she said, hanging up.

Mike quickly called the quarterdeck and told them to ring him off. He looked at his watch. No time for changing clothes, or sprucing up, he thought. Just go. The four bells and "Goldsborough, departing" rang over the ship's announcing system. He walked quickly down to the quarterdeck, hoping there would not be the usual queue of officers with last minute paperwork. He returned the salutes of the OOD and was halfway down the brow when the Exec came trotting down the main deck. Mike cursed mentally, but paused on the brow to wait for the Exec, who gave a perfunctory salute to the OOD and hustled out to where Mike was standing.

"I just got a call from Commander Barstowe; the Commodore wants to see you at 0900 tomorrow morning. He thinks it's to discuss our little project, as he called it."

Mike paused for a moment, aware that the quarterdeck watch personnel were watching curiously.

"Did he elaborate?"

"No, Sir, just said 0900."

"Then make damn sure that Chief MacKensie gets over to Deyo tonight," said Mike. "And if he hits any kind of brick wall, do what you have to do to break it down. Or call me and I'll call Pierce at home if I have to."

The Exec nodded. "Chief MacKensie doesn't anticipate any problems; he knows the senior chief over there in Deyo—they served at sonar school together. He'll get the dope, if there is any. You'll be on the boat tonight, Sir?"

"Right; I'm headed there now. Give me a call if you need me to help with the Deyo stuff, and have the CDO or Chief Mac call me with the results of his little look-see."

"Aye, Aye, Sir. I'll probably call you, myself. I'm kind of curious. Have a real good evening," he concluded, saluting.

Mike returned the salute, and hurried down the rest of the brow to the pier, wondering fleetingly if the Exec meant anything more than his routine, end of the day farewell. Ben Farmer was a pretty perceptive officer, and Mike did not normally bolt off the ship like this. Time was, however, short. He reached the Alfa and got in, glancing over to the ship to see the small knot of people on the quarterdeck watching him go as he gunned the car down the pier. No way, he thought; there was simply no way they could know. And it had better stay that way, too.

FORTY

The Mayport Marina, Wednesday, 30 April; 2030

"You better git," Mike said, without conviction.

"You throwing me out of your bed, Sailor?"

Diane lay on her side, her upper body propped up on one elbow. Her right breast was level with Mike's right eye. He spoke again; the breast appeared to be paying attention.

"That plane came in at least an hour ago, and you are going to have some questions to answer."

"It's not like I don't have all the answers," she said. "I think I could say with a straight face that I'd been out fucking my brains out, and J.W. would give me a condescending smile and say something clever about going to a brain fucking contest unequipped."

Mike adjusted the level of his right eye and made a tentative probe with his tongue.

"Looks like you're equipped to me. From this aspect, that is."

The bedside phone began its electronic trilling. Diane swung herself out of bed and headed for the bathroom.

"If that's for me, I might as well stay here," she said as she closed the door.

"Captain," grunted Mike, pulling the phone across the bed from the bedside table.

"Yes, Sir, Captain, Ben here," came the XO's voice. "I think it's not over."

Mike groaned, and switched on the bed's reading light. He could hear the sounds of the shower coming from the bathroom. He looked at his watch. Woman liked to live dangerously, he thought.

"OK, what'd Chief Mac find out?"

"Uh, I think it might be better if you saw this stuff for yourself, Sir. Can maybe we come out to the boat?"

Mike glanced over at the bathroom door. The shower noises had stopped.

"Yeah, uh, sure, XO," he said, thinking quickly. "But make sure you bring along the presentation stuff we gave the Commodore, though."

The Exec seemed to hesitate for a second.

"Uh, Aye, aye, Sir. I think Linc's got that squirreled away in his room; we'll have to go find it. We'll be out in about twenty, maybe thirty minutes."

"That's fine, XO. See you here. You get chow?"

"Yes, Sir. I had dinner on board. Meat loaf."

"Meat loaf, hunh? Thirty-weight or forty-weight?"

"Forty weight at least."

"OK, I'll have some decent Scotch ready. See you in a bit." He hung up as Diane came back out of the bathroom, drying her hair vigorously with a towel. She retrieved her various articles of clothing, and put them on while continuing to rub the towel through her hair. Mike lay back and enjoyed the show of dexterity and wondered what might be accomplished in five minutes or so. She caught his look and smiled, picked up her purse and went back into the bathroom to tend to her makeup. She was back out in three minutes. Her eyes were shining; she fairly exuded an aura of well being.

"I'm impressed," said Mike, looking again at his watch. "But you need to dim that glow a little; the whole world will know what you've been doing."

"Not to worry," she said. "J.W. hasn't seen that glow for ten years. He wouldn't recognize it even if he did notice. I'll have my machine call your machine."

She blew him a quick kiss before he could say anything else, and slipped through the bedroom door. Hooker gave her a wolf whistle as she went through the lounge. "Hooker needs a girl friend," she called in a sing song voice from the hatchway.

Mike got up and headed for the shower himself. He figured he had about twenty minutes to get cleaned up and dressed in something that might suggest to his two visitors that he had been doing something more Captain-like than fucking *his* brains out for the past few hours. The Chief would probably not be fooled. He hoped that they would not pass Diane on the two lane road that led from the base to the marina. He was also grateful for the size and layout of the houseboat, which made it possible to separate the bedroom cabin from the main lounge. Maybe he would take them straight back to the back porch deck, at least for long enough to let the A/C system clear out the redolence of sex.

He was tempted to linger in the shower as he let the hot water soothe his muscular body. They did by God make the music together. He wondered now why the hell he had always sought out the younger women among the beach bunnies. Diane had to be close to forty, and yet she was infinitely more satisfying in bed than any of the nubile young lovelies. He acknowledged to himself that he still had much to learn about women. He chased away a disturbing tendril of thought about the possible consequences of an affair with the Chief of Staff's wife with the rationalization that the Chief of Staff would have more to lose from public exposure than he, an already out of favor Commander. Sounded good, anyway.

He was dressed in slacks, loafers, and sport shirt when the Exec and Chief Mackensie picked their way across the piers to the Lucky Bag, their khaki-clad figures appearing and disappearing through the circles of light shining down from walkway lights atop the pilings. The Chief was carrying several charts rolled up under his arm, and the Exec carried two briefcases. He greeted them at the gangplank, and escorted them back along the main deck to the screened porch overlooking the intracoastal waterway, thereby avoiding the interior of the boat. The waterway was quiet, with only a few boats plodding down the channel. The air was beginning to cool off after the heat of the day.

He set out three glasses, a silver water pitcher, an ice bucket, and pointed the tip of a bottle of Glenlivet at each in turn.

"I have club soda if you prefer," he said.

"A little water's fine, Cap'n" said the Chief.

"Fine for me, too, Sir," said the Exec.

Mike poured out the whiskey, and then sat back in the wicker arm chair while the other two adjusted their drinks.

"OK, guys. What did we learn from the good ship Deyo?"

Chief Mac leaned forward, putting his drink down on the edge of the glass topped table. He reached down to the floor for his collection of rolled up charts, scattering them around his chair until he found the waterfall print he was looking for. He unrolled it on top of the table into the circle of yellow light from a brass standing lamp. The paper was flimsy, like the variety used in a facsimile machine, and the light breeze from the water lifted the paper. The Exec pinned down one corner, and Mike another. The Chief reviewed with them what the lines meant, and then showed Mike the little red tick mark on the side of the waterfall.

"Right here," he said, "The passive operator saw that all the lines were beginning to draw together, makin' a mess. So he changed the frequency scale, which means that individual frequency lines are now separated by more physical space on the paper trace. You can see that here. Now, look right below this area."

"Those thick lines?"

"Yes, Sir. They start up right about here on the timeline, and they're way over here on the left, that's the low freq side. These are primaries, these here are harmonics. See how close the harmonic lines are together? That's another indicator of low freq noise: second harmonic of 10 Herz is only 20 Herz, whereas the second harmonic of 50 Herz is a 100. If the sound source is a big thumper, the harmonics all draw real close to the base freq."

"Which means?"

"Which means a big fuckin' diesel came on line right about the time the passive operator spread out the trace. And stayed on line: nice and stable, see—" He unrolled more of the scrolled trace. "You look down the trace for another hour and you see the smaller engines changing up and down—fishermen changing their boats' position a half a mile or so, and then slowing back down. This thing stays the same."

"Like a big diesel generator," said Mike softly, staring down at the line trace.

The Chief leaned back in his chair, nodding his head, but holding up two fingers, and staring at Mike.

"Two? Two engines?" said Mike.

"Yes, Sir. Two."

"But the trace only show one set of lines."

The Chief nodded, reached for his drink, took a hit, and then put it back down, and reached under the table again. He unrolled a second trace chart on top of the first one.

"I had me a talk with the guy who was on the *active* console that night. Because they were doin' passive search, they of course had the big SQS-53 shut down, so he didn't have anything to do but stay awake. The passive guy made a head call right about when the big engine came up, so it was actually the active guy who marked the trace. Now, the Deyo bein' a fancy ASW boat, they always record on mag tape what the array is drawing on the paper trace."

"So?" asked Mike.

The Exec leaned forward, joining the discussion.

"It means that they can replay the whole thing after the fact, anytime they want. So Chief Mac had 'em replay it, and he sent the replay to the paper trace again."

"Only this time," continued the Chief, "I had the passive processor do a frequency diversity algorithm on the signal coming off the mag tape before it went to the paper. The computer takes the broadband signal and breaks it down into all of its parts, and does a statistical comparison between what it's listening to and the normal statistical distribution of individual frequencies in a sound like that. If there's a difference, it concludes that there are two sources, so it does a sort to see if it can construct two sound lines, each with the correct distribution of frequency components and harmonics. If it can, we get this—" He unrolled a new paper trace. "You can see right here that the two big black lines are separated by an RCH, which equates to two sound sources, similar, but still two separate sources."

"Two generators."

"Which, if it's a diesel sub, would indicate a Foxtrot," said the Exec. "They have three main engines; they'd snort with two, and keep one lined up for a crash dive."

"So what we gotta do now," said the Chief, "Is get a training tape of a Foxtrot on the diesel, and make some comparisons."

Mike sat back in his chair, and considered the enormity of what they were telling him.

"What else could it be?" he asked.

"It could also be a medium sized merchant ship with twin diesel main engines, going either up or down the coast beyond radar range of the Deyo, but within a convergence zone of the Deyo's passive sonar," the Exec said.

"Were the water conditions right for convergence?" asked Mike, already knowing the answer. "Not deep enough is it?"

"You got it, Skipper," said the Chief. "But shallow water will sometimes channel sound for a long way, especially coming over the continental shelf. They coulda been listening in a sound channel; without radar contact, they'd have nothing to correlate this source with. That sound coulda been coming from sixty miles away, and their radar is good for about twenty-five. So it could be surface noise."

"But you don't think so, do you?"

"No, Sir. It's real unlikely."

"And the lines show almost no bearing drift," interjected the Exec. "A merchie underway in steady state steaming conditions would move across the bearing circle. They only go in two directions out here: into or away from port, and up and down the coast. Into and out of port directions would have eventually produced doppler; parallel to the coast would have produced bearing drift. We've got neither."

Mike nodded thoughtfully, swirling the ice cubes around in his drink. Then something else occurred to him.

"Why didn't the Deyo report this?" He looked from the Exec to the Chief.

"That's also kinda interestin'," the Chief said. "Seems like the two operators told their Chief, and the Chief told the ASW officer, and the ASW officer took it up the line, and then came back and told the Chief to forget about it. So he forgot about it, until I come askin' around."

Mike looked at the Exec. "Comment?"

The Exec shook his head. "All I can figure is the Deyo CO was predisposed to ignore anything that came out of this search drill."

"Or he was told to bury it, maybe," speculated Mike.

"Possible," said the Exec. "But not likely. It was the Commodore who tasked him to do this, and I don't think the Commodore would have told him to record the diesel band but ignore the results, if any."

"I wasn't thinking of the Commodore," replied Mike as he leaned back in his chair, his face in the shadow outside of the lamplight.

"Pierce Marshall keeps himself pretty well plugged in to the Group Staff, because that's where the nearest Admiral is. I'm wondering if Group didn't know about Deyo's little project, and if someone on the Group staff didn't instruct Deyo on how to play this one."

The Chief studied his glass, as he realized that the discussion was rapidly getting above his paygrade. Mike noticed his discomfiture, and shut it off.

"OK, XO, tomorrow, you, the Chief here, and Linc redo our presentation, and fold in this new data. I'm apparently on the Commodore's calendar first thing tomorrow, so I'll give him the gist of this, and suggest that the four of us go over it with him again, in his office this time. I'm also going to suggest he get Commander Barstowe into it. He's a level head and a straight shooter. Maybe when he sees it cold for the first time he can find a hole in this deal."

"Aye, aye, Sir," said the Exec, finishing his drink. The Chief did likewise and began to gather up the trace charts.

"Chief," said Mike, "Can you get those comparison tapes from the local ASW training office here on the base?"

"No, Sir, they won't have 'em, but the Spruances carry a collection of those tapes for their mag trainers; I'll go to one of the other ships and ask to borrow the use of it."

"Can we play those tapes?"

"Goldy? No, Sir, no way. But I can get them to run the tape and push it to the trace paper; it's the paper we want, anyway, so's we can compare it to these waterfalls."

"Good man," said Mike. "Keep it discreet—I think you can see we have two problems here."

The Chief grinned. "Gotcha, Cap'n. Long as we can go back out there and go find this sewer pipe, I don't care what kinda games we gotta play ashore."

Mike grinned back. "That's exactly what I want to do," he said. Beyond the porch screens, the waterway was lost in the moonless darkness.

FORTY ONE

The Submarine Al Akrab, Jacksonville operating areas, Wednesday, 30 April;
2100

The officers stood up around the metal table in the tiny wardroom
as the Captain and the Musaid came through the curtained entrance. The
Captain slid sideways into his chair at the head of the table, and nodded
once. All of the officers except the Deputy sat down together. The
Musaid remained standing behind the Captain.

The wardroom was hot and stuffy, as was the entire boat, and three
small electric fans mounted on the bulkheads did nothing more than dis-
place the stale air. The Deputy stood by a briefing easel at the end of the
table, to which he had appended some navigation charts. His face shone
with a layer of perspiration, and there were large dark circles on his shirt
around his armpits. The Captain looked at him expectantly. The Deputy
cleared his throat.

"Sir. My briefing this evening concerns the reconnaissance we shall
make on the entrance to the Mayport naval base river in preparation for
the mine laying operation. I have three charts. The first is the ocean
approach chart to the St. Johns river and Jacksonville, Florida. The
second is the harbor chart of the entrance to the naval basin itself, and
the third is a schematic. If this is satisfactory I shall continue. Sir."

The Captain nodded again; he glanced through the crack in the
curtain to his left and saw the steward and motioned to him with his head.
The steward pushed a cup of hot tea through the curtain and hastily withdrew, not wanting to see any more guns. The Deputy waited patiently
until he had the Captain's attention again.

"Sir," he began. The other officers watched attentively. "I will
recommend a straight-in approach to the river entrance at about 0100,
three nights from now, on a rising tide and a new moon."

"Why that particular time?" asked the Captain. He anticipated the
answer, but he wanted to verify the Deputy's tactical reasoning.

"Sir. The new moon gives dark conditions. The rising tide counter-
acts the river currents and minimizes the cross current at the entrance.
And if we ground, the water will be coming up and not down, so that we
might pull ourselves off."

"We will not ground, Deputy," said the Captain with a chilly smile.
"Because you will, of course, do a perfect job of piloting us in and out,
yes?"

"Sir." The sheen of perspiration on the Deputy's forehead was
bright in the fluorescent light.

257

"But the timing is correct, Deputy. If the sea will cooperate and make escape routes available, only fools would not take advantage of it. Continue."

The Deputy brightened.

"Sir. There is a prominent, lighted range on the north shore of the St. Johns river that allows for good visual navigation during an approach. The range consists of two towers, one with a white light and one with a yellow light, in line, with a quarter mile separation. I shall fix the periscope on that range, and make course recommendations left or right to maintain us on the range against the currents."

"Do you propose that we enter the river itself?" asked the Captain.

The Deputy was aghast.

"No, Captain. Absolutely not. As I understand it, we need only to approach within 500 yards of the actual entrance, turn, and fire the mines into the channel."

"That is correct, although we need to get a bit closer than that, because the river current coming downstream will shorten the actual distance travelled by the mines upstream. We need to come into about 250 yards of the defined channel junction, turn completely around, and then fire the mines into the junction. And when I say junction, I am referring to the junction between the river channel and naval base channel. The carrier will stick to the defined channel area, so we must be precise."

"Sir," asked the Weapons officer. "When do we intend to plant the mines?"

The Captain looked around the table at their expectant faces. So far, he had not revealed any of his plans. Perhaps it was time.

"The night before the carrier returns to port," he announced. "We await a report from our intelligence services as to which day the Coral Sea will return. We have indications that it will be within a week."

There was a murmuring of anticipation around the table. The end of the mission was within sight. A week!

"This must still be confirmed," warned the Captain. "And we must be even more vigilant than before. The Americans may raise security precautions around their base with the imminent return of such a large ship."

"Would it not be better to fire the mines on this reconnaissance run, than to come in so close two times?" asked the Chief Engineer.

"It would be safer, yes," replied the Captain. "But there are many large ships that use this channel. We take the chance of having the mines go off under a tanker or one of those automobile carriers if they sit there for five or seven days."

"Can they not be set to lie inert for a set number of days, and then turn themselves on?"

"They can," interjected the Weapons officer. "But the Captain does not trust the delay mechanisms. If they fail, or malfunction, the mines might not activate for days or even weeks. Or worse, they might activate at once with zero delay."

"This is true," said the Captain. "If this practice run into the coast goes well, we could indeed fire the mines and set their delay circuits. But there is a more fundamental problem, Engineer. We do not know for sure what day the carrier returns; even if we did, it might be changed in the course of a week's time. Once the delay circuits are set, and the mines deployed, there is no way to go back and reset the mines. Thus I wish to wait until the last night to lay the mines, and, since that operation must proceed flawlessly, we will conduct a practice."

"Sir," the Engineer persisted. "I do not mean to offer objection. But we risk much to conduct such a practice: we must come in on the surface right up to the enemy's coast. He must have guards at the base, and radar surveillance of the approaches to the river and the base. Surely somebody or some thing will detect a darkened surface contact and raise the alarm. I recognize we must do this once, but twice?"

The Captain sat back in his chair, looking down the middle of the table. He had thought long and hard about these very points. It was extremely risky, and the Engineer was right: they had to do it once, but twice?

"I acknowledge your opinion, Chief Engineer," replied the Captain. "And I value your concern and questions. Here is my reasoning: the Americans do not guard their naval bases from the sea. They only guard them from the land. We have good, firm intelligence of this. There is no radar surveillance of the entrance to that river, or any others. Yes, the ships in the harbor may have a radar on for maintenance, but a destroyer radar's minimum range is beyond where we will be operating; we would be in their radars' shadow zone. But more importantly, the Americans dismiss any threat coming from the sea, because their Navy is vast and powerful. They appreciate no threat, therefore we approach with some impunity." He paused to sip some tea.

"Second, when we go in to actually deploy the mines, the operation must succeed. There will be no room for surprises or last minute discoveries, such as the water depth is not sufficient, or the current too strong, or the presence of a physical barrier of some kind. We have charts and intelligence reports, but until we go there and see with our own eyes, we do not know the ground truth of the situation in the river mouth. If we

259

discover impediments on this reconnaissance, we will have time to withdraw and several days to think of solutions, time we would not have if we wait until the last minute to try it for the first time."

The men around the table nodded at the Captain's arguments. The Captain did not enunciate the third reason, which was that he wanted to test himself, to confirm that his nerve held. He was tired; they were all tired. The waiting, the hiding, the four hour battery rechargings every other day from twelve to four in the morning, short rations of water, and the humid heat had all begun to exact a toll on human endurance and morale in the submarine.

He himself had spent too many hours iron-eyed in his bunk wondering, worrying, and, worst of all, doubting. He was going to have to push his submarine's nose right into the American Navy's complacent face, not once, but twice. The more he had thought about the mission, the more important the mines had become. He was no longer quite so sanguine about their chances of success with the torpedo attack. There were so many unknowns: from which direction would the carrier approach? The carrier only had to be lucky once to get by them; he and his submarine had to be lucky every time he made a choice about where and when to set the ambush. How many escorts would she have, and of what type? Would there be the accursed aircraft? Would the Americans make their passage in bright, broad daylight, or would the Al Akrab have the mercy of darkness? There were so many variables that their chances were less than even. But the mines only had to lie in wait in the mud of the river bottom to tear the bottom out of the first very large ship that came across them. And the mines heaped a double insult on the torpedo attack: it would be doubly egregious when the Americans finally deduced that he had sailed right up to their doorstep to plant them. The Musaid cleared his throat discreetly behind him. He realized they were looking at him. He sipped more tea.

"Deputy, continue: show us the charts of the approach, and your schematic of the maneuver."

"Yes, Captain. We can approach to this point on the chart from virtually any direction, right up to the area of this buoy which the Americans call the sea buoy. It watches five miles offshore, and marks the seaward end of the river channel. On a clear night, the lighted range is visible from the sea buoy, so we would turn on range course and close in. We will need to surface nine miles from the sea buoy because of shallow water."

He flipped over the sea chart and unrolled the approach chart.

"From the sea buoy in to the actual river entrance there are six buoys, alternating in number on either side of the channel. They are lighted, and the channel is four hundred yards wide. If we could use radar the channel would be clearly marked, but we will, of course, be radar silent. On a visual approach, we must depend on the lighted range ashore, and confirm our track when we see the buoys on either side. We shall drive in at low power, on the battery to reduce noise, to this point here, which I have marked point A, twist in place, lay silent for the time it takes to fire the mines, and then exit at high speed on a reverse of the approach course."

He stopped and looked expectantly at the Captain. The Captain nodded slowly, studying the chart and the proposed track. Then he spoke.

"I have one change. Submarines cannot twist on their engines very well in the best of circumstances. We will be in the mouth of a river, with currents, eddies, and cross currents, and shallow water. It might take us five minutes to twist around, during which we would be set down in some unknown direction. No. Deputy, set up the track so that we execute a turn in the channel entrance, and then we will back in to the firing point, stop, come ahead slowly, simulate deploying the mines, and then escape at high speed."

"Very well, Sir," said the Deputy, making notes on a piece of paper.

"Sir." It was the Engineer again.

"Yes, Engineer?"

"Sir: what do we do if we encounter civilians, or a fisherman, or even a merchant ship.?"

"We will fly an American flag, and pretend that we are an American submarine. We will, of course, do a surveillance before we start in, and let any fishing boats or merchants out or in as the case might be. But once we surface, we will be an American submarine. You made a good point on being darkened: that would attract attention. We will show dimmed running lights, and a dim white light on the American flag. That will not fool any military people, but, as I said earlier, they do not watch the sea. Civilians will want to believe it. There should not be much traffic at 0200. It is as safe as we can make it, Engineer."

"Shall we flood down so that the decks are awash, Captain?" asked the Weapons officer. "That would do away with the distinctive silhouette of a submarine."

"I will have to think about that. We can do that if we are surprised by something coming down the river. But we are going to be in shallow waters; flooding down changes our effective draft, and raises the risk of grounding on a sandbar. It also makes the boat very much harder to maneuver. But, your point is well taken. I will keep that option open. Now, Weapons, describe the mine launch procedures."

The Weapons officer consulted his notebook for a moment.

"Sir," he said. "For safety purposes, the mines are never activated while still in the tube. We will access their computers with the test set to double check settings, and then activate the memory battery. This can be done one hour before launch, but no earlier. The lanyards have already been attached when we loaded the mines. After we verify settings with the test set, we pressurize the flasks and fire them as we would any torpedo. They are expelled from the tubes at an effective speed of about thirty knots. They will go as far as gravity allows and settle to the bottom. As soon as they are fired, the setback activates their clocks, the clock turns on memory, the computer sends the settings to the sensors, and they are ready for business even as they land on the bottom. Effectively, there is a short delay to allow the submarine to get clear. Except for the fourth mine, whose computer does not seem to be functioning properly. That one I worry about."

"Which is why we will hold that one back for an emergency situation at sea," the Captain reminded him.

"Yes, Sir, but even then, I worry that it might arm at once and blow our stern off. These are very large mines."

"Yes, it might arm at once, but it should not fire at once if the magnetic field is decreasing, as it would be after being fired out the stern tubes."

The Weapons officer seemed to want to argue, but decided to return to his briefing. He consulted his notes again.

"Normally we would fire the mines at 1000 yard intervals, so that they would be spaced far enough apart to prevent countermining the entire field when one mine goes off. In this case, however, we want them to countermine, to triple the explosive power of the blast under the carrier's hull. I recommend, therefore, that we fire them at quick intervals so that they group together on the bottom."

The Engineer, who had been mentally chewing on the remark the Weapons officer had made about he fourth mine blowing the submarine's stern off, had a question.

"Regarding the fourth mine, Captain?" asked the Engineer.

"Yes," nodded the Captain, patiently.

"I understand that you have decided not to deploy the fourth mine because its computer is unreliable, and that you are keeping it to act as a torpedo if we are being pursued closely by an enemy ship. But it seems to me that, if the computer is unreliable, we have no way of knowing what it will do if fired. It might indeed arm and fire on even a decreasing field. I seem to recall that the firing decision is based upon first sensing a rising field, and then the decreasing field, which means the target is passing overhead. It might—"

The Captain raised his hand, his expression showing exasperation. "There are four mines. The fourth would not accept the settings for the carrier; it would only accept a setting of first ship, first encounter, any tonnage. I elected to keep that one back from the channel mining so that it would not go off on the first fishing boat that came down the channel, with the possibility of setting off the other three in sympathetic detonations. Now: remember that we had to give up our four defensive torpedoes in the after tubes to load the mines. This mine will serve as a substitute in an emergency, since it can be fired into the path of a pursuer and get his attention while we escape. I would order such a firing only in a desperate emergency, and I will ensure that we are moving away at high speed before doing so. That is my decision."

The Engineer flushed and looked down at the table. The Captain glanced at the Deputy and saw that he was finished with his briefing.

"Now," he continued. "This is what I wish to be done: Deputy, you shall construct a navigational exercise which simulates going to the channel, turning, laying the mines, and withdrawing. I want all the navigation aids plotted out, and a trial paper run made for bearings, turn points, and turn times. Weapons, I want the firing consoles manned so that we practice the firing of the mines at the appropriate time. We will surface tonight to recharge batteries, and I want the diving team to participate by exercising the flooding maneuvers to hold the boat with decks almost awash without actually submerging. Musaid, I will want the special team to be positioned up forward, ready to go on deck to deal with any close up surprises we might encounter in the channel."

He looked up at them. "We have three days to practice this operation, and I want to take maximum advantage of that time. Deputy, leave the charts. That is all."

The officers arose immediately and filed out of the wardroom, one at a time due to the constricted space. Finally, only the Captain and the Musaid remained. The Captain turned in his chair to look up at the Musaid.

"Well?" he asked.

The Musaid walked around the table and examined the charts. The Captain got out of his chair and passed his empty cup out to the waiting steward, who refilled it and passed it back through the curtain at once. The Captain walked up to the charts.

"Do you think we should lay the mines the first time?" he asked.

"No, Effendi. I think you are correct in going in to take a look. Who knows what surprises the Americans might have for us."

"I am more concerned with what surprises the river might have for us," muttered the Captain, studying the chart. "I also need the rehearsal to imprint the operation on my mind. That way I can react to unexpected threats or emergencies on the night we actually plant the mines against the background of having done it once. That is important, Musaid."

"Seven days," mused the Musaid, quietly. The noise of the three fans almost buried his voice.

"It is difficult to believe we have come this far and may yet strike the treacherous Americans. It astonishes me that no one has found us."

The Captain sipped his tea before meeting the Musaid's eyes.

"We must not underestimate the American Navy," he cautioned. "But it is difficult to respect them when we have been able to prowl at will in their own waters. The Colonel was right: they are supremely arrogant, Allah be thanked."

"And what of this fourth mine business?" asked the Musaid.

The Captain remained silent for a minute.

"It would be risky to use it," he replied. "But even if it armed and fired right away, our hull would be as a pencil, pointing at the shock wave. The surface ship, on the other hand, would be right on top of the shock wave. The explosion will be vast, but so will the confusion that follows, which would allow us to get away. I shall simply have to judge the situation and decide."

The Musaid nodded. "I shall prepare the diving team's part of the rehearsal plan," he said.

"Very well."

The Musaid stood back, but did not leave the wardroom. The Captain remained, staring down at the charts. He could say all he wanted to about using that mine as a close range torpedo: the fact was that a warhead that large would probably do quite a bit of damage to the submarine if it went off prematurely. The fourth mine was an unknown. To fire it might indeed invite self destruction. On the other hand, if he were in that serious a situation, the final paragraph of their mission orders, known only to him, would be invoked as the Lieutenant Colonel had reminded him. The order made it explicitly clear that he was to sink the Al Akrab rather than give up any physical evidence that would point to the origin of this operation should it go wrong. And if he had to do that, he was determined that he would take any American naval pursuers with him. So the fourth mine might solve two problems for him. He studied the close-in chart and tried to visualize what the enemy's front door might look like.

FORTY TWO

Destroyer Squadron Twelve Headquarters, Mayport Naval Station, Thursday, 1 May; 0840.

Mike sat in an armchair in Barstowe's office waiting for the Commodore to finish a meeting with three other Commanding Officers. The DesRon 12 staff was humming again now that the Commodore had returned from Norfolk. Mike noted that there was much coming and going through the suite of offices in the old building. Barstowe had taken a quick briefing from Mike on the status of Goldsborough's engineering repairs, and was now on the phone with the base police about a traffic accident involving a staff yeoman.

Life goes on, Mike thought. He was always struck by the diversity of responsibilities imposed on senior officers in the Navy, whether ashore or afloat. Every facet of everybody's life was somehow mission related and therefore the Command's business. He turned over for the hundredth time in his mind the whole business of the submarine, shutting out the intermittent stream of petty officers and junior officers coming in to see Barstowe.

Beyond the previous facts, what did they know: Deyo's tapes revealed the presence of what could be a diesel powered submarine recharging her batteries on or near the surface. The ASW school had evaluated Goldsborough's tapes as "possible". Diane really liked to have the hollow of her throat kissed.

"Captain? The Commodore will see you now, Sir."

With a mild flush rising across his face, Mike got up and followed the yeoman down the hall to the Commodore's office, passing the three Commanders as they came through the batwing doors. They exchanged greetings, sizing each other up as CO's did, and then he went into the Commodore's office.

"Mike, sit down," barked the Commodore. He continued to scribble on a yellow legal pad for a minute before putting it aside and looking up.

"So Deyo drew a blank, hunh?"

Mike took a deep breath. "Not quite, Commodore."

Captain Aronson's face began to gather in a frown. Mike went on to explain what his Chief had found out from the Deyo tapes. The Commodore had set his mouth in a flat line by the time Mike had finished.

"Lemme get this straight," the Commodore said. "Deyo's message said nothing there, but the tapes show the sound line of a snorkeling submarine?"

"What *could* be the sounds of twin main engines on a diesel boat, Commodore. And it could also be a distant merchie with a pair of big diesels transiting offshore and propagating the sound lines through an unusual convergence zone or sound channel. The point is that amongst the fishing boats out doing their thing in the Mayport opareas, two big diesels came up on the waterfall screen at around 1 in the morning, and ran for about three hours without bearing drift or doppler, and then faded off the displays."

"Sonofabitch!" exclaimed the Commodore. He leaned back in his chair and studied Mike's face before continuing.

"We both know that there's not enough depth excess out there for convergence zones," he said. "And the normal deep sound channel is at 3000 feet. So what's your take on all this?"

Mike paused for a moment, glancing out through the large, tinted plate glass window at the forest of ship's masts along the waterfront.

"I'm not sure what to make of it, Commodore," he sighed. "If you want to believe that there's been an unident lurking around the Jax opareas for the past couple of weeks, then you can make a lot of these things support the proposition. On the other hand, there's ambiguity associated with each factor in the case."

"Why do you suppose Deyo didn't report the sound lines from the big diesels?"

"I'm not entirely sure, Commodore. According to my Chief, the presence of the sound lines were purportedly relayed up the chain in the ship, but the command ruled that it wasn't worth reporting. The Chief got that from his counterpart in Deyo. Last night I suggested to my XO that maybe Deyo had been told to bury this whole deal, but the XO pointed out that you were the one tasking Deyo to go have a look in the first place."

"And?"

"And, it's not beyond the realm of possibility that one of the I.V.'s buddies up at Group told him to put a lid on it."

The Commodore looked at him for a long moment, and then swivelled around in his chair to look out the large window himself. Without turning back, he began speaking, almost as if he were musing aloud.

"Something doesn't quite add up here. We get this hare-brained report of a U-boat sighting, we go look for something, find nothing, then a fishermen goes down for no apparent reason, leaving behind an oil slick and a nameboard with a bullet hole in it, the boat ending up on the bottom with no visible fatal damage, so we go out looking again, get a contact this time, lose it, get another one that acts a lot like a decoy—and I talked to the Master Chiefs up there at the School, by the way, and they think the decoy contact was indeed a decoy—lose that, give it all up for Lent, and now Deyo comes back in with a negative report, but their sonar gang has a waterfall that might be a pigboat on the snort. If it's not a distant merchie..."

Mike spoke to the back of the big chair.

"The thing that I keep hanging up on is what XO has been calling the motive. If there is a gomer hiding out in the opareas, why the hell is he here? I mean, Chief Mac thinks it's a Foxtrot. OK, say it's a Foxtrot—is it reasonable that the Soviets would deploy a diesel electric antique into one of our fleet operating areas? It simply doesn't wash. We speculated that it might be a test of some kind, something the Fleet Commander set up to see if we would notice, you know, his big readiness kick. Like the Barry business with the EW signal. But the USN doesn't have any conventional boats. I'm stumped."

The Commodore remained silent. Outside his office three phones began ringing at once. Monday morning. Except it was Thursday, Mike thought irrelevantly. The Commodore swivelled the chair back around again. It occurred to Mike that the Commodore suddenly looked older.

"So what do you recommend, Captain?" he asked softly.

Mike recognized the ploy—when you don't know what to do, ask your subordinates for a recommendation. They might even come up with something. He took a mental deep breath.

"I recommend that Commander Barstowe come over to Goldy later on today and listen to the whole pitch, from start to finish. I presume he's reasonably cold on the subject, so maybe he can give us an unbiased look. Maybe even come up with a course of action. I, for one, am not ready to go to the Group with this—there are too many technical ambiguities, even if we could get past the biggest question of why would this guy be here."

The Commodore nodded.

"I concur. And, yes, Bill Barstowe is cold on it because I've kept him out of the loop so that at some point he could do just this kind of an appraisal. He knows we're working an issue, but not the details. And I guess I have to go do some snooping up at Group to see who might be playing the backfield on this issue. When can you go to sea again?"

"The snipes tell me they'll have that pump set back together by tomorrow, so we can light off probably Monday, and if everything tests out, get out to sea by Wednesday. We can go faster, but we'd have to work all weekend—"

The Commodore shook his head impatiently.

"No, no, I don't want to get into that. It's not like we're talking about a deployment here. Keep an even strain going, but don't bust your guys' humps. Meanwhile, I'm gonna have to go scratch around on this submarine deal. The thing is, if we all decide down here that there might in fact be an unidentified boat out there, the next question is who do we send out. I mean, we have the world's supply of heloes here, P-3's over in Jax, Spruances—the best ASW forces in the Lant fleet. If it comes to it, we can probably find this gomer and smoke him out."

"In shallow water, on the margins of the Gulf Stream, Commodore?"

The Commodore opened his mouth as if to speak, and closed it again. He paused, thinking.

"Yeah, you're right. This whole deal's been over the shelf, hasn't it. What we're talking about here is active sonar. Shit, Goldy's the only straight stick active pinger we've got down here—all these other guys would just blow each other out of the water with those monster, low frequency sonars. But the heloes, now, the heloes could catch his ass, 'cause they can dip an active sonar into the water or drop active buoys. But I'm getting ahead of myself: we still haven't concluded that there is a boat out there. Or why."

"The why bit is the hard part," said Mike, getting up. "You want me to talk to Bill?"

"No, I'll brief him. Plan on this afternoon. I may even come along. Your people keeping this under wraps for now?"

"Yes, Sir, although we gained some more converts to the cause once Chief Mac showed the Deyo's waterfalls to the other sonar girls."

"OK; we'll take a look this afternoon. You do understand that, if we all agree there's the possibility of an unidentified submarine lurking in the opareas, we'll have a *national* issue on our hands, not a local problem?"

"Yes, Sir," said Mike glumly.

"OK. And before we get to that, of course, we'll have to go up the mountain to see your good buddies at Group."

"Yes, Sir. But I thought you were going to mention it to them up in Norfolk."

The Commodore shook his head.

"The time wasn't right—we were so wrapped up in budget drills and scheduling fights that I couldn't bring myself to raise a Weird Harold like this. And before you say anything, yes, basically, I procrastinated—I wanted to see what Deyo came up with. This whole thing remains so ambiguous. But now I think we have enough data points that I have to take it up the line."

"I can hardly wait," said Mike.

"I don't want to, either. But maybe Bill can see the flaw in this mess."

Mike shook his head. "I feel like we ought to be going to GQ over this, not just sitting here talking about it. I realize that—"

"Yeah, that's the problem," interrupted the Commodore again. "We have barely enough steaming hours and flight hours allocated these days to keep basic readiness up to snuff, and nobody would give this story the time of day unless we have a very convincing case—like you said, we can make the various data points fit the curve, but the data points themselves don't necessarily produce the curve."

"And the basic question—if he's there, why is he there?"

"Beats the shit out of me," said the Commodore with a sigh. "But when we figure that out, then we may go to GQ."

"I just don't want to find it out the hard way," said Mike.

"I'm open to suggestions, Captain. But until you or somebody thinks of something, let's take another look at the ASW data. Absent the smoking gun, we'll have to take this thing one step at a time. I'll have Bill come over this afternoon."

FORTY THREE

USS Goldsborough, pierside, Mayport Naval Station, Thursday, 1 May; 1700

The DesRon Twelve Chief Staff Officer leaned back in his chair and rubbed his eyes. Sitting around him at the wardroom table were Mike, the Exec, Linc Howard, and Chief MacKensie. They were waiting for Barstowe's reaction to their two hour presentation. The voices of the sweepdown crew could be heard on deck outside; the announcing system on the ship next door called away supper for the crew. The smells and sounds of evening meal preparation in the wardroom galley could be sensed through the pantry window.

They had gone through the whole thing, from the first reports of sighting to the Deyo's passive sonar tapes that suggested a possible snorkeling submarine. Mike had watched the Chief Staff Officer, trying to gauge his reactions as the briefing progressed. A nagging thought had been twitching at the back of his mind about the whole subject, something that Diane had said, but he could not get his mental claws on it. Barstowe had asked few questions, preferring to concentrate on the data being presented. He had made only a few notes, which Mike had tried to read from the head of the table, but Barstowe wrote in the tiny script of the professional meeting goer. He leaned forward now, consulting his notes.

"I'm inclined to believe that there is—maybe was is more precise—something there," he began. "I'm still hung up on the why question, just like everyone else."

Mike and the Exec exchanged glances. Bingo, Mike thought, as Barstowe continued.

"Most of the data is, as you've pointed out, ambiguous. It is possible that the Deyo contact is a merchie at long distance, and that the sound carried through some anomaly in the waters offshore. But we all know that you don't normally get convergence zones over the continental shelf, nor can we see a deep sound channel—the water is simply too shallow. The other thing I noticed is the timing and the placing of the Deyo's sound contact: three hours, more or less, from start to finish, and the source is somewhere along the western, inshore margins of the Gulf Stream, in the vicinity of the Mayport fishing fleet. Right where and when a guy would choose to snorkel if he wanted to mask what he was doing, and timed to catch any potential listeners at the ebb of human effectiveness. I also note that everything that's happened in connection with this business has been in this same general area where we have permanently turbulent sound conditions. The fishing boat went down in the same longitudinal area. This suggests to me a chain of related events, not coincidence."

He looked up. "I think there's somebody out there."

The other four men around the table let out a collective sigh.

"I'm still curious why Deyo didn't see it that way—" began Mike.

"That's a separate issue," interrupted Barstowe firmly. "Let's stay on the Soviet sub issue for the moment."

Mike was surprised at the sudden authority in Barstowe's voice. Barstowe was supposed to be cold on the submarine matter, but it sounded as if he knew something about the Deyo's reporting discrepancy. The Exec spoke up.

"You suppose this is some kind of test?" he asked. "You know, the Fleet Commander gets a guy to hang around, and he sees how long it takes all these Mayport ASW hotshots to tumble to the presence of an unident in the area?"

"No, I don't," said barstowe, shaking his head. "First of all, we don't own any more conventional subs, except for one on the west coast that they use for oceanographic research. The US submarine force is a nuclear Navy. It would probably have to be a Canadian or a Brit to be enlisted for such a scheme, but that would be really risky—one of our guys might get trigger happy, and then we'd have a real mess on our hands."

"The rules of engagement wouldn't permit somebody to just launch an ASW torpedo," offered Linc.

"Yes, but you could never be too sure about that," said the Exec. "Catch an unident in our territorial waters, a U.S. destroyer might shoot first and ask questions later, especially if the submarine did something to make the destroyer think he'd been fired on."

Mike and Barstowe exchanged patient glances, acknowledging to each other that neither the ASW officer nor the Exec had it quite right.

"It's a little more complicated than all that, guys," said Mike. "There are standard procedures for dealing with an unident or even a Soviet sub caught in home waters, and there are a lot of steps to walk through before anybody can start shooting. But back to the proposition: if this were a test, too many people would have to know about an operation like that in advance, especially if they were introducing a foreign submarine. I think at least the Group Commander would have been cut in, and then we would not ever have been sent out the way we were."

"And if you believe that the fishing boat incident was a part of all this, the exercise idea goes out the window," added Barstowe. Mike nodded, and then addressed Linc Howard.

"Linc, you and Chief Mac gather all this stuff up and put it in a safe place."

Howard quickly understood that the Captain wanted to talk to the CSO and the Exec alone. He and the Chief gathered up the briefing materials and left.

Mike got up and stared out one of the portholes. He tried to remember what it was that Diane had said their first night together that had lit a small fuse in his mind. He turned around to look at the other two officers. Then he remembered: it wasn't just the Russians who had Foxtrot class submarines.

"This whole business has gone on over a period of a few weeks," he began. "This would imply that, if there is a guy out there, he's waiting for something. Now if this is a Fleet Commander's drill, and it's a Brit, Canadian, or other friendly, he's waiting to be "discovered", and the Fleet Commander is waiting for a report. But if this is not a test, then what is this guy waiting for."

He paused for a moment.

"What do submarines always wait for?"

"Targets?" said Barstowe, studying Mike's face.

Mike turned to look right at him. The elements of a very disturbing idea had begun to take shape in his mind.

"Right," he said. "Targets. Or in this case, maybe one target in particular."

Barstowe frowned.

"A target?!" he asked, incredulously. "Shit, Mike,, you're talking an act of war here. We're not at war with the Russians or anybody else, for that matter. And if he wanted to shoot somebody, he sure as hell has had the chance for all this time he's been out there, if we count the first reports as accurate."

"Maybe the target he's waiting for isn't here yet," said Mike. "And that's the distinction I'm making here: a specific target, not just any old ship that comes along. Something that would be worth all the waiting, and maybe even being caught afterwards."

Barstowe was silent for a moment, thinking.

"Like one of the carriers," he said, finally.

The other two men looked at each other.

"Well," continued Barstowe, "The Saratoga has been inport for the whole time, and isn't going to sea again for another month. The Forrestal is in the yard in Philly, and that leaves the Coral Sea, who's down in the Caribbean. Now I can see a Soviet sub maybe wanting to bag a super-carrier, but Coral Sea? She's a training carrier, older than Goldy, and probably going out of commission pretty soon."

Mike walked over to the counter to refill his coffee cup. Diane had maybe hit the nail on the head. It's not a Russian sub.

"If it's a Foxtrot, you're automatically assuming it's a Soviet Foxtrot," he began. "I agree that proposition is ludicrous. But what if it's a third world gomer?"

Barstowe looked at him blankly for a minute. Mike pressed on.

"Coral Sea's a training carrier now. But she hasn't always been a training carrier. And I know one guy who has a reason to do something dramatic to the Coral Sea. The guy in the green sheets over there in Libya, Muammar the K. Coral Sea was the carrier that bombed that phony tent he had set up in his headquarters compound, remember? Killed his adopted daughter or niece, or something. And created a bad day out at the capital's airport and various parts of the city. Now, Libya has Foxtrots. Right, XO?"

The Exec, startled, scrambled up from the table and went to the bookshelf.

"I think so, Captain, but let me check Jane's."

He flipped through the pages of *Jane's Fighting Ships* for a minute, and then nodded.

"Yes, Sir, six Foxtrot class submarines, although Jane's says most of them are questionable in terms of being able to go to sea."

He looked up.

"But a fully operational Foxtrot could get here, no sweat. Those diesel boats have long legs. The Germans did it routinely."

Barstowe let out a long, soft whistle.

"You think maybe the Libyans have sent one of their subs over here to get even for something that happened, what, three years ago? Mike, we're really reaching here."

Mike put down his coffee cup and began slowly pacing the length of the table.

"I know, I know," he began. "That's a big jump to make with what little evidence we have, but look at it this way: we think we had a submarine out there, based on the contact and the decoy business. We think it's a diesel boat—the "U-boat" description fits. The Deyo's tapes suggest, not prove, but suggest it's a Foxtrot, based on engine configuration. Now—Foxtrots: only the Soviets and their Third World clients have Foxtrot class submarines. It's been one of their more popular export items. The Russians wouldn't do this; the stakes are much too high right now for them to be screwing around in our waters with any kind of submarine, much less a diesel boat. *If* it's a submarine, and *if* it's a Foxtrot, and *if* it's not a Soviet, that leaves Third World. From our perspective, the Third World has good guys, neutral guys, and bad guys. Eliminate good guys and neutrals for a minute, and focus on the bad guys. Cui bono, as the cops say, right, XO? Who stands to gain? What country with Foxtrots would come to Mayport? Big Chief Greensleeves over there makes a pretty good candidate. He has the motive, revenge, he's got the ego to dream it up and then do it, and he has the means: six Russian Foxtrot subs, only one of which has to be seaworthy to pull this off."

He paused for a moment to gather his thoughts, oblivious now to the expressions on the other officers' faces as they watched him silently. He reached for his coffee, drained it, and put the cup back down.

"What's happened on this end also makes sense in this scenario. Everything we have is ambiguous, admittedly, but: if there were a pigboat lurking out there waiting to attack just any old thing, it would have already happened. But nothing's happened, except that we continue to get whiffs. This sucker's waiting for something, and it's not a destroyer, because he's had several chances to bag a tin can, yours truly included, now that I think of it. It has to be something big, something worth all the effort of covertly sending a boat 6000 miles. And why Mayport? Because *the* target lives here in Mayport. She's gone now, but will be back soon. Real soon."

He stopped as a sobering realization hit him. Coral Sea might be back in a week.

"Ipso almost facto," he concluded with his eyebrows raised. "Now all we gotta do is sell this to the rest of the Navy and then go get the bad guy."

"The rest of the Navy is going to ask what we've been smoking," said Barstowe. "And who's going to pitch this little fable to the Group Commander?"

"Who's junior man at the table," said Mike with a grin, eyeing the Exec. The Exec began to look worried.

"Just kidding, XO. But when's the Coral Sea actually coming back to Mayport?" asked Mike.

"I don't think anybody knows yet," replied Barstowe. "They're still doing the investigation after the collision at Roosevelt Roads, and then they'll come home after that. I'd guess end of next week, maybe beginning of the week after. Like that. I can check with Carrier Group Six."

"So between now and maybe a week from now, we have to convince the powers that be that there might be a hostile submarine waiting in ambush for the Coral Sea," said Mike.

"I think the Coral Sea is on her own," muttered the Exec.

"I think it's time to call in the Commodore," said Barstowe. "He's the best guy to decide how to present this whole deal to the Group, if at all, and maybe higher than that, if it comes to it."

Mike sat back down in his chair, and looked at Barstowe. "This whole deal is pretty much what the Commodore called it, a Weird Harold," he said. "I'm not sure I want to be the champion of the proposition."

Barstowe nodded thoughtfully.

"I know. But I have to admit that the concept makes some sense out of otherwise nonsensical events."

He looked around the table.

"And for now, Gents, this whole situation just became top secret, OK? XO,—you're going to have to convince your troops to go silent on this without making it such a big deal that they talk. The official word is that we're holding meetings on what's happened so far, but we can't get our hands around what's going on. Nothing about a possible Libyan connection can go out of this room."

"I'll put a lid on it with our people," said the Exec.

"If the Commodore agrees with our hypothesis," Barstowe contin-ued, "He'll take it up to Group. If they agree, it will become a national issue right away. This would be terrorism on a grand scale. Although it's interesting, isn't it: from a legal perspective, what's the difference between our air attack on Tripoli and their setting up a submarine attack on the carrier that did it?"

"They started it, for one thing," growled the Exec.

"I'm not sure they see it that way, XO," replied Barstowe. "But in any event, if the Admiral agrees that we may have something here, it will be escalated to JCS right away, and they'll call in a coordinated air-sea ASW search of the area. Especially if the intel weenies can confirm that one of Quadaffi's boats is unaccounted for. But right now the Captain and I have to take this plot up the line and see whether we can get respect or orders to go see the shrinks over at NAS Jax. OK, XO? So do keep a lid on it, no shit. Captain Montgomery, Sir, let's go see the Boss."

FORTY FOUR

Destroyer Squadron Twelve headquarters, Thursday, 1 May; 1845

Commander Barstowe came into the Commodore's office and nodded once at the Commodore, who was sitting at his desk in his big chair. Mike followed and sat down in one of the armchairs at the Commo-dore's conference table. The Exec, Linc, and Chief MacKensie sat in straight chairs against the office wall. A PC was set up on a moveable table, along with Chief Mac's tape player. Outside, the deepening orange light of sunset glinted on the sides, masts, and funnels of the warships clustered along the piers, the light still bright enough to penetrate the shaded window. The Commodore stopped arranging papers on his desk and looked up.

"OK. He's agreed to come over. Alone, right, CSO? Good. Mike, you get to walk through the whole thing one more time. Just relate the facts—no advocacy, no passion, no Perry Mason. Just go over what you got. Mr. Howard, you and the Chief be prepared to turn on the sound and light show at the appropriate moment. Mike, you just tell the story, and I think I know him well enough to predict that he'll ask the magic question of why, and then you can drop the Libyan theory on him. After that we'll see where he wants to go with it, OK?"

"Aye, Aye, Sir. May I ask a question?"

"Yeah?"

"Do you believe it ?" asked Mike.

"Let's just say I think we have enough to warrant a more serious look, no offense to Goldy intended. If there is a goddamned Libyan submarine loitering in our opareas, I think the proper mix of helicopters and specialized ASW ships could flush his ass out. We can put a small task unit out there, three Spruances, each with a helo, and some more heloes on stand-by here at Mayport—you disagree, Chief?"

Chief MacKensie shifted uncomfortably in his chair.

"Well, Sir, you're talking about getting the first team, ASW-wise, out into the problem, and that's logical and everything, except for the waters we're talkin' about."

He paused and looked over at Mike, as if asking whether or not he should continue. Mike nodded at him.

"Go on, Chief, we're all regular Navy here," said the Commodore, who had detected the Chief's discomfort.

"Well, yes, Sir, like I was sayin'—the Spruances got too big a sonar to go active in these shallow waters. Anything less than a coupla thousand feet for those big ass, low frequency sonars, be like climbin' up in the steeple and banging on the bells with a fifteen pound sledge—you're gonna make a lotta noise, but you won't hear shit for all the ringin' in your ears. And I know they got really slick passive stuff, but if the gomer stays on the battery, he won't make any noise. Not one squeak. A diesel boat with amps in the can's gonna hover on his trim tanks out there in all that swirling plankton and shit on the edge of the Stream, and a dozen shrimps gonna make more noise'n he is. Or he can go sit on the bottom for ten days. And he will, soon's he hears the first Spruance go active. Which means you gotta put a large crowd out there for a coupla weeks at least, make him expend the battery, make him snorkel, and maybe get a line on him. And when he hears that crowd coming out of the harbor on day one, he's gonna go slip-slidin' away, other side'a the Stream, and we got nothin'."

"But the heloes, they'd have a much better chance," retorted the Commodore. "They have precise, albeit short range sonars."

"That's just it, Commodore," said the Chief. "You can't use a helo until you've localized the target to a reasonable area; then they're good at getting him into the killing ground. But they're useless for general purpose search. This guy—"

"What guy is that, Chief," asked Admiral Walker, stepping through the bat wing doors.

Everyone in the room, including the Commodore, stood up. The Admiral waved them back into their seats. He went over to the leather couch against the opposite wall, sat down, stretching his long, lean frame out comfortably, and looked around the room.

"OK, Eli, you called. Here I am. Who's going to tell me what this is all about?"

"Mike, go ahead," said the Commodore.

"Yes, Sir," Mike said, clearing his throat. "Admiral, this concerns that phantom submarine we've been screwing around with—"

"I thought it might, Captain. I suppose you're going to tell me you think it's really there."

The Admiral did not pose this as a question, but rather made a flat statement, his face impassive and, to Mike, unreadable.

"Yes, Sir, we are. Permit me to review some facts and some assertions."

The Admiral gave Mike a neutral look.

"I'm glad to hear you categorize what you're going to say into facts and assertions, Captain. I have a feeling we're going to have more of the latter than the former."

Mike did not say anything for a moment, and the Commodore gave him a warning look. Mike looked down at his feet before continuing, applying control.

"Yes, Sir, that's correct. We have a great deal of ambiguity here, and connecting it all is one underlying assumption, that all of the events tied up in this problem are related. And I admit from the start that the whole thing is unlikely."

"Good. We feel the same way. Go ahead."

Mike reviewed the entire story from the first report of a submarine sighting through the developments of the Deyo's passive search mission. He was careful to segregate factual events from logical conclusions. The Admiral listened carefully, asking no questions. He listened attentively as the Chief and Linc Howard presented some of their acoustic data. Mike found himself nervously rubbing his face under the older man's direct concentration.

"We conclude from all of this that there's a good chance that there is a conventional submarine that's been lingering in our fleet operating areas the entire time," he concluded. "Which surfaces two questions: who and why."

"I assume you have some proposed answers?"

Mike took a deep breath and wished for a glass of water.

"Yes, Sir: we think from the technical evidence, such as it is, that it's a Foxtrot class diesel boat. Chief MacKensie here can amplify that if you'd like. But we know it's not USN, and we're pretty sure it's not an allied submarine. If it's not USN, and it is a Foxtrot, then it's either Russian or Third World. We assume it's not Russian because they don't ever send their Foxtrots across the Atlantic; there's no conceivable mission for them, not to mention the political implications if they did so at this particular juncture in our mutual relations. If it's not Russian, then it's Third World; the only Third World country that has Foxtrots and also has a credible reason to send one over here is—Libya."

"Libya?!"

"Yes, Sir." Mike took a deep breath. "The U.S. Navy had the major role in bombing Quadaffi's headquarters, and we think he's cranked up one of his boats to come over and get even by torpedoing the carrier that did the bombing, the Coral Sea."

"And?"

"Uh, that's it, Admiral. I guess it sounds a little farfetched—"

"A little? A little?! The whole thing is preposterous. Eli, I'm a little surprised at this. You don't have any facts here—it's all gross conjecture. And I also did not know that Goldsborough had ever made a contact with something through all of this—when did that happen?"

The Commodore looked embarrassed.

"Well, Admiral, Mike here didn't believe what he was seeing at the time, so he did not make a report for fear of crying wolf until he had had some time to look at and analyze all the data. Once he did, he came in and told me about it right away, but to tell the truth, I had the same problem with it. I didn't believe it. So I didn't say anything about it until *I'd* had a chance to get some expert help. When I went up to the Norfolk conference, I had them run the acoustic data by the ASW analysis center; they concluded that the contacts on Goldy's tapes were 'possibles', and that the decoy contact, or the one we call the decoy, did in fact look like a transponder."

"Did they give you this in writing?"

"No, Sir. It was an informal look, so the answer was verbal."

"Hell's bells, Eli, everything is always a "possible" to those people," snorted the Admiral. "That doesn't prove anything one way or the other."

He was ignoring the others in the room and focusing directly on the Commodore.

"Yes, Sir, I know," said the Commodore, getting out of his chair. "As Mike has said, no one element of this business stands up very well to the light of day. That's the main reason I haven't brought it to you before this, and it's why I asked Deyo to do a passive probe. And even Deyo's data on the traces of the three hour diesels were ambiguous."

"Yes. I think Captain Martinson mentioned that Deyo was doing some kind of acoustic tasking for you in conjunction with her sea trials. And reported that he found nothing, as I recall. And of course they're ambiguous. Those engine noises could be anything at all and anywhere at all. I agree with Deyo."

Mike looked over at Barstowe. They had their answer about the I.V. The Commodore leaned forward.

"But the sequence of events, Admiral. It's very suggestive of something more than pure coincidence. Fisherman sees a 'U-boat', as he calls it. Another fisherman is sunk for no apparent reason, no bodies, almost no floating debris, a bullet hole in his nameboard. The police confirmed that. No other marks on the boat to indicate why it went down. Then Goldy goes out and gets two active sonar contacts, using the only sonar here in the basin that's fit for doing active ASW in these local waters. They're evaluated by the pros at the ASW analysis center as 'possible', which means that they did not conclude these were spurious contacts. Deyo gets a sound gram that could be construed as a diesel boat on the snort, in the same general area of Goldy's contacts, running for three hours, at zero dark thirty and in good masking position...yes, it could be a merchie in some subsurface acoustic anomaly, but there's no doppler and no bearing drift. You see what I mean? It's the chain of events that has me wondering."

The Admiral shook his head.

"And how on earth do you make this wild leap to Quadaffi? You say that the Soviets have never deployed a Foxtrot over here—well, neither has Quadaffi. So likelihood of deployment is no argument. In fact, the Sovs do have Foxtrots that go to Cuba from time to time, so they do deploy diesel boats out here in WestLant."

"Not to Mayport waters, Admiral."

"Not that we've known about, OK, because they're supposedly always on transit to Fidel's workers' paradise. They have no reason to come to Mayport."

"Precisely," muttered Mike. The Admiral shot him an exasperated look.

"What's that supposed to mean?" he asked.

"The Libyans have a reason to come to Mayport," answered Mike.

"Oh, right. I forgot: to torpedo the Coral Sea. Can you just imagine the repercussions if a Libyan sub torpedoed an American carrier in U.S. coastal waters, or anywhere else, for that matter? That's an act of war, at a minimum. The U.S. would go over there and pound the dogshit out of Quadaffi and every raghead within five hundred miles. We'd do to Libya

279

what the Romans did to Carthage, only our salt would glow in the dark. Quadaffi might be a looney, but he has also survived a long time, and he's done it by not ever going so far over the top that a superpower might have had to take formal notice and whack him seriously. And I think everyone agrees that he got the message when President Reagan had the balls to whack him semi-seriously."

He stood up, reaching for his hat. Everyone else rose with him.

"No way, Gentlemen. No frigging way. And even if I were convinced that there was something to all this, and I am most certainly not convinced, I'd have to get ships and aircraft underway for unprogrammed at-sea operating time. There's no money for that. Hell, we're fighting every day for the dwindling number of at-sea days that we do get. This is simply preposterous, and I can't go forward with it, and I want you to drop it altogether. I'm sorry I ever sent Goldsborough out in the first place."

"If I may, Admiral," said Mike. "Suppose it were true? Suppose Quaddaffi construed the attack on his country by the U.S. as an act of war? Suppose the Coral Sea gets ambushed, gets torpedoed, and we never find the guy who did it? Who would we go whack then? There's every probability that any escorts coming in with Coral Sea, as well as the carrier, will be rigged out for return to port and liberty call and not be at a state of readiness high enough to detect or even to deal with a submarine, especially if Coral Sea was blowing up all over the approach lanes to Mayport. Any escorts would be trying to avoid running into her and the rocks at the same time. They wouldn't even have charged flasks in their torpedo tubes, so what would they do to a submarine even if they did detect it? And when you think about it, you can't even fire an ASW torpedo in water that shallow. How much egg would the U.S. Navy have on its face if it worked out that way, the Coral Sea torpedoed and the U.S. Navy without a clue as to what the hell had happened ten miles from a major ASW base?"

The Admiral stared at Mike. The Commodore diplomatically looked out the window, and the other officers tried to get small in the suddenly close room. The Admiral put down his hat.

"Eli, I want to talk to you. Alone."

Mike and the others gathered quickly by the door and filed out of the room. Barstowe shepherded them down the hall, away from the batwing doors. The staff offices were quiet, the rest of the staff having gone home except for the duty yeoman. They filed into Barstowe's office.

"I've got to admit, I was siding with the Admiral until you asked those pungent questions," said Barstowe. "Now, I just don't know what to think. And you didn't ask the one question that I think actually cleared the room."

"What was that?" said Mike, his heart heavy with foreboding.

"How would anybody here ever explain those awful events you conjured up in there having had a warning beforehand..."

"I think all we did was really piss him off."

"No doubt of that, but you told it like it is," said Barstowe.

"Like it might be, you mean. Hell, I want to line up with the Admiral, too," said Mike. "I don't want to believe any of this. But if it did happen, and there was an investigation, and it came out that we knew or thought something was out there beforehand, and did *nothing*, I think a lot of American heads would roll, not Libyans. As well they should, for that matter. But I guess I'm condemned to be the perennial devil's advocate on this little deal."

"Yeah, well, I'll spot you that. In the meantime, keep a hand on your own neck," said Barstowe with a mirthless grin.

They heard the batwing doors squeak and the Commodore speaking rapidly to the Admiral as he escorted him out the front door of the staff offices. The final words from the Admiral as he went through the door were "No way, Eli. No way." Then the door closed, and there was a moment of silence in the darkened hallway.

"Bill?" called the Commodore.

"They all went home, Commodore," called out Barstowe from within his office. "The CSO, the Goldsborough troops, everybody. Nobody here but us chickens."

"Get your asses in here, all of you," growled the Commodore as he banged through the door to his office. They filed back into his office and remained standing. The Commodore sat down at his desk.

"OK, you heard him. He was, as they say, underwhelmed by the force of your arguments. In other words, he thinks we're all nuts. He told me to drop the whole thing, and to ensure that none of you ever mentioned this again, and that no further expenditure of Navy assets or resources was authorized."

Mike stared down at the floor, his stomach churning.

"Captain?" said the Commodore, softly.

"Yes, Sir?"

"I know you disagree, but we've done what we're supposed to do here. You brought the matter to me, your boss, and I took it to the Admiral, my boss. We've presented the facts, our conjectures, and our conclusions, and the next senior guy in our chain of command is not convinced. He has the authority and the responsibility to make a decision, and he has decided that this is a fairy tale. He has ordered all of us to drop it. That's a legal order, and it's also not unreasonable."

"But it may be dead wrong," said Mike.

"Yes, it might," nodded the Commodore. "But then we did our best to convince him, and it didn't fly. Remember that old rule about following orders: the guy giving the orders we disagree with might know something we don't know. Anyhow, that's it."

"Can we make one last check of something," asked the Exec.

"What's that, XO?" asked the Commodore.

"Can we check with the intel world to see if all of Muammar's pig-boats are in their pens?"

The Commodore thought for a moment.

"OK, I'll do this: I'll have my staff intelligence officer make an informal call to the N2 up at Surflant or maybe LantFleet. Informal sort of thing. Somebody will tingle a friend in Washington, somebody who prepares naval force locators, and they'll have the latest pictures from the appropriate satellite. But that's it, guys. Now let's go home."

Mike said good night to Barstowe and the Commodore, and he and the rest of the Goldsborough officers went out the front door of the staff office. The entire Mayport basin could be seen from the front steps, the ships illuminated for the night, with bored little knots of watchstanders lounging around each quarterdeck. It was almost fully dark, and Mike paused at the top of the steps leading down to the waterfront street.

"OK, people, I guess that's that. Linc, take all the tapes and other materials and lock them up somewhere safe. I still think we were right, but, orders is orders, as they say. Thanks for all your efforts, and let's hope the Coral Sea doesn't go boom in the next few weeks."

The Exec shook his head.

"I don't understand why they won't even go out and take a look—we're always doing drills and exercises, why not make this an exercise?"

"Because there's barely enough money for the regularly scheduled underway ops; all the exercises are planned out and funded a couple of years in advance. The Group Commander just can't get a ship underway for more than a sea trial anymore on his own authority, certainly not without explaining it up the line. I think the Admiral's coming at this from a different point of view—he's got an entire Cruiser-Destroyer Group to operate and keep at a specified level of readiness. What did the I.V. call this? A firefly? They can't go getting a task unit underway to chase a firefly, I guess. And you know, I felt quite strong about this when we worked it out in the wardroom, but I felt kind of dumb in there when I pitched it to the Admiral. Think how he'd feel pitching it to the Fleet Commander. I think he's wrong, but I can sure see his point of view."

"I wonder if they'll even alert the Coral Sea group to be on the look-out?" asked the Chief.

"I don't think so, Chief," said Mike. "The Coral Sea would have to come back and ask what they want him to do about it. Anyway, I guess we get back to concentrating on boilers and feed pumps. I'm going to go home and have a beer."

"Sounds good to me, Cap'n," said the Chief. "Thanks for taking this up the line." Linc Howard nodded his agreement.

"Yeah, well, I don't think I had too much to lose, based on the way the Admiral was looking at me when we were excused. But that's why they pay me all this terrific money. Hang in there, Guys. I'll see you tomorrow morning at whatever inspection inbriefing we have on tap."

The Chief and Lincoln Howard said goodnight and walked down the steps. Ben Farmer remained behind.

"Damn, damn, damn!" swore Mike softly.

"Yes, Sir," said the Exec. "Are we just going to drop all this?"

"I think the Commodore isn't finished yet, Ben. I think—I hope—he's gonna find a way to keep probing. It'll depend on what the Admiral said to him when they chased us out. I keep saying to myself we did our best, but that doesn't cut it, somehow. I think Coral Sea might be in real danger."

"Now who's believing this shit, Cap'n?" said Farmer, softly.

"Yeah, yeah, there you go being insolent again, XO." grinned Mike. But then his face grew serious.

"We need to put our thinking caps on. There has to be some way we can keep going on this thing until we either prove ourselves right or wrong."

"I wouldn't mind being all wrong on this one," said Farmer, staring out over the quiescent basin.

FORTY FIVE

Mayport Marina, Thursday, 1 May; 2130

Mike stretched out on the chaise lounge in his bathing suit and sneakers and watched the boats go by on the intracoastal. The back porch of the boat was hot and humid in the early darkness. He sipped the remains of a gin and tonic, absently letting the cold glass sit and sweat on his bare midriff. Two piers over a couple was having an increasingly loud argument over whether or not one of them was going to leave in the morning. One of you leave tonight, he thought, and then we can restore the peace. He wished Diane were there; he badly needed somebody to talk to. The Admiral had probably gone back to his office and called the Bureau to get a new CO for the Goldsborough. Or, better, had Martinson do it. Martinson would like that.

He wondered about the Commodore, giving up so easily; it wasn't like him. He had seemed genuinely convinced that there was something worth looking into. But he had folded like a napkin when the Admiral dismissed the whole thing. Preposterous. OK, maybe it was preposterous. But what if it were true? What if Mrs. Quadaffi's bouncing baby boy, Muammar, had sailed a submarine to Mayport to exact some vengeance. So it wasn't a modern, atomic powered submarine. But after the Second World War the Russians had modelled their F series class on the last (and best) class of the German U-boat fleet. German submarines had sailed with impunity to the east coast of the United States, and farther than that during the war. They had lingered for forty-five day patrols, without support ships, and then sailed all the way back to occupied France. Routinely. Less capable American submarines had sailed all the way across the Pacific to conduct long patrols off China and Japan. The diesel boats were capable then, and more capable now. It was feasible.

But was it likely? That's the rub, thought Mike. Would he do it? Would he risk war? Or was this simply a very high tech Arab suicide squad, steeled to deliver one fatal attack and then implode the boat at depth to guarantee anonymity and entrance to raghead heaven? Depending on where they made the attack, the boat would only have to evade for two hours at full underwater speed to reach the edge of the continental shelf, and then go down in 10,000 feet of water, to be lost forever in the ancient slime at the bottom of the sea.

It would be a terrorist attack on a grand scale, unless the Navy could find them and force them to the surface almost immediately in order to produce a suspect in hand. Otherwise, big explosions along the carrier's side, mass confusion outside and in the harbor, escorts going everywhere, not knowing what had happened – which of the current skippers had ever seen a submarine torpedo go off under a ship? And the bad guy snaking seaward on his silent electric motors, hugging the bottom until he reached the acoustic safety of the swirling biomass of the Gulf Stream. If he actually got away into the Atlantic, all the guy had to do was get into the shipping lanes and go back to the Med among the hundreds of ships that traversed the Atlantic.

It was feasible. He kept coming back to it. It was feasible. It was possible. They ought to go out and take a look. They sure as hell ought to warn the Coral Sea group that there was the possibility of trouble when they came home.

No way, the Admiral had said. No frigging way. We don't have the money, we don't have the assets, and I might look stupid. I might be wrong, but I will not look stupid. Mike shook his head in the darkness. The appearance of things had become so important. We don't have any problems here, Boss. And if we do, tell 'em we don't, and fix them, out of sight and behind the scenes, but we never, never, let it show. You gotta look good, regardless of whether or not you are good. Look good and everyone would smile, and say, yeah, good looking ship, smart crew, must be a top skipper. Unlike that weirdo that thought there was a submarine hiding out offshore. Some poor toad who had command of the oldest ship in the basin, the one they were going to decommission, the guy who never had to deploy and show his stuff with the first team overseas. So he dreams up this little fable about a submarine, gonna get some attention, some visibility. Gonna get relieved early and sent ashore was more likely. He drained the rest of his drink, and headed back inside to make another. He wished Diane would call.

FORTY SIX

Mayport marina, Thursday, 1 May; 2345

Mike lay awake in his bed, uncomfortable in the air conditioned darkness. A thunderstorm had passed over a half hour ago, waking him with its sharp cracks of thunder and a sudden, sweeping rain across the deck above. He had awakened with a headache from too much gin, a queasy stomach, dry mouth, and zoo dirt breath, as the Boatswain Mate Chief liked to call it. He had never had a big capacity for alcohol, and he knew that his age was showing. He had taken a quick shower, popped two aspirins, rinsed out his mouth, gone back to bed, but could not go back to sleep.

He could feel the oppressive weight of the humid night air even through the air conditioning, the atmosphere not quite wrung out in the wake of the thunderstorm. There was another episode of heavy rain, punctuated by rumbling thunder in the distance over the ocean. His bedroom was washed in a dim, half light from the pier lights.

He thought about the submarine. Was there another Skipper out there even now, lying awake in his bunk, watching the clock and waiting for his big day. Going over the mission plan again and again, looking for the holes, waiting for the signal to get ready, to come up to periscope depth on a sunny afternoon amongst the Chris Crafts and the fishing boats to let loose a spread of Russian torpedoes? As he tossed and turned, he felt that he, they, *somebody* ought to be doing something. He recalled that terrible night on the bridge, the Captain yelling, the bridge watch fumbling around in the dark, and that terrifying black shape filling the windows just before the crash. Somebody ought to have done something; *he* should have done something.

As the rain subsided, he felt the boat move under the unmistakable weight of someone coming aboard. He sat up in the bed, looked at his watch. Twelve thirty five. He kept a gun taped to the back of the night table, and was trying to decide between the gun and simply calling the cops when he heard a female voice swear softly out on deck. He grinned in the dark as he felt the "intruder" walk back to the midships hatchway, obviously making no attempt to be stealthy, open the door none too surreptitiously, and come down the stairs into the lounge. What was this crazy woman doing out here in the middle of the night.

Diane slipped into the bedroom. She was wearing a stylish full length, white cotton raincoat, buttoned all the way to her throat. She carried a pair of sneakers in one hand, a small, clutch purse in the other.

"You always go breaking into peoples' boats in the middle of the night?" he asked.

"I didn't break in; I just walked onboard. Even your guard parrot didn't care."

She stood at the foot of the bed, hands on hips. They looked at each other for a few seconds in the semi-darkness.

"Well," she said.

He threw aside the sheet, indicating a space for her on the big bed. She looked at his naked body for a few long seconds, and began to unbutton the raincoat. She wasn't wearing anything else. She let him look, and then slithered onto the bed and into his arms.

"Needed to talk to someone, is that it?" he murmured into her ear. She covered his mouth with hers in a fierce, demanding kiss. Didn't want to talk, after all.

Afterwards, she still didn't want to talk. But he was awake, and all the anxieties about the submarine flap flowed back into his mind. His headache was also gone, helped on its way by rapid blood circulation. He asked her how in the hell she had managed to get out of the house in the middle of the night. She mumbled something, snuggling closer. He partially sat up.

"Hey, Diane, what did you do, slip him a mickey?"

She opened one eye, closed it again. "Yes, actually, I did. He had a bad headache, so I gave him a couple of bufferins, only one was a valium."

"A valium? You keep valium around?"

"It's a prerogative of almost-forty year old women to keep valium around. J.W. never takes anything stronger than aspirin, so it put him out like a light. What time is it?"

He snapped on a bedside light. "One thirty."

She snuggled in again. "Turn that off and set your alarm for five."

"I don't believe you drove through the gate with no clothes on."

"Seemed like a good idea at the time."

"It did have a certain effect."

"Yeah, well, I had the raincoat on. My flasher uniform. I don't think the gate guards are going to mess with a car with Captain's stickers on the window. Besides, I cheated; I had a bikini in my purse just in case the stupid Volvo went swimming again."

He laughed and hugged her. "I'm glad you came."

"Well that's good. I was beginning to wonder. Now, tell me what's that bad dream sitting on your shoulder."

He told her about the day's events, including the Admiral's black look as he left.

"Don't worry about it, the Admiral, I mean. Wasn't he the one that sent you out on this wild goose chase in the first place? After the fishing boat sank?"

"Yeah, but—"

"So he can't fire you for concluding that there might be something out there without revealing that he's the one that started it. He's not going to do that. Trust me."

Mike realized that, politically speaking, she was right. Captain's wife, Dummy—what do you expect?

"He sure looked like he was going to fire my ass by dawn's early light."

"It's harder to do that than you think. Do you really think there's a submarine out there?" she asked, turning around to look at him.

"Yeah, I kinda think there is, or has been, anyway. I think the Navy ought to at least go out and take a hard look. Too many little indicators point to more than coincidence. I guess we'll find out when the Coral Sea comes home."

She sat up at last, tossing her hair away from her face. Her heavy breasts swayed as she tried arranged her hair with her fingers. He sat behind her, and wrapped his hands around her front.

"You're not helping."

"Helping myself, sort of."

287

"You worry too much about your career, you know that? If he's going to fire you, look at it this way—you can get on with your life. You're obviously not having a very satisfying command tour anyway; he might be doing you a favor."

"I guess that's one way of looking at it."

"What would you do—you've got your twenty, haven't you?"

"Yes. I hadn't thought about it."

"You should. J.W. is very sensitive about the subject of retirement. If he doesn't make flag I think he'll just spin in place somewhere, become even more unpleasant than he is now, and hang on until they throw him out at thirty. There's a whole world out there outside of the glorious Navy, and most of you serious lifers don't even want to look at it."

"Just a lot of civilians out there. I've never talked to civilians. I don't know what the hell I'd do."

"That's what I'm talking about. It's ironic—the Lieutenant Commanders who don't make it to command spend their last five years setting themselves up for civilian life when they hit their twenty. The guys who do get command never give it a thought, and then when the grand career peters out, they're suddenly confronted with the possibility that they're not going to make Captain or Flag. None of you guys ever think past the Navy."

She turned to face him.

"You're not married, no kids in college, no mortgage—you could probably live right here and not even have to work, except when I come sneaking around after midnight."

"That's not work."

"But you could make it a second career. Think of the benefits. Why don't we practice."

"Right now?"

"Yeah. It has to beat thinking about submarines. Or is that a periscope?"

FORTY SEVEN

The Officers Club, Mayport Naval Station, Friday, 2 May; 1205

"I'll have the veggie-burger, no fries, a small salad, diet coke," said the Commodore. He handed over the menu.

"I'll have the Navy bean soup and some French bread, iced tea," said Mike.

The waitress took their menus and departed to get the next table's order. The dining room was full with the usual lunch crowd, which was about the only time the Mayport O-Club dining room was full. Everyone knew that evenings were heavily dependent on microwave cookery. There was the normal mix of ship's company officers, shore pukes, staffies, and even some techreps in shirts and ties who were trying not to look like civilians. Mike and the Commodore were seated in a corner table near the seaside windows. The bright white sand of the Navy beach stretched a quarter mile to the Atlantic over low dunes dotted with sawgrass.

Mike had arrived onboard at a little after eight o'clock, his usual arrival time. The Exec had informed him that the Commodore had invited him to lunch at the Club. Mike and the Exec had speculated over coffee in the wardroom on the reasons for lunch, with Mike feeling sure that there was going to be some more fallout from the disastrous meeting with the Admiral. The Exec took the opposite tack, saying that the Commodore would do dirty work in his office, not at the O'Club.

"Have a good night's sleep, did you, Michael?" asked the Commodore. He had not missed the signs of a mild hangover, compounded by not much sleep.

"I've had better, Commodore," said Mike, smiling inwardly at the half-truth. Started off shitty but had a lovely finish. Diane had slipped away at just after five and presumably made it home without incident. Mike had wondered what the gate guards thought. Woman was getting out of hand.

"Yeah, well, don't let it bother you," said the Commodore casually. "I went to the usual morning staff meeting at Group. Two of the operations staffies were sitting behind me on the back benches. One of 'em put a handkerchief over his head and pretended to operate a periscope. I could see his reflection in the window. After the meeting I cornered them in the passageway. Told them both that I looked forward to seeing them in the Fleet someday."

The Commodore gave a wolfish grin.

"Made my morning to see their expressions. But Himself seemed normal, and I didn't sense any lingering animosity."

"You mean he's having Martinson call the Bureau instead of doing it himself?

The Commodore laughed out loud, a short barking noise.

"You take yourself too seriously, Mike. Maybe I gotta stop lecturing you about your career. You're centering on yourself instead of your ship. Admiral wants your butt offa there, he simply says the word and you turn over to your XO and pack your seabag. He doesn't have to call the Bureau. I'd have to call the Bureau. Besides, this submarine deal has the potential of being embarrassing, so public executions are not in order. I really think he would be most appreciative if we would just bury the whole notion and go back to normal ops."

"Cover it up, in other words."

The Commodore shook his head.

"Such words you use," he said, going into a Jewish corner grocer routine. "So dramatic. Everyone wants to be part of a Watergate. We were told to bury it. It's now officially buried. We were never told to do a cover-up. We're not going to do a cover-up. At least *I'm* not going to do a cover-up."

He looked directly at Mike, his expression suddenly no longer part of a routine lunch.

"*You're* not?"

"That's right, Sunshine. And neither, I hope, are you."

Mike drank some iced tea to cover his confusion. If he understood Captain Aronson correctly, the Commodore wanted Mike and Goldsborough to pursue the phantom submarine matter without the Admiral's knowledge. Which meant that the Commodore thought the threat was sufficiently real to risk throwing in his lot with a CO who was now firmly in disrepute with the Admiral. The Commodore watched Mike's face as he worked it out.

"You game?" he said.

Mike grinned. "You bet I am. Sir. But you're taking a walk on the wild side, if I may say so."

"You may say so."

The Commodore broke off as the waitress brought their food. "But what the hell," he resumed, after she left. "I figure if we do it right, which is to say very discreetly, and we come up empty, and nothing happens, then nothing happens and life goes on. And if we turn up a bad guy, prove we were right all along, who knows?"

"There'd be some awfully embarrassed people up at Group if that came to pass."

"Yeah, there would. And well above Group, for that matter. But don't go thinking that embarrassment at high levels is necessarily a good deal for the guys who cause it. Remember the Flag protection circuit."

Mike knew that in the Navy, as in other familial bureaucracies, the Admirals tended to close ranks when one of their own screwed up. When the Flag protection circuit operated, it usually spat out a sacrificial Captain or two and the matter was quietly closed. Mike also knew that the Commodore understood the system probably better than he did, and thereby knew full well the risk he was taking.

"You're doing it for the satisfaction?" he asked, watching the Commodore carefully.

"I'm doing it for the integrity of the system," said Aronson, the kidding gone from his voice. "Hell, from the Admiral's perspective, he's doing the right thing. He gets leaned on to conserve operating dollars, and to keep things on an even keel. But: recall my little homily in your cabin. The Navy is getting out of the habit of calling things as they are. Dog craps on the rug, I'm of the opinion that that's dogshit on the rug, not circumstantial and temporary evidence of a defective canine house-training program. Deal like this might shake the Navy up a little, knock some of that Washington E-ring varnish off our image and get us back to being straight shooters. And yeah, maybe just a skoshii of satisfaction."

He looked over at Mike, his expression tinged once again with amusement. Mike was impressed. The Commodore's decision to keep on with the submarine project was a refreshing demonstration of principle.

"I'm still having a little trouble distinguishing between burying something and covering it up. How do we work it, Commodore?" he asked.

Captain Aronson finished his salad before replying, and then looked around the room to make sure no one was paying attention to them. He leaned forward.

"Burying something means putting it in a deep hole and forgetting about it because it's a dead issue. Covering it up means putting it a deep hole because we don't want to see it or have anyone else see it, even though it's a *live* issue. Cover-ups are OK sometimes—they serve our purposes occasionally. But you shouldn't ever execute a cover-up unless you know you can control all aspects of it. In this case, if there's a submarine out there, he controls what happens when the Coral Sea comes back, not us. Based on the Admiral's orders, we have to be seen to be putting it in a hole. But because you and I think it might be a live issue instead of a dead issue, I feel obliged to kick it around a little bit more until we're convinced it's really dead. Then we can and will forget about it, as directed."

He glanced around the room again before continuing.

"So: what we do is sail Goldsborough on a sea trial next week as soon as you've got the engineering repairs done and the plant checks out. We'd do that anyway after major engineering system repairs, so it won't cost the Navy anything it wasn't going to pay for anyway. No further expenditure of assets, like the Admiral said. Besides, I happen to know that there will be some extra at-sea days in the budget because Goldy isn't going on the FleetEx. Now: you can't stay out there forever, so what we gotta do is make sure you go out there for your sea trial on the day when the Coral Sea returns to Mayport, because if something's going to happen, that's when it's going to happen. I figure she'll come back next Friday or so. If we're right about the submarine, we can use the old convoy tactic to flush the bad guy: put the escort next to the target, and since the submarine has to come to the target to do business, the escort doesn't have to go find the submarine—it comes to him."

"There's still a lot we don't know, Commodore. Like when Coral Sea will return, exactly, and whether or not she'll have escorts of her own, or even if one of Quaddafi's boats is unaccounted for. We'll have to time this sea trial pretty carefully."

"Exactly. But I have the staff assets to check on some things. For instance, I told you I'd have my intel weenie pulse the system to see if Muammar's sewerdogs were all in the kennel. I mentioned doing this casually to the Admiral. Admiral said forget about it. OK, so I don't formally pulse the system. But my intel weenie can make an informal call to a buddy on the SurfLant staff, and he can call a guy on the LantFleet staff, and that guy can call the right place in D.C. and ask the pregnant question. Actually, we could just read the weekly intel summary, but I'd like to ask the guys who actually read the satellite imagery directly if we can. Kinda like the Deyo deal: there was nothing there but there was, until somebody who shall go nameless told the I.V. to blow it off."

"Yes, Sir. And you'll know from the daily meeting at Group when Coral Sea's coming in."

"Yeah. Now, we can also get that from port operations—you know they freeze all harbor movements when a carrier's coming back to this little fishbowl of a base. So there won't be any special inside information."

The waitress came back to clear away the dishes and brought coffee and their checks. The Commodore again surveyed the dining room before continuing.

"Now, we can work this little deal without causing even a ripple, but it depends on your not lighting any more fuses up at Group. I told you earlier that the Admiral is not likely to take you off Goldsborough just over the submarine thing. But I do think he'd like to make you go away, and I know Captain Martinson would love to make you go away. Martinson's been keeping a book on you, did you know that?"

Mike felt a flash of alarm, but was not entirely surprised. "No, Sir, I didn't."

"Well, he has—he called me in for a little chat this very morning and went down a list of your supposed sins. The pretty bastard's clever, for a

292

staff puke. I believe his dislike of you is personal more than professional, but the notes in his little book are all couched in professional terms: ship doesn't meet her operational commitments, their traffic safety program is ineffective, the Captain leads a very unconventional life style, the Captain displays a 'screw it, I got my twenty in' attitude, the Captain tends to be flippant and even occasionally insolent to senior officers, the Captain sends intemperate messages when the repair establishment screws up, shit like that. Martinson's a pattern man, and he's painting the kind of pattern that only needs one dramatic incident to make his case. So, for the next week, cool it, OK? No vitriol in the message traffic, make sure you pass your 'surprise' maintenance inspection, and so forth. OK? This submarine thing may be a total wild goose chase, but if it's not, you're the only guy I can put on it, because the whole idea has been officially discredited. So please don't do anything to attract attention until Coral Sea is safely home."

"In other words, don't fuck up never no more," said Mike. He could not disguise a trace of the bitterness he felt about how his career was going, or not going.

"Right. For a week, anyway. That's not so hard. And, look—this whole deal between you and the shore staffs isn't personal, as the Sicilians say, Martinson not withstanding. It's just business. Peacetime business. And it's been peacetime for a long time. The Navy gets pretty hidebound and conventional when all it has to do is look at its own image. You've read U.S. naval history: every war that's come along, the Navy always has had to fight its way out of its own inspection manuals before it ever got to the enemy. It's just the way it is; it's a good outfit, with more than a few fine people. But you're a member of pretty rarified group right now: a Commander, USN, in command at sea. We only have, what, 450 ships? Which means 450 some CO's out of what, sixty thousand officers in the whole Navy? You step up to the command box, you step right into a big spotlight. You are not a bad guy—you're just a bit of a non-conformist, and that's OK if you're willing to pay the price in a conforming society. If I thought you were a slacker or a non-hacker, I wouldn't be here talking to you, nor would you still be in command. The main thing is, Oldy Goldy may end up being the only thing between the five thousand guys on the Coral Sea and a boatload of raghead terrorists, if in fact there's something out there. So I want you to forget about the career shit and focus hard on getting your plant fixed in time to get to sea before Coral Sea shows up in the Jax opareas. After that we can resume the image wars. OK?"

"Yes, Sir. Got it," said Mike with a sigh.

"Good," replied the Commodore, not missing the dejection on Mike's face. "Think of it this way: think what a message you could send if you bagged a terrorist sub that was about to attack a U.S. carrier. Think of the new heights of sarcasm you could reach. It would be the Montgomery-gram to end all Montgomery-grams. I'll do my part and find out what we gotta find out."

"Suppose the Group finds out what we're up to?"

"They won't. This is between you and me, and your guys. Your guys are good guys. Goldy won't be doing anything that she wouldn't be doing anyway after a big engineering repair; everybody will expect a one day sea trial. We're just mucking around a little with the timing of it, and you're gonna groom your ASW teams a little bit between now and then, and maybe do some tactical warfare exercises with your CIC staff. Good inport training, like we tell you to do all the time."

"The Group seems to have its ways of finding shit out. What then?"

The Commodore smiled. "Fuck 'em if they can't take a little joke, right?"

Mike laughed then. That was an attitude he understood.

FORTY EIGHT

USS Goldsborough, inport, Mayport Naval Station, Friday, 2 May; 1320

Mike returned to the Goldsborough after lunch and sent for the Exec. They went over the status of the engineering repairs, and then went down to the wardroom for the weekly meeting with the department heads. Afterwards, back in the Captain's cabin, Mike debriefed his lunch with the Commodore. When he was finished, the Exec gave a low whistle.

"I'm surprised," he said. "I wouldn't have thought Captain Aronson would persist with this. I thought he was bucking for Flag pretty hard."

"Maybe we underestimated him. I think he's a team player up to the point where a real threat presents itself, and then he's regular Navy and damn the consequences. I was just as surprised. But what we have to do now is some planning, first on these repairs, and second on how we're going to approach our little ASW problem."

"Yes, Sir, but are we gonna tell the troops what's going on?"

"No, at least not yet. The Commodore was specific: I was to keep this between us chickens. But as Exec, you are part of my official self, and besides, I need your tempering influence. He told me I couldn't light any fuses for a whole week."

"Golly, Gee, Cap'n, a whole week...?"

"Yeah, wiseass, a whole week. But keep in mind that I'll just save it up."

"Now that's a comforting thought."

"Right. First the engineering plant: can they fix those valves and the steam leaks in time for us to run pierside tests by, say, Wednesday of next week?"

The Exec consulted his notebook. All Exec's carried the ship's entire lifestream of events, problems, issues, and crises in little green notebooks. It was an Exec's job to know everything, and the green notebooks served as a memory flywheels.

"It's going to be tight for the lube oil purifier—not the fix, but the parts. The ETA on parts is Tuesday. On the other hand, there's not much of a test for that repair. The main steam systems require hydros, some X-rays on the key welds, and then a light off for the real test. When might we have to go to sea to do business?"

"Friday, I think. No, Friday, we ought to be at sea. Which means Thursday underway, say, late in the afternoon. If the carrier comes in on Friday, they'll try for a morning arrival so they can get people ashore that afternoon. You know what a zoo that is when 3500 guys hit the beach."

The Exec thought for a minute.

"Actually," he said, "They'll come in when the tide is high and we have slack water in the basin."

Mike gave himself a Polish salute with a slap to his forehead.

"Of course. What was I thinking about. Of course—high, slack water in the basin. Which is, what, an hour after high tide in the river?"

"Yes, Sir. About that. Lemme make a quick phone call, if I may."

He picked up the phone on Mike's desk and called Port Operations.

"Yes, this is Lieutenant Commander Farmer, XO on Goldsborough. When's high slack in the basin this week? Yeah. Right. Advancing fifteen minutes each day, right? Much grass."

He hung up the phone.

"Port ops says high slack is 1700 today, advancing about 15 minutes a day. So for next Friday, it'll be around 1900 in the evening. Seven o'clock—almost nightfall. Which is good, because, if they're coming back Friday, that effectively gives us another day inport if we need it."

Mike thought for a few moments. "1900 Friday means Coral Sea has to be ten miles from the river entrance by 1730, to give her time to make her approach to the river, pick up her tugs, and be entering the turning basin by 1900."

The Exec agreed. "And that means her approach window to the ten mile point happens between about three thirty and five thirty in the afternoon."

Mike felt the first tendril of apprehension wrap around his vitals. If there indeed was a submarine lurking out there, he and the Exec had just fixed the attack window at around five in the afternoon. The submarine could not come in any closer than ten miles because the water was too shallow. She would not operate much farther out than thirty miles because she could not know the precise approach track of the carrier, and a diesel boat could not afford to get into a long, submerged chase situation. The attack position, therefore, had to be between ten miles and thirty miles from the river entrance to minimize any pursuit maneuvers and yet keep the submarine hidden. Mike could see that the Exec was thinking the same thing.

"We need a chart, XO. We need to figure a great circle track from San Juan to the Jacksonville approaches, and then a rhumbline from the end of the great circle to the river. That rhumbline will be the axis of the attack zone. Then we need to look at the hydrographic characteristics in the attack zone. And we need to figure this out in a way that doesn't alert the rest of the officers or the crew."

"Yes, Sir. I'll just do it myself. If anybody asks, I'm doing the initial planning for the sea trial next week. No biggee."

"OK. We'll do the geography planning first, and then we're going to have to figure out both our search tactics and our attack plan. Again, just the two of us right now; we'll cut the weapons and ops officers later. Once we get to sea we'll brief the crew. Now, I hate to say this, but can you work up something tomorrow, maybe bring it to the Lucky Bag? We can skull it there in privacy."

"No problem, Cap'n."

"Right, good. I'll square it with Mrs. XO, somehow. And another thing—I've heard there's going to be a surprise ASW ordnance inspection week after next. You might alert the weapons officer to spruce up the torpedo tubes, check out the sonar fire control, the depth charges, etc."

The Exec grinned. "Gotcha covered, Cap'n. How 'bout the guns?"

"Shit, Ben, we have to use guns we'll be in pretty desperate straits."

"It has happened, Cap'n."

"Yeah, OK, tell the guys it's either an ASW or a gunnery inspection—we're not sure which. Tell 'em we'll do some practice firing on the sea trial. That'll do it. Those gunners mates love to shoot those things. And in the meantime, make sure the plant gets fixed, all the paperwork gets done, everybody gets paid, you know—the little shit."

The Exec stood up and put away his little notebook, into which he had copied the Captain's latest instructions.

"Piece a cake," he said airily. "Piece a cake."

"You're bragging again, XO."

"Hackers never brag; we just chop it up and get it done. And, by the way, you'll need to change into whites for the reception tonight."

Mike abruptly sat forward in his chair. "What fucking reception?!"

"Group Twelve hosting the Chambers of Commerce from Jax Beach, Neptune Beach, and Ponte Vedra at the Club. All CO's inport command performance. CO's only, no XO's. You're gonna love it, Cap'n."

Mike closed his eyes and began to count to ten. The Exec wisely fled.

FORTY NINE

The Mayport Officers Club, Friday, 2 May; 1830

Mike arrived at the Officers Club ten minutes after the reception began. He joined a stream of officers in tropical whites and civilians in business suits at the front door, and passed through the reception line a few minutes later. Admiral Walker and Mrs. Walker were receiving; Captain Martinson, and the base Commander, Captain Johnson, were the other senior officers in the receiving line. Mike could see the Commodore across the room, talking to two other CO's. The civilians passed through the line and then congregated in small, uncomfortable looking knots around the main reception room until one or more naval officers made their approach.

As soon as Mike saw the Chief of Staff, he looked for Diane, but was surprised to see that she was not there. The Admiral said hello pleasantly enough, as did Mrs. Walker, and then they both turned to the trio of businessmen right behind Mike. Stepping to the right, he said good evening to the Chief of Staff. Captain Martinson was aloof, as usual.

"Good evening, Captain. How's the plant coming along?"

"Slowly, but surely, Chief of Staff. We're welding on top of welds at this juncture."

"Yes, well that's the price we pay for keeping antiques around." He dismissed Mike by turning to greet the civilians next in line.

And I hope someday soon to show you what the antique can do, thought Mike as he headed for the corner bar. He got a beer while wondering fleetingly where Diane was. The Commodore saw him and signalled him over as the room filled up with more civilians. Soon he was part of the process of making the luminaries of the Chambers of Commerce feel at home in the Club. After a while, the Admiral, his wife, and the Chief of Staff began a tour of the room, joining each conversation group for a few minutes. When they arrived at the Commodore's group, Mike listened to the pleasantries for a few minutes, and then felt an urge to ask the Chief of Staff where Mrs. Martinson was this evening.

"I actually don't know," admitted the Chief of Staff. "She left me a note saying she might drive down to Orlando to see some friends. By the way, thank you very much for rescuing her the other day at NAS Jax. That was most kind." Martinson sounded unusually human for a change, Mike thought. Look out. A tentative thought about where Diane might really be began to form in his mind.

"No problem, Captain. For awhile there, I thought your Volvo was going to be totally submerged."

"It might as well have been, although fortunately the engine compartment apparently didn't go under. There's still a faint whiff of wet sawgrass inside, though."

The Chief of Staff turned further away from the group of civilians.

"Tell me something: where really did that crazy idea about Libyans come from?"

Mike looked around to see if the civilians or anyone else were listening before answering.

"It was and is a wild guess, Chief of Staff," Mike sighed. "It's not hard to make a case either for or against it. But the Admiral has quashed it, and so that's that."

"Yes, well of course he had to. We'd all look like flaming idiots if we surfaced a notion like that at headquarters in Norfolk, remarkably imaginative though it was. You need to understand that we're under a great deal of pressure these days on such issues as operating funds, days-at-sea money, you know—the budget wars. The Admiral invests a lot of his personal prestige on claiming our fair share down here in the toolies. A report like this right now would hurt everybody. Now, I could see how one might think there was something out there, although it's all pretty thin gruel in the cold light of day. But making the leap to Libyans, as it were, was just a bit much. I mean, really, Colonel Khaddafi has been threatening to attack western surface shipping for years, like the QE II threat a few years ago; and yet he's never once actually sailed a submarine for more than three days. *Jane's Fighting Ships* says that his boats are not really operational."

Mike hid his surprise. The Chief of Staff may have been dismissing the whole idea out of hand, but he had consulted the world standard reference.

"Yes, Sir, but a Foxtrot class could certainly go that distance and stay out on patrol for a long time, if they wanted to do it. The German diesel boats went all the way around Africa and out into the Indian Ocean during the Second World War."

"Yes, yes, everyone knows that. But I just can't see it, for two reasons: one, I can't see the Arabs ever getting that organized, and, second, if he made such an attack he risks war with the United States of America, which gains him nothing but destruction."

"Yes, Sir, if you could prove that *he* did it. You'd have to catch the submarine, physically, and even take some prisoners; otherwise, he could just deny it. As things stand, we won't even have any grounds for making the accusation if in fact the Coral Sea is attacked."

The Chief of Staff appeared to think about this for a moment, and then the Admiral began to move on to the next group. Martinson gave Mike a brief, strange look, and hurried to join the Admiral. The Commodore broke up the conversation group by making a refill maneuver to the bar, and then he caught Mike's eye. They moved over to a window away from the crowd.

"What was all that about, Michael?"

"He thanked me for rescuing his wife from the drainage ditches over at NAS, and then we got on to the submarine thing."

"Oh, yeah? What'd he have to say?"

"How ridiculous and unlikely and improbable, etc. But he apparently thought enough about it at one time to go look up Quaddaffi's sub force in *Jane's*."

"Hmmm," grunted the Commodore. "I wonder if they really have dismissed it, or if they have someone working it on the Q.T."

"If they do, what are the chances of your Q.T. running into their Q.T.?"

"That's what I'm afraid of. Or he could be thinking about how to cover his ass if trouble materializes. By the way, my intel guy has asked the question, but it's Friday, so we won't get any feedback until Monday. He couldn't exactly go in with fire bells ringing."

"Yes, Sir, I appreciate that. The XO and I have started planning on two fronts." He went on to describe the work planned for the weekend.

"Good move," said the Commodore, eyeing some new civilians who were making their approach. "Let's plan to meet Monday night. And good evening, gentlemen, I'm Captain Aronson, ComDesRon Twelve, and this is Captain Montgomery, CO of the Goldsborough. How do you do?"

Introductions were made all around, and one of the civilians, whose name tag said he was President of the Jacksonville Beach Seafood Restaurant Association, asked Mike if Goldsborough was the ship that found the sunken fishing boat.

"Yes, we did, or rather we found the oil slick and the Coast Guard actually found the Rosie III on the bottom. It was a sad discovery—I knew Chris Mayfield."

"So did I. He used to come to our meeting sometimes. His sister—do you know her, too? She gave me a call the other day. Said the fishermen are pretty upset. There's lots of talk going around about some kind of submarine out there. The fishing people still think the Rosie wasn't an accident."

"Well, it's just most unlikely," the Commodore interjected before Mike could answer. "It just doesn't figure that a submarine would be hiding out in our fishing grounds taking shots at commercial fishing boats, does it."

"Well that one fella is insisting that he saw a submarine out there, and that it looked like one of those old U-boats. He says he's been told the Navy doesn't have any subs that look like that, and so it must be a foreigner. He's saying the Navy's covering something up."

The others began to listen in interest.

"There's nothing to cover up, I'm afraid," replied the Commodore, patiently. Mike kept his eyes on the carpet, letting the Commodore carry the water.

"If we were covering something up, we'd have never reported finding the Rosie's oil slick, would we? Anyway, the Coast Guard is investigating the Rosie III sinking. They'll probably pinpoint something that's going to make all this submarine talk sound pretty foolish. Captain Montgomery lives out there in Mayport, and knows several of the commercial fishermen, don't you, Mike. Some of those guys hit the bottle pretty hard, from what I've heard."

He laughed to take the sting out of his insinuation, and most of the group laughed along with him, but the one man would not let it go.

"I think maybe you'all are making a little light of this thing, Captain," he said defiantly. "There's some people's upset out there in the Mayport community."

"I can appreciate that," said the Commodore, with a hint of exasperation in his voice. "We get upset when we lose a plane or have an accident aboard one of our ships. But the Navy is not allowed to get into the Coast Guard's business, and the loss of the Rosie III, if not an accident, is a law enforcement matter. All this talk of a submarine makes for interesting bar talk, but there's simply nothing to it. Now, Sir, tell me about your Association."

The conversation moved on to other things. An hour later, Mike managed to extricate himself from the reception and the O-club, and headed for the Lucky Bag. He found himself driving faster than usual, in anticipation of finding Diane at the boat. But when he arrived, only Hooker was present for duty.

"Well, Bird, where the hell is she?" he asked, stripping off his uniform whites in the cool of the lounge.

Hooker declined to answer, and went into a whistling jag instead. Mike promptly dropped the cover over the cage; he hated it when Hooker started in on one of his random collection of melodic fragments, as the noise tended to go on for hours. He shifted into boat clothes and went down to the fishing piers to scrounge a fish for dinner. Later that night he was reading in the lounge when the Exec called.

"Sorry to bother you, Sir, but the CDO called me a few minutes ago," said Farmer.

"What's up?"

"The quarterdeck got a call from a woman who would not identify herself, but who insisted on having your home phone. The OOD wouldn't give it out, and referred her to the CDO; he also refused to give it to her; he did get her number, it's long distance by the way, and then called me."

"No idea who this is?"

"No, Sir. But the OOD said she acted like she was somebody important; she apparently got kinda pissed off at the end of the whole deal."

"Curiouser and curiouser; maybe she's pretty—lemme have the number."

The Exec gave it to him, noting that it was the south Florida area code. Mike said he'd give her a call and see what it was all about. Sometimes irate divorced wives called the Captain to find out why sailor John wasn't paying his child support. He dialled the number.

"Hello? This is Mary," was the reply at the other end.

"This is Commander Mike Montgomery calling," Mike began. "Someone called—"

"Oh, yes, hang on a second." He could hear the woman calling someone. She sounded excited. Then the sound of Diane's voice came on the line. Mike had forgotten all about Martinson's comment.

"You've got a pretty effective screen on that quarterdeck, Captain," she said, mock exasperation in her voice.

"Yeah, well they have their instructions. CO's get a lot of strange calls."

"How about obscene calls, Captain?" said Diane, her voice coy.

"Not as many of those as I'd like, I'm afraid, Ma'am. Where the hell are you, anyway?"

"Do you miss me?"

"Well, I'll survive, but Hooker's gone on a whistling jag; he might be pining. Wants to see a little leg, I think."

She laughed, a delightful, throaty sound over the phones.

"I'd forgotten the houseboat number. I'm in Orlando with Mary Jackson; she's now officially an accomplice. She caught her husband playing around two years ago, divorced him, and now is in advertising at Disney World. We've been friends since Washington, five years ago. I told J.W. I was coming down here for the weekend to visit."

"And just how does that solve Hooker's problem?"

"Well, here's the plan—I'm calling J.W. tonight from here, and I'm going to let Mary say hello. I'll tell him that tomorrow we're going shopping all day, just to spoil his weekend, only I'll drive back up there tomorrow. If he calls tomorrow night, which he probably won't, Mary will stall him and call the boat; she has three-way calling, so we can make it sound like I'm still here. How's that sound?"

"Complicated. Why don't you just come back here tonight."

"Hooker that bad off, hunh?"

"He might not be the only one, but there's all that goddamn whistling..."

"Well I do really have some shopping to do; maybe I'll buy some interesting outfits and we can see how Hooker likes them. Besides, Mary wants to visit. She wants to hear all about you. Aren't you proud?"

"Everybody's right; I don't understand women," he sighed. "But half a weekend is better than no weekend. I've got lots to tell you."

"You mean we'll have time to talk?" she asked, that teasing tone returning. "Mary thinks we won't. Isn't she awful? So, I'll see you sometime tomorrow afternoon. You have all the beach bunnies off the boat by the time I get there."

"All of them?" he complained. "That's going to affect my reputation, you know."

"Yes, but it'll do wonders for mine. Bye!"

Mike hung up. Hooker, who had gone silent under his cover during the conversation, resumed whistling. Mike yelled at him to shut up, but Hooker ignored him. Mike went back to his book. She had sounded like a schoolgirl, teasing, flirting, and one hundred percent into her little conspiracy. And happy. He wondered not for the first time what the hell he had gotten himself into, but was feeling fewer regrets all the time.

The submarine intruded into his thoughts. He wondered again if it could all be true. And if it is true, what the hell am I doing here reading a book and making plans for the weekend. Up to now, it had all been hypothetical, an interesting theory with enough questions and ambiguity to make it implausible. If it's implausible, we can toy with it. But Coral Sea was coming back. Next week, maybe. Coral Sea provided several new elements: the target, the motive, and the consequences. And then it might not stay hypothetical or implausible. It could get real in a heart-beat, real in the worst way, with smashed ships and hundreds of casualties spilling into a stunned sea on a late Friday afternoon. He stared out the porthole at the darkened marina. What should he be doing now, if some bastard is really out there?

FIFTY

The Mayport marina, Saturday, 3 May;

Mike spent the next morning doing boat chores and cleaning house after a week of domestic neglect. Hooker had begun the day with another siege of whistling, but Mike had turned the vacuum cleaner exhaust on him. The mini-hurricane that followed required the bedraggled parrot to spend the rest of the morning settling all the severely ruffled feathers, effectively shutting him up. Mike's thoughts strayed continuously to Diane's impending arrival, until he remembered that the Exec was coming out to the boat that afternoon.

He paused to work it out. Orlando was about three, four hours from Mayport. If she went shopping until mid day, then had lunch with her friend, and then drove up, it would be about four, five o'clock before she arrived. But maybe earlier. He'd better go see Max.

He found the Marina owner up at the front office, explaining the joys of boat ownership to a pair of urban sophisticates. Maxie was being polite, but his hackles were up just a little. Mike watched in amusement as the two explored every nuance of the marina lifestyle. One of them began giving Mike the eye behind his friend's back, so Mike wandered out to the back pier porch until they were through. Maxie joined him in a few minutes.

"Just what we freaking need," he growled. "Some more girls."

Mike laughed out loud, and then told Max he had a problem.

"Yeah, what?" said Max, giving him the look. "You've invited two women down for the same weekend, am I right? And you want old Max here to shunt one of 'em off."

Max was older than Mike, but still reputed to be quite active amongst the local ladies.

Mike laughed. "Not quite, but it is something like that; I've got one woman coming down for the weekend, but I've also got my XO coming out here for some business. I've got to make sure she doesn't come tripping aboard while he's still there."

"This that tall brunette I been seein'? She's too good lookin' to be single, which means you're doin' somethin' really dumb, and I ain't gonna get involved in somethin' that produces husbands showing up in the office with shotguns lookin' for wayward women, unh-unh!"

Mike explained the situation about the husband and his girlfriend, and how it was a Navy triangle, so to speak. Max, who genuinely liked Mike, shook his head in wonder.

"You like livin' dangerously? Is that it? You bored with no war on?"

Mike shook his head. "It's more serious than that, Maxie. I think she's going to split, and I'm actually entertaining the notion marrying her if she does."

Max whistled. "Man, this is some serious shit. Lemme make an observation, and then I'll shut up. Married woman who plays around is unfaithful; what makes you think she's going to become faithful just because she's married to you? Think about it. OK, look, she shows up, I'll tell her to go get a drink over at Hampton's. Maybe I'll take her into the back bar; those ole geezers over there need a shock. I'll call you if you haven't already called me, and you can get your XO home where he belongs on a Saturday anyways. How's that?'

"That's perfect, Maxie. And you're right, of course, I'm probably waterskiing in a minefield."

"But she's worth it, right? And she's gonna leave her husband for you, too. And the check's in the mail, and I won't come—"

"Awright, awright!" said Mike. "Any more shit and I'll sic Hooker on you; he'll whistle you to death."

"That bag of feathers is usually too drunk to whistle. Hang loose, sport. And watch out for guys wearing raincoats on sunny days."

The minor details arranged, Mike returned to the boat and called the Exec on the ship. Ben promised to be out at noon. Mike, knowing the usual level of cuisine on the ship on the weekend, called over to Hampton's for a carry-out cold seafood platter.

The Exec arrived promptly at noon, carrying charts rolled up under his arm and a briefcase. He was somewhat conspicuous in his khaki uniform among all the denizens of the Marina, who typically dressed in as little as possible. Not a few of the boat owners stared at the Navy officer in uniform as if he were a man from Mars. Mike saw him coming across the floating piers and called Maxie to remind him that under no circumstances was Diane to be allowed into the marina until the guy in khakis had gone home. Maxie said he would see what he could do, as long as the lady was reasonably cooperative. Mike worried about that.

The Exec came aboard and was delighted to see a decent lunch. Mike took him to the porch where they spread out the planning materials. They then shared the seafood platter and some cold beer on the porch, talking about inconsequential things during their lunch. The inland waterway was filled to capacity with boat traffic, and the noise of engines, boom-boxes, and the occasional horns of boats trying to obey the inland rules of the road punctuated the bright sunlight. It was already getting seriously hot, with a promise of thundershowers unfurling in heavy, white cumulus towers to the west. Mike tried to relax over lunch but was aware of the clock ticking in the background and wondered what crazy old Max might really do if Diane showed up before the Exec left. He cleared away the remains of lunch, popped open two more beers, and they got down to business.

"I felt a little nervous about bringing these classified pubs out here, Captain," said the Exec, putting the two plastic binders on the floor. "They're not supposed to leave the ship."

"Operational necessity, Ben. We'll make sure nothing goes adrift, OK?. Put them on that chair, there, so we keep them separate. So, how's this problem shape up?" Mike said.

"Yes, Sir," said the Exec, spreading out the large area chart. "Initially, the carrier will approach from the southeast. I constructed a notional great circle track from San Juan, with an end point here on the chart. From there, a rhumbline to the sea buoy is a straight shot, 300 degrees. Assuming an estimated time of arrival of 1730 at a point ten miles from the sea buoy, which I call point Bravo, the Coral Sea should be right here, at point Alfa, at 1530. This allows her time to slow down and enter the channel at a little before 1900, to meet slack water in the basin at 1900. Her track to the sea buoy looks like this, from Alfa to Bravo, assuming a speed of about fifteen knots."

"Now, you can see from the chart that the water depth would allow a diesel boat free range anywhere between Alfa and Bravo, so that's where I would expect an attack. It ranges between 350 and 450 feet. His periscope depth is sixty feet, so he has on average around 300 feet of water to maneuver in. The bottom is pretty flat, except for a couple of wrecks and one large pinnacle along the track. This is the silt area from the St. Johns, so it's a mud bottom, mostly. This large canyon is the result of a few millennia of the St. Johns digging out the Shelf, and its tributaries show up in the attack zone as lots of smaller canyons and ravines, with layers of river mud piled up along their rims. We hear mudslides all the time when we listen on the sonar. Inshore of point Bravo it starts to shallow up markedly."

Mike examined the track lines on the chart. He could find no obvious errors, and the Exec's logic seemed to be correct.

"OK. That looks reasonable to me," he said. "The good news is that this whole attack zone is well inshore of the Gulf Stream, so we shouldn't have the acoustic problems we've been looking at during our search excursions. We will have shallow water, though, which means reverberation for the active sonar, and it also renders our torpedoes almost useless with the bottom that close. You know, a lot's going to depend on whether or not Coral Sea's bringing any escorts with her."

The Exec produced a piece of paper. "According to this, she's coming north with three escorts. But all three are from Norfolk, so I figure she'll detach them out at sea and be coming into Mayport all by her lonesome."

"Incredible, when you think of it," said Mike. "And yet, why not? It's peacetime, she's within fifty miles of her home port, in U.S. waters. There's no threat, so why have any escorts, especially when they have another day's trip to get home."

Two boats got into a hooting match out on the waterway, prompting much vocal derision from the boat people in the marina. There were several suggestions called out from the marina to the larger of the two motorboats, but in the end, the smaller one gave way to the law of gross tonnage. Mike and the Exec watched the interplay for a few minutes, and then resumed their study of the ASW problem. The Exec reviewed the search tactics that applied to shallow water, confined hydrography situations, and then walked Mike through the attack tactics for depth charge and, in an emergency, given the water depth, the use of the torpedoes in bottom-close situations. Mike thought aloud about the timing.

"We have to be out in that tactical channel between Alfa and Bravo by fairly early in the morning, so we can work it over acoustically and also take a look at the bottom features," Mike observed.

"Yes, Sir. And, ideally we would be between the sub's potential attack position and the Coral Sea. But there's no way to know if the sub will be north, south, or even along the track."

"That's why I want to get out there early, by Thursday evening, if possible, so we can start working the area. Maybe spook him into a wrong move; hell, we might even gain contact. If we could keep him involved in dealing with us, the carrier might slip through. Can we expect any other traffic in that area?"

"Well, it is the most direct route for any ship coming up from the Caribbean to go to Jax; the big oil tankers that go up to the northside refinery would be on that track. Those big Toyota car carriers also come up that way, from the Panama Canal."

Mike reflected. That might be a good news, bad news factor. Good news in that the sub would have to come up to take a look at a big tanker or a car carrier coming through, in case it was the carrier; bad in that a tanker would plow through the area with no regard for what a destroyer might be doing in an ASW problem.

"OK, let's say we get out there in the Alfa-Bravo channel area by first light Friday. How would we start the search?"

The Exec moved the area chart to one side and laid down a tactical chart he had drawn up, using tracing paper from the CIC. He pointed to the eastern end of the tactical box.

"I figure the sub will lie in wait at the deeper end of the box, out towards Alfa, rather than inshore where the water begins to shoal. You see this ridge on the track—it's more of a sea mound, really, but it comes up almost eighty feet off the sea floor, and it's a half mile in diameter at the base, with lots of canyons around it. If I were the sub CO, I'd get on the western, inshore side of that mound, hugging the bottom, in case the carrier did have escorts pinging out ahead. That would put the sub in the sonar shadow zone created by the ridge; when the escorts and then the carrier passed overhead, she could come up and put six torpedoes into the carrier from behind all of them."

Mike nodded thoughtfully. "But we know there won't be escorts. And if he did that, we'd have to meet the carrier head-on so we could illuminate the western side of the sea mound with our sonar."

"Yes, Sir. And that raises another problem: what do we do if we gain contact? By the regs, we're required to conduct an identification drill, to find out who he is. And we can't determine that he's hostile until he does something. And then, in this tactical geometry, we can't go firing anti-submarine torpedoes directly into the path of the carrier—one of them might acquire the carrier. And we can't run in there under the bird farm's bows so we can drop depth charges. How in hell do we attack this guy?"

"I think we have to assume that, if we find this guy on the carrier's approach track, he's not there to take pictures. We'll do the standard identification procedures, and then lock on to him with the sonar and make sure he knows we have his ass boresighted."

"But to shoot at him, we'd have to make the carrier maneuver somehow."

"Well," said Mike. "What do we do, tell him over Fleet Tactical that there's a sub waiting in ambush for him? I think they'd report us for smoking dope on the high seas!"

They both sat back in their chairs to think. Mike knew that the Exec was right. They would need to think up something that would make the carrier move almost reflexively, without question, if Goldsborough gained contact along her track.

"I've got it," said the Exec, leaning forward. "Mines. We could say we've sighted a floating mine ahead of him, and request he move right or left. We can call the direction at the time according to what we see on the tactical plot. Nobody screws around when they hear mines."

Mike nodded. That would indeed work. All you had to do was say the word mines, and ships would maneuver at high speed in the away direction. It would also relieve them of the burden of trying to explain to the Carrier CO just what they were doing out there.

"And, otherwise, we just apply our regular fleet tactics; search, gain contact, classify, hold him, and shoot his ass before he shoots ours," said Mike.

The Exec nodded thoughtfully.

"That's yet another loose end that bothers me," he said.

A sudden breeze sprang up off the waterway, and there was rumble of thunder in the western distance. The sunlight had taken on an orange hue. A sudden, hot breeze lifted the chart paper off the table momentarily, spilling the classified publications and the other charts onto the floor in every direction.

"What's that, XO?" said Mike, grabbing for the charts.

"The business of shooting. So far this whole thing is conjecture on our part, that there's even a submarine out there, waiting for the Coral Sea. And that it means to attack the carrier. Under peacetime rules of engagement, we have no authority to shoot anybody without making a pretty substantial effort to identify him first and then prove that he was hostile. I mean, suppose this is a colossal screw up, and that's a Canadian sub out there, practicing shallow water ASW under a NATO OpOrder for the defense of the eastern approaches to U.S. harbors?"

"Surely we'd have known about a friendly foreign submarine operating here, XO. Hell, they would have provided some live sub training time for the Spruances as quid pro quo for letting him operate here."

"You have to admit that it is feasible that there's something we don't know, Captain. It's more likely that this guy is a Canadian or a Brit than he is a Libyan..."

Mike gave a short laugh. The Exec had a point. He piled the papers into a stack on the deck, and put one of the classified pubs on top as a paper weight.

"OK, but if this guy is what we think he is, he may solve the problem for us. Under the rules of engagement, if he takes a shot, either at us or the carrier, then we're weapons free on his ass. And that might be how we in fact classify him in the end analysis."

"Yes, Sir. We probably ought to talk to the Commodore about the R.O.E. before we leave port at the end of the week."

The thunder rolled again, closer this time. Mike glanced at his watch. It was three-thirty. There seemed little left to discuss. What was required now were the actual search plans, the various attack patterns that could develop, and an acoustic prediction analysis of the area of operations. The Exec saw Mike looking at his watch. He stood up.

"I'll work the details tomorrow; Sunday's are dead quiet on the ship, and I can get to the pubs I need without attracting attention. I'll tell the CDO I'm working up fitness reports."

Mike stood up, lunging for the papers as the wind blew again, spilling his neat stack.

"Ben, I appreciate this very much; you call me if you hit any snags. Tell your wife we'll get you a couple of long weekends after this is all over."

The Exec gathered up his materials and the charts. The wind was visibly picking up across the surface of the waterway, and the rumbles of thunder were more frequent. The western sky was turning deep purple. Mike helped him gather up the charts and the pubs into an armload, and they went forward to the gangway. The Exec had to grab his hat in the stiffening breeze. Around them, the weekend sailors were busy stowing gear and deck chairs in anticipation of the approaching squall. Shroud lines could be heard clanking against their masts over the wind; some of the girls looked faintly ridiculous in their skimpy bikinis as they grabbed loose gear to get it below.

"You go on home, Ben," said Mike. "Start again fresh tomorrow, and call me around noon, let me know how it's going. And maybe we ought to think about going out quiet, not pinging at all, until the carrier does show up. It occurs to me that a pop-up destroyer act might be more effective in screwing up his attack on the Coral Sea than an all night pinging operation."

"Yes, Sir, you may be right," said Farmer. He was having to shout over the wind. "If he knows we're there and we don't gain contact, he'd have all night to hide out. If we delay, and go out quiet, we might be able to take him by surprise, and then make him do something that allows us to classify him and short circuit the rules of engagement problem. I'd better mosey," he concluded, eyeing the approaching thunderstorm.

He peered at the pile of charts and books in his arms. "I hope I got everything."

"If not, I'll bring it in Monday. But think on it; we'll talk some more tomorrow," said Mike.

"Yessir," shouted Ben into the wind as he walked down the pier toward the marina office.

Mike went back into the lounge and called Maxie, who answered on the third ring.

"She show up yet?"

"No sign; I see your guy is leaving. So if she shows up, she comes straight through, right?"

"Right. I hope she beats this storm."

"Yeah, I gotta go secure some shit."

"You need a hand?"

"Nope; as long as I git off this phone, I'll make it."

"Thanks, Maxie."

Mike hung up, and went topside to make sure his own porch furniture was secured. The screens kept out most of the weather, but a good blow could knock things around, and from the looks of the darkening sky across the waterway, they were in for a good blow. As he stacked the chairs, he found one of the classified publications wedged between the couch and a chair. He looked quickly over to the parking lot, but Farmer's car was just pulling out of the sand lot. Mike carried the pub to his briefcase and locked it inside. He wondered where Diane was.

310

FIFTY ONE

Mayport Marina, Saturday, 3 May

Ben Farmer was almost all the way back to the base when he realized that one of the two classified ASW publications was not in the stack of materials spilled on his front seat. He pulled over into a convenience store parking lot and made a quick inventory to make sure. The wind was whipping up clouds of dust and sand around the parking lot, and the proprietor, an elderly oriental man, was pulling in signs from the front porch area as the afternoon sky darkened.

He knew that he had brought two classified references, both with white, plastic covers. Only one was on the front seat. He remembered putting both of them on the floor under the table on the porch. But the Captain had used one to weight the paper stack. He checked under the seat, and in his briefcase without success, and then looked out the window. The edge of the squall line was visible over the tops of the trees to the west, but that main bang still looked to be about five miles west of the river. He might just have time to go back.

He turned his car around, waited for a white, four door sedan to go by, and pulled out onto the highway back to Mayport. The woman in the sedan had looked familiar, but he dismissed the thought as he kept an eye on the approaching storm. It took him five minutes to get back to the Marina parking lot, and the squall line seemed much closer now that he was back on the waterway itself. The palm fronds were standing straight away from their trees, and there was a lot of sand blowing around the parking lot. The sky looked and sounded ominous.

The white car he had been following had preceded him into the parking lot. As he was gauging whether or not he could make it to the Lucky Bag before the rain started, the woman got out of the car. The wind whipped her summer skirt up around her knees, and she clutched a small overnight bag and a wrapped package under her arms. He watched her make a run for the Marina office; she had a dynamite figure. He could not see her face because she was wearing sunglasses. As she made it to the Marina office door, however, she took her glasses off before going inside, and then Ben recognized her. Mrs. Martinson. The Chief of Staff's wife. What the hell was she doing at the Marina?

The wind began to gust, rocking his car, and the first few fat raindrops cratered the sandy dust in the parking lot. There was a washboard of whitecaps standing up across the intracoastal waterway, and all the boat traffic had disappeared. The sky was dark enough that the buoys had begun to blink in the channel. Ben decided he would make a run for the office and call the Captain. The Captain could bring the pub up from the boat and meet him halfway. He could barely see the Lucky Bag, three piers over from the office. He had just opened the car door when he saw the Captain come running across the piers towards the office. Then to his astonishment he saw Mrs. Martinson make a similar dash from the office. They met halfway, she crouching under the protection of his broad shoulder while they both turned and dashed, laughing, back to the Lucky Bag. The rain swept across the waterway at that instant and drew a noisy curtain over the entire Marina.

Ben Farmer closed the door and sat back in his seat in shock as the rain drummed on the roof of his car. The windows fogged over after a minute, completing the obscuration of everything outside. A flash of lightning speared the waterway to his right, and the clap of thunder made him wince.

The Exec had been happily married since he was a junior Lieutenant. He and his wife had three children, and lived in quarters on the base in the CO-XO housing area near the beach. He had, of course, noticed Diane Martinson. Every adult who lived in CO-XO housing, male and female, had noticed Diane Martinson at one time or another. His wife had caught him looking for just a shade longer than marital propriety permitted and had pinched him just above his belt line for staring. Diane's arrival at the Marina, on a Saturday afternoon, complete with an overnight bag, was evidence of a situation that he fervently wished he did not know about. The rain drummed louder.

Navy ship wardrooms had a well defined hierarchy among the wives. The Captain's wife was socially in charge, and organized, usually with the help of the Executive Officer's wife, most wardroom functions such as the annual Christmas party, charity events, cocktail parties, and homecomings when the ship had been away. The CO and the XO's wives also handled a myriad of family problems, officer and enlisted, that inevitably cropped up when the ship was out of home port for extended periods.

When the CO did not have a wife, the "duties" of the CO's wife fell upon the Executive Officer's wife, as was the case in Goldsborough. The Captain contributed funds for many of the functions, and Ben's wife, Carol, ably ran the show. The fact that the Captain was a bachelor lent spice to some of the social occasions, as the wives were always eager to see what he might bring along as a date. Some of the bachelors' dates had found the Captain to be more interesting than their escort for the evening, which usually caused the Captain some acute embarrassment.

As Exec, Ben kept himself in the know about which officer's marriage was in trouble, who had a chronically sick child, and which of the ship's bachelor officers was in danger of getting himself hooked. But Ben had carefully eschewed knowing anything at all about the Captain's private life. The Captain kept all of that to himself, which was just fine as far as Ben was concerned. And now this little discovery. His CO was seeing the wife of the Chief of Staff, and from the way he had sheltered her from the squall, their relationship was well advanced.

He decided to get the hell out of there while it was still raining. The Captain could bring in the pub, and he recognized that the only thing worse than knowing what he now knew would be for the Captain to know that he knew. The bulk of the rain squall was passing, and he could just begin to see across the parking lot again. Just when you think you've seen all the problems that an XO tour can throw at you, something bigger and better smacks you in the face, he thought. He started the car, turned the wipers on high, and began to navigate his way through the downpour very carefully across the parking lot and out onto the road back to the base. He wondered how long he could keep this from Carol.

FIFTY TWO

The Al Akrab, seaward approaches, St. Johns River, Sunday, 4 May; 0100

The Captain wiped the rain out of his face and tried to clean the optics on his binoculars. He was wedged into the conning tower cockpit, bent low behind a makeshift plexiglass windscreen which did very little to keep the weather out of his face. The two lookouts perched above and behind him on the periscope shears were shapeless bundles of raingear in the dark. A warm wind streamed over the conning tower as the submarine plowed steadily through a heavy chop, the air redolent with the scents of the shoreline ahead. He had decided to bring the Al Akrab in partially flooded down after all, so that the usual shape of the bows and the foredeck ahead of the conning tower were missing, revealed only when larger waves broke over the black, rounded hull like the roils of water in a river over barely submerged rocks. The rain came in intermittent sheets, followed by slack periods when the night sky opened to reveal a large thunderstorm booming its way out to sea to the south. The lights of Mayport and the naval base were visible as an orange glow against the base of the low flying clouds up off the port bow.

The Captain was grateful for the shield of the foul weather, but he knew that the Deputy, as Navigator, would be not so grateful. He could hear the periscope swivelling in its tube as the Deputy in the attack center attempted to take bearings on the navigation aids ashore. The Captain peered again through his Russian binoculars. The lighthouse at Mayport

313

was clearly visible, beaming a strong flash of white light every twenty seconds from atop its man-made hill on the base. But he had not yet detected the two river range lights. Without radar, and without those lights, their position was essentially a guess. They knew that they were somewhere on a line of bearing from the lighthouse, but the all critical factor of range from the river's entrance was missing. They had to find at least one more light for a cross bearing. He felt a tightness in his gut as the submarine advanced inexorably on the darkened shore at four knots.

"Navigator, Captain," he growled into the intercom box.

"Sir," replied the box, barely audible over the noise of a new squall of rain and wind rattling on the plexiglass shield.

"Can you see the river range lights?"

"No, Sir. Not yet. We are searching on high power, but there is too much weather."

"When was our last good fix?"

"Uh, some time ago, Sir. We have now only an estimated position. We are using a dead-reckoning plot, bearings from the lighthouse, and the depth sounder. The range to the river's mouth is estimated at ten thousand meters, and there is sixty feet of water beneath the keel. We need—"

"Yes, yes, I know what we need—another light!" the Captain said. He brought his binoculars back up to his eyes and continued to sweep the shore, or at least the sector of the horizon ahead where the shore ought to be. He realized that the navigation team was doing the best it could. The wind was from dead ahead, but the local currents along the Florida coast set northerly. With the submarine flooded down, the current's effect would predominate over the wind, and the nearest shoal waters were to the south of the channel, away from the direction of drift. He glanced at his watch. If they could not get a fix within the next twenty minutes, he would have to break it off. He needed one accurate fix to give him the intercept course to the sea buoy; after that they could buoy hop their way into the channel. He scanned the shore again, starting with the light-house and moving right, to the dark sector to the right of the naval base lights that had to be the river, and then searching inshore of the river's mouth. One of the lookouts gave a low shout.

"Stay on it!" ordered the Captain, craning his neck to see which way the man was looking. The man's binoculars were trained well to the right of where the Captain had been looking. He put his glasses up to his eyes, swept right, and saw the blinking red light, down low on the surface. A buoy. They were going to pass it close aboard to their starboard side. Very close.

"Left full rudder!" he shouted into the intercom box. "Navigator we have a buoy close aboard to starboard!" He watched as the rudder angle indicator dial, a green blur on the rain soaked instrument panel, swung left. The boat ploughed on for a few heart stopping moments before finally answering the helm. He looked up anxiously as the buoy came down the starboard side, only some thirty feet away. They could hear the metallic clank of its buoy bell as it bounced in the windswept chop.

"Shift your rudder," he ordered, to swing the stern and the screws back away from the buoy now that the boat had begun to swing. "Steady 270." He yelled to the lookouts to get the buoy's number if they could.

"Two," called the starboard lookout, as the submarine's head swung slowly back to the west.

"Mark buoy number two abeam to starboard," yelled the Captain into the intercom. His whole body listened anxiously for the rumble of a propeller hitting the buoy's anchor chain, but they slipped safely past. The wind whistled around the conning tower, as if in appreciation. The rain suddenly stopped in a final sweeping gust of wind, and moments later the periscope stopped swinging.

"Contact on the river range," called the Deputy from below. "Stand by for course recommendation."

The Captain straightened up as the Al Akrab came out of the squall line, and let out a long breath. There were many lights suddenly visible ahead as the air cleared; they were closer in to the shore line than he had thought. He scanned ahead to find the range, aligning his binoculars with the glass face of the periscope, and found it almost at once. They were to the right of the range. As he prepared to make a course adjustment, the intercom sounded off.

"Recommend come left to 267 to regain track," said the Deputy. "We hold ourselves 7200 meters from the turn point, and we have a good fix."

"Very well; come left to 267," replied the Captain. He turned around to the lookouts. "We have found the river range; search now for small boats coming down the river; look for running lights."

The lookouts acknowledged, and the Captain resumed his own surveillance of the river's entrance. He could see the pattern of red and green buoy lights now that the rain had passed, and the channel into the river was clearly marked, even against the brightening backdrop of the shore lights.

"Depth beneath the keel?" he asked of the intercom.

"Depth is forty five feet beneath the keel and conforms to the charted depth," replied the box. Behind the conning tower the rumble of thunder and lightning was diminishing in the distance as the storm cell passed out to sea. The wind had freshened in its wake, veering around to the submarine's starboard quarter as she approached the shoreline, returning to the normal on-shore breeze pattern after the squall line. The submarine was dead quiet, running on the battery with electric propulsion.

"Turn on the navigation lights, dim position," ordered the Captain. If there was radar surveillance, the only substantial echoes would be returned from the conning tower, as the rest of the submarine's shape was awash. The dim navigation lights, red and green on the sides and one dim white light on the front of the sail, would look like a fishing boat to any watching eyes. So far, the electronic surveillance console had reported no radar signals sweeping across the Mayport approaches. He continued to watch for several minutes while the submarine thumped and bumped its way through the choppy waters.

"Based on a good fix at time 24, range to the turn point is 4200 meters; recommend come back right to 271," spoke the box.

"Very well, come right to 271," replied the Captain. Another buoy was shaping up in the darkness, to port this time, its green light winking comfortably in the rapidly clearing night air. The squall seemed to have scrubbed the coastal atmosphere; all of the lights ashore were now unnaturally bright. The Captain suddenly felt very exposed. He could make out the red aircraft warning lights atop the masts of the ships bunched together in the Mayport basin. He could even make out the vast bulk of the aircraft carrier moored to the bulkhead pier along the river. It was incredible: they were within a few miles of the American Navy's largest southern naval base, and operating on the surface with total impunity. The Captain felt a surge of pride at their achievement.

"Look at them," he mused aloud. "Dozens of destroyers, all asleep even as we bring our scorpion to their very doorstep."

The lookouts grunted their acknowledgement, surprising him. With the wind no longer blowing in their faces, the Captain's every word could be heard at the top of the conning tower. The Al Akrab pressed on, even as the shimmering rays of amber light from the sodium vapor streetlights on the base began to reach out for them across the surface of the St. Johns river.

"1500 meters to turn point," spoke the box.

The Captain detected a note of apprehension in the Deputy's voice that penetrated even the fuzzy sound of the intercom. He imagined what it looked like on the chart below, as the submarine crept into the outer channel along a series of small, pencilled X's on the chart. He could see in his mind's eye the tight knot of officers surrounding the plotting table in the red light below, looking fearfully at the chart's depiction of the naval base. Into the lion's den. He scanned the river range through his glasses, and saw that they were back on track. At 1000 meters he would come right to allow room to make the turn in the river entrance.

A mile and half ahead to port lay the junction between the St. Johns main channel and the dredged channel into the Mayport naval basin, which slanted off to the left in a Y intersection with the river. The junction that was the target for the mines. The Coral Sea had to turn left into that basin channel at precisely the right time to avoid the sandbar just upstream of the junction. He would plant the three mines in the river channel just downstream of the turn; they would tear the bottom out of the carrier and send her careening across the channel to run aground on the opposite shore, thereby blocking the entire river exit. Perfect.

"950 meters to turn point; recommend come right to 280 to offset for the turn."

"Very well;" replied the Captain. "Navigator is to take control of the conn in the attack center and position the ship to make the turn; use power for standard speed to twist the boat."

The Deputy acknowledged; with their navigation plot now accurately updated by the half-minute with buoys, the range lights, and the lighthouse, they had a much better picture on their chart than the Captain did perched in the darkness at the top of the conning tower. They could shoot bearings with precision through the periscope, determine their exact position on the chart, and maneuver the boat to come right into the mouth of the river, turn sharply, stop, back up if they had to, simulate firing the mines, and start back out. The submarine began swinging to the right.

The Captain looked at his plastic, Japanese watch; the lights from the shore were almost bright enough to read it without hitting the light button. 0155. An excellent time for this night's work. He wished he could fire the mines tonight, but they still did not have a precise arrival time from fleet intelligence. He studied the layout of the river approaches, the lights, and the position of the stone breakwater. He had noticed the long wake each buoy was carving through the water, a wide V pointing upstream, indicating a stiff current from the river. They would have to note that current when they put the mines down; it would not do to have them shoot out the stern torpedo tubes and go only twenty meters in the face of the current.

317

"Surface contact, bearing 350 relative," sang out the port lookout. "I have running lights, and a red over white combination on the mast; contact is coming downstream."

The Captain cursed, and then informed the Deputy.

"Begin the turn now," he ordered. "We have company."

Almost at once the submarine steadied, and then began her turn to port, although it seemed to the Captain to be exceedingly slow. Ballasted down as she was, and in shallow water with a river current on her head, Al Akrab seemed reluctant to swing through the turn. The Captain was reaching for the intercom when he felt the sudden rumble of a propeller shaft as the navigator increased the power on the opposed shafts to bring her around. He scanned ahead again with his binoculars, and finally picked out the dim red and green lights, low on the surface of the dark river ahead of them, upstream of the naval base. The boat was coming quickly, her speed augmented by the downstream current; her top lights indicated a fishing boat. Someone had waited to get underway until after the squall lines had subsided.

At long last the submarine began to swing with authority, as the current caught her starboard bow and shoved her around. After another minute and a half, she was pointed seaward.

"Increase speed to twelve knots; turn off all running lights," ordered the Captain. "We will simulate the mine firing at high speed."

He wanted very much to get away from the fishing boat that was bearing down on them from behind. The boat looked to be about two miles distant, enough distance to cover them, although her skipper might be curious about the contact coming upriver that had suddenly turned around. He had decided not to back up into firing position; having seen the current, he knew what he would have to do next time.

The Al Akrab began to move out now, her ballasted hull pushing up a large bow wave that revealed her forward decks intermittently. The Captain noticed that the submarine was also beginning to porpoise a bit. The planesmen were trying to counteract the effect of the ballasted down hull as it met the incoming swells from the sea.

"Blow ballast tanks to full surface condition!" he ordered into the intercom.

The last thing he needed was to inadvertently dive in only sixty feet of water. He moved over to the side of the conning tower cockpit and swept the river behind them with his binoculars. It was very hard to make out the fishing boat's lights against the glare of the base lights.

"ESM reports commercial radar set on the air, bearing 271," spoke the box.

"Very well," replied the Captain.

The fisherman had turned his radar on as he approached the sea channel; they would hold contact on the Al Akrab, but there would be no lights. He felt the submarine lighten as the ballast tanks were blown clear. The submarine stabilized on the surface with a rumbling rush of compressed air and sea foam along the sides as the bows and foredeck rose clear of the swells rolling in from the east.

"Increase speed to fifteen knots," he ordered.

He knew that the fisherman would not be making much over eight knots at best, with some additional knots of push from the current; fifteen would open them handsomely. He looked back at the dim running lights behind them, and wished for a radar. There was no telling how far the lights were behind them. They should have mounted a commercial radar in place of the distinctive Russian submarine radar set.

The Al Akrab was throwing up a good wake now, a wide V of white water standing out from her sides, creating a broad wake astern which was clearly visible from his vantage point. He wondered if the fishermen would also see it, or if the lights behind them would put the submarine's wake in shadow.

"Range to the shoreline is now 3500 meters and opening," reported the box. "Sir: do you wish to light off the diesels—we can make almost twenty knots."

"Negative," the Captain replied. "Stay on the electrics; I want to turn south off channel axis as soon as we clear the last channel buoy; once the fisherman goes by, we will bring up the diesels and recharge the battery while we move offshore. Turn off all the lights."

The Deputy acknowledged. They both knew that running at fifteen knots on the battery was draining precious amps at an alarming rate. But the Captain did not want a trail of diesel exhaust to combine with the radar contact held by the fisherman and thereby confirm to the fishermen that something was out there ahead of them. He would slow and disappear into the darkness along the south shore, and then use the fisherman's engine to mask their own main engines. He looked at his watch again.   •

"Time to run out of the channel?" he asked of the box.

"Time remaining on this leg is nine minutes, Sir."

The Captain nodded in the darkness. Ahead of them the thunderstorm rumbled and glimmered on the distant horizon. He looked back at the fishing boat, whose lights were dimmer now as she was left behind by the submarine's urgent burst of speed. He had momentarily forgotten all about the mining exercise, but thought now that the practice run had been well worth making. They had not considered the weather sufficiently during their planning. The rain squalls had made for excellent cover, but they had almost caused them to abort the run into the beach. They would need to allow more time to make their approach, and they would need to find other reference points to help with the navigation problem.

"Six minutes to turn point," spoke the box.

The Captain looked again behind them, but the fishing boat's lights were no longer visible against the backdrop of the lights ashore.

"Very well," he said. "Turn on time, and prepare to light off the mains; we will run offshore on the diesels and recharge while we open the coast."

Farewell for now, Mayport naval base, he thought. We shall return soon, and turn your river into a charnel house.

FIFTY THREE

The Mayport Marina, Sunday, 4 May; 0230

Mike awoke suddenly, as if sensing an intruder. The sound of thunder rumbled across the darkened river. Lightning flickered against the windows of the cabin, and the rain from the latest squall line continued to drum on the deck above. He could feel the persistent slap of small waves against the transom of the boat.

Diane lay asleep in the crook of his arm, her legs wrapped over his, her breathing deep and regular. His arm was asleep, but he did not try to move it, choosing instead to look at her as she slept. After their first frantic coupling on the couch, he had carried her back to his bedroom, where they had tried it all again, pacing themselves this time. He had been touched by her murmurs of need as he brought her to climax a second time. When she was spent, he held her on top of him, wrapping his arms around her and kissing her hair until they both fell asleep. She moved.

"Oh," she said, opening her eyes and finding him awake, looking at her.

"Oh, indeed," he replied. They kissed, and he felt himself stirring again.

"Unh-unh," she moaned. "I have to be able to walk out of here tomorrow."

The thought of her having to leave deflated him at once, as the real world intruded. She rolled away to the side of the bed.

"Is the bathroom still in there?"

"Sure is."

She groaned as she got up from the bed, moving gingerly.

320

"Want a light?"

"No; it would spoil the glow." He smiled in the gloom as she closed the door to the bathroom.

He got up, thought about putting on his robe, and then decided against it, and looked out the portholes at the river junction. Occasional spears of lightning painted photo flash pictures of the choppy water and the masts of the fishing boats weaving from side to side in the rainy gusts outside. It was the back of the storm, though; the dark mass of clouds was moving rapidly offshore. Diane emerged from the bathroom.

"All yours," she said, as she flopped onto the bed.

He went in and took care of business, and then came back out to the bedroom. She was lying on her stomach across the bed, her head turned sideways on her folded arms, her buttocks white and round in the flickering light of the storm. He went over to the bed, and carefully straddled the backs of her thighs, holding most of his weight on his knees and hands. He kissed the back of her neck, and pressed himself between her thighs, insistent, searching.

"You promised," she murmured.

"No, I didn't."

"You are going to have to carry me from here on out, Captain," she sighed, as she moved with him at last.

"Least I can do," he said, before he found her again and went inside in one smooth thrust. She groaned at the feel of him, and he lay there for a long minute, savoring the exquisite warmth of her body. He drew back, and, holding her hips, pulled her up onto her knees, and then entered her again, deep this time, gradually building his rhythm, trying to make it last but finally letting go in a surge of powerful stroking until he came so intensely it almost hurt. He held her when he was done, his arms locked around her waist and his face on her back. He could hear the hammering of his heart, and realized he was out of breath. After a few minutes she straightened out on her belly again, pulling away from him, turning over on her side, and reaching for him, cradling his head in her breasts until he was still.

"I can't get enough of you," he said, after a while. His voice was muffled by her arms.

She stroked his cheek. "In case you haven't noticed, I'm having the same problem."

He looked up at her, trying to see her face, but it was in shadow.

"I knew I was in bad shape, ever since the O'Club," she continued. "The O'Club?"

"When we collided in that doorway. Your hand touched my stomach. I felt like I'd been branded for the next week. Just an inadvertent touch. I didn't realize how badly I needed a man to just love me, like you did just now."

"One way Charlie, I'm afraid."

She giggled. "So you'll owe me."

"I always pay my debts, Madam."

"See that you do, kind Sir, only not tonight, please."

He looked up at her face in the half light.

"Did you hear the one about the sex survey guy who knocks on this lady's door one morning, tells her he's conducting a sexual practices survey, and asks if she would be willing to answer a few questions for their statistical records. She says yes, so he goes through a whole long list of stuff, and then finally asks her if she smokes after making love. She thinks about it for a moment, and then says, I don't know; I've never looked..."

She hooted, falling back on the bed and laughing with him until they both had tears in their eyes. He moved up alongside her, looking into her eyes, tracing her features with his fingertips.

"You really are lovely," he said. "We're both kinda out of control here, but the more it goes on, the less I care."

She stared back at him, her eyes wondering at her own feelings. A multitude of expressions fled through her mind, each of them sounding more trite than the last one. I've never done this sort of thing before, she wanted to say, except that it sounded so ridiculous. He watched her struggle for words, and put a finger on her lips.

"I know. I've been a bachelor all my life. I wasn't kidding about my hangup about married women. But you, well, I just had to have you. You've swept me away, and I don't even think you meant to do it. It's completely crazy, but, God, it's wonderful. Now, don't say anything. That way you're free to do whatever you want."

Her eyes misted over, and she pulled his face down to her lips. They held each other for a while longer, alone with their thoughts but not alone in their need. Then his stomach growled, and she started giggling again.

"OK, OK, people, it's chow time in the city." He got up from the rumpled bed, and pulled his robe on.

She swung her legs out of the bed, and sat unsteadily on the edge of the bed for a moment. He laughed and brought her a robe, and helped her into it. She leaned against him, her arms wrapped around his neck for support.

"Rubber legs, I'm afraid," she said softly.

322

"All in a good cause, Madam."

He walked her out to the lounge and lowered her down gently on the leather couch, and turned on some more lamps. Hooker grumbled at being awakened. Mike went to the bar, and pulled a bottle of Riesling out of the refrigerator. Opening it carefully, he filled two wine glasses, and brought them over to the couch, and went into the galley to make dinner.

"I want you to know that I had to lay out a screen before you arrived," he called from the galley.

"A screen?"

"Yeah. I forgot that my Exec, Ben Farmer, was coming out here this afternoon. I had to alert Maxie Barr—he's the guy owns this marina—to watch for your arrival and divert you if Ben was still here."

Diane had a fleeting image of another car following her into the parking lot, but she had not really paid attention to it when she made the dash for the marina office. She did remember the older guy in the office, but he had made no visible effort to divert her from seeing Mike after she asked him to call the Lucky Bag.

"I guess he must have been gone by the time I got here," she said.

"Yeah, he'd left about fifteen minutes before you called from the office. If you'd been five minutes later, I'm not sure the phones would even have worked."

"You must be a mean man to make your XO come to work on Saturday," she said.

He came out with the wine bottle and sat down. The aroma of shrimp drifted into the lounge.

"I guess I can tell you about this," he said, sitting down. "It's a little operation that the Commodore and I are running. Nobody at Group knows about it, and we'd both be in the shit if they did."

She sat forward, interested. Mike once again made the mental observation that this was a Captain's wife. It seemed to him that there were two kinds of Navy wives: those that knew a hell of a lot about the profession, and those that knew almost nothing. Diane was obviously of the former variety.

"It's that damned submarine thing," he began.

"I'm surprised," she said. "J.W. told me the Admiral had squelched that whole business. He said that you all thought it was a Libyan sub? Waiting to ambush the Coral Sea?"

"Right; I know it sounds farfetched, but actually you gave me the idea when you noted that other countries have diesel subs besides the Soviets."

"And you and the Commodore briefed the Admiral? J.W. was a little miffed that the Admiral came by himself, by the way. But he said once the Admiral heard the story, he decided that the whole thing had gotten out of hand and was just a pipedream, and that the mystery submarine issue was now officially over. Are you saying it's not?"

"Officially, yes, it's over. Unofficially..."

Mike took a long pull at his wine before continuing.

"Basically, the Admiral said we were all nuts and ordered us to drop it. The next day the Commodore calls me to the Club for lunch and says he doesn't want to drop it. He believes—and so, somewhat reluctantly, do I—that there might in fact be a Libyan sub waiting out in the Jax opareas for the Coral Sea. Might is the operative word. At least we think there's enough evidence to warrant timing my next engineering sea trial to coincide with Coral Sea's arrival sometime around next Thursday or Friday."

"My God," she said. "And Group doesn't know this? What happens if you're right?"

"We'll have us a little gunfight at the OK corral, Ma'am, and everybody'd better hope Goldsborough wins."

She thought about that for a moment. "And if it's not true?"

"Then no big deal—Goldy went to sea to conduct engineering sea trials, saw the Coral Sea go by, paid her respects, did her trials, and came back in to gather some more rust, with, hopefully, nobody the wiser. Right now only three people know we're even thinking about it—four, I guess: you, me, the Commodore and my Exec."

She shook her head, and gathered her robe closer as if suddenly chilled.

"I'm having a little trouble with this," she said. "You're telling me you may go out to sea five, six days from now, with no help from all these other ships and air squadrons at Mayport, in search of a hostile submarine, and, if you find one, you're going to try to sink it, and, presumably, it will try to sink you, and try to torpedo the Coral Sea?! How can you be just sitting here!?"

"Shucks, Pilgrim, it ain't nothing," Mike said in a passable John Wayne imitation.

"Mike, for God's sake, get serious. You've got to tell somebody!"

"We did, remember?" he replied, his voice sharper than he meant it to be. "They all laughed. What's worse, they were embarrassed by our 'preposterous' conjectures. And now, even if something happened between now and when the Coral Sea comes back in that substantiates our theory, I don't think they'd go forward with it because they've sat on it for so long. They'd all look twice the fools."

Diane stood up and walked slowly around the room. She suddenly looked to Mike like a woman who needed a cigarette. Mike felt a sudden flare of passion for her, not so much sexual wanting as a thrill of possession. Diane caught his look.

"Oh, stop," she said, peremptorily. "There must be some way out of this box. All I've ever heard about ASW is that one ship versus one sub is no contest, that it takes a bunch of ships, airplanes, intelligence, sensors, and even then, good luck to find a submarine who doesn't want to be found."

Mike nodded, sitting back on the couch. "That's all true," he said. "Except this case is a little different. For one thing, assuming he continues to wait offshore, we know roughly where he has to be in order to make an attack on the carrier, and also, about when. All he will know about Coral Sea is that she has to come from the sea to Mayport. He may or may not know when, although if they have spies here, it's hardly a secret when a carrier's coming back. But that's really all he has to know. So all he has to do is hang around the Mayport approaches, which is what this guy's been doing, we think, and wait for the target to come to him."

"Second, he can't just stay hidden on the big day—he has to come in and make an attack. That means he has to move, and he probably has to show a scope. The water is not deep, and Goldy happens to have a pretty good sonar for that kind of situation. We'll probably go out there quietly, and then light off and make no secret about being there once the bird farm shows up, and hopefully complicate his attack a lot."

"Sure," she interrupted. "Until he torpedoes the Goldsborough."

"Or we torpedo him. Either way, the carrier will be warned and hopefully will get away. Coral Sea can outrun a diesel submarine—not a nuke—but a diesel-electric on the battery? Piece of cake. The trick is to warn him in time."

"I know Jack Farrington, the CO of Coral Sea," she mused, looking out at the remains of the rain squall through the porthole. The lights from the marina played a calico pattern across her face. She turned to look at Mike.

"He's an aviator. He'd care a lot more about protecting his ship and his crew from a terrorist submarine than he would about the possibility of looking silly. Why don't you send him a personal message?"

Mike shook his head.

"The Commodore has ordered me to tell no one. He feels that the only chance we have of even getting Goldy out there is if we keep the whole operation in very deep cover. If even a hint of it gets out, Group would see to it that Goldy stayed in port, and then Coral Sea arrives with no escorts. The best I'll be able to do on-scene, assuming we gain some positive indication that there is a bad guy waiting out there, is to do something really extreme, like issue a floating mine warning to the carrier. Farrington might wonder what the hell, but the first thing he would do would be to turn out of the area, and that will allow us time to deal with the submarine. That way it'll just be the two of us to duke it out."

Diane gave him a long look.

"Now that's a comforting scene, Oldy Goldy mano y mano with a submarine with all her torpedoes left and her primary target hauling ashes over the horizon."

Mike grinned weakly. "Yeah, well, that's the idea, isn't it?"

She came back to the couch and sat down with him again.

"Mike, this thing scares me. Mayport is a peacetime base; everybody here is much more interested in politics and promotions than in real combat at sea; let's face it, combat at sea is a pretty remote possibility. The battles here are all fought in the message traffic, by the achievement of face time, and with successes in the inspection schedule. Sure, on deployment it gets a little more real, but even that is mostly for the Captain's fitness report. You're talking about going out on a sea trial, with a patched up steam plant and a twenty-five year old destroyer, and taking on a submarine that's come, what, five, six thousand miles with one burning objective, to destroy an aircraft carrier, and the only thing that's going to be in his way is you? Are you really ready for this? Are your crew, your officers ready for this? I mean, I know I'm just a dumb Navy wife, but you're talking about the real McCoy here: when a destroyer gets torpedoed a lot of people die—that's why they call them tin cans, remember?"

Mike's face grew serious.

"And when a submarine gets torpedoed, or depth charged, everybody dies, and yes, I've given this matter some thought. Remember—there's a decent chance that we're all wrong and that there is nothing there. Or there is something there but it has nothing to do with Coral Sea. It could still all be bullshit, and the Commodore is still checking out a couple of things. All we have to go on so far are disconnected hints, just a couple of sniffs that there's something out there. On top of that, the top brass have dismissed the whole notion. That's their prerogative, and they didn't get to be top brass by being wrong all the time. They've applied their best professional judgement and decided that it just isn't so."

"Their best *political* judgement, you mean," Diane said.

"Well, I don't know that. At the Admiral's age and station in life I'd guess his professional and political judgement are the same thing. Whatever, it's their job to call it, and they've called it. Captain Aronson and I think differently. He's willing to take the political risk, so I don't think it's unreasonable for Goldsborough and all of us sailors who've taken the King's penny all these many years to go out and take the tactical risk. So we're going to go out prepared to look, and if need be, fight this guy. If he exists. If, if, if....It's the best we can do, Diane."

She moved over to be close to him, and he put an arm around her.

"Hey, I'm one of the good guys, remember? But promise me that the first hint you get that he's really there, you'll blow the whistle long and hard so that you get some help," she whispered.

"Count on it, although I'm not convinced the higher ups would be predisposed to listen. But I think the Commodore will be sitting on one of his ships inport, and we'll have a special circuit set up between us so that we can sound the alarm. The main problem is that it's going to go pretty quick—the sub won't show himself until the attack geometry is pretty mature, and then we're all going to be very busy."

Diane snuggled closer. She suddenly decided that she might not just sit back and wait for this little game to play itself out. But she would have to be very careful about how she approached the problem.

"When's dinner ready," she asked, with a smothered yawn.

"Excitement's overwhelming you, isn't it; lemme go check."

Twenty minutes later he brought back a tray of fresh shrimp baked in seasoned butter, hot French bread, and a spinach salad made with mandarin oranges and almonds. They ate hungrily, enjoying each other's company, the submarine pushed back from their thoughts for the time being.

After dinner they cuddled on the couch for another hour, talking and being close. She talked some more about her years as a Navy wife. She admitted expecting a guilty conscience, but in fact she felt better, more complete than she had for years. Neither of them spoke about love, preferring to let it build without the help of words for awhile. A final band of showers passed overhead, and they sat in silence with their thoughts as the rain drummed on the deck above. The submarine hovered at the perimeter of both their consciousness, like a faint but disturbing sound in a house late at night.

FIFTY FOUR

USS Goldsborough, Mayport Naval Base, Monday, 5 May 1530

"Attention on Deck," said the Exec as Mike walked into the wardroom for the 1530 department head meeting.

"Sit down, gents, sit down," said Mike. He fixed himself a cup of coffee and joined his officers at the table. It had been a long day. He looked down to the end of the table.

"OK, let's start with the snipe: how goes it, Engineer?"

The Chief Engineer launched into a fifteen minute report on the status of the main plant repairs, which were actually going fairly well for a change. His men had worked over the weekend opening up the steam systems, and the parts for once had been ready when the actual repair work began.

"So what's your ETR as of today, assuming no major hiccups?" asked Mike.

"We could have it buttoned back up by tomorrow night," said the Engineer. "But then SIMA has to x-ray the level one welds, and we have to hydro. Thursday morning to be safe, Captain."

Mike looked at the Exec before acknowledging this estimate. The Exec looked down at the table. The Department heads were still unaware of the Goldsborough's secret time bind. Mike wanted to sail Thursday evening, to be out in the opareas and prowling the Coral Sea's approach track late that night and all day Friday.

"OK, Engineer," Mike said. "What I want to do is get underway Thursday evening if we can. That would give us Thursday night to warm up the plant and chase leaks, and then we can do a modified full power run for about an hour Friday, and come back in for the weekend, hopefully with these major steam leaks corrected once and for all. If we have to wait until Friday to go out, we may have to stay out until sometime Saturday, which, I think, everybody'd like to avoid."

There was a chorus of agreement around the table.

"So what I need is steady effort—I want you to aim for Wednesday night to have the plant lined up and all the systems restored and everything ready for a lightoff on Thursday morning. Give everyone a break, get a night's sleep, and then we'll do a light off by the book with everyone fresh. That'll give us all day to screw around with emergent problems, and still maybe make it underway by dark. Now, Weps, you got the word on this inspection rumor?"

"Yes, Sir. We're going to do a general groom of all the records and admin this week."

"Well," said Mike, "What I really had in mind is a groom of all the actual weapons machinery: the torpedo tubes, flasks, control lines, the depth charges, the five inch guns—"

"Yes, Sir," interrupted the Weapons officer, "But these combat systems inspections are usually aimed almost exclusively at the admin."

"I know, Weps, but the word I'm hearing is that the Commodore wants to change that. He's going to hit the paperwork as usual, but then take a hard look at the actual gear. He's making noises about perfect paper programs that mask equipment that's not so perfect, see?"

The Weapons officer nodded. "OK, yes, Sir, that's a little different. I'll have to change my instructions to the Chiefs, then. Any idea of when this might hit?"

"No, although I had the impression that it would be this week. It's supposed to be a surprise, so you may only have two days, especially if we're trying to get out of port Thursday evening."

"Wow. Sir, may I be excused? I have to catch the Chiefs before everybody bails out. It's almost sixteen hundred."

"Go to it, mate, although I assume," Mike said drily, "Since it's not sixteen-thirty that at least some of your department is still aboard..."

The Weapons officer colored a bit as he got up from the table.

"Yes, Sir, they are and they will be once I put this word out."

He banged out the wardroom door in search of the Chief Petty officers for sonar, gunnery, fire control, and the underwater weapons battery.

"Wouldn't want to interfere with the deck apes' liberty," muttered the Engineer, whose main hole snipes worked twelve hour days just to stay even, and who resented the fact that the above deck personnel were able to trudge happily over the brow at liberty call every afternoon. The Exec grinned.

"All right," said Mike, glancing at his watch. They all knew his distaste for wardroom meetings. "Ops, you're next."

"Yes, Sir," said the Operations officer. "If we're serious about a Thursday night departure, we'll have to get clearance from the squadron for an out of hours departure—that's overtime for tugs and port services stuff."

"I'll take care of that," interjected Mike quickly.

He did not want a request like that filtering through normal channels up to Group. He would call the Commodore directly and get permission for the out of hours departure. The operations officer raised his eyebrows, but then continued.

"And I'll need to do a notional movement report, Sir, probably just a modloc fifty miles out for engineering trials."

"Make it a hundred miles," said Mike. "If we go full power we'll run out of a modloc of only fifty miles."

"Right, Sir, will do. You really think we'll do full power?"

He glanced sideways at the Engineer with a sincere expression on his face. The Engineer, who was used to this kind of abuse, shook his head.

"Cut off his hot water, Snipe," offered the Exec.

"One might not be able to tell," sniffed the operations officer.

Theirs was an entirely friendly feud, except when the engineers dropped the electrical load and zapped some of the operations department's equipments.

"OK, guys," said Mike. "The XO's got a load of paperwork in my in-basket, so if there's nothing else, let's get back to it. XO, I need to see you in my cabin."

Mike got up, as did everyone else. The Exec accompanied him to his cabin. One of the Division officers was waiting for the Captain, with one of his junior enlisted in tow. The man had a personal problem and wanted to see the Captain. Mike took care of this problem while the Exec and the Division officer waited outside his door. Anybody in the ship could make an appointment with the Captain by putting in a chit that went up through the chain of command, from Chief, Division officer, Department Head, the Exec, and finally to the Captain. By the rules, the chit had to make it to the Captain the same day it was put in. Sometimes the intervening levels of the command could fix the problem, but sometimes the men really wanted to talk to the Captain, and Mike made sure they had their opportunity to do so. The Exec came back in and closed the door after the man had left.

"He wouldn't say what he needed to talk about, Captain, other than it was a personal problem," began the Exec.

"Yeah, no biggee," said Mike. "He wanted to work out some advance leave—he and his wife are having problems, and he doesn't have any leave on the books."

"That he could have simply asked for," said the Exec.

"Yeah, but this way he's got a lot better chance of getting it. He doesn't want the whole crew to know about his problem, especially since he thinks she's maybe seeing another guy in the crew."

"Oh," said the Exec, suddenly at a loss for words.

"Yeah, well that's kinda delicate," said Mike. He failed to notice the strange expression on the Exec's face.

"Anyway, I haven't heard from the Commodore as to what the intelligence guys found out. Now: I want to make sure you ride herd on the engineers—I don't want a panic push, but I need that plant back together for a Thursday morning lightoff. Sure as hell, we'll have some emergent problems, and we'll need all day to chase them down so we can get underway. Also, you better keep an eye on Weps and make sure they do both sides of that system grooming—any hints of problems, let me know. The Commodore can get us parts, even if he has to cannibalize somebody."

The Exec was writing furiously.

"Yes, Sir," he said, without looking up. Mike's outside phone line rang, and he picked it up.

"Captain," he said.

"I've got another piece of ambiguous news," the Commodore's voice began.

"Yes, Sir?" said Mike. The Exec stopped writing in his notebook.

"It seems that my intel guy talked to another guy, who talked to yet another guy who was able to get through to the appropriate office in Washington. The first time, he asked if all the Green Hornet's pigboats were accounted for. Guy told him wait, put him on hold for five minutes, and then came back with an affirmative. Said he had had to check with the analyst that works Africa, and that the analyst was a pain in the ass, sorry for the delay. But, yes, everybody present and accounted for. Except our guy hears a woman in the background making bullshit noises. So he, being a clever intel weenie, asked by the way who was the girl giving this guy such a hard time. Guy said it was Maryann something or other. So our guy offers him some sympathy, hangs up, waits a little while, and calls back and asks for Maryann. She's gone to lunch. So he tries again later, this time, he gets a hit. Asks her about the subs. She says, funny, second time today somebody's asking about these subs. Confirms they're all accounted for. Our guy asks if there's anything else. Any additional information. She says no, except that one of them is a different color from all the rest. Says her boss, that's one Harry Somebody, apparently, said the color is not relevant to their reporting, just whether or not all the worms are in the sandbox."

"Yes, Sir. And—?"

"Well, our guy is persistent, so he asks her why she cares about the color. And she says she doesn't except she's been instructed to report changes. The color is a change. And then the kicker: our guy asks what color is it. She says, well, it's not a color really, it's an infrared photo, which really means black and white, with white representing hot and black cold. What's different, she says, is that one of the subs is showing no heat patterns, while all the others do. And, they weren't that way on the last set of pictures."

"Did she offer any explanation?"

"Nope; all she does is note changes, and if her boss doesn't give a shit—her words—then she's done her job. But: the guy at Fleet headquarters tells the Surflant guy who tells my guy that what it means is one of their subs has probably been inactivated, there's no cooling systems operating or anything going on in the boat, so it shows up on the take as a homogeneous temperature. Of course, he wants to know why the question, but my guy has a little fable prepared and puts him off."

"Yes, Sir. I guess that's not much help, then," said Mike.

The Commodore grunted in exasperation.

"Then again," he said, "It just might be. Those guys know we have satellites; their Russian "advisors" probably even have the surveillance time-on-top for them. Now suppose you wanted to sail a sub, but didn't want the satellites to know—what would you do?"

Mike thought for a moment, and then it hit him. "Build a decoy."

"Right on, Michael. Make it out of wood and sheets of aluminum, get the topside shape right, put it on a long raft or a barge, paint it, float it out to the pier, and park it. Satellite comes over, counts six Foxtrots in the nest, everything's OK."

"Except because it's a fake, the whole thing heats up in the desert sun evenly, so it displays no coloration patterns in the infrared spectrum," Mike said.

The Exec was sitting forward on the bunk bed, obviously dying to know what was going on.

"Right again," said the Commodore, softly. "I think one of their sewerpipes is AWOL."

"Jesus, Commodore," said Mike. "Shouldn't we maybe tell somebody now? I mean this is another indicator that we might be right."

The Commodore was silent for a long moment.

"No, I don't think so, Mike. Not yet. I mean, think about it: officially, the Navy intelligence world has spoken—all the subs are there. If we asked a question like that, we're effectively calling them on their position, and we'd have the entire intel world snapping their bras at us. Like every other aspect of this drill, we're speculating. An impartial observer could even say that we're vigorously making every data point fit the curve. The other intel guy could be right—a sub that's been inactivated, and maybe even sealed up, would also look like that. Like I said, it remains ambiguous. You and I might be convinced, but you didn't hear all of what the Admiral had to say after our little meeting the other night. He was, to say the least, vehemently opposed to going any further with this. He questioned your judgement in general once we laid out the idea of who this might be, and my judgement for entertaining the notion. Well, now it's my judgement that we can't broach it again until we have at least one oil soaked, squirming Libyan on deck, and even then, they're not going to want to hear it."

It was Mike's turn to be silent. The Commodore filled in the silence.

"We have to keep the objective in sight, Mike, and that's to disrupt what you and I think is a possible terrorist attack on the Coral Sea. Given the rest of the Navy's not unreasonable verdict on the subject, our only chance, if there is a real threat out there, is to get Goldy to sea so that she can be in the right place at the right time. If we're all wet, we get a sea trial out of it and nobody's embarrassed. If we're right, well, we'll have to play that eventuality as it comes. Or you will, to be more precise about it. I may be wrong, but I think this is still the best way to go. I'll make sure there's no follow-up questions about our little probe. I think the intelligence bureaucracy is so big and so convoluted that nobody will notice, but we took a chance with that question. You guys going to be ready?"

Mike gave him a debrief of the engineering status, and also asked him to clear an out of hours departure on Thursday. He told him about their efforts to groom all the weapons systems without alerting the crew, and about the fictitious inspection.

"I can throw a little gas on that fire, if you want," said the Commodore. "I can also get you parts if something comes up broke."

"Yes, Sir, I think both efforts are in order. Maybe through the Chief's circuit."

"Yeah, I'll turn on a couple of my guys to drop a hint at the Chiefs' Club. It'll get back to your guys. And my material chief will be primed to get you parts if they're a problem."

"Thanks, Commodore."

The Commodore hung up, and Mike debriefed the Exec.

"Wow," said the Exec. "I gotta tell you, Captain, I'm beginning to think we may be getting in over our heads."

Mike was reminded of Diane's words Saturday night.

"Well, XO, we said we were bored with Mayport routine. Here comes a chance, maybe, to go out and take somebody on. We're supposed to be able to do that, you know."

"Yes, Sir, but our doctrine says you stack the deck when you go after a submarine. One on one is not very good ASW tactics."

"Look at it from the Coral Sea's perspective: one submarine against an unescorted carrier is the alternative. We squeak now and they'd keep us inport. Let's just get ourselves ready as best we can and go out there

333

Thursday. We've got a shot at it—the bad guy expects Coral Sea to be running alone and un-alerted. We'll at least screw up his attack geometry for him."

After the Exec left, Mike took a tour of his ship. It was after liberty hours, but most of the weapons people were still onboard. On the torpedo decks under the bridge wings, the torpedomen were opening and inspecting the torpedo tube machinery and running communications checks with the anti-submarine torpedoes nested in the tubes, their stainless steel noses glinting in the orange light of sunset. Below, on the forecastle, the gunner's mates had mount fifty one lit off, and were doing transmission checks with gun plot down below decks. Back aft, on the fantail, Mike found the sonarmen checking over each of the five hundred pound depth charges, greasing up the plug caps where the hydrostatic fuzes would go when the order came down to arm them, and cleaning the accumulated salt out of the antiquated launch mechanism hanging out over the stern.

Below decks he found the engineers in both firerooms and the forward engineroom, fitting in the new steam seals and preparing for level one, high pressure welding to close the steam admission valves back up. The main engine lubricating oil purifier was in a hundred pieces on the deck plates of the forward engine room, with three machinists mates ankle deep in parts and shiny bits of metal, putting it back together. Down on the second deck in the after berthing compartment, he peered through the hatch to Mount Fifty Three's magazine and found the junior Chief Gunner's mate directing two gunner's mates in rearranging some five inch powder cans, bringing specific lots of powder cans forward in the bins so that they would be loaded first. Mike asked him why he was doing that. The young Chief, who had only made Chief a year ago, moved away from the sweating sailors.

"Senior Chief said to get this lot of powder up close to the loader drums; some of that other stuff has caused jams, and he said we didn't need any jams this Friday."

Alerted by this response, Mike asked why Friday was special.

"Don't know, Cap'n, but Senior Chief, he seems to think we got somethin' cookin'. All those guys polishing up the torpedoes and the depth charges, and the sonar girls tweakin' and peakin' the gear...Senior Chief don't think it's just an inspection."

Mike smiled. He should have known better than to try to fool his crew. Especially the Chiefs. But he decided to maintain the facade.

"Senior Chief is just suffering from a bout of wishful thinking, I'm afraid, Chief. Friday's just a sea trial. If we're lucky, we'll get out to sea before the inspection goes down; if we're not, we get to do them both."

The Chief's expression was non-committal. "Yes, Sir, Cap'n. Anyhow, I gotta move the rest of this powder."

Mike went back up to his cabin as sundown began to paint the harbor a reddish orange. There was a quiet hum of activity about the ship, in contrast to the normal silence of empty spaces, offices, and passageways. He reflected not for the first time that the ship was a living thing, animated by its crew of three hundred fifty men. He had disturbed the routine by pressing the engineers for a Thursday evening sailing, and by the instructions to the weaponeers to go over all their equipment. Two thirds of the crew was still on board instead of tearing up the gin mills along Mayport Road. His guys were not fooled. Mike was suddenly certain of it. And more than a little proud of them.

He had been in command for nearly two years, with only months to go before his change of command. Pretty soon his relief would be named. The new guy would take it through decommissioning and mothballing; now, there's a good deal. You think you have it bad, he mused. He had been surprised that they didn't just leave him onboard to finish out Goldy's career along with his own. But the system didn't work that way. The new guy would take Goldy through a year of decom procedures, decommission the ship, and then he'd be given another ship for a regular two year CO tour. That way he'd hang two sets of plaques in his I-love-me room, showing two destroyer commands. Mike smiled. The system. Designed by a few geniuses to be run by many fools, someone had said. Mike wasn't sure about the numbers, but the system sure did run. And ran right over anyone who didn't want to play ball, too.

He felt a pang of regret, sitting there in the darkening solitude of his cabin. Not like you didn't know the rules, Hoss. The Navy selected only a very few for command, and then gave every one of them a free scope of chain to produce his own command persona. He had chosen to be an independent. Ah, well. Again he felt the familiar thrill of impending action in his belly, followed by a hollow pang of fear. He realized that he had not felt that kind of physical fear since Vietnam and the river gunboat days. You should be afraid, he thought. Hell, you should be scared shitless. This ship is not ready to go out and duke it out with an attack submarine all by herself—she's too old, has the wrong gear, the wrong weapons, and almost no edge on her. So whose fault is that, Captain? She's *supposed* to be ready. Did you possibly get seduced by all this peacetime, too? You bitch and moan about the staffies and the politics—could you have maybe done a little more about battle training? What if this thing is real? His mind whirled. What if there is a goddamned submarine out there, a tightly trained professional killer submarine, who has come 6000 miles to do a bloody job of work? Is he going to swat Oldy Goldy aside like a fly? Unlike yours, his torpedoes will work just fine in shallow water. Big, Russian torpedoes, fifty miles an hour and 2000 pound warheads; tear a tin can to pieces. Was he going to take his troops out to die in a boiling, bellowing sea?

Mike turned in his chair, his throat dry and his eyes wide open, staring through the gloom of the cabin at the porthole and the waiting Atlantic beyond the breakwater.

FIFTY FIVE

USS Goldsborough, Mayport Naval Station, Wednesday, 7 May; 2250

Mike sat at his desk in the cabin and rubbed his eyes. It was nearly twenty three hundred, and the day was not quite over yet. He had to call the Commodore at home one more time and give him an update on the main plant repairs. As he reached for the phone, however, it rang. He hesitated for a second, and then picked up.

"Captain," he announced.

"Captain, indeed," said a throaty voice. "I might have known you'd be on the damn ship."

"Diane. Jesus, did I forget—"

"No, silly. I made an escape tonight. I'm on the boat. Max told me you hadn't been home since Sunday. I got him to let me in so I could check on Hooker; your poor bird is not happy. He said some awful things to Max."

"Max is used to it; he usually says awful things back. Damn, I'm sorry I missed you. I'm missing you right now."

"A likely story. You haven't even called."

"We've been pretty wrapped up getting ready for, well, you know."

"Yes, I do," she said, her tone more serious. "You're really going to go forward this with this crazy scheme? Alone?"

Mike took a deep breath and let it out, a sigh of fatigue tinged with frustration.

"No way around it. We even have another indication that it might be true, but the Commodore is still keeping the whole thing under wraps. The way he sees it—but we've been through this. Right now I've got my hands full getting ready. Some of the crew is getting wise, I'm afraid. I just want to get her out of Mayport before somebody runs his mouth."

"No chance of your coming back to the boat tonight?" she asked.

"Well, hell, yes; the engineers are about done with preparations for light off; I've just got to sign the light off orders for tomorrow morning. I was going to hit the sack here, but, if there's a future in it..."

"There's a future in it, sailor."

"Uh, what about—"

"J.W.? Didn't you know? He flew down to San Juan Monday afternoon to oversee the final report of the collision investigation. And, here's the interesting bit: he's going to ride back in the Coral Sea."

"Holy shit!"

"Yeah, I thought you might find that an ironic note. Think of how proud you'll be if the submarine shows up after all. You can write I-told-you-so in the water with depth charges."

Mike laughed weakly. It made a pretty image, as long as the good guys had something to crow about.

"I'll be there as soon as I can. I really want to see you."

"Getting cold feet?"

"Cold pit in my stomach is more like it. I'm beginning to think I know what the knights felt like, suiting up in their tents before dawn. Just a little bit scared."

"You probably should be," she said softly. "You should also be going out there with some support."

"Too many people have painted themselves into a corner, Diane. We squawk now, and you can come visit me in the rubber room at NAS Jax hospital. And then Coral Sea might drive directly into an ambush."

She was silent on the phone for a long moment. "Hurry out here," she said finally.

Mike went down to the wardroom where the Engineers were preparing the main plant light-off orders. The Executive Officer handed him a cup of coffee, which Mike dutifully carried to his seat. Mike was glad he had decided to let them spend all day getting the plant ready and everything picked up in the main spaces after all the repairs, some of which had required around the clock work. The engineering people were tired. He wanted everyone to get a good night's sleep, breakfast, and then proceed with light-off with all hands rested and alert. With the final status report in hand, he made a call to the Commodore and reported in. Then he called for the light-off orders.

The light-off orders were a formality carried over from the nuclear navy. They specified which boiler would be lit off first, the main and support machinery that would be placed on the line to bring up half the ship's propulsion power, and named the supervisors who would be in charge of the main spaces for the light-off. The conventional surface engineers took a dim view of the procedures, but Captains appreciated the discipline the procedure brought to major engineering evolutions. Many of the navy's worst boiler fires and explosions had taken place after a long siege of repairs, when tired people made mistakes. He read through the orders book carefully, asked a few questions, signed off on the approval line, and went over a few last minute details with the senior engineering people. When he was through, the senior boiler tender asked if he could ask a question. Mike shot the Exec a look before answering.

"Yeah, Chief, what is it?"

"Scuttlebutt is that there's more than a sea trial going down tomorrow night, that maybe there's some real business to be done."

The senior BT was a leather tough old man of thirty six, who had almost eighteen years in steam plant firerooms. He was well known in the ship for going directly to the point in any conversation.

Mike stood up, and looked at his watch. "I never shit the troops I march with," he announced. "I'll be back aboard at 0700. Good night."

As everyone stood up in some confusion, he left the wardroom without looking at anyone, and headed aft for the quarterdeck. After the wardroom door banged behind him, there was an awkward moment of silence. The Chief BT looked across the table at the Exec.

"Was that an answer, XO?"

The other engineers watched and listened carefully.

"Just get her lit off safely, Chief," said the Exec, his face set in a blank mask. The Chief Sonarman had obviously been talking.

"But we really do have to get out to sea tomorrow night. Take it from me—that's a no-shitter."

The Exec's mind was on the Captain as he walked aft to his own cabin. The Captain had said he'd be staying aboard tonight, but now he was headed for the beach. The bells rang four times announcing his departure over the 1MC. Going to see her, no doubt. Talk about playing with fire. He felt a flash of male admiration, and then felt it subside when he wondered how he would feel if it was his wife waiting at the Marina. The Chief of Staff's wife, for Chrissakes!

FIFTY SIX

The Al Akrab, submerged, Jacksonville operating area, Wednesday, 7 May; 2245

The Captain sat erect in his steel chair at the head of the wardroom table. The officers watched him attentively as he re-read the message from naval headquarters. The Musaid stood behind him as always, his eyes focused on the other end of the wardroom. The Captain cleared his throat.

"The evening of Friday is confirmed," he announced. "The day after tomorrow."

"We will conduct a daylight attack, then?" asked the Engineer, his eyes intense.

"I think a twilight attack better describes it," replied the Captain. "The intelligence report indicates the carrier must be in the basin by 1900 to ensure sufficient depth of water. So some time between 1600 and 1900, probably closer to 1730, we will make the torpedo attack. But there is more."

The officers leaned forward.

"The agents report that the three ships escorting the carrier are based in Norfolk in the state of Virginia, to the north of Mayport; our agents in Norfolk confirm the names."

He looked up at them with a cold smile.

"This means Coral Sea will be alone."

"An easy target, then," observed the Weapons Officer. "We know the most likely approach route from the sea, we know the area which she must pass through to make the sea buoy, and we know the arrival time in the basin. We can kill her at sea," he said with an excited grin on his face.

The weapons officer had little faith in the mines, and wanted the torpedoes to succeed. The Captain appreciated the Weapons Officer's blood lust. They were all excited by the prospects of finally making the attack. But there were still risks. He held up his hand in admonition.

"What we do not know is whether any escorts will be sailed from Mayport," he began. "And we do not know if the carrier herself will put up helicopter screens. They could make this very difficult because the water is quite shallow along the attack area. But the report analysis indicates that since she is coming home after a month in the Caribbean, the carrier's airplanes will all be flown off and dispersed to their bases around Jacksonville that morning, and that the concentration will be on getting safely in and their people ashore."

He permitted himself another wolfish grin.

"But, yes, this may succeed beyond our best dreams."

"When shall we plant the mines, then," asked the operations officer. "Tomorrow night?"

The Captain nodded.

"Yes, tomorrow night. We have reviewed the practice run, and we will allow another hour to make the approach. The field will be planted at the same time, around 0200; the weather will be what it will be. The Navigator has found two other lights which can be used for rough cross bearings in case we cannot see the river range. We did not really get to practice the firing of the mines the other night, but that is a relatively simple detail once we put the Al Akrab in position. Open the outer doors, fire three tubes, close the outer doors and run for the sea. Deputy, brief the approach plan."

The Deputy unfurled the approach chart on the wardroom table; the other officers stood and gathered around him to look down at the chart.

"Sir: we are currently fifty miles out from the base," he began, pointing with his finger to their current position. "We will begin a submerged approach this evening, aiming for a point here, where there is a shallow, submarine canyon. We will spend the entire day there tomorrow, and then begin a submerged approach to this point, twenty miles out from the river. Our plan is to surface at midnight, run in on the diesels for an hour and a half in the darkness while recharging, flood down and switch to electrics for the final approach at 0200. We have established that there is no radar surveillance of the base and river approaches. Once the mines are laid, we will withdraw on electrics, switch to diesels and run on the surface while recharging batteries until 0430, submerge in this area here, and then commence a slow, submerged transit to the attack corridor, which we estimate to run from here to here."

He pointed to a long, trapezoidal shaped box drawn on the chart, beginning with its wide end some fifty miles out from the base, and narrowing down at the seaward end of the river approach channel.

"Why this shape, Deputy Commander?" asked the Weapons Officer.

"Because she can enter the box from many directions, and thus there is uncertainty at that end. There is no uncertainty about where she must be when she finishes transiting the box. Thus it narrows."

The Captain put his finger about two thirds of the way down the box.

"Here would be ideal. The water depth is sufficient for a submerged approach and for some, but not much, maneuvering room. There is this gradual ridge running north-south, behind which we could loiter and be masked from sonars looking inshore. The box has begun to narrow, which means that the probability of Coral Sea being in the box has begun to rise, and thus we ought not to end up in a pursuit maneuver. That is important—we cannot pursue on the surface, and there is limited depth for any submerged maneuvering. The essence of this plan is that he must come right by us."

"Sir. You will fire from ahead?" asked the Engineer.

"No. I will fire from the quarter, as he goes by. Remember these are steam driven torpedoes and they leave a wake."

The mission planning in Tripoli had been specific on the torpedo type. The Russians had the best electric anti-shipping torpedoes in the world, but their older, straight running, steam driven torpedoes packed the largest warheads in the world in a torpedo that went better than fifty miles an hour. They had decided to trade off the detectability of the World War II type torpedo wakes for the lethality of those 2000 pound warheads. The Deputy stood back from the chart.

"Are there any questions?" he asked.

The officers continued to study the chart. There was not much to ask; the plan was straightforward.

"This is a simple plan, but there are many things that can go wrong," said the Captain, leaning back in his chair. "The weather, the schedule of the carrier, passing escort vessels, an equipment casualty here in the boat, interference from merchant shipping, both in the river tomorrow night and in the operating areas the next afternoon. We cannot plan for all of these things—we must simply be alert, aware, and ready to deal with the unexpected."

He looked around the table at his department heads, making sure he had their attention.

"I want all of you to go through your spaces in the next twenty-four hours. Prepare the boat for battle. Prepare the boat for underwater damage, for silent operations. Prepare the men to fight. Review with them damage control procedures, isolation procedures, medical first aid. We did not come out here to die for the Jamahiraya; we came out here to exact justice from the Americans, to execute a smashing success against the American Navy, and to return as heroes to our homeland. The outcome of this battle shall be as Allah wills it, but if the enemy continues his sleep, we shall do all of these things. That is all."

The officers stood, waited for a moment to see if the Captain was going to leave, and when he did not, they filed past him. Their voices rose in excited tones as they scattered to their various compartments to make final preparations. The Captain put his head in his hands, his arms akimbo on the table. The silence in the wardroom was broken only by the sounds of fans and the air vents as the submarine loitered 300 feet beneath the surface.

"Well, Musaid, we are nearly there," he said, lifting his face out of his hands and rubbing his eyes. "How long has it been—six weeks?"

"Nearly that, Effendi," rumbled the Musaid, who remained standing behind the Captain's chair.

"I think we actually have a good chance to do this outrageous thing," said the Captain. "The Americans are truly asleep. What we must watch for now is the chance thing, the unexpected thing, the hissing thing that emerges from a sand dune and strikes your foot while your eyes are fastened upon the horizon. We have had an abundance of good fortune so far; I fear for the day of battle that we may run out of it. Make your way through the boat for the next night and day. Sharpen the men's edge, build their confidence. There are still those who think this is a suicide mission; make sure they understand that I do not feel that way and that I will make every effort to get all of us home."

"As you command, Effendi."

FIFTY SEVEN

Mayport Marina, Wednesday, 7 May; midnight

Mike parked the Alfa in the nearly empty marina lot; Diane's white four door was parked up by the office, under one of the pole lights. The office was dark, as was Maxie's forty two foot sloop, which he moored right next to the ramp leading down to the piers from the office. As Mike walked across the floating pontoons, the cool air from the river junction eddied around the boats, clinking the rigging on some of them, and making others bump and creak against their pilings. It was a clear night, with only a sliver of a moon. Only the sounds of the kitchen fans from Hampton's disturbed the night air over the waterway. The Lucky Bag was also in darkness as he walked down his pontoon.

He went aboard, and headed aft to the porch deck. Diane was in the chaise, her long figure draped demurely in a white bathrobe. She silently handed him a gin and tonic as he sat down on the foot of the chaise. He took it and set it aside, and then pulled her into his arms for a long kiss. She sensed that he needed strength more than loving, and held him against her for what seemed like a long time. He pulled away finally and kissed her again, and then recovered his drink.

"I stink of ship," he announced. "I'm going to take a quick shower. Be right back."

He went below and stripped down, pitching his khakis into the hamper and headed for the shower, where he stood for a long time, trying not to think about anything. Diane joined him after awhile and they made love awkwardly in the shower, laughing afterwards at how difficult a slippery, wet shower stall made everything. They dried off and went back out onto the porch deck. Diane gathered her robe tighter, as the light breeze after midnight was almost chilly. They sat together on the long, rattan couch at the back of the porch, completely in the shadows. Out on the waterway a lone Chris Craft motor cruiser rumbled south, all of its windows dark and only side lights reflecting across the light chop in the channel.

"This is so perfectly—I don't know the word," Mike said at last, nuzzling her thick, damp hair. "If you'd come to live with me we could do this every night."

He surprised himself with what he had just said. She felt him tense up as he waited to see what she would say, whether she would let is pass by as an offhand comment or address it seriously.

"Did you plan to say that?" she asked, softly.

"I think my subconscious just said what I didn't have the nerve to say," he replied. "I know it's probably a totally impractical proposition, but I wish you would."

"I don't think we could just set up house here in Mayport," she murmured. "This is altogether a Navy town."

"Boats move," he replied. "I could put an engine in this old girl and we could go anywhere it suited us to go. I've got plenty of money saved up; I wouldn't even have to go to work for a couple of years. We could do the intracoastal, see a lot of the country from the perspective of something besides Navy orders. Whatever, as long as we're together."

She turned to face him, her eyes shining, the features of her face indistinct in the darkness. He traced the line of her cheek with his fingers, seeing like a blind man, combining touch with memory to see her face.

"I mean it, Diane," Mike persisted. "I love you and want you. I'd really like to marry you if you'd consider it. I know we're talking divorce and all that hassle, which is easy for me to talk about but a bitch for you to go through. But: I think your marriage ended a long time ago, and I don't think J.W. Martinson gives a damn about anything but his career and occasionally his girlfriend up there in Norfolk. You don't even have to marry me if you don't want to, I'll settle for just having you here, however you want to work it, I'll—"

She put her fingertips on his mouth to shut off his increasingly urgent flow of words.

"OK," she said, so softly he almost didn't hear it.

"OK? Did you say OK?!"

He gave out a loud warwhoop, which echoed around the Marina. Diane clamped her hand over his mouth this time, but he was laughing and hugging her and kissing her all at once. She finally calmed him down, and then sat up on the couch to look him in the eye.

"There's a condition," she announced.

"Oh-oh," he said, in mock fear. "She wants a church wedding. Her mother will have to live with us. She wants—"

"Will you shut up," she said. She ran her fingers through her hair for a moment.

"My condition is this: I will handle the business of separating from J.W., and you will stay out of it until it's a done deal. I know you're going to want to help and be supportive and all that, but you've got to let me do it, my way, and my rules, OK?"

"Whatever you say, Diane, but I'm not sure—"

"Because if the Navy finds out that you and I have been seeing each other, you will get sudden orders out of here, that's why. My husband and I can call it quits privately and discreetly, and the Brass'll smooth it over. But if I run off with one of the destroyer Captains, there'll be all hell to pay. So—my way, OK?"

"You got it," he said, wonderingly.

A woman who thought ahead and who understood consequences was a new phenomenon in his life. God, what a catch. Diane felt another warwhoop coming on, and smothered it with a kiss. Mike was so happy he forgot all about the submarine.

But it came back when they were nestled in bed below. It was a little past one in the morning, and Mike had set his alarm clock for 0600, which had brought the entire reason for their sundown departure tomorrow—today—back in a flood of concern. He lay awake, with Diane cuddled in the crook of his left shoulder. Her breathing indicated that she was asleep. Mike stared at the dark ceiling of the cabin as he worked through the possibilities of the next seventy two hours. Light from the channel buoys winked on and off the ceiling, first green and then red. The waterway made small noises under the transom of the boat.

It would be a close run thing, as Wellington had described his adventures at Waterloo. On their side was an element of surprise, in that the Libyans probably thought they were undetected and might get a free shot at the Coral Sea. Just by showing up, Goldsborough complicated the submarine's problem a lot. The water was not very deep, so Goldy's sonar had a good chance of getting contact, as long as Mike managed to place his ship in the same part of the ocean the Libyan picked.

That was the rub: the Libyan CO could hide anywhere, just lurk on the bottom or very close to it, and come in from any direction at all when the carrier hove over the horizon. Maybe, he reasoned, the Exec was right: Goldy ought to go out covertly, not pinging, quiet ship, operating on only one screw instead of two, and using only her commercial radar. Don't turn into a destroyer until late afternoon Friday when we get radar contact on Coral Sea. But where? Where along that thirty mile long approach track to Jacksonville would the sub be? At the seaward end? If so, they had little chance—too much ocean to search. But then, the sub had the same problem. The only area where the sub CO knew he would find the carrier would be at the Jacksonville end of the approach corridor; the carrier could come *from* any direction, but she had to end up at the St. Johns river. The sub was going to get only one chance; once the carrier got into or even near the river channel, she was safe from torpedoes.

What if the carrier ignored his warnings and kept coming? Maybe she would be safer if she did—if she turned away back to sea, the sub would get another shot at her, or as many as she wanted until Mike got lucky. It all depended on whether or not Goldy gained contact before the carrier first entered the torpedo danger zone. Maybe, he thought, maybe the thing to do is warn him to do a big zig zag around the "mines" and then continue into Mayport and safety. If Mike had the sub engaged, that might be the best maneuver. Yeah. Get Coral Sea inport or at least inshore and then it'll just be Goldy out there. Alone in the open ocean with a submarine full of fanatics who'd just been cheated out of their primary target. He wondered how fast he could get Goldy into Mayport if that happened. Horseshit, you stay out there, find the bastard, and bag his ass. Right, John Wayne. And the rest of the Navy will be behind you. Way behind you, as they used to say in 'Nam.

The other thing was that they had to shoot fast once they gained contact. This meant that he would have to break the conditioning of years of peacetime ASW practice. Any time a Navy ship was given a sub to exercise with, the objective was to gain and hold contact for as long as possible, to maximize training for the sonarmen and the CIC plotting teams. But in a real fight, you had to make your classification very quickly and then fire, before the other guy did the same thing to you.

Fire. Fire what? The torpedoes would be next to useless in shallow waters. They'd go screaming down into the depths, turn on their homing sonars, and see the bottom. Oh, shit, they'd have to use depth charges! That meant Goldy had to literally run over top of a maneuvering submarine that was hardly going to stand still long enough for him to drop depth bombs.

He felt the urge to get up and walk around while he sorted out all the possibilities. Diane stirred in the crook of his arm, but then went back to sleep, which ruled that out. My God, she said yes! He thought about that for awhile instead of the submarine. However this whole deal came out, she had said yes, she'd leave the jerk and come to live with him. He fantasized about taking his Navy retirement and spending a year or so wandering the coastal waterways with Diane at his side. Have to put an engine in the Bag. He considered the engineering details of that project and was soon asleep.

FIFTY EIGHT

USS Goldsborough, Mayport Naval Station, Thursday, 8 May; 1530

Mike stood sweating in the control console booth of the forward fireroom, and listened to the satisfying whine of main feed pumps, forced draft blowers, and the underlying roar of 1B boiler making 1200-pound steam. The amplified intercom circuit between Main Control in the forward engineroom and the rest of the spaces blared intermittently with orders from the Engineering Officer of the Watch, abbreviated inevitably as "EE-OW" by anyone speaking on the circuit. The rush of air from the 16 inch ventilation ducts added to the noise level, but it kept the temperature at a bearable 95 degrees. The fireroom smelled of steam, lagging, fuel oil, and ozone in about equal proportions.

"She came right up, Cap'n," shouted the BT Chief over the noise of the machinery. "Nary a wisp of steam, either. First time we've had a dry hole down here in a long time."

The Chief Engineer stood behind him, a big grin on his face for a change.

"Looking good, Chief," Mike shouted back.

So far, the main plant had come on the line like clockwork, almost as if the old girl knew she had a job to do. He had conferred with the Commodore earlier that morning, and they had discussed tactics and several what-if's. The Commodore had explained the arrangements he was making to have someone on watch back in the harbor. Mike had promised the Commodore a call at noon to report status. He glanced at his watch.

"Gotta go call my Boss, Engineer. Keep her turning and burning, but if something does pop, make sure I hear about it right away—don't try to handle it on your own."

"Got a time bind, do we, Cap'n?" shouted the Chief, with a knowing grin.

Mike looked at him for a moment. "Yes, we do, Chief."

He climbed up the short stub ladder from the lower level to the upper level, where the temperature was approaching 105 degrees. The water check-man saw him from across the upper level deck gratings and waved; Goldy's snipes were an informal bunch when they had their boilers on the line. A fireroom was hardly the place for saluting. Mike waved back and then climbed up the twenty foot, stainless steel ladder to the main hatch, eased his bulk through the hatch, and headed for the more reasonably angled ladder-stairway up to the 01 level and his cabin. He went into his tiny bathroom and washed the sweat off his face. The air conditioning in the cabin felt like a winter breeze after the fireroom. He dialed the Commodore's number, and was answered by the Chief Staff Officer, who put him on hold. A minute later, the Commodore picked up.

"OK, Mike, whatcha got?"

Mike gave him a quick update on the success of the repairs, and was able to report that Goldy was lit off forward and aft and that, so far, everything was holding.

"Good. Very good," grunted the Commodore. "Better than we all expected, given the past history of some of those problems. What time you want to go?"

"I'd like to let her steam for the afternoon, Commodore, make sure we're tight and right, and then get underway about 1630. I just need one tug to pull us away from the nest, so the pilots can't claim overtime."

"OK, do it. Coral Sea is still due in tomorrow, in the basin at around 1900. Now, as we discussed: I'm going to post an operations watch in the Deyo starting at 2000 tonight. I'll have a watch officer and one enlisted on watch in the Deyo's CIC. He'll be joined by the CSO at daybreak, and I'll be onboard at the first sign you have something. I've told the CO that I'm running a command and control test with you and Coral Sea. I've also asked him to have his passive electronic warfare suite manned up. Deyo's gear is more sophisticated than what you have there in Goldy; if this gomer pops a radar, you'll have another set of ears on the air. He can give you a bearing, although that won't be too much help, coming from Mayport. My guy will be up on a secure UHF freq, and my comms Chief will contact you with callsigns and backup frequencies before you take off. OK?"

"Yes, Sir, sounds good. Did the I.V. seem curious?"

"A little, but I told him that you were going to combine a sea trial with a little exercise with the Coral Sea, and he seemed happy. Your crew figured out something's going down?"

"Yes, Sir, some of the Chiefs have. The weapons groom for a possible inspection story didn't wash; I think the Squadron chiefs were less than convincing."

"I'm not surprised. Some of my guys are giving me funny looks. I suspect Chief Mackensie may have said some things. I wish Goldy had a unit commander's cabin, because I'd be coming along if you did. But you're gonna have to handle this one solo, Cowboy. You said you were sick of peacetime routine."

"You heard it here first, Commodore," said Mike with a grin. "But is there any chance of having a helo or two on alert thirty tomorrow, like around 1500 onward?"

"Yeah, CSO and I talked about that, but the problem is weapons: the only weapons they can carry are torpedoes, but their torpedoes will have the same problem your torpedoes are gonna have: bottom acquisition. And if we set them with a real shallow floor, they're as liable to lock on Goldsborough or Coral Sea as they are the sewerpipe. Neither of you need that kind of problem."

"Yes, Sir, but I was thinking, if they came out loaded with buoys instead of weapons, they might make a crucial difference in my localization search, especially if they could localize any sonar contacts we gain on the 23. Once the bird farm shows up, I'm not going to have much time to localize and whack this guy."

The Commodore thought about that for a moment. A request for forces outside of the destroyer force would have to go through channels—from the Cruiser-Destroyer Group to the local Air Wing commander. He would be very hard pressed to explain why he wanted a helicopter to go out and play with Goldsborough when Goldy was supposed to be on an engineering sea trial. He was already amazed that no one at Group or higher up had tumbled to what they were doing.

"Mike, I'll try to think of something. Maybe talk to one of the helo squadron CO's. But I can't go through channels or we're gonna get caught. But I'll try. I know Mike Sinclair from a couple of golf games; he's got a LAMPS helo squadron. He might be able to send a guy out, but he'll have to come out there ignorant."

"I'll take anything I can get, Commodore," Mike said.

"Hey, don't forget the carrier—he has heloes, too,"

"Yes, Sir, but they usually fly the airwing off before they come into port. He might be fresh out of fling-wings by the time I see him." He paused for a second. "At this juncture I'm still hoping we're both entirely wrong."

"I know, Mike. I hope we're wrong, too. But the more I think about it, the more I don't think we are. And if we're not wrong, you and Goldsborough are all that's between Coral Sea and a major tragedy for the U.S. Navy. What do the snipes call it—a no-shitter? I'm afraid you're going to have to forget the past two years of admin, politics, paperwork, and liberty weekends and pare down to the bleeding bone. Get on the 1 MC and brief your crew as soon as you're clear, and then get into Condition Two right away—tonight. Button her up like you were at Condition One, and keep a damage control team manned up at all times; the first hint you get of a contact, get your entire damage control organization into Condition One. And—but, shit, I'm telling you your business. Gimme a call just before you sail if you need anything."

"Aye, aye, Sir," said Mike, and hung up.

He called for the Exec to come up so he could pass on the Commodore's arrangements and review their plan for bringing the ship's readiness up as soon as they were clear of the channel. He reminded himself to call Diane if he could before they sailed. As he waited for the Exec, he thought about the upcoming operation. The Commodore's warnings on damage control readiness had brought home the grim possibility that things could get nasty out there in a hell of a hurry. He recalled the vivid images from the Victory at Sea documentary films, of bigger ships than Goldsborough blown in half by a single submarine torpedo, their seemingly impervious armored steel hulls being punched up effortlessly by a thundering sea, bending first upwards in the middle before settling back down into the fatal, V-shaped sag that preceded a swift slide into the deep, with everybody aboard still able trying to get to their feet even as the sea sucked them down to spend eternity, entombed in sealed, flooded steel compartments.

He knew, without ever having experienced it, that the reality of a sea fight was a far cry from the antiseptic play-acting of the annual fleet battle problems. He wondered how the crew would react. The typical Navy destroyer went to sea with last year's high school class, the average age aboard ship being around nineteen. Outside, in the passageway, he heard the 1MC order the crew to set the special sea and anchor detail, and the familiar cold worm moved in his guts. It was one thing to be Captain at the head of the wardroom table. It was quite another to be Captain on the bridge, getting underway for what might be the battle of his life, of his ship's life.

The Exec knocked on the door and came in. Mike briefed him on the Commodore's arrangements, and went through the details of how they would tighten up the ship's readiness as soon as they were clear of the river entrance. The Exec, as usual, wrote everything down in his little green notebook.

"Now," said Mike, "I have to figure out how much to tell the troops—how much or how little."

"Yes, Sir," said the Exec. "I think they need to know what we think is going on. Maybe hold back on the Libyan aspect, but the rest of it—I'd just tell 'em right up front."

"I agree, XO," Mike said, nodding his head. "I'm going to lay it out for them, tell 'em we may be full of shit, but then again we may be right, and, if so, that we'll be the only thing between Coral Sea and a very bad afternoon."

"Operationally, nothing beats the whole truth, Cap'n," the Exec said, closing his notebook. "I'd tell 'em the "evidence" too."

"Yeah, I will. I think what I want to do is get on the 1MC and brief the whole crew, but then have a meeting in CIC with the principal officers to lay out our search and attack tactics."

The Exec got up. "I'll make an announcement that you're going to speak to them about fifteen minutes after we secure from sea detail. We going out in a deception mode?"

"Yes. I think you were right about that. I'll want to lock one shaft, shut down the military radars—just use the Raytheon, and keep the sonar and fathometer silenced until the right time.'

"When is that, Sir?"

Mike looked up at him. "I'm damned if I know yet, XO, but it'll probably come to me."

The Exec grinned. Mike threw up his hands.

"Probably when we have a confirmed contact on the carrier," he said. "Right now I need to study the hydrographic charts very carefully, and I'll need Linc's PC. The sub can't know yet, or shouldn't know, anyway, that the carrier's escorts are all going to leave her when she turns west, so the bad guys should be hiding, initially. In that water depth, they'll need to use the bottom topography, and my guess is that they'll be on the west or inshore side of any good shadow zone. Let the carrier approach, which they can easily hear and classify, go over top, and then rise off the bottom and fire. If she had escorts, they would all be looking out ahead of the carrier, not behind her, especially one hour out of home port. It's not like there's been any warning."

The Exec nodded. "That's the part I really don't like about this whole deal. For fear of looking silly, nobody's willing to tell the carrier he may be walking into something."

"It may indeed be silly, XO. Part of me is hoping that we are indeed a bunch of dummies who've talked themselves into a wolf in the woods. We're taking a chance that we may look quite the fools come tomorrow night, especially to the crew."

"That's why we get paid all this extra money, Cap'n," the Exec said. "To take all these chances."

"There you go, XO. Now, I gotta make a phone call."

The Exec nodded and slipped out the door. Mike dialed Diane's home phone number. She answered on the first ring.

"Yes?" she said anxiously.

"That's what I like to hear," Mike said. "A pretty girl who says yes."

"Oh, stop," she said. "I was afraid you'd leave without calling me."

She paused for a second, and then let it all out in a rush. "Mike, I'm scared. Oh, shit, I'm sorry. I was determined to keep a stiff upper lip, pretend this is just an ordinary underway. But you guys could get hurt, or worse. I couldn't stand that, not now, not after—"

"I know, Diane, I know," said Mike softly. "If it makes you feel any better, I'm a little scared too, but I have to tell you, I'm more scared of fucking it up than I am of getting hurt."

"Oh, Mike, you need to stop worrying about how your actions are going to look. You just focus on getting that bastard out there before he gets you, your ship, and your crew. Don't let all the Commodore's lectures about getting along politically interfere with your instincts. If all those ribbons you wear mean anything at all, they show that you have a fighter's instincts. Listen to them."

"Yeah, I know. But Vietnam was a long time ago. And this whole thing may yet be a phantom of our imaginations."

"But if it isn't, a lot of guys are depending on good old Goldsborough and Mike Montgomery, and the hell of it is, they don't even know it."

"Including, I guess, even your husband."

"He's not my husband," she said defiantly. "Not any more. Not for a long time. I had to meet you to find that out, and now you're going off to sea on this crazy mission. Oh, listen to me. I'm sorry. I sound like I need a widow's walk up on the roof of these quarters so I can pace around up there until I see you coming back in. Oh, Mike, I'm so glad you called."

"I love you, Diane," he whispered.

"I love you, Mike. Please, please keep safe and come back to me."

351

"Count on it, Love."

There was a knock on the door, and the IC-man stuck his head in. "Outside line coming down, Cap'n," he announced.

Mike waved his acknowledgement and the IC-man closed the door. "Gotta go," he said to the phone.

"I heard him," she said, her voice under tight control. "I've hated those words for too many years. I'll be right here, waiting."

"I know. I love you," he said, and then the line went dead as the IC-gang disconnected on the pier and pulled the line aboard.

FIFTY NINE

USS Goldsborough, Mayport approaches, Thursday, 8 May; 1715

Mike sat in the Captain's chair on the bridge, his mind paying only half attention to the departure navigation. The forced-draft blowers whining steadily atop the number one stack made a comforting sound. The Executive Officer was conning the ship, and they had finished the tough piloting part, the turn out into the river channel from the basin channel. The Exec had managed to swing the ship directly onto the river range course in one competent turn. They were pointed fair for sea, buoys on parade on either side, and a fresh sea breeze was already blowing the stale heat and humidity of the basin out of the ship as she came up to fifteen knots. With the setting sun behind them the eastern sky was deep blue, and the sea the color of indigo ink, with pillowy white clouds bunched along the far horizon. There was a deep swell which lifted the bows rhythmically but not uncomfortably; Mike could see the bosuns on the forecastle adjust their stance to ride the bow up and over each swell like old hands.

The sea detail crewmen in the pilothouse were quietly excited; rumors had been flying around the ship ever since she had cleared the pier. Mike had put on a severe face and made himself remote in his chair. The officers on the bridge had been closemouthed, and had kept their distance from the Captain. Even the bosun mate had backed off, sparing Mike the necessity of drinking the bosun's miserable, salty coffee. The Exec had been all business, with none of the usual getting underway repartee, and the bridge crew picked up on this as yet another sign that something was indeed up. They covertly watched the Captain and the Exec for hints of what was going on, ready to pass along the word over their soundpowered phone circuits to their buddies at other control stations in the ship. Mike looked at his watch.

"XO," he called. "I'll speak to the crew at 1800, or as soon after you've secured from special sea and anchor detail as possible."

"Aye, aye, Sir," replied the Exec, formally, taking a bearing on the next approaching buoy to see if they were being set down on it by the current. He decided that they were. "Come right to 091."

Mike got out of his chair and headed aft for his cabin, paying no attention to the flurry of mumbled messages being sent around the ship over the phones by the bridge talkers. He needed to compose his thoughts, think about what he was going to tell the crew. The closer that little chore got, the more uncomfortable he felt about it. They had so very little to go on, almost nothing in the way of concrete evidence. The Exec had tried to bolster his confidence earlier.

"They trust us absolutely, Cap'n," he had said. "If it's our judgement that there might be some bad guy out there, then they'll trust us to tell them and to get the ship ready to fight. The only crime would be to keep quiet and then get surprised by the bad guy. And if it's all bullshit, they'll laugh about it, roll their eyes, talk about dumb-ass officers, but they'll know you were erring on the side of being ready, which in the long run, aims at saving their asses. Besides, this is go nowhere, do nothing Goldsborough. Give these guys a chance to do something for real and the big problem will be holding them back."

Mike went into his sea cabin, and automatically looked around for Hooker, but then remembered the bird had been left behind. He analyzed his thoughts about that, and it was a little bit scary. Didn't bring the bird because they might lose this little gunfight; no sense in killing off the parrot just because they didn't do their ASW right. Real vote of confidence in what was coming. He flung himself down on his bunk, rolled over on his back, and closed his eyes. He thought at once of Diane. Finally find the right woman, and she's married to someone else, and I'm headed into God knows what. To do battle with a terrorist, a Libyan submarine, to save the carrier that's carrying her husband home to Mayport. Where she's going to tell him that she's leaving him. If we get through this little deal in one piece. And if we don't, well, it was a blast while it lasted, one of those marvelous things, etc., etc. He wondered if she'd leave El Jerko even if Goldy was trashed. He thought not. Right. You were a one of a kind, Man. Die young and leave a beautiful memory. This is total crap, he thought, finally. He swung his legs off the bunk as the phone buzzed.

"Captain," he grumped.

"We're about to secure from sea detail, Captain. The IC-room has activated your 1-MC microphone. If you'll let me know when, I'll have the bosun pipe all hands," said the Exec, the wind in the pilothouse making puffing sounds over the sound-powered set.

"Yeah, OK," replied Mike. "Tell you what: don't secure from sea detail, that'll just have everybody milling around while I try to talk to them. Make sure there are no contacts close by, and go ahead and pipe all hands now."

"Aye, Sir." the Exec hung up, and moments later the long notes of attention, all hands whistled through the ship. Mike knew that people would automatically expect the word, 'Secure from special and anchor detail' to follow, but instead, they heard Mike asking them for their attention, this is the Captain speaking. He very rarely used the 1MC himself, so he knew they would indeed pay attention.

"Gentlemen, as some of you have already been speculating, Goldsborough is underway for something more than a sea trial," he began, hearing his voice echoing in the passageway outside his cabin. "We have a most unusual situation on our hands, a situation that may not even exist, or one which may mean that there is a hostile diesel electric submarine lying in ambush for the Coral Sea who, as some of you know, returns to Mayport tomorrow afternoon from Caribbean ops. The complication is that Goldsborough is the only ship that may be able to do something about the submarine. If it's really there, that is. Let me explain to you what's been going on."

He went on to give the background of the case, speaking slowly and methodically, leaving out some of the details of the Admiral's reaction to the entire hypothesis, but not his conclusion that the whole thing was a figment.

"The bottom line is that the Commodore has dispatched Goldsborough to rendezvous along the approach track with Coral Sea tomorrow afternoon, and to search the area for submarines, and to attack and sink this guy if he shows himself to be hostile or makes an attack on the carrier. The Admiral and his staff do not think there's anything there. They may well be right; the Admiral didn't get to be an Admiral by being a dummy. If they are right, we'll go out and ping around, find nothing, and Coral Sea will go on by and no one will be the wiser. On the other hand."

He paused to gather his thoughts.

"On the other hand, the Commodore may be right and there may well be a terrorist submarine waiting out here, waiting in our own backyard, where we think he's been waiting for more than three weeks, waiting for the chance to put six torpedoes into the Coral Sea and send her to the bottom not ten miles from home."

"So here's what we're going to do: tonight, we're going to set battle readiness condition two throughout the ship. As soon as we secure from sea detail, we're going to set material condition zebra from the main deck and below. We're going to lock one shaft, turn off all the radars except the commercial navigation radar, turn off the fathometer and the sonar, rig the deception lighting on the masts, and go on out to sea tonight pretending to be a slow, single screw merchie headed for points east. Once we get into the area of probability, and that's the area where Coral Sea has to drive through to get home to Mayport, we'll wait until we actually make a radar contact on the Coral Sea sometime tomorrow afternoon, and then we'll become a tin can again and go into an active search mode. If this guy is out there, he'll hear that sonar and know somebody is on to his ass, and he will have to deal with us before he can attack the Coral Sea."

"Now, that brings me to the important part. If this guy is who and what we think he is, he *will* try to take us off the board if we get in his way. If we're right, he has come a long way and waited a long time for his one shot at the bird farm, and he will probably not hesitate to try to kill us and then kill the carrier. If we're right, this is a transplanted Russian submarine. A Foxtrot class. They carry great big, steam driven Russian torpedoes. Just one of his torpedoes would break this old girl in half. This is real guys, not 'hit alfa' from the battle problem. His fish go fifty miles an hour and put 2000 pounds of explosives into their target."

"So from now on out, until Coral Sea is safely inport, Goldsborough is at war. I want you to secure from sea detail, and then go through your spaces and get them ready for a shoot out. Lash stuff down as if we were going to go through a hurricane. Get all the fire hazards and flying missile hazards taken care of. Just like we've trained to do, only now it's for real. We're going to lay out all the damage control gear, and we're going to arm the torpedo flasks and the depth charges, and we're going to put live ammo into the gun mounts. If we're right, by mid-morning tomorrow we're going to be in the torpedo danger area, and we're going into battle readiness condition one at sunrise and we'll stay there until Coral Sea enters the river."

"Now, I know this comes as something of a shock. And I reiterate that we may be wrong and that this all may be for nothing. But I don't want to find out that we were right and not be ready to defend ourselves and the carrier. Because the authorities ashore don't believe it, the carrier has not, repeat, not been warned. And we'll have no help for the same reason. We're hoping the bad guys think they have a free shot, and that when we show up, we'll screw things up for him for long enough that the carrier gets by him. But as I said before, there is something he can do about that. If he attacks us, we'll finally have proof that he's there, which is good as long as we get the time to holler and warn off the carrier. But right now, everyone ashore thinks we're out on a one day sea trial. There are no other tin cans standing by, no heloes, no P-3's, no nothing. If our theory is true, it's going to be entirely up to us. Now: I want to see all officers in the wardroom in fifteen minutes, and all Chiefs in quarters thirty minutes after that. That is all."

He clicked off the microphone and put it down in his desk. He found his forehead damp with perspiration. The phone buzzed, and in the passageway he could hear the bosun piping secure from sea detail.

"Yes," he said to into the phone.

"That was perfect, Cap'n. You should see their faces up here."

"I can just imagine, XO. You should see mine. Call me when you have everybody in the wardroom. You have the charts and stuff ready?"

"Yes, Sir, all set. We've got all night to get CIC set up and the weapons ready. We ought to be ready to go by sunrise, barring any surprises tonight."

"Yeah. OK. What speed do we need to be in the middle of the box at around 1000 tomorrow?"

"No more than about eight knots, which is good for our deception profile. We'll slow to five now and start rigging the lights and reconfiguring the plant."

"How is the plant, anyway?"

"Engineer says everything is right and tight; so far so good. The water chemistry in 2B is a little shaky, so he'd like to shut down aft when we lock a shaft until he chases down the problem, but otherwise, no steam leaks."

"Super. OK, call me when you're ready to brief."

SIXTY

The Al Akrab, surfaced, the St. Johns river approaches; Friday, 9 May; 0200

The lights ashore fairly blazed in the night's crisp, cool air; the channel buoys seemed to be beckoning the submarine as she moved silently between them under the cover of a new moon. This time the Captain could see the two lights of the river range without his binoculars. The sea dazzled with reflected light, its glossy black surface fragmenting into a million shards of undulating mirror with each passing wave. The darkened sector between the lights of the base on the left and the silver gray sand beaches to the right was the river itself, and there were no lights indicating downstream traffic. This time, in place of the confusion and uncertainty of the last approach, there was a calm stream of positional information coming up, with crisp course recommendations.

The practice run had been well worth the time, he thought. He scanned the naval base, the clustered sodium vapor lights almost painful to his night adapted eyes. The yellow lights of a car driving along the carrier pier perimeter flashed into his glasses, and then away as it turned around to return to the main base. A security patrol, he thought; you are not secure, you Americans. One of the lookouts above called a number as a buoy went by to starboard.

"Buoy four abeam to starboard," he relayed into the intercom. Below, the Deputy acknowledged the report.

"Navigator, aye, and request permission to open outer doors aft," he replied.

"Permission granted; open outer doors aft on tubes 5, 6, and 7. Do not open door 8."

The Deputy acknowledged. Tube 8 contained the defective mine, and had been locked out of the fire control system. The Captain wondered for a moment if he should fire tube eight anyway, but again dismissed the idea. It would not do to have the thing detonate under the first fishing boat to come along and alert the Americans that something dangerous was going on. Let the other three detonate under the first really big thing that came along, like the Coral Sea.

"Range to turn point is 3500 meters," reported the intercom. "Request conn control."

"You have conn control," responded the Captain.

He now had to become like one of the lookouts, content to scan the waters ahead, watching for any sign of movement or alarm on the shore, while the navigation team in the control room turned the boat, steadied her against the current, and then fired the three mines up into the channel junction. The Captain found himself holding his stomach in tightly as he waited for the maneuver, first to starboard, and then the swing to port, just inshore of the last two buoys. It was unnatural, not to be in control. But they had the precise navigation picture, and he did not. He waited.

They were now no more than a third of a mile from the firing point. The lights seemed incredibly bright now; he could see individual sets of masts on the destroyers in the basin. How could they not be seen! Because no one is looking. But suddenly, one of the lookouts called to him urgently.

"What," he said, impatiently, turning to see where the lookout was pointing his binoculars. At the long, dark breakwater that ran down the left side of the river channel. There. He saw it, too. The flare of a match, a cigarette lighter. He scanned the rocks with his binoculars. Great God! There were people on the rocks. Fishing from the breakwater, their poles jammed into crevices between the great, black stones. He could just make out the white blobs of faces, the shine of metal ice coolers perched on the rocks. He had not realized that the breakwater jutted this far out into the sea channel, or that the authorities would ever permit people to be on the breakwater at night in a security zone. He numbly counted more than a dozen shapes along the rocks, and caught the sound of a music as a gust of the night breeze swept over them.

He thought frantically, unwilling to report what he was seeing to the team below: they needed their full concentration on making the swing maneuver. Would they see him? Would they understand what they were seeing? The submarine was ballasted down again, with only the shark's fin of the conning tower jutting up above the water; the smaller dorsal fin of the rudder assembly would not be visible in the darkness. He had ordered no lights to be turned on unless another vessel was sighted, so there would be no lights to attract attention, and there was not much light on the opposite shore to backlight the fin. A man would have to have keen eyesight to see the big, black conning tower cutting across the river. And yet...He swallowed nervously as he swept his glasses ahead, feeling almost naked. He sensed the submarine begin the swing-right maneuver, and then scanned the breakwater again. The shapes along the rocks were not doing anything different, no alarms, no arms waving and pointing, no sudden stab of searchlights from the base. Thank God they had come in on the battery: the big diesels would have had everyone looking.

The submarine checked her swing to starboard, and then came around to port, the screws rumbling and thumping the structure of the conning tower as opposing power was applied to bring her around. He kept his glasses steadied on the breakwater, watching for any signs that someone saw something out on the river. He felt the boat steady up as she pointed seaward again, the vibrations pause as the direction was changed on the screws, and then the strain of both screws backing now to steady her against the current, the sea breeze fresh in their faces.

"Preparing to fire the after tubes," reported the Deputy.

"Yes," said the Captain, his throat dry. "Fire the after tubes when the boat is on bearing. Wait until the turbulence from the screws has subsided."

"Navigator, aye."

He looked over the side as the wash from the beating propellers came swirling up the sides, casting great sheets of gray water over the submerged bulk of the afterdecks like waves over a reef. The stink of river bottom washed up to them from the foam. The submarine began to gather sternway as the Navigator backed her upriver to the precise firing point. The Captain scanned the upstream channel and the breakwater, but there were still no changes. He was beginning to fear that the boiling wash from the screws would be seen and heard ashore, but apparently no one was looking out into the mouth of the river.

Finally, the screws stopped their urgent drumbeat, and the wash subsided aft. Then a thump and a roiling wash of air and water broached the surface astern; a second thump, and a third. There was no sign of the mines as they shot aft, arcing down through the black water to the mud and silt below. Then the screws again, this time kicking out a wash astern, and the boat gathering headway, her bows pointed out to sea and safety. The Captain scanned the breakwater again, but there was still no sign of anyone seeing them. He glanced around to see where they were, and noted the junction buoy watching just upstream. He conjured up the 900 foot long hull of the carrier as she nosed into the river, and swung her bows to make the left turn into the basin. He looked again at the junction buoy, disappearing rapidly now as the Al Akrab jumped ahead under full power. Yes. Very good. There was no way the carrier would avoid the mines. He keyed the intercom.

"The placement looks perfect, Navigator. Well Done!"

Three hours later and many miles from the enemy's shore, the Al Akrab shut down her main engines, switched over to the electrics, and submerged, levelling off at a depth of two hundred feet. The Captain held a short meeting with his department heads, and then returned to the control room, the Musaid as ever at his side. The steward's mate offered tea, but he had had enough and needed sleep. He checked with the sonar station.

"One significant contact only," reported the young sonarman. "A single screwed vessel, a steam ship, since there is no diesel engine noise. She is headed east on a bearing of 120. Barely down doppler. Distance probably beyond twenty thousand meters. Two fishermen on the trawl to the north, small diesels; winch machinery noises. Nothing else."

"Is the steam ship a warship?"

"We cannot tell, Captain. There are no sonars or other military indications, and she proceeds east. More than likely a merchant."

"Very well," replied the Captain, relieved that there were no warships. He dismissed the Musaid and headed forward to his cabin for some much needed sleep. Tomorrow was going to be another long day. With any luck, the last long day.

SIXTY ONE

Mayport Naval Base, Friday, 9 May; 1230

Diane sat in her kitchen, staring at a cooling cup of coffee as she had for most of the morning, squinting against the harsh sunlight streaming through the windows from the beach. Her eyes hurt from the glare and from the fact that she had spent most of the night awake, worrying about what Goldsborough might be facing, what might happen to Mike and his crew if this submarine thing were true after all. The contrast between the peaceful morning routine of the base, the sounds of car doors closing and officers going off to work, the occasional honk of a ship's horn and the hooting of tugs as they went about their chores in the basin, weighed heavily on her mind every time she thought about Mike out at sea, the hours drawing near when he might have to fight for his life.

Might. That was the rub. As Mike had said more than once, this whole thing might be a fairy tale. Or it might become bloody truth with the roar of torpedoes tearing apart the afternoon's sunny silence. She could understand Admiral Walker's reluctance to accept even the possibility, although J.W. had seemed reluctant to discard the notion completely, at least for awhile. It was clearly a difficult proposition for the staff. But Commodore Aronson had acted. Eli Aronson was an ambitious, tough, and experienced surface warfare officer of the classic, eat-your-young-if-they-don't-measure-up school, not an officer to be taken in by fairy tales. He obviously thought that if it were possible for the Libyans to do this thing, then the U.S. Navy ought to go take a look, take some precautions until they were proved wrong. How many times had she heard J.W. talk about the first rule of intelligence: concentrate on capabilities and not on intentions. That's what they always did when they discussed the Soviet Navy. It's the politicians' job to figure out the enemy's intentions, he would pontificate; it is our job to cast a clear, cold eye on their capabilities, and to be ready to deal with all of those capabilities if the politicians get it wrong. The conventional wisdom in 1941 had been that the Japanese *would* never attack Pearl Harbor, but every late 1930's Navy study of their capabilities had shown that they *could* if they wanted to.

She twisted in her chair, absently stirring the muddied coffee. Her instincts told her that there was more to this than met the eye, and her years of marriage to both J.W. and the Navy way of life had taught her to trust her instincts. Something was off the tracks here with this submarine thing. Something that smelled profoundly of Navy peacetime politics, a fear of being the first to take action in an ambiguous situation. No one on the staff wanted to be the first one to broach the possibility that a hostile submarine could be operating in the Navy's own backyard, or that it might have been there for maybe a couple of weeks.

She recognized that the senior officers at the Group staff, her husband chief among them, were reflexively observing the cardinal rule that one doesn't make waves until one draws considerable water. The problem with that rule was that by the time they were big enough players in the system, many of them no longer knew how to make waves, having spent too many years pouring oil on the waters to ensure that waves disappeared.

She knew in her heart of hearts that J.W. had a better than even chance of making Admiral. She also knew that he would fit the mold only too well. He was adept at pleasing his superiors, smoothing over problems, and keeping the bright image of his boss of the day intact. But she was also convinced that, if he were to become an Admiral, he would no longer know what to do about a situation like this mysterious submarine other than to take whatever precautions were necessary to keep any potential consequences from splattering on his own reputation. He took the same approach to his marriage, she thought with a sudden stab of bitterness.

The revelation that he had been seeing another woman still hurt. She felt again the venomous surge of anger that had nearly overwhelmed her when she first found out about the Wave Commander in Norfolk. The real insult was that the son of a bitch took his wife sufficiently for granted that he could afford, emotionally, to be involved with another woman and think absolutely nothing of it. And it wasn't as if she'd gone to fat or booze. Given the way other men reacted to her, it would never have occurred to her that he would even want to stray, and old J.W. had depended on that hubris to keep her from suspecting. He also depended on other senior officers to look the other way; the rest of the staff had to know about his Norfolk playmate, which made it doubly humiliating. How many times had she endured the endless Navy cocktail parties, putting on a pretty face and being so terribly interested in yet another story of some man's career triumph, all the while surrounded by staff officers who knew her husband was seeing another woman on a routine basis.

She picked up the coffee cup, and then put it down again. Her hands trembled with anger and apprehension. Now Mike was out there at sea, looking for a terrorist submarine, in an antique destroyer with no help and none likely other than the Commodore's single radio watch in the harbor, while the routine of the Navy base getting ready for a weekend transpired gently towards 1630 and liberty call. Who was the Commodore going to call if Mike radioed in that he had made contact? The fabulous Group staff?

She glanced up at the clock on the wall. It was nearly 1 p.m. The hot sun outside was directly overhead, casting the shapes of the tropical plants around the house into deep shadow. The house and the quarters area were silent except for the rush of the air conditioners working full time to defeat the sticky heat outside. She took a deep breath. She could no longer just sit there, and do nothing. Three times during the morning she had made her decision, and each time the doubts had pushed her back into her chair. This time, for the first time in her life as *Mrs.* J.W. Martinson, she was going to go light a fuse.

She got up from her chair and went to J.W.'s study, and sat down at his large desk. She began to go through the neat piles of papers stacked up along the left side of the desk, looking for the Navy directory for the Norfolk area. She paused when she came across one file marked MFR. Memorandums for the Record, she remembered. The staff officer's device for covering his backside, as J.W. had described it. If you disagree with a policy or a decision, but are unwilling to challenge or argue with the Boss, or you have been overruled, write an MFR. That way if the issue turns to worms, you can always produce the MFR as proof that you never did agree with the decision. She opened the file, and was surprised to find that the top MFR in the stack dealt with the submarine issue. She read it and felt her face go red with embarrassment as she realized what he was doing.

J.W. had outlined the background of the submarine problem in three neat paragraphs, and then concluded that the proper course of action was to dispatch a three ship ASW force to the area for a period of time longer than the submarine's estimated capacity to stay submerged without snorkeling. He acknowledged the problem of limited budgetary assets, but concluded that the Navy ought to look into the possibility that there was something there. He further concluded that the decision not to forward what information they had on to Naval headquarters in Norfolk was an error, and that he had advised the Admiral in the strongest possible terms that they should tell headquarters.

Diane snorted out loud. I'll just bet! She could not visualize her dear husband "advising in the strongest possible terms" for or against anything, and especially not to an old hardcase like Admiral Walker. But the memo carried his signature block, was machine date-stamped, and his signature was scrawled through the date and signature block to prove that it had been written on the date in question. J.W. had covered himself neatly in case something happened to the Coral Sea. She suspected that a copy was in the files at Group, and the original here at home for safe keeping. Well done, J. W. She wondered if he knew what Eli Aronson was up to. She wouldn't put it past him to let that game play out; either way, he was protected from any career consequences. Well, screw that. Finding the MFR had made up her mind.

She dug through the rest of the stack until she found the Navy phone book for Norfolk. She leafed through the directory until she found the section for the Atlantic Fleet Command. She ran a pencil along the listings until she found the Atlantic Fleet Commander's office, and wrote down the number for his Executive Assistant. She picked up the handset on J.W.'s Navy secure telephone console, and dialed the number.

"CincLantFleet headquarters, Admiral Denniston's office, Yeoman first class Michaelson speaking, this is a non-secure line, may I help you, Sir?" intoned a faintly bored male voice on the other end.

Diane took a deep breath. "I need to speak to the EA," she said, with as much authority as she could muster.

"And may I ask who is calling, Ma'am?"

"Yes. This is Diane Martinson. My husband is Chief of Staff to Group Twelve in Mayport."

"Uh, yes Ma'am, and the subject, please?" The voice not bored now, but curious, cautious.

"I'll tell that to the EA," she said haughtily. "And this is fairly urgent."

"Uh, yes, ma'am," replied the yeoman. "I'll see if he's available. Please hold."

Silence. No music, no cute little advertisements for careers in the Navy, not even the clicking, you're-on-hold sound. Silence. Diane began to wonder if she's have the nerve to tell them what was going on. Mike had confided in her, told her everything, and she would probably have to use it all. Including, ultimately, she realized with a sudden chill, the source of her information. She wondered how Mike would react if he knew. She took a deep breath, and let it out as the line opened again. An exceptionally smooth, baritone voice came on the line.

"Mrs. Martinson, this is Captain St. Claire. What can I do for you?"

The voice projected a sincere interest in what Diane had to say, and enough warmth to infer that they were old friends, overlaid by the faintest suggestion that her calling instead of her husband was somewhat peculiar. She took another deep breath.

"I realize this is unusual, Captain St. Claire, but this is an unusual situation. How do you make this telephone secure?"

"You're calling from a STU-III?" he asked, the surprise evident in his voice.

"Yes, I think so. They put a secure telephone in the quarters when J.W., er, my husband, took the job as Chief of Staff."

"Right. And you want to go secure. Very well. See the red button at the top left of the telephone? Push that down and hold it for two seconds, then let go. When the word "secure" shows up in the data readout panel, we're secure. Push it—now."

Diane did so, and heard a faint trilling sound like a facsimile machine in the earpiece, and then Captain St. Claire was back on the line. The requisite word showed up in the display above the dial panel. His voice was no longer quite so clear, but otherwise there was no difference.

"Are you there, Mrs. Martinson?"

"Yes, I am."

"Very good. Now, how can I help you?"

His tone of voice inferred now that he thought he was about to become embroiled in a domestic dispute or some other tawdry personal matter, but was ready to do his manful duty.

"Yes. Well, I'll get right to the point: this is about a submarine, a Libyan submarine, as a matter of fact, that has apparently been operating in American waters off Jacksonville for a month, waiting to ambush the Coral Sea in revenge for the bombing of Libya three years ago. The Coral Sea is due home from Puerto Rico this afternoon, so an attack is probably going to happen this afternoon, and the only thing between the Coral Sea and the submarine is an old training destroyer, the Goldsborough, who has been sent out by his Commodore to prevent the ambush. And apparently nobody else in Mayport or anywhere else, for that matter, even knows that all this is going on."

She ran out of words suddenly, and felt a slow burn of embarrassment rising up her face as the silence on the other end of the line grew, an incredulous, I must be talking to a drunk or a psycho case silence from the other end.

"Captain St. Claire?"

"Uh, yes, Mrs. Martinson. I'm afraid you've caught me somewhat flat-footed. This is most—"

"I know," interrupted Diane. "You think you've got a nut or a drunk wife on the phone. Let me walk you through what I know about it, and then you can call COMDESRON Twelve's office, that's Commodore Aronson, and simply ask him what's all this about Goldsborough and a Libyan submarine, OK? I've been awake all night trying to decide whether or not to make this call, so I'm only going to give it to you once, and then it's all yours, all right? Can you tape this line?"

"Uh, well, actually, yes we can, but—"

"Get your tape running, Captain. Time is shorter than you know."

There was a one minute delay while someone set up the tape, and then Captain St. Claire came back on the line.

"Mrs. Martinson? We're taping now, all right? Is it possible that we can talk to Captain Martinson? I don't mean to imply anything by that, but it—"

"Forget it," said Diane. "He's on the Coral Sea; that's one of the reasons I'm making this call. Now, I want you to listen without interrupting me."

"Mrs. Martinson,—"

"Just let me talk, Captain St. Clair, and whoever else is on the line. You really don't have much time."

Diane had heard a few clicks on the line while waiting for the tape recorder to be set up. St. Claire putting someone else on the line so that there would be a witness. Fair enough. Diane knew she was lighting a fuse; the more sticks it lead to, the better Mike's chances were.

She then went through the entire story, from the first incidents, to the slow accretion of evidence, sparse as it was, to the Group's skepticism of the whole theory, to the first and second explorations by Goldsborough, the sound recordings of the Deyo, the Admiral's emphatic denunciation of the idea that there might be a submarine out there hunting the Coral Sea, and then the Commodore's secret decision to send Goldy out covertly to rendezvous with Coral Sea. It took a half an hour, and Diane found herself perspiring when she was finished. She waited for a reaction.

"Uh, stand by, Mrs. Martinson, this is, uh—we'll be right back to you, Ma'am," said St. Clair.

Probably calling the little men in the white coats, she thought. She took another deep breath to steady her nerves. If that's the way they were going to react, then that was all she could do. They'd been warned. She drank some cold coffee, unaware that it was cold.

"Mrs. Martinson?" inquired a new, older voice.

"Yes?"

"This is Vice Admiral Bennett. I'm Admiral Denniston's Chief of Staff. I've been listening to what you had to say on a speakerphone in my office. I apologize for eavesdropping, but my EA said this was—important."

I'll bet he didn't say important, thought Diane. Bizarre, maybe, but not important.

"Mrs. Martinson, your—story, uh, this report, is extremely disturbing. You are exactly correct that we have no knowledge of anything like this going on in Mayport, or of any Libyan submarine operating out of area. In fact, if I recall my morning briefing, our intelligence—Mike, is thing secure? It is? OK, thanks. Mrs. Martinson, our intelligence has all the Libyan submarines in their base or otherwise accounted for. I—"

"Call Washington," interrupted Diane. "Talk to the people who do the photo analysis of the North African coast. The satellite reveals that one of the submarines at the base is a decoy. That is, Mike—we, uh, they think it's a decoy. That the real sub left port over a month ago."

There was another stunned silence at the Norfolk end. Then the Admiral came back on the line.

"Uh, Mrs. Martinson, national satellite photography is extremely sensitive material," he began, sternly. "I have to ask you: how in the hell do you know what you're telling us? Is this something that Captain Martinson—"

"No!" She almost shouted.

"No," she continued in a softer voice. "Captain Martinson thinks the whole thing is untrue." So much for your MFR, dear. "He is as convinced as Admiral Walker is that there is no submarine. They both feel that the whole idea is preposterous, and that it wasn't worth reporting up the line. Admiral Bennett, they may even be right. But if they are wrong and the Commodore and Mike are correct, the Navy is about to experience a very bad afternoon."

"I have to ask, Mrs. Martinson—who is your source for this? The Commodore? And if not, is it this—Mike?"

Diane took a deep breath.

"No," she said. "It's not the Commodore. My source is the Captain of the Goldsborough, Commander Mike Montgomery."

There was a strained silence, as the unspoken but obvious next question vibrated down the phone lines.

"Look," she said quickly, to fill the silence, suddenly beginning to run out of courage. "I'm not going to explain the circumstances. They're not relevant right now, anyway. Call Commodore Aronson's office. Warn the Coral Sea. Get some ships out there to help Goldsborough. You're almost out of time. You've been warned. Do something. Don't sit there on your high ranking tailfeathers and be part of another Pearl Harbor, OK?"

Then she hung up the phone, and sat back in her chair, J.W.'s chair, she thought irrelevantly, her heart pounding. The secure telephone rang back immediately, but she did not answer it, staring at it instead, willing it to stop ringing. Finally it did. You've had your warning, big shot. And now, more than one cat is out of the bag, besides.

She went limp in the big leather chair. Oh, Mike. I told you I'd handle our situation my way, and now God knows what they're going to do. I just hope and pray they don't play politics with this. It would be just like them to focus on the indiscretions of a Navy wife and not on the submarine. She leaned forward, grasping her knees, and huddled in the chair. Outside, the normalcy of the beach, the base, the rolling surf sounds flowing through the beach side windows above the sounds of the air conditioning, concentrated her fears in the empty house.

The secure telephone began ringing again, but she ignored it.

SIXTY TWO

Atlantic Fleet Headquarters, Norfolk, Virginia, Friday, 9 May; 1320

Admiral Bennett and Captain St. Claire looked at each other blankly after Diane hung up.

"Get her back on the line," ordered the Admiral, running his hands through his thinning hair.

The Admiral stood by the yeoman's desk while St. Claire pushed the retrieve circuit button, but the STU-III in Mayport was not responding.

"No joy, Admiral."

"But she was definitely calling from a STU-III?"

"Yes, Sir, and the ID was correct: quarters unit for the Chief of Staff at Group Twelve. Sir, I've met Mrs. Martinson. At a reception down there. It did sound like her."

"She must be something to look at if you remember her, Mike," said the Admiral drily.

"Uh, yes, Sir, as a matter of fact she's a memorable lady. But this bullshit about a submarine—"

"Yeah, I know. Run that tape back for me. I want to hear this all again. And then I want to talk to Eli Aronson. If it were any other name but that one, I'd go on to lunch. He and I were golfing buddies when he was on the SurfLant staff here a year ago. Super officer, but he's also fully capable of getting mixed up in some squirrely thing like this. Must be something in the water at Mayport," he said, shaking his head.

St. Clair rewound the tape quickly, and then they put it back on a speaker in Admiral Bennett's office and listened to the whole conversation again. The two yeomen in the outer office tried to look like they were not paying any attention. St. Claire switched it off when they got to the point where Diane had hung up.

"Do we need to tell the Admiral?"

St. Claire did not have to distinguish between Admiral Bennett, who was a Vice Admiral, and Admiral Denniston, a four star who was the Commander in Chief of the Atlantic Fleet. The CinC. Admiral Denniston was the Admiral. Bennett shook his head.

"Not yet. But get the N2 up here—I want him to pull the string in the intel system on the possibility that the Libyans have planted a decoy. And get me Aronson on the phone—I'll take it in here. Why does shit like this always have to break loose on a Friday," he asked no one in particular.

Bennett walked back into his office, while St. Claire instructed the yeoman to get Commodore Aronson in Mayport on the horn for Admiral Bennett. He went over to his own desk, ready to pick up the silenced handset on which all EA's listened in to their bosses' conversations in order to keep records called memcons, a memo of conversation. He arranged a pad and pen as he waited. He heard the yeoman say yes, Sir, a few times, and then the yeoman punched a button transferring the call into Bennett's office and gave St. Claire a signal to pick up. The yeoman scribbled down something on a yellow gummy, and passed it to St. Claire. Commodore not there; this is CSO. St. Claire nodded and listened.

"Commander Barstowe speaking, Sir," came a nervous voice over the line.

"Commander, this is Vice Admiral Bennett; where's your boss?"

"Uh, Admiral, he's over on the Deyo right now, Sir. Can I help you with something?" There was a distinct note of anxiety in Barstowe's voice now.

"Yes, Commander," replied the Admiral in a patient but increasingly threatening tone. "You can get your boss on the phone. Secure. I want to ask him a question."

"Uh, yes, Sir, right away. I'll have him call you right away, Sir. Secure, Sir."

St. Claire, realizing that there would be no conversation to record, hung up his phone. Prematurely, he found out, as he could still hear the Admiral in the other room.

"The subject?" said the Admiral in a voice that was getting louder. "Yes, I can tell you the subject. It's a one word subject. It's *submarine*. Make it two words, as in *Libyan* submarine."

A pause. Then St. Claire heard the Admiral get up out of his chair.

"What did you say?!" the Admiral shouted. "Just what the hell do you mean by 'Oh, shit', Commander?!"

Out in the front office, St. Claire hurriedly grabbed his phone and punched in the number for the duty officer at the Atlantic Fleet Operations Center.

SIXTY THREE

USS Goldsborough, Jacksonville Operating Areas, Friday, 9 may; 1145

Despite the air conditioning, it was becoming hot in the Combat Information Center. Mike sat in his Captain's chair near the central plotting table, surrounded by almost two dozen men at their various general quarters stations. Everyone was wearing battle dress, which included fully buttoned, long sleeved shirts, trousers tucked into their socks, gas masks in their hip pouches on one hip and a CO_2 inflatable lifejacket on the other, protective flashburn hoods and gloves, and steel helmets. The extra gear made it awkward to move around the crowded CIC, especially with all hands present. The men were quiet but alert, doing their surveillance jobs with an intensity Mike had not seen before in Goldsborough.

The operations officer perched on his stool at the head of the plotting table, while the trackers plotted a radar contact closing them from the southeast.

"What do you think, Ops," asked Mike from his chair. There was no room for him at the plotting table.

"It could be him, Cap'n," replied the Operations officer. "The radar contact on the Raytheon display is big enough, and he's coming in at about twenty knots. But ESM isn't holding anything out there but a commercial surface search radar. No TACAN, no GCA radars, no nothing that indicates an aircraft carrier. Passive sonar says it's big and moving down the highway, but can't give any other clues. Right now he's out there at twenty two miles, so we'll get a look at him pretty soon. The lookouts have been alerted, as has the bridge watch."

"OK. If it is the Coral Sea, we'll come up to fifteen knots, turn around and parallel his course, and open up the active sonar. We're far enough out now that I think the best ambush area is west of us, towards Mayport."

"Yes, Sir, we're ready with search plans. The PC indicates that that submerged ridge line is about ten miles back to the west, so we're in good position."

Mike nodded, and reached down for the intercom unit to the bridge, customarily called the bitch-box.

"XO, Captain."

"Yes, Sir, Cap'n," replied Farmer.

His GQ station was on the bridge when the Captain came into CIC. His primary duty was to take over command if CIC were knocked out, and to act as general maneuvering safety officer if things got hot and heavy during an action. He was supported on the bridge by a full GQ watch team, which included an Officer of the Deck, Junior Officer of the Deck, a tactical communicator, three quartermasters, a bosun, a messenger, three additional phone talkers and three lookouts.

"XO, this big radar contact continues to close from the southeast. Keep a sharp eye for a visual ID; we need to know if it's Coral Sea."

"Aye, aye, Sir. Bit early, though, isn't it?"

"Yes it is, and no corroborating ESM, either. May be a big merchie. He's going twenty knots."

"Sounds more like a Toyota carrier than a Navy carrier," said Farmer. "Those guys haul ass."

"Yeah, well, anyway, keep your eyes peeled. What's the weather?"

Mike had been in CIC all morning. He could walk twenty feet out through the front door of CIC and see for himself, but did not want to lose his red lighting adaptation.

"Bright sunlight, light high clouds, sea state zero, wind calm, temp is hot, sweat is everywhere," said Farmer.

"People pay money for cruise conditions like that, XO; enjoy."

"XO, aye."

Mike punched out the intercom buttons. They waited.

Fifteen minutes later, the lookouts on the signal bridge, one level above the pilothouse, spied the oncoming ship low on the horizon. He called the description down to the CIC via the sound powered phone circuit.

"Looks big and looks like a box," relayed the operations officer.

"OK, that's probably a merch; XO was right, I'll bet it's a Toyota boat."

Ten minutes later, the lookouts and the Exec confirmed that the contact was one of the big automobile carriers. Shaped like a shoebox with a narrow bow, a squat, overhanging stern, 100 foot high slab sides, swing ramps at the stern, two small stacks at the very back, and a pilothouse built into the front of the box over the bow, the 850 foot long car carriers transported over 2000 new automobiles on seven drive-through decks. They were modern, fin-stabilized, and fast ships especially designed and built to feed America's unrelenting appetite for high quality Japanese cars and trucks.

"Contact is tracking 285 at twenty-two knots," reported the surface supervisor.

"Pretty good for a single screw ship," remarked the operations officer.

"Especially one that displaces around fifty, sixty thousand tons," said Mike. "Leave it to the Japanese to make a ship as modern as their cars. Tell sonar what the classification is, and tell the bridge to keep us in this general area, five knots, random course changes every ten to fifteen minutes."

As the operations officer passed the word down to Linc in Sonar Control, Mike decided it was time for a tour of the ship. His large body was never meant to sit for hours on end even in the comfort of the Captain's upholstered chair. He left CIC, and headed down the interior ladder to the 01 level, one deck below the bridge. He walked aft past radio central and his own cabin, and out through the watertight hatch onto the midships deck area. Bright sunlight reflecting off an aquamarine sea dazzled his eyes, and it took him a few minutes to get his full vision back.

He walked aft past the after deckhouse with its gun director perched on top, and came around the corner by the boat decks to Mount Fifty Two. The mount's two steel doors were open, and the amplidyne motors shut down to prevent overheating. A gunner's mate was sitting in each door. They got up as the Captain approached, and Mike motioned for them to sit down again.

"How's GQ treating you guys," he asked as he walked up to the big gun mount.

"OK, Cap'n," replied the senior gunner. "We're just waiting around to shoot somebody."

Mike could see the brass fuse tips on the five inch shells gleaming in the transfer trays. The big gun's automatic machinery could load and shoot forty two rounds of five inch diameter shells in one minute, and Goldsborough sported three of these mounts.

"Well, hopefully, you'll get your chance, if this bad guy comes up on the surface."

"You really think there's a A-rab submarine out there, Cap'n?" asked the gunner's mate.

"We think there's a chance, gunner, just a chance. All of this may be for absolutely nothing, but as long as there's a chance, it's our job to try to get in his face and prevent an attack on Coral Sea."

The gunners nodded.

"When's the carrier coming?" asked the younger one.

"We expect the carrier to pass through this area on the way into Norfolk around 1600. But the submarine might be here right now, for all we know. We have to sit here quietly so's we don't spook him out to some-place were we can't get at him; when we see the bird farm come over the horizon, we'll come up active and go looking."

"So he could be drawin' a bead on us right now, for all we'd know it," observed the senior gunner, looking anxiously at the horizon.

"Well, he could," replied Mike, "But if he took a shot at us before the carrier got here, it would reveal that he was here, and that would warn off the carrier. He's only going to get one opportunity, and he's not here to get a tin can. Way we see it, he has to wait, just like us."

Both gunners looked around nervously at the calm, pristine sea.

"Sure hope you're right about that, Cap'n," said the senior gunner.

"Well, once the carrier comes over the horizon, we'll probably find out. That's when I'll need all the eyeballs that are topside looking for periscopes, feathers, or torpedo tracks. If it stays flat calm like this, you guys will be as valuable as radar."

Mike left them thinking about that, and headed aft down the ladder to the main deck. He continued aft along the main deck, glancing himself at the horizon, walking past Mount Fifty Three, greeting its gunner's mates, and stopping at the depth charge racks. The racks were cleared for action, with each of the 500 pound depth bombs fuzed with bright brass fuse rings, and the stainless steel caps of the power supplies and depth sensors inserted. The two sonarmen who operated the rack stood to attention as Mike walked up. They were both dressed out in full battle gear, with one man wearing an oversized helmet to accommodate his sound powered phone circuit.

"At ease, Guys," said Mike, taking in the dark patches of perspiration in their battle gear. It was hot back here on the fantail in the bright sunlight. "Got these hummers ready to go?"

"Yes, Suh," replied the petty officer in charge, in a deep drawl. "You git us on top of that gomer, and we'll open his ass up to underwater southern living."

Mike smiled. These guys were ready to believe there was a submarine out here.

"That might be hard to do, guys," he said. "The submarine isn't going to just sit there while we drive over top of him."

"We kin allays roll one or two if he's nearby; guys at school say that sceers the shit out of 'em, and sometimes screws up their machinery to boot."

"You ready to set fuzes quick-like?" asked Mike.

"Yes, Sir," said the other petty officer, brandishing the Y shaped fuse wrench.

Each depth charge had to be set by hand for the detonation depth, which ranged from 50 to 500 feet. The fifty foot setting had to be set twice, because a detonation at that depth would likely damage the ship dropping the depth charge. As a matter of course, the charges were all pre-set for 200 feet; that way, if the men on the fantail were incapacitated, the bridge could operate the release machinery remotely, drop them and get some effect. The rest of the Navy had long since given up depth charges, because they required the destroyer to maneuver right on top of the submarine. With the advent of high speed nuclear submarines, it was now the submarine that could out-maneuver the surface ship, thus making the depth charge attack almost impossible. Most ASW experts, however, still yearned for the depth charge capability, if only for the psychological effects of a five hundred pound bomb going of at depth, down there where the submarine lived. Very few submariners alive had ever been subjected to the sheer terror of depth bombs.

"We may have to do some fancy setting this afternoon," said Mike. "The water depth here is around 300 to 350 feet, and this is a diesel boat we're after. He can ride down to the bottom if he wants to, or be operating at sixty foot keel depth. But remember the basic rule, if I say roll one now, I mean now, and don't take time to change the standard setting—just roll that bastard and assume the position."

They grinned at him. The 'position' was a deep knee bend held in the flexed position—a depth charge at 200 feet could still hammer the stern hard enough the break legs if the ship had not moved far enough away.

"Won't be using any torpedoes at all, Cap'n?" asked one of the petty officers. He was a sonarman, and thus was privy to the weapons briefing conducted the night before.

"We might," replied Mike. "Chances are the fish would acquire the bottom and attack that before it acquired the pigboat. But if we set it too shallow, it might acquire us instead of the pigboat—we're the bigger target in the eyes of its sonar. I know they've got the fifty foot lockout but I wouldn't want to bet my ass on that feature, not after that one jumped out of the water at a helo about ten years back. But I still might use one, especially if he shoots a fish at us—I'd fire back down the bearing of the incoming fish and let him take his chances while I try to get out of the way of his screamer. Either way, you can count on our using these beauties back here to get his attention away from the bird farm, if he shows up. So you guys be ready; from now until about 1800 is the attack window."

They assured him that they and their deadly charges would be ready. Mike walked forward up the port side to the forward breaks, the weather shield structure underneath the pilothouse that protected the main decks from waves coming over the forecastle. He climbed a short, vertical ladder to the port torpedo platform, finding it harder to keep his balance with the steel helmet on. On the platform he found two torpedomen waiting for him at attention. He smiled mentally. The word was getting around the sound powered phone circuits that the Old Man was making a tour; the torpedo decks had obviously been alerted.

The two torpedomen saluted Mike as he climbed through the chains at the top of the ladder. Mike returned their salutes and talked to them for a few minutes, answering questions and exhorting them to be on their toes for this afternoon's possible engagement. Mike found out that one of the air flasks had a slow leak, and that the torpedo decks were having a problem getting 3000 pound air from the forward engineroom. Nothing beats personal reconnaissance, he thought, making a note of the problem.

One of the men pointed over towards the starboard side. The Toyota car carrier was steaming by, carving a creamy wake some 6000 yards away. Mike decided to get back up to the bridge and CIC. He'd yell at the snipes about the HP air. It was getting on to noon. He wondered briefly what Diane was doing.

SIXTY FOUR

The submarine Al Akrab, Jacksonville operating areas, Friday, 9 May; 1205

The Captain stood behind the sonarman, his face intent. Everyone in the control room was listening to the sounds of the approaching ship, a steady beating noise coming from the speaker above the sonar console. The Captain shook his head.

"Single screw; this is not the carrier," he pronounced, and the control room crew relaxed slightly.

"Depth," he asked.

"Depth is sixty five meters," responded the Musaid from his chair behind the planesmen. "On course 090; speed is four knots."

The Captain tapped the sonarman on one shoulder.

"Evaluation," he inquired.

"Sir, the contact is east of us, bearing 145, exhibits up doppler, single screw, making high speed. A power screw, which indicates a large ship."

"Could this be a deception?" asked the operations officer from his position near the attack director. "The Coral Sea on one screw?"

The Captain frowned. It was possible, but unlikely. Why would the carrier be operating in a deception mode? If she had been warned of Al Akrab's presence, there would be a mob of escorts out here, and very likely no carrier at all. He shook his head slowly, still concentrating on the hydrophone effects coming over the speaker. The big ship was going to come fairly close to them; the bearing had been steady and then had begun to drift right only slightly in the past five minutes. But what was it? Who was it? He decided they had to take a look.

"No. This is something else. What is the CPA?"

"Sir. The closest point of approach will be to starboard, approximately 3000 meters, based on passive bearing analysis."

"Very well. Secure the speaker. Musaid. Go to periscope depth."

"As you command, Effendi," replied the Musaid.

He touched the shoulder of the depth control planesman, who nodded and pulled back on the yoke. The submarine tilted slightly up at the bow, and began to rise silently on electric propulsion. The members of the control room battle stations team made way for the Captain as he took his position at the periscope well. The control room was steamy in the heat of the tropical sea; the ventilators fought a losing battle with all the main compartment hatches latched shut. The Captain watched the depth gauge in front of the planesmen as Al Akrab came up to a keel depth of sixty feet. As the bow levelled off and the deckplates returned to horizontal, the Musaid nodded at the Captain, who turned once more to the sonarman.

"Report," he ordered.

"Sir. The large ship is almost abeam, bearing 195, and passing down our starboard side; I have no estimate of range, but the bearing drift indicates she is not close aboard. There is something else."

"Yes?"

A sudden silence in the control room, all eyes on the young man sitting the sonar stack, as he listened carefully, his hands clasped over his earphones. The silence became prolonged.

"Sir. I think there is another ship. Very quiet, but something I can hear. Also east Bearing 095. Distant. I could not hear it over the noise of the large ship, who now exhibits down doppler—she is going past us."

"Classify," ordered the Captain.

"Sir. I cannot classify, other than one screw. I may be wrong. But I think there is something there. East of us, and very quiet."

The Captain took a deep breath. They had made their approach into the attack zone from the north, slowly and silently, on the battery, well below the acoustic layer. They had detected a couple of fishermen and small craft on the way, and then, an hour ago, the large ship, a steady drumming sound coming from the southeast, headed in toward the Jacksonville approaches. The intelligence report had said Coral Sea was due that evening, but it was only mid day. Had there been a change of plans? A warning? And now the report of something else out there. His hackles rose.

"Depth control is stable at periscope depth," reminded the Musaid.

"Sonar, what is the sea state above?" asked the Captain.

"From the sound, it is flat calm. I hear no waves," replied the sonarman.

"Up scope," ordered the Captain. "Hold at fifty five feet for manual control."

The periscope came up swiftly, but stopped short of its full height, its bronze tip remaining five feet beneath the surface above. The Captain took a switch cable in his hand, and lowered the periscope control arms, squatting down on the deckplates to meet the eyepiece. He pushed his forehead against the eyepiece headrest, and then closed the trigger switch. The periscope started up again, but very slowly. The Captain took little duckwalking steps around the compass as the scope came up. At first he could see nothing, and then light, a blue haze everywhere, and then a lighter blue as the optics neared the actual surface. He released the button for a moment.

"Make minimum speed," he ordered. If there were no waves, the periscope would be visible to the naked eye, and even more visible to a surface search radar.

"Minimum speed," acknowledged the watch officer. "Setting for three knots."

"Can you hold depth at three knots, Musaid?"

"Yes, Effendi. I must pump two trim tanks, but we can hold depth control."

"Permission granted to activate trim tank pumps. I'm breaking the surface—now," he declared, pushing his forehead tightly against the headrest, revolving the scope quickly, and then pulling it back down one meter below the surface.

"Some kind of large merchant ship," he announced. "Not the Coral Sea."

There was a collective sigh of relief in the control room from everyone except the weapons officer, who was staring at the Captain, aware of the pained expression on the Captain's face.

"Sir. How big a merchant ship?" he asked the Captain.

376

The Captain gave him a slight nod, acknowledging the weapons officer's acumen in asking the important question.

"Very large, weapons officer," replied the Captain in a tight voice. "Very large indeed."

The Deputy, who had been watching this interchange intensely, suddenly figured it out,

"The mines," he said.

The Captain turned to stare at him, and then trained his cold eyes around the control room.

"Yes," he sighed. "The mines. Now it is up to us. If that ship is going to Jacksonville, it will eat the mines. Now it is entirely up to us. Prepare yourselves."

"Sir," called the sonarman. "I have heard it again. Bearing east, by a half south. Something is there, Captain."

The Captain rotated the periscope to 120. He waited. Two minutes later the swell made by the passing car carrier began to gently rock the submarine.

"His wake is passing by; I will expose the periscope," the Captain said.

He squatted again, and pushed the control button at the end of its wire, timing the periscope to come up out of the sea coincident with the passage of the merchant's wake. To a radar, the sudden return would be taken for the wake. He hoped.

He turned the periscope to high power, and stared as it neared the surface, the image of the turbulence right at the surface causing him to blink. Then daylight, bright sunlight, flashed through the optics. He drew back reflexively, and the control room crew could see the bright ring of sunlight around his eyes for an instant. He pressed his face against the optics again, and stared, rotating the scope right and left ten degrees. Again. Nothing. Right and left twenty degrees. And hold.

There. On the horizon. The unmistakable shape of a warship's top hampers, the dark, lattice masts and the multiple radar antennas. Hull down. A destroyer. Not moving, keeping quiet. A chill filled his belly.

"Periscope down," he ordered. "Make your depth sixty meters, course 180, speed five."

He looked up at the faces of the control room crew as the periscope sank into its well, the deckplates pitching forward and down as the Musaid took her below.

"It seems," he announced, "That we have company."

SIXTY FIVE

Atlantic Fleet headquarters, Norfolk, Virginia, Friday, 9 May; 1430

Captain Larry Desantes, the staff intelligence officer, was standing in front of Vice Admiral Bennett's desk. He was not having a particularly good afternoon. The Admiral was reading a secure telefax obtained from Washington ten minutes ago. Admiral Bennett was shaking his head from side to side, as if to will away the information in the fax. He looked up at the staff intelligence officer.

"According to this, N2, the senior photoanalysis committee has met in emergency session and are now saying that one of the six subs tied up at Ras Hilal may not be a real submarine."

He pitched the piece of paper down on his desk, and swivelled his chair to stare out the window, where he had a fine view of the Navy Exchange across the parking lot.

"And then, of course," he continued, "In the inimitable fashion of all intel weenies everywhere, it may, on the other hand, be a submarine and the photo might be bad. Or it may be a fox terrier and the satellite is bad, or it may be a rainy day in Washington and the weather is bad!"

He swivelled back again.

"What the hell am I supposed to do with this?"

Before the perspiring N2 could answer, the Admiral yelled past him to the open doorway.

"Mike, where the hell is Aronson—I want to talk to him now, goddammit!"

"Working on it, Admiral," came the voice of the EA.

The Admiral looked back at his intelligence officer.

"Well?"

"Well, Sir," he began, nervously. "I listened to the tape of the phone conversation. She said they had several scraps of "evidence", but no one thing that's conclusive. I would say that this estimate could be considered another scrap, and one that's just as ambiguous as the rest of them. But the whole thing, Admiral, is so—I mean, Quaddaffi would have to be out of his fucking—"

The Admiral's flat stare cut him off.

"Muammar Quaddaffi," he said. "Out of his mind. What a novel concept."

The EA appeared in the doorway. "Line two, Sir. Commodore Aronson."

The Admiral punched a button violently on his phone console, pointing the red faced N2 and the EA into chairs, and putting line two on his speaker. The Admiral wasted no time with polite preliminaries.

"Eli, what in God's name have you got going down there in Mayport? What's all this shit about a submarine and the Coral Sea—you guys been getting downwind of all those dope smokers down there in Florida, or what?"

"Hello, Admiral," replied Aronson in a subdued voice. "And, no, we're not doing any dope. I almost wish we were. Bill Barstowe told me you called and said the magic word. Before I tell you our side of it, may I ask a question of my own—what prompted your call?"

"A very disturbing, thirty minute phone call from one Mrs. Diane Martinson, wife of your Group Commander's Chief of Staff. How she knew about this is a second Mayport mystery, but it involves the CO of the Goldsborough somehow. I'll leave that little problem to you Mayport types; I suspect that's going to be easier to solve than this submarine mystery. Now lemme have it—what's going on? I haven't told the CinC anything yet, but I'm getting the feeling that I'm going to have to go see him pretty soon."

The Commodore sighed and went through the story from the very start to their current situation. He covered his and Mike's joint presentation to Admiral Walker in detail, and described the net result of that presentation. He reviewed all of the tendrils of evidence indicating that there might be a threat to the Coral Sea, and then, to preserve balance and to show that they had thought of other possibilities, postulated alternative explanations for each one of them.

"As you can see, Admiral," he concluded, "Each of these little indicators is pretty flimsy; it's the fact that there were so many of them that gave me pause. It has cost me nothing to send Goldy out there, because she had to do a sea trial anyway. I would have preferred to get a crowd out there for a real look, but, well, my boss thinks it's all bullshit, and he's the boss."

Admiral Bennett thought for a moment.

"And if you guys are right, and there is a Libyan pigboat out there, then what happens?" he asked.

It was Aronson's turn to be silent for a long moment.

"Mike Montgomery is a pretty good guy," he said. "No E-ring ballerina by any stretch of the imagination, but he had a solid, combat operations record in Vietnam over several tours. He's one of those warriors we talk about a lot but don't promote so much, you know? And Goldsborough? Well, Goldy is a bit of an antique—she's going out next year, you might remember—but she's got a good, medium power active sonar, and this situation needs a medium power active sonar more than the fancy, new passive stuff. If we're right—big if, I admit—this is a diesel-electric boat. Not even the Spruances would have much of a chance hearing him when he's on the battery, and the reverberation from their own active sonars would blow their own sonarmen out of their chairs in that shallow water. But, still: one tin can versus one sub is bad odds. I just didn't know what the hell else to do, except that I couldn't sit back and do nothing. I guess that says it all."

Admiral Bennett nodded thoughtfully to himself. He respected Aronson's instinctive approach to an ambiguous problem, and, given the circumstances, was rapidly concluding that he himself might have done the same thing, but with one important difference. He would never have done it on his own.

"When's Coral Sea due in?" he asked.

"At 1900 tonight in the basin, to make the high slack water. Which means sometime in the next three hours we ought to know if this was a drill or for real."

"And you say the Group Commander doesn't know anything about this?"

He heard Aronson sigh.

"About Goldy being out there looking? That's correct, Admiral. If it's a drill, I figured no one had to be the wiser, and if it's not a drill, then there's going to be hell to pay anyway you look at it."

"Eli, Eli—basic rule," intoned the Admiral in a chiding voice. "Gotta keep the boss informed. Now there's going to be a rocket coming down from CincLantFleet, and we're going to catch ComSecondFleet, ComNavSurflant, and ComCruDesGroup Twelve all off base."

"They had their chance, Admiral," said Aronson stiffly. Across the room, the EA rolled his eyes. He knew the sounds of political suicide when he heard them. The Admiral stared down at his desk.

"I think on the face of it," he declared after a moment, "We need to send a warning message to Coral Sea, but I'm going to have to get to the CinC before I do that. And we also have the minor problem of figuring out how and what to tell those bit actors in Washington like JCS, the Secretary of Defense, and the President."

"Yes, Sir," said Aronson. "I realize that. I think that was the major underlying part of our problem down here. We are postulating that a foreign power is going to attempt an act of war against one of our largest ships. That's a lotta water to carry to Washington, and I just didn't feel there was anybody in my chain of command who would be willing to carry it. I should also point out that even if something happens to Coral Sea, or Goldsborough, or both, we probably still won't have any proof it was the Green Hornet over there that did it unless we pick up a boatload of Libyans. The way I see it, we're all going to have to wait and see if anything happens out there, and then figure out a way to explain it if it does."

Admiral Bennett shook his head.

"We might have been able to get away with doing nothing if Mrs. Martinson hadn't called, Eli. But now that we know, and now that it can be shown that we knew about the possibility in advance, we gotta do something. How long would it take you to get a couple of Spruances and some heloes out there to where you think this action might take place?"

"I'm sitting in the Deyo right now, waiting for word from Mike that he's turned up something. I guess I could—"

His voice was drowned out by the sound of thunder rumbling over the amplified speaker phone. The three officers in Norfolk sat up in their chairs as another and then another thundering blast echoed in the room.

"Eli? Eli? What the fuck is that?" yelled the Admiral.

"Hang on a minute, Admiral. It sounds like something's just blown up out on the river. Wait one!"

They could hear the sound of a phone being dropped on a desk, and then a hubbub of voices in the background. Admiral Bennett began to get a cold feeling in his stomach.

"Did you turn on a crisis action team down at the Command center?" he asked the EA, holding his hand over the phone.

"Affirmative, Admiral, right after you heard the CSO say 'Oh shit'."

"Good man."

After a very long minute, a new voice came on the line.

"Uh, Admiral Bennett, Sir—this is Ensign Purvis, Deyo CIC? Are you still there, Admiral, Sir?"

"Yes, Goddammit!"

"Uh, yes, Sir, sorry. There's a big merchie in the channel junction—one of those Japanese car carriers? She's on fire from stem to stern, and looks like she's rolling over in the river."

"What were those explosions, Mr. Purvis?"

"Sir, the XO of the Fife—she's nested alongside?—said it looked like the merchie got torpedoed. He told the Commodore up on the bridge just now that there were three big fu—, uh, real large explosions under the merchie, just like in the movies?—as she came into the channel. He said they lifted her right up out of the water, and these car carriers are fifty, sixty thousand tons!"

"What's happening now, Ensign? Quickly!"

The EA had run out of the room to call the Command Center again. "Buncha people running around topside, Admiral. They—"

His excited voice was interrupted by the sound of yet another blast, big enough to buzz the little speaker on the Admiral's desk, and then the sounds of people yelling 'Take Cover' in the background.

"Uh, Admiral, there's shit landing all over the basin—pieces of the merch, it looks like. Whoa! Goddamn!"

There was a loud, metallic banging noise, and then the line went dead. The speaker hissed impotently in the office.

Admiral Bennett found himself on his feet, along with the N2. Another phone line buzzed, this one the red phone from the LANTFLT command center. The Admiral grabbed it.

"Bennett!" he said. He listened for a minute.

"Does the CinC know this? OK. Thank you very much."

He hung up the phone as the EA came back into the office. He looked at the other two officers.

"That was the duty officer, reporting a major incident in the entrance to the St. Johns river. The river is apparently completely blocked, and so is the base channel. I'm going down to the Command Center. The CinC is on his way down, too. Mike, get me that tape and meet me downstairs. You, too, Larry."

Admiral Bennett left the room, his face grim as he pulled on his service dress blue blouse and headed for the Atlantic Fleet Command Center in the basement.

SIXTY SIX

Mayport Naval Station, Friday, 9 May; 1535

The Commodore and several other officers stared out the windows of Deyo's expansive pilothouse at a scene from hell. Huge clouds of black smoke were rolling in over the base, obliterating the afternoon sunlight and making it appear that many ships in the basin were on fire. The smoke was so thick that its source, the partially submerged wreck of the car carrier, was visible in the murk only as a brilliant, pulsating orange glare. An entire sector of the horizon along the carrier piers was obscured, and the towering pillar of black smoke was pushing itself into a mushroom shaped cloud above the base.

The sound of police and ambulance sirens could be heard all over the base. Men on the ships moored near the Deyo were scrambling to help injured shipmates who had been hit by the hail of metal raining down out of the sky when the car carrier, packed with over 2000 partially filled automobile gas tanks, had blown up on the river. It was plain that there was now a major problem on the base as well as in the river junction, with scores of people injured. The Captain of the Deyo hurried in through the back door of the pilothouse, and walked over to where the Commodore was standing.

"Sir, I've got some people injured out on deck, and there seem to be a lot of injuries on the ships all around us. My medical people are helping our guys, and then we're going to send a team out on the base. The base command center has apparently sent out an operational incident report. If you don't need me right now—"

"Yeah, go ahead," interrupted the Commodore. "But make sure I still have that circuit up with the Goldsborough. I need to talk to Mike right now."

"Yes, Sir, base shore power is stable, so we shouldn't have lost comms, unless an antenna got hit. I'll verify you're still on the air."

He stared out the windows for a moment. "What on earth do you suppose happened out there?"

"I have the inkling of an idea, Captain," said the Commodore, shaking his head, his face grim. He hurried below to CIC. The IV looked at his Exec, who shrugged his shoulders in a beats-me expression, and hurried back down the ladder.

The Commodore took the handset from the anxious looking watchstander and called the Goldsborough. A radio talker in Goldsborough's CIC answered at once.

"This is Charlie Delta Sierra One Two," said the Commodore. "Pass to your Charlie Oscar that a large merchant ship has blown up in the St. Johns river channel. An eye-witness reports that the merchant was torpedoed, I repeat, torpedoed. Tell you Charlie Oscar, Heads Up, we may be right after all, over?"

"This is One Sierra, roger, copy all, out."

The Commodore put down the handset. Mines, he thought. Fucking mines, not torpedoes, not in sixty feet of water. The bastards laid down mines, right on our front fucking door!

SIXTY SEVEN

USS Goldsborough, 1610

"Captain, surface radar has a contact we believe is the Coral Sea, bearing 140, range twenty miles, closing on course 310, speed twenty three knots; ESM confirms, Sir."

There was a stirring among the bridge watch team. Mike leaned forward in his chair on the bridge, and keyed the bitch box.

"Captain, aye. I'll be right in."

He turned to the Exec, who was looking wilted in the afternoon heat. Everyone was looking wilted. The strain of waiting was beginning to tell.

"XO, we're about to turn into a tin can again. I'll speak to the crew from CIC as soon as I've seen the picture in there. Make a quick tour through the ship and let everybody know we may be in action soon. Wake 'em up if they're slacking off. I know it's been a long wait."

"Aye, aye, Sir," said the Exec, taking off his binoculars.

Mike got out of his chair and hurried into CIC. As hard as the air conditioning was working, it was still only ten degrees cooler in Combat than out on the bridge. He went directly to the plotting table, putting his sunglasses away in his shirt pocket.

"OK," he said, approaching the plot. "Where is he?"

"Right here, Cap'n. Good solid contact, and ESM holds a GCA radar on that bearing. We're pretty sure it's the bird farm. I've projected his track, and we've laid out the search plan on that axis."

"All right. Come around to match her course, speed fifteen. We'll let her overtake us while we sweep out ahead of his track. Tell Main Control to release the locked shaft, and get the sonar going in omnidirectional mode. Make sure they've taken a BT drop in the past half hour. Let's go find this guy if he's out here. Are there any other contacts?"

"Only two fishing boats, about 12,000 yards away to the south and west. They're no problem to our track or the carrier's."

"OK. Ops, activate the 1MC for me."

The Operations officer handed him a long cord microphone and threw a switch, and then nodded at the Captain. Mike stood by the side of his chair.

"Gents, this is the Captain speaking. The carrier has been sighted, and we're going to begin our hunt. We're going to sweep the waters ahead of the carrier's track for the next hour or so, until we flush this guy or until we're into the beach and the Coral Sea is safe. I know it's been a long day of waiting around. Look to your gear, and check your spaces, and figure out what you're going to do if we take some damage. I've said it before, and I'll say it again: we don't know for sure that there's a bad guy out here, but if there is, Goldy is the only thing between him and the carrier, so pay attention. That is all."

"It'll be a couple of hours before he overtakes us," said the operations officer, looking down at the track geometry.

"Not really," replied Mike, "Once we begin the search plan, we'll be maneuvering on various courses and speeds on either side of the carrier's track; our net effective speed of advance will probably only be ten knots or so relative to his twenty three. He's going to be on us like stink on shit before we know it. I just hope we shake something out before he runs right past us."

"Sonar going active," announced the 29 MC speaker.

"Find his ass, Linc," muttered the Captain.

"And if we do get a contact, Captain, we're to tell the carrier something about a possible floating mine, and recommend he turn away?"

"Right. I'll do that myself so they pay attention. Get a radio check on Fleet Common with the bird farm in the next five minutes."

The radio messenger came through the door a moment later and handed Mike a message board. Before he could read it, the CIC radio talker took off his headset, and gestured for Mike to come over.

"Captain, I've got a message from ComDesRon Twelve himself."

"Hang on a minute, messenger," said Mike, handing him back his board. He headed for the communications console.

"But, Sir," said the radio messenger, this is a—"

"Hang on, this is our boss calling here."

Mike picked up the message pad with Commodore's message about the Toyota carrier and read the message. He whistled once. He handed the message pad back to the operator, and then took the message board from the anxious radio messenger.

"That was the Commodore," he announced to the officers at the plotting table, as he scanned the board. "Remember that big Toyota car carrier that went by this morning? It apparently blew up all over the entrance to the St. Johns river a few minutes ago. First reports are that it was torpedoed! Gentlemen, we may be in business after all. Now, what's this."

"Sir," began the messenger again. "It's a flash message to the Coral Sea, info us, warning him—"

"OK. Lemme me read it," said Mike.

He finished scanning the message.

"Well I'll be goddamned," he said, finally. "This is from CincLantFlt, warning Coral Sea of a possible submarine threat in its path into Mayport. He's been ordered to divert back to sea at best speed until otherwise directed."

He looked up at their eager faces.

"I wonder what the hell triggered this? Maybe the Commodore tried again."

"Are they sending any additional forces out, like heloes?" asked the operations officer.

"This message doesn't say anything about help, and I suspect nothing's getting by the river entrance right now. A helo or two would sure be useful, wouldn't they. What's the carrier doing on the scope?"

"Sir, the carrier is continuing to track straight in."

Mike shook his head.

"Typical aircraft carrier; sometimes they act like a dinosaur: smack 'em on the ass and it takes fifteen minutes for the head to get the message. You watch, it'll take ten minutes to get the message up to the CO from radio, and then another five for the aviators to decide there's no pictures in it and then someone will have to read it to them."

There were grins around the CIC. Destroyer officers did not think much of the fly boys.

"OK, everyone, let's settle down and let's get to work finding this sewer pipe, preferably before the Coral Sea tramples all over both of us. Ops tell the XO about what's happened back at the base."

"Yes, Sir, but if the Toyota-boat got torpedoed back there, it means we don't have a submarine out here..."

"Those weren't torpedoes, Ops. Nobody would shoot torpedoes into the mouth of a river—they'd go out of control in all those shallow water currents and blow up on the bottom. Those were mines. Which means somebody had to put 'em there. And I'm betting that somebody is within our sonar range. Now tell the XO, and then get me comms with the carrier. We need to make him believe that flash message from CincLantFleet."

SIXTY EIGHT

The Submarine Al Akrab, 1610

The control room was darkened down to red lighting to conserve electric power and to reduce heat from the noisy, Russian fluorescent lights. The officers and petty officers of the battle team were pale shadows in the half light, clustered over their instruments and consoles. The hum of electrical machinery permeated the compartment. The Captain watched the visual display of the sonar console intently.

"Classify," he ordered.

"Sir. Multiple screws, high speed, up doppler, closing from the east. The surface duct carries it clearly, thus deep draft. No merchant ship has that many screws. Classify as target Coral Sea."

The Captain straightened up and took a deep breath.

"Very well. Track target Coral Sea. Attack director, flood torpedo tubes, open outer doors, forward; open outer doors aft on tube eight."

"Attack director, aye. Establishing track on sonar target channel one. Opening all forward outer doors. Flooding torpedo tubes one through six and eight."

The Captain turned and walked over to the plotting table. They were at sixty meters, on the battery, and rigged for silent running. The Captain thought for a moment. What was the accursed destroyer doing? They had remained well clear of the warship, not willing to take the chance of a detection. The destroyer had remained passive, not pinging on his sonar. He ached to take another look at him, but had to steel himself to stay hidden. It was an ominous sign that there was almost no sound from the destroyer. Loitering speed, no engine noises, not even a fathometer.

The presence of the waiting destroyer had thwarted his plans to use the electronic listening buoys. And now he could not know about radars without putting up the ESM mast, and with these flat seas, he was not going to put up anything he did not have to. The destroyer was waiting—but for what? The carrier? But why then the silence?

Twenty-five minutes ago they had heard the deep booming sounds of explosions reverberating along the bottom from the west. The mines had found a victim, probably that large merchant ship. Now the base would be alerted, but, hopefully, unable to dispatch forces with the wreck of the ship littering the river channel junction. The mines had claimed the wrong victim. Inshallah. At any rate, it was more than twenty five miles to the base. With the carrier already approaching, nothing but an aircraft could get out here to interfere. And there should be no obvious tie between what had happened at the river and the Coral Sea. After an explosion that could be heard underwater for twenty five miles, he thought that the base itself might not be operational for a while. Which brought him back to the mysterious, silent destroyer.

"What is the layer?"

"Sir. The layer is at twenty meters, refractive."

Twenty meters. Effective shielding against a destroyer's sonar, but not as good as the double and triple layers of the Gulf Stream margins. The plotting team had begun a passive bearing analysis on the carrier; in forty minutes they would have her course and speed, enough to set up the basic firing solution. He would rise to periscope depth just before firing to confirm with a few, quick looks, and then release six steam driven torpedoes down the carrier's path.

He regretted the loss of the mines. That would have been a nice touch. But then a happy thought struck him: if the base had been neutralized when the merchant ship had struck them, then the carrier could not go home. She would have to stop and wait. In his attack zone.

"Any preliminary estimates of range?" he asked.

"No, Sir," replied the Deputy from his position at the plot. "It is too soon. The bearing plot shows almost no, perhaps slight right drift, so we should be off axis and in good position. We need—"

The Deputy was interrupted by the sudden sound of the destroyer's sonar ringing throughout the control room. It sounded very close. Too close. Everyone looked up.

"Bearing of the sonar."

"Sir: the sonar bears 110."

"Make your depth 90 meters, and come left to 090," ordered the Captain. Depth accentuated the effect of the layer, and coming to an easterly heading put the submarine's narrowest aspect facing the probing sonar, and also helped him close the range to the carrier.

If the destroyer had begun a search, it might mean that he was running out of time to make his attack. The danger was that any maneuver to close the carrier also closed the submarine into the destroyer's sonar beams.

"Set up a second firing solution on the destroyer," he ordered.

If he had to, he would smash the destroyer and then attack the carrier.

"Attack director, aye. Establishing second track on sonar channel two."

"Sir," reported the sonarman. "The destroyer is occasionally cavitating; his speed is probably right at or above fifteen knots. His screws are nearer than the carrier. His sonar is in the omni-directional mode. I estimate the range to the destroyer by ping stealing to be about 14,000 meters. Sir. We have heard this sonar before. It is the old destroyer."

The Captain's eyebrows rose.

"Is it indeed," he said. "Very well, that is better for us than a Deyo."

He looked over at the attack director, where the weapons officer was entering and monitoring the two data streams coming from the sonar system. Finally, the weapons officer activated the computer, and the dials began to swing on the attack director. The weapons officer studied the readouts for a moment, and then shook his head.

"No solution, but we are close," he declared. "I need a stable estimate of course and speed of the target in channel two, and a range estimate for channel one, the carrier."

"Sonar?"

"Sir: according to the doppler, the destroyer is changing aspect. I suspect base course is westerly, but it is not steady. He is now left of the bearing of the carrier. A few minutes ago he was coincident."

"Very well."

The Captain went back over to the paper plot. The passive bearing analysis on the carrier, which was being carried out by one plotter, was a spider web of lines occupying one side of the tactical plot. Passive bearing analysis was always a time consuming process, typically taking one or more hours to compute a refined solution. He did not have the time. The course change to the east, the direction from which the carrier was approaching, would not help the analysis. If anything, the submarine needed to move off the bearing axis in order to develop cross bearings, but that would put her full beam aspect in the path of the probing sonar.

A second plotter had begun a track on the destroyer, taking the bearings from the sonar console as the sonar operator locked in on the point source of the pinging. A destroyer's sonar in the active mode was always a beacon for a submarine. Better yet, knowing the velocity of sound in the present water conditions, they could make a rough range estimate by timing the individual sonar pings from source to their own hull. But the destroyer was not steering a steady course, which made firing on him a very uncertain proposition.

Tension rose in the control room. The sudden appearance of the destroyer had everyone on edge, especially now that she had begun a sonar search. It was one thing to creep around avoiding detection; it was quite another to set up an attack on a target while a destroyer was hunting you. This was supposed to be an ambush of an unsuspecting, capital warship in peacetime. The persistent pinging from above indicated that the other side might be aware that there was danger here.

The seams of the submarine began to creak as she descended to 280 feet. No one was worried about crush depth. The problem now was the proximity of the bottom. The Musaid perched on his stool, his legs spread in front of him to keep from sliding forward as the deckplates dipped, his gnarled hands gripping the stainless steel seat of the stool as he fixed his eye on the depth gauge and the diving plane indicators.

"Depth is 90 meters," he announced softly. "Request permission to trim aft."

"Permission to trim."

The Captain continued to study the nascent plot. Too soon to develop a clear picture. He began to conjure one up in his mind. The big carrier plowing westerly towards her base. Ahead of her a destroyer had begun his screening work. If indeed he was screening, then he would generally match the carrier's expected route. Track the destroyer and obtain attack geometry on him, and that would also serve as a good estimate for the carrier. As long as the destroyer did not detect the Al Akrab.

"Bring me the most recent BT trace," he ordered.

The senior sonarman collected a piece of paper from the sonar console and presented it to the Captain, who studied it carefully. A bathythermograph, or BT trace, was a plot of temperature versus depth, obtained by firing a thermocouple probe attached to a wire out of the submarine into the depths. It recorded the thermal structure of the ocean until the wire broke off. Kinks in the trace indicated thermal layering, and thereby the depths of relative safety for submarines. This plot showed only one layer, and not a strong one at that, fifty to sixty feet below the surface. Better than nothing, he thought. Some of the destroyer's sonar energy would be refracted back up, creating acoustic shadow zones underneath the layer where strong returns would not materialize.

But he could not count on that for very long, especially as he was headed towards that sonar. At some point, the energy levels of the returns from the boat would break through the acoustic mirror surface, and they would be in trouble. He stared down at his shoes in the red light. He would have to deal with the destroyer, sink him if possible, or disable him at the least, in order to get a free shot at the carrier. If the destroyer made a detection, the carrier would be warned and would speed away, out of range, wrecking the mission. But timing was crucial—a premature attack on the destroyer would produce the same results.

"Is the carrier continuing in on her original course?"

"Sir," said the Deputy. "We cannot tell her precise course, but the rate of her bearing drift is fairly constant, which would indicate—"

"Yes, that she has not changed her course; I understand the basics," interrupted the Captain, annoyed by the pedantic response from the Deputy.

"Make ready tubes one and two; I intend to fire at the destroyer as soon as we have a reasonably good solution on him, *and* some idea of the range to the carrier. Give me a southerly course recommendation that will put the destroyer and the carrier on the same bearing; when we achieve that geometry, I will fire two torpedoes on wire guidance at the destroyer. If they miss, or he evades, I want them redirected down the bearing of the carrier. Set the running depth for one and two at four meters; select wire guidance. Retain the settings on the remaining four tubes at seven meters. Make haste!"

The Captain walked back over to the sonar console, and studied the bearing traces. The weapons officer set up the running depth settings for tubes one and two, transmitted them to the torpedo guidance systems, verified continuity between the wire and the guidance modules, and initiated warmup power to the computers in the two torpedoes.

The Deputy and the operations officer scrambled to work a maneuvering board solution. They could estimate the range to the destroyer, but not to the carrier. In order to start the problem, the operations officer postulated that the carrier was twice the distance of the destroyer. If the destroyer was about six miles away, and closing, then the carrier was about twelve miles away, also closing. They looked across the table at each other and agreed on the assumptions; with hard data absent, they made estimates in order to set up trial geometry.

The Captain watched the bearing traces, and listened to the audio from the passive sonar. From the sounds of the screws, the carrier was going faster than the destroyer. She would also be overtaking her because the destroyer was changing course often as she worked her search pattern out in front of the carrier. He walked back over to the plot.

"What is the best range estimate you have on the carrier," he demanded.

The Deputy looked up at him and shrugged. It was far too soon. The Captain leaned forward and put his thumb down in the middle of the spiderweb of bearing lines.

"What *is* that range? Now!" he hissed.

"Sir, that range is—"

The Deputy measured quickly with the protractor arm.

"—approximately thirty-two thousand yards. But—"

"Yes, I know. Keep refining it. And the range to the destroyer?"

"Sir. From ping stealing we have 12,000 yards. But his course is unstable. Widely unstable. It would be useless—"

The Captain spun away from the plotting table, and went to the attack director's console. The persistent pinging of the sonar was getting louder. It was only a matter of time before there would be a shift to directional pinging and the dreaded click of contact.

He stared down at the weapons console. The submarine's sonar was feeding direct bearing inputs to the weapons console for both targets. The big torpedoes could go fifteen miles at their best speed of almost 55 miles per hour. They knew the destroyer was closer than that. As long as they had the bearing information, they could steer the big fish using the wire guidance system right down that bearing towards the source of the pinging. As long as the wire did not break, they could not miss. But the range to the carrier was uncertain. If they hit the destroyer, or missed and alerted him, the carrier could run back out of range faster than either the submarine or the torpedoes could catch her.

"We must wait until the carrier is closer," muttered the Captain. "I did not come out here for some ancient destroyer. What is the bottom depth?"

"Sir, the bottom depth here is 140 meters, and there is a ridge 4000 yards to the east of us that is 120 meters."

"Very well. Musaid: make your depth 125 meters! Deputy, I need that course recommendation, now."

There was a stunned silence in the control room. The Captain was ordering a depth that was within fifty feet of the bottom, with a ridge ahead that stuck up off the bottom higher than their ordered depth. The deputy blanched, and consulted quickly with the operations officer.

"Sir. We recommend 190 to make the carrier and the destroyer tracks coincide." And to miss the ridge.

"Very well, come right to 190. Deputy, refine your calculations as the bearings develop. Musaid. Report when your depth is stable at 125 meters."

"Sir. Flooding trim tanks forward to achieve 125 meters while we turn. Trim should be sufficient."

"Very well. Now: we wait for a few minutes, to let the carrier get closer. Then we will attack the destroyer. I will have some tea."

The messenger of the watch gawked at him for a second, along with several of the officers. It hardly seemed the moment for a cup of tea. The Musaid smiled at the Captain's insouciance, understanding the gesture. He prodded the messenger with a boot to go fetch tea. Everyone else waited and watched in silence, as the depth gauge crept around to 375 feet, and the pinging from the destroyer's sonar grew inexorably louder.

SIXTY NINE

USS Goldsborough, 1615

The Captain stood at the head of the plotting table, surrounded by his ASW battle team of officers, plotters, and phone talkers. The plotting table looked like a surgical suite, with the team bent down over the backlighted NC-2 plotting table, it's stark white circle of light projected up on the glass top depicting the ship in relationship to all other contacts, the light reflecting into the part of their faces visible through the flash hoods.

The plotters muttered into their telephones, and reached out onto the plot with different colored pencils, making their marks to indicate Goldsborough's own track, the track of the carrier, and, almost as an afterthought, the two fishing boats away to the southwest. The submarine target plotter, who would mark any sonar contacts with a red pencil, stood idly by the table.

Mike eyed the plot and reached for the bitch box talk switch.

"That carrier still coming on, XO?"

"Yes, Sir, Cap'n; I guess they're having trouble understanding a don't-come-home message."

"Probably wondering if somebody isn't pulling their chain, and I can sympathize with that."

He punched out the button to the bridge, and punched in the one to sonar control.

"Linc, how're the conditions?"

"Standard Jax opareas, shallow water, some reverberation, a sixty foot layer, but not too much marine life, and a lot better than along the Stream, Captain. The bottom comparison program is working four-oh. If he's out here, we ought to get onto his butt pretty soon."

"All right. We're keeping the courses random to maximize your chances for looking through a hole in the layer. Keep your powder dry, Linc. And listen carefully for hydrophone effects."

"Roger that, Cap'n."

There was a stirring in the CIC. 'Hydrophone effects' was Navy parlance for the sound of incoming torpedoes.

Mike looked over at the operations officer. "How far away is that bird farm? And did we ever get comms with him on fleet common?"

"No, Sir. I guess we could try channel 16, bridge to bridge. They must have secured everything over there for coming into port. And he's into thirteen miles now."

"OK," said Mike.

He keyed the bitch box again.

"XO, try bridge to bridge with Coral Sea, see if we can get comms, and see if he has anything to say to us."

"XO, Aye."

There was a pause. The Exec came back on the bitch box. "Cap'n, I got her, and her CO wants to talk to you ASAP."

"Shit," muttered Mike.

He headed out for the bridge. The bridge to bridge radio was a VHF circuit set up for collision avoidance by the international rules of the road. In theory, any ship could call any other ship on channel 16 and get

SCORPION IN THE SEA

an answer, and settle any uncertainties about which way they were both going to maneuver to avoid collision.

Mike winced at the afternoon sunlight streaming in through the windows as the ship swung through a westerly heading. There was almost no sea breeze and it was stinking hot in the pilothouse. He felt for the watch members, who had to wear flak jackets in addition to all the other paraphernalia of general quarters. He walked over to the chair and picked up the microphone for bridge to bridge.

"Coral Sea, this is Goldsborough, Charlie Oscar."

"This is Coral Sea, Charlie Oscar. Captain, did you receive a high precedence message about thirty minutes ago?"

"That's affirmative, Captain. We are, uh, working that problem right now. Recommend you turn around ASAP, Sir."

There was silence on the circuit, interrupted by a distant conversation in Spanish which clobbered the net for a full minute. Then Coral Sea came back.

"You mean this isn't some kind of a joke?"

"Sir, we're not positive, and I can't explain it on this net. But you need to get your ship out of here, preferably to the east. At max speed. Now. I say again, now. And there's been some kind of disaster at the river entrance, so I don't think you can get in for awhile, anyway. I strongly recommend you turn around now and buster out of here, Cap'n."

"OK, I hear you. Request you meet me secure on 256.1 and maybe you can cut me in on what's going on here. And I have no traffic on any problem in the river."

"Roger that, Captain. We'll come up 256.1 secure and I'll have my XO brief you."

Mike put his binoculars up to his eyes and trained them on the carrier. As he feared, the flight deck was empty except for what looked like a pair of SH3 anti-submarine helicopters. The carrier was also not yet turning. Mike decided to prod him.

"Coral Sea, this is Goldsborough, we have sighted what I believe to be floating mines ahead of you, over."

There was a three second silence. Then the carrier came back.

"Did you say mines, over?"

"That's affirmative. Strongly recommend you turn now, over."

"Roger that. Message understood. Turning now. Out."

"And, Captain," Mike continued, "I desperately need an SH3 if you've got one on alert, over?"

There was another short silence before the carrier responded.

394

"We flew everybody off this morning at first light. I've got two heloes on deck; I can get one airborne with some buoys, but if you want him fast, he'll have no weapons."

"I'll take anything I can get, Cap'n."

"Roger that, and we'll scramble him ASAP. I'm gone."

"Captain," called the Officer of the Deck, peering through his binoculars at the horizon. "Carrier's coming left and making a bunch of smoke."

"Very well, and about frigging time" said Mike. "I'm going back into Combat. XO, I'll have them patch that secure circuit out here; you give them what we know, and emphasize that they haul ashes AND get us a helo right fornicating now!"

"Aye, Sir. They know it's a submarine problem, then?"

"The message warned them of a sub, but since he wanted to talk instead of maneuver, I gave him the mine story. That did it. But you brief the sub problem."

Mike turned to the rest of the people on the bridge.

"And you guys who aren't doing anything, get out on the wings and watch for torpedo tracks. If this guy is out here, we've just spoiled his whole show and made ourselves the only available target."

Mike hurried into CIC, and instructed the communications console operator to patch the secure circuit into the bridge. He called for an anti-submarine air controller to set up shop on a radarscope and wait for a helo.

"When you get one, I want an active buoy pattern put in 5000 yards ahead of and to the west of wherever we happen to be at the time."

"Active, Sir? Without contact?" asked the air controller.

"Yes; I want to add another distraction to this guy's picture, hopefully before he shoots something."

Mike stared down at the plot, noting the absence of the red lines that would indicate contact. He now had a stone cold, certain feeling in his gut that there was a submarine down there, and that they were very close to getting some proof of that.

"Ops, exaggerate the course changes from the search pattern; I want big, wide changes from here on out. And activate the fanfare noise-makers," he ordered.

"Aye, aye, Sir;" said the operations officer, turning to the ASW phone talker.

"Talker, tell sonar to activate the fanfare. Captain, if you really want to put some shit in the game, we could roll one depth charge. We're not going to hit anything, but it would shake up 'em down there; maybe spoil their solution if they're setting up on us."

Mike stared at him for an instant, and then nodded. He keyed the bitchbox to sonar control.

"Linc, in addition to having fanfare on, I'm thinking of rolling a depth charge. I have this feeling we're in somebody's gunsight, and I want to fuck with his mind. The carrier's clearing out now, so it's just us and our phantom left to do business."

"Aye, Cap'n, just give the word."

Mike walked back over to the plot. The carrier's plot was tracking in broad data points now as he opened to the east. His speed track was showing 27 knots. I'll just bet he's making smoke, thought Mike. Coral Sea was even older than Goldsborough.

He thought fast. By making his course changes more radical, it would be harder for the submarine to set up a firing solution on Goldsborough. By turning on the towed torpedo decoy noise-makers, he introduced yet another sound line into the submarine's passive command and control system. A beacon, for sure, but something else to think about. A depth charge would frighten his enemy, and maybe provoke him into doing something that could lead to contact.

The radio messenger came hustling into Combat again, waving a message form. Mike took it, read it, and shook his head in wonder.

"The system absolutely slays me sometimes. We've been designated a Task Unit and told to defend Coral Sea from possible hostile submarine attack. And, get this. Help is on the way. Two Spruance destroyers will be out here in two to three hours, depending on whether or not tugs can get the remains of the Toyota carrier out of the channel junction. One of the Spruances will have ComDesRon Twelve embarked, who will then relieve me as Commander of the Task Unit..."

He threw the message on the deckplates.

"Fuck it," he declared. "Let's go fishing, backwoods style. Weapons control, roll one depth charge, depth setting two hundred feet, now."

"Weps, aye, rolling one on standard setting. Now."

Mike grabbed the 1MC microphone.

"All hands be advised that we are rolling one depth charge as a distraction device. Brace for shock."

Everyone in CIC grabbed on to some standing part of the structure, and waited. Finally there was a large thump that resonated through the ship all the way up from the keel, rattling the loose equipment in CIC, followed by a roaring noise astern as the plume broke the surface. The Exec's voice came in over the bitchbox.

"That was a pretty impressive blast, Cap'n, even at 200 feet. We trolling?"

"Yeah, XO, Georgia fly fishing. Throw some dynamite, see the fish fly. I've activated the noisemakers, too. Once he figures out that the carrier is outbound, we ought to get a sniff. And by the way, we're now officially a task unit. I guess they're believers back on the beach. They're sending some Spruances out."

"Spruances?" said the XO. "No aircraft? Ships will take a couple of hours to get out here."

"My guess is that, having ordered the carrier out of the area, the problem's not so urgent."

"I hope they're right about that. I wonder what the hell changed their minds."

"That car carrier blowing up in the channel probably influenced their thinking, but there must be more to it than that. Anyhow, keep alert. Let's see what that depth charge produces."

"So far, a helluva lot of dead fish. I'll bet those fishermen over there are going ballistic."

Mike sat back down in his chair. That depth charge would blank out a sector of the underwater search scene, so he had taken a chance letting one go. He focused his mind on what to do next. Keep searching for the sub. The carrier was outbound, and unless the sub were east of Goldsborough, between the destroyer and the carrier, Coral Sea was getting safer by the minute. Goldsborough had already swept those waters with her sonar, so the sub should not be there. Should. If they had really guessed wrong, the carrier could be running like hell right into the jaws of a trap. But Mike didn't think so.

What to do next. We're still headed west. Hopefully we're between where we think the sub is and the carrier, right where we should be. We have weapons ready. We're making a large zig zag pattern, which should make it very tough for a sub to set up a solution. Unless he's got wire guidance. A chilling thought.

"Sir, the secure circuit is up with Coral sea, and the XO is transmitting."

"Very well."

OK, so the carrier's skipper would be getting the picture. Probably add a knot or two to his departure.

"Ops, what course is the carrier tracking?"

"Sir, Coral sea is going due east, 090."

"Tell the XO to break in and recommend he come left to 060."

"060, aye, Sir," said the operations officer, relaying the message out to the bridge via sound powered phones.

Why did I do that, Mike mused. Something about torpedo geometry and woods sense. He couldn't put his mind right on it, but he knew that a steady course away was still a steady course. The Libyan would carry Russian torpedoes, which could go for miles and miles in pursuit of a target. A steady course made for an easy shot. So make the carrier turn. Instincts. Don't stand still in the woods. The feel of crosshairs on his back.

His stomach was churning, although outwardly he just sat there in his chair. You should be doing something. What's the next step. Search, evasive steering, decoys active astern, weapons ready to go, a random depth charge to fuck with the guy's mind—can't do that again; not enough depth charges left. He stared hard at the backs of his people around the plotting table. This isn't an inspection, man. What if that bastard wasn't here—could he be east of them instead of west?

SEVENTY

The Submarine Al Akrab, 1630

The Captain sipped his tea, not tasting it, hardly feeling it in his mouth. His eyes were intent on the depth gauge. He held his face immobile, while trying to still the seething tension in his stomach. He watched the depth gauge as the Musaid directed the planesmen into a smooth level transition at 125 meters. The pinging sound from above was grating on everybody's nerves, the incessant pinging physical evidence of their enemy's acoustic energy field advancing through the black depths, probing for them, reaching out to touch just once the steel hull of the submarine that was now slipping south a bare fifty feet off the ocean floor. The depth was not extreme, but neither was it comforting. The old hull made occasional soft popping sounds, and the compression mist was beginning to form around the overhead of the control compartment.

"Sir," announced the sonarman from his console. "Coral Sea's doppler has changed."

"What?! Are you certain?"

The Captain threw the mug of tea into the trash can as he moved quickly to the sonar console.

"Sir. Yes. It is certain. The propulsion noises are about the same, perhaps louder. Screwbeats are up, too. But the doppler line has changed. He is moving away from us. It is certain."

The Captain's face tightened. The mission was dissolving in his face. He had one option left.

"Attack director, set tubes three, four, five, and six to slow speed, long range. Prepare to fire on bearing only. We will make a pursuit shot."

The weapons officer hastily entered the settings. The "slow" speed for the big, Russian torpedoes was thirty five knots, but the twenty knot speed differential allowed them to run for almost twenty miles. They still had no accurate range information on the carrier, but they had a chance of a hit if they fired now and let the big fish rush down the bearing as the carrier hauled away to the east, transmitting a clear beacon of sound back to the submarine's sonar and the torpedoes' own guidance systems.

"Torpedoes are set; tubes are ready, Sir!"

"Very we—"

The Captain's order was interrupted by the sudden rattling, buzzing noise of the destroyer's torpedo decoy noise makers. It was a sound none of them had ever heard, including the Captain. The Deputy panicked.

"Torpedo!" he yelled. "They have fired a torpedo at us!"

"Silence, you fool," yelled the Captain, whirling on him. "That's not a torpedo! Sonar, quickly, what is the bearing?"

"Sir," shouted the sonarman, "The bearing is coincident with the destroyer."

"Steady bearing!" croaked the Deputy, his fingers in his mouth. "It comes straight for us!"

The Deputy was clearly unnerved, and the Captain could see that the Control room crew's composure was shaken by the loud buzzing noise erupting over the speaker. The speaker! He reached up and turned it off. The buzzing noise stopped, and he leaned down again to look at the trace on the sonar. It was broadband noise, loud, deliberate. But definitely not a torpedo. He had heard the sound of American destroyer's electric torpedoes at the Soviet ASW school. They sounded like an electric drill, but nothing like this. He put his hand on the sonarman's shoulder to steady him, and was about to order the release of the pursuit torpedoes when the depth charge went off.

The underwater blast was huge, hammering the submarine violently, knocking all the lights out for an instant as switches were dislodged, and producing a cloud of dust and small debris in the control room. Several men screamed in panic when it hit, only to look around sheepishly once it was over. The only real casualty was the sonarman, who was disabled, his ears ruined by the huge audio overload, his face in tears from the pain. The Chief sonarman pulled him off the console at once and took the phones himself. At the diving planes, the Musaid held onto the shoulders of both planesmen, urgently coaching them to hold the depth level.

The sonar showed a massive blur of amber light to the east of them as the depth charge plume broke the surface and generated yet more noise into the water. The Deputy was yelling again.

"It was a torpedo! It was a torpedo! It hit the bottom instead. We are—"

He was silenced by a wicked, backhanded slap to the face from the Captain, the force of which sent the Deputy off his chair and sprawling onto the deckplates. The Captain towered over him amidst the confusion in the control room.

"Control yourself, or I will put you in a tube and fire you into the sea! That was a depth charge, you idiot. The old destroyer carries depth charges. Her torpedoes cannot work in shallow water."

He straightened up, his face dark with a rage.

"But mine can. Attack director, verify the settings on the pursuit torpedoes. Musaid, get damage reports from engineering!"

"Settings verified. The system is in order!" yelled the weapons officer.

"Fire tubes three, four, five and six in pursuit mode, on channel one fire control data. Prepare to fire tubes one and two on wire guidance. This destroyer needs to die!"

The submarine jolted once, twice, and twice more as the fish were fired by water impulse into the sea. The Captain reached up and turned the sonar audio speaker back on. Above the buzzing decoy noise everyone in the control room immediately heard the harmonic whine of steam turbines spinning up as the torpedoes came alive instantly, surging forward and up towards the surface as the guidance systems took control, turning left in great arcs to the bearing of the target, the carrier to the east.

The giant steam fish were not stealth devices, which was why submariners called them screamers. Once fired, they broadcast approaching death in a howling whine to anything listening in their path. Four thousand pounds going at nearly forty miles per hour, they were capable of smashing a ship even without their one ton warheads.

"Bearing to the carrier!" barked the Captain, crouching over at the sonar console. The plot was forgotten now.

"Sir. Bearing is 095. Fish appear to be in pursuit; no circle runners," reported the chief.

The young sonarman with the best ears, what had been the best ears, huddled next to the console, rocking back and forth on his haunches. A medic had been summoned to give him demerol against the pain shrieking in his head.

"Bearing to the destroyer. Quickly!"

"Sir, the bearing is 080, but changing."

"Keep that bearing data on channel two. Attack director, prepare to fire tubes one and two on wire guidance, data on channel two! We will wait until he steadies."

SEVENTY ONE

USS Goldsborough; 1642

"Hydrophone effects, bearing 255! Multiple screws! Screamers inbound! Screamers inbound!" yelled an excited voice over the 29MC speaker from sonar control.

The report galvanized everyone in CIC, including Mike, who jumped out of his chair.

"What's our course?!" he shouted.

"240!" yelled the surface supervisor.

"Bridge, Combat, torpedoes inbound! Come left with hard rudder, flank speed, to 210!" Mike yelled over the bitchbox to the bridge.

Basic rule: torpedo coming from ahead, turn across the bearing, and steady up within thirty degrees of the bearing. If the torpedoes were aimed ahead, they had to miss. Unless they were active homers or wire guided.

The report of torpedoes inbound was repeated over the ship's announcing system, and Goldsborough shook herself violently as the snipes poured on the steam, her propellers kicking out huge gouts of white water from under the stern, the rudder barely able to hold over in the face of seventy thousand shaft horsepower beating the water. Men who were not strapped into their console chairs were tossed over to one side of CIC as the ship heeled and then dug in to come up to speed.

"Hydrophone effects increasing, sharp up doppler, bearing 253!" reported sonar control.

Mike had a horrifying thought. The bearing drift was now left, and he had turned left. He had assumed the fish were aimed at Goldsborough. Was he turning right into them?

"Mark your head!" he called.

"Sir, our course is 215, coming to 210, speed is twenty two, and increasing."

"Captain!" yelled the weapons officer. "Recommend we fire one torpedo down the bearing, initial search depth 200 feet!"

The weapons officer held his finger over the firing button.

"Permission granted, fire one torpedo down the hydrophone effects bearing, set for 200 feet."

There was whooshing sound from the starboard side as the air flask propelled the MK 46 torpedo thirty feet over the side. "Hydrophone effects bearing 249, amplitude increasing!" reported sonar again, the speaker's voice rising in pitch.

"Bridge, Combat, emergency flank bell. Tell the snipes what's coming!"

"Bridge, aye, we did. We can't see any tracks yet, but we're looking!"

Mike felt a momentary surge of relief. If the torpedo tracks were not yet visible, they might have another minute to cross the tracks. The guy had fired way off. Unless. Unless—he had fired at the carrier!

"Bearing to the carrier," he called.

"Sir, carrier bears 135 from us, range thirty six thousand and opening!"

Mike did the arithmetic. Shit! That's what he'd done. Fired at the carrier. A pursuit shot! Mike grabbed the bitch box switch.

"XO! Tell Coral Sea to make an emergency turn due north, torpedoes coming in his wake now!"

Then he punched in the bitch box button to sonar.

"UB, prepare to roll three depth charges, set for shallow, repeat, set for shallow: fifty feet. Linc, I want to drop them in the path of the torpedoes—he's fired at the carrier. Go, man, go!"

Goldsborough was shaking from stem to stern as the she came up to 27, then to 28 knots. In his excitement, the helmsman had overshot the ordered course, and was throwing everyone around as he compensated.

"Hydrophone effects bearing 248, amplitude increasing!" reported sonar. "Charges set for fifty feet, ready, Cap'n."

The hydrophone effects bearing had steadied. Goldsborough was crossing their track just about now.

"Roger, roll three in ten second intervals, now, now, now!"

"Sonar, Aye; rolling one!"

Mike grabbed the 1MC microphone.

"This is the Captain speaking! We're avoiding a torpedo attack. The submarine has fired torpedoes at the carrier, and we're going to roll three shallow depth charges in their path to disrupt the attack. Stand by for—"

There was huge, blamming sound, and the ship vibrated even more violently as the first charge went off, close enough to punch a swell of hydrostatic pressure under the destroyer's stern and lift her screws nearly out of the water. Astern an enormous blast of dirty gray water erupted into the sky.

"Rolling two!"

This time everyone braced, and were again treated to a wrenching whump, followed by the eruption in their wake. Over the noise, Mike heard the ominous sound of a forced draft blower winding down. Something must have given way down below under the shock of the depth charges.

"Rolling three!"

Mike closed his eyes in a tight grimace as the ship was hammered again.

"Combat, Bridge, Coral Sea acknowledges and is coming left. He says a helo is lifting off in three minutes."

"Roger that, XO. Have the OOD get an OpRep out ASAP; tell the beach this guy is here, no shit. Positive sub!"

"Here, no shit, positive sub, aye!"

"Hydrophone effects bearing 255! Right bearing drift, we're across—"

The 29 MC was drowned out by one, two, three booming blasts astern of the destroyer as three of the torpedoes ran into the boiling vortices of the depth charges, went tumbling out of control, and exploded as their guidance systems decided that they had made a contact hit on their targets. Goldsborough again lurched as the shock waves came in from astern, although they were not as powerful as the depth charges had been. The ship was vibrating badly now as the screws became unbalanced, one turning at twenty eight knots, the other losing power rapidly.

"Goddamn, Combat," yelled the Exec from the bridge over the bitchbox. "End of the world back there, Cap'n!"

"What's happened in the plant?" called Mike.

"Hydrophone effects, bearing 030," reported sonar. "And we've lost the fanfare!"

"Shit! One got away," Mike said through tight lips. he punched the bitch box switch.

"XO, call the carrier. Tell him we intercepted three of the torpedoes, but one got away and is chasing him. Tell him to continue due north, emergency bell!"

"XO, Aye, and we've lost vacuum in number two engine room after the depth charges went off; Cap'n, we're gonna have to slow down and lock that shaft!"

"Combat, aye. Ben, he's gonna fire at us next. Come to speed fifteen, and come back west to 250. We've gotta get contact on that bastard. Tell the Engineer to do what he has to."

"Hydrophone effects diminishing to the east, Combat. That thing's still running, but with marked down doppler."

"Is our fish running?"

There was a pause, as the sonar operator below shifted focus to the west.

"Affirmative, our unit is in search mode, bearing 245. In search mode. Wait one, our unit has exploded, Sir!"

"Did it acquire?"

Mike waited while they checked with the acoustic operator.

"Negative, Sir, the unit's sonar never changed mode. She's probably hit the bottom, Cap'n."

"All right, maybe it kept him off balance. Look hard, guys, and be ready for more torpedoes."

SEVENTY TWO

The Submarine Al Akrab, 1649

The sonar Chief signalled for the Captain's attention.

"Sir: the pursuit torpedoes are running hot, straight and normal, down doppler, no bearing drift. But, Sir: the destroyer is much closer; by ping stealing I estimate the range at around 8000 meters."

The sonar chief held his earphones hard against his left ear, his better ear, while punching buttons rapidly on the sonar computer console with his right hand. The Captain bared his teeth.

"Attack director," he ordered. Enter 8000 meter estimated range on channel two. Course west, speed fifteen! Make ready tubes one and two for wire guidance on channel two. We—"

"Torpedo inbound! Torpedo inbound!" yelled the sonar Chief. "Electric, bearing 085! Up doppler, in search mode!"

"Right full rudder! All ahead full!" yelled the Captain.

The helmsman punched out the order to engineering, and the submarine jumped ahead, and then leaned way over to port as the rudders took effect.

"Fire decoys aft! Fire both at once!"

The sonar operator armed the decoy tubes and punched out the firing orders. One hundred feet aft, two metal filled canisters were ejected into the sea and exploded almost at once, filling the water with a dense ball of air bubbles that grew into a maelstrom of broadband noise covering the search frequencies of the approaching torpedo, the boiling turbulence created by hundreds of pellets of gas-producing chemicals.

The submarine turned off the approach axis of the homing torpedo, leaving the decoys to suck in the oncoming torpedo's sonar.

"Captain! Recommend we change depth to 100 meters—at this speed we are too close to the bottom," called the Musaid.

"No! Stay where we are; rudders amidships, slow to ten knots! Depth saves us, Musaid. He is not in contact. That was a reflex shot in response to the pursuit torpedoes. Maintain depth. Come all the way back to the east as soon as the speed comes down to ten knots."

The torpedo was still too far away to be audible in the control room, but everyone stood rigid in silence listening for it. The sonar operator could hear it clearly, as revealed by the expression on his face, but the Captain had switched the speaker off, mindful of the panic the last time. Finally, after a tense minute, one of the officers spoke up.

"I hear it!" he said in a soft voice.

Everyone listened, and then they could all hear it, the sound like someone was outside, walking toward them with an electric drill going. The Al Akrab had circled rapidly all the way around, across the path of the approaching destroyer, and was now turning back east.

The whining noise was not getting louder. The Captain listened carefully. The decoys had it. Boiling away only fifty feet off the bottom, they would suck it down to the bottom. They waited, and there came the rewarding sound of the small, shaped charge warhead on the Mark 46 banging into the mud of the bottom. There were audible sighs of relief, and the Captain turned back to the attack director.

"Now," he growled. "Status of our torpedoes!"

"All are still running, Sir."

"Very well. Now: we must kill this destroyer. Attack director, as soon as we are steady on 090, we will fire. Make—"

But once again the submarine was hammered by the blast of a depth charge, followed by a second and then a third. Even at 8000 yards distance, the 500 pound depth bombs punched out a hefty pulse of hydrodynamic pressure into the sea, physically shaking the submarine. For one, heart-squeezing moment, her bow plunged downward, throwing everyone in the control room to the deck except for those strapped into their console chairs. Then there were three more explosions, even more violent than the first three. It was the sonar chief's turn to arch back in his chair, screaming as he held his ears, the earphones dangling by his chair. The submarine had settled into a down angle.

The Musaid reached over the planesman's shoulders and hauled back on the after planes in a frantic effort to keep her off the bottom. The bow jerked up and the Captain sprawled between the sonar console and the attack director, trying frantically to get back up, but was thrown down again when the submarine's bow caromed off the mud bottom at a shallow angle and shuddered to bare steerageway.

Realizing what had happened, the Captain shouted an order to the Musaid.

"All engines stop! Blow after ballast! Instantly! Blow it! Blow it!"

There was rumble of compressed air aft as the after ballast tank was purged of seawater. This had the effect of making the stern more buoyant, and ensuring that the vulnerable propellers and the rudder stayed off the bottom even as the bow bumped softly along the mud bottom.

"All back together two thirds! Secure the blow!" ordered the Captain.

He was upright now, his eyes blazing in the gloom of the emergency lighting, his arms rigid against the periscope well as he tried to keep himself upright at the unnatural down angle. At first he had thought the destroyer had run into the spread of torpedoes intended for the carrier. Then he realized that his enemy had countermined the torpedoes with depth charges.

His face turned white with fury. The rumbling noise ceased as the diving officer slammed the air valves shut. The Al Akrab hung suspended, her bows pushed down into the silty mud of the bottom, her stern thirty feet off the bottom, the entire boat pitched down at a twenty degree down angle. He could hear men yelling and things crashing down off shelves in the forward part of the ship. Then the propellers took effect, and her bow came unstuck. With a great lurch she came off the bottom, but her bow remained pitched down as the screws backed her toward the surface, aided by the abnormal buoyancy in the after ballast tank.

"All stop. All ahead together, one third. Musaid, get her level!"

The old chief had jammed his stool between the two terrified planesmen, and directed them urgently as they fought to get the boat under control. The diving officer partially flooded the after ballast tank again, and she finally came level. As the confusion in the control room died down, they heard the destroyer's sonar again, without the speaker, this time in directional ping. The Captain listened carefully. The American was in contact!

"All stations, report damage to Control!" he ordered.

The compartments reported in. Engineering reported no damage to main propulsion other than two leaking pipes, but they were investigating two chlorine alarms from after battery. Forward torpedo reported that the outer doors on tubes one and two were not responding to control signals.

"Attack director!"

The Captain's voice was frantic, close to screaming.

"Prepare to fire tubes one and two. Prepare—"

"Sir! I cannot. The outer doors were open. The tubes are surely filled with mud. We cannot—"

"Yes! Yes! We will! We must! This cursed American must die. He has cost me the carrier. I must kill him. Then we shall pursue the carrier! Do as I say! Report your solution!"

The weapons officer was aghast. If the tubes were choked with mud, the torpedoes might not leave the tubes. But once the firing key was closed, they would start. Once started, the screws turned. Russian torpedoes armed themselves by counting screw revolutions. After the first few thousand turns, the warheads, including their magnetic detectors, would energize, under the assumption that the torpedo was well clear of the submarine. If the torpedoes were still inside the submarine's tubes when the magnetic detectors energized, they would sense the boat's own magnetic field and blow the front of the submarine off.

"Sir, I cannot!" screeched the weapons officer. "The torpedoes will arm in the tubes if they do not launch. We must not do his!"

"Report your solution!"

The others in the control room were frozen in fear. The weapons officer hesitated for a fraction of a second, swallowed hard. and then looked down at his console. The sonar was still sending in bearing data, locked onto the Goldsborough's sonar. He needed a range.

"I have no range data. Course and speed are unreliable. No solution!" he shouted.

The Captain scanned the sonar console himself; the sonar Chief had joined his mate on the deck, ears useless after the multiple underwater blasts. He would have to provide an estimate.

"Estimated range 7000 meters. Enter! Now!"

The weapons officer reluctantly punched in the data.

"Course and speed data unreliable," he repeated.

"Course is west-270; speed is fifteen! Enter!"

The green solution light came up. The weapons officer shook his head, pushing back from the console.

"Sir, we must not—" he began.

The Captain jumped over to the weapons console, lifted the plastic protectors over the glowing lights for tubes one and two, and pushed one, then two. To everyone's horror, there was only a half-hearted thump from the bow, not the full discharge reaction. A red icon flashed onto the control screen over tube one, and then over both tubes. The icon showed a torpedo in the tube, with its propulsion end red hot. The white-faced weapons officer sat frozen in his chair, staring at the icons.

"Recharge and fire them again, Effendi," shouted the Musaid. When the Captain, himself momentarily frozen in shock, just stood there, the Musaid jumped over to the weapons console, shoved the paralyzed weapons officer aside, and punched the button for the torpedo compartment intercom.

"Forward torpedo room: cross connect HP air to tubes one and two; fire both tubes as soon as the pressure reaches one thousand pounds. *Instantly! Or we all die!*"

Once again the submarine lurched downward as one of the planesmen overcompensated, and the Musaid clawed his way back to the diving station. The Captain stared at the red icons, holding his breath, the tactical picture above totally forgotten. Finally there came a pair of thumps, these sounding normal, and the icons blinked out. The ring of the destroyer's sonar grew louder. The Captain grabbed the shaken weapons officer by the shirt collar, and shoved him back in front of the console.

"Guidance, you idiot. Operate the guidance! Kill the destroyer before he is upon us!"

The Weapons officer grabbed the joystick that sent rudder angle and dive angle orders through a thin, tungsten wire that should have been unreeling from the torpedoes' propeller hubs as they roared through the water in the direction of the Goldsborough. Then he realized that the torpedoes had been fired on a bearing of 087, but that the sonar was holding the destroyer's sonar now at 095. He jammed the joystick to the right. Nothing happened on the readout. He looked over at the feedback panel. The lights showed nothing but digital eights. Horrified, he realized what had happened. The initial attempt to fire the torpedoes had jarred them forward in the tube, and the wire had probably begun to deploy, but with the spinning screws right there, it had been cut into a million pieces. He tried to report, but could not get the words out. The Captain was shouting at him.

"Status! Why are those bearings different?!"

"Sir: the wires—I have no control over the torpedoes. They are straight runners! We should have set a pattern, but—"

"May Allah curse you to the pit!" screamed the Captain. The destroyer was in contact, and he was out of torpedoes. There was no time to reload.

"Left full rudder, flank speed!" he shouted. "Make your depth 100 meters! Course west!"

He would have to maneuver quickly to get away from the approaching destroyer; they could not stand a depth charging close aboard. And then he remembered the mine.

SEVENTY THREE

USS Goldsborough, 1701

"Sonar contact, bearing 265, range 5500 yards, echo quality sharp, classify as possible submarine!"

"Yeah, Linc!" exclaimed the Captain. "XO, come right to 265, prepare for depth charge attack. How many we have left, anyway?"

"Sir we have four depth charges left. And Captain, that helo is airborne and coming to our control on button five."

"Very well."

The antisubmarine air controller, hearing the report of an inbound helo, slapped on his headset, punched up the frequency, and began to call the incoming helicopter.

The weapons officer was tugging on the Captain's sleeve.

"Sir, recommend an urgent attack down the bearing with a 46; it's a doubtful shot, but we might bag his ass."

"No. The last one went right for the bottom. I want to run over him and put one of these 500 ponders right between his ears. Tell sonar to be alert for hydrophone effects."

"Sonar, aye, and Captain, this contact is stationary. It may be a decoy. There's a lot of clutter on the scope around the contact, but we can still see him in there."

"Keep on him; we're running in on the plot. Get your depth charges ready."

"Sonar, aye. Wait one! Hydrophone effects! Hydrophone effects. One, possibly two torpedoes inbound, bearing 260!"

"Combat, aye, bridge, come left emergency to 240, speed twenty knots!"

"Aye, Cap'n," came the Exec's voice back over the intercom. "We've got the rudder over, but we're stuck at about fourteen knots until they get vacuum back on number two; number two shaft is locked, and number one is making turns for twenty right now. She's coming around."

"Hydrophone effects, bearing 261, doppler up, amplitude increasing, make it a pair!"

Mike grabbed the 1MC microphone as Goldsborough came around to the southwest, grudgingly with that one screw locked.

"All hands, torpedoes inbound, starboard side. We're maneuvering, but brace for impact, brace for impact!"

"Hydrophone effects, bearing 262—they're drawing right, Captain!"

Every man in CIC stared at the plot while their brains feverishly broadcast the same message—draw right, draw right!

"Combat. Bridge, Cap'n we see 'em! Big fucking wakes coming up the starboard bow! If they're not pattern runners, we're gonna be clear, they're right on the bow, and there they go, two wakes, down the starboard side."

Mike could hear the sounds of cheering out on the bridge. he keyed the 1MC again.

"All hands, the torpedoes have cleared, the torpedoes have cleared. We're going in for an attack of our own, and we have a helicopter now to help out!"

He bent back over the plotting table. The Operations officer was calling the course changes now, as Goldsborough limped in at fourteen knots in the direction of the submarine.

"Captain, Sonar," called Linc over the intercom. "We're not closing this guy—he's kicked it in the ass. We're showing down doppler, and a course that's westerly. Request eighteen knots."

"Can't give it to you Linc, the snipes have a problem; we're maxed out right now until they get vacuum back on number two. When the helo gets overhead, we'll put active buoys down; that should make him change course and maybe we can get closer."

"Captain, recommend we shoot a torpedo down that bearing; he might turn to avoid it, and we'll get closer."

Mike thought about that for a moment. It was better than sitting back here and taking a chance on stern tube torpedoes from the submarine. They had been extremely lucky the last time.

"OK, weps, let one go, on the current bearing of the contact; set it for 150 feet, maybe it will see the submarine before it sees the bottom this time."

"Weapons, aye, firing one MK 46 to starboard, on bearing 264, snake search, initial search depth 150 feet; torpedo away!"

The whoosh of the air flask was audible above the din of voices as the plotting team kept the picture going on the NC2.

"Evaluator, the helo is marking on top the contact, and is dropping active pingers on a line from 090 to 270, spacing 500 yards. He has no weapons."

"Evaluator, aye, inform him we have a weapon in the water, headed down bearing 265 from us."

The controller hurriedly passed this word to the helicopter, who promptly climbed out to 500 feet from his buoy dropping low pass, while Goldsborough drove in behind her torpedo.

Mike stared down at the plot, standing shoulder to shoulder with his tactical team around the plotting table. Everyone stank of sweat and fear, their eyes white with adrenaline. The contact data flowed up from sonar control, and the plotters acknowledged, making their marks on the trace paper.

Mike stared hard at the plot, thinking furiously. What do you do now? Think! Guy's running away from you, you've got a torpedo chasing his ass, he's got stern tubes. He's fired two at you. He fired four at the carrier—we got three and a fourth kept going. Which means he's empty forward. But what's he got in his tail tubes. Four more? And we're right behind him? He looked at the plot. They were headed west.

"Come right to 300," he ordered. "Quickly!"

The Operations officer relayed the order, and then looked at the Captain, a question forming on his lips.

"Stern tubes, Ops. Like chasing a guy who's carrying his rifle over his shoulder—pointed right at you. We'll lose ground, but zig zag across his bearing every two, three minutes. Try to keep it random. I don't want to give him a sitting duck solution. And have radio get another Oprep out: tell 'em we are in contact, two more torpedoes fired at us, and give a position in case this all turns to shit!"

"Aye, Sir."

The Operations officer relayed the order to the bridge to execute a broad zig zag, and then called radio central.

"Status of our torpedo!"

"Sir, our fish is still running, but the range is extreme. Still in search mode. No acquisition."

Mike continued to watch the plot. The torpedo would probably do what the last one did, look down, acquire the ocean floor, and zoom down to go bang in the mud. The submarine was getting away to the west, slowly opening the range, but he could not keep that up. To the west was shallow water, and two Spruance destroyers.

"Ops, once you get your amplifying OpRep out, find out where those Spruances are, and whether or not they can vector their heloes out here now. And get our helo back in front of the contact, dropping active buoys. I need to herd his ass back east, so we can have a go with depth charges.

"Ops, Aye."

The Exec's voice sounded over the bitchbox.

"Combat, bridge, the carrier wants to know what's going on."

"Tell him we are in contact and trading torpedoes with this guy. Tell him to go east some more, stay out of range."

"Bridge, Aye."

"Combat, sonar, torpedo at end of run. No acquisition."

"Fire another one, Sir?" asked the Weapons officer. "Keep him busy?"

Mike thought fast. Goldsborough's torpedoes were useless in this shallow water. Good maybe for psychological warfare, but not much else. Why hadn't the guy taken another shot? He had four stern tubes. Had they damaged him?

"Sir, the contact is changing course," announced the red plotter.

SEVENTY FOUR

The Submarine Al Akrab, 1711

"Control, engineering! We have a chlorine alarm validated in after battery; there is seawater intrusion in the compartment. Request permission to secure after battery!"

"Negative," shouted the Captain.

That was half his battery supply, and he had the boat going max submerged speed.

"We need one hundred percent power, you idiots: there's a destroyer pursuing us, and we have no more torpedoes. Isolate the compartment; secure ventilation if you have to, but do not secure that battery!"

"Engineering, aye," replied the engineer, sounding doubtful.

The Captain swallowed hard. Sea water in the battery compartment was a potential disaster. Any sea water that got into the cells would mix with the sulfuric acid electrolyte and produce chlorine gas. If it went on too long, the boat itself could fill with the deadly gas; they would have to surface or die of asphyxiation. He immediately thought he could already smell the chlorine in the boat's vent system. He watched the speed indicator as the submarine maintained almost fourteen knots in his flight to the west, away from the destroyer.

He thought frantically. His men forward were attempting to reload tubes one and two; the other tubes were out of commission. He knew that

412

he could not outrun a destroyer, although the sound of the pinging sonar did not seem to be getting any louder, and he wondered about that.

"Musaid, are we stable on depth?"

"Sir, we are at 100 meters, depth is stable."

"What is the water depth?"

"Sir," said the Deputy, who had regained some of his composure. "The water depth is 120 meters, but will shoal to 80 meters about 4000 meters ahead, or in nine minutes at this speed. Recommend we come up to sixty meters in five minutes, or turn out back to sea—"

The third operator to take the sonar console jumped up in his chair.

"Hydrophone effects, hydrophone effects. Mark 46 torpedo inbound, bearing 082! Starboard quarter, search mode!"

The Captain cursed. Somebody had forgotten to tell his opponent that antisubmarine torpedoes were useless in shallow water. Unless of course the torpedo got lucky, or he was shooting something new. Now he *must* hug the bottom. Once the torpedo looked down at the bottom, it would see the biggest contact of them all, and, hopefully, drive straight down into it.

"Make your depth 115 meters; all ahead slow, make turns for five knots; sonar, prepare decoys."

"Sir: decoys ready."

"Fire decoys. Left full rudder. Musaid keep her level. We cannot afford to hit the bottom again."

The control room crew tensed at their stations. The torpedo was not yet audible in the control room. The Captain held his breath, and watched the depth gauge out of one eye and the sonar operator out of the other. He saw the man's knuckles whiten on the console controls. *He* could hear the torpedo. The Captain decided to add a knuckle in the water to the decoys' noise.

"Now: right full rudder. Steady 270."

The Musaid acknowledged, nodding his head in agreement with the Captain's tactics. The submarine, which had barely started its turn, now steadied, and then began to swing back to the west, leaving a knuckle of dense turbulence in the water behind them that was strong enough to attract a homing torpedo if the decoys failed.

"Sonar, report!"

"Sir the torpedo is closing, still in search mode. Doppler is up and high, amplitude increasing. Snake search."

The fish should see the decoys soon, complemented by the knuckle created by the submarine's full rudder turns; the decoys, blooming along the bottom, should seduce the torpedo into a dive straight down through

413

the bubbling clouds into the mud. He grabbed the spare sonar earphones, unwilling to turn the speaker back on with his control room crew in their current unnerved state. The electric drill sound was clear, coming nearer and then drifting away as the torpedo did its snake search across the firing bearing 100 feet above their present depth. But then he heard a new sound in the background, a rapid pinging noise above the frequency of the running torpedo. He thought for a moment. The destroyer had turned its main sonar off momentarily when he fired the torpedo, so as not to confuse the torpedo's homing sonar. This pinging was different.

Then with a start he realized what it was. A sonobuoy. An active sonobuoy. The buoy, floating on the surface with its own hydrophone suspended on a thin wire fifty feet below the surface, had joined the hunt like an acoustic robot. Sonobuoys meant an aircraft. The accursed destroyer had help. They were now in real trouble, and he could do nothing until his forward torpedo room crew reloaded their two operational tubes, which they had better be working on frantically. He longed for the torpedoes he had thrown away to accommodate the mines. With a helicopter up there, he now had little choice. It was time to let the crazy French mine that wanted to kill the first thing it saw have its day in the sun. He spun around and fixed his gaze on the still trembling weapons officer.

"You! Go to after torpedo, make ready tube eight. We will use the mine! Put a mask on, there's chlorine in after battery. Report when you are in position. Go!"

He turned back to the sonar console, as the operations officer relieved the weapons officer as Attack Director.

"Sonar, report!"

"Sir the torpedo appears to be going aft of us, to the decoys."

"Good, remove your headphones: I need your ears intact."

They could hear the torpedo now, first strong and then weak as it snaked back and forth along its search axis. Moments later, the electric drill noise ceased. They waited for an explosion, but none was forthcoming. End of run. The Captain nodded in satisfaction. As long as he could put out decoys and hug the bottom, the enemy could not get to him with their torpedoes. But they must be farther away from the destroyer than he thought. The destroyer's main sonar pinging resumed.

Now he had to avoid depth charges and the bottom itself, while positioning himself to use the mine. He had to lure the destroyer right over the mine. Two choices: slow way down, deploy the mine, and let the destroyer overrun him, taking a chance on being depth bombed if the American did not set off the mine. This would take time, but it was a safe move. The mine would probably destroy the surface ship before he could get to his depth bomb release point.

But then he remembered the helicopter, whose presence had been announced by the high frequency pinging. Slowing down would make him easy meat for the helicopter. So: the second choice—turn around, run right at the destroyer, head to head, deploy the mine at the right instant, and turn off axis at the last minute. The destroyer would keep coming, certain that the submarine had made an error, and run right over the mine before she could detect the submarine's turn off axis. And the helicopter could do nothing because her torpedoes might endanger the surface ship. Risky, but quicker. He made his decision.

"Left full rudder, come left to 090, slow to ten knots. I want to run right at him. Attack director, how long on tubes one and two?"

"Sir, they report difficulty with tube one. They could not line up the reload trays with tube one. They have switched to tube two as the reload tube. It will be several minutes."

Useless. They had lost valuable time trying to load a tube that would not load. The torpedo tubes would never be ready in time. He had made the right decision: the bold maneuver, something quick, decisive, and very soon, before the forces above combined to overwhelm him, or the slowly rising chlorine gas problem drove him to the surface and ignominy. Run under him and stab him from below, as befits a scorpion.

As if in response to his thoughts, the destroyer's sonar switched to directional, again ringing its message of death through the submarine. The Captain looked around the control room at their taut faces.

"This is my plan," he announced to the control room, speaking in a loud voice to make them listen to him and not the pinging. They looked at him fearfully. There was desperation in the air. He stared at each of them in turn, steeling them with his hard and confident expression. The Musaid sat up straighter when the Captain looked at him.

"We are turning back east. To the west is shallow water. Above us is a helicopter. To the east is the destroyer. He will be attempting to depth bomb us, since his torpedoes are defeated by the bottom. He must pass over top of us to use his depth bombs effectively. I will permit him to close us by running straight at him at ten knots. Just before he is in position to drop his depth charges, I shall accelerate to maximum speed right in front of him, release the last mine, turn and go out from under him. If Allah is with us, he will detonate the mine before he can react to our turn or release his depth charges. If not, well, so be it. We are out of time and options."

The Deputy spoke up from behind the central plotting table.

"Sir: that mine is too large for this—the warhead will damage us as well as the surface ship!"

The Captain stared at him in exasperation. Yes, the man might be correct. But there were no other options.

"Effendi."

It was the Musaid.

"Effendi, make the maneuver. A hard right turn immediately after launch of the mine will separate us and minimize our aspect to the blast. Climb towards the surface as we turn. It will work."

The Captain looked at both of them. As long as he did not wait until the destroyer was too close, it should work. The range was the key.

"I shall proceed with my plan. Prepare yourselves."

SEVENTY FIVE

USS Goldsborough, 1720

"Goddammit, I thought that fish would get him," Mike swore.

He took off his helmet and scratched his head. The report from sonar that their fish had gone to the bottom told the tale. They just could not use torpedoes.

"They just weren't designed for shallow water," declared the weapons Officer. Mike nodded.

"OK, gang," he announced to the team in Combat. "We're going to have to run right over the bastard, or drive him so close to the beach that he has to surface. Set us up for depth charge attack. Ops, have that helo keep a tight cloverleaf pattern of buoys on this guy. I want him to think there's an air dropped torpedo coming."

He keyed the bitch box.

"XO, what's the status on the plant? I need to go faster if we're gonna get on top of this gomer."

"XO, aye, they've located the problem—busted air ejector line; ETR is twenty minutes to 27 knots available, Cap'n."

Mike shook his head. Twenty minutes was too long; he was stuck with his slow boat. Sonar came back on the line.

"Combat, Sonar control, contact regained, and he's showing null doppler, Captain; we think he's turning."

Turning. He knew he was running out of water, then. The chart showed less than three miles to water that was only 250 feet deep.

"What's the contact's bearing right now?" he asked.

"Sir, she bears 265," said the surface supervisor. "Sonar is tracking him on a turn to an easterly heading. If he keeps coming, he's gonna walk right into us."

Mike thought for a moment. The submarine CO had to know that Mike had depth charges; they'd undoubtedly shaken him pretty badly already. Why on earth would he turn east to avoid the rapidly shoaling water. Why not north, or south? Maybe he had reloaded? It had not been that long since the first brace of four torpedoes had been fired. But maybe the first batch had come from his stern tubes. Shit, he could be staring four, maybe six fish right in the face.

"Range? And what's the water depth?"

"Sir, the range is down to 4800 yards; we're closing pretty fast. Depth of water is about 330 feet."

4800 yards. He would have fired by now. Hell, he can fire off axis if he wants to. So maybe he doesn't have torpedoes. Maybe he thinks I'm out of depth charges. Maybe he thinks I won't roll 'em because the water is too shallow and I'll hurt myself.

"Range is 4200 yards, closing. Up doppler," said the Operations officer. "He's coming right towards us. What the fuck's he doing?"

"Might be going to try to break contact by running under us and into our baffles," said Mike.

What's he doing, what's he doing...he hadn't fired any more fish, so maybe he can't fire any more fish. He has to run for it. He's probably spotted the fact that we can't go fast. He knows my fish can't hurt him, but he must know I have depth charges. If he can just get by me once, he can outrun me until I get this plant fixed...if he can get out to the Stream, he's gone. That's what he's doing: he's taking his shot—the quickest way past us is head to head. But he's forgetting the helo.

"Ops, break off that helo and put him east of us on the 5000 yard fence; Weps, get your depth charges ready, set for 250 feet. Unless this guy's got a nose full of torpedoes left, he's making a big mistake."

Mike stood back from the plot, mindful of the building tension. They were going head and head. The submarine might be preparing for a down the throat torpedo shot. But he'd fired six fish so far, and nothing out of his stern tubes when he had a clear shot. It was like counting cards in a life and death poker game: how many aces were face up? Would he try a down the throat shot? The submarine had fired only straight runners so far; they might not have pattern fish. In that case, Goldsborough's best aspect was straight on—if he lost his nerve and turned, he would present his whole broadside to the enemy's torpedoes. But if he were going to fire, the guy should have fired by now. He's tapped out. This is a run.

"Range, Ops?"

"Sir, the range is 2200 yards. Steady up doppler, steady track. I can't believe this shit. He's gonna run right into the depth charge pattern."

Mike called sonar.

"Linc, what do you make of this? Are we on him for real?"

"Yes, Sir. Unless this is a super big decoy, we've got the guy nailed. Sharp, metallic contact, smooth track, around eight to ten knots, steady depth, same definition against the bottom clutter, and he's coming straight into us. I keep waiting for hydrophone effects, but he's awfully close now. His fish couldn't even arm—"

"Right, that's my take. OK, stand by your DC rack. Shoot 'em all, 250 feet, at my command."

"Sonar, aye; roll four, 250 feet, at your command; standing by."

"Range?"

"Sir, 1400 yards."

Mike stared down at the plot. Something was tugging at the back of his mind. Instinct. Something wrong here.

"Wait," Mike said. The plotters looked up at him.

"Sir?" asked the ops officer, looking first at Mike, and then at the weapons officer, as if to say, what the hell? The plotters had stopped plotting, and were staring at him.

Mike tried to concentrate, but could see only the tiny red pinpoint of light on the NC2 plotting surface. Coming right at them. Just like the night of the collision, years ago. That red light. That sudden, awful silence when everyone knew that they weren't going to make it. That the Captain had given the wrong order. Do something, a voice was saying, this isn't right.

"Sir?" asked the operations officer again.

"Sonar reports depth charges are ready. Set for 250 feet."

"Sir, range is 1000 yards."

1000? That was a big jump. Mis-plot, or had the submarine increased speed?

"Bridge, Combat, this is Sonar Control. Doppler is marked up. He's kicked it in the ass, Captain, I think he means to run out from under the depth charges. I think he's coming right. Captain, we need to come left to hit him!"

Mike thought quickly.

"Range is 800 yards."

Linc was right. They had to turn. Turn left!

"Combat, Sonar Control, we need to turn with him to keep the sonar on him. Sir, we need to come left."

418

Mike stared down at the plot, at the little red light. Linc was right. Turn with him, keep the sonar pointed at him. If they went right, the target would pass behind the destroyer, through his sonar's dead zone. The depth charges would miss. He might get away. But there was something wrong here. Something very wrong. He felt an awful sense of dread rising in his belly. His mind flashed back to the collision. He had said nothing. He had just stood there. His instincts then had been to go the other way, but he had been afraid to contradict the Captain. Only now he was the Captain. They were looking at him. Don't go left.

"Captain, Sir? We need to come left. Right now, Sir!"

"Range is 600 yards."

Listen to your instincts, Diane had said. This will be for keeps, not for show. Don't go left.

"Captain?"

Mike stood up and grabbed for the bitch box, punching in both sonar and the bridge.

"Sonar, check fire on the depth charges!" he shouted. "XO, *right* full rudder!"

"Sir," cried ops, "That's the wrong way—we'll put him through the baffles!"

But the Exec did not hesitate. Goldsborough heeled over sharply to port, biting into a hard right turn to the north. Mike could feel her swinging, and something in his gut was urging her on. Go, ship, go. He felt her dip her nose into a wave, hesitate, and lunge back out of it, as if she was listening to him.

"Sonar has no echoes! Last bearing 190, last range 280 yards. Contact is entering the baffles. We've lost—"

A horrendous blast plunged CIC into a maelstrom of darkness, flying objects, and screaming men. Mike felt a punishing hammer blow in both his legs, and then a blinding red arc of pain in his head, before everything roared away into blackness.

SEVENTY SIX

USS Goldsborough, 1732

What saved Goldsborough from being blown completely in two was the right full rudder ordered forty seconds before the mine exploded. She was heeling to port and her keel was at an angle of about sixty degrees to the detonation point. The mine, fired from tube eight as Al Akrab passed under where she thought Goldsborough was, had not even reached the

419

bottom when it sensed the blooming magnetic field of the destroyer and exploded its 4000 pound, gas boosted warhead.

Goldsborough drifted to a stop as the enormous tower of gray seawater from the mine blast subsided back into the sea, having sent a twenty five foot wave crashing down over the main deck and up the port side of the ship. In CIC, as throughout much of the ship, nearly every man who had been standing had had his legs or ankles broken by the force of the blast which had hammered the hull with a single, massive shock. Men were crawling around the deck in Combat through a toxic haze of smoke from small electrical fires, dust blown out of the overhead panels, sprays of water from the broken cooling coils of the consoles, and the cries of injured men. The ship ploughed ahead briefly, almost surfing on the receding plume of the explosion, rocking slowly from side to side as she shook off tons of water, and then subsiding into the shocked sea to a fitful stop.

Mike came to as the ship drifted to a stop, revived by a blast of refrigerated water from a broken NC2 cooling coil spraying directly into his face. He shook his head, producing a jag of pain, and tried to extricate himself from the jumble of chairs, steel cabinets, and struggling bodies all around, only to collapse immediately with a yell of pain when he tried to stand up. It felt like both of his ankles were broken, and the stab of pain brought tears to his eyes. He realized he was not the only one so injured. He also realized that the ship was beginning to list to port.

Using his hands, he dragged himself backwards across the jumbled deckplates, his useless feet dangling out of his trouser legs like dead chickens being dragged on a string. He tried to move towards the front door of CIC. He was having trouble seeing and wiped his eyes, and realized that he was bleeding from a head wound. He could not feel any pain in his scalp, but there was enough blood streaming down over his forehead to obscure the vision in one eye completely. Through the light of the battery operated battle lanterns, he saw the operations officer bent over on the deck, retching next to the remains of the NC2 plotter, the weapons officer next to him, also bent double with pain, his forehead cut open to the bone and his feet sticking out at unnatural angles to his legs.

Mike continued to drag himself towards the door until he ran up against a tangle created by an overturned file cabinet and the surface search radar repeater. Above the sounds of moaning men and spraying water lines, he could hear a rush of steam from the forward stack, which was just behind CIC. The radar operator lay unconscious or dead across his path, his head lolling at an unnatural angle.

"Hey," he yelled into the gloom. "This is the Captain. I've got to get out to the bridge. Can anyone walk?"

The sonar contact plotter emerged on all fours from the smoke and noise. He had been sitting on a padded stool, and thus his feet had survived the bonecracking blast. He was bruised and had cut his hand on something, but was ambulatory.

"Lemme help you up, Cap'n," the sailor said.

He was obviously very frightened, his face ashen and his bleeding hand shaking as he reached for Mike.

"Can't walk, son. I think my ankles are broken; get this guy out of the way; clear a channel for me so I can drag myself out to the bridge. Then help your buddies."

Mike's own hands had begun to shake from the shock and pain; he saw the sailor staring aghast at the bleeding cut on his head.

"No big deal, sailor," Mike said with a confidence he did not feel. "All head wounds bleed like stuck pigs. I'll get it dressed on the bridge, but I gotta get out there right now, OK? Gimme a pull."

The sailor cleared a path through the debris, coughing as the smoke began to thicken, and wincing at the inert form of his shipmate lying at the base of the radar repeater. He put his hands under Mike's arms and pulled him over the hatch coaming and into the afternoon sunlight flooding the pilothouse. Mike nearly passed out when his broken ankles dropped off the hatch coaming. The sudden blaze of sunlight hurt his eyes.

The bridge was also in chaos, but not so badly damaged as CIC. The people, however, had suffered the same fate as their mates in CIC. There were a dozen men lying around the pilot-house, some bleeding from head and face cuts, and most of them down with broken limbs. The deck in CIC was a false deck, to allow cables and cooling lines to be routed to the equipment; it had absorbed some of the shock wave from the mine. The deck under the pilothouse was solid aluminum, and had transmitted the full force of the explosion. Several of the men were weeping; one was hysterical with the pain of compound fractures of both legs just above his feet. The pilothouse deck was awash in seawater and was covered in shards of glass; all of the windows had been blown out when the ship's structure deformed under the force of the undersea blast.

The sailor who had carried him out had reappeared with a large, green medical dressing, and was applying it to Mike's head, even as Mike tried to look around. The Exec appeared beside him, miraculously walking.

"Been sitting in the Captain's chair again, XO?" asked Mike in a shaky voice.

"'Fraid so, Cap'n. Only this time it saved my ass," he said, his face trying to disguise his own shock at the carnage around them.

"More importantly, it saved your legs," said Mike. "Now I need to get to the chair, and you need to do some mighty fancy damage control. I sense a list to port."

"Yes, Sir, we're still getting reports over the sound powered phones; all power is out, and I've lost comms with the engineers."

He nodded back in the direction of the stacks, from which low pressure steam was still escaping.

"We have smoke and steam out of both stacks, and I don't hear the blowers anymore, so I suspect the boilers are off the line. My guess is we have a zillion small leaks instead of one big hole—the explosion was off on the port quarter about 250 to 400 yards. All this water here, it came in when the plume fell back into the sea. I thought we were going to turn right over from that wave. Lemme get you up into this chair."

One other man on the bridge, the bosun mate, had legs and feet intact. He had been sitting on his usual roost on the chart table, which had collapsible front legs. The table legs had buckled, absorbing the force of the blast. Everyone else standing in the pilothouse had been disabled.

"XO," said Mike, weakly, once they had heaved and hoisted him into his chair, "In the land of the blind, the one eyed man is King. You've got legs. You're gonna have to take charge of the damage survey, send info up here, and I'll try to run damage control from here. Get me somebody who can function as a phone talker, and the damage control diagrams. Get yourself some walking help from Combat—there's a coupla guys in there who can walk, but not many. The objective is to plug as many leaks as we can: flooding control, then we'll deal with any fires; see if we can keep her afloat. We need an emergency radio on the air as soon as the snipes get a diesel running; we're going to need a tow—after that blast I suspect the shafts are broken. And we need lots of medical help; God only knows if the Doc and his gang can walk or not. But, first, stop the flooding. As soon as you can get some power back in the ship, get me the 1MC. I'll direct anyone who can walk to gather amidships so you'll have a working pool. OK?"

"Yes, Sir, got it. Cap'n? What the hell happened out there? We had that guy dead to rights! And then we turned away—and thank God we did. But what was it?"

"I don't know, XO. He let something go, I guess. Fucked us up pretty good, too. Probably took him off the boards as well, but right now, we've got to get going on DC. Go, man."

"Aye, aye, Sir."

The Exec grabbed the bosun, and they went out of the pilothouse through the door back into CIC. Mike shifted in his chair, and realized the list to port was getting worse. He craned his head around, and felt a wash of nausea. He studied the inclinometer, blinking his eyes until he could see it clearly, and read a four degree port list. Not too bad. Goldsborough could stand about forty degrees in a damaged condition before capsizing.

He looked around at the injured men on the deck. The OOD gave him a weak, gray-faced nod; both his legs were broken, and he was slipping into shock. Mike suddenly felt a profound sense of guilt. His ship had been badly damaged, and many of his people, most of them from the looks of things, shattered along with the ship. What the hell had he done wrong? What the hell had blown up next to them? It hadn't been a torpedo—they would have heard it coming. He felt a deep chill as he realized what would have happened if he had turned left. At least he called that one right.

He heard a noise and looked out the gaping windows. The helicopter was approaching, its nose high and its big blades whipping up a cloud of spray and noise on the surface as it transitioned into a hover. It came within 100 feet of Goldsborough while the pilots took in the scene: the old destroyer listing to port, oily clouds of black smoke interlaced with bright, white steam rolling out of the funnels and down onto the water, injured men lying everywhere topside while those who could crawl tried to provide first aid. The noise of the helicopter overwhelmed all the noises in the pilothouse.

There was *his* radio, Mike thought. Those guys would take one look and yell for help, lots of help. They had to have seen the explosion from five miles away, and their sonar operator was probably bleeding from the ears because of it. They would have already called the carrier for help. Good. That took some of the pressure off. And the Spruances were coming. Maybe.

The helo edged closer, the noise of the rotor blades and the engines drowning out everything and throwing a wash of salt spray over the forward part of the ship. The pilot hovered on the port side, and then walked the big, white helicopter around the bow. Mike could see the bug eyes of the pilots' helmet visors, saw them pointing. They drifted around to the starboard side, blowing the black smoke aft in whipping sheets.

They were high enough to look into the bridge wing hatch, where they must have been able to see all the injured lying around on the deck of the pilothouse. Then they banked away, backing off. The silence in the pilothouse was loud once the noise from the helicopter died out.

We must really be a sight, Mike thought. They won't know what to do next. Hell, I don't know what to do next, especially if the XO can't find enough guys with feet. They had to find all the leaks, the split seams, the broken fire mains and water lines, the cracked seachests, and patch and plug very quickly. Otherwise, Goldy was going to go down, with most of the crew unable to swim. At least they had their lifejackets. If they could get topside.

He wondered where the submarine was, and his sense of apprehension deepened. He could take small comfort in the fact that Goldy had achieved her mission; hopefully, the carrier was long gone, out of range, and thus safe. But the submarine had escaped. No more questions about whether something was there or not, he thought with a grim smile. Wonder what J.W. Martinson was making of all this, safe on the bird farm. Mike had another black thought. Maybe the bastards would circle back, reload their tubes, and put Goldy on the bottom with one screamer while she lolled helplessly on the flat surface. Or wait until rescue ships showed up and attack all of them. He sighed. They were fucking helpless. Lose an ASW action and this is what you get. You get dead.

He shook his head to clear the haze of depression that was settling into his eyes. Large mistake. His head responded with a jolting lance of pain that made him grunt aloud and almost made him pass out again. He took a deep breath, squeezed the tears from his eyes, and looked around again. He could not just sit here like the rest of the wounded. He was the Captain. He had not relinquished command to his Exec. Yet. Maybe he'd better do that. He had to get his brain going. The injured men were quieter now while they waited for help, many were in shock, and some had slipped into unconsciousness. Some of them were watching him. He had to stiffen up or they would lose all hope.

"I need a phone talker," he announced into the unnatural silence on the bridge. "My ankles are busted; I need somebody who can crawl to get a set of phones and crawl over here."

Many of the injured men just stared at him or down at the deck, lost in a fog of pain, but two looked at each other, nodded, and began to crawl. They took sound powered headsets off more seriously injured men, and crawled painfully over to the foot of the Captain's chair.

"See that phone jack down there? That's 1JV—engineering. One of
you get on that circuit. The other get on this circuit here, X1J, and maybe
we can get some DC going."

While the sailors grappled with the phone cords and jacks, Mike
risked another look at the inclinometer. Six degrees. The distant blue
horizon through the window frames was higher on the port side than on
the starboard side. Some of the men saw him glance at the inclinometer.
Their fear was palpable. They had better get some DC going real quick,
or Goldy would not see another sunrise.

SEVENTY SEVEN

The Submarine Al Akrab, 1745

The colossal explosion that had broken Goldsborough's bones did
not spare Al Akrab, who ended up being even closer to the blast than the
hapless destroyer. The mine had been expelled out of tube eight with a
full impulse charge and had armed almost immediately. The magnetic
field from Al Akrab was decreasing as the two ton mine spun out into the
darkness. She should have been safe. But Goldsborough's field was an
increasing field, and the mine had detected it even as it rejected the
submarine's field. Al Akrab's attempt to turn right had been late, due
principally to the submarine's lack of knowledge about the range to the
destroyer. The Captain had estimated 1500 yards; the true distance was
less than half that. The enormous warhead had gone off between them.

Water is incompressible. An explosion underwater creates a spherical pressure wave in all directions, but especially towards the surface, the
area of least or decreasing pressure. The mine had exploded somewhat
below and on the starboard quarter of the submarine, only 180 yards distant. The blast created a ball of rock solid hydrodynamic force that
punched the stern of the submarine up, flattening her stern planes and
rudder, and dislodging her propellers. The sudden up angle on the stern,
combined with her burst of speed, had driven her down with stunning
force to the bottom, with enough impact to bury her hull almost all the
way back to the sail into the mud on the side of a small canyon. Al Akrab
caromed off the side and banged down seventy five feet onto the bottom
of the canyon. The sudden impact of the submarine caused mudslides on
both sides of the canyon, and a silent flow of ancient mud and slime
buried the Al Akrab's hull over three quarters of her length. Only the top
third of her conning tower, and the battered remains of her stern
projected above the mud when it all stopped moving.

The submarine hit so hard that every piece of machinery that was not shock mounted came off its foundations, wrecking her engineering plant, her air compressors, and most of the hydraulic equipment in the boat. The forward torpedo compartment was crumpled and flooded instantaneously, the interior a jumble of dislodged torpedoes, weapons handling gear, and crushed bodies. Two fuel tanks under the bow split open and would have sent great gouts of diesel oil to the surface had it not been for the deep layer of mud that swiftly encased her hull.

The after torpedo room and steering engine compartment had also been split open by the force of the blast and the destruction of the outside appendages. The weapons officer had been stepping back through the after torpedo room hatch when the world ended. The open hatch crushed him against a bulkhead as the sea slammed into the auxiliary motor generator and switchboard compartment, shutting down all AC power in the boat, leaving only the DC emergency circuits.

The primary salt water cooling main ruptured in the electric motor room; at nearly 300 feet of depth, the pressure from the six inch diameter pipe blasted a column of icy seawater off the overhead strong enough to tear down the cableways running along the length of the compartment. Those who could get to their feet after the crash clawed their way through the bobbing beams of the battle lanterns and the surging, chest high tide of water and oil towards the forward hatch into the diesel engine room. It took ten men in the engine room to close the hatch against the pressure of the air being compressed in the motor room by the rising water, and they managed it only just in time, straining and sweating with all their might on the hatch, closing their ears to the screams of the injured left behind to die in the swirling, drowning tomb that had been the motor room. One man opened the hatch at the forward end of the engineroom leading into after battery, but slammed it shut instantly when he saw the choking green cloud of chlorine gas illuminated by the single battle lantern in the compartment.

In the control room, the Captain and every other man had been pitched headlong down the length of the compartment by the crash, fetching up in a tumble of arms, legs, bodies, and dislodged equipment heaped up against the forward bulkhead. The Al Akrab was jammed into the canyon with a fifteen degree down angle, her attitude created by the weight of the flooded forward compartments jammed into the mud, and the offsetting buoyancy left in the engineroom. Her down angle was solidified by the mudslides that followed the crash.

Four battle lanterns in the control room remained on their mountings after the impact. Their dim beams illuminated the wreckage of the control room, the periscopes hanging out of their foundations, the big fire control consoles jammed at odd angles against the cylindrical hull, deckplates upended everywhere, and some small streams of water hissing into the compartment from small cracks in the interior piping.

The Captain's trajectory to the forward end of the compartment had been broken by the body of the sonar chief, who had been catapulted against the bulkhead an instant before the Captain landed on him. The Chief was unconscious, the top of his head a bloody mess of fractured skull and blood-matted hair, with thin trails of blood coming from his mouth and ears. The Deputy was obviously dead, his head caught in flight between the periscope shaft and a stanchion in the middle of the control room. The Musaid was slumped into the space between the two planes-men's chairs; the planesmen were motionless in their seat, their smashed faces bleeding over the remains of the control consoles. They had been belted in, but the impact had broken their necks on the control yokes.

The Captain came to amid the sounds of a deep rumbling noise all around the hull. The submarine shifted slightly towards a more even keel, sliding him off the inert form of the Chief, and rolling him onto the grid that had supported the deckplates. His left arm hung useless by his side from a numb shoulder socket, and his lips were a puffy, bloody mess, as if someone had smashed him in the face with a pipe. He tried to get up, but his feet were tangled in the maze of pipes and cables ordinarily covered by the deckplates. No one else seemed to be moving, and the air in the compartment was already becoming heavy and wet. He tried again, and this time managed to pull himself out of the wires, and onto a single deckplate that had not been broken loose. He crawled over to the diving station, and touched the Musaid, who groaned. The Captain tried to turn the senior chief around with his good arm, but then realized that both of the older man's shoulders had been dislocated by the impact. His arms were dangling straight down; in the gloom they looked longer than they had been. The senior Chief's head slumped back down on his chest, his breathing shallow and ragged.

The Captain turned away. He tucked his useless left arm into the waist of his trousers, ignoring the beginnings of a throbbing pain from his shoulder. He crawled through the wreckage of the control room to the intercom box, which was hanging by its cable from a stanchion. Someone stirred and made a groaning noise in the jumble of bodies piled up against the forward bulkhead, but he ignored the sound. He keyed in the engineering spaces.

"Engineering, Control room," he croaked. His battered lips made it difficult to speak.

"Control, Engineering," replied a frightened voice. "Thank God. We thought we were alone. We are trapped back here!"

"This is the Captain," he replied, trying to put some authority in his voice. "Report."

There was a moment of silence, and then the Engineer came on the line.

"Sir. We have lost after steering, after torpedo, after auxiliary generator, and the motor compartment. We are in engineering control; the compartment is flooded up to the foundations of the diesel engines. The after hatch is shored and holding. There are fifteen men surviving here. We cannot come forward. After battery room is filled with chlorine gas."

"Is the engineroom holding watertight integrity?" asked the Captain.

"Sir. There are some small leaks, but we are plugging them. There is a lot of oil vapor in the air, and we are having to tap the ballast air cylinders to keep sufficient oxygen. Sir. We cannot stay here for very long."

The Captain paused. The engineers had one of the sub's two escape trunks in the overhead of the diesel room. They were at 350 feet, which was on the edge of the free ascent envelope, but it was feasible, using the Russian variant of the Momsen hoods.

But now there was the larger, strategic question. If the men escaped, and survived the ascent to the surface without exploding their lungs, they would be captured and the plot exposed to the world. He shook his head to clear it. He needed time to think.

"Maintain watertight integrity; bleed air as much as you need. I am sending someone forward to determine the status."

"Engineering, aye."

The Captain switched off the intercom. He had a pretty fair idea of the conditions forward of the control room, and had no intentions of opening any of the hatches, especially not the hatch leading forward from the control room. The steel hatch was blowing a fine spray of water around the hatch clips. The passageway to the forward berthing and weapons compartments was obviously flooded, which meant that everything forward of the control room was probably flooded. He knew without even checking that there was probably no one left alive up there, but he wanted the engineers to believe that he still had access forward. He did not want them panicking and using the escape trunk. He glanced up at the overhead, to where the spherical, bronze hatch to the forward escape hatch chamber was visible in the dim light of the battle lanterns.

He sat back down in the wreckage of the control room, adjusting his dangling arm with his good arm, and then rubbing his face. It was over.

The mission had failed. He had failed. All those months of training, the weeks of stealth, the dread of detection, the heart in mouth operations to plant the mines in the river, all for nothing. He should have listened to the weapons officer when he had recommended dumping the accursed French mine into the mid-Atlantic. The geometry had been wrong; the destroyer had been much closer than he thought, and the damned thing had gone off practically at their back.

There was only one element of the mission remaining: the Americans must not be able to prove who had done this. There was no way he could allow those men in engineering to make their escape. The mission had failed, and now it was their duty to bury the evidence of the conspiracy with the Al Akrab. He limped back over to the intercom unit.

"Engineering, Control,"

"Engineering."

"This is my plan: it is still light up there; we do not know if the destroyer survived the explosion. My estimate is that he did not. But there was a helicopter. Soon there will be more American naval forces in the area. If any of us try to escape now, we will be shot as soon as they see us on the surface. We will wait until late tonight. We still have full ballast air tanks, and forward battery power to operate the blow system. We will wait until 0100 or thereabouts, and then blow all the ballast tanks and bring her to the surface. With only those end compartments flooded, she will come up. Then we will escape into rafts and take our chances."

"But, Sir: surely the forward compartments are also flooded—that impact—"

"Only forward torpedo is lost," interrupted the Captain quickly, the lie coming smoothly. "And some of the fuel tanks in all probability. We hit mud. There are thirty of us still alive up here. I have brought the survivors into the control room area and sealed the forward hatch in case the berthing compartments forward let go, but for now they are holding. Many are injured, and there is not enough air for everyone to use the escape trunks, so eventually we must bring her to the surface. The rest of the boat remains intact, and we can use the torpedo air flasks to blow some of the water out of even the forward torpedo before we attempt to surface with the main ballast tanks. You can attempt to do the same thing with the electric motor room. The other compartments are small. If we cannot bring her up with ballast tank air, then you can use the after escape trunk, and we will attempt to do the same from the forward trunk. But for now, we must remain quiet until darkness falls. Only then can we make our escape."

There was a long moment of silence. Then the engineer responded. His voice sounded tired.

"Engineering, aye, Sir," he said. "We will await your orders."

The Captain switched off the intercom, and looked around the wrecked control room with its jumble of bodies. Across the room the Musaid stirred again, moaning in pain. Everyone else was still. He realized that he had been hearing a strange slithering sound outside on the hull. He wondered about it briefly, and then realized that they must have landed in some kind of canyon or wadi. That slithering sound had to be the sound of sand and mud. The sea was burying them. He nodded to himself. It was fitting.

He looked at his watch. It was just past 1800. If he waited for seven hours, the shifting mud of the St. Johns canyons would solve his final problem, hopefully forever. He sat down, resting his back against the periscope well casing, and closed his battered eyes.

SEVENTY EIGHT

USS Goldsborough, 1815

A very light breeze came up a few minutes after 1800, and Goldsborough slowly aligned herself with it, her bow acting as a large weathervane, pointing her settling stern into the wind. The smoke from the funnels had stopped, and now only a diminishing feather of steam was escaping from the forward stack.

The list to port had become more pronounced. There was a haze of acrid, grayish smoke coming from the central super-structure aft of the bridge as dozens of small electrical fires continued to smoulder in the debris of wrecked electronic equipment. Except for the moans of the injured, the ship was eerily quiet.

Mike sat in his chair, fighting to keep his concentration on damage control and away from the increasing pain in his legs, pain that had begun as a throbbing lance in each ankle and that was now spreading, up his lower legs, his thighs, and into his abdomen, as if it were trying to rendezvous with his pulsating head. His two phone talkers scribbled furiously as reports came in from various stations about cracks in the hull, broken fire main piping, leaking tanks, and residual electrical fires. The after emergency diesel engine had been dismounted, and the forward one had had a fire in the switchboard, thus there was no electrical power in the ship. The ship's four steam powered turbo-generators had died with the engineering plant.

Mike could not find a comfortable position in the chair, and regretted getting into it. The battle dressing on his head was heavy and sodden. He occasionally wiped drops of blood off his forehead, and was having trouble keeping his head up. His useless feet were propped up on the chair's footrest, but they were not up where he would like them. His ankles echoed each heartbeat with a stab of pain.

The Chief Hospital Corpsman, known as Doc, had made it to the bridge about forty minutes after the explosion, accompanied by two volunteers who still had operational legs and feet. The Doc had been dozing on the examining table in Sick Bay when the ship was hit. He had been thrown into the overhead of sickbay, but had landed on the table mattress as he and it hit the deck at the same time. He had a large black eye and a bloody nose, but was otherwise unhurt. His assistant, known as the Baby Doc, had been sitting on a pile of soft, kapock life jackets up on the mess decks, and was unhurt.

The Doc had seen to the men lying around the pilothouse deck, especially the moaning man with compound fractures, and then had offered a morphine shot to Mike. Mike had declined. He had never been one to take medicine, and he knew the morphine would knock him out. He needed to remain not only conscious but competent. He had settled for some heavy duty Tylenol. The Chief Corpsman tied a couple of soft splints around Mike's ankles, while Mike tried unsuccessfully not to cry out.

"How bad are the injuries?" Mike had asked, his voice a strained whisper after the Doc had finished working on his ankles.

The Doc was one of those old-young men that seemed to inhabit the Chief Petty Officer ranks of the Navy. He was only thirty four, but looked about forty five. After the past hour, he looked about sixty. His face was haggard behind the multicolored hues of his black eye, and his eyes barely disguised his shock at the scale of the injuries.

"We have four dead above decks, at least four dead in the main holes, and easily one hundred fifty serious injuries, Cap'n," he said with a sigh. "I'm not counting superficial injuries like mine—but broken limbs, concussions, burns. The Baby Doc is working with a crew of four volunteers, and I've got these two guys. But we're running outa stuff pretty quick, especially morphine and the other pain killers. I hope to Christ we got some help coming."

He adjusted his stance on the wet deck to remain upright, and saw Mike glance over at the inclinometer. Ten degrees to port.

"I think we do, Doc. The helo that was with us has undoubtedly been on the radio to the carrier, and there were supposed to be two Spruances coming out in the next hour if they could get them past the wreck in the channel. I'm still waiting for the snipes to get me a diesel generator so we can use a radio."

The Chief Corpsman shook his head.

"The snipes are pretty fucked up, Cap'n," he said. "Anyone who was below decks is either busted up or walking around in shock. I saw the XO trying to round up people to patch and plug, but a lot of them just looked at him, even though they weren't busted up. The four guys who died below were in two fireroom, where a steam line let go and—well, you can imagine. Nobody's been down there yet—the temperature in the space is still over 300 degrees. One fireman got out by diving into the bilge and coming out the escape trunk, but the steam got the others."

He looked around.

"It's kinda weird—the ship don't look that damaged, but she's literally had the slats kicked out of her. I've seen hundreds of little leaks."

"Yeah, I'm very worried about the hundreds of little leaks," Mike said, scanning the horizon again for signs of help.

The two fishing boats who had been southwest of them were small specks on the horizon, and there were no pleasure craft around. The sun was slanting into the low western horizon. He looked back at the Doc.

"As you make your rounds, get people to stuff something in the leaks, any kind of thing to slow down the water. Get 'em to tie rags around the busted piping, and stuff anything that'll stick in any leak below the waterline. I've had no reports of a big hole anywhere, and I know they're doing some shoring in Mount Fifty Three's magazine, but it's the little stuff that's putting this list on. If it keeps up, we go down. It's that simple, Doc. You're ambulatory. Spread the word."

"I will and I have been, Cap'n," said the Doc, somewhat defensively. "But people are dazed. They pick up a rag or some shit to stuff in a crack and they just look at it. But we'll keep on it."

"Thanks, Doc, I know you're hard pressed."

As the Doc hurried down below, Mike was startled by the sound of a gasoline engine starting up on the main deck. Mike realized that the Exec must have organized a portable fire pump gang. The P-250 fire pumps were gasoline engine driven, and could either pump water into fire hoses or suck water up out of a flooding space and pump it overboard, or both at the same time. Mike was comforted to hear the ragged little engine running at full blast. Goldsborough carried two more of the P-250's, and he found himself waiting impatiently for the other two to light off.

He leaned back in the chair. He was in the peculiar position of having almost nothing that he could do. Ordinarily he would have been

Handy Billy?

432

sending a stream of orders to organized damage control teams, but with so many casualties, the DC organization had broken down completely. The Exec was out in the ship somewhere, organizing small teams of men who could function to attack the flooding problem below decks. The two Docs were trying to cover the ship to treat the wounded. The rest of the crew was dazed, crippled, or lying in shock at their stations. Mike kept passing down orders to anyone they could contact to work the flooding problem first. Beyond that, there was little he could do but wait.

He had tried moving, but his head hurt so badly he could no longer even lift it. He wondered if he had suffered a concussion. The bandage on his head felt like a wet mattress, and from the looks the men on the bridge were giving it, he must have been a sight.

The situation was indeed weird, just as the Doc had described it. Normally there would be a throng of men scrambling all over the ship, fighting the flooding problem, digging through debris, dewatering and de-smoking, and helping out the injured. There would be noise and confusion and officers milling around trying to restore order. But the ship was almost silent except for the noise of the firepump engines. There were too many injured men lying about the decks in small clumps, some bandaged, but most with their legs up on blankets as the two medical teams made their way through the ship and tried to make men comfortable and to fight off shock. Beyond the blown out windows and the mess on the deck, the bridge equipment had not suffered much. Mike remembered the wreckage of CIC, where large equipments had been bolted to a false deck in some cases, but topside, at least the part of it he could see, the guns were in place, the radars still on the mast, the lifelines tight. Only the clumps of men lying against bulkheads, or supine on a nest of extra lifejackets showed the scale of the disaster.

"Captain," called one of the signalmen from the signal bridge. "I think I see a coupla heloes coming."

"From which direction, Sigs?" asked Mike.

"From the east, Sir."

The carrier was east of them. The helo must have gone back, dumped its sonobuoys, and hopefully loaded up with doctors and medical supplies. The big SH3's could carry up to eight men in the passenger compartment if they had to.

Mike scanned the horizon. He tried to lift his binoculars out of their case, but the movement sent his head spinning. He finally saw the two dots coming in, low off the water. As he was watching, the Exec came back up on the bridge. His uniform was wet, filthy, and stank of fuel oil. He looked exhausted, and more than a little afraid.

The dots materialized into heloes, who began their flare to a hover, approaching the port side, sliding back down towards the stern, and then they came sideways back up the port side to hover near the bow, slow dancing with each other as the pilots sized up the situation. Mike grabbed the Exec's wet shirt, and pulled him nearer.

"The fantail must be clobbered," he shouted over the noise of the rotor blades. "Can you go forward and direct them to put their stuff on the fo'c'sle?"

"Yes, Sir," shouted the Exec.

He took a deep breath, appeared to be about to tell Mike something, but then turned and disappeared out the back door to the pilothouse. Moments later he appeared on the forecastle, and helped to drag injured men back behind the gun mount. He then climbed up the steel rungs on the side of the Mount Fifty One and positioned himself where the pilots could see him, waving his arms slowly up and down to attract their attention. His wet shirt and trousers were whipping hard in the rotor downblast. He held his arms level like a crucifix, and then bent them inward, making the signal to advance.

The first helo moved right in, as the Exec used arm signals to bring him up, advance him, and then hold him level over the deck that the pilot could no longer see, while the winch-man began to lower khaki clad men wearing life vests and protective head gear down to the destroyer's deck. The first helo unloaded ten people, an emergency load, and then banked away to stand off. The second helo came in and unloaded three more people, and then several loads of medical supplies in gray boxes with red crosses stencilled on their sides. Both heloes then banked away back towards the darkening skies in the east.

Mike watched from the bridge as the Exec gave the medical team a quick briefing, and then they all fanned out and began administering to the wounded littering the decks. The Exec came back up on the bridge with a doctor wearing the eagles of a Captain, Medical Corps, USN.

"Cap'n," said Farmer, "This is Captain Worthington, senior medical officer on the Coral Sea."

Mike blinked weakly at him, afraid to move his head very much. The Doctor's eyes widened when he saw the Captain's blood smeared face, bandaged head, and ballooning ankles. When Mike leaned forward to greet him, he saw that the back of the Captain's chair was soaked in blood. He did not shake Mike's hand, but bent down immediately to examine Mike's ankles while he talked.

"Skipper," he began, while undoing the splints, "The helo that was operating with you radioed in about an hour ago that you had been torpedoed by some kind of submarine out here, and that the explosion looked like a small nuke. They did a—sorry about that," as Mike gasped in pain—"they did a quick survey, saw bodies and smoke everywhere, and the ship listing, and came running back to the farm to get some help for you. They're on their way back now for some more people—how bad are your casualties?"

Mike took a deep breath. "Eight dead and over a hundred fifty with serious injuries," he said in a small voice. His vision was beginning to blur.

"Jesus H. Christ!" exclaimed the doctor, stopping what he was doing with Mike's bandages. He stood up, and unsheathed a small portable radio from his belt, pulled up an antenna, and spoke into it.

"Big Mother 501, this is SMO, over?"

He put the radio up to his ear, and then back to his mouth.

"501, this is SMO, inform Mother that there are over one five zero, repeat one five zero casualties here, and we need all the medics we can get!"

"And morphine-pain killers, and plugging and patching gear," added Mike weakly from his chair. "And—"

The Doctor nodded at him silently while he listened to the radio, and relayed the additional requirements. He listened again, said, "Roger, wait one," and then turned back to Mike.

"The CO has asked me to ask you: is your ship in danger of sinking? Apparently the beach is bugging the hell out of him."

Mike took a deep breath, and looked at the Exec. The heloes had arrived before he could get a briefing from Farmer, but Goldy was continuing to list to port, and she was not rolling in the light chop that was beginning to blow up. She felt like an old, rotted, watersoaked log in a lake, responding to the wave action about half a wave late.

"Yes, she is," interjected the Exec, forcefully.

He turned to Mike, his face tight with concern.

"We have more casualties than that, Captain, more like two hundred fifty. All the same kind of injuries—broken legs, feet, ankles, or concussions. The people who can walk are zombies. They're mostly in shock."

He shook his head as if to clear away all the bad news.

"I'm sorry, I haven't had time to brief you. We're trying desperately to find able bodied men to plug holes and dewater the spaces, but all the machinery's been dismounted down below—all the pumps, the fire pumps—we have no eductors, only the portable gear to dewater with. We've got lots of little smoky fires, and we've got fuel leaking into the main spaces."

He turned back to the Doctor, whose mouth was agape as he tried to take it all in.

"Tell Coral Sea that if we don't get about a hundred able bodied guys aboard here in the next hour, Goldsborough will capsize with two hundred fifty guys with broken legs onboard."

The doctor swallowed hard, nodded, and then stepped out on the bridge wing to relay the message to the heloes, who were once again just white specs on the horizon.

"Bad as that, XO," said Mike weakly.

"Yes, Sir, although I think she'll go more than just an hour. The problem is this list. As the water gets deeper in the main spaces, more shit rolls down hill and she goes over more, and more water comes in—you know the problem. I've got some small teams trying to find leaks, but they're mostly cracks in the hull, not big obvious holes. The shaft alleys are flooded, and two engineroom has a cracked main condenser—water's halfway up to the upper level. We can't get into the firerooms, so God knows what we've got going on down there. You can't see it from here, but the stern's way down; water's near the lifelines. The after MG room is flooded, and the storerooms along the port side. I had a guy safe the depth charges—remember that ship in World War II that didn't, and killed all their survivors?" He paused.

"I'll tell you what. I think we better get the CO2 life rafts down off the racks, inflate them, and tie them alongside and start getting these wounded over the side."

"We can't save her?" cried Mike in an anguished voice.

The Exec looked down at the deck.

"No, Sir," he said softly, "I really don't think we can. If we had the whole crew, or most of it, we could give it a try. But if the few able bodied guys we do have work on the flooding, and lose, the wounded don't stand a chance. I don't have enough guys to fight the flooding and get the wounded into rafts. I guess it's your call, though."

"Thanks a bunch, XO," said Mike, trying for a little levity, but not succeeding.

He looked over at the inclinometer, eleven degrees now, and then back at the eastern horizon. There was nothing out there, no contacts, no merchants, no fishermen, no pleasure boats. Just the waiting sea, shimmering in the fading sunlight, and darkening to the east as the sun went down behind them. Eighty percent of his crew were casualties. And he still did not know what had hit them.

The Doctor came back into the pilothouse. Two of his team came through the door and began to treat the injured on the deck.

"I've relayed the essence of that back to the carrier, Captain," he said. "I'm sure the heloes can run relays; it only took thirty minutes to fly back here. They're gonna try. And they said there are two ships coming out."

He looked around the bridge, and then back at Mike, trying to gauge Mike's condition from the pallor of his face, and trying to judge the amount of pain from Mike's voice.

"Your Doc give you something for the pain?"

"I took some tylenol," said Mike.

"That's not going to do shit," said the doctor, reaching for his bag.

"I can't take anything stronger; I'll pass out, and then this young man will be in charge, and he'll probably fuck it up," said Mike with a weak grin. "Besides, I've got a decision to make."

"Yes, Sir," said the doctor, closing up his bag. "Let me look at these guys up here, and then I better change that dressing on your head, or you'll pass out from loss of blood. You guys keep this radio. It'll beep if someone calls you."

He handed the radio to the Exec, and turned to join his team. He looked around at the bridge again.

"Sweet Jesus," he muttered.

Mike leaned his head back on the soggy chair. He had to sit at an angle in the chair due to the list. He closed his eyes for a moment.

"Captain," said the Exec, quietly. "We gotta decide."

"Yeah, I know. OK. Get all the wounded moved out onto the 01 level, amidships, or onto the main deck forward. Two groups. Have some guys break down the inflatables, and get them opened up along the port side, like you said. She's at eleven degrees now. If she gets over to twenty, we'll start getting everybody off. We can use the stokes litters to put twenty men to a raft; they won't be in them long, and once she gets to twenty degrees, we may not have much time. But I don't want to abandon her just yet; let's see what the carrier comes up with. They got 4000 guys on Coral Sea. And two Spruances coming. The Navy didn't believe us before, but it's usually pretty good at coming to the rescue. Tell the troops we're getting them assembled in one place so the docs don't have to look for them all over the ship. Use Chiefs, if we have any left, to get the rafts down. Tell that Captain medico what we're doing. Go on, you better get on it. When the heloes show up, we'll peel a couple of guys off to help with the liferafts, and the rest of them can go do some damage control. Now: hand me the deck log before you go down below."

The Exec retrieved the deck log from the tilting chart table and handed it to the Captain, along with a pen. Mike promptly dropped it, and the Exec retrieved it after chasing it across the sloping deck.

"Thanks, XO. You've done great, as always. Go get people set up."

"Aye, aye, Sir," replied the Exec. He looked as if he wanted to say something else, his face working, but then he turned and went out the starboard bridge wing door.

Mike flipped open the deck log, and found the last entries of his hold fire order on the depth charges and the full rudder turn. There had been no other entries. He clicked on the pen, and began writing. He wanted to explain the final, right turn. It was suddenly very important. His battered brain told him that his final maneuver had saved his ship, although what he saw around him put a whole new meaning to the word saved. Half an hour later, the pen slipped out of his hand as he passed out; his head drooped onto his chest, and drops of blood from the soaked bandage began to drip down onto the pages of the deck log. In the gathering darkness on the bridge, no one noticed.

SEVENTY NINE

USS Goldsborough, 1930

Mike awoke to noise, a great deal of noise. There were many people around him, moving around his chair, and some of them were talking to him. He was bewildered by all the noise and the fact that he could hear all of them but understand none of them. He was unable to move his head at all, and had to look up the figures around him from under his eyebrows. It was both dark and light inside the pilothouse, the darkness of night stabbed by the dazzling beams of carbon arc spotlights blazing on both sides of the ship.

He tried to move but several hands restrained him, voices saying, easy, easy, Jesus, look at his head, we need to get that thing offa there, and then they were picking him up and putting him down in a steel meshed Stokes litter, a stretcher molded to fit the human body and made of wire mesh instead of canvas fabric, with the frame of the litter draped in kapok floatation material. Hands strapped him in while other hands changed the heavy bandage on his head. He was amazed that there was no pain when they picked him up; he could no longer feel his ankles, and his head felt like a wooden block, even when they pulled the bloody bandage out of his matted hair. He could hear it, but not feel it. No pain at all. He tried to talk, but his lips were stuck together, his face felt crusted, even his eyelids seemed to stick together. He could hear the noise of a helicopter outside, maybe even two, and as they strapped him into the litter. By turning his head slightly, he could see the darkened bulk of a ship right alongside out the starboard pilothouse door, a bright red running light shining steadily amongst the dazzle of the blue-white spotlights. He moved his head slightly the other way, and saw the massive shadow of what had to be another ship out the port side door, the edges of its silhouette sparkling with lights.

Above the noise of helicopters he could hear the raucous buzzing of what sounded like several P-250 engines, and the hubbub created by dozens of men working, chain saws cutting up shoring timbers, sledgehammers banging baulks of timber up against sagging bulkheads, the rush of seawater going over the side from the black P-250 dewatering hoses, the clatter of diesel engines from the boats alongside, and much shouting.

The stretcher team lifted him up and he was carried out the port side door, the downhill door it appeared, because the stretcher bearers had to struggle to keep him level against the list on the ship. He could not tell if the list was worse or not. He could barely see anything at all in the blinding lights from all the spotlights on the ships alongside. The noise of the damage control teams echoed up between the slab sides of the big ships alongside like echoes in a canyon. Again he tried to talk, but his lips would not work, and his mouth was very dry.

After they got him down the two ladders to the main deck, he thought he saw the Exec talking to another officer, the two of them standing in a cone of white light, but he was unable to call over to him, and then the Exec was gone. A powerful stink of gasoline engine exhaust fumes, fuel oil, steam, and salt water swept over him as they landed on the main deck. He had smelled it on the bridge, but it was much stronger down here, and he could see other stretchers lined up on the main deck, each with an attendant. The men carrying Mike did not stop, however, walking aft, stepping over the forms on the deck, until they reached the area of the after officer's passageway door. Mike was amazed to see that the main deck aft of that point was awash; the stretcher bearers were standing in water up their knees, and the ship's lifelines were sticking up out of the black water, drawing a curving line showing where the hull was under water, disappearing where the quarterdeck and the fantail should have been. A motor whaleboat was tied alongside to a lifeline stanchion, and before Mike could take it all in, he was lifted over the partially submerged lifeline and the stretcher set down in the boat, which cast off right away. He heard another boat making its approach as his pulled away. He closed his eyes against the dazzling confusion in his brain.

Minutes later he was being loaded aboard a helicopter which was turning up on the flight deck of one of the ships alongside. The helicopter was white and had a broad orange diagonal striped painted down it side, indicating it was a Coast Guard helicopter. Once again, he was surrounded by officers who were talking to him, and thought he recognized the I.V., of all people, but the lights and the noise overwhelmed him and he closed his eyes. He heard the deepening roar of the helicopter engines, and felt the helo lift off, hover for an instant, and then bank away into the darkness. There were other stretchered forms on the deck of the helicopter cabin, and two young women in uniform tending to some IV bottles. One of them saw him watching and came over.

"Everything OK, sailor?" she shouted above the din of the rotor blades overhead.

He tried to nod, but his head was strapped in. He still could not open his lips. She saw his predicament, and brought a damp cloth, wiping some of the dried blood off his face and his lips, and then offering a small water container with a bent, steel spout. He drank some of the water gratefully and then lay back. It hurt his teeth, and it tasted salty. Just like the bosun's coffee. She slipped a small pillow under his head, easing the straps around his forehead, and then went back to the men with the IV's. Mike drifted off again, wondering curiously who was taking care of the ship.

EIGHTY

Jacksonville Naval Air Station Hospital, 2130

"Mrs. Martinson," said the pretty young Corps Wave from the Admission's Desk. "I think that guy you were asking about is being brought in now. They're radioing in the names as the helicopters come in. We're trying to, like, keep a list. The next one to land has a Montgomery on it."

"Thanks, Sally," said Diane.

She hurriedly finished stacking the pile of sterile bandage packages on the steel trolley table, pushed it out into the hall, and then hurried down the hall towards the ER. The hospital was at general quarters, with all staff and every volunteer on the list called in to handle the avalanche of casualties from the Goldsborough. The official story circulating within the hospital was that the ship had struck an old, World War II mine and had nearly sunk. There were supposedly over two hundred casualties. Coming on top of some of the injuries transported earlier from the Mayport Naval Station, the hospital was approaching saturation. As Diane hurried down the green hallway, she could see that every room had its lights on, and there were dozens of people, staff and volunteers, scurrying about to make them ready for incoming casualties. The hospital's announcing system was going continuously, paging doctors and directing the movement of medical equipment and supplies. The announcing system was competing with the urgent instructions being called from desk to doorway along the hallway. There was a sense of barely controlled pandemonium in the air.

As Diane arrived at the ER vestibule she saw a large crowd of dependents milling about outside the double glass doors, pale faces trying frantically to see into the ER operations area, which had been screened off with several portable screens. There was a hastily painted sign saying "Triage", with a red arrow indicating the holding area in the north wing. There were several security police standing around both inside the ER vestibule as well as outside in the ambulance driveway, trying to keep people from coming into the ER. There was a pair of officers in khakis surrounded by a small mob of anxious dependents while they consulted clipboards.

She thanked God that she was a volunteer; only her Gray Lady uniform would gain her access to the mob scene inside the E.R., but what she really wanted to do was get to the triage area. She scooped up a stack of blankets from a waiting trolley, and pushed her way through the glass doors. A harried looking orderly intercepted her immediately.

"These have to go to the triage area," she said authoritatively from behind the stack of blankets, not stopping for questions.

"Uh, OK, Ma'am-triage is right through there. They're using the whole north wing, I think."

"Thank you," she said in a sing song voice, trying to sound like the nurses, hurrying around him before it occurred to him to ask why triage needed blankets on a hot night. She glanced into the ER itself as she went by and saw barely organized chaos in there behind the screens, with dozens of doctors and corpsmen working over patients, standing amidst piles of bloody dungarees and other clothes on the floor as they processed each casualty. The normal four bays of the ER had been drawn back, and there were at least twenty gurneys all rolled together haphazardly, leaving only enough space for the medical people to work and for corpsmen to dodge the debris on the floor as they grabbed for bandages, drips, IV stands, and instruments. She caught a brief, shocking glimpse of bare, bloody skin amongst all the green gowns and bandages.

She hurried through another set of double glass doors, and into what was normally an infrequently used medical holding wing. A set of metal double doors was opened at the end of the hallway in the back, and the buzzing sound of a helicopter out on the pad next to the hospital could be heard echoing down the hall. The rooms on either side were filled with more people, four beds shoved into rooms designed for two, and two triage teams going from room to room deciding who was next into the ER and who could be sent upstairs to wait. She saw the red faced, overweight CO of the hospital, gowned up as if for surgery, steering a small knot of interns from gurney to gurney, pointing to injuries and making his decisions while the interns poked and probed the lumpy forms under the sometimes bloody sheets.

All the lights were on, and Diane found herself blinking rapidly in the sudden, hot glare. Medical corpsmen and nurses brushed and bumped by her without noticing her, shouting to orderlies and junior corpsmen to bring this or that equipment or medicines. She threaded her way down the hall past rolling gurneys, loaded with gray, young, pain filled faces, some with their eyes open, most with them shut. Many had their heads bandaged with green dressings, some of these showing large, dark stains. Diane held on to her load of blankets, trying not to stare while fighting down a rising sense of panic, and made her way steadily through the traffic to the end of the hall nearest the helicopter pad. She gripped the blankets tightly, keeping them between herself and the horrors all around, trying not to panic.

As she got closer, the helo on the pad changed its pitch, and the roaring, buzzing craft lifted into the dark sky, a rotating red light under its tail painting the open doors with scarlet flashes. It was replaced by the next helo almost at once, a flare of noise and the blaze of its landing lights dazzling the doorway. A new crowd of orderlies swept past her, headed for the pad, pulling squealing gurneys behind them into the square perimeter of amber ground lights outlining the landing zone.

Trying to stay inconspicuous, she put the blankets down in a corner, and waited by the side of the doors. She was terrified that someone would give her an urgent order, that she might miss him. The helo touched down with a light bounce, the rotors changed pitch, and the gurneys were rolled up to the sliding hatch, a rectangular dark hole in the white sides of the helicopter. After a minute, the gurneys began to stream back in from the pad, each propelled by one corpsman. Diane watched frantically, her heart in her mouth, where it had been for most of the afternoon, ever since the car carrier had blown up in the river and the subsequent call from the Commodore.

She had been talking on the phone to her friend in Orlando when the first blast boomed over the peaceful, Friday afternoon routine of the base, followed by two more in quick succession, the explosions bellowing across the flat expanse of the naval station. She had been startled enough to drop the phone, and, oblivious to the squeaking shouts of her friend, she had raced to window to look towards the basin. The officer's quarters were on the beach area south of the carrier basin; the river was on the north side. She had seen the gray-black column of writhing smoke pushing skyward above the palms like some kind of movie monster, dwarfing the distant masts of the ships, growing impossibly large by the second, looking like the cloud that had come off the St. Helens volcano. A long minute later, there had been another blast, which drove a bright orange fireball up into the cloud, making it even bigger and giving it the shape of an atomic cloud rising into the afternoon air.

The second explosion had been followed thirty seconds later by the sound of a metallic hail rattling through the palm trees and onto the flat, tar and pebble roofs of the quarters. She had grabbed the phone and told her friend that she had to go, that something terrible had happened on the base, and hung up as the sound of sirens began to rise from the area of the carrier basin.

She had wanted to get in the car and drive down there, but realized that this would be foolish. The huge cloud of now all black smoke continued to boil up from just beyond the carrier piers, punctuated by dull thumps which produced smaller orange fireballs. From her kitchen door she could no longer see the top of the smoke column. She heard voices out on the lawns as her neighbors gathered on the grass to watch and pick through the glittering debris. It was evident by now that whatever had happened had happened out on the river and not on the base.

She slipped out the back door, and found twinkling bits of what looked like confetti all over the lush grass, with some pieces of metal almost big enough to identify. Realizing she was barefoot, she went back into the house to get shoes, and then hurried out onto the beach behind the house, and started down the white sand beach towards the river junction. It took her twenty minutes at a fast walk to get down to the stone jetties, where the rumbling, towering cloud of smoke and flames began to fan her face with its hot, burning petroleum breath. There were sirens sounding all over the base, and dozens of flashing blue lights visible down on the destroyer piers. The beach was littered with progressively larger pieces of debris as she got closer to the jetties, most of it metal, but also a great deal of glass and what looked like bits of automobiles. From one of the big rocks on the jetty she could see what looked like the blackened remains of a large ship at the base of the firestorm, the flat stern recognizable because of the funnels and the rudder jutting up out of the water. The funnels leaned in towards each other, looking as if they had been made of lace, with bright orange flames rippling through the latticed steel.

As other people came down the beach to see the wreck, a security pickup truck came bumping out over the sand dunes, the driver angrily ordering everyone to get off the beach and return to their quarters. A fresh series of explosions from the river impelled all the sightseers to obey the orders.

She had returned to the quarters and watched the smoke column boil and rumble for the next hour, trading theories with her neighbors, some of whom had figured out that there must have been damage and injuries down on the piers. Finally the phone had begun to ring inside. Diane was not alarmed, as she knew her husband was safe at sea onboard the Coral Sea. She had answered on the fifth ring, and was surprised to hear the voice of Commodore Aronson. She felt a thrill of guilty fear in her stomach as she thought quickly about her call to Norfolk. She realized that the Commodore must have been having less than a really nice day, even before something went bang out on the river.

"Mrs Martinson? This is Eli Aronson."

"Yes, Commodore?"

She had tried to think of something else to say, but could not. He let her hang there in silence for a few seconds.

"I understand you made a call to CincLantFleet this morning," he said.

"Yes, I did." She swallowed. "I'm sorry if—"

"No matter; this thing was bound to come out anyway, and it appears to me that what's just happened might be part of it."

"Exactly what did happen out there, Commodore?"

"Our picture is pretty fragmentary, but we know one of those big Toyota car carriers came into the river junction on what looked like a routine transit upriver. We have witnesses who say that it looked like she was torpedoed—three big, underwater blasts along her port side that were big enough to shove her halfway across the river. She began to roll to port right after, turned over within seconds, and started to burn from stem to stern. She was packed with cars, which means a couple of thousand gas tanks all crammed inside, and we think that's what finally blew her to bits. We've had a lot injuries on the piers and around the base, and the station dispensary is going to be pretty busy. But that's not why I called."

Diane swallowed again, but did not say anything. In a sense, she had probably wrecked the Commodore's career with her phone call.

"Are you there, Mrs. Martinson?" His voice was hard. "I'm calling because I think that ship out there was mined, not torpedoed. The river entrance is much too shallow for torpedo work. Which tells me that our little submarine theory is probably not a figment. Thanks to your call, the Atlantic Fleet commanders are grappling with that little problem as we speak. It also means that Goldsborough is probably going to turn over a nasty rock out there in an hour or so. If we're all lucky, Coral Sea will be warned in time to divert, but we can't count on it. That's up to Norfolk. But the Admiral, that's CincLantFleet, Admiral Denniston, is certain to order a full investigation if he hasn't already done so. I wanted to alert you to the fact that whatever relationship you have going with Mike Montgomery is bound to be dragged across a long green table, Mrs. Martinson. From the way the big guys were talking up in Norfolk, it won't be a pretty process. For either you or Mike."

"I understand," she replied in a small voice.

"Do you? I don't really think you do, but I've got problems of my own just now, as will Mike."

"Thanks to my call."

"Well, I admit I indulged in some creative language when I found out about the call. But I've been telling myself it's for the best; I would have had to tell them what we thought was going on when the Toyota carrier went to heaven. But I'm going to offer you some advice: when Mike gets back in, there's going to be hell to pay. I like the guy, and had hopes of getting him promoted. That's still possible, depending on what happens out there. But it's not possible, not even thinkable, if it becomes known that he was involved with the Chief of Staff's wife. If ever you planned to take a trip, go visit your mother, whatever, this would be a good time to do it. I don't know anything about the status of your marriage to J.W. Martinson, but if you take a powder, it might help young Michael get through the shit storm that's coming."

Diane was silent. She truly could not tell if the Commodore had Mike's best interests at heart, or had figured out a particularly vicious way of getting back at her for spilling his secret into official navy channels. The sound of some more secondary explosions boomed in through the kitchen windows. She could think of absolutely nothing to say.

"Goodbye, Commodore." she said, and hung up.

She had sat in the kitchen for almost two hours, letting her emotions range from a flood of tears to red faced anger at the whole Navy system. Mike was going to be pilloried somehow for being right about the submarine, and the club they would use on him, if no other weapon could be found, was going to be his affair with her. Somehow she knew in her bones that Navy officialdom would rally around J.W., the wronged husband, never mind that he had been carrying on with another woman in

Norfolk for God knows how long. She had mixed herself a strong drink, and then poured it down the drain. Maybe the Commodore was right; maybe she should just get out of Dodge until the whole thing was resolved.

But what about Mike? How would he feel when the shit hit the fan and she was gone?. He had said he loved her, and she felt the same way about him. He had brought her back to life, revived her as a woman and as a person after her long stint in the unemotional, one dimensional desert of life as Mrs. Chief of Staff. Where she really wanted to run to was the old houseboat, to be there when he got in, and to hell with what the Navy establishment thought about it. But that might, no, certainly would, make it extremely tough on Mike. She was still fretting about it when the phone had rung again. She had just stared at it for the first four rings, a feeling of apprehension growing in her stomach, and then she had snatched it up.

"Yes, hello?" she answered breathlessly.

"Diane? This is Margaret Forrest at the gray lady office at NAS. Diane, can you come in to the hospital? We've been receiving a lot of injured people from that accident on the river, but now we've been told that apparently something awful has happened to one of the Mayport ships out at sea, and we've been told to get every able body we can down here right away."

Diane's mouth went dry. Her heart began to pound. She could hardly get the next words out.

"Which—ship?" she asked in a whisper.

"The Gold-something, I can't remember the name. But they're talking about two hundred casualties, so it's very serious. Can you come in?"

Diane had almost fainted.

"Yes," she had said weakly, "Yes, right away."

The third gurney bumped through the doors, its passenger unconscious and connected to an IV that was being carried alongside by a corpsman. She looked back out into the darkness, and saw them wheeling the last gurney in from the pad as the helicopter made ready to take off. The wind from its rotor blades almost blew the doors shut and flung sharp bits of sand in her face. As the gurney rolled through the doors, she caught a momentary glimpse of Mike's face, and she had to bite her lip to keep from crying out.

His face, or that part of it that was visible, was black with encrusted, dried blood, one eye puffed and shut tight, his head covered in a huge battle dressing that was itself black with blood, with two thin, scarlet streams of bright red blood visible running down his neck. At the other end there were two round cylinders of splints and dressings where his lower legs should have been.

The corpsmen rolled the gurney down the hall, with Diane following them like a robot, her face ashen. One of them turned to see why she was following them. She pointed down to the inert form.

"That's the Captain," she said.

They stopped rolling the gurney, and the other two corpsmen turned around to look at the obviously distressed, pretty woman in the Gray Lady uniform following them.

"What's that?" one asked.

"That's the Captain of the ship. Captain Montgomery."

"Holy shit," said the corpsman. He looked around for an officer.

The triage team headed by the CO of the hospital was backing out of a room nearby. The corpsman called to the CO.

"Sir, this is the Captain of the ship," he said.

The tall doctor walked over swiftly, and did a quick, professional appraisal. There was a tag in a plastic page protector tied to the stokes litter, containing the field diagnosis. He studied it briefly, lifted the bandage on Mike's head, and shook his head.

"Probable skull fracture, both legs and ankles fractured, possible sub-dural hematoma, considerable blood loss," he intoned, while an intern wrote it all down.

He glanced over at Diane for a brief instant, and then back at the senior corpsman.

"Upstairs. OR. Stat.," he ordered.

The corpsmen started back down the hall, and Diane tried to follow but the florid faced Captain stepped in front of her.

"We need you down here, Mrs—?"

"Martinson," she replied blankly. "But—"

"I understand, Mrs. Martinson, and I assume you know the patient, but we need the help down here, all the help we can get, as you can see, and you won't be able to see him where he's going right now, possibly not for several hours. Perhaps you can find his wife out there and inform her that he's here in the hospital. But then, please come back. OK?"

She nodded silently, fighting back sudden tears, as the triage team swept away again into the next set of rooms. One of the interns gave her a curious glance as they left, and then a nurse grabbed her and asked for help getting a patient off a gurney and into a bed.

EIGHTY ONE

NAS Jacksonville Hospital, Saturday, 10 May; 0530

Diane was awakened by the sound of the night call bell on the counter of the intensive care suite waiting room. She had fallen asleep on the sagging, imitation leather couch in the dark corner of the waiting room. Her entire body was stiff and aching. She sat up slowly and looked around the darkened room. The other three women who had been waiting in the room with her had gone; they had probably turned out the lights when they had seen she was asleep.

She tried to remember details from the night before. After Mike's gurney had gone upstairs, she had been swept up in the press of tending to the flood of casualties for two and half hours before breaking free to try to find Mike. The exhausted OR staff on the fifth floor had told her that Mike had undergone three hours of surgery and was now in ICU on the third floor. She held back in the ICU lounge while several other dependents, legitimate dependents, she remembered thinking, had sought after news of husbands and sons. Finally she had steeled herself to step up to the desk and ask. If the corpsman had had any curiosity about why she was asking, he had given no sign. Commander Montgomery was stable, following major surgery. Was she his wife? Only a spouse or other close next of kin would be allowed bedside; she was welcome to wait and ask for reports throughout the night if she liked. The last report she was able to wring out of the ICU staff was that he was stable, and barring complications, would pull through. She heard the bell again.

An officer was at the darkened counter, obviously looking for the corpsman on duty. The waiting room and the adjacent hallway were darkened down to night lights. She stretched and yawned, fighting off her fatigue and the stiffness of sleeping on a couch. The officer rang the bell again, impatiently, but still no one came out of the stainless steel, swinging doors leading into the ICU. She switched on a table lamp.

"They'll come out when they can," she called across the room. "Sometimes they get busy."

The Gray Lady speaks, she thought irreverently. Support the staff.

The officer turned, and she recognized the Commodore. He was in khakis, and his face was shadowed by the beginnings of a heavy, dark gray beard. His uniform was rumpled, and he looked like he had been up all night. He stared at her for a moment, and then walked over, pitching his heavy, gold braid encrusted hat onto a chair. He examined the coffee pot as he walked over, but it was long since empty. The waiting room and the hallway were dead quiet.

"Well," he said. "I see you didn't take my advice." His voice sounded weary, but he spoke without rancor.

"I was called up," she said. "They needed everybody."

"I can believe that. Christ, what a night. What a day and a night. What's his status?" he asked, sitting down heavily on the other end of the couch.

"Fractured skull, legs broken, ankles broken, lost lots of blood, beat all to hell."

"Sounds just like Goldsborough," he said, sadly.

"They finished surgery sometime after midnight," she continued. "They told me that he was stable after surgery, and that they were watching the head wound. I drifted off sometime after two, I guess. They said they'd call me if there was a change."

She shook her head to clear the cobwebs. She desperately wanted a shower and some coffee. She got up from the couch, partly to get away from the Commodore's disapproving gaze, to see if the makings for coffee were in the cabinet beneath the pot. They were.

"How about you getting the water, and I'll make the coffee?" she said.

He nodded. "First useful thing I'll have done in the past twenty-four hours."

He took the pot up the hall to the men's room. She fixed the filter basket, and started up the pot when he brought it back. They both sat down again to watch the coffee maker go through its cycle, the smell of freshly brewing coffee bringing a ray of life to the dreadful room. Outside, the first hints of daybreak began to dilute the stark blackness of the windows. There were still no sounds from the ICU.

"So," she said. "What in God's name happened out there?"

He closed his eyes and leaned back into the couch. At first she thought he was ignoring her question and going to sleep. But then he began to tell her.

"They got the Goldsborough back in. By the skin of everyone's teeth, and she still may have sunk at the pier by now. Because the seas were flat calm, the two Spruances decided not to wait for any tugs but simply made up double lines to Goldsborough, made a Goldy sandwich, and steamed back in at five knots with guys holding axes standing by the lines in case she went down on them. The ship is apparently shattered, literally—hundreds of cracks in the hull, most of the main machinery dumped on the deck, and damned near all hands here in the hospital or downtown at Duvall General."

He looked over at her. "And we don't know what did it."

"Surely the submarine did it," she said.

He smiled at her, closing his eyes again.

"Ah, yes, the submarine. The mysterious, improbable, most unlikely, hardly credible, submarine."

He was silent for a moment, as if waiting for her.

"They're going to cover it up, aren't they," she said.

He laughed this time, an unhealthy sound.

"You're as smart as you are good looking," he said admiringly. "Right to the heart of the matter."

He sat back up and rubbed his eyes again.

"Because that is the heart of the matter. I spent a very unpleasant few hours yesterday, last night, between the first reports of the action at sea and the beginning of the full scale medevac and salvage operation. Got to participate in several politically toxic conference calls between Norfolk, the Type Commander, the Fleet Commander, the Joint Staff in Washington, Group Twelve, and us little fish in Mayport. Your husband, by the way, is back—flew in on a helo from Coral Sea. The carrier's coming in around seven or so this morning, but your husband could not wait. No matter that they needed the seat for some of the injured."

"That's my J.W.," she murmured.

"The submarine that wasn't there," he continued, as if he had not heard her. "We have reports from the Coral Sea helicopter pilots who were assigned to Goldsborough when he gained contact. They confirm that torpedoes were fired. They confirmed some electric torpedoes from Goldsborough, which they could hear on their dipping sonar, and some great big fucking torpedoes, their words, excuse my French, which they could see from some unknown source fired at the carrier. Apparently Mike turned his ship across their track and laid a pattern of depth charges in their way, and countermined three of them. One kept going, and the helo pilots saw its wake heading over the horizon in the direction of the carrier."

"Then the helo got a contact on its dipping sonar—a good contact, according to them, running west at high speed. Just like sonar school, they said—a good, solid contact. Another torpedo was fired by Goldsborough—they heard it running, and they heard it fizzle out, probably on the bottom in that shallow water. The helo didn't have any weapons onboard. Then the contact turned around east towards Goldsborough, and the helo was ordered to break contact and position itself between Goldy and where the carrier had vamoosed to. They broke dip, got out on the 5000 yard fence as ordered, and then somebody set off a small nuke, that's the way both of them described it—a small nuke, underwater, on

Goldy's port quarter. The explosion was so big that Goldy disappeared in the water plume, and you need to keep in mind Goldy's masthead height is 117 feet. That's how big the plume from the explosion had to be. The pilot activated his wire cutter, jettisoned his $200,000 dipping sonar, and lifted the helo off the surface to avoid the wave getting him too. Big fucking wave. Big fucking underwater blast. You know what I think?"

"What?"

"I think the bastard had a mine left after his little visit to the river. Because the mines that got the Toyota Maru in the river picked that 60,000 ton ship up, 60,000 tons, that's fifteen times the size of Goldsborough, and nearly threw her out of the channel. We have Navy witnesses to that. That plus the fact that no one could find any big holes in Goldy. Just a zillion little holes and cracks, and everyone onboard with busted legs and heads, like Mike in there. A massive shock wave. Mine guys said that big mines can deliver a 20 to 30 G-force shock wave if they're placed right."

"A mine," she said. "But from the submarine. Who also laid the other mines in the channel."

"Yeah. I think the mines in the channel were insurance, or maybe even the primary weapon. The whole bit about attacking the carrier was always risky—she could have been expected to have escorts, and it was only a fluke that she didn't. And the water is really shallow for submarine work—300, 400 foot out there. Not much room to maneuver a sewer pipe. I think the mines were meant for the carrier, only they got the wrong carrier. And thirty seven Nipponese along with it—nobody survived what happened out there on the river.

"I saw that thing go up," she said. "It was terrible."

"Yeah. I was in Deyo in the CIC, and it rained car carrier for a full minute when all the gas tanks let go. Big mines. We sent a minesweeper out, after it was all over, naturally. They didn't find any more mines, but the river is ninety feet, that's ninety goddamned feet deeper than it used to be where it happened. The mine guys say these had to be monster mines, three, maybe four thousand pounds, more than likely gas boosted explosives, to make those kinds of holes. And that's what I think this guy fired at Goldsborough as Mike went in to kill him with his depth charges, the only weapons he had that might work against this guy, because our side's torpedoes had locked on to the bottom."

"But what would happen to the submarine if he was close to an explosion like that—wouldn't it be just like a much bigger version of a depth bomb?"

The Commodore smiled again.

451

"You want a job?" he asked. "I take it back—brains are dangerous on a staff. Yes, of course. The submarine, being completely submerged, would have taken just as big a hammering as the tin can did, maybe even worse. It probably went down within a mile of Goldsborough."

"Which means that the Navy can truthfully say that a mine got the Goldsborough, just like the Toyota carrier, but that all this talk of a submarine is fiction, because we don't habeas a submarine corpus."

"Precisely. Although they are looking. Boy, are they looking. They've got one of the new minehunters down from Charleston, got five sonars on him and frogmen, too, sailed an hour after the Toyota went up, and the Coast Guard has the tethered eye out there. The water depth is between three and four hundred feet, plus or minus, and they are looking very hard indeed. But the bottom is riddled with canyons and ravines, so it's going to be very tough."

"But, either way, they're not going to find anything, are they?"

"I suspect they are not."

"And how will they explain the mines?"

The Commodore looked up at the ceiling.

"If I were a public affairs officer, I would speculate, not announce, mind you, but speculate that a cluster of World War II mines, from some long ago minefield, have been bumping along the bottom inshore of the Gulf Stream, where there's known to be a counter current, for lo, these many years, and that they finally did some damage. There will be a great deal of minehunting along the northeastern coasts of Florida for awhile."

Diane got up to check the coffee, and poured them each a paper cup. She sat back down, and eyed the Commodore over the rim of her coffee cup.

"And what will happen to Goldsborough?"

"She'll be decommissioned; she's beyond repair. And then she'll be scrapped."

"And Mike?" she asked softly.

The Commodore drank his coffee in noisy little sips for a minute.

"That's a hard one, and it kinda depends," he said finally. "He saved the Coral Sea. There's no doubt about that. If those were Russian steam torpedoes, and they probably were, they had plenty of legs to run out there and chase down the bird farm. But Mike called the Coral Sea when the radio message from Norfolk warning the carrier first came out, confirming it as Coral Sea first showed up in the kill zone, mentioning mines by the way, and got him going in the away direction. He also sent them a critical warning to turn north when the torpedoes were detected, which took the carrier off axis enough to escape detection when the one survivor made it out to where the carrier had been. And, of course, Mike's maneuver with the depth charges was decisive in thinning out the spread to one fourth of its original size. And if Goldy hadn't been out there in the first place, the gomer could have hit Coral Sea with a spread of six torpedoes, and the mines might yet be waiting for the survivor of that."

"But by saving Coral Sea, he's demonstrated that the Group not only guessed wrong, but kept silent when the possibility that there was a submarine out there surfaced."

He nodded slowly at her, his eyes lidded.

"And that, politically speaking, career-wise speaking, is a major crime," she said.

He nodded again, sipping his coffee, watching her work it out.

"Compounded by the fact that he was having an affair with his Group Chief of Staff's wife, another major crime in terms of his professional judgement. So let me guess: they'll offer to balance it out. Assuming he lives through all this, and provided he keeps his mouth shut about Libyan submarines, he'll get a medal, one of those given in the privacy of some Admiral's office, and then he'll be helped to retire."

"Bingo," said the Commodore.

"And, let me see: I'll bet my job is to go in there when he wakes up, and gently explain all this to him when he's a little better, and if I do that, successfully, and we simply fade away, presumably together, then nobody will come after me, or Mike either, especially his highness, the Chief of Staff."

The Commodore nodded again, watching her carefully.

"I love it," she said bitterly. "The Navy way. Right way, wrong way, Navy way. But tell me: what about all these people, practically the whole crew of the Goldsborough, the hundreds of injured? What happens to them?"

"Victims of an act of God. A stray mine from a war forty years gone. The investigation will determine who were heroes and who were not. The Exec of the Goldsborough was a big hero—he kept her afloat until the Spruances got there. He's going to come out of this with an early selection to Commander and a command of his own. He deserves it. Many others will get medals, everyone will get a unit citation medal for saving the carrier, and the injured will get purple hearts and a big commendation in their records, something vaguely worded as to how so and so made a gallant sacrifice when his ship saved a carrier by throwing itself on a mine. Something like that. Beyond the pain and suffering, what happened to Goldsborough will actually be a bigger boost to their careers than anything else they might have done on that ship."

"The career; above all the career," she said bitterly.

"Most of them are careerists," he pointed out.

"But many of them knew there was a submarine. How will they cover that up?"

"There will be two kinds of witnesses. The great bulk of the crew, the engineers, the gun mount people, the fire control guys, people in the magazines and in auxiliary spaces, they had no role in this other than as victims. The investigating board will tell them that their CO was mistaken. After all, nobody saw a submarine. They *thought* they had a contact. They heard what they *thought* were torpedoes. It was a mine, all along. And the second category of witness will be the officers on the bridge and in CIC, who will be told that the mine story is a deception, a deception vital to national security."

"How, for God's sake, could they justify that?"

"You really don't know? It'll go like this: Gentlemen, we need to bury this incident because it is the right thing to do. This whole Navy, this whole Defense Department, operates on the theory of deterrence. Successful deterrence is heavily dependent upon image. The other side has to think you're ten foot tall, that, if not perfect, you are close to it, and to try you on means *certain* defeat. The Navy simply can't admit that a third world submarine came all the way over here, undetected, either at sea or by our superior intelligence systems, operated in our fleet opareas for weeks, successfully planted mines in the entrance to a major seaport, and almost successfully ambushed one of our carriers, who was, ahem—regrettably operating unescorted. And worse, that the local chain of command suppressed the warnings of a CO who caught on to what was going on and wouldn't leave it alone."

He leaned back in the couch, eyes closed, delivering his 'speech'.

"It's a major fuckup, all around. But not one we can have becoming public. Believe me, Gentlemen, there will be repercussions at very high levels over this, and some high ranking people are going to lose their jobs. But it is absolutely vital to national security that a thing like this be handled behind closed doors. We simply have to, or the thousands of officers and men of the Navy who are doing a superb job, day in and day out, would be tarred, and worse, would lose their confidence in the judgement of their national command authorities. We ask you to bury this whole incident, accept your medals with grace, and get on with your careers, which are now more promising than they were because of the outstanding contribution you and your ship made."

She stared at him for a long moment. He raised his eyebrows, as if to ask, was that not convincing? She realized that his little speech, or something very much like it, was probably being polished by professional speechwriters even as they waited in the hospital waiting room.

"And what happens to you?" she asked, finally.

"I will not get a medal and I will also retire, but not right away. I was the real instigator and the chief accomplice in the major crime of embarrassing their lordships. I have to go because I should have known better than to put the Admirals in an embarrassing position. I should have 'handled it' better. Mike was in his first command, so he's being given the benefit of the doubt. I was in my major command. The point of major command is to demonstrate that you're one of them, or can be one of them, and I guess I demonstrated just the opposite. But they'll be nice about it, because they know I'm old enough to maybe someday run my mouth."

Diane shook her head slowly, in silence. He leaned forward.

"It takes something like this, usually in peacetime, to shake the tree. And believe me, if the tone of their voices yesterday, or last night, or whenever it was, is any indication, the whole forest is shaking. Mike and I are going to be down in the noise level, in the grass, as they say. And please believe me when I say that's precisely where I, and where Mike and where you want to be."

Diane put down her coffee cup and hugged herself, her eyes on the floor, while she thought about it.

"Will you be reassigned?" she asked, almost idly.

"If they have any sense of irony, they'll make me the Group Twelve Chief of Staff," he replied.

Diane found that funny. She began to laugh, softly at first, but then louder, with an hysterical edge. She was still laughing, with tears in her eyes, when the duty corpsman came out of the ICU. He had never, ever heard anyone laugh like that in the ICU waiting room. He stood uncertainly by the steel doors.

"Mrs. Martinson?" he called. "Commander Montgomery is awake. We told him you were out here, and he's asking for you, Ma'am. The Docs say he's going to be OK, barring all the standard stuff. I'll take you in, if you'd like."

He caught sight of the Commodore. "Sir, can I help you?"

"No, young man," said the Commodore. "Take this lady to see Commander Montgomery. Mrs. Martinson, Diane, will you think about what I said? Will you try to convince him? Anything else will be like sweeping against the tide."

Diane stood up, smoothing out the wrinkled Gray lady uniform, running her hands through her hair. She put her arms straight up and stretched, revealing in one smooth gesture her beauty and intelligence and vitality all in one graceful motion. The Corpsman looked on admiringly. Then she smiled at the Commodore, a radiant, 50,000 watt smile, and turned without answering to follow the corpsman into the ICU.

EIGHTY TWO

The Submarine Al Akrab, Saturday, 10 May; 0545

The Captain awoke slowly, prompted back to consciousness by the throbbing pain in his shoulder and a sensation of breathlessness. He was stretched out on the sloping deckplates, his legs wedged into a grid space to keep from sliding on the wet deck. He was not quite stuporous, but close to it as the oxygen levels shrank in the humid, dark confines of the wrecked control room. He could now definitely smell chlorine gas. His eyes felt like burning coals in the hollowed sockets of his face. The light from the two battle lanterns that were still working was very weak.

During the course of the night, he had maintained contact with the surviving engineers in the engine room, shifting over to sound powered phones when the intercoms died for lack of power. They had begun preparations for escaping to the surface after darkness fell above, at around 2200, but the sudden appearance of minehunting sonars had aborted their preparations. The sonars were close enough to be heard through the hull. At 0130 they drifted away, but at 0150 there had been another mudslide, and the Al Akrab had slipped further down the canyon's slope in a long, groaning rumble of metal, ending up still pitched nose down and canted over to port. The mud had continued to move outside the hull for an hour after the submarine stopped moving.

The Captain had listened to the mud and tried to visualize where they were. He was convinced they were in a ravine or canyon cutting the bottom. He was almost sure that the reason the sonars had drifted away was because the submarine had been buried by the mudslides. If that were true, the escape trunks were already useless. He wondered if the engineers realized that. They were further aft; perhaps they had not detected the moving veil of mud. He looked over at the diving control console, at the still figure of the Musaid, who had died sometime around 2100. It was now almost daybreak on the surface. It was time to put an end to it.

He pulled the sound powered phone headset over to him, and slipped the earphones over his head. His movements were slow, and it took a few minutes of fumbling before he could snap the chest strap holding on the earphones.

He glanced up at the pressure gauges of the main air banks. Both he in the control room and the survivors in the engine room had been tapping the primary ballast air banks to restore oxygen to their compartments. The gauges for the forward group showed less than fifty percent air remaining. The Captain had decided hours ago how to put an end to the Al Akrab. He called the engine room. The Engineer answered.

"What is the pressure remaining in your air tanks?"

"We are at forty-two percent, Captain. We must begin the escape procedure very soon, or there will not be enough air to bring her up. The oxygen levels are very low. We are all getting stupid back here."

"I understand," replied the Captain. "The forward tanks are at sixty percent. We can blow the ballast tanks at this depth with thirty percent of the air tanks, so we have enough air to try it once, and to let it blow for a good minute. But you will need more oxygen to get your wits about you. We can share some of our excess air with you. Open the interior ventilation valves on the main induction pipe. I will cross connect one of our air tanks to main induction, bleed down some of our extra air, and we can refresh your whole group. Then we will begin the escape procedure. We will just have to take our chances on the surface with the Americans. It will be daylight in one hour."

"As you command," said the Engineer, with the first hint of enthusiasm. The Captain sighed, and took off the headset, and crawled over to the bank of valve operators on the port side of the control room, past the bodies of the Musaid and the two planesmen.

The valve bank was on the downhill side of the boat, so he had to climb up onto a hull strake to reach the valves. The pain in his shoulder brought him wide awake. He had to rest for a minute until his head stopped spinning. The main induction pipe ran from the snorkel mast in the control room straight back into the engineroom to the diesels. There were two additional large valves that allowed snorkel air from the surface to be bled into the boat while feeding the diesels, to refresh the crew's atmosphere after weeks of submergence. One of these valves was in the engineroom; the other was in the control room. They were hydraulically operated valves, but they had handwheels as well. Upstream of the two ventilating air valves was the main induction valve itself. Above main induction was the snorkel mast, with its bronze float ball seated firmly at the top of the snorkel tube, held fast by tons of seawater pressure.

The Captain watched the valve indicator panel, which was still lighted by the battery circuit, although growing dim. He saw the indicator change showing that the engineroom had opened the ventilating valve off the main induction line. It was a large valve, six inches in diameter. His plan was simple. He would now open the six inch ventilation valve in the control room. Then he would crawl forward and release the dogs on the forward hatch of the control room. Seawater would thunder into the control room, flooding it in less than a minute. As the control room filled, the remaining air would be driven back up into his ventilation valve, down the main induction pipe to the engineroom, filling the engineroom with new air.

They would never suspect. They would sit up on the deckplates, turning their faces to the stream of air flowing in, and they would still be sitting there when after about a minute the air was followed by a six inch stream of seawater at full depth pressure. Not a hundred men could close that valve against such a stream, and it would be all over in a minute.

He took a deep breath, and struggled one handed with the hand-wheel. Slowly, the wheel turned, and there was a faint hiss of air as the pressure equalized between the engineroom and the control room. He slid back down the bulkhead, and pulled himself over the pile of stiffening bodies to the forward hatch. He positioned himself at the bottom of the hatch, facing the vertical steel door with its six hatch clips jammed down onto bronze wedges. The steel surface of the hatch was sweating visibly, as the cold seawater on the other side condensed the stagnant humidity in the control room. There was a faint halo of seawater mist around the hatch, as water at depth pressure leaked by the hatch seals. He had to pull two bodies away from the hatch to get at the bottom clips.

They had almost pulled it off, he thought, as he placed an undogging wrench on the first hatch clip, and pulled down with his good arm. It barely moved under the intense pressure from the other side. He had to lift his whole body and hang on the wrench to make it begin to move off the wedge. The whole hatch groaned, and the mist of water hissing around the edges of the hatch grew into a hard spray as the clip slowly rotated. He stopped it while there was still a quarter inch of metal to metal contact.

They had done so well, staying undetected for weeks, silencing the fishing boat, evading the old destroyer, placing the mines in the river. He moved the wrench to the other side of the hatch, and fitted it to a second clip. Again he had to put his body weight onto the wrench to dislodge the clip. But the old destroyer had become his nemesis. He had dismissed it at first as being an unworthy foe, but it had returned twice to probe the waters of the Gulf Stream, and then again on the last, decisive day. The second clip began finally to move, and the hatch groaned again, the heavy steel beginning to deform. It began to bulge at the top, and the spray of water was now strong enough to reach all the way to the overhead of the control room. His right arm was soaking wet, and his eyes stung from the salt. He left the second clip barely attached like the first one and placed the wrench on the third clip.

But at least they had made the attack. Two actually, as the river mines had caught something in their jaws. The old destroyer had frustrated their attack on the carrier, although one torpedo had evaded the depth charges and hauled away to the east. He would never know if it found *its* target. But the final mine had found its target, even though it had killed the Al Akrab in the process. We will die like the scorpion we are.

He was sweating heavily now, his breath coming in short gasps in the oxygen depleted atmosphere. The hatch was bulging and creaking ominously now, and there was water streaming around half of its knife-edge coamings. The third clip would do it. He held the wrench on the third clip, and pulled himself right up to the hatch, face to face with it, the icy seawater streaming down his face now, washing his hair into his eyes, stinging his eyes with the salt, a cold ablution before death, a cleansing of his unworthy body and his eager soul. He took a deep breath, and called out for the last time "Allahu Akbar!", and pulled hard on the third clip.

Ninety tons of sea pressure slammed the hatch into his face and flooded the control room in thirty thundering seconds. The engineers, waiting for the air pressure to rise, heard a rumbling thump forward and then felt the sudden stream of air blowing out of the ventilation valve. The Chief Engineer was sitting on the oily deckplates of the engineroom, closest to the ventilation valve. His oxygen deprived brain tried to tell him that the noise from the control room was somehow wrong, that this was not the sound or the feel of oxygen rich air from an air tank, that it was something else, the sound of a ballast tank flooding, flooding, water not air, water was coming! He gave a shout and tried to untangle his legs and get up to reach the valve just as the column of water erupted out of the valve. The engineroom took a full minute to fill, the roaring black water snuffing out men and battle lanterns with equal efficiency. The maelstrom subsided when the sea pressure had compressed all the air in the engineroom into a tight, hot pocket up against the overhead. The submarine, now completely flooded out except for one battery compartment, rolled completely over on her beam ends, and slid further down the sides of the canyon, followed by another avalanche of mud that buried her fifty feet deep.

Two miles away, onboard the brand new minehunter, the USS Avenger, the audio frequency passive sonar operator listened carefully, and then signalled for his supervisor.

"Is there volcanic activity along this area, Chief?"

"Nope," said the Chief, complacently. "The bottom contour map shows lots of canyons and ridges, so we probably get some seismic, but you gotta go to the mid-Atlantic Ridge to get volcanic. You're probably hearing a mudslide, sort of a low rumble with what sounds like gravel chasing after it?"

"Yeah, that's it. I heard a big bubbling sound, and then just what you described. Bearing 100, range medium. It's all quiet now, though."

"Yeah, that shit happens all the time. Disregard; it's just mud. Things that go bump in the night, you know? It don't mean a thing."

EIGHTY THREE

Naval Air Station Hospital, Saturday, 10 May; 0630

The orderly lead her into the ICU, past the charge desk, and into the central bay area. The beds were lined up abreast in temporary bays, each bed nestled into racks of life support equipment surrounding the bed on three sides. The ICU was full, with every bed taken, and a double sized shift of green garbed men and women on duty. The air was cool, almost cold, and filled with the sounds of electronic monitors, respirators, and heart-beats of varying strength and intensity. The overhead lights were out, but each bay had a bedlamp. There were other visitors, some sleeping in chairs alongside shrouded figures in the beds. Diane wished for a sweater, and realized her chill was not all due to the ambient temperature. They walked down the line of beds to the last one in the line, to where Quigley had been.

"Here we are, Ma'am," the orderly said. "Nurse said you can stay as long as he stays awake; then you gotta leave."

Diane nodded to the orderly, and looked down at the battered figure on the bed.

"Hey, sailor," she said gently, trying not to cry.

Mike's normally large features looked small underneath the biggest bandage dressing she had ever seen on his head. He was hooked up to various machines via tubes and wires on both arms. An ugly drain tube ran out from under his head bandage. She noted that his heartbeat seemed strong and regular on the oscilloscope above his bed. His feet were elevated on a stainless steel contraption and bandaged heavily. His puffy eye was less swollen than when she had first seen him, and the skin of his face was pale but clean. A bronze band of Betadine stained his forehead. She sat down in the single metal chair provided with each bed. He looked at her, and then she saw a tear forming in each eye.

"Oh, Mike," she said, reaching for his hand. "It's OK. It's OK. Don't cry." She found herself weeping now.

"All those guys," he whispered. "Everybody beat to hell. Ship all beat to hell. All my fault."

He closed his eyes and took a deep breath. Then he opened them and focused on her face.

"Did they get the ship back?"

"Yes, they got the ship back. She's in Mayport, and everyone's safe. And it's not all your fault. The Navy should never have sent you out there all by yourself."

He gave a small laugh, and winced.

"Navy didn't send me out. Matter of fact, Navy said stay in and forget about it. Commodore and I did this one all by ourselves. Where is he, anyway—nurse said he was outside."

"He went home. We had a talk. He told me some of what happened out there. And the Navy is very damned glad you did go out. They know you saved the carrier. They know there was a submarine out there, too. But—" She hesitated.

"Yeah, but," he continued for her. "Lemme guess. Nobody ever found the submarine. And we're gonna hear very little in the future about a submarine."

He closed his eyes again. She wondered if he'd gone back to sleep. She did not want to leave. But then he opened his eyes again.

"He talk to you? The Commodore?" he asked. His voice was getting weaker.

"Yes. We talked for quite awhile outside before they let me come in."

"And he didn't come in, so you must be the designated messenger, the bringer of the "deal", right?"

Diane held her breath. She was suddenly afraid of how Mike might react, that he might feel she was one of them, arrayed against him and not with him. Even in his sedated state, he caught her anxiety. But he also seemed to know what was coming. He squeezed her hand.

"As long as you and I walk out of this mess together," he said. "I love you, Diane."

Diane felt a rush of warmth in her heart. She wanted to hug him but was afraid to even touch him. Such a big man, and yet he looked eggshell fragile lying in the ICU bed. She put both her hands to her lips, and laughed and cried at the same time.

"And I love you, Mike. Nothing's going to change that."

"Look," he said, "There's gonna be shit all over the walls over this one. I suppose they're offering me a graceful exit as long as I keep my mouth shut about the submarine. They'll take care of the crew, hand out some medals, some good assignments, and spin some tale to explain what happened out there. Am I close?"

He actually tried to sit up, but she gently pushed him back into the bed covers.

"Yes," she said. She watched him carefully, saw the small spasms in his face as the pain reached for him. She pressed her fingers along his brow, but then felt him frown.

"But there's more, isn't there?" he whispered. "I keep my mouth shut, and they let *you* exit gracefully. That's the other club. The sonsabitches—"

He tried again to sit up, but gave it up with a grunt of pain as soon as his head moved.

"Shsshh," she whispered. "We don't have to do anything right now. You have to rest—"

He lay back in the bed, seeming to shrink a little. His eyes stayed closed for a few minutes while she stroked his arm. Then he was looking at her again.

"Your call, Diane. You're the one who's going to see the really ugly stuff, getting snubbed by everyone on the base, listening to other wives. They won't do anything to the crew, and my career no longer exists anyway. But they can walk all over you. You say the word, and I'll turn my back on the whole bunch."

She gave him a long look. "I think I'm made of stronger stuff than that, Michael," she whispered.

"Then we'll tell 'em no," he said in a fierce whisper. "Tell 'em I promise not to talk to anybody about a submarine except Sixty Minutes, Twenty-Twenty, the BBC, NBC, ABC, Dan Rabid—"

She grinned, putting her finger to his lips.

"Why don't you," she said, "Tell the Navy nothing at all?"

He stared at her.

"They're going to want to know If I'm going to play along," he warned. His voice was raspy and weak.

"Don't tell them," she said. "And you don't talk to the press. You're the Captain. If you say nothing at all, your silence is going to get very loud. Every time a reporter asks you a question you just give him an enigmatic smile. The longer that goes on, the more pressure there'll be on the Navy to come clean. With a ship broken, and all these people hurt, the press will shake this thing like a terrier with a rat. They'll talk to other people on the ship, on those helicopters. The Admirals aren't fools—they'll see pretty quick that a cover up is going to fall of its own weight. They'll eventually have to come out with it, and that really is the best outcome, because then they're going to have to decide how to keep it from happening again."

"The Commodore is always telling me to pipe down," Mike said with a weak grin. His eyes kept opening and closing. She stroked his cheek.

"Maybe I'll try it," he whispered a few minutes later. "As long as you can stand all the B.S. that'll be coming your way. Hell, the CinC's staff in Norfolk might even get on your case."

Diane smiled then, knowing it was going to be all right.

"Somehow, I think I can probably handle the CinC's staff, Mike," she said. But Mike had drifted back off to sleep.

—THE END—

About the Author

P.T. Deutermann's naval career spanned twenty six years. An Annapolis graduate, Deutermann commanded a gunboat in riverine operations in Vietnam in the early sixties, and subsequently was Captain of a guided missile destroyer and Commodore of a squadron of destroyers. All of his sea service was in cruisers and destroyers; ashore he was a politico-military policy specialist in Washington, completing his service as the chief of an arms control division on the staff of the Joint Chiefs of Staff. He published one text on naval operations and several professional articles during his career; this is his first work of fiction. He is working on his second novel.